“Praise be to the Lord, My rock,
Who trains my hands for war,
My fingers for battle.”

~ Psalm 144 NIV

Other books by Iain McLachlan

Moon Dancing Volume 1 (Silver Bow Publishing 2019)

Moon Dancing

Volume 2

Iain McLachlan

720 Sixth Street, Box # 5
New Westminster, BC
V3C 3C5   CANADA

Title: Moon Dancing (Volume 2)
Author: Iain McLachlan
Publisher: Silver Bow Publishing
Cover Design: Candice James

www.silverbowpublishing.com
info@silverbowpublishing.com
© 2023 silver bow publishing

Library and Archives Canada Cataloguing in Publication

Title: Moon dancing / Iain McLachlan.
Names: McLachlan, Iain, 1969- author.
Description: Second edition. | Contents: Volume 2.
Identifiers: Canadiana 20230561004 | ISBN 9781774032824 (v. 2 ; softcover)
Classification: LCC PR6113.C49 M66 2023 | DDC 823/.92—dc23

5

Foreword

A journalist knows *'they'* are real, a former police officer has found out he is one of *'them'* as is his closest friend, but an un-believing world just will not accept what it knows to be fiction.

Dedication

For Peter McLachlan, one of the original 'peace people' in Belfast 1976 and to his wife Jill … who first called me 'Iain'

I wish you both could have read this.

Acknowledgements

I would like to give a big howl out to all those who allowed me to use them as the basis for several of the characters in the story.

Chapter 1

Portstewart Strand, New Year's Eve 2008

The sun had set over three hours ago, and the end of the year was approaching. He had dug a small pit for the fire, which still burned, warming them and illuminating their faces. His car was parked behind them in the darkness. Kris Martin smiled - 2008 had been a good year and 2009 was looking to be even better. He gazed at the woman who was snuggled in beside him; her long, dark hair tied back in a ponytail that reached down her back. Niamh Beckett laughed at what had just been said, but Kris had missed it. She glanced up at him; happiness shone in her eyes. Yes, he would ask her to marry him before the end of next month.

Adam Dickson and Ryan McCommiskey were opposite them, sharing a loving glance. Kris had known Adam for years and had met Ryan through him. Adam laughed at something Ryan had just said, his large frame rippling with the laughter. The light from the fire glowed on his unshaven face. Ryan seemed smaller when sitting beside him, but he had speed where Adam had power.

Kris looked over to his right. The fire illuminated the happy faces of Jonnie Swain and his other half, Sarah. They had only been dating since October, but this was looking like it was going to be long term. Jonnie's glasses reflected the fire, but it was his smile that lit up his round face. His short, dark hair was cut in a flat top, currently in style, which contrasted with the startling blondness and length of Sarah's hair. Sarah had a natural beauty that attracted people to her. He could see what Jonnie saw in her; the question was, what did she see in Jonnie? Kris had often joked about it. It was good to see his friend this happy.

A gust of wind blew around them, throwing sand over the group. Kris and Niamh had been sitting on a small blanket. The food from the daysack had been consumed earlier in the evening, as had the tins of beer, leaving only the partial box of cheap white wine. The sand swirled among them. Adam jumped up and began to dust himself down, brushing grains of sand over Jonnie.

"Oi, watch it!" Jonnie exclaimed. Adam laughed as he sat back down beside Ryan, Jonnie took off his glasses and started to rub them on his tee shirt. Ryan lifted his arm and placed it around Adam's shoulders, Adam looked at him and smiled.

"I think we should," he said.

"What? Now?" answered Ryan.

"Yes, why not?" Adam extended his hand towards the others, "We are among friends, are we not?" They shared a giggle and then a small kiss.

"What do you think you should do?" asked Kris from the far side of the dwindling fire. The two men looked at each other and giggled again.

"Well," started Adam.

"Well, what?" asked Sarah, impatiently pushing her hand through her hair.

"Well," Adam started again, "We have something to tell you all!"

"You're pregnant!" Sarah exclaimed. The group burst into laughter.

"No ... but we do keep trying there," Ryan said playfully.

"Well, don't keep us in suspense! What is it?" Kris asked. Ryan looked affectionately at Adam as he spoke,

"You say it," Adam nodded.

"Okay .... We are going to London in January."

"So? Why is that big news?" Jonnie asked, taking a drink from the plastic glass in his hand. Adam and Ryan looked at each other again. Their excitement was growing. They nodded at each other, then looked at the rest of the group.

"We are getting married!" The group exploded with joy. Hugs and congratulations were exchanged among all six of them and, as they all sat down again, Kris lifted his glass.

"Right then," he started, "this calls for a toast." Everyone reached around and found their glasses, "to the happy couple!"

"To the happy couple!" they all responded.

"Will it be recognised over here?" Niamh asked, Adam shook his head.

"No, not yet, but at the magazine, we are fighting the equality fight." Adam had looked down sadly when he had answered, Kris sat forward.

"Adam," he said. Adam looked up; Kris lifted his glass again.

"To equality!" The group responded again,

"To equality!" Adam smiled and took a drink. He lowered his glass and looked past Kris into the darkness.

"What time is it?" Sarah asked. Jonnie looked at his watch.

"Nearly midnight," he said, excitedly.

"Congratulations," came the female voice out of the darkness. The group turned towards the tall woman with short, blonde hair who was walking towards the group. None of them knew who Alison Wallace was.

"Err, thanks," said Ryan. Alison stopped just short of the small circle of friends.

"A bit of an isolated place to bring in the New Year..." she mused. The smile on her lips had no warmth to it.

"Yeah," Kris started, "we do this every year - come down to Portstewart Strand and watch the last sunset of the year." Kris turned towards the male figure that had emerged from the darkness and stopped beside Alison.

"Sounds lovely," the accent was American. His skin was pale, even in the dark. He was dressed head to foot in black; other figures moved behind them. Kris stood and turned towards them.

"Yeah, it is." There was a pause, the happiness of the moment lost. "Are you not doing the same?" he asked. The rest of the group moved slowly as the figures came closer.

"Sort of ..." Alison started, "we are planning our own party." She looked at the American. "We just weren't expecting to find anyone down here on this cold night." She looked back at Kris, who extended his arm towards the slowly dying fire.

"Well, you are welcome to join us if you want."

"Oh, we have already decided to," smiled the American.

∞∞∞∞

Mike Dear looked at his phone while he was eating his breakfast. He had left the Special Branch party just after midnight but knew it would still be going strong well into the night. They wanted to outlast the soldiers who were in attendance. It had become a pride thing - who was the last one standing!

"Who is texting you on New Year's Day?" his wife asked, as she walked into the kitchen. Mike glanced up as she adjusted her dressing gown. She had only just woken.

"It's Darren Forester," he answered, opening the message.

"Are you not on days off?" she asked as she started to refill the kettle. Mike read what was on the screen. "Six murdered on Portstewart Strand, they all had their throats ripped out." She stopped what she was doing and glared at him.

"You are not M.I.T. anymore," she paused, "so... not your problem!" Mike looked up, then continued to read. "Kris Martin 32, Niamh Beckett 27, Adam Dickson 23, Ryan McCommiskey, Jonnie Swain and Sarah Allen 22." She replaced the kettle and turned to walk out of the kitchen. She stopped and looked back at him.

"As in the Kris Martin, the guy who was on the news the other day about gay rights and overturning the ban on gay marriage?" Mike looked up at her and shrugged.

"No idea, I am not M.I.T. anymore, so not my problem." She glared at him and slammed the door of the kitchen behind her. Mike read the message again, then forwarded it to Sean Parrish, adding to it before he sent it. 'I KNOW YOU ARE RETIRED BUT HAVE YOU HEARD ABOUT THIS ???'

∞∞∞∞

The room spun, then slowed, and came back into focus; Kyle Foster was breathing heavily. He fought to regain his breath. A thin film of sweat covered him, he lifted his right arm and covered his eyes as he gradually relaxed. Moving his arm, he looked around the bedroom of the farmhouse. Amanda was face down in the bed beside him. He glanced over at her, watching her naked back rise and fall. His body was calming down. The heat of Africa was replaced by the chill from the frost outside the small window. He wondered if it would snow. Amanda's long, dark hair moved, then she rolled over onto her side, taking the thick duvet with her and leaving Kyle exposed on the bed. He did not mind - the chill was helping him cool down. Slowly he turned and, with deliberate movements, stood up and walked over to the door. He slid the thin dressing gown over his shoulders and tied it at the front, stopping to look back at the sleeping woman. He stared for a few moments before opening the door. Quietly, he made his way down the stairs. The kitchen was what you would expect in an old farmhouse. The cast iron cooker dominated the far side of the room, giving it a warm, cozy feeling. It did not take long before he was sitting at the heavy wooden table with a mug of tea, a bowl of cereal and a small plate of hot buttered toast. His mind wandered. A lot had happened over the last few months; his world had been turned upside down. Everything he thought he knew about his life had changed.

Change. The word covered a lot - from where he had been this time last year to where he was now. For a moment, he wondered, at this rate, where he would be this time next year. Last year, he had lived alone and had a job he knew was not going to be a lifelong career. He'd missed his life in the Legion. In the last year, he had fallen in love with someone who had not loved him, found out what was only supposed to exist in fantasy actually existed, and that he was not who he'd always thought he was. Now, he was in charge of a large, successful business and there was a beautiful woman, whom he hardly knew, in his bed.

Oh... and his best friend occasionally turns furry and grows fangs. How could he explain that to anyone? And, as if that was not enough, these creatures lived all over the world and were in a strange death match with an enemy that was also not supposed to exist .... but did. Yeah, a lot had changed. He was sipping his tea as the kitchen door opened and Paul Hawkins walked in.

"Oh great, you're awake." Paul said as he took a seat on the opposite side of the table. He was now dressed for work on the farm, not the way he had been for the celebrations they'd all enjoyed last night. Kyle and Amanda had left the party just after 1am. It had still been in full swing and looked like it would be for some time yet.

"I am, yes," Kyle said, Paul looked serious as he took out his phone.

"We've got a problem," he said, and started tapping the buttons.

"What is it?" Kyle asked, lifting a slice of toast to his mouth.

"Six dead up on Portstewart Strand." Paul was reading from the small screen. "Got their names."

Kyle swallowed, then took a sip of his tea. "Any of ours?"

"Nope... sapiens," Paul answered.

"So, how is that a problem for us?" Kyle asked.

"They were killed by a group of Nocs we didn't know about."

"Go on."

"Well," Paul continued, "five Nocs we know about are all accounted for: three in Belfast, one in Bangor, one near Lurgan," Paul paused. Kyle straightened up in his chair.

"How many are we talking about?" he asked.

"More than one," Paul answered. The door to the kitchen opened and a very sleepy woman walked in. Her hair was dishevelled, and the thick woollen dressing gown was wrapped tightly around her in an attempt to keep the morning chill out, both of them at the table turned and looked at her as she stumbled towards the kettle.

"Good morning," Paul greeted her. Amanda cast him a glance as she reached for the still warm kettle and mumbled an unintelligible response.

"So," Kyle spoke to Paul, "what can we do about the vampires killing six sapiens on Portstewart Strand?" he asked. Amanda dropped the kettle on the floor.

ooooooo

Cara-Marie looked at the ringing phone. She stretched under the duvet. She was warm and still tired, and her head throbbed as the bedroom slowly came into focus. The phone continued ringing. Slowly she reached out and looked at Mark's name on the screen. She pressed the small green button and retreated back under the duvet,

"I thought you were not allowed to phone me." She could hear the gruffness in her own voice. She'd not had a lot of sleep after seeing in the new year.

"Cara!" there was an urgency in Mark's voice that woke her senses. "This is work. Six people were murdered on Portstewart Strand - their throats have been ripped out!" She sat upright in bed as he continued, "Kevin wants to meet us in the office as soon as possible." he coughed, "I think your furry friends are back." She could hear a car starting in the background. "I'm on my way there now; you'd better be, as well." Cara-Marie McKenna, of the Coleraine Herald, was now wide awake.

Chapter 2

Sean Parrish looked at the message on his phone again. He felt his mood drop. He was no longer in the police and was having issues with retirement. Yes, he'd had to leave a few months early after the bodies had been found up at the Mussenden Temple; and yes, it was widely known the higher echelons of the police force wanted the case wrapped up as soon as possible. The *'werewolf'* case had come to a sudden stop. All their evidence and lines of inquiry had been archived and most of the team moved to other M.I.T.s. The police disliked having a *'werewolf squad'*. Mike had been received with open arms by Special Branch - Sean had no doubt Darren Forester made sure of that. Whatever happened, they'd managed to shut Mike up properly. In all the years he'd known him, Sean had never seen him react in that way. Like the way he himself was reacting to not being in the police anymore.

Suddenly he had time, and it seemed to move very slowly. No, he was not enjoying his retirement. Everything now seemed to get under his skin, everything annoyed him, and life with his wife had become strained. Once his gardening leave had ended, he had gone to headquarters to formally hand in his weapon and his warrant card. Then he'd solemnly signed the form that released him at the end of thirty years as a police officer. The final interview with the chief constable had been a joke. Of course, the top man had no idea what he had done, apart from what was on the news. He did not know about his time as a constable, the terrorist attacks he'd survived, the funerals of those who had not. How could he? How could an English police officer come in and -just take over? That afternoon, he had gone home, intending to go out for a quiet meal with his wife. He hadn't expected over thirty, mostly ex-police officers, and his last team, led by a smiling Mike Dear, to be waiting in a function room of the hotel in Ballymena. He listened to, and was embarrassed by, the stories of his first days on the job. He laughed along with everyone else at the amusing anecdotes that were told by several of the older men. They all enjoyed the meal.

"Aye, there was this one time when Sean ...." All the stories were good-humoured and received by those listening with much laughter before Sean had the final word. His short speech ended with all in the room on their feet applauding. He'd received several gifts, including a new coffee machine for his kitchen. There was little mention of his last case. That had been two days before New Year's Eve. New Year's Day had been a very quiet one, except for Mike's text.

Today was Wednesday, the first day back at work. He had woken up, gone through his morning ritual - showered, shaved, and enjoyed a quiet breakfast. With the sweet taste of a hazelnut latte still in his mouth, he walked outside and got in his car. It was only when he started to reverse that he suddenly remembered and stopped. His hands were shaking, and his breathing had become shallow. He started to sweat .... Where was he going? He was not in the police anymore! Confusion swirled around in his head. His hands and arms were trembling. He looked up at his wife, who was standing in the open doorway of their house. She was speaking, but he could not hear her. She had wrapped her dressing gown around her and was beckoning him back inside. It took several seconds before his mind made the decision to turn the car off. He made slow, deliberate movements: getting out of the car and quietly closing the door, looking around.

The interior of the house was warm in comparison with outside, but he still felt a chill as he slowly sat back down at the kitchen table. He was in his suit and his hands were on the table, still trembling. His body, his mind, had completed this ritual nearly every weekday morning for thirty years. His wife was at the sink, she started to wash the dishes from his breakfast and was speaking to him. He could see her lips move, could see the anger on her face, but could not hear the words. He looked at the back of his hands...then turned them and stared at his palms. These were still his hands. His wife stormed out of the kitchen, slamming the door behind her, and suddenly he was alone. The silence closed in around him, suffocating him. He wasn't 'Inspector' anymore, he was an ex, a former. He was nothing. His head bowed slightly, and he slowly leaned forward, lowering his face into his hands. His body started to shake again, and he wept. When his wife returned to the kitchen, dressed for the day, she was still angry. Thankfully, she would be going out soon.

After two hours of sitting alone in the living room with the tv off, his phone started to ring. He looked at the screen, not recognising the number. Part of him did not want to answer, but he forced himself to press the green button. He had reread Mike's text several times yesterday. He picked up the phone and held it to his ear.

"Hello," he spoke quietly. There was a pause before a man with a very upper-class English accent spoke,

"Inspector Parish? Hi, good morning, Rupert Baskerville here," Sean's mind raced. Then he remembered the phone call in the car, months ago. The Earl of Baskerville had wanted to meet him face to face but Sean had insisted it only happen after he had left the police, and the investigation. The Englishman had agreed. Now, he wanted to meet. It only took a couple of minutes to settle the arrangements. "Right, so outside the front of City Hall, here in Belfast, in one hour," the Englishman repeated back to him.

"Aye, that will be grand," Sean answered.

"First class! I'm looking forward to meeting you, Inspector. We do have a lot to discuss, after all." There was a slight laugh as he spoke, but Sean couldn't think of anything he found amusing.

"I am sorry, your Earlship, but I am not an Inspector anymore. Please call me Sean," there was another chuckle down the phone.

"I am sorry, Sean, but I'm only called Earl when I'm being formally introduced to someone, I would usually be addressed as Lord Baskerville ... but please, call me Rupert." Sean felt himself cringe at the formality.

"Okay, *Rupert.*"

"Excellent." There was a pause in the conversation before Rupert continued, "See you in an hour then." It was an accent Sean could not even attempt to mimic and suddenly he had the thyme tune to a child's tv programme, from his childhood, in his head.

"Aye, see you then," and the phone call ended. Sean placed the phone down and stood up. It was the motivation he'd needed. He now had something to do.

∞∞∞∞∞

There he stood, facing the two-storey building. The dome at the top of the central tower seemed to shine brighter in the sunlight, the pillars around the circumference looking like bars on a cell. He entered through the open black metal gates and followed the tarmac to the large circle of grass, in the middle of which a marble Queen Victoria towered above everyone, sightless eyes towards Belfast. The statue stood on a plinth at the top of three well-crafted steps, raising her even further above him. Sean stared at her. The sun shone. He felt its warmth, but there was still a chill in his body. He glanced over to his right at the large, grassed area, which looked so pristine - well-groomed and tidy. He could still picture the Christmas Market that had been here only weeks beforehand. All trace of it was gone. Small groups of people dotted the grass. They were chatting, drinking beverages, smiling; seemingly oblivious to the winter chill that hung in the air.

"Excuse me, Inspector Parrish?" The English voice came from behind him. He turned and watched the aristocrat, hand extended, walk towards him.

"Yes," Sean unconsciously replied as his hand was grasped in a firm handshake. The tall man was smiling. He had a prominent forehead with swept back hair that had once been dark but was now fading. The smile filled a surprisingly rugged face - this man had an experienced look about him. The dark green Barbour jacket covered his slim torso. Underneath was a navy-blue shirt, which had obviously not been ironed. The colour of the shirt matched the dark blue of his jeans, and he wore scuffed walking boots, he seemed out of place in the city. This was a man who was more at home in the country.

Sean was the opposite, dressed in a pressed, light grey suit, and a shine on his black shoes. Rupert stepped to one side and extended his hand to guide Sean away from the statue and the people walking past it. The side of the main building was somewhat private. Rupert led the way, distancing them from the small groups of people on the grass. Obviously, he required a very private chat. Sean was positioned between him and City Hall. Rupert's eyes moved continually; he was totally aware of his surroundings.

"Well, I must say," Rupert started, "it is first class to finally meet you." This English gentleman was smiling, as the pace of their walk decreased. "I have heard so much about you," he stated, Sean glanced towards him.

"Great," Sean paused, "I have heard nothing about you." Rupert looked up, then around himself again, the grin turned into a self-deprecating smirk.

"Well, I am used to being around people who know who my family is."

"I try and keep the opposite," Sean replied. Rupert nodded once and made a 'mmm' sound. They walked on for a few seconds before Sean spoke again. "What is it I can do for you, Rupert?" Rupert came to a stop.

"It seems we have been tackling the same problem, but from different angles." Rupert looked around them again. There was no one close enough to hear what was being said. Sean could guess what Rupert was talking about but did not want to say the words.

"And what problem is that?" he asked. Rupert's head snapped around to look at him, the smile was gone.

"Come now, Inspector, we both know what we are talking about.... I watched the crime watch programmes." Rupert turned away slightly, "and was very impressed by your Sergeant .... Dear, isn't it?"

Sean nodded once, and Rupert continued, "the Furry and Fang Club!" Rupert let out a short laugh, "I really liked that one."

"I am not with the police anymore," Sean stated. Rupert stopped.

"Yes, you said," he paused, "but we both have had the same problem, and ..." he looked pointedly at Sean, "from recent news reports, they have not gone away." Sean felt his insides churn, the same way they had when he'd received Mike's text. "Wasn't that what you were investigating last year?" Rupert's eyebrows lifted. Sean paused and thought about how he could answer.

"Our investigation came to a conclusion following the deaths of the main suspects of the multiple murders." Sean held the stare of until Rupert turned his head.

"Yes, I heard. What was it? Eastern European gang warfare that ended in a cliff- top battle? Come, Inspector, I know a cover story when I hear one. I did spend twenty years as a squadron commander in Two One." Rupert smiled and took a step forward. Sean was confused.

"What, may I ask, is 'Two One'?" Rupert looked around, answering in a lower voice.

"Sorry, Two One SAS," Rupert glanced over his shoulder, "United Kingdom's Special Forces Reserves," He turned away and stepped forward again.

"Does the name, Steve Minister, mean anything to you?" Rupert stopped at Sean's question. He turned and smiled at him.

"Yes, of course. When I was Staff Sergeant, he was one of our instructors, before he went back up the road to Two Two." Rupert turned away and Sean stepped forward to join him.

"Since you know him, I conclude he is back over here again .... good for him." Rupert nodded as he spoke. "Now that I have passed your little test and I am who I say I am, shall we get down to business? You have a werewolf problem ... and I can help."

"I never said anything about werewolves." Sean looked ahead as he continued to talk. "We were investigating several brutal murders, carried out by a group of people who had to be brought to justice for their crimes."

"Yes," Rupert straightened up, "as I said, I heard... eastern European organised crime gangs hacking each other up with chainsaws and gun battles on clifftops. Come, come, Inspector, do you really think that was what killed one of your own?" Sean felt his body tense up at the reference to Simon. He'd still not gotten over his friend's death.

"That murder was fully investigated ..."

"And those responsible were found at a National Trust site following a shootout involving persons unknown. Yes, I read the report." Rupert had cut in before he had a chance to finish speaking. He'd just quoted the official report of the incident at the Mussenden Temple. "But do you, as an Inspector with your vast experience, believe that report?" Rupert glanced over at Sean who had stopped walking. Rupert continued, "No, I didn't think so."

Rupert stopped and turned towards him again, "Look, they have been on my family's land for over a hundred and fifty years. They have been nothing but trouble since they arrived. Thankfully, since the truce, there have not been any more murders, but they still make their presence felt. All the local farmers are constantly losing livestock to them."

"Truce?" Sean asked, his interest piqued. Rupert responded with a smile. "Yes, that was my grandfather's doing." There was a pause, Sean still looked confused, so Rupert continued. "It was in 1940 and we all had to prepare for a German invasion at the time. He negotiated a truce with their clan leader, and we all helped the country get ready for what everyone thought was about to happen. Before that, we'd killed several of them and they'd killed several of us .... including members of my own family." Rupert's eyes were intense. He was gesticulating with his hands, explaining, "I mean, for a while they seemed to have a thing about putting heads on poles in people's front gardens .... terror tactics .... it happened here also, yes?" Sean pictured what had happened to Simon. His throat was dry, he could not form words, as Rupert continued, "Yes, that's what attracted me to the events here."

"What do they want?" The question was almost a whisper from Sean.

"What they want, is our moorland for themselves. And that, as you can imagine, is certainly *not* going to happen. This land has been in my family since the 1400's and it is my responsibility, as the custodian, to maintain the land for future generations. I am certainly not going to just hand it over to the 'Furry and Fang Club'." Rupert responded.

"I mean, what do they want here?" Sean's question was louder than before. Rupert smiled a warm smile and stepped towards him.

"That, Inspector, is what I intend to find out." There was a long pause before Sean asked the next obvious question.

∞∞∞∞

Minutes later, as Sean was walking away, his phone bleeped in his pocket. He slowed as he reached the metal gates at the entrance to Belfast City Hall. The message was from Mike: 'PHONE ME', he pressed the green button and lifted the phone to his ear as it began to ring.

"Hiya," Mike answered, cheerfully.

"Hi," Sean replied, walking through the gates. He turned to the right and started towards the law courts. Mike paused before he spoke again.

"You okay? You sound really pissed off."

"You are not going to believe who I just met." Sean slowed down, as people walked past him in both directions, totally immersed in their own worlds.

"After the last six months, I would believe anything," Mike said, wryly.

"Yes, I suppose." Sean paused, thinking about what he was going to say. "Do you remember Rupert Baskerville?" Mike was thoughtful, "cannot say that I do. Who is he?"

"The English Earl who phoned us in the car just after the O'Brien post-mortem." Sean looked around, there was no one close enough to hear what he was saying.

"Ahh, yes .... wait, he is here in Belfast?" There was surprise in Mike's question.

"Yes, we just had a chat outside City Hall," Sean answered.

"And what did he want?" Mike asked, abruptly. Sean stopped walking.

"He wanted us to join forces, as we are tackling the same problem from different ends"

"He what?"

"Yeah, I got a story of how his family has been fighting them for over a hundred years,"

"Fighting whom?" Mike asked.

"Werewolves," Sean replied. There was silence, and he continued, "Yeah, I kept telling him I am not on the job anymore, but he kept going on about *same problem, different ends.*"

"What did he want from you?" Mike's question was not what Sean had expected. There had been no werewolf putdown. Mike was now in a different environment.

"Well," Sean stated, "all he wanted was a copy of the complete case file." He let out a short laugh at the thought. "I had to tell him again I was not in the police, so could not help him there. I don't think he liked that very much." Sean glanced up at the rooftops of the buildings around him. His eyes caught sight of a passenger jet climbing into the clouds away from Belfast City Airport. He wished he was on it.

"No, I am sure he didn't. What was his name again?" Mike asked. Again, not the question Sean would have expected from him.

"Lord Rupert Baskerville, Earl of Baskerville," Sean looked around himself again. Mike was writing the name down.

"Right, I will see what I can find out. Is it okay to call around this evening?"

"Sure, no problem." Sean smiled. "Text me when you are on your way."

"I'll see you later." The phone went dead, and Mike was gone. Sean felt uneasy. There was something about this whole thing he did not like. This had not finished on the cliff top and, even though he was out of the job, he was still involved. He pushed the phone into his pocket and started back towards his car and home. He had to prepare for seeing his friend again; he had something to do now and that felt good.

Rupert Baskerville watched the former police detective walk away. Someone had gotten to him and shut him up properly. It was clear the powers at the top of the police force, and the government, still refused to admit these creatures were, in fact, very real. Different people, but the coverups were still the same. Rupert took out his phone and scrolled through the numbers. He stopped at the name, 'Unholy Steve', and pressed the green button. He looked down the side of City Hall at the large memorial to the fallen from conflicts in the 20th century. It was an impressive sight. The ringing in his ear was soon answered,

"Hello." Rupert recognised the voice of Steve Minister.

"Hi, Stevie, Rupert here," he announced himself, and got an instant reaction.

"Boss! Hi there, how are things with you?" Steve was pleased to hear from him.

"Yes, not bad, not bad."

"So, what are you up to these days? Still running around your moor in that old, battered Land Rover of yours?" Steve asked.

"You mean, the one I used to get you off the moor and into hospital after your little fall?" There was a hint of mischief which got the desired laugh from the other end of the phone.

"And I was NOT lost.... I knew exactly where I was.... just did not see that obstacle any decent landowner would have removed before inviting people onto his property."

"Yeah, yeah, putting the *Special* into Forces!" There was a mutual camaraderie that anyone looking from outside could admire, but never understand. "Anyway, the reason I am phoning .... I am currently outside Belfast City Hall and wondered if you fancied lunch...my treat!"

"You are over here?" Steve's voice raised in volume.

"Only for a couple of days, yes ... But I would rather chat face to face."

"Well, there will be at least two others as well, since you are paying," Steve answered.

"Good Lord, do not tell me all three of you are over here? Isn't that dangerous?"

"Yes, Boss, right cogs for the right machine, and all that," Steve answered. "We can be down there for two .... Do you know the Wig and Pen?" Steve asked.

"I do and will there by two, see you then."

Chapter 3

Cara-Marie was scanning what she had written. She was re-reading it after the shouting down she'd received from Kevin, the editor. 'Just write what you know.' There was to be no reference to werewolves or any other mythical creatures running around the coast of Northern Ireland. All her stories from last year had been rubbished, Dr Burns' theory had been disproved, and it wasn't werewolves that carried out the murders in Coleraine, Limavady and Belfast, but a violent eastern European *mafia* gang that was having its own turf war... even though there were witness statements... and a photograph. The police investigation results had been made public.

"There are no werewolves in Northern Ireland." Chief Inspector Anderson had repeated several times at the press conference. The in-fighting within the gang had spilled over, and they were removing witnesses who had observed their activities. They had even obtained several experts on organised crime to back up the story. But Cara-Marie was still not convinced, and she knew she was right. The whole northwest was enjoying a boom in tourism and various 'werewolf hunter experiences' and 'werewolf tours' had sprung up. There was now such a demand for hotels and rooms that local people had gone into the bed and breakfast business... and business was booming! The mayor was loving what it was doing for the economy, however, a lot of the existing local attractions which had seen initial increases were starting to have problems with visitors constantly searching for evidence of werewolves. The largest golf club had lodged official complaints with the local council regarding several incursions onto their fairways by teenagers and young adults searching for clues about the werewolf killings. Tempers were flaring.

Cara-Marie knew she was right. All she had to do now was prove it. Kyle Foster had been made Alpha of the northern den of An Rua, a clan of wolves that had existed for thousands of years in Ireland. Unlike other myths and legends, the werewolf stories in Ireland were different. They were not about the random attacks on people, not the fear-induced delirium and 'kill them all' tales that prevailed over much of the rest of Europe. They told of pairs and packs of wolves defending children and helping lost and injured travellers. Cara-Marie had also found stories from the great kings of Ireland, when Ireland was five provinces and not the four it is today. The fifth had been 'Tara', the high seat and high kingdom that ruled all of Ireland. In times of war, the great kings had employed the wolves to fight for them and one king had made them swear to always 'defend the lands, and not govern them'. The wolves had agreed. These had just been legends, but aren't all legends based on tales of real events, like the stories of King Arthur and Robin Hood? The Hollywood film industry had totally corrupted these stories far away from reality, and she hated that.

Real. They were real, and she knew it. She heard Kyle had moved from his bungalow and onto the farm. He was now hard to get a hold of and, since both he and Tony had left the police, two of her best sources inside Coleraine police station were gone. They were both being quiet about what was happening on the farm. The notebook hit her on her shoulder, abruptly bringing her back to the present. With an annoyed look on her face, she glanced over at Mark, the photographer.

"Hello ... Cara .... Earth calling Cara ..." he said mockingly.

"What?" she demanded, Mark pointed with his head towards his screen,

"I said .... which you did not hear ... have you seen these?" Cara-Marie pushed with her feet and the wheels of her chair propelled her around the desk, so she was beside him. Mark moved the mouse of the desktop computer and the screen jumped to life. The first picture was of a young, thin male whose body was twisted and contorted in the sand. His head was tilted to one side, a look of terror frozen on his face. His skin was marble white, and his jeans had several blood-stained tears in them, as had the thin tee shirt; but it was the injuries around the throat that grabbed her attention. There had been massive force in his death. Cara-Marie stared at the picture.

"Who is it? she asked. Mark read from the notebook on his desk.

"This is Kris Martin, 32 ......"

"Where did you get these?" she asked, and Mark looked at her.

"An unconfirmed police source," he answered. She knew what that meant, they could not use them. "The injuries are totally different from the others; they all had mass trauma to nearly all of their bodies, whereas with this one, it was mostly just around the neck." Mark continued to talk but she was not listening as her eyes moved over the mutilated neck, the parts of the larynx, trachea, neck veins.... she studied each detail. Yes, this was different from the others, Mark poked her in the side. "You do know what this means?" he asked. She looked puzzled.

"No, what?" she asked. Mark leaned back in his own chair and pointed towards the screen.

"That ...." he paused, "wasn't done by your 'Furry and Fang' club. That was done by someone else!" Cara-Marie looked at him, then back at the screen. He was right. That was certain. This *was* totally different.

"There is a new bad boy in town."

"Oh, for goodness' sake," shouted one of the reception staff as she walked by pointing at the screen, "Do you have to?"

∞∞∞∞∞

Kyle was sitting in the large chair in the front room of the farmhouse. He had an open laptop resting on his knees. Tony was just walking through the door from the kitchen with a mug in each hand when the main door opened and in walked Paul Hawkins and Dermott McMurragh. Paul was holding a large brown envelope, which bulged with its contents. He seemed relaxed; Dermott was not. Kyle looked up and smiled in greeting as Dermott closed the door behind them.

"I suppose I'd better make two more of these, then," said Tony as he passed one of the mugs to Kyle.

"Great idea," said Paul, taking a seat opposite Kyle, Dermott moved over towards the empty fireplace.

"So," asked Kyle as he closed the laptop and placed it on the floor beside the chair.

"So," repeated Paul, emptying the contents of the envelope onto the small coffee table. "Which do you want to do first?" he asked. Kyle glanced at Dermott, then back at him.

"Farm business," Kyle replied. Paul nodded and started to sort through the pile of paperwork in front of him. He chose a paper and started reading,

"We have finalised three supply contracts with new vendors ...." Kyle was already bored as Tony returned with the mugs of hot liquid for the two men. Once he'd handed them out, he deposited himself on a chair at the far side of the room. Kyle was not the businessman Paul was. He watched as Paul went through the details of each contract in turn until Kyle held up his hand. Paul stopped, "What?" he asked, and Kyle sighed.

"Paul," Kyle slouched in the chair, and Paul looked towards him. "How long have you been running the business?" Kyle asked. Paul glanced at Dermott before he answered,

"Nearly twenty years."

"And how has the business progressed?" Kyle inquired. Paul sat upright, then he answered,

"The business has shown growth every single year." A proud smile appeared on his face and Kyle nodded. Tony and Dermott shared a glance - no one knew where Kyle was going with this.

"And how often would you discuss business dealings with Carl?" the smile dropped from Paul's face. Carl had not been mentioned since the funeral.

"Every day," Paul's eyes darted around the room, and Kyle slowly nodded.

"Was Carl involved with all aspects of the business?" Kyle asked.

"Yes," replied Paul, and Kyle nodded again.

"Honesty is a big part of me," Kyle said as he stood up. Paul and Tony stood, as well. Kyle stepped towards Paul and extended his right hand, which Paul took.

"Paul Hawkins," Kyle started. Paul straightened his posture, sensing he was being given a command. "I am not a businessman, but you are ..." Paul looked Kyle in the eyes and waited, "You are to take over the complete running of the business, all decisions are yours. If there is a problem, then let me know .... I will not interfere with your management of that side of the farm. I want a monthly briefing from you, the accountancy contractor and the legal team." Paul nodded; the smile was back. He lowered his head before responding,

"Thank you, I accept." The two men shook hands and when Paul looked up, Kyle was smiling at him.

"I will learn from you, but I am not ready to run a business that I know nothing about. Given time, I will be ready but for now, no need to fix what isn't broken." Kyle almost laughed as Paul's smile widened. He was a happy man. Kyle stepped forward and the two men hugged. Dermott and Tony stepped forward and shook Paul's hand, in turn. The atmosphere in the room had lifted, and everyone knew this was the right decision. As Kyle sat down, Paul gathered the paperwork and stuffed it back into the envelope.

"Well," he started, "I certainly have enough to do now."

"Aye," commented Dermott, "it will keep you out of my face for a while." There was a shared laugh before Paul walked towards the door of the farmhouse. Kyle motioned with his eyes to Tony to sit where Paul had been, then extended his hand to the other chair for Dermott.

16

"Don't forget about your trip down south. That has to be done in the next few days," said Paul, and Kyle's eyes widened.

"Yeah … I had forgotten about that," Kyle said. Paul smiled and nodded towards Tony,

"Good thing I didn't… sort that, will you." It wasn't a command from Paul, it was direction. Paul was still higher in the pack than Tony. He was just doing what he was supposed to do - keep Kyle where he was supposed to be. Tony smiled and nodded as Paul closed the door behind him.

"So," Kyle started, "tell me what you have found out about Portstewart Strand, then …." Dermott looked serious as he sat down and began to speak,

"Well, judging by their injuries and cause of death, it was done by Nocs. After the Mongols took out that teenager on the hill near Castlerock, they all went into hiding. Good thing we know where they are all sleeping."

"And, thanks to all that lot from Salisbury coming over last year, we have found their biggest site," added Tony. Dermott nodded. Kyle did not move, he just listened.

"Yes, we could take them all down in less than an hour." Dermott was not hiding what he thought they should do. Tony looked over towards Kyle, who took a deep breath before he spoke.

"So, this new lot, do we know anything about them?" Kyle asked.

Dermott shook his head, "No. Nothing."

"Any idea where they could be sleeping? They are obviously somewhere around the north coast," said Kyle, and Dermott nodded again.

"Yes, they must be close, but no, not yet." Kyle glanced over at Tony, then back at Dermott.

"What do you need to find them?" Kyle asked, as Dermott straightened up.

"Four teams of four and an assault team at the farm on thirty minutes notice."

"You have it. Confirm with Paul which people you are using so it doesn't affect the running of the farm too much," said Kyle,

"Done," Dermott smiled, "I will find them for you." Kyle stood up and the others followed. He reached out his hand, which Dermott took. "See it is done, Dermott. I want to know everything about them: who they are, how many, any contact with sapiens, who is guarding them as they sleep …. the whole thing,"

"It will be done." Dermott lowered his head.

"Within our laws …. we defend these lands, not govern them," Kyle repeated the law. Dermott looked up. He understood what he was being told. He nodded, and Kyle released the handshake. As Dermott turned and walked out of the farmhouse, Kyle and Tony re-took their seats.

"Well," said Tony.

"Well," replied Kyle.

"How does it feel to be in the 28-day club?" Tony asked, and Kyle smirked.

"Well, I could ask you the same question!" Kyle relaxed back in the chair, "28 days after resigning and being out of the police … yeah, it feels good." Tony looked over at him.

"Yeah, a lot has happened since then." The sadness on Tony's face said it all. Kyle knew he was thinking about his wife and the miscarriage she had suffered. His heart went out to his friend.

"Tony?" he asked quietly. Tony looked up. There was a pause before Kyle spoke.

"I have not seen her in a while…How is she?" Kyle asked.

"Yeah, she is on the mend," Tony paused as he lowered his eyes again. "Her mum is 'round a couple of times a week now, just to make sure." Kyle looked at the top of his head. He knew Tony still had not fully come to terms with the fact that his child had been murdered and they'd nearly killed his wife as well, just to get to him. Yes, he'd had a father's revenge, a husband's justice …. but that did not heal everything.

"How did counselling go?" Kyle asked. Tony looked up. There were tears in his eyes as he shook his head. Kyle guessed it had not gone well; he heard Karen stormed out of the last session.

"They are not sure if she can ever have a child again …." Tony said. "And she is not taking it very well." Tony shifted uneasily in his chair; she was not the only one who had taken it badly.

"They will never hurt you again!" Kyle stated. Tony's head shot up. He looked Kyle in the eyes, then lowered his gaze again,

"I know." It was almost a whisper. Suddenly he stood up and moved towards the door. "Well, if we are heading down south, I'd better organise the transport, then." Kyle watched his friend walk across the room and open the front door of the farmhouse. Tony turned back towards him. The smile on his face was as fake as the humour he tried to inject. "I'll sort out a decent room for you two also … can't have Amanda roughing it, can we?"

"No, we can't." Kyle returned the fake smile as Tony closed the door behind him, leaving Kyle all alone. Slowly he felt anger rise within himself. It became strong enough to make him stand and clench his fists. His anger was directed at the Mongols; at what they had done. Not just to the pack, but to his friend, to his family, the ones he most wanted to protect. His mind flashed back to how they had found Karen, the blood, the smell, her anguish and the pain in his friend, a pain very much still there. He felt himself bare his teeth, his body tensed, his breath forced its way out of his nostrils. The anger grew, yearning to be released. Kyle took a step forward and almost collapsed, he knew what had nearly happened - his wolf wanted to come forth, wanted the freedom, wanted to attack. He fell back into the chair behind him and, as the tension subsided, the wolf retreated. He fought to control his breathing. No, this was not the time. His body had begun to shake slightly. He started to curl up in the chair just as Amanda came down the stairs.

"OH GOD, KYLE .... HELP ... SOMEONE, HELP!" she screamed.

Chapter 4

Cara-Marie slowed her car down as she approached the turn-off to Kyle's house. She had only been there once before, but remembered it well, she glanced over at the house as she slowly turned into the driveway. The lights were off. Part of her wanted him to be in, the other part wondered what she would do if she found him there. She had questions; she wanted to talk but was hesitant. Her car stopped in the driveway. The house was in darkness; his car was not there, and the curtains were drawn. She'd heard just before Christmas he was leaving the police - a '28-day man', meaning he had signed the forms and given his 28 days' notice to leave. She had messaged him just after Christmas and they had what she could describe as a brief message chat, but she'd not really heard from him since then. Her heart was still beating loudly as she got out of the car. Slowly, she walked up to the door and pressed the doorbell. She could hear the chime echo inside. There was no movement, no lights suddenly switching on. She waited, then rang the bell again. The only sound was the wind blowing past her. She stepped back and tried to look beyond the curtains of the living room. Nothing.

Normally, if this had been anyone else's house she would have just turned and left, but something stopped her. She moved closer to the window on the far side of the front door. The sheer drapes were still there but the curtains were gone. She could just make out what had once been the spare bedroom - it was empty. She stepped back and took in the front of the bungalow. Without thinking, she started walking around the side of the building. She reached through the wooden gate that was part of the fence surrounding the back garden. There was no padlock and the gate swung open. The evening grew darker as she walked into the back yard, which was empty. She looked around. Her eyes darted over to the back door ... It was slightly ajar! She moved slowly towards it. There was some damage to the handle and the frame - it had obviously been forced open. She stopped in front of the door, and pushed it, using the back of her hand. If this was a crime scene, she did not want her fingerprints to be found among the others. The door gently swung inward, and she stepped into the kitchen. It was empty and looked like it had been for some time. She looked down. On the floor were two sets of muddy footprints. They were large and, from the pattern, she guessed they had been made by walking boots or something similar. They led towards the front of the house.

She slowly walked towards the door leading into the hallway. Cara-Marie moved quietly through each room - all were empty and, apart from the back door, there was no other damage to the house. Every room had been stripped bare. He was not here. Her mind flashed with memories of the two of them on his sofa in the living room, a glass of wine in her hand, both laughing. He could make her laugh, she knew that, and she missed it. He had only become defensive when she asked about 'the northern den' and 'An Rua'. He had not answered her questions and he'd made it clear he wasn't going to. But that was at the beginning of December, and they hadn't met up since. She hoped she hadn't scared him away.

Suddenly it seemed like the house grew darker. She looked around the empty living room, then turned and walked back out the way she'd come in. This was not a crime scene. She closed the back door behind her and shut and locked the side gate before getting into her car. The door slammed shut and she looked around in the darkness of the night. She sat there motionless and wondered where he was; what he was doing. She had not believed the story about Carl O'Brien's death or the other stories about eastern European gangs and gang warfare at the Mussenden Temple. Kyle was obviously sticking to his story and that intrigued the journalist in her; he was hiding something. Deep down, she knew he was somehow the key to what happened last year ... and if she was ever going to be able to prove it, she needed him.

She had started a blog online, under a different name, about searching for werewolves and she was already getting quite a response. Most were nerds and wolf fans who just wanted anything to do with the craze sweeping the tourism industry in Northern Ireland. But she had received a few messages offering support, and, a couple of times, guidance. One was from an American woman who stated her whole family had been killed by them and another was from a German man who survived an attack; their descriptions of what they'd seen and experienced fit with her own. Most of the rest were nonsense. She took out her phone and tapped in a message. She re-read it before she sent it to him, 'HIYA, BEEN A WHILE. FANCY A COFFEE AND A CHAT SOMETIME? IT SEEMS LIKE AGES.' She watched as the screen changed and 'message sent' appeared. Her car roared to life and she was soon on her way back home, listening to her phone for an answer that would not come tonight.

∞∞∞∞

Rupert Baskerville had gone back to his hotel. He looked impatiently at his watch again. It was now after 7pm and they still had not arrived, but then Steve Minister had a reputation for being late. Rupert stared at the glass containing a soft drink, sitting on the low table in front of him. He was seated in the lobby, not far from the front doors. Every time they opened, he studied those who passed through. The bar was to his left and the seated area of the restaurant was behind him. He had booked a table for the four of them and knew they all would eventually be here; a free meal would never be passed up. Rupert knew the stories from Scotland and knew Alan Dukesby had taken the fall for whatever really happened. The four dead had not perished in a helicopter crash and his posting to Northern Ireland was a lateral move, not upwards to Commanding Officer, as was expected.

Rupert had seen the pictures from the crash; everyone in that aircraft had walked away. He had listened to two others who'd been on that exercise towards the end of a squadron function. Yes, he had been buying them drinks. Of course, he would, he had been a squadron commander. Yes, he had waited until it had started to take effect and tongues loosened. Yes, it was indeed a cover story, and yes, four guys had died. The photos of heads on poles had all been removed. Non-disclosure orders were in place and all communication with the Americans who'd been on the same exercise were abruptly stopped. No, the two soldiers had not seen what had killed their friends, but they had seen the photos and heard *that* noise, '*like a long wolf howl*' in the night. Rupert had not pressed them - he did not have to. He knew *that* sound well enough.

The entrance doors opened, and a familiar figure walked in and looked around. Rupert stood up and caught Steve's attention. They were joined seconds later by Chris Abbey and David Priest. The smile on Steve's face spread as he walked towards him; Rupert stepped forward and the two friends shared a familiar hug. There was mutual trust and respect between them. Rupert shook the hands of the other two and they all took seats around the small table. Rupert had a drink in front of him already, so David asked what the other two wanted then headed towards the bar. Steve relaxed back in the chair.

"So, how is life at the Manor?" Steve asked.

"Good, good, things are progressing." Rupert shrugged as he continued, "The financial crash hit everybody, but we were able to protect most of the farms on the estate. Rupert looked between them, "One old problem still remains … but …" Steve looked up.

"But what?" Steve asked.

"But *they* seem to have their own problems, so they've been mostly keeping to themselves over the last year and a bit." Rupert noticed Steve and Chris exchange a glance, neither wanting to join the current conversation, but both seeming to know exactly what he was talking about. Rupert changed tack. "So, how long have you been over here?" he asked. There was obvious relief in the other two, as David returned.

"Well," Steve began. David balanced the three glasses, nearly dropping them on the table.

"Hey, don't spill it!" protested Chris.

"I paid for them, so I can do what I like with them," retorted David as he lifted one of the glasses and walked behind Chris's chair, deliberately knocking into it as he passed. David took his seat, and the banter between the two men continued for a moment, before Rupert brought it to an end. Steve reached out for his glass and lifted it to his lips.

"Well," said Rupert, "you were saying?" Steve looked over at him.

"Yeah... just over a year. Things have been busy, as you know." Steve nodded slightly towards him. Rupert knew what it meant... 'don't ask'. He was no longer in the military and everything Special Forces do is secret. No former member would ever ask a serving member anything about what they were currently up to. What they had done in the past was, however, fair game.

"Yeah," Rupert replied, "So how is Alan getting on?" Steve smiled. Alan Dukesby and Rupert had been friends for years.

"Not too bad," Steve replied,

Rupert noticed neither David nor Chris added to the conversation.

"So, tell me," Rupert asked, "what happened in Scotland? I know what was in the papers was absolute tosh." There was a ripple through the three men, and they all sat up and paid attention.

"I wouldn't believe the date printed in any of the tabloids." David stated. There was a chorus of understanding. The newspapers had a thirst for stories about their regiment, but 99% of what was published was out of date or just plain wrong. It always caused consternation. They had no way to reply - they all knew what it would mean if they did.

"Yeah, I want to stay off the 'naughty list'," Chris said. There was a collective laugh from the group. The 'naughty list': ex-members who had spoken with the press or written books and revealed things they should not have or just plain lied in order to generate income. To be on the 'naughty list' meant being removed from the regimental association. Serving members and a lot of ex-members would cut all contact with them. They were not to be offered employment, advice or guidance, and not to be told about reunions or other gatherings of ex-members. The association has a lot of members in nearly every level of business and commerce. To be on 'the naughty list' meant you were on your own.

"It wasn't a chopper crash then, was it?" Rupert asked, as the three men glanced at each other, then back at Rupert.

"There was a chopper crash, yes, engine failure, that happened the day after …."

"But that isn't what took down three of ours and one of the yanks, was it?" Steve shook his head, and again the three soldiers shared a glance.

"None of them died where we found them," Chris stated, and everyone looked at him.

"Were the bodies laid out beside each other?" Rupert asked. Steve looked surprised. "Like you were meant to find them?" Rupert concluded.

"How did you know that? Who have you been speaking to?" Steve asked.

"Were their heads displayed on poles, as trophies?" Rupert asked. The comedy from the group was gone; this was serious. David sat back in his chair with his drink, Chris stared at Rupert, and Steve looked around them all.

"Yes, yes they were," Steve answered.

"They won't be doing it ever again," said David.

"Why?" Rupert asked.

"We took them down," stated Chris, and a satisfied smile spread over his face. David looked over at him and nodded, an answering smile on his face. Rupert did not have to ask anymore. He knew what that meant.

"Good, good lads," he paused, "glad about that." Rupert looked at each of them in turn before speaking again, "So, do you believe me now?" Steve looked up from his drink.

"Yes, Boss." Steve looked at the other two, then back at Rupert, "I'm sorry I didn't believe you before." The group relaxed once again.

"So," Rupert began, leaning forward, "let's eat, then go somewhere to talk shop, eh?" Smiles broke out amongst the group. Rupert had an idea, but he knew they would immediately say no. He wanted to know exactly what happened in Scotland and on the clifftop, but now was not the time. This was the time to bring them in, make them comfortable around him again. Then, and only then, would they open-up. This meal was going to be expensive, but he did not mind. It was the next step in getting what he wanted, and he would need men like those presently around him to be able to get it.

∞∞∞∞

Kyle's eyes slowly opened. He was laying on top of the bed, it was dark outside, and he was confused. Slowly, he rolled off the bed and stood up. He was still fully dressed, but his boots had been removed. He looked at the worn pair of trainers that were sitting near the door. It did not take long for him to gingerly make his way down the stairs. When he walked through the door at the bottom into the living room, the light seemed to be brighter than usual. Amanda stood up from the chair he had been sitting in earlier. Tony, Paul and two others were also in the room.

"Yay, he is awake!" Amanda slowly pushed her arms around his neck and pulled him in close. Kyle reached his left arm around her, but his right stopped on her shoulder. The hug only lasted a few seconds before she let go and stepped back.

"Finally," said Tony who remained seated. Paul turned to the two farmhands,

"Okay, you both know what to do?" he asked. They nodded. "Right, off you go and let me know when it is done." Both nodded again and left without speaking. Amanda moved behind the chair as Kyle slowly walked around it and sat down.

"What time is it?" he asked. Tony looked at his watch before answering.

"Nearly nine … you were out cold," he stated.

"What happened?" Kyle asked. "What happened to me?"

"Well," Tony started, as Amanda stepped forward on his left, blocking his view of Paul.

"You collapsed, and …" she stopped. He looked up at her.

"And? And what?" his voice raised in slight annoyance. He stretched out his hand and gently pushed Amanda back, so he could look Paul in the face.

"And your wolf tried to come out. That can't be allowed to happen, not yet anyway."

"This is part of me, yes?" he asked.

"Yes," Paul confirmed, "but you do not have control of him yet and an out-of-control wolf running around isn't something we want to deal with." Kyle looked down, then up at Tony before looking back at Paul.

"I will ask you again… what happened?" Paul paused before he answered,

21

"You became angry at something and your wolf tried to emerge. Presently, you cannot control this, and you need to learn how."

"And learn fast!" interrupted Tony.

"Precisely." Paul continued, "If you cannot control it, then there is only one option," Paul glanced at Tony, then back at Kyle, "and we can't afford that situation to arise." he paused, "She can teach you how to control him."

"Who is 'she'?" Kyle asked.

"Tyler," answered Tony, "and this needs to happen before you go down south."

"Agreed," Paul said. "If you go south and that happens, they will put you down and send someone else to be alpha here ... and we don't want that, either."

"Tyler? The lass on the Isle of Skye?" Kyle asked.

"Yes, and no," replied Tony. Kyle's eyebrows raised, and Paul answered for him.

"Yes, Tyler Reynolds. She is the best trainer I have ever known and no, she does not live on the Isle of Skye anymore. She had to move .... suddenly. She's just getting settled on Rathlin Island, presently." Paul continued, "I have spoken with down south and they are happy to wait the couple of weeks before you are ready to go."

"Why is it so important for me to go to her? Why can she not come here?" Kyle asked.

"Everyone goes to her," Paul answered. "You need to learn 'control' and she is the best to teach you." Kyle paused as he was about to say something when his stomach rumbled.

"Someone is hungry," Amanda stated.

Kyle smiled as he glanced over at the clock above the fireplace, "Some of us have not eaten all day." Amanda affectionately placed her hand on his shoulder, then walked towards the kitchen.

"No probs, I will sort something out for you." She glanced over her shoulder as she was going through the doorway. "You guys want something?" There was a moment of surprise and Paul and Tony looked at each other. Tony spoke first.

"No thanks. Karen will have something sorted for me when I get home."

"Ahh, yes please," answered Paul, "that would be lovely." Amanda smiled, then closed the door behind her.

"Speaking of which, I need to be heading home," announced Tony, as he stood up. The other two stood as well, and Kyle held out his hand, which Tony took.

"Thank you for today," Kyle started, "and give my love to Karen." He was smiling as he said it, and Tony smiled back.

"Yes, yes I will, thank you." Tony shook hands with Paul and headed out the front door of the farmhouse. A blast of cold air rushed in as he opened the door but was cut short as he closed it behind him. Paul was staring after Tony.

"He still isn't in a good place," he stated.

"Hardly surprising ... Now what can you tell me about this Tyler person ... and why the move from Skye to, of all places, Rathlin?" Kyle's stomach made another noise. Paul paused and got himself comfortable.

"Well, where to begin with Tyler Reynolds..." Paul smiled, "First of all, she is fast, amazingly fast, in fact ... I don't know anyone who has actually beaten her." Kyle relaxed back into the chair again. He was about to be given a lot of information. It would be the following morning before he would notice the text message from Cara-Marie.

Chapter 5

Sean was in his living room with the TV on, but it was only moving wallpaper; he was not taking in anything on the screen. He looked at the empty mug in his right hand - he could not remember drinking from it. He looked up, as the sound of his wife walking across the bedroom above him thudded through the ceiling. Not being at work was getting to him. It was also getting to her. For nearly thirty years, every time she came home, the house would be quiet, and she would have some time to herself before his arrival. Sometimes she had hours, but now …. he was always there. He had been outside today. After the meeting at City Hall with the English Earl, he had driven down to Shaw's Bridge and gone for a walk along the towpaths around Minowburn. It wasn't until he spotted a small National Trust signpost that he realized he was on one of their sites. 'I must join someday,' he had thought to himself at the time; but it did not change the fact that he had nothing to do. He was retired, and that was not going to change. The work that would normally be open to him was not being offered. Each of his approaches had been met with very polite 'we are not looking for anyone at the present time'. He knew what that meant - they were not looking for *him*. During one call, he had actually been asked about the 'werewolf squad'. His retort that they had been investigating eastern European organised crime; not indulging in fantasy, had not answered the question asked. But he understood. No one would touch him. He knew the 'werewolf squad' would remain with him forever and there was not a damn thing he could do about it.

The mobile phone in his pocket started to ring. He glanced at the clock on the mantlepiece above the open fire. It was nearly nine in the evening. His face lit up with a smile as he read Mike Dear's name on the screen.

"Mike, how the devil are you?" Sean sat forward and placed the empty mug on the small coffee table.

"Hiya, yeah, not too bad."

"What have you been up to since I last heard from you?"

"You mean since we spoke on the phone earlier? Yeah, loads!" Sean knew Mike was making a joke.

"Yeah, yeah, whatever," Sean replied, smiling.

"Yeah, some of us have work to do, not spending our days lazing about and enjoying a life of leisure, you know."

"I will have you know I have been busy today, myself," Sean retorted defensively.

"Yeah, right…visit every coffee shop in Belfast and try to consume as much coffee as possible in one day?" Mike was being sarcastic, and Sean knew it. He missed this kind of banter.

"Well, after my business meeting this morning, I took in the National Trust site at Minowburn, so yes, I've been out and about." There was a small laugh from Mike.

"Anyway," Mike continued, "the reason I am phoning…"

Sean sat back in the armchair, "You've hit a brick wall in your investigation and want my advice and guidance to help you out of a pickle…again." There was another laugh from Mike.

"No, I have info on that fella you met this morning." This made Sean sit up straight.

"Really? That was quick," he replied.

"Yeah …. Are you sitting comfortably?" Mike asked, and Sean knew this was going to be important information.

"Yeah, go for it … who is he?" Sean asked. Mike was obviously reading from whatever was in front of him.

"Right, Rupert James Baskerville, 27th Earl of Baskerville Hall," Mike paused.

"Sounds like the Sherlock Holmes novel," Sean said.

"Yeah, apparently that book was based on a farmhand who brought a big dog over from Europe. Turns out it had rabies, then started attacking people."

"Based on real events," Sean started to laugh at his own joke.

"Yeah, how many times have we heard that, *based on real events* and it is nothing like what actually happened." Mike joined in.

"So, what else do we know about him?" Sean asked, and Mike continued,

"Well, he certainly has quite the background. He was in Two One SAS, the Special Forces Reserves for over twenty years; got to the rank of Major."

"Well done, him," interjected Sean.

"It appears he had to."

"Why, 'had to'?" Sean asked.

"It was in his grandfather's will that, in order for him to get the full inheritance, that is what he had to do," Mike replied.

"That sort of thing still goes on, does it?" Sean inquired.

"For the gentry, apparently, yes."

"What else?" asked Sean. "So far this is nothing really of interest to us."

"Well, the next bit might be," replied Mike.

"Why?"

"Listen to this... Apparently, over one hundred and fifty years ago, a group of travellers from 'a far land' arrived and promptly set themselves up on the northernmost part of the Baskerville estate, which then started a feud."

"Travellers? Like gypsies?" Sean asked.

"No, nothing like travellers today, this lot arrived and decided they were *taking* the northern part of the estate. There was a long-running fight, which went on for years," Mike continued.

"What kind of fight?"

"The 'kind where people turn up dead' kind of fight .... It seems the 25th Earl formed his own little 'band' and took the fight to them ... it went on for years."

"And why is this of interest to us?" Sean asked the obvious question.

"Well, legend has it ...." Mike started.

"I am not interested in legends Mike, I want facts!" Even though he was out of the police, it was still in his blood.

"Yeah ... yeah, I know, but I think I found out why he is interested in what was happening over here," Mike replied.

"Okay, go on..."

"It was reported in local newspapers, over a period of forty years, that the travellers were a pack of werewolves who had been chased out of continental Europe and managed to escape to southern England; and his Earlship's grandfather ...."

"His title is Earl, he is addressed as 'Lordship'," Sean interrupted.

"Yeah, whatever," Mike chuckled at Sean's comment. Sean smiled, then went back to listening. "His grandfather managed to negotiate some kind of truce in 1940 as there was a real threat of invasion by the Germans at the time ... and the truce has stuck. This fella, Roger..."

"Rupert," Sean corrected.

"Rupert," Mike stated, "has been an open voice for some time about werewolf sightings and organising events trying to prove they are real. The events over here last year...." Mike paused.

"...Would be all he would need," Sean finished off the sentence.

"Yeah, he's made it clear he wants them recognised. Then he can drive them from his family's land, once and forever."

"That sounds like a quote," Sean said.

"It is," Mike replied, "from press coverage of a local council meeting near his estate just over two years ago."

"I am beginning to see why he is so interested in our stuff." Sean did not notice that Mike didn't answer. He'd nearly said, 'police stuff, you're not a copper anymore', but had stopped himself. There was a slight pause before Mike continued.

"If he was to get copies of my statement about Simon's death..."

"Or any of the witness statements," Sean added.

"Precisely!"

"Then he could hold it up publicly saying PSNI has been investigating werewolf attacks!"

"And that is the last thing we need," Mike said resolutely.

"What happened to Dr Burns from the labs?"

"He was placed on early retirement with a massive gag order ... He is not allowed to speak to anyone about any cases he dealt with during his time there, including ours."

"Wasn't his paper disproved in the end?" Sean asked.

"Yeah, it got shredded by the yanks and the Chinese. I think it has destroyed his career, which is a pity."

"Why pity?" Sean asked.

"Okay, he was barking mad ... but he was good at what he did. He always wanted each murder he investigated prosecuted, and he would go out of his way to help ... He just went a bit left field with the last one." Sean heard Mike give a low chuckle.

"Yeah, that would do it."

"So, short version ..." Mike paused again, "I do not think our Earl is going to be a problem for us. Just stick to what was released and I doubt we will hear from him again," Mike said.

"Yeah, I doubt we will." Sean leaned forward, then propelled himself upwards. "In that case, it is time I made myself a coffee.... Are you two still coming around for dinner next weekend?"

"Next weekend?" Mike paused, "Yes, as far as I know that is still the plan." Sean smiled. It would be good to see Mike and his wife again. He knew the four of them would enjoy the evening together.

"Until then, Mike."

"Yes, see you then." Sean took the phone away from his ear and pressed the red button, then turned and headed towards the kitchen. It would soon be filled with the smell of strong coffee.

Mike turned and looked at Darren Forester, who had Alan Dukesby sitting beside him. Darren pressed a red button on the console, and they stopped recording the phone call that had just taken place.

"He isn't going to say anything," Mike stated, and Alan started to nod.

"I agree." Alan's accent seemed very out of place, compared with the two Belfast men.

"Well, I hope he doesn't," answered Darren, who looked over at Alan. "We just need to sort your Earl out next." Alan Dukesby gave Darren an iron look. Mike had only known them a short while and there was obvious history, but it was clear Baskerville also had history with Alan Dukesby.

"Life around here is seldom dull," Mike whispered. Neither heard him as they stood up and headed out of the control room.

∞∞∞∞

Kyle's eyes slowly opened. He was in the main bedroom of the farmhouse. He was lying on his back and Amanda was lying face down beside him. He could hear the sounds of people moving around the farm; every morning was a busy one here. But there was something about this place, something he could not explain; he felt comfortable, he felt safe; it did feel like home. Every day he learned something new about the running of a deer farm and the people who worked on it. It was a family way of life and had been for such a long time. Many of the older ones would openly speak about his father and his exploits; some funny, others serious, but all came with respect. Kyle wished he had known his father as well as these men and women had. He looked at his phone for the exact time. There was a message from Cara-Marie. He opened it, glanced at the invite for a coffee and then closed it. He would answer later. He thought over what he'd been told the evening before about this person called 'Tyler'.

She had been married to a sapien and they had moved to Canada. The marriage was outwardly a happy one. The sapien had known she was a wolf and kept her secret. She was out running when five Nocs had gone to the house. When she returned, the house was on fire and the police were there. Her husband's body was staked out in the back garden and with his heart cut out in some sort of ceremony. The police managed to recover the CCTV footage from their security cameras but were not able to identify the five young men. Tyler did not know them, but knew what they were; so, she hunted them down and killed them. That had been over twenty years ago. She moved to the Isle of Skye and bought a small holding and kept her favourite pets - capybaras. Kyle had to use his laptop to do an internet search for what they were: officially rodents, but the size of large dogs; they, lived in or near water, and made strange sounds. One by one, every member of the pack had been to see her for training, and the northern den was stronger for it.

Paul said she had known Kyle's father and was the only person who had ever beaten Carl O'Brien one on one. Paul had laughed at that. He also laughed when he recounted what Tony had said about cooking one of the capybaras for a barbeque.... she had kicked him in the head for it.

They had known for some time the Nocs wanted revenge on her for the ones she'd taken down in Canada, but they could never find her. Paul went on to explain there had been two female orphans, both young wolves who had been living with her; one called Catherine, and the other called Rhydian. Catherine had been killed in what was initially thought to be a quad bike accident. They found out very quickly the Nocs had discovered her and it was they who arranged the crash. The night after Catherine's funeral, they'd attacked her farm. They killed the animals outside and nearly got Tyler, but Rhydian helped, and they fought back. Tyler tied the four remaining vampires to posts on the fence in her back garden and drank coffee as the sun came up. She watched them burn. Rhydian told Paul they were screaming at her to kill them quickly, but she just sat there and drank her coffee. Rhydian had watched from the farmhouse, knowing how much Tyler hated them. That same day, Tyler had spoken with Paul and was already packing for a move. She chose Rathlin Island. She could not stay where she was. The Nocs had found her. They would be back, and in greater numbers. She could not fight them all, but she could definitely 'kick some ass', as his Canadian friends liked to say.

Kyle heard how Paul had made arrangements to send a security team over to protect Tyler and the young teenager during their move. The pack was there for them. The southern pack had been informed

25

but did not get involved - it was northern business and did not affect them. Kyle had to go to her. She could teach him how to control his wolf; this had to happen. If his wolf got out, he would have to be taken down. Paul had stated this several times. They could not have a wild or rabid wolf running around, or they would appear just as they'd been portrayed in so many werewolf films already. Kyle would make it happen. He felt an unusual ache as he got up and padded over to the shower. Amanda did not move. Today was going to be a long day. He could feel it in his bones.

Chapter 6

Cara-Marie looked at the clock on the wall. It was nearly lunchtime and she could feel her hunger growing. The morning had been a usual one, not overly busy but not dull either. They were still fending off news outlets from around Europe who mostly wanted to try and link the New Year's Day Murders, as they were now known, with the werewolf attacks last year. It was obvious they were not linked, but the conspiracy theories were certainly rampant on the internet. Some made her laugh, others made her angry, and some were just plain ridiculous. She became aware Mark had just spoken to her. She turned her head, so she was looking straight at him.

"I didn't think you were listening," he said, as he went back to studying his monitor.

"What?" she asked. His eyes darted over towards her, then back at his screen.

"I said, let me know when you have finished the story of the classic car show at the weekend, then we can do an early lunch." She relaxed and looked back at what she had written. The 'Mini Owners Club' had their annual meeting at Portstewart at the weekend. There had been over 7,000 people in attendance, most driving their classic Mini cars from the 1960's and 1970's. Every owner of a Mini had to be able to quote from their favourite film from the 1970's about a gold robbery in Italy. Mini Coopers had been used in the film as getaway cars and it was a must-watch for every new Mini owner. Cara-Marie did a short interview with a retired firefighter from Lisburn. He had over twenty years' service but was retired through illness. She towered over the short man, who was losing his hair. He could not contain his excitement when she asked him about the immaculate car he was standing beside.

"She is 'British racing green'," he smiled broadly. "The chrome is original from the factory." He was very proud of his clean car. She had been introduced to the short woman at the far side of the car who was smiling but seemed more aware of the cold than he was. "My wife loves coming to these just as much as I do," he stated. Cara-Marie noted the small smile on the wife's face. She doubted that and continued to ask about the car. "She is a classic 1973 Mini Cooper ..." Cara-Marie had been scribbling down notes, most of which meant nothing to her, but she could see the joy and excitement in the interviewee. That interview made up most of the article on the screen. She added more details from the press release that had been put out prior to the event, and the article was done. She saved it in the editor's dropbox. They could then add all the photos Mark had taken. Most of those who'd attended would just be looking at the pictures and not really reading her words. That done, she could concentrate on the story she really wanted to work on. Her phone beeped with a text message. Her eyes widened as she saw Kyle's name on the screen.

"So, still with the new boyfriend then?" Mark was smiling as he pushed his chair closer to her. He had spotted the name, as well.

"He *isn't* my boyfriend," she replied.

"Not through lack of trying," Mark replied, just as a notebook hit him in the side of his head. Cara-Marie pressed the button on the phone as she stood up. She pulled her thick coat from the back of the chair. Mark started to do the same. It was a short message. 'JUST HEADING AWAY FOR A FEW DAYS BUT LIKE THE SOUND OF A COFFEE WHEN I GET BACK.' She read the message a second time, then pushed the phone into her pocket without replying. She would do that later. She wanted to know where he was going. He had already told her about leaving the police. Well, that was to be expected once you'd inherited a multi-million-pound business. Traipsing around Coleraine in the rain would just never match up. She began to zip up her coat. Mark was following behind her, but as they got to the back door, Kevin, the ever-present editor, appeared in the doorway of his office.

"Oi! You two," he motioned with his head that he wanted them to come into his office. Cara-Marie and Mark just looked at each other.

"Lead on, conqueror; your quest awaits." Mark bowed towards Cara-Marie and swept his hand towards the open door of the office.

"Oh, for God's sake, grow up, man." Cara-Marie barged past him and stomped towards the office door, Mark right behind her. She walked in and stopped in front of the desk. Mark stood beside her, and Kevin looked up.

"Right, I just heard that one of the bodies from the New Year's Day murders has gone missing from the morgue." He was looking at the screen of his desktop, and the landline phone on his desk started to ring. He looked up at the two of them. Both looked shocked. "Get onto all your sources. This is not public knowledge yet. I want everything you can find on this, and Cara ..." he paused. She was already fumbling for the phone in her pocket,

"Yes," she looked up.

"I want confirmed sources, exact details and people willing to appear in print." She nodded. She knew what she was being told. "And Mark..." Mark looked up, awaiting instructions. "I want recent pics of him, etc.... you know what to do, right?" Mark nodded.

"Um..." Cara-Marie butted in.

"What?" Kevin asked, his face showing annoyance.

"Do you know the name of the body that's gone missing?" she asked, "That would be a massive start for us." Kevin turned back to his screen as he reached for the still ringing handset. He read, "Yeah .... Kris Martin," as he lifted the handset and brought it to his ear. "Editor!" He looked at the two of them and, with his eyes, ordered them out of the office. "Yeah hi, Debbie, long time no hear ... how are things in Birmingham?" Cara-Marie closed the door to the office behind her.

"Well," Mark started, "so much for lunch." Cara-Marie walked back to her desk. Her own mobile was in her hand and she was scrolling through the names. Stopping at one, she looked at Mark, who was taking off his coat. "What?" he asked.

"If anyone can find out, she will." she held the now ringing phone to her ear.

"Who will?" Mark asked as Cara-Marie landed back on her chair.

"Hi Fiona, it's me ...... yes I am good ...... how are things with you? ..." Mark hung his coat on the back of his chair and reluctantly dropped himself back into it. Cara-Marie was now chatting away as he logged back into his desktop computer. His ears perked up when she started asking about the reason for the phone call. "Yes, we just heard ... that fella, Martin ... yes .... Disappeared? Really? ..... When was that??" Her face suddenly scrunched up, then she spoke loudly, without meaning to, "What? Two days ago? ...'any idea who took it?" Cara-Marie sat forward and placed her elbows on her desk. She was listening to every word from whoever 'Fiona' was. It was not a name he recognised. "Really? ... wow ... when? ... oh, my God! ... are you sure? .... that is astounding ..." Mark continued to listen, but she had now reduced to 'Mm...uh-huh... wow...err'.

Mark's monitor came to life, as the conversation beside him continued, "Well, I can get to Belfast this afternoon, if you like..." There was a smile on her face, he had seen it before - she was onto something and she knew it. "Okay, tomorrow is good for me, as well ..." 'Fiona obviously had work to do today. "Yes, same place as before? Great, what time best suits you?" she was nodding, and an excited smile broke over her face as she hung up and dropped the phone on her desk. Sitting back, she kicked the chair so it spun around to face Mark. He looked over his shoulder at her.

"Okay, who is 'Fiona'?" he asked. Cara-Marie picked up a pen and tapped it on her teeth. She was grinning.

"She works in the forensics lab. She's given me stuff before; we went to uni together!" Mark paused his typing and thought for a moment.

"Didn't she work for that mad doctor down there?" he asked.

"The very same," she replied.

"And wasn't it she who got you those reports about werewolf DNA and bits?"

"The very one," she was triumphant, as she spun around again.

"And wasn't that the doctor whose research was completely rubbished and nearly got himself committed?" Mark raised his eyebrows as he spoke. She sat up in her chair and nodded. Mark looked at his screen. "Will she go public with whatever she has?" he asked.

"Probably not," she replied.

"So, after what Kevin has just said ... what have you actually got?" he asked. She smiled before answering,

"I have a police investigation that is going on after a body was stolen with no signs of a break-in. In fact, it looks more like a break-out, from what she just said. I am going to find out everything tomorrow afternoon." She was still smiling. Mark smirked.

"Rearrange these words into a well-known phrase: 'Chase, Goose, Wild'," he said, and turned back to his keyboard.

"Rearrange these words into a well-known phrase: 'Off, Piss, Can, you'." She turned back to her desk just as an empty paper cup passed in front of her face. Her eyes darted over to Mark who was innocently working away with an 'it could not possibly have been me' look on his face. The hole punch that flew past him only missed by a small margin. He glanced over at the very busy journalist who was engrossed in her work. The notebook did hit her on her right shoulder. Mark was typing faster than he ever had before, as an accurately aimed stapler connected with his ear.

∞∞∞∞

He was cold; his whole body was cold. He wrapped his arms around himself and curled up into a ball to try to reduce the shivering. His eyes slowly opened. The morning light was blasting through the windows and the holes in the walls of the old barn. He was lying on straw near some hay bales, but it was of no comfort to him. The ground was covered in mud, but it was dried mud; the cattle from the farm had not been in here in a couple of days.

His mind flashed, his body shook. The fingers of his right hand slowly made their way up and felt his neck, finding the broad scars from the wound. Images flashed in his mind from the night it happened; the way the one with the American accent had suddenly lunged at him. He had tried to fight him off but couldn't; had felt his own strength fade as this man had bitten him; had felt his own arteries burst into the mouth of the American. He could hear the screaming of the others at the shapes that had emerged from the darkness. The darkness. How quickly the darkness had come; but so had the cold. He had woken up in a cold, white room, so confused. What had just happened to him? His body was so cold. He was lying on a metal table and he was naked. Ryan was on another table beside him - his face was marble-white, his lips had changed to grey. The life had gone from him; Ryan wasn't there anymore. He had found a plastic bag with clothes that were not his and dressed hurriedly. It had come quickly, the fear. The fear was there, he had to get away from here. He panicked. Then the darkness came again. He remembered running, running across a field, it had been cold, so cold and now he was here. The fear and the panic returned as his fingers jumped away from his neck. This could not be...confusion reigned as he turned over and tried to warm himself.

"Good morning." The accent was American, and his eyes darted to where he was standing. The American was staring at him. The fear returned. It was the same American who'd attacked him. He was confused; what was happening?

"Get up!" Kris felt compelled to do what he said. He was still shaking as he forced himself to stand up.

"Okay," Kris's answer was tentative.

"Do you know who you are?" The American's question was direct.

"What? Err ... ... yeah."

"Good, tell me what happened?" The American was staring at him. Kris dropped his gaze to the ground.

"I ... err..." Kris's mind fought for the words to try and describe the flashes of memories, "...woke up in a mortuary ... err ..." How could he rationally describe what had happened? "...and... everyone I was with up at the Strand was lying around me... dead, aahh." The American just stared, "...pretty panicked and ...." Kris looked around him. The American did not move, he just listened. "...and, ah .... just grabbed any clothes that were there, and ... ..."

"Do you know what you are?" the question stopped him. *What he was?*

"No," he blurted quickly. The American moved slowly to the side of the barn, as he spoke,

"You have joined a family with a long past. It has a remarkable history." The American glanced over at him. Kris had stopped shaking.

"That seems strangely ... familiar," he stated.

"Yes," the American smirked, "we have a family bloodline that goes back centuries. You have now joined this family ... you are now a member of our coven."

"Coven? What coven?" Kris asked.

"You are no longer the man you once were; you are no longer sapien-kind; you have become one of us .... you are now Noctrailis!"

"What?" The American smirked again, before leaning up against the side of the barn and folding his arms. The smile remained on his face.

"Most have a strange idea about us, the film industry in Hollywood ... you were a homo-sapien. Some call us 'homo-noctrailis' but that is incorrect ..." Kris was still confused; his mind was racing at what he was hearing; this could not be! The American continued, "To give us our correct title, we are 'Noctrailis Vampiri'. The smile spread across his face as Kris fought with the words.

"So, ... I'm .... a ..." he paused before he finished the sentence, "...a vampire?" his own face contorted with the words. The American glanced around the barn, then looked back at him.

"That is what some call us, yes."

"I don't really .... um..."

"The makeup of your blood has changed," the American continued to explain. Kris was still confused. "Normally, with what happened to you, sapiens die ..."

"I should have died?" Kris asked.

"Normally, yes," Kris stepped back, the words hitting him like boulders. "but when we heard you had awoken.... that filled me with great joy." Kris stared at the smile beaming back at him.

"But .... how did I survive .... what you did to me?"

"Your blood changed, and. You joined our coven." That didn't answer his question.

"It seems strange ... to me ... to join ..."

"Well, Hollywood calls us 'Vampires' .... like Latin, but it isn't. It is a dialect of old Russian, 'Noctrailis-Vampiri'." Kris still looked confused. "'The man who walks by night'," the American continued. Kris just stared. "You are one of us, now!" Kris turned slightly and tried to walk away, but his feet stopped after a short distance. The voice of the American brought him back. "You *are* one of us and we will bring you into our family. We will show you how to sleep. We will show you where we walk." Kris turned his head as the American repeated, "You are one of us now."

"Err, ...I just don't think ... I don't believe ..."

"Of course, you don't," the American cut him off. "Up until half an hour ago you thought that our kind was fake, that it was fantasy; you thought that *'you'* ..." the American pointed at him, as he spoke, "don't exist for real, only in films, and that it is *cool* to be one of us. They are the latest model: nice shirts, nice ties, going around casually, everyone is gorgeous. Life is not like that, at all."

"None of that is true, then?" Kris asked.

"Look in a mirror!" came the quick reply.

"Ha, fair point ... are *any* of the myths true?" Kris asked.

"What has happened to you is this: ... You are now infected with a blood disorder called haematophagia."

"What?" Kris was even more confused now.

"Haematophagia is a condition in which drinking blood is part of the dietary requirements of the subject. It is found in nature when mammals and creatures have to survive by drinking blood. I have some good news ... and some bad news for you... Which do you want first?"

"The bad news." Kris felt himself sink at the thought of what he was going to be told next.

"Your body can no longer produce enough red blood cells; it can no longer produce, or store, vitamin C or vitamin D." Kris looked around the barn, his mind trying to process everything he was being told, and tried to imagine how this all would affect him. "At the moment, as you are recently turned, you can still go out in sunlight, which is good news for me because, for the immediate future, I can use you to do tasks in daylight. For a time anyway, you will not be harmed by ultra-violet light."

"So, I, ... will ... get burned?"

"Not yet, but given time, yes."

"But ...."

"But your body will, unfortunately, change." Kris looked down at his feet as the American continued, "Do not believe the myths - you are not immortal, you cannot turn into a bat, you cannot fly; your lifeline has just been reduced by a third."

"What?" Kris looked up, shocked.

"You have twenty, possibly twenty-five years before you die."

"Aah, okay." Kris fought hard to understand, "...Strange. I thought ..."

"Your body now degenerates. It cannot produce what it needs to survive, which is why you have to take in. You have to drink ... you have to feed ... almost daily ..." Kris looked up again. This was not him; he did not do these things.

"What do I feed on?" He already knew the answer, but he had to ask.

"Blood,"

"From where?"

"You now have to hunt the kind of person you used to be," Kris shook his head,

"I have to hunt humans?"

"Sapiens, only *they* call themselves 'human'."

"I can't get it from animals?"

"The type of red blood cells you need are only found in sapiens. Animals are nice for a treat, but you cannot live off them." The American looked around the barn, then focused back on Kris. "Sapiens are now your cattle, they are now your prey. We will show you how to hunt, how to kill, and ..." the American glanced down at his feet then looked back up, "we will show you what to do with what is left."

"So, feeding will increase my life?" Kris was fighting for a way out.

"If you don't ..." and Kris's eyes widened, "you will be dead in less than two weeks." His eyes fell to the ground.

"Wow, I ... ." his voice trailed off.

"You will still have to eat; you will still have to take on nourishment. Your body still needs food and fuel. Blood is not the only source of this, but your lifeline, the very thing that keeps you alive ... is blood." Kris took a step back, slowly shaking his head as the American continued. "And there is only one way to get that now."

"I think ..." Kris started, but the door of the barn opened, and a tall blonde woman appeared, dragging a scruffy young male by the back of his collar along the ground. "Hey, I know you ..." Kris pointed towards her as she dropped the teenager in the middle of the floor of the barn. She looked at the American, who motioned with his right hand towards the barn door. She turned and closed it behind them, shutting them in. "...you were on Portstewart Strand at the new year, as well!" Kris looked down at the obviously drunk teenager. He was looking around, his words slurring incoherently. Suddenly Kris realised what was about to happen, and he was afraid.

"Yes, this is Sabine and yes, you have met before," explained the American. Sabine took off her outdoor jacket and tossed it to the side. Kris looked her up and down: brown leather walking boots, blue jeans and a dark cotton top. She wasn't wearing any jewellery. She smiled at the American, who spoke to her in a language Kris did not understand. Then, Sabine stepped forward. "Watch," the American said. "We have something to show you." Kris looked over as the American moved to the far side of the barn. "You are to watch closely, do not divert your eyes; pay attention, you are looking at a master." Sabine smiled at the comment and placed her hands on her hips. The American folded his arms and started speaking again, in the odd language. Kris was confused - he had heard many different languages but nothing like this.

"What is that?" he asked, as the American and Sabine looked at him, then at each other.

"You will learn it one day ... it is the ancient language of our kind."

"We have used this language for centuries," Sabine stated. Kris looked at the beautiful woman standing there; her hair was tied back in a ponytail and she had an almost perfect body. Surely, she could not be one of these? She looked over at the American and spoke in the strange language. The American nodded. Sabine looked at Kris and opened her mouth. Kris could only stare as the incisor teeth in her upper gum started to move... not much, but they moved, and became longer. She breathed through her nose as she fixed her gaze on Kris.

Suddenly, she threw herself on top of the teenager, like an animal pouncing on its prey. Kris was shocked by the speed and force of the attack. The teenager tried to fight back but was overpowered in seconds. He yelped like an injured puppy, and after a few seconds, his body went limp. Sabine's head was attached to the right side of his neck. The teenager's legs and arms were pinned to the ground as her head started to move in a slow, rocking motion. Kris felt his feet move. Slowly, he walked around what was happening in front of him, his eyes transfixed. He stopped when he could see her face. Her eyes were closed, her face alight with ecstasy. The teenager's eyes had rolled to the back of his head. Sabine moaned; Kris was mesmerized. He did not notice the American walk forward.

"Welcome to the coven, Kris. Now you know what you are - you are a hunter."

Chapter 7

The road into Ballycastle had been quiet until he entered the town, where the streets were suddenly filled with bumper to bumper traffic. Kyle slowly made his way past the marina on his right and into the small car park next to the ferry terminal. Over to his right, in the distance, he could make out the island of Rathlin. He had never been there before and wondered what lay ahead.

He drove around and found the last available parking space, reversing into it. He retrieved his rucksack from the back of the car and walked towards the single-storey terminal. Parked cars lined the route as he approached. The double doors were around the side, facing the main road which led into the car park. Outside the doors, there was a wooden bench, and on it sat two teenage girls, engrossed in their mobile phones. Neither looked up as he approached. Kyle glanced at the markings on the road that led away from the terminal towards the jetty: *Foot pas x only*, the yellow painted letters were between the marked path for foot passengers. He glanced around, then walked inside. On the wall to his right were several maps; most were of the northwest and a larger one was of Northern Ireland. All had marked out places of interest and tourist destinations.

Kyle walked up to the counter. The middle-aged man seated behind the clear plastic screen did not look up. Kyle ordered a single ticket, and the man leaned forward and tapped at a keyboard. Pushing the ticket under the plastic towards Kyle, he nodded at the payment device that was attached to the side of the wall. Kyle paid and left without hearing the man utter a single word. He walked outside and followed the marked pathway towards the waiting ferry. The low cloud from earlier had lifted, and there were gaps where he could see the blue sky above. The red ramp of the small car ferry laid out like a large tongue protruding from the mouth of the blue-hulled ship. He followed a line of other foot passengers up the ramp where a member of the crew stood, dressed from top to bottom in luminous jacket and trousers. Kyle thought she looked about twenty. Her woollen hat was pulled down around her head so only her face was visible. She directed them to the door leading up to the passenger deck. He walked on.

The deck of the ship was painted red, and the sides, white; she was very clean and obviously well-maintained. The other passengers quickly found seats, but Kyle walked over to the side and stood by the rail. He could see over Ballycastle marina and off down the coast. It was beautiful. He had heard on a brief just before he'd left the police that there were location managers for a large American tv and film production company scouting about this area. They were interested in Ballintoy and its old harbour for a tv show; something about dragons and knights, set in the winter. Kyle wasn't interested in fantasy like that, his own life had turned the supernatural into reality, and dragons were just not something he wanted to entertain right now. The Inspector had told the officers if they met any of the production crew to be polite and courteous, but not to get involved in any discussions with them as things like that had to go through the station.

An alarm sounded, and the engines of the ship shuddered to life. He looked over the side at the wash roiling up at both ends of the vessel. Commands were shouted between the crew on the lower deck and the ship slowly moved away from the dock. Kyle glanced over the few cars that were on the lower deck and wondered why he had been told to leave his car and travel as a foot passenger.

The vessel turned and headed out of the small harbour. He was now looking down the coast towards the causeway. The clouds were high and, once the ferry was underway, the wind picked up. The strong smell of the sea that filled his senses, mixed with the wind in his face and gave him a feeling of freedom. He looked in the direction the ferry was headed; the island was slowly growing bigger and a smaller craft was heading towards them. He glanced back at Ballycastle - the stone walls of the harbour seemed darker than they had before. The tanoy of the ferry crackled to life; it was a message for the crew.

"Why didn't we bring our car, Daddy?" a young female voice asked. He glanced over at the child, who was leaning over the opposite side of the passenger area. Daddy was zipping up his thick outdoor jacket, trying to shelter from the wind.

"Only people who live on Rathlin are allowed to have cars there," 'the Daddy' answered Kyle's earlier thought. The child began to ask more questions about the vessel they were on, but Kyle was not listening anymore. The sea was relatively calm, as the small fishing boat passed them. There was a brief acknowledgement from one of its crew to the ferry, and they carried on their way towards Ballycastle. Kyle returned to his thoughts. Why was it so important for him to meet this woman? Everyone spoke of her with respect and awe. He had been told different stories about her feats; some, no doubt, had an element of legend added to them, enhancing the impressions, but the overall theme was one of loss and vengeance against the Nocs for what they had done to her family.

The island grew closer. The edges of the cliffs rose straight up, in dark contrast with the blueness of the sea. Different shades of green cultivation covered the tops of the cliffs. As they drew closer, he could see that parts of the cliffs were white, like a darker shade of chalk. Bobbing between the ferry and the white cliffs was a large marker. The base was black and the top, yellow. There were two large black arrowheads pointing down towards the base. Kyle remembered from a sailing trip once that this was called a Cardinal, denoting a submerged danger. The arrows pointing down were indicating that it was safe to pass to the south of the marker. He smiled in surprise at the long-forgotten memory. The ferry slowed; they were approaching the small harbour on Rathlin island.

The marina housing the privately-owned boats was on the right as the ferry began the docking procedure. The other passengers started to make their way out on deck. The brisk wind had subsided as the vessel entered the small harbour. Ahead was a single road lined by a row of buildings: some were houses; others, small shops. A few people were gathered, waiting for the ferry. None fit the description he had been given of Tyler. The ferry shuddered and, as the engine died, he followed the last of the passengers. He took his rucksack off his shoulder and carried it in front of him until he was off the ferry. It would not fit through the narrow passageway, nor the hatches of the ferry, hanging on his side. He walked along the stone harbour wall, as other passengers were greeted by friends or relatives. The obvious tourists were armed with cameras, already recording as much of the island as they could. He walked on. The road ran from east to west. There was a low stone wall separating it from the harbour on his right as he walked along, perusing the single-story buildings on his left. They were a mix of tea shops and gift shops - tourism seemed to be the main industry here.

He took his phone out and tapped in a message announcing his arrival. He'd expected to be met and was annoyed. He scrolled through his phone to her name, saved as 'TYLER R', and pressed 'send', then replaced the phone in his pocket. He walked on, and the low wall gave way to a hedgerow. The narrow road was only wide enough for one vehicle at a time; obviously, there wasn't a lot of traffic. The bay curved around, and he glanced down at the small peninsula, clearly making out the only pub on the island, which was already busy. He moved to the side to allow a family with a pushchair to go past. They seemed to be in a rush, heading back towards the ferry.

The phone in his pocket bleeped; the message had clear instructions. 'FOLLOW THE ROAD FROM THE FERRY AND TAKE THE FIRST LEFT, CONTINUE ON THAT ROAD UNTIL YOU SEE THE FARM' There was no greeting, no 'Hi, sorry I could not get there', just instructions. Grudgingly, he moved forward, past a play area with swings and other apparatus for children to play on. The left turn was up ahead. The message had not said how far the journey was going to be, so he pushed his right arm through the strap of the rucksack and made it comfortable on his shoulders. His pace quickened as he set off - it couldn't be that far. His walk became a speed march as he turned and headed up the road. The sun was setting behind him and slowly the land started to darken with the approaching night.

∞∞∞

Cara-Marie was walking with purpose. The security guard at the supermarket had engaged her in conversation and again, she could not remember his name. She had seen several people there whom she had previously spoken with and, yet again, they all wanted to tell her about various things that were going on in their lives, none of which interested her. But that was part of her job. The New Year's Day murders were high on the topic of conversation, but most people just wanted to gossip; there was nothing she could use. She found out quite a bit about Kris Martin over the afternoon: he'd been living with a girl called Niamh and had been very vocal about gay rights in Northern Ireland for some time. Cara-Marie had found several interviews he'd given in the past, but that didn't seem a reason to have him killed. Judging from his injuries, it wasn't wolves either. This was something different.

She fumbled in her pocket for the keys and it seemed to take ages before the door of her flat slammed behind her. She turned on the light and struggled out of her outer coat. It would be several more minutes before the shopping was stored, the glass of wine poured, and she flopped down on the sofa. The tv burst into life. The glass of wine in her left hand was one of the larger glasses – 'size does matter' she had joked with one of the reception staff. 'No one wants a small glass of wine, now do they?' She sipped at it and let the taste swirl satisfyingly around in her mouth. The remote control in her right hand she flicked through the different channels and settled on a programme about families from the UK emigrating to Australia. It was not something she was interested in, but it was better than what was on the other channels, and she did not have to think about it too much. The phone in her pocket started to ring. She dropped the remote and placed the wine glass down on the coffee table. She had to move so she could get the phone out of the pocket of her jeans. She'd been expecting her mother and was surprised when she saw the name on the screen.

"Hi Fiona, aren't we meeting tomorrow?" she asked. The voice at the other end was subdued,

"Yes, yes we are ... Same place as before?" Fiona inquired. Cara-Marie sat upright; something was wrong.

"Yes, same place as before." She paused, then asked, "Are you okay?" There was a pause, and she could hear her friend breathing into the phone.

"Yes, all good." She knew instantly it was a lie but let her continue talking. "I just wanted to let you know before I see you tomorrow that I heard your name mentioned at work earlier." This made Cara-Marie sit up.

"Why? What was said?"

"Well, it was Dr Ferguson. You know, Dr Burns' replacement after ... well ... you know ...." Fiona let the comment hang in the air. Yes, she did know what had happened to Dr Burns. She did know that none of his former colleagues would even take calls from him anymore. All his research had been rubbished, and his career and reputation were in ruins.

"I can't say I know the man," she heard herself saying.

"Woman," replied Fiona.

"Pardon?"

"Dr Rachel Ferguson is a woman." Cara-Marie cursed herself. Of course, why not? "But anyway, that is why I am calling ..."

"Yes," Cara-Marie queried, "What was said?"

"Well," Fiona coughed, "we were having a staff meeting about what happened the other day with the missing body ...." Fiona began. Cara-Marie's earlier weariness had left her. This was the very subject she had wanted to talk to Fiona about, but face to face, not on the phone. "The police were back this afternoon and after they left, Dr Ferguson made mention of you and another journalist from the Telegraph. She said you were trying to find out what happened." Fiona paused, "So, we have all been advised if either of you approach us, we are to say nothing." Cara-Marie thought for a moment before answering.

"Well, isn't it a good thing that two friends from university had already arranged to meet up for lunch, or it may look a bit suspicious." Fiona got where she was going with this.

"Absolutely!" There was excitement in her voice now.

"So, we are still on for tomorrow, then?" Cara-Marie started to relax back onto her sofa.

"Yes, yes we are." She could almost hear her friend smiling down the phone.

"So, until tomorrow then."

"Until tomorrow." The phone in Cara-Marie's hand went silent, then she heard the dead tone when Fiona hung up. Cara-Marie stared at the blank screen and, using her thumb, she started to scroll through the numbers until she got to Mark's.

"What?" His voice sounded defeated.

"That is no way to answer a phone," she replied. There was a grunt back at her, "you're starting to sound like Kevin."

"Okay, I give in ... what has changed in the precious few hours since I saw you last?" he sounded downbeat.

"What is wrong with you?" she demanded.

"What?" His voice increased in volume.

"What is wrong with you?" she repeated. "You were fine earlier. What has happened between then and now?" Part of her didn't want to know. She had news for him!

"Well, if you must know," he replied. *'not really, but I did ask'*, she thought to herself, and he continued, "my pregnant ex was 'round with a list of demands ... none of which I can, or even want, to agree to. She is already threatening to take me to court." That suddenly made sense to her. Cara-Marie had not liked the way things had gone with his previous girlfriend. She had been shocked at the speed with which they'd split up and how quickly things had deteriorated between these two. The fact she hated Cara-Marie was only part of the equation. She lost count of the number of times she and Mark had been accused of sleeping together. It had gotten boring and tedious very quickly.

Mark started going over his earlier conversation; his ex wanted him to give her half the value of his flat; he had pointed out that they were not married and had not actually lived together; he wanted to be a part of the baby's life, but the soon-to-be mum and her parents were already saying that there would be no contact of any kind between father and child. This was going to end up in court - something he really did not want to happen, but he could see that it was going in that direction.

"They cannot stop you having access to your baby; you have right of access just as much as she does!" Cara-Marie exclaimed.

"Yeah, well, I will have to wait and see what happens." He was dejected and there was nothing she could do about it. "So, what were you ringing about?" he asked in an obvious change of subject tone. She had to think for a second before she answered.

"Oh, yes. You know I am meeting Fiona tomorrow?" There were a few seconds of silence before Mark spoke.

"Sorry, I give in, who is Fiona? And do I know her?" he asked.

"Err, my source from the forensics lab who I am meeting for lunch tomorrow in Belfast!" She paused, then continued, "I did tell you earlier."

"Really? ... Yes, I think you said something earlier about it ...." Mark was not in a good place, so she let it go this time without the verbal ribbings she would normally have given him.

"Yes, well she phoned me a few minutes ago."

"So?" Mark asked.

"It was to say that they have all been warned about speaking to me." There was a hint of excitement in her voice, but Mark's voice remained neutral.

"I warn people not to speak to you all the time," There was a brief chuckle from him, which she thought was good.

"Yeah, I wish that worked. Pity, it seems that everyone walking around Coleraine wants to speak to me - all at the same time, in fact."

"You cannot account for taste." he retorted. "So, they were told not to speak to the press. What is different about that?" he asked. She stared ahead, as if he was sitting in front of her.

"Don't you see? Something has happened, and they want to keep it out of the public eye." A smile spread across her face as she finished speaking.

"They have lost a body from a multiple murder and it makes them all look bad!" His put down made her sit back on the sofa - she had not thought about that.

"Or maybe they are trying to hide something, something important," she replied.

"Like losing a body. Mmm, yeah, I can see it now." She was feeling deflated. He was right, it could be as simple as that.

"But what if it isn't?" she asked.

"Then, when you meet ... what is her name again?"

"Fiona!"

"When you meet Fiona again, you can ask her!" he was right.

"Anyway, if Kevin or any of the others ask, can you remind them where I am?" It was a simple request.

"Didn't you book out in his dropbox?" Mark asked.

"Yes.... but since when does he look at his own calendar?" she replied. There was a short chuckle down the phone.

"Yeah, fair one."

"'Til tomorrow then," she said.

"Aye, see you then." With that, the line went dead. Cara-Marie dropped her phone on the sofa, turned up the volume of the tv and lifted the glass of wine. Mark had been right, it could just be something as simple as that but, she thought to herself, what if it isn't? The question intrigued her, and she refilled her large wine glass.

Chapter 8

Tony was sitting at one end of the sofa in his living room, looking outside over the landscape. The weather had closed in and he knew there was a storm coming tonight. He had spoken with Paul earlier. The decision not to take Kyle down south was probably a good one, and he had chosen to drive himself over to Rathlin. Tony looked over at the entrance to the room. Karen was slowly walking in with two steaming mugs. She looked scruffy, her hair wasn't tied back, and she wasn't wearing any make up... none. She had not smiled properly for months. Christmas had been an issue. Her family all descended on their place and everyone was asking how she was after the miscarriage. They kept asking about the one subject she did not want to talk about. That all stopped near dinnertime on Boxing Day when she finally exploded. He hadn't heard her shout and scream like that in years; a plate of food was smashed against the far wall, as it all came out of her.

The false happy atmosphere was gone. She had been almost hysterical. He'd not been in the kitchen when it started – he'd been in the living room with her dad. It took some time for everything to calm down. Most of the family left soon afterwards, but her parents had stayed overnight and left after breakfast the following day. They had laid on top of their bed and he held her. She wept for over an hour before finally drifting off to sleep. She would say later, 'in your arms is the only place I feel safe anymore'. Tony repeatedly told her no one would ever harm her again, and she knew he meant it; and so did the Pack. The Pack was there for them - a security team stayed around the house until after the Mongols had finally been dealt with. Some of the girls helped with the household jobs and the shopping. Two of the guys offered help but she had joked with them, 'What do you know about housework? I have seen inside your farmhouse!' She appreciated the offer but at that exact moment, apart from Tony, she felt more comfortable in the company of other women.

They went to the Christmas Moon Dance but had not stayed long. It was Christmas, so there was no hunt. Tony thought at the time that Kyle had handled it well. Amanda was all over him and let every woman in the room know to not even try and approach without her being there. She had clearly marked her territory, and the thought made him smile. Tony's wife walked towards him, smiled, and held out the mug. "I thought you would like some tea." It was her old familiar smile, but there was still a sadness in her eyes. Tony felt his soul turn; he hated seeing her like this, but this feeling, this process, was going to take time. It was time he would gladly give her. He sat forward and extended his hand, smiling at her.

"Yes, that's great, thanks," he took the mug, and she sat down beside him. Tony sipped at the hot liquid, closing his eyes. Karen got herself comfortable and tucked her bare feet under her legs, leaning into him as she did so. Tony sat back and lifted his right arm, allowing her to snuggle in. She rested her head on the side of his chest.

"I love listening to you breathing," she said softly.

"Yeah, I am taking that as a good sign .... It's when you want me to stop breathing, I should begin to worry!" She lifted her head and the two of them shared a laugh. She could relax around him. Sipping her tea, she looked out the large window,

"It looks like there's a storm coming."

He surveyed the darkening landscape, "Yeah, just in time for Kyle's little trip over to meet Tyler." Karen looked up at him,

"He has gone to Scotland?"

"No, she just moved over to Rathlin. She's setting up her little training camp there. Apparently, the old farm she found is ideal!"

"On Rathlin Island?" Karen sat upright.

"Yeah," Tony replied.

"Why the move? Did she finally get sick of living in the middle of nowhere?" Karen snuggled back into Tony.

"They found her."

"Who did?"

"The Nocs." Tony felt his wife's body react.

"But she is obviously alright?"

"Yeah, not totally sure what happened but, from what I heard, five of them attacked her wee place and one of the orphans helped her fight them off." Tony was smiling as he spoke.

"Did she bring those funny dog things with her?" Karen asked.

"Her capybaras? No, the Nocs killed them first; and they are not dogs, they are actually rodents from South America."

"They were the same size as dogs."

"And she loved them like dogs."

"I bet that pissed her off."

"Well," Tony took another sip of tea before he continued, "legend now has it that once she fought them off, she tied the four that were left to posts in her back garden, drank coffee and watched the sunrise." Karen raised herself up and looked at him. There was a real look of happiness there, and she did not have to ask him what happened to the vampires. For a second, she had a mental picture in her head of Tyler drinking coffee as they screamed and burned.

"Wow, that girl can still *kick some ass!*" She smiled as she spoke.

"Yeah, she was the only one I ever knew of who beat Carl hand to hand,"

"I still wish I could have seen her kick you around for wanting to barbeque her pets."

"Well, I never said it again!" Tony joked.

"So, our new Alpha has his hands full, then?" she asked. Tony slowly placed the mug on the floor with his left hand and turned his head, so he was directly in front of her.

"Yes, he has. But I am sure he can handle her." Karen smirked at what he had said.

"I wonder how long it will be before she makes his nose bleed."

"Not long, probably." Tony smiled, as Karen sat upright and reached towards the floor.

"I found something and thought of you," she said. He lifted his arm out of the way.

"Err, okay." He had no idea what she meant. She picked up a small book, he couldn't see the title on the cover so tilted his head, trying to read the words. "Poetry?" he asked. She looked meaningfully at him when she found the page she'd been searching for.

"Yes, now sit back and listen." She sat upright and composed herself before she started to speak. Tony looked at this amazing woman, who spoke softly as she started to read. It was a poetry book. She made the words dance. Tony could feel his heart thumping inside his chest; the hair on his arms stood up. She took a soft breath, and Tony hung onto every word. "If there were such a man as this ..." she looked over at him and finished reading, "he'd win my heart and have my kiss." He looked straight into her eyes. He could feel his emotions building as he moved towards her, stopping only inches away from her face.

"I love you," he whispered, she pulled a funny face back at him.

"Well, you'd better, or this marriage is in serious trouble." The two of them laughed with each other. Tony brought his right hand up and gently caressed her cheek with the tips of his fingers. She closed her eyes as he did so. He carried on past her ear and around the back of her head, pushing her hair back over her shoulder. He could feel himself well up inside as he closed his eyes, slowly leaned forward and placed his lips on hers.

∞∞∞

Kyle followed the unlit road, darkness enveloping him. There was no traffic. The only sounds were those of the wind and the ocean crashing onto the rocks over to his right. He could not see beyond the countryside to the edge of the island, but he knew it was not far away. The road made a sharp left turn which, if he had been in a car, he may have missed. He passed through a metal gate which opened to a dark field. He could hear the sound of the ocean. He paused and looked around; there was a small light on a building in the distance, but this was not what he was looking for. He carried on. His pace quickened, the weight of his rucksack having no effect on his speed. It was not quite a speed march, like he had done so many times in the Legion, but he wanted to get there now. The sides of the road were lined with stone walls which, in the darkness, looked like they had not been put together by a stone mason, but by someone just building a barrier to their land.

The road continued; a small building with no lights came into view on the right side of the road. This was in a different field, and the wall was a more modern one. It was higher and had been cemented together, unlike the previous field. He came to the T junction at the end of the road. He read Tyler's message again – JUST FOLLOW THE ROAD. Tony mentioned the farm was near a lighthouse. The road signs pointed in both directions, but 'East Lighthouse' directed him to the right. He headed in that direction. The quality of the road diminished as it became a country lane. Kyle could smell the purple heather as the wind blew past him. His nose filled with other smells of the island: the sea, the gorse. He stopped to take it in and smelled animals - he had no idea what kind, but something had been there recently. The road rose up a small hill and, in the distance, the lighthouse came into view. The brilliant light cut through the darkness, scanning out to sea.

Suddenly a small row of lights came on, lighting up the lane to the farm that had been in darkness. As he was looking at it, several more lights came on. This was the place. His phone buzzed with the arrival of a text message. He reached into his pocket and looked at the name on the screen: 'Tyler R'. He pressed the green button and the light of the phone lit up his face. It was a simple message - GOOD YOU FOUND US.

Kyle looked at the front door that was only illuminated by a small light. There were no obvious security systems in place, but he guessed there must be. He did not reply but closed the phone down and headed towards the door. He could not see anyone, but he knew at least one person was watching him approach. He glanced over at the 4 x 4 which was parked beside the house, facing back down the lane. It looked new and clean. Reaching out to press the doorbell, he was surprised as the thick wooden door swung inward.

The exterior lighting illuminated him where he was standing. As the door opened, he noted the interior was in darkness. Their security was good. Around the door, the face of a girl slowly emerged. She had a round face that looked at him through dark- rimmed glasses. Long, straight, fair hair hung over the teenage face. Her dark blue eyes stared at him, and she kept her body behind the door. She did not speak.

"Hi," he paused. There was no reaction from the teenager. "I believe you are expecting me?" he heard himself say. The door slowly moved back, and she stepped around it. A smile spread over her face. It was a smile that lit up her eyes. She held out her right hand, and he stepped forward through the doorway, taking her hand in his. She had an extraordinarily strong grip - stronger than one would expect from someone so young.

"Hello," she smiled as she spoke, "I'm Rhydian." He stepped forward and she moved to the side, allowing him to move past her, then closed the front door.

"Hello," he repeated back towards her, "I'm Kyle." He looked into her eyes and she nodded in acknowledgement.

"Yes, I know. Mum said." She turned and headed into the hallway. She was wearing a plain, baggy sweatshirt, which was far too large for her, and jeans. She wore fluffy slippers on her feet. She was only slightly shorter than he was, and she was stocky but neither thin nor fat. She had an exercised body which reminded him of a rugby player's; strong, yet subtle.

Down the hallway, he saw outdoor coats hanging on hooks on the right-hand side and cardboard boxes waiting to be unpacked, on the left. She reached up and flicked a switch, lighting up the hallway. She stopped halfway and looked back over her right shoulder, "Well, come on then, Mum's in the kitchen." She nodded her head towards the end of the hallway. She had not offered to take his bag - there was no submissiveness here. She turned and led the way; he was expected to follow.

Chapter 9

Cara-Marie looked up at the sky over Belfast City Hall. It had rained, earlier, and the clouds were slowly separating. The darkness of the night sky above contrasted with the greyness of the cumulus clouds. She studied the people around her. They walked by, engrossed in their own worlds and, for a moment, she wondered what was going on in their lives... what struggles did each one had? An older man shuffled by the front gate of the massive building. At the end of a leather leash was a small dog. Cara-Marie did not recognise the breed. The man was in a foul mood, constantly waving his arm and raising his voice at anyone who came too close. He wanted them all to stay away from his dog but, the way the dog was behaving, it just wanted to make new friends.

"Cara!" she spun around at the voice of her friend, who was coming towards her. Fiona was well-wrapped up; boots, dark trousers, a thick outdoor jacket and a small woollen hat that was pulled down so only her face was visible. Cara-Marie smiled in recognition, opening her arms, and the two friends shared an affectionate hug.

"Hi Fiona, how are you?" she asked. Fiona smiled back.

"Yeah, not bad," she replied. "Sorry you had to wait until I finished work. I just couldn't get away at lunchtime." Cara-Marie turned slightly towards City Hall, and the two began to walk.

"Not bad?" Cara-Marie asked, acknowledging only the first part of her comment. Fiona looked at her friend.

"Yeah, no point in complaining," she started, and the two friends spoke at the same time, "No one listens anyway!" They both laughed and bumped shoulders.

"So," Fiona started.

"So," Cara-Marie replied.

"So, tell me about your new guy!" Cara-Marie scrunched up her face at Fiona's question.

"There isn't a guy," she replied wistfully.

"Oh, I thought you had found someone?" Fiona looked at her friend; this was obviously not a comfortable subject.

"No, there was someone but that just turned out to be a few nights, either at mine or his." She looked at Fiona wryly, "His heart just wasn't in it." Fiona closed in towards her friend again.

"Sorry,"

"Pity, ... he was kind of cute," Cara-Marie looked up and shrugged.

"Kind of cute?" Fiona asked with a smile, and Cara-Marie smiled back.

"Okay ... he was gorgeous ... but his eyes were elsewhere," both smiles faded. "Anyway," Cara-Marie continued.

"Anyway," said Fiona, "the first thing you should know is that the family of the body that was taken will be doing a press conference this evening. They are going to make a public appeal to have the body returned."

"Really?" Cara-Marie exclaimed, and Fiona glanced over at her.

"Don't worry, no one knows about it yet. It was only decided this morning. We were advised just as the police were leaving the site." They slowly walked on. Cara-Marie had to ask,

"What were the cops doing there this morning?" Fiona looked over at her.

"Trying to find out how they got in, then out again. It is weird." Fiona paused. Cara-Marie did not speak as she let her friend do the talking. "There is no sign of a break-in, or break-out for that matter ... It's like he just walked out!"

"What about CCTV? Surely that showed something?" Fiona gave her a serious look. "What?" Cara-Marie asked.

"As it turns out, the cameras at the entrance and at the front are still real, but ..."

"But?" Cara-Marie asked.

"But all the ones around the rest of the outside are duds." Cara-Marie looked shocked. "Budget cuts, and no one is saying how long it has been like that." Fiona continued. The journalist in Cara-Marie went into overdrive; that, in itself, was a story. "But please don't say anything as we only got told yesterday, so if that comes out ... well, it's a short list of where the leak would be." Fiona gave her a look that reinforced what she was saying: *Do not use what I just said!* She nodded in agreement.

"So, someone," Cara-Marie started, glanced at Fiona, then finished her sentence, "could have gotten in and out without anyone noticing." Fiona nodded.

"But that isn't the weird thing," Fiona stated, Cara-Marie looked at her.

"What is the weird thing?" Cara-Marie asked, and Fiona frowned. She glanced around them both -even though there wasn't anyone nearby. Fiona lowered her voice.

"The body was the only one that hadn't had the post-mortem done on it; all the others had. Dr Ferguson was due to complete it the following morning." Fiona's eyes darted everywhere except at Cara-Marie.

"So, what was the official cause of death?" Fiona briefly looked at her, quickening her pace. "Well, all the others died of massive blood loss from traumatic injuries to their necks in which the main arteries were severed .... Death would have occurred in less than two minutes." Fiona had gone back to her *at work* formal voice.

"What was the cause?" Fiona looked down.

"Dr Ferguson is not sure, but it looks like a bite." Cara-Marie's eyebrows shot up.

"What? Like the Castleroe murders?" she tried not to sound excited, but she was. Fiona shook her head.

"No, no, they had massive trauma to nearly all parts of their bodies. These were different, totally different. Those were caused by an animal - the New Year's Day murders were different." Fiona walked on; Cara-Marie had to quicken her pace to catch up.

"How? How are they different?" she asked. Fiona glanced around uncomfortably.

"It's what she is saying caused the injuries," Fiona slowed down and looked at the ground.

"What is she saying?" Cara-Marie asked quietly, and Fiona looked up, almost in despair.

"Human ... they were human bites; the mouth structure was totally different from the casts from last year." Fiona shook her head. "Sorry, it isn't the wolves you are looking for. Even the police are saying the Coleraine/ Castleroe murders are not connected with the New Year's Day murders; plus, they are adamantly saying the Coleraine case is shut." Cara-Marie's mind was racing but, looking at her friend, she knew she did not want to carry on this conversation; plus, she had enough to go on, for now.

"Well, that can wait, and..." Fiona looked at her with a slightly puzzled look on her face.

"And what?"

"And since you have been banned from speaking to the press, but are not banned from meeting a friend for dinner, and ... it is my turn..." They both shared a smile, and Fiona nodded. They headed towards one of the side gates.

Now came the hard part...to find somewhere for dinner in Belfast that they both liked to eat at. Fiona did not notice that Cara-Marie had taken her phone out of her pocket and, keeping it by her side, scrolled to Kyle's name. She began to type a message with her thumb. The two old friends chatted as only old friends do. She would head to the deer farm tomorrow and speak to Kyle Foster, face to face.

∞∞∞∞∞

Rupert Baskerville had his phone in his hand. He looked at the screen and scrolled through the numbers. Pacing up and down the hotel room, he stopped at one number, pressed the green button and held the phone to his ear. He waited for the ringing tone to start. It rang and rang again. He breathed slowly. Just as he was considering ending the call, it was answered. The male voice had a local accent and just said 'hello'. There was no name, or any other information given. Rupert spoke first.

"Inspector Parrish? Rupert Baskerville here." There was almost a joyful tone in his voice, like an old friend speaking to someone he had not spoken to in years. The friendliness was not returned.

"Mr Baskerville, I have repeatedly told you in the past, I am not with the police department anymore!" Rupert took a deep breath in at the retort.

"Yes, yes of course, sorry. Now the reason I am phoning," he paused, but Sean did not say anything, so he carried on, "I would like to know if you would join me for a spot of lunch tomorrow?" Rupert stopped pacing and waited for a reply. He heard Sean exhale before he answered.

"Well, ... okay, but I am not sure what help I can be ..." Sean did not say the exact thought that was in his head.

"It isn't help that I am after, Mr Parrish. I would just like to meet for an informal lunch, that's all." There was a mumbled response back down the phone, "It would be my treat," Rupert was pushing the sale.

"Okay, no harm in it, I suppose," Sean replied.

"Excellent! Shall we say, meet outside City Hall tomorrow at 2pm?"

"Aye, no problem."

"Looking forward to seeing you, Mr Parrish." Rupert was being formal. Sean wasn't.

"Aye, tomorrow at two, then." Sean ended the call, as Rupert turned and walked over to the window. His hotel room was quite high and had a good view over Belfast city. He smiled; he might yet get

40

what he came here for. He jumped at the heavy knock on the door. He walked over and, looking through the spyhole, was elated to recognise the man standing there. He flung open the door, a smile spreading over his face, and thrust out his hand. It was taken in a very firm and familiar handshake.

"Alan!" he exclaimed. Alan Dukesby returned the smile and placed his left hand on Rupert's shoulder.

"Ru, so good to see you." Rupert released the handshake and backed into the room. He stepped aside to allow his old friend to enter.

"Come in, come in." Alan walked past him towards the window. Rupert shut the door and walked over to stand beside him. Alan turned as Rupert spoke. "It is really great to see you; how long has it been? Three years?"

"Four," Alan replied. The two men looked thoughtful. "It was after that exercise when one of your patrols ran across the runway in Cyprus."

"Just as the American U2 was trying to take off." Rupert finished the sentence, and they both laughed at the memory. "The Americans were not best pleased." Alan looked out the window.

"The RAF base commander was furious!" Alan pointed out, and Rupert smiled as he reminisced.

"Yeah, the rest of that exercise was really good. We were hosting the Swedes at the time." Alan nodded and smiled at the thought. Rupert continued, "And then we did that beach reconnaissance that caused a bit of a stir, as well." Alan let out a short laugh.

"Yeah, someone forgot to tell twenty tourists that the spot they had picked for their nudist sunrise 'get together' was part of a military training area, and about to have a load of heavily armed special forces swimming ashore." The two men shared another laugh at the memory.

"Yeah, that was funny." Rupert looked over towards Alan. "So, I do not even have to ask how you found me." He was still smiling, Alan dropped his eyebrows and glanced over at him, then looked back out the window.

"You are not hiding yourself very well," he pointed out.

"I am not trying to hide; I have nothing to hide." Rupert explained, and Alan nodded again. "So," Rupert looked at his friend. "To what do I owe the pleasure? I'm fairly sure this isn't a social call." Again, Alan glanced over at him, then looked back out the window.

"No, Ru, it isn't." Alan paused for a second, then spoke again, "Have you got your mobile phone on you?" he asked, as the joy on Rupert's face slowly disappeared.

"Yes, of course."

"Right," said Alan as he turned and started towards the door of the hotel room. "Leave it here." Alan stopped and looked back over his shoulder. Rupert was staring at him.

"One of *those* chats, is it?" Rupert asked. Alan glanced at him and answered,

"Yes, Ru, one of those. We need to chat … and not here." Rupert Baskerville knew what that meant. Alan opened the door of the hotel room and looked back. "Well, come on then." Rupert was fully aware he had been given a command that could not be refused, and immediately he followed Alan through the door and down the hall.

ооοοо

Sean Parrish was standing in his kitchen looking out the window over the rear garden, his phone still in his right hand. He looked down at it, listening to his wife moving around upstairs. He scrolled through the numbers and pressed the green button. Raising it to his right ear, he waited impatiently for the ring tone to end. Suddenly it was broken by the sound of Mike Dear's voice.

"Hi Sean." Mike sounded cheerful. "How'z you?"

"Aye, not too bad." Sean paused while he considered making small talk with his friend but changed his mind and went straight to the reason for the call. "Mike, I have had another call from that Baskerville fella."

"What did he want?" Mike asked quickly.

"Well," Sean started, "he wants to meet for lunch tomorrow."

"Does he?" Mike questioned. There was noise and muffled conversation in the background of wherever Mike was, and Sean waited. "Okay, we can have a look at that …. How are you otherwise?" Sean picked up on the conversation change. He knew that they did not need anything else from him, and that when he arrived at the lunch tomorrow, he would not be alone. He was glad.

Chapter 10

Rhydian disappeared into the kitchen, so he followed through the doorway. The smell was already filling his nostrils; a meal was being prepared. As he passed through to the kitchen, he noticed a door at the far corner of the room, the bottom half of which was wood and the top half, paned glass. It led outside. He noticed the shiny, new bolts at the top and the bottom of the door. To his right was a wooden sideboard nearly at waist height, under which were light-coloured cupboards full of plates, pots and other items for cooking. The cupboards lined the circumference of the room and were only broken by a door in the far corner, and a white fridge freezer next to it. The wooden table in the centre of the room looked brand new, like it had come from a large chain store specializing in flat-packed furniture. There were two chairs of the same design on either side of the table, the top covered with the contents of a recent shopping trip that had not been put away yet. He guessed he would learn the layout of the rest of the house very quickly. There was a small CD player in the corner. He recognised the song; it was good old-style rock and roll, and he liked it.

She had her back to him as she stood at the cooker, either side of which brickwork formed a wall that reached all the way up to the roof. This old house once had an open fireplace here, but it had been modernised. She was wearing thick, white woollen socks, no footwear, loose jeans and a red cotton top, the sleeves of which reached halfway between her elbows and her wrists. Her dark red hair was tied back in a ponytail, and she was concentrating on what was on the stove. Rhydian walked around the kitchen table and spoke quietly to her.

"Mum..." She reacted to the single word, first looking over her left shoulder, then turned and looked directly at him. Kyle stepped forward and held out his right hand in greeting. She turned back to the cooker, tapped a button and turned a dial. Then she fully turned to face him. He could see her shirt had a zip opening, and she was wearing a dark blue round-necked top underneath. A smile broke her thin face and her grip of his handshake was firm. But it was her eyes. Kyle looked into the grey, piercing eyes that did not just look at him, they studied him intensely.

"Hi, it's nice to finally meet you. I'm Tyler," her tone was light, and she blinked once as she released his grip.

"Hi," he answered, lowering his eyes. For once, he did not know what to say. "That smells good." He felt himself cringe as he said it. Tyler's eyebrows shot up and the smile was replaced by a smirk. She looked over her shoulder to the stove.

"Thanks, it should be ready in about an hour." She stepped back, and Kyle's eyes darted around the room. "Rhy, can you take Kyle up to the spare room?" Rhydian nodded and crossed behind Kyle, as Tyler continued speaking, "Sort your stuff out, and I will make a pot of tea." Her head tilted slightly to the right. Kyle looked at Rhydian who smiled at him, then disappeared back out the doorway they'd come through. Tyler smiled at him and turned back to what she had been doing. For a moment he felt like he was back in the military. He had just been summarily dismissed. There could be no doubt who was in charge here. Kyle smiled to himself, then followed the teenager back into the hallway.

The single staircase was open wood. He picked up his bags, there being no offer of help, and was led up the stairs. He'd noticed another doorway under the stairs and was sure he would find out soon enough what was on the other side.

"Bathroom is in there." Rhydian was pointing towards the open door on the left at the top of the stairs. "Simple rule: if the door is closed, there is someone in it." Kyle nodded as she walked on. "You are in here," she said, approaching the next room on the right. There was only one other door on the landing, and it was closed. Rhydian stood back to allow him to enter the room.

"What's in there?" he asked, nodding with his head. She looked over her glasses at him. The smile was still there, but there was menace in her voice as she answered,

"My room .... and if you ever go in there uninvited, I *will* dismember you." Her smile was re-enforced with raised eyebrows. He had stopped abruptly in the doorway of his room. He'd never had anything like that said to him before. Well, not by a teenager, anyway. Rhydian spun on her heels and disappeared back down the stairs at speed. He walked into the spare bedroom and flicked on the light switch.

The room was square and sparse. the bare walls were a neutral colour. A plain wooden wardrobe was next to the door and the double bed took up most of the room. The only other piece of furniture was a small set of three drawers. The wood was a light colour and unstained. He dropped his rucksack to the floor with a thud. It would not take him long to unpack. Then his phone bleeped with a message. He smiled when he saw Amanda's name on the screen. It wasn't long before he was making his way back down the staircase. The door to the kitchen was not quite closed, and he slowed as he approached. He could hear gentle sobbing coming from inside. Using one finger, he slowly pushed the door. It only moved a short distance, but enough for him to look inside. Tyler had her back to the door and Rhydian was embraced in a hug. The sobbing was coming from her, and Tyler was stroking her hair comfortingly.

"I...miss... her..." she sobbed. Tyler lifted her face and kissed her forehead.

"I miss her too .... They paid for what they did."

"But why Catherine? What did she ever do to them?" Rhydian's body shuddered as she coughed an anguished cry. Kyle retreated and turned away, as the sound of the sobbing continued. He tried to be as quiet as possible going back up the stairs.

Kyle took out his phone and laid back on the bed. He typed out another message to Amanda, then started to scroll through all the others he had not answered. He spotted the one from Cara-Marie inviting him for coffee. Reading it a second time, he felt himself breathe deeply. He knew what she wanted, but he would never tell her, of all people, what had really happened at the farm the night Carl died. He had been reading her blog posts about gathering evidence of the existence of werewolves. Some of it had been good, other parts had made him cringe. He tapped in a short reply about being away, but yes to coffee when he got back. When the screen indicated the message sent, he read his reply again and realised that it would cause more questions than it answered.

There was a soft knock at the door. As he propelled himself upwards, Rhydian's voice came from the other side of the partially open door,

"Tea is ready." There was no sobbing or emotion of any kind and, as he opened his door, he saw the door to her bedroom close. She would not be joining them. Kyle made his way back down the stairs again and, without knocking on the kitchen door, walked straight in. Tyler was at the stove and looked back over her shoulder.

"Grab a seat. Tea is coming now." Kyle glanced around the kitchen. The table had been cleared and two blue mugs sat in the middle. There was a matching bowl of white sugar with a spoon in it, and a small creamer of milk beside it. He took the chair at his side of the table, as Tyler turned around, holding a large metal tea pot. He had not seen the type in several years. As she started to pour the dark liquid into the cups, Kyle spoke,

"That is a lot of tea for two people." Tyler glanced at him, then concentrated on what she was doing.

"It isn't full. Besides, if you did drink all of it, you wouldn't sleep tonight."

"It isn't decaf tea, then?" he asked, smiling as he did so. Her face relaxed as she turned and placed the teapot back on top of the stove.

"No, no it isn't." She poured milk into her and pushed the jug towards Kyle. There was no offer to pour, he could do that himself. All was quiet as Kyle added milk and one teaspoonful of sugar to his mug. He used the spoon from the sugar bowl to stir it, then placed it down on the table and lifted the mug to his lips. Tyler was already drinking hers. She held the mug in front of her face, her elbows on the table and her arms forming a pyramid in front of her. She looked at him over the rim of the mug. "Thank you for not coming in earlier," she said quietly. He was about to ask how she knew he was there, but he discounted it as soon as he thought it, guessing the answer already.

"No problem. Is she okay?" he asked. Tyler's eyes darted over to the door then back again.

"She is strong, but she's still dealing with losing Catherine." Kyle recognised the name, but he thought he had better ask,

"Who was Catherine?" Tyler looked at him, paused, then placing her mug on the table. She stood up and reached over to pick up a small framed picture from the side near the fridge. She handed it to him and sat back down. There were three people in the photo: Tyler in the middle with Rhydian on one side, and another young woman on the other. Everyone was smiling. They were outdoors, and it looked like they were hiking on a mountain.

"This is Catherine." Kyle took the picture and looked at the happy, smiling faces. Catherine had short, dark hair, and there was excitement in the clean, round face. Her eyes were wide, as was her smile, very much in contrast to Rhydian.

"She doesn't look very old."

"She was only 15 when that was taken." Tyler sat down and raised her mug again.

"Where and when was this taken?" he asked.

"Just over a year ago. We were in the Cuillin hills on Skye." Tyler drank more tea before continuing, "We used to go walking at least once a month. We all loved it." Kyle could sense the feeling of sadness enveloping her.

"What happened to her?" he asked. Her eyes darted up and narrowed with anger at the question. Kyle did not move. He just watched as she spoke.

"They made it look like an accident, but I found out they had tampered with the quad bike. She didn't stand a chance." There was venom in her words, and he let her continue. "She was found by the family from just down the road. The paramedics pronounced life extinct at the scene," he could clearly see they had been close.

"Both orphans?" It was a question, but he already knew the answer. She stared into her drink as he placed the frame down on the table.

"Yes, both of them came to me when they were only ten years old."

"Is that why she calls you 'Mum'?" Her eyes shot up, the anger was there again, but it subsided just as quickly.

"You will have to ask her that... So, I hear you are very good with a sword." The question was an intentional change of course. He shrugged.

"Well, I would not say 'good'...."

"What would you say?" she almost cut him off.

"I would say I was 'lucky'."

"Lucky? An untrained sapien taking down a Mongol alpha in less than twenty seconds? That does not sound like luck to me." This time the smile on her face opened her mouth, and Kyle let his smile widen as he relaxed back in the chair.

"What else have you heard about me?" He reached forward with his right hand to lift his tea. She looked at him, raising her eyebrows, then relaxed, gathering her thoughts.

"Former police officer, has a knack for being around trouble, ex-something military ..."

"Legion," he cut in.

"Sorry?"

"Ex-French Foreign Legion." He lowered his head, admonishing her like a teacher speaking to a pupil at school.

"Which part?"

"What?"

"Which part of the Legion were you in? What did you do?" she asked.

"I was a sniper in 2 ReP, the Legion's parachute regiment; then, two years in the special forces element."

"Nice .... So, you know how to hunt, then?"

"Stalk," he corrected her. "A sniper 'stalks' a target. It is not a hunt - it requires patience and accuracy. 'Hunting' is fast killing."

"'Glad you know the difference." The smile was back. "I also hear you lived in Canada for a few years. I was there myself. Where were you?"

"Ottawa... well, Petawawa to be exact." He drank again from the mug.

"On the shores of the Ottawa River," she commented. He paused, then nodded.

"Yeah, very few people outside of Canada have ever heard of it."

"True. I was mostly around Calgary. You know, Medicine Hat, Okotoks...places like that."

"Okotoks?" he exclaimed. "The Rockies?"

"Yeah, I moved closer to the mountains after ...." She looked down, then back at him again. Common ground: trust had been established. "I only met your father once." It was his turn to feel uncomfortable, but he did not interrupt her. "It was at the farm; can't say I knew him well .... but Carl thought the world of him." She sipped from the mug as Kyle replied,

"Yeah, I saw the picture on the wall of the bar."

"That's still there? Wow, I thought that would have been replaced long ago."

"It's still there."

"So, tell me about you taking down the Mongols?" Kyle paused, then began to describe the challenge made against Carl, their fight, and the challenge that he took up. "What made you do that?" she asked, as she finished the last of her tea.

"I don't know," he answered. She tilted her head as he spoke, "I guess something in me knew I had to at least try."

"It could have ended badly for you...very badly, in fact."

"Yeah, I think Tony was more surprised than I was."

"Tony!" she let out a short laugh at his name.

"Yeah." Kyle sat forward, placing his arms on the table. "I hear you made his nose bleed once?" he was smiling as he asked the question. She was relaxing more. This was good.

"Well, if he had not said what he had, then ...."

"Then you would not have kicked him in the side of the head?"

"His fault," she smirked. Kyle laughed, just as the door opened and Rhydian walked in. Her face was clean and there was no evidence that she had been crying.

"Hi," she said, as she passed behind Kyle. A look of concern passed between the two girls.

"Hi," Kyle answered.

"Did you get all that sorted?" Tyler asked her, as she sat down. The girl nodded in response. Tyler lifted her mug. "'Cuppa?" Rhydian smiled and nodded in reply. As she was standing up, she pointed to Kyle's mug and asked, "'Fancy a fresh one?"

"Yeah, sure." Tyler lifted both mugs and turned away from them. Kyle glanced over at Rhydian, who was staring at him.

"So," he said.

"So," she repeated. Tyler glanced over her right shoulder, laughed, and went back to what she was doing. "You are the new Alpha of the Northern Dun, then?" Rhydian asked. Kyle tried not to smile as he looked around the kitchen.

"Yeah, it appears I am," he acknowledged.

"But you are not yet a full wolf?" She was direct with her question. Kyle glanced at her, then looked away.

"No, not yet. Apparently, that is why I am here." He forced a short smile and the teenager's face contorted slightly.

"And you are .... 'dating' Amanda?" Kyle had not expected that question from Rhydian. Tyler turned around with a half-smile. Placing the full mugs in front of first Rhydian, then him, she reached for her own and sat down.

"Yes, yes we are 'dating'. You know her?" Kyle explained, Rhydian let her smile spread across her face.

"Yes, she texts me." That made Kyle's eyebrow rise, Amanda had not mentioned that she even knew anyone here.

"Really?" Kyle was genuinely surprised. "And what else did she say?" Kyle had now turned in his chair to look directly at her. Tyler did not say anything, she let the conversation go on, clearly enjoying it.

"Girl talk." Rhydian smirked; Tyler laughed at that. The two girls looked at each other and laughed again. There was obviously a story there that he would have to ask about sometime. Suddenly, a chugging noise came from the rear of the farmhouse, and Tyler stood up.

"We are going to need a new generator - that one is crap!" she pushed her chair back and headed out the far door. Rhydian watched her go.

"We have had problems with that since we moved in," Rhydian explained.

"You have a generator? Are you not on mains power?" he asked, Rhydian shrugged.

"Well, apparently the island only got mains power in 1992 when the turbines were built, and this is one of the few farmhouses that still does not have it. Before that, every building had its own generator." Kyle did not know any of that. "I hear you can really *kick ass!*" she exclaimed. He smiled at her comment.

"I hear you can as well," he replied, her head tilted. There was a bit of a smile, but also a mix of emotions in her eyes. Kyle carried on, "So what happened that night on Skye when the Noc's came for you all?" Rhydian glanced over at the door that Tyler had walked out of, then back at him. There was a pause, then she shifted in her seat, she decided to tell him.

"Well, we had guessed there was at least one Noc around. Kat was very good on a quad, and that...was no accident." Kyle let her talk as he reached out for the fresh mug of tea in front of him. Rhydian followed, lifting her mug. After a long sip, she spoke. "I woke to a crashing sound. There was a fight going on. I knew someone was in the house." As she was speaking, a rolling image of what she was describing appeared in his head. "So, I grabbed my ninjato and headed into the hallway," she drank again from the mug.

"Ninjato?" Kyle asked, she shifted in her chair.

"A short, straight Japanese sword. You probably have a Katana, a curved Japanese sword?" she questioned. He smiled again and nodded once; he could feel himself warming to this teenager very quickly.

"Yes, yes I do."

"Great," she glanced down. When she looked up, she carried on, "The ruckus was coming from Mum's room and when I got to the door, I could see all five of them. I knew exactly what they were, cheering and shrieking." She did not have to say 'Noctrailis'. "Mum was on her knees at the side of the bed, one of them was pushing her head down into the duvet and another had her hands high up her back, the third was tearing at her jogging bottoms. She couldn't breathe," she explained. Kyle listened as she continued, "There was one with his back to the door .... big mistake, and the other one was at the far side of the bed pulling off his trousers ..." She sipped more of her tea.

"So, what did you do?" Kyle asked. Rhydian looked at him and with a sly grin.

"Well, the one with his back to the door he got a surprise when I burst in. He got my sword through his back and out his chest!" Her face lowered as did her eyebrows, in a very intense look. "In fact, he got one *mutha-fooka* of a surprise!" Kyle shared the smile at her pronunciation. She looked him in the eyes, and said, "He dropped like a stone!" She drank some more. "The one with his trousers down actually tripped and fell over. That was hilarious!" She was grinning at the memory; she was excited and angry at the same time. "When I saw what they were about to do to Mum, I just wanted to kill them all!"

"What happened next?" Kyle asked. Rhydian leaned forward placing the mug on the table.

"Well, the first one was dead, no question, the one on the floor wasn't a threat, and the ones that had Mum all let go at the same time and jumped at me!" Her excitement had taken over, flowing from her as she recounted the events. "I jumped back so I was in the doorway - they could only come at me one at a time. They had knives but I was able to keep them back. They had forgotten about Mum at that point - their *last* mistake!" There was almost a laugh from her, as she looked into Kyle's eyes, "and once mum got up .... well .... all I had to do was keep them in the room. It was amazing." Rhydian sat back with the mug in both hands. Kyle could see that she was remembering the events clearly, but she had stopped speaking. He wanted to know more.

"So," he paused, "what happened next?" Rhydian looked at him with a confused look of 'isn't it obvious?' Her face shone with pride.

"Mum battered them senseless!" She laughed as she spoke, and Kyle felt himself join in.

"Then?" He raised his eyebrows leaning towards her, he wanted the conclusion of the tale.

"Then we tied them up and dragged them into the back field." The excitement fell from her face as she remembered another detail. "That is where we found what they had done to the capybaras." Rhydian looked over at him. "Mum had them for years, she loved them." There was another short pause, then "they had gutted them ... gutted them wide open .... I have never seen Mum so angry." She shrugged before she spoke again, "So they got what they deserved."

"Tied to fence posts?" Kyle tried to picture it.

"Yes. I had never seen anything like it, each one sitting with their hands tied behind a post of the perimeter fence, including the dead one ... I had heard what sunlight does to them but had never actually seen it." The excitement was back, there was no remorse from her.

"And she drank coffee," Kyle stated. Rhydian smiled again.

"Yeah, when they started waking up. Mum sat in one of the garden chairs and had one of the metal screw top mugs that we take walking." Rhydian drank the last of her tea. Kyle had hardly touched his. "She was near the far one, talking to him. I could not hear what they were saying, but they all started crying, the wimps, when they realised what she was going to do .... so, she gagged them." The teenager looked out the window of the kitchen. She was deep in her memory. "The view out the back of the house was beautiful, there were mountains on the left and the lough to the rear, each sunrise was stunning." She had a starry look in her eyes, but refocused and looked over at him as she finished her story. "And there was Mum, just sitting there, arms folded, watching them wriggling and struggling, muffled screaming." The smile was back. "I watched from the kitchen as each one started smoking, then, one after the other, they burst into flames." There was another pause as she breathed slowly through her nose. She glanced down at the table, then looked up and repeated, "and Mum just sat there, watching them .... burn."

"Well, she doesn't like them." said Kyle.

"She *fookin* hates them!" Kyle again smiled at her terminology.

"She has reason to." The door opened, and Tyler walked in, hands black up to her wrists.

"You suppose what?" she asked, as she used the back of her foot to shut the door and walked over to the sink. Using her elbow to turn on the tap, she began to wash her hands.

"He says you have reason to hate the Nocs!" Rhydian exclaimed. Tyler turned her head over her right shoulder and looked at the two of them.

"And what, exactly, are you two talking about?" The half a smile was back. Kyle and Rhydian looked at each other and shared a smile. It was Kyle who spoke.

"I was just hearing about you enjoying a coffee and a sunrise on the Isle of Skye." Kyle could not help the smile on his face as she started to dry her hands on a small towel, turned and leaned up against the sink.

"Well, life is too short to drink bad coffee." The three of them laughed, then, "Have you got everything sorted for tomorrow?" Tyler's question was aimed at Rhydian, whose shoulders sank.

"No, Mum." she was more subdued now. Tyler raised her eyebrows and Rhydian nodded. She knew what she had to do. Excusing herself, Rhydian walked behind him and placed her right hand on his shoulder. Kyle looked over his left and looked her in the eyes. Then she passed behind him and headed out the door. Tyler retook her seat.

"She trusts you," she said quietly. Kyle looked over at her.

"Really?"

"Really. I've never seen her react to anyone, especially a man, like that before."

"I am honoured."

"Blessed, would be a better description," She sipped her tea.

"So, tell me," Kyle started. Tyler lowered the mug to the table as Kyle asked his question, "The one bit I don't get, how did they overpower you to begin with?" He looked at her as she stared down at the table. Rhydian had been keen to talk about it; Tyler wasn't so much. She sipped more of her drink before she answered.

"They used a taser. I heard the break-in and, when I got into the hallway, there were two of them near the door to the kitchen, the third one was in the doorway of the spare room," she shrugged. "They took me down. If it had not been for Rhy, I would not be here today." Kyle listened to her. There was a sadness, a reluctance.

"Good job she was." Kyle glanced over to the window, then looked back at her. There was an intense look on her face.

"They were sent."

"Sent? By whom?" he asked. She shook her head.

"The older one said they didn't know. They were only told who I was and where I was. They knew about one of the girls, but did not expect two... plus, they were all youngsters." Kyle thought for a moment.

"What do you think it was about?" he asked, she shifted in the chair. She took a breath in before she replied.

"They were not from anywhere near there, which means they were brought up. They were not trained, so it wasn't a professional attempt, but ..."

"But someone still wanted you dead," he stated. She looked at him,

"And I wanted all of them dead."

"Has this happened before?" he asked, there was another pause from her.

"No, not in twenty years," she spoke quietly before taking another mouthful.

"So why now?" Kyle asked out loud. The half-smile re-appeared on her face.

"Well, 'Alpha of the Northern Dun', that is for you to figure out. We, in the meantime, have got work to do!" She finished her drink, then pushed the chair back and stood up. "And you ... will need your sleep."

"But what about dinner?" he asked.

Chapter 11

It was still early in the morning and Cara-Marie was looking at the screen of her mobile phone. Her mum had bought it as a Christmas present, and she was the first one in the office to have a touch-screen phone. The message she had sent to Kyle last night still had not been read. She was sitting in her car at the side of a country road. She looked down the road that led towards the deer farm, the road was empty. She could see the tops of the farm buildings in the distance. There was something going on at that farm and she wanted to know more about it. There had to be a connection with the wolves; all her research into the 'An Rua' was coming up against walls; no one was talking, but there were stories of sightings that went back nearly two centuries. She had watched the family of Kris Martin at their press conference last night. She hadn't learned anything from it. She knew the body would probably never be found.

The phone in her hand suddenly started to ring. She looked at the screen; it was a UK mobile number. She had learned very quickly not to answer international numbers, as they were nearly all conspiracy theorists who were looking for things that were not there: 'no, she did not think that werewolves were actually aliens from another world', or 'no, this was not the next stage of human evolution'. She had grown tired of them, but they were not as bad as the ones who just turned up at the office. Kevin had to lock the back door so all public had to enter via reception, and the reception staff were getting good at 'she is very busy right now so, if you fill out this contact form, someone will get in touch with you'. Her bin was full of them nearly every day. She pressed the green phone symbol and held the phone to her ear.

"Hello." She did not say anything else. If this was another waste of time, the call would be ended very quickly.

"Hello," the male voice was English. "May I speak to a Miss Cara-Marie McKenna please?" He wasn't just English, he sounded aristocratic. She paused before answering. He had been very formal in his request, which normally meant broadsheet newspaper or other media outlet. Her guard was up.

"And who is calling?" she asked in her best office telephone voice.

"This is Rupert Baskerville," the name meant nothing to her.

"And who do you work for Mister Baskerville?" There was a pause.

"Sorry ... I ... don't work for anybody," he replied. It was not the answer she expected but he carried on, "I'm still not used to speaking to people who don't already know who I am ... well ... let's change that. I am Rupert Baskerville, Earl of Baskerville Hall." Her eyebrows shot up. 'Well, he definitely isn't another journalist,' she thought to her herself. She'd never met a 'journo' who pretended to be an Earl before.

"And what can I do for you, your Lordship?" her reply was a test. She had addressed him in the correct way. If he was an Earl, he would respond to that.

"Please, no need to address me by my title, please just call me Rupert." He passed! This guy was probably a real English Earl!

"So, Rupert, what can I do for you?" she asked.

"Well," he started, "I have been reading your blog and your stories and I would like to meet you face to face, as it appears, we have much to discuss." Her defences were back up again; she did not like the possibility of meeting more conspiracy theorists, plus, how did he find her from the blog? It was a false name!

"And what is it, precisely, you'd like to discuss?" She was more assertive with her question and his reply left her in a state of shock.

"Quite simple really, these creatures have been plaguing my family for nearly two hundred years and I can tell from your work that you do believe they are real. Are you free for lunch tomorrow? I can be in Coleraine for 2pm."

"Yeah .... sure .... 2pm."

"First class! Looking forward to finally meeting you. I will phone you when I get into town," and the phone went dead. He had hung up. He had not used the word, 'werewolves' but she had known exactly what he was talking about. It would be later in the day before she realised that they had not organised a place to meet. Her fingers tapped away at the screen, then she held the phone to her ear. It rang twice before it was answered.

"Coleraine Herald, photography."

"Mark, stop what you are doing and listen to me!" she almost shouted.

"What's up?" His voice had gone from passive to concerned very quickly.

"I need you to research someone for me." She quickly passed over the details of the call she received. Mark repeated bits as he wrote. "I need you to find out as much as you can about him."

"Okay, I will see what I can do ... Are you actually going to meet this guy?"

"Well, that depends on what you dig up," she heard a laugh down the phone.

"Yeah, okay, I'm on it." The excitement was back. She looked up at the farm in the distance, switched the engine on, and soon she was turning into the lane that led up to the farmhouse.

∞∞∞

Mark looked around the office of the newspaper, hearing the normal buzz of conversation. He turned to his desktop and brought up a search engine on the internet. He read the name he had written down, typed it in and, in seconds, he was scrolling through the results. He selected one and printed it, then clicked on another: it was a story from a newspaper he had never heard of. He read the title, 'LOCAL EARL AND HIS STRUGGLE AGAINST THE WEREWOLVES.' He glanced over the story - whoever had written it had not believed a word. There was a picture of the Earl and the story followed.

"So, what valuable work are you doing at the moment to contribute to the next edition of our newspaper?" Mark looked over his right shoulder at Kevin, the editor, who was now leaning over him and reading what was on the screen. He did not look at Mark.

"Something for Cara-Marie, she is apparently meeting this guy tomorrow." Kevin tutted.

"If she wants to indulge her fantasy then, as I have said many times, she can do it on her own time!" Mark looked back at the screen and shrugged.

"Yeah, she just phoned and asked me to find something out about this guy, so I did." The printer beside his desktop hummed to life when he clicked print. Kevin straightened up.

"Where is she now?" he asked. Mark glanced over at him, then collapsed the screen. She would have booked out on the editor's dropbox, and Kevin would have known this.

"She has gone out to the deer farm to see if she can get any more details about the fella who died there a few months ago." Mark glanced at Kevin again, then back at his screen.

"Mmm," Kevin walked away. That was what she booked out to do, so if she was doing something else, then that was anyone's guess. Mark picked up his phone and sent a short message about the conversation he'd just had.

∞∞∞

Sean Parrish was sitting near the window in the café. He was looking out at Belfast City Hall and could smell the fresh coffee in front of him. His mind was wandering. If anyone asked him how he was doing the reply was always the same, 'fine, things are good' etc., but things were far from that. He was missing being in the police, missing being at the station; retirement was not working for him. He had worked all his adult life, and he now understood why so many former police officers ended up in alcohol rehabilitation. Their marriages would break down and, in some cases, they'd find themselves homeless and their life not making sense anymore. Everywhere he looked he saw the same, smug people going about their daily lives. All with a point, with a reason - they were going to achieve something today... like what he used to do. Who wanted to employ a 52-year-old former police officer and, in this case, one with a caffeine addiction? That thought made him smile. Both Simon and Mike had always commented on how much coffee he drank.

He liked that Mike was staying in touch, but chat about work had become vague since he had moved over to Special Branch, and it didn't happen often, Darren Forester had been up to his old tricks again. Sean had enjoyed the phone call last night, and the fact that Mike knew about this meeting. He cast his eyes around him at everyone in the café and wondered how many of the other customers were undercover police. No one fitted the stereotype, but then, they shouldn't. Sean glanced out the window, watching young people, old people, walking hurriedly to the left, to the right, more and more of them, these days, walking around staring down at the phones in their hands.

"Mr Parrish?" The English accent brought him back to where he was. Rupert Baskerville was walking towards him with his right hand extended and a smile on his face. He was wearing a dark blue cotton shirt with matching trousers, neither had been ironed, and he carried a small backpack in his left hand that had an outdoor jacket slung through the handle. Sean stood up and took the hand of the unshaven Earl.

"Mr Baskerville." Sean noticed that Rupert had not addressed him by his former rank, so he did not use the title. There was a warmth to this English aristocrat, but this meeting would decide if he would like him or not. They shook hands and Rupert dropped the small backpack beside the empty seat.

"Please, call me Rupert." Sean extended his hand towards the empty chair.

"Thank you," Rupert stood by the small table and looked around. "Let's get lunch sorted first." Rupert pointed to the mug on the table. "What would you like?" he offered. Sean glanced down; he had not noticed that he'd nearly finished the coffee in front of him.

"Ah, may I have a hazelnut latte, please?" Sean looked up, Rupert was looking around the room, then returned his attention to Sean.

"Well this is lunch, so would you like something to eat as well?" Sean sat back in the chair and shook his head.

"No, no thank you, I am fine," just before he finished speaking, Rupert turned and walked away. Sean looked around again, he knew they were watching but he could not see them. He would guard his words very carefully when the Earl returned. It seemed like only a few moments before Rupert was back, but it must have been longer. He was precariously balancing a small metal tray with two large mugs and a small plate holding assorted traybakes. Sean leaned forward and moved his mug out of the way so Rupert could place the tray in the middle of the small table.

"Here we go," he said, as he lifted the coffee for Sean and placed it in front of him. Sean smiled and nodded as Rupert took the other seat. They both drank tentatively from the large cups. Sean would normally find this relaxing, but in this current situation, it wasn't. He watched the Earl once again scan the room... he obviously did that a lot.

"So," started Sean.

"So," repeated Rupert, replacing the mug back on the small table.

"I am not quite sure how I can help you. I told you all I could when we last spoke," stated Sean. Rupert looked into his eyes, then around the room again.

"Yes, yes you said," Rupert started, "but I'd like to tell you what I want to do, then you can decide if you want to help, or not." Sean knew his answer even before the English Earl continued. He shifted in his seat - he was sure that Rupert noted his body movements.

"Well, I am not sure how I could possibly help you any further, as I have already said," Sean started. Rupert cut in.

"Yes, you are no longer a serving police officer and the case is closed." It seemed like Rupert was getting a little annoyed. "May I ask you something?" Rupert lifted the mug to his lips, holding it there. Sean looked at him and nodded.

"What do you know of the Noctrailis?" Sean's eyes darted around; he sat back.

"The what?" he asked. Rupert sat forward and placed the mug on the table.

"The Noctrailis." Rupert paused as he sat back into the deep chair, "the 'ones who walk by night'." Sean looked confused at what he had just said.

"The what?" Sean started to shake his head, "I can't say that I have heard of them. Who are they?" Rupert now knew he was telling the truth.

"That is what the vampires call themselves."

"Vampires!" There was an instant reaction from Sean

"Yes, vampires," Rupert leaned forward again.

"But," Sean almost stuttered, "they are not real." Rupert smiled before answering.

"Six months ago, you did not believe in werewolves, but here we are."

"I still don't." There was a change in Sean's expression. Silence hung between the two men, Rupert had his answer, Sean would not help him. He believed Sean knew nothing of the Nocs. If he didn't, then the police didn't. It had not been a total waste of time. Rupert reached for his coffee.

"Okay, no problem, got that from the top, shall we just enjoy a good coffee then?" Rupert smiles. Sean nodded and returned the smile, as he lifted his mug drank from it.

"Not sure if good coffee is an accurate description, but certainly not bad." Rupert relaxed a bit and took a large gulp of the steaming brew.

"Yes, I'd heard that you are a coffee connoisseur." Sean smiled at Rupert's comment. His eyes darted around again; his accent was totally out of place here.

"And who told you that?" Sean asked, Rupert smiled again.

"Steve Minister did. He was telling me about helping you guys last year." Sean's eyebrows raised, then relaxed as he glanced at the floor and back up towards Rupert.

"You have seen him?" Sean asked. Rupert nodded, and drank more. He was finishing his coffee as fast as he could now.

"Briefly, it was good to catch up with him,"

"Next time you see him, tell him I said hello."

"I will," replied Rupert who finished the contents of the mug and stood up. Sean did so too and took the proffered handshake. "Thank you for meeting up with me today."

"Thank you for the coffee, sorry I could not be any more help," replied Sean.

"No problem. Well, all the best." Rupert broke off the handshake and lifted his bag.

"You will have to let me know how you are getting on." Sean stated as Rupert stepped away from the table and looked back at him.

"Yes, yes I will." Sean sat down again and watched as the Englishman started to walk away. Suddenly, he stopped and tapped another customer on the shoulder. The man was sitting on a high stool in front of a small bench alongside the wall. He was casually dressed and had a laptop in front of him. He was wearing headphones, but Sean noticed he had small speakers attached as well, and one of them was pointing towards where they had been sitting. "Excuse me." Rupert's accent stood out even more. With a surprised look, the man removed his headphones. Sean spotted the small flesh-coloured earpiece in his left ear. Rupert tapped on his own watch. "I think my watch is broken. Would you be able to tell me the correct time please?" Rupert was standing close to the sitting man, who still wore a startled look on his face.

"Err, yeah, yeah, hang on." The man exposed the watch on his wrist and confirmed the time. Rupert again tapped his own watch and gave a huge grin.

"Excellent. Thank you, old chap." Sean sat down as Rupert walked away. He had not heard Rupert talk like that before, but he understood what he had just done. Sean sat back in his chair, as the compromised surveillance officer started to pack his laptop away. Sean looked out the window and watched as Rupert darted across the street. He secretly wished him well.

Chapter 12

The sky was a blanket of grey, with no break in the clouds. It was completely overcast. It had rained earlier but had stopped for now. Dani looked up, then glanced around the rows of terraced houses that lined both sides of the narrow street. She had passed a tree on the corner - it had been her marker to look for, according to the bus driver, who'd had the thickest accent she'd ever heard. He had been nice enough and dropped her off at the junction with the main road. He'd directed her down the street, then 'take the left turn at the tree on the corner, that wee hotel is on the left-hand side - can't miss it.' She had learned that Irish directions that end in 'can't miss it' normally meant that you probably would, as the instructions were usually vague. She passed two young men who looked like they were in their late teens. She walked on and knew they'd turned to watch her walk away. If she concentrated, she could have heard their lustful comments. She chose not to. She did not think she was much to look at, presently. Yes, her jeans were skin-tight, but the thick outdoor jacket hid her figure and the heavy rucksack on her back just made sure of that. She wasn't wearing any make-up and knew she looked tired, but then she had not slept much on the ferry from France. It had been eighteen hours, and she had paid cash so there would be no trace of her boarding. Salisbury thought she was on her way to Italy - exactly what she wanted them to think.

It had not taken her long to find a truck driver with a cabin. The bar had opened just as they had set sail. She knew it had flattered him that a woman with her looks was interested in him, even bought him a drink. She had been deliberately leaning into him to speak into his ear, rubbing her breast up against his arm as she did so. It had not taken her long after the third drink to suggest they go back to his cabin. He'd even carried her rucksack for her. She had spotted the CCTV cameras in the bar when she had first walked in and she had stood in the only part of the bar that wasn't covered by them. Yes, he had been easy prey, but then men like him would always be taken in by good looks, a smile and a little flirting. The sex, for her, had not been that good. In fact, she was bored, but she'd made enough noise to make him think he was the best she'd ever had. It did not take long before he was sound asleep. He slept for an hour before waking. Then they'd had sex again, and he'd fallen asleep just as quickly. Then she fed. She did not bite him in the neck but somewhere less obvious - she had fed and fed well. She then slept for a few hours.

When she awoke, the body was already cold. She washed and packed her things. She went through his stuff and took all his cash, leaving the credit cards, as she could never use them without leaving a trace. For a long-distance driver, he had quite a lot of cash on him. She would be off the ferry and long gone before his body was found. It would take even longer to find out that he had not died in his sleep. She stopped. There were three carpark spaces in front of the nondescript building. The sign on the wall advertising the hotel was so small that if you were not looking for it, you'd miss it. She smiled and walked in through the thick front door. It slammed behind her. To her right was a single glass-panelled door; the room beyond had round tables covered in white cloth and set out for evening meal. To her left was another door leading into the hotel bar. It appeared empty. The hallway in front of her was split; the right-hand side was taken up by the heavy wooden staircase; the hallway on the left was narrow, allowing only one person to pass at a time. The walls had small landscape prints on them, none of which she recognised.

There was a rectangular sign on the wall with the single word, 'Reception' and an arrow. She moved down the hallway and, when she reached the end, an Asian face peered up from behind the cheaply built reception desk. It would be another ten minutes before she was given a room - 'No, she had not pre-booked... no, she did not have a credit card... no, she did not want to join their gold club membership scheme'...

The door of the small room closed behind her and she threw the rucksack onto the double bed. She tore off the jacket and tossed it towards the open wardrobe - it fell onto the floor. She sat down on the bed and unzipped the ankle-high boots and, with a flick of each, they landed on the floor in front of the open wardrobe. She unbuttoned the inside pocket of her jacket and took out the small plastic bag with the brand-new mobile phone in it. The battery and sim card were separate. She had been given it just before she had left Salisbury. It would be nearly untraceable, but she would only be able to use it for a short time. It took a couple of minutes before the screen lit up. No, she did not want to register it online. Once she had got it working, she tapped in the number she had memorised; then, holding it to her ear, she stood up to talk when the phone was answered.

"Hello." She recognised the voice of the American straight away.

"Hi, it's me," she replied.

"Dani!" There was an initial exclamation of surprise in his voice. "So good to hear from you." He paused before asking his first question, "have you arrived yet?" She picked up that he did not say the name of the city she was in.

"At the first place we discussed, yes."

"Good, good," there was another pause, "have you found a place to stay?" she felt a sudden anger rise in her. He was asking the wrong questions!

"What? Of course, I have, I can take care of myself!" she snapped at him. "But that isn't my concern now. My concern is, what were those fucking idiots doing?" Her anger was apparent, but the American remained calm.

"No, that did not go as planned, not at all," he responded.

"Not go as planned?" Dani was shouting now. "They were supposed to kill the bitch, not try and rape her. What the fuck were they thinking? Nearly every wolf in Europe is talking about it!"

"Dani!" His voice had a stern tone to it. "Do not raise your voice - others may hear you." Her eyes darted around the room. Yes, it was a small room and no doubt the walls were not very thick; a raised voice could be heard. She took a deep breath and sat back on the bed.

"But exactly what were they thinking? Were they not told exactly who it was and how dangerous she is?" She had lowered her voice now.

"Yes, yes, they were, but they paid for their mistake, that will not happen again."

"But she will have gone by now." Dani looked up at the mirror on the wall in front of her. She could see the anger in her own face.

"Yes, of course she has. We sent a second team once we heard what had happened, but the place was empty."

"That was our best chance to get her in years," Dani spat. "How long will it take before we find her again? And how much protection will she have?"

"Do not worry about that, leave it to me .... You have your own work to do." Dani looked at her reflection again.

"Yes, yes I do," she thought for a few seconds. "It will take me a day or two to get everything I need for the first part."

"No problem. Message me the address where you are staying, and I will get the point of contact to you for the next step." She smiled an anticipatory smile at the very thought of what she was going to do next.

"Yeah, sure .... I am already looking forward to it!"

"I bet you are." Then he hung up and the line went dead. Dani dropped the phone on the bed and stared at her face. After a while, she walked over to the small window and looked out over the rooftops of Dublin. She did not have much time to get what she needed, and she had to be discreet. She was going to enjoy doing this. She turned away from the window. The shower would feel very good indeed.

∞∞∞∞

Kyle was running as fast as he could, but he could not catch her. The distance between them was increasing. Even Rhydian had overtaken him once already. They had run to the far end of the island, where the Seabird Centre was. It was a single-story stone building and the road up to it was a single track. If anyone had been coming the other way in a car at speed, they would have been hit. They were nearly back to the farm. Tyler was now at least fifty yards ahead of him, and she stopped by the entrance to the lane that led to her house. She turned and began to pace, waiting for him to catch up. Her hair was tied back in a ponytail, her black leggings stopped just above her ankles and a loose top covered her torso. She had her hands on her hips, and was, at least, out of breath.

He stopped when he reached her and almost collapsed. His body fought for breath, as Rhydian arrived not far behind him. She had a level of fitness that greatly exceeded her appearance. He had expected a gentle run, but this had been punishing. Yes, he had run farther in the past, carrying weight as well, but that had been years ago. He'd often felt that he was one of the fittest members of the police force, but that was nothing compared to what he'd just been through. Tyler was grinning excitedly; she had enjoyed that. He fought to control his breathing, as his body demanded oxygen. He glanced at Rhydian, her hair had come out of the tie that had been holding it back and now covered her face; she, too, was fighting for breath. Tyler spoke. Kyle straightened up and placed his hands on his head. He looked at her, slightly confused. She had just spoken to him, but he had not heard.

"Sorry?" he asked, his breathing was gradually slowing down.

"I said .... there is someone to see you." She nodded with her head towards the house. To the right side was one of the 4 x 4 vehicles from the farm. The driver's door opened, and Dermott climbed out. He shut the door and lifted a hand in greeting. Tyler smiled and waved back. Dermott stopped at the rear of the wagon. Tyler started walking towards the house and the other two followed. Dermott and Tyler met in a brief hug. They obviously knew each other; there were smiles and warm greetings on both sides. She stepped back and introduced Rhydian. Dermott and Rhydian shook hands and exchanged formal greetings. "So," she started, "How is the head?" she was smiling as she spoke, and Dermott smiled and looked down.

"Yeah, it's fine," they shared a laugh at the common joke. Kyle butted in,

"My main man getting head injuries, anything I should know about?" His breathing had returned to normal, but he was still sweating in the cool morning air. Tyler and Dermott shared a look, then she extended her hand towards Kyle.

"I will let you tell him!" She turned to Rhydian. "Right, Rhy, let's get ourselves sorted and let them talk business," she nodded towards the front door. Tyler walked off; Rhydian politely excused herself and followed Tyler into the house. As the door shut, Dermott looked over at Kyle,

"Having fun?"

"Well, I would not call that run we just did *fun* but so far, no problems," Kyle stated. Dermott shrugged,

"Well, give that one time."

"Hey, how come you got to drive the land rover over? I thought it was residents only?"

"Tyler sorted a resident two-day pass for it," Dermott shrugged again, "she did it online, I just had to pick it up at the ferry port!"

"Nice for you...too bad she didn't do that for me... you must have pull, but since I don't believe this is a social call...." Kyle let the sentence trail off, and a look of concern rose on Dermott's face.

"No, no, it isn't." Dermott pointed towards the front of the 4 x 4 and walked back to the driver's door. He opened it and lifted out a brown A4 envelope that had been on the passenger seat. Dermott closed the door and walked to the front of the vehicle. Opening the envelope, he extracted a single photo and laid it on the bonnet. Kyle walked over beside him and looked at the group of people in the photograph. There was a tall, slim blonde whom he recognised, another woman and two men he did not. One of the men was younger, with short, dark hair and, for some reason, seemed out of place with the others.

"I know that face," he pointed to the blonde, "but who are the others? Dermott nodded.

"Her name is Sabine and I believe you met her with Tony in the carpark last year." Kyle's mind flashed back to the meeting when they'd handed the princess back.

"Yeah, I remember. Who are the others?" Kyle asked. Dermott took a short breath in.

"These are the Nocs that carried out the New Year's Day killings on the Strand ..." Dermott pointed to each one in turn. "This is Sabine, the one in the back may be called Matt."

"Maybe?" asked Kyle.

"Maybe. He's part of the protection for this guy who we only know as 'the American'..."

"No name?"

"No name ... That is how he is known ...No one can find any details about him."

"What do we know?" Kyle asked

"Well, he is a Noc, and has nothing to do with the Nocs we have here already, that much we do know ... No friend of the lot that were over from Salisbury either." Kyle's eyes focused on the face of the American as Dermott continued, "I have a team on them so it will not take long for us to find where they are sleeping." He straightened up, "then, if you want, we can take them all down." Kyle glanced over at him; Dermott was letting him know what he thought the next course of action should be.

"Who is the younger guy?" Kyle asked pointing at the picture.

"That," Dermott took a breath in, "is one Kris Martin." Kyle looked at the face that seemed out of place.

"Martin ... I recognise that name," Kyle said.

"You should," confirmed Dermott. "He was one of those killed on New Year's Day and,"

"And?" Kyle looked over at Dermott again.

"And his is the body that has gone missing from the mortuary in Belfast." Kyle straightened up as he looked at the picture.

"When was this taken?" he asked.

"Yesterday."

"So, he survived then." It was more of a statement than a question.

Dermott responded, "Survived? No... turned, yes."

"Turned?"

"Yes, turned, they turned him .... He is now a Noc!" Kyle sensed the rising anger in Dermott, "According to the truce, they are not to do that. They've broken the law."

"Where are they?" Kyle asked.

"Once we know that, I will let you know... but this has to stop!" Kyle could sense Dermott's hatred.

"Right," Kyle turned towards him. Dermott straightened up, awaiting instructions: "Confirm where they are sleeping, how many, external security, et cetera. Do a full Close Target Recce on them. Plus, I want to know all about their feeding, who, what, where... I don't want any surprises when we act." A broad smile broke over Dermott's face. This was direct action, and he liked that.

"Oh, have we got the stuff from that fella, Dukesby, yet?" Kyle asked. Dermott shook his head. "Right... when we do, give them this." Kyle pointed at the photograph. Dermott smiled. The two men shook hands and exchanged a friendly farewell. Dermott climbed into the 4 x 4 and reversed back down the lane. Kyle glanced into a small window in the side of the wall. It was one of the windows of Tyler's bedroom - she had been observing the whole conversation. When she realized that he had seen her, she turned back into the room. Dermott beeped the horn and sped away. Kyle thought about what he had just been told. Soon it would be time to act, exactly the way they had acted in Africa. An excited smile broke on his face as he walked around the old house, then pushed open the front door.

Chapter 13

Kris Martin was standing by the rear door of the small house, which led into the basic kitchen. He was leaning up against the wall and looking out over the fields. Anyone driving past would see a small bungalow with a garage and a very small front garden which had been well kept in the past, but certainly not recently. No one would guess the true nature of what the unregistered basement was being used for. He folded his arms and gazed upwards. The rain had stopped. He watched as a kestrel circled, then dived towards its prey. The back door opened, and Alison appeared with a plain blue mug in her right hand. Steam rose from the contents. She smiled and handed it to him. He nodded and nestled it between his hands.

"It's colder today," she mused, and closed the door behind her. She was holding a red mug with an emblem on it that he did not recognise. Returning his gaze to the distant fields.

"Is it? I hadn't noticed," he replied, Alison stood against the wall at the far side of the door, slowly sipping from her mug.

"Is something troubling you?" she asked. Kris quickly turned his head and glared at her. She stared straight ahead and drank some more, he relaxed and looked away,

"Yeah, there is." There was a pause before she asked the obvious question,

"Well, what is it?" she glanced over at him. He turned his head and their eyes briefly met; he looked away first. Her blue eyes were still piercing him. He felt she could see right through him.

"Are you getting used to what you are, now?" She noted that his body slightly shivered at the question. He took a deep breath in, relaxed his shoulders and, with the mug in his right hand, placed his left in his pocket. He looked up to the sky, searching for the kestrel, but it was long gone.

"There is no way back, is there?" his question was almost a whisper. She looked at him.

"No." There was a pause, and a gust of wind blew around the enclosed backyard. "Are you wanting to go back to your family?" she watched him. "They saw your dead body, and from now on, you will need to feed." He glanced at her, then back at the sky.

"So, I am dead to them?" he asked.

"You are."

"But ...." he stopped. He faced forward, his eyes darting around as he fought to find the words, she did not interrupt him. "But, what if, like, the police catch me? What will happen then?" She laughed. "What?" he asked, she shifted where she was standing.

"Put it like this... *if* you were caught, what have you done? You were murdered, your body was declared 'life extinct' by two paramedics, then declared dead by a doctor." Kris listened, and memories of the beach came back to him: the screaming, trying to fight off what was attacking them, seeing his friend, Jonny, fighting for his life and then screaming in terror as it was being drained from him, Alison continued, "You have not actually ... committed a crime."

"So, they would just let me go, then?" he asked, and Alison raised her eyebrows.

"A living witness to five unsolved murders? Haha! No .... they would keep you and interview and re-interview you ... I mean ... how would you explain to them what you are now?" she was smiling as she spoke. He looked at her, then away, as she returned to sipping from her mug.

"But ..." he started, this time she cut him off,

"But what?" She straightened up and slightly turned towards him. "Look, if they did detain you, how long would it take them to find out that you are not a sapien anymore? They would take a DNA sample from you, that would go through toxicology, etc." They met eye to eye again, "and you need to feed ... You cannot control that ... If you were confined, you would attack ..." Kris looked down at his feet. His head shot up and his eyes searched the sky as the haunting screech of the bird of prey echoed around them. Alison looked in the same direction, "and speaking of hunting, it sounds like something, at least, has just been successful." The sound ceased and silence fell over them. Alison slowly sipped her mug; Kris wasn't drinking from his. His eyes still searched the countryside. Matt approached, from around the side of the building. He was much taller than Kris. He had a heavy build and would not look out of place on a rugby pitch. He had short, dark hair with a small bundle of curls just at the fringe, and his pale skin retained a youthfulness about him. He had a thin shirt on, and his boots were covered in a thick layer of mud. He had not stopped walking around and around all day. Matt did not talk much... he didn't have to. Kris nodded towards him, and Matt answered him with the same. He had a canvas bag slung over one shoulder, and Kris knew it held the side by side shotgun. Matt did not seem to notice the weather. He walked on, smiling boyishly at Alison, and blushing slightly at the same time. She smiled back as he walked towards the back of the yard. "He will patrol around here until sunset," she whispered.

"I think he likes you," Kris commented, a cheeky smile lit Alison's face.

"He has a crush on me," she replied, as her eyebrows jumped. They looked at each other as she finished the sentence, "and I would eat him alive!" She let out a short laugh as she watched Matt walk steadily across the field at the back of the bungalow.

"Really?" Kris turned his head towards her and asked, "Do we feed off our own?" it was Alison's turn to glance down before looking over at Kris again.

"No, we don't... figure of speech," they both smiled, as Kris got what she meant.

"So, what is he doing? He hasn't stopped all day." Kris watched as Matt, having reached the far side of the field, turned and carried on down the side of the hedge that separated the next field.

"His job." Kris looked over towards her. She glanced at him, replying, "He is part of the protection squad." Kris looked confused, so Alison continued, "they keep the coven safe during the day, and stop the wolves from slaughtering us while we sleep." Alison was watching Matt as he disappeared from view.

"Wolves?" Kris asked. Alison's eyes shot over to him, and Kris noticed her body tense up.

"Yes, the werewolves. If they found this place, they would slaughter us all." Kris half laughed, but the smile soon dropped from his face as Alison glared at him.

"You are kidding ... Really? .... You're telling me werewolves are real?" he was slightly joking with his question, but the stern look from Alison continued.

"What do you think was doing all that killing around Coleraine last year?" Kris looked away; he was dumbfounded. "We fought a war against them for almost two centuries .... It was nearly the end of everything. The truce has been in place since way before my time."

"Truce?" Kris asked with a quizzical look on his face, and Alison smiled back.

"Yes, Matt and the rest of the protection unit look after us while we sleep. Wolves don't like us, and we don't like them," Alison lifted the mug and poured the last of its contents into her mouth.

"So, how come Matt can walk around during the day? I thought that slowly I would become more averse to UV light?"

"You will, the condition has not fully taken you yet, but it will."

"But what about Matt?" Kris asked.

"Because Matt .... is still sapien."

"What?" Kris shot upright. Alison smiled at him, as she shook the last few drops from the mug onto the ground.

"Yes, most of the protection unit are sapiens whom we control. They *want* to work for us." She smiled as she looked towards where she had last seen Matt.

"So, what about you? How come you can still walk around in daylight?" Kris asked, Alison smiled and slightly tilted her head as she answered.

"Because my young apprentice ... I am not fully Noctrailis!"

"What are ..."

"I am something else," Alison cut him off. "Besides, if you are to join the protection unit, you will need to be trained," Kris looked confused.

"Trained? Trained to do what?" he asked.

"Trained to be a bodyguard. We are not just going to give you a gun and let you lose," she was smiling as she spoke. Kris's head slightly dropped, and she could see his eyes darting form side to side; another question was coming. He looked up at her.

"Before that happens, there is something I want to do," he stated.

"What?" she asked, and Kris fumbled in his pocket for his phone. It was one of the new touch-screen ones; Alison still had her old keypad phone. She watched as he started going through pictures on it. He stopped at one and held the phone in front of her. The picture was of a couple; the man was a bodybuilder with tattoos on his arms. He was bald and had a very tight top on; his thin legs were out of proportion to his over-developed upper body. To his left was a much shorter woman who had shoulder-length blonde hair. She was wearing skin-tight gym wear and, judging from the pleasing proportions of her body, was no stranger to fitness. Alison looked back at the male.

"Who is he?" she asked.

"Her husband," he replied, Alison looked at the anger in his eyes.

"Who is she?" she asked.

"Her name Nicole," Alison looked back at the screen and Kris continued talking, "and they don't live too far away from here." Alison stared at the picture.

"Well, if you are after her, I know someone who will really like him." She smirked as she spoke, "...just his type." Kris did not have to ask; he knew she was talking about the American.

Chapter 14

She was seated, facing the entrance to the room at the top of the stairs, and Cara-Marie was trying hard not to engage anyone in conversation; she did not want to be distracted. It was still raining, and it was constant and oppressive. The sky was a thick blanket of grey, indicating there would be no reprieve for some time to come. Mark had certainly done his research; she did want to meet this English Earl who, if the stories were to be believed, had gone public about a pack of werewolves near his family land. She looked around. It had been a few months since she had been in this same coffee shop when Rachel Boyd had her meltdown and threw the glass at the far wall. Kyle had been great in with dealing with it. She could think of other police officers who would have arrested everyone in sight! She looked over at the mother, smiling down at the baby in a very new-looking pram. She had silver streaks in her hair so she could have been the grandmother, or she might just have had the child late in life. Cara-Marie was trying not to stare as the woman lifted the tiny baby out and cuddled her. She looked over at the only other person there, a woman whose hair was tied back in a ponytail. She had a thin face, wore glasses and small white headphones which were connected to the laptop on the table in front of her. She appeared to be in her forties, and it looked like her next stop was the gym; her thin black top contrasted with the very brightly coloured leggings she wore. There were dark pink and light purples in the pattern. She was engrossed in what she was doing. Cara-Marie glanced around her; her own coat was over the chair behind her and her handbag was placed on the seat to her right. The only other seat was directly in front of her. She had moved the fourth chair away so she would be able look directly at him as they spoke.

"Excuse me," the polite English accent made her look up. She had not seen him enter the room. "but you must be Cara-Marie McKenna!" The face held a smile, Rupert Baskerville looked much like his photograph.

"Good afternoon, and you must be Lord Baskerville," she answered. He seemed relaxed as he stepped forward and held out his right hand, which she took. He had a very firm grip. His hands had worked the land; they were rough. She'd known enough farmers to be able to tell the difference between them and someone who worked in an office.

"Yes, but please, call me Rupert." They both exchanged pleasantries as he removed the dark-coloured waxed jacket that fitted the stereotypical image she'd had of him, then hung it over the side of the seat that held her handbag. He took the seat opposite her, his back to the entrance. She felt sure he did not normally do that, and she noticed that he did not have a drink with him. She looked at her coffee,

"Would you like me to get you a coffee?" she offered,

"No, that is very kind of you, but I do have one coming up. There was a bit of a queue downstairs." She thought for a second - it had been almost empty when she had come in, but she did not pursue it. "Would you like a fresh one?" he asked. She smiled and tried to relax.

"No, thank you, this one is still quite fresh." she said as she pointed with her eyes towards the mug in front of her. Rupert glanced towards the window.

"Still a bit wet out there," he remarked. She glanced over and looked out the window – the rain was pouring down.

"Well, it is Ireland, after all," she casually remarked.

Cara-Marie looked over his shoulder as one of the staff members appeared at the top of the stairs carrying a tray with one mug on it. She caught her eye and motioned that it was for their table. The girl nodded and walked towards them. "Looks like your coffee is here!" she said. Rupert turned in the seat and thanked the girl for the coffee, and she quickly left. Cara-Marie noticed the older mum at the other table replaced the baby back in the pram and started to pack up her things. She pushed the pram to the small elevator, and the door closed gently behind them.

"So," he sipped at his coffee as he spoke.

"So," she answered, "what does the 27th Earl of Baskerville want with a local journalist from Coleraine?" Rupert's face relaxed, he lifted his right hand and perched his chin on it. She studied the shape his hand had formed; the thumb was under the chin and his forefinger was up against the side of his face with the other fingers tucked away in support. He was studying her, as well.

"Well, not 'just' a 27-year-old journalist from Coleraine. One with a degree in criminology from Queen's University, Belfast for starters. You have many talents!" Her eyebrows shot up and she took a quiet breath in to calm herself.

"What else did you find out about me?" she quizzed. Rupert adjusted his position and sat upright, lowering his right hand.

"Cara-Marie McKenna, 27, youngest child with an older sister and brother, both married; been with the Coleraine Herald for nearly three years; witness to a brutal murder in Coleraine last year and, well …" Cara-Marie stared at him as he spoke, "very outspoken critic of both the police investigation and how the recent series of violent attacks that happened around here late last year were reported in the wider press." She studied his face. He wasn't boasting, just being very 'matter of fact' with what he was saying so far. "And …" this time he paused before finishing, "author of several, very accurate articles on the truth behind what was actually committing these crimes." He looked directly into her eyes as he spoke. "You notice I said "what" not "who". She looked back at him and she saw it. *He believed her.* She did not feel her pupils dilate, but he saw it. There was a brief silence between them. The woman who was plugged into her laptop answered her mobile phone. Cara-Marie watched without speaking as she closed down her laptop and, keeping the phone to her ear, walked out. They were left alone, upstairs in the nondescript coffee shop.

"So, what do you know about me?" he asked. She took a long breath in before speaking. It was her turn.

"Rupert James Baskerville, 27th Earl of the vast Baskerville estate in southern England;" He watched her as she continued, "became Earl at the age of twenty after the sudden deaths of his parents; only child; married a debutante, in what was possibly an arranged marriage." She watched the small smile spread across his face. "Served in the Special Forces Reserves, 21 SAS to be exact, for nearly twenty years and reached the rank of Major," he glanced down, then back up at her; both were now smiling at each other. "'Has led a public campaign for nearly all of his adult life against a group of travellers who currently occupy a large area of one of the Baskerville estate moorlands and which, you claim, …" she paused, blinked, then finished her monologue, "are a group of werewolves; you have tried several legal challenges to have them removed, all of which have been, so far, unsuccessful." The silence returned; mutual respect was apparent. They both sat there for a few seconds before he answered her,

"A campaign that was started by my great grandfather - a campaign that has lasted nearly one hundred and fifty years and cost my family dearly." She could see sadness in his face and hear it in his voice; this was painful for him but, she could also see, it was the truth.

"And you are sick of people not believing you, stating these things are not real, and he needs to stop living in a fantasy!" she was quoting one of the stories she'd recently read about him. He shifted in his seat.

"Ahh, and that particular mayor then had to deal with one of his own teenage children being torn apart by them." He reached forward and lifted the mug of coffee.

"A farming accident…" She did not move as she spoke.

"Yes, it was reported that he had fallen into 'farmyard machinery' …. but there isn't anything on his farm that does that much carnage to a human body." There was anger in his voice. He sipped at the hot liquid and continued, replacing the mug on the table, "but I am not the only one who has not been believed." He sat back and watched her unconscious reaction as her body slightly twitched, "and by writing the articles that you have, you've opened yourself up to public ridicule and condemnation." She nodded. "So," he continued, "that is something else we have in common." Cara-Marie scanned the empty room. He had just touched a nerve.

"Apart from the fact we both know werewolves are real, and they kill people, what else have we in common?" she inquired. He drank more coffee without answering.

"What exactly do you want from me?" she asked. "You wanted to meet me, and I am very glad that we have done so, but I am not sure what I can do for you"

"Well, I have been organising a response to finally deal with the trespassers on my family land. I do not want this going on for another one hundred and fifty years."

"What are you going to do?" she asked.

"Doing!" he corrected, "what am I doing! Quite simple, really," he began to outline his plans, "I have been creating a Fire Force that I can use against them."

"What exactly is a 'Fire Force'?" she asked,

"I have been recruiting a force of rangers who are mostly ex-military with 'specialist' backgrounds. They can track, observe and deal with them." He looked around, "I want my family land back. They have taken land and lives from family and friends, and it is time we took it back, once and for all."

"How are rangers going to deal with the wolves?" She placed both her hands around the mug in front of her but did not drink from it. "You have seen what they can do, you cannot go up against them with just people." She tried to picture what he was saying.

"Oh, they are armed of course!"

"Armed?" she quickly sat upright, "Isn't having your own little army illegal?" she asked, and Rupert smiled.

"They are armed with legal weapons, shotguns, stalking rifles, etc. All of them are very professional at what they do." He was smiling as he spoke, "They take and take; now finally we are going to take from them." She could see he was determined and meant what he was saying.

"Okay, I get that, but I still don't see how that affects me. What do you want me to do?" He could see that she was genuinely puzzled. Rupert placed the mug down on the table and, reaching over to his jacket, removed a brown A4 envelope from an internal pocket. She saw that it was blank on the outside.

"Actually, not much. I am here to help you. It seems we have been fighting the same fight, but from different positions." He pushed the thin envelope across the table. She glanced at him, then slowly opened the envelope. There was a single A4 colour picture in it. The picture had been taken at night, but she could see a middle-aged man with swept- back hair; his clothes were very dark, and he looked pale. Beside him was a tall, slim blonde who was wearing mostly leather clothing. She had a very stern look on her face. The other woman in the photograph was older; her hair was short and also blonde, and she wore jeans and a hooded top. There was a glimmer of recognition there. Cara-Marie also recognised the face of the other young man but could not place him.

"And who am I looking at?" she asked.

"These are the ones who carried out the New Year's Day murders ... well, except for the younger one," she looked up at him, then back at the picture.

"Who are they?" she asked. Rupert leaned forward and pointed to each one.

"This one is called 'Sabine', this one is Alison Wallace, former police officer right here in Coleraine," Cara-Marie reacted.

"I know her!"

"Yes, yes, I am sure that you do. We don't know this one's real name - he is only referred to as The American". She looked up,

"The American?" He looked at her and nodded,

"And this one, you should recognise. His name is Kris Martin. He was one of those murdered at the new year." He could hear her breathing heavily now.

"And his body was stolen from the mortuary! Yeah, I know him." He could see her face fall as she studied the photo. "When was this taken? It was obviously before Christmas! How do you know, and how can you prove they did it?" she asked, without looking up.

"That picture was taken last week," her reaction was instantaneous.

"WHAT?" she almost shouted, as she sat bolt upright, clutching the picture in both hands. "But that isn't possible! He is dead!" Her eyes darted over every detail that she could make out.

"No, it isn't impossible .... not for what they are," he answered. She slowly looked up and lowered the picture to the table.

"They are not wolves - the injuries were totally different from the wolf attacks last year!" she stated, and he nodded in agreement.

"You are right, they are not wolves, quite the opposite in fact." Rupert was leaning his elbows on the table, and there was a small smile on his face. She stared at him, not having to ask the most obvious question. He carried on, "They are Noctrailis, the wolves' greatest enemies!" he exclaimed.

"Knock-what?"

"Noctrailis ... 'man who walks by night' is what it means." She slowly shook her head,

"Man ... who ... what? What does that even mean?" He smiled again and looked down at his nearly empty mug.

"*Man who walks by night*' ... or '*vampires*' as they are more commonly known." Cara-Marie sat there with her mouth open in disbelief. "Do you know the name 'Yelina Gurin'?" he asked.

"One of the Latvians who died in a gun battle at the Mussenden Temple in a feud between eastern European organised crime gangs," she answered. He nodded.

"Yeah, I did not believe that story, either." He saw in her eyes that she agreed with him, so he carried on, "What if I told you, she .... was actually killed by a vampire, in the car park, and... the police have video evidence of it."

"How do you know all this?" she asked.

"Well, that one is going to take some explaining, so before I do ...." he drank the last of his coffee and placed the now empty mug on the table, "we will need more coffee." He was smiling as he stood up, "What would you like?"

It would be another hour before a stunned journalist walked out of her favourite coffee shop in Coleraine. Her biggest concern now was how the hell was she ever going to prove any of this... but she was glad that the Dictaphone in her handbag had recorded the whole conversation.

Chapter 15

Tony was sitting on the sofa in his living room, listening to the sounds echoing from the kitchen - Karen was making such an effort. He was proud of her and smiled at the thought. She walked in with a mug in each hand, careful where she was stepping, and smiled as she approached. Her hair was tied neatly back in a ponytail and she was wearing a running top and leggings. She wasn't going to go for a run - she just felt comfortable wearing them.

"Thought you could do with a cuppa."

"You thought right," he smiled as she approached. Reaching forward, he took one of the mugs from her.

"Dinner will be an hour, at least." She sat down beside him, and they both shifted until they were snuggled up to each another. Tony felt a surge of love and adoration for his wife, as he watched her. She sipped from the mug, then looked back at him. "What?" she asked.

"Do I need a reason to look at you?" he said playfully.

"Look, no... stare, yes!" He looked away. The news was just starting. "So, how long is Kyle going to be away on Rathlin?" she asked. Tony shrugged.

"That depends," he answered.

"Depends on what?" she asked. Tony was about to answer when the first news story began.

"A married couple have been found brutally murdered in their family home near Cushendun." He glanced at her, then back at the news story. Live footage of a cottage filled the screen. A police car blocked the entrance to the property and two police officers were standing nearby. The voiceover continued, "Gavin and Nicole Summers only moved to the area last year. It is understood that Mr Summers was known to the police." Tony thought for a moment; he did not recognise the name. A photo appeared on the screen. Gavin Summers was a bodybuilder and the very tight top was worn deliberately to make himself look bigger. He was smiling at the camera. Tony glanced at the trophy wife standing beside him: near-perfect looks which had probably cost a fortune. The report kept going back to the savagery of the attack and the fact that they were found in separate rooms in their house.

"Oh God, how awful," Karen exclaimed. Tony lifted his arm and placed it around her in a reassuring embrace. The screen switched to a young female reporter, the house in the background.

"The two deceased were found by a family friend this morning when they failed to turn up at an arranged meeting. Gavin Summers had served two prison sentences in the past for possession and supply of controlled substances and the alleged assault of Mr Henry Coast several weeks ago, in which Mr Coast was left in Intensive Care. Police are currently investigating whether this was in possible retaliation for that attack."

"Now, I know him." Tony said out loud.

"Who?" asked Karen.

"Coast .... He does not deal drugs; he supplies them in vast quantities. If it's going down in the northwest .... he is involved. Drug squads have been after him for years."

"Do you know the other guy?" she asked, as the screen changed to a still from one of the CCTV cameras around the house. The resolution was bad, but he could make out the blurred figure of a man dressed head to foot in black, and a tall woman with long, blonde hair and leather clothes.

"No, I ...." He stopped and suddenly sat up as the female reporter continued,

"...and police would like to interview these two people, who were picked up on CCTV the night before. Police have said there were at least three others, but they could not be identified from the footage. The public are asked not to approach them as they are considered extremely dangerous." Tony almost dropped his drink as he sprang up. Karen jumped back, turning her head and closing her eyes. Tony was up close, staring into the TV.

"Oh shit!" he exclaimed.

"What? What is it?" Karen demanded. Tony hurriedly placed the mug down and struggled to get his phone out of his pocket.

"It has nothing to do with drugs," he said, as he began to pace up and down with the phone to his ear, "come on, come on... answer ..." He spun around, "Dermott!" he was almost shouting. Karen stared at him. Fear was growing in her, she did not like this at all. "Dermott, have you seen the news? .... Yes, yes, the couple that were murdered .... No, it isn't, it is nothing to do with drugs." Tony spun on his heels, "I have just seen the CCTV .... It was the Nocs!" There was another pause. Tony had his free hand in front of him, clenching it into a fist. "No, no, no... because I recognise one of them. The blonde is called Sabine .... Yes, from the carpark." Tony turned again. Karen could tell where this was going. "Yes, I can be there in less than an hour." Tony was nodding at whatever he was being told, "...sure, no problems, I am on my way."

Tony saw the look on his wife's face. He paused, and spoke again, "Can you send a small team to look after the house while I'm out?" There were a few seconds of silence, then he nodded, "great... thanks."

Karen Fallon would be eating dinner without her husband tonight.

∞∞∞∞

She walked out through the sliding doors of the terminal at Belfast City Airport. Looking up at the sign, she took a second to translate it. She nodded to herself, then reached into her pocket for her phone. She started to press buttons on the keypad. It was a cheap phone, but then, that was all she needed. People walked past her; most ignored her, but one didn't. He stopped about ten feet away and looked at her. She was a very attractive woman. There was a natural curl to her shoulder-length blonde hair that bounced as she walked. She had been in the row in front of him on the flight, and he had tried to speak to her, but had been ignored. He had heard her speak to the attendant and he picked up that she was speaking German first, then English, but with a very heavy accent. She was wearing thick-rimmed glasses and she was transfixed on the phone in her right hand. The large, brightly coloured outdoor jacket hid her shape, but by the way she had picked up and swung the heavy rucksack onto her back, he knew she had physical strength. She had the legs of a body builder and those jeans did not do her justice... his mind wandered.

She glanced up at the guy who was staring at her and felt the venom rise. He looked to be in his early forties with a bald head and unshaven face. His jeans were too big for him and he slouched inside his open jacket. He carried a small bag in his left hand. She could tell he wanted to speak to her, so she glared at him. He didn't get the hint. He strode towards her, holding out his right hand,

"Hi, I'm Tim ...."

"Geh weg!" she spat at him, he looked confused,

"Sorry, I ..."

"GO AWAY!" This time it was a shout, followed by a shove from her right hand into the centre of his chest that sent him flying backwards and skidding over the ground. He had dropped his bag and there was a look of shock and hurt on his face. He was about to say something else, but she was already marching away. She was not interested in anything from him. She needed to find the train station and make her way into Belfast where the second-hand car would be waiting for her. She had things to do, it was dark, and she was already hungry.

∞∞∞∞

Kyle was breathing hard. He fought to control his breath once the onslaught had stopped. Tyler had been working him hard all day. Just after breakfast, he had been told to be dressed for training .... but he wasn't told what the training was. The morning run had been just as fast as the first one. He was still surprised that Rhydian could run as fast as she could.

He had been led through the door under the staircase: the short hallway had a door at the end on the left, that was Tyler's bedroom. He was not given a tour. At end of the hallway was a small square window looking out over the side of the house, where the 4x4 was parked. The door on the right was close to the hallway entrance and led into a surprisingly large room that he thought had once been a garage but was now a gym. The floor was covered in thick mats and the walls were painted a neutral colour. Beside the doorway, on the wall were three small wooden panels with motivational quotes carved into them. '*Relentless in the pursuit of excellence*' was the first one. He guessed that she believed that 99% would never be good enough. On the second one was carved '*Humour and Humility*'. That made him smirk; he had seen very little of her humour so far, but he understood the last one perfectly: '*Strength and guile*'. As a pack, they had to be strong, but they had to be very clever with their strength. There was a difference between 'wisdom' and 'knowledge'.

Several plastic containers held fighting gloves and other training aids; a punch bag was up against the far wall and had not been hung yet; but the rubber human torso had been unpacked and its stand had been affixed to the floor in one corner. He recognised the long fighting staffs, or 'Bo'. In the Legion, they had used brush handles. She said that some of the other things they would be using had not been unpacked yet. What followed had been fast and fun and had taken place mostly in the gym...an extremely intense workout. They had started with unarmed combat: 'It is the basis of all combat - only an idiot relies solely on a weapon' was how she started. She had changed from the run and had showered in between. He noted a pleasing feminine scent from her shower gel as she had walked past him. She was barefoot and wore leggings and a sleeveless black top. Her hair was back into a tight ponytail. She'd had a determined look on her face all morning. She was fast, extremely fast. In fact, he had not even got close to her.

Just after lunch, she timed him for two minutes punching the rubber torso as fast as he could. Two minutes may not sound like a long time, but it is when you are at maximum output straight away. She was counting the number of landed punches on the strike marks. That test would no doubt happen again. He went from that straight into a one-minute spar with her. She had him wear headguard and a body protector, although she didn't. He never even had a chance. She had landed several punches and kicks on him, and he was thankful that they had not been full force. Each time, there was a short comment on his performance:

"You are dragging your left foot there." "Don't overextend your reach, ... do not waste your energy." They were little things, but it was obvious she was very good at this. He could see why she'd had no problem fighting off the four Nocs who'd attacked her. She stepped back and pointed towards the door. He turned and looked at the smiling face of Rhydian in the doorway. She held the handset for the landline in her right hand, extending it towards him.

"It's for you," she said.

"Thanks, who is it?" he asked, she contorted her face at the question.

"How many people actually know where you are?" She let out a short laugh as he took the white phone. She was right; there were only those at the farm who knew he was here. She turned and walked away as he stepped into the hallway. The phone was an older model from the mid-nineties and must have come with the house. The metal antenna extended out of the top of it. He placed it against his right ear,

"Hello." It was Tony, and he wasn't happy. This was not a social call.

"Hi, have you seen the news?" There was an urgency in his voice. Kyle thought for a second: he had been shown the living room, but they had not watched any TV since he had arrived.

"No, nothing. Why?"

"Turn it on. There have been two sapiens murdered. It's being reported that it was a drug hit ... but it wasn't!" Tony was not himself.

"Whoa, calm down. What happened?" Kyle walked past Rhydian and headed towards the living room.

"What's going on?" Tyler asked Rhydian. Kyle did not hear the reply.

"It was the Nocs, the ones we've been looking for." Kyle pushed open the living room door and walked inside, as Tony continued, "They have to be stopped, and we have to do it!" Kyle reached down for the TV remote and pressed the power button.

"How do you know that?" he asked.

"Because Sabine was there!" Tony almost shouted his answer. Kyle had to think for a second as he scrolled through the news channels.

"Sabine?" he asked, stopping at the channel he was looking for. The volume on the TV was down and there were two solemn looking presenters. The main news was still the financial crash from the previous year.

"Yes, you know, the tall, blonde one. She was at the carpark when we handed the other one back." Kyle suddenly remembered.

"Yeah .... How do you know she was there? By the way, there isn't anything on the news," he said. Kyle did not notice the other two standing by the doorway, watching and listening intently.

"They were picked up by CCTV. So was that fella, Martin... the one they turned." Tony was getting impatient now. "It will be on the local news."

"So, what happened and where?" Kyle asked as he read the reports that were scrolling across the bottom of the screen. There was nothing he was interested in, so far.

"It was at a bungalow near Cushendun .... and by the sounds of it, it was pretty extreme."

"In what way?" Kyle asked. He could hear voices and movement in the background; Tony was obviously at the farm.

"Well," Tony started, "it looks like that fella, Summers, was the subject of a brutal male rape before he was murdered." The news changed to another story, the main headlines still scrolling across the bottom of the screen. Kyle was speed-reading.

"I heard from the police that there were signs of torture on him, as well." Kyle listened, but kept reading. The news story ended and another one began, but still not what Tony was talking about. "...looks like he was bitten a couple of times." That made Kyle wonder, and ask a question,

"Why would he be bitten more than once?" The question stopped Tony's flow,

"Simple, that means there was more than one feeding... drank him dry by the sound of it, which means it also took a long time, but it was the girl .... that is horrific!" The news story changed again, and Kyle interrupted Tony,

"Hang on, looks like this is it." He stepped forward and turned up the volume. Tyler and Rhydian were now standing right behind him, listening and watching intently. Tony had stopped talking. The screen changed to an outside shot of a bungalow with two police officers standing beside a single strip of police tape, the voice-over talked about the double murder. A face that Kyle did not recognise filled the screen. The title of 'Inspector' and an unfamiliar name appeared under it. He wore a pressed police uniform and was being questioned by a reporter.

"Who are Gavin and Nicole Summers?" Kyle asked. There was the sound of more background movement behind Tony,

"Nobody of interest to us, but it was a Noc attack. The girl suffered what is being described as 'a prolonged and very vicious sexual assault', which lasted several hours .... There was evidence of torture, as well, but she was only bitten once," that got Kyle thinking,

"Why only once?" Kyle asked, Tony paused; someone at the farm had just spoken to him.

"No, I'm talking to Kyle now .... hang on .... Yeah, she was only bitten once because it was probably a first kill for our wee friend Martin."

"The one they turned?"

"The one they turned," Tony answered, "and under the truce, they are not allowed to do that...We have to do something about this!" The news story was continuing.

"The news is saying that the police are looking at drug connections and there has been no mention of any torture." Kyle stated, "have we told them about the Nocs?"

"Not to my knowledge, nope."

"Okay, have we had anything from them, yet? They did say they were going to send us what they had!"

"Nope, nothing."

"Okay," Kyle had made a decision, "only share if they share with us, first. After all, they said they were going to."

"Yeah, they did," Tony confirmed.

"Is Paul there?" Kyle asked.

"Standing right in front of me," Tony replied.

"Right... get him on that. I want to know everything about them .... Am I on loudspeaker?" he asked.

"Hang on .... you are now."

"Okay. Paul, has Dermott told you about our chat when he was here?" he asked.

"Yes, he is on that already. It shouldn't take him and his team long to find them."

"Right," Kyle continued, "any help he needs with that, make sure it happens. Also, find out if the military are involved, but," Kyle paused, "we don't give them anything unless they give us something, first." There was a chorus of agreement. Kyle ended the call and looked over at Tyler, who was staring at him.

"Don't wait... kill them all," she said. The anger in her voice was matched by the hatred in her eyes. There was no smile on Rhydian's face.

"Did you hear all of that?" he asked. Tyler turned to walk out of the room,

"Yeah, and I can guess exactly what happened," she said.

"What is that?" He turned to look at her as she stopped in the doorway. She looked over her shoulder at him, and said, with venom in her voice,

"The one they turned ...his first kill would have been someone he knew, someone he wanted to get back at. Get your boys to look there; that will be the connection."

"Why do you think that?" Kyle asked. Tyler spun around. She placed her hands on either side of the doorway, and there was a look of near rage on her face.

"Because, once they realise that they can do *whatever they want* and know that they can get away with it, they will go after someone from their past, someone who has hurt them, someone they want to get back at! That is what they do! .... Oh, for fuck's sake, don't you know *anything* about what you are up against?" There was a pause. She stared at him, then turned and stormed off. A door slammed, and Kyle turned back towards the TV.

"She hates them," Rhydian said. Kyle glanced over at the sullen teenager.

"Well, I suppose she has reason to." Kyle looked at the TV; the news story had moved on again. Rhydian moved almost without a sound and stopped by the door.

"Kyle ...." He turned. She was standing in the doorway, her body facing the doorframe. She was looking back at him, with a pleading look on her face.

"What?" he asked. She looked down, then back up at him,

"Do what she says .... kill them all .... don't wait. They are evil - never forget that!" Kyle nodded and Rhydian turned and left. The phone in his pocket buzzed with the arrival of a message, and he looked at Dermott's name on the screen. He pressed the green button and the message opened. It was only one line.

'WE HAVE THEM.'

Chapter 16

Dermott studied the sunrise and, for a moment, he was at peace. He was sitting in the Land Rover. The coffee perched on the dash was cold – it had hardly been touched. He had purchased it with breakfast when he'd stopped at a garage attached to a small supermarket. The breakfast hadn't been that great either. He looked out the windscreen at the landscape in front of him; the countryside was beautiful. The small radio on the seat beside him suddenly crackled to life. He recognised the voice as a member of one of the teams he had deployed.

"Delta, November, that is second Charlie on red and passing red nineteen." He did not do anything - he didn't have to. A second vehicle was coming down the road towards where he was parked in the layby. The first car had just done a drive-by to confirm that he was there; at least they'd got that bit right. He glanced over at the forest block on the far side of the road. Though he could not see them, he knew there were two more men in a subterranean observation post. Their camera would record the SAS Major arriving and the electronic countermeasures equipment, also pointing towards him, would ensure that he could not be recording their conversation. The voice spoke again. "Delta, November, two mikes." He was less than two minutes away. He picked up the small radio.

"November, Delta," he had got the message. He turned it off and set it down on the seat beside him. Dermott picked up the large A4 Envelope and got out of the 4 x 4. He looked down the road, knowing Alan Dukesby was approaching. It did not take long before the small, red hatchback crested the hill, slowed down, turned into the layby and parked behind him. He was alone. Dermott waited as the engine died and silence fell over the area. The Englishman seemed to be doing something inside the car, and Dermott studied the vehicle. A trained eye could spot the minute indicators which gave away the fact that it was a surveillance car. The Major was still busy with something on the front passenger seat, and his expression showed he was not 100% happy. A small grin came over Dermott's face. The car was facing where they would be talking, and the major had just discovered that all his electronic equipment was not working.

Alan opened his car door and got out. He was wearing scuffed walking boots, baggy jeans and a thick woollen jumper with a shirt collar visible. He smiled as he straightened up.

"Good morning Dermott," he said, Dermott walked towards him as he closed the car door. "Mornin', how'z you?" The difference in their accents was vast.

"No problem, I am good,"

"So," Dermott stated, "What have you got?" 'This guy gets straight to the point', Alan thought, with a smirk. He reached into the pocket of his jeans, pulled out a USB stick and held it out. Dermott took it and offered him the envelope. "So, what is on this?" Dermott asked. Alan scanned around them, then looked at Dermott.

"Video footage from the car park at Mussenden Temple. The Latvian called 'Yelina' wasn't killed by us." Dermott looked at the USB stick, then up at him.

"So, who did it?" Dermott asked. Alan shifted his stance. "I think it is more of a question of 'what' than 'who'." That concerned Dermott, "Another wolf?"

"No, not at all .... From what our O.P. recorded, it looks like some sort of vampire." *Alan really didn't know.* Dermott did not move.

"Noctrailis."

"What?" Alan asked.

"Noctrailis, they're only called vampires in movies." Dermott saw Alan's eyes darken.

"So, they are real as well, then?" Dermott nodded and held up the stick.

"Is this all the police have?" he asked.

"Yes, that and the requested CCTV from the bungalow the other day." Alan gave a shrug, "But why are you interested in a drug problem?" He looked around them again. Dermott stared at the stick, then raised his head.

"Because the Nocs who carried out the New Year's Day murders are the same ones who did the bungalow." He did not have to ask what Alan was thinking; the look of shock and horror was gradually replaced by a determined stare.

"So .... you lot are, like, at war with them, or something?" Dermott let out a short laugh as Alan continued; the military officer's mind was back working. "How many are there, where are they, and how do we take them down?" Dermott smiled at him and motioned to the envelope that he had given him.

"There are a few already here. We .... keep an eye on them. No, we aren't *at war*. There has been a truce between our kinds throughout Europe for over a century .... And *we* take them down, not you," Dermott explained. "Plus, this is a new lot; we keep an eye on the few who are left here in the north."

"Over Europe?" Alan asked with surprise.

"Aye, our kinds have clashed a wee bit over the centuries, but there haven't been any problems here in a while." Dermott pointed towards the envelope again. "Everything we have about New Year's Day. And we will need everything you have on Kris Martin." Alan glanced at the envelope, then back at Dermott.

"You say that like I am supposed to know who he is." Alan said, which made Dermott's eyebrow raise.

"The young fella they turned after the New Year .... you know, the one who escaped from the mortuary in Belfast." Alan Dukesby actually took a step back,

"I thought that body was stolen?"

"Nope, they turned him..." Alan could see this made Dermott angry, "and they aren't supposed to do that. They didn't steal him; he walked out, ... against the truce, like, you know?"

"So how do you know that it was them at the bungalow?" Alan asked. Dermott looked up and gave a short nod before he spoke,

"From the CCTV footage that was on the news... we recognised him. We think it was Martin's first kill. The others went along to take down the guy. Tell the cops to look for a link between the girl and Martin .... It's all in there," he pointed again at the envelope, "It's nothing to do with drugs!" Alan stared at the information in his hands.

"I will." He took a deep breath, "Well, thank you for this." He waved the envelope and Dermott raised the USB stick. Alan suddenly thought of something else. "Oh, do you know about the journalist?" Dermott stared at him.

"Which one?" he asked, Alan shifted where he was standing.

"Cara-Marie McKenna of the Coleraine Herald!"

"Aye, we know her." Dermott smiled and relaxed.

"She is still looking at all of you at the farm," he said.

"Aye, we read her blog." Both men laughed at that.

"Also, have you ever heard of Rupert Baskerville?" Alan asked. Dermott looked at him.

"Can't say I have. Who is he?"

"Earl of Baskerville Hall .... He has been campaigning against a group of travellers on part of his family land ...." Alan stopped speaking, as there was a reaction from Dermott.

"Aye, yeah, 'heard about that. 'Been going on for quite a wee while." Dermott looked up, "'Not our problem."

"He is over here, and he had a meeting with the journalist yesterday in Coleraine," Dermott shrugged his shoulders.

"So?"

"He is trying to link what happened here to what has been happening on his land for the last while," Alan explained, and Dermott shrugged.

"'Nothin' to do wit' us."

"Well, that's all on that." Alan said, as he pointed to the USB stick.

"Aye," Dermott confirmed, Alan Dukesby relaxed a little. He really wanted to see what was inside the envelope now, but it would have to wait. Dermott relaxed as well, then offered his hand. Alan took the firm handshake. "You and your boys will have to come out to the farm sometime," he offered. They released each other's hand, and Alan nodded.

"Thank you, I will pass that on .... Some of the police might be able to, but I am not sure what the CLF would do if he found out we were spotted at a farm of wolves," he smiled; he was trying to lighten his rejection of the offer.

"CLF?" Dermott asked, Alan blinked,

"Of course, ...sorry. CLF, Commander Land Forces .... my boss," both men smiled.

"We all have them!" Dermott joked.

"That we do." There was a pause, then Alan turned back towards the car. "Right then, I'll need to get this back to the police."

"Aye, right then. Until next time..." Alan got back into his car and Dermott walked to the driver's door of the 4 x 4. In seconds Alan's car was started and reversed in a well-practiced move. Dermott watched it take off back down the road before climbing back into his vehicle. The radio burst into life.

"Delta, November, that is Charlie two mobile back down red route towards red 19." Another voice came on,

"Delta, Tango, that is Two Bravo Foxtrot, back along the hedgerow towards Charlie One." Dermott smiled. The soldiers from the first car had deployed in an overwatch; little good it would have done them if it all had gone wrong. Dermott picked up the radio.

"All stations, Delta. Well done, thank you. Pack up and meet back at the petrol station." Several clicks confirmed everyone had heard and would start to move. As he got comfortable, he opened the window and tossed out the contents of the disposable mug. The mug would go into the bin, and he would never buy it from there again! The Land Rover roared to life.

Alan Dukesby pressed the send button on the covert communications system that was in the car, once he was over the rise.

"Zero Alpha, now mobile." The response was instant.

"Zero Alpha, Three Three, roger. All good?" Steve Minister wasn't far away.

"Three Three, yes. As suspected, they used ECM, but the live letter box was no problem."

"Roger, Boss. They had three teams out, one across the road from you, another on overwatch and a cut off near the junction." Alan smiled. These guys were good, very good in fact, but they were better.

"Roger, Three Three. Was our decoy picked up?"

"One Nine, Three Three." Steve was calling the two who had done the drive by.

David Priest's voice was clear, "Three Three, One Nine. Yes, their overwatch took the bait. Two Zero, did you have eyes on?"

"Two Zero, yes, all complete." It was the voice of one of the newer members of their squad. Then Chris Abbey's voice came over the air,

"All stations, all stations, this is One Zero. Task complete. Collapse your tasks and meet at the FRV, One Nine, Two Zero and Three Zero, acknowledge." Alan relaxed as Chris controlled all the deployed call signs. There was a lot to talk about once they got back to their compound.

∞∞∞∞

It would be nearly lunchtime before there was a knock at Tony Fallon's front door, with a copy of everything the police had given them. There was some 'filling in the blanks' to be done.

Chapter 17

Bloody Bridge Carpark, 9am.

She was sitting in the car and she was angry. In this country, they drive on the wrong side of the road, and it made her furious. She had backed the car into the space. Behind her was a wooden table affixed to the ground; the benches on either side of it were attached to the legs. This was for people to have picnics on. Behind that was a short, stone wall, and the sea beyond. Her car faced the hills. The carpark only had two other cars in it; both were empty and had been since she'd arrived. Over to the left, was a single-story, white building that looked unused. Between the carpark and the base of the mountains was a very busy main road. There seemed to be a constant flow of traffic both ways. She was still angry; she could feel the rage welling up inside her. She struck the steering wheel with the palms of her hands and screamed in anger. She hated this little car, as well - the wheel was on the wrong side, it did not handle well and there was no power in the engine. She looked over the rims of her glasses at the silver hatchback that pulled into the car park and slowly drove past. She stared at the smiling face of the sole occupant. The car made its way to the bottom of the carpark and then reverse parked beside the white building. She could feel herself salivate as she watched him getting out of the car.

Craig Keegan stood up and looked towards the mountains; he loved it here. His hair was a mess, but he didn't care; 'windswept' was how he would describe it. His hair was light brown, and he was unshaven. He only shaved once a week but could not be bothered with a full beard. He was forty-eight and could easily pass for much younger. He was thin, and fit; he could run up to the top of Slieve Donard, the highest peak in the Mournes, in less than an hour. He was in the hills at least twice a month. He walked around to the rear of the car and opened the boot. He pulled off the fleece he'd been wearing and tossed it inside; the skin-tight fitness top showed off his frame. He was not a bodybuilder, but what he had was developed and defined, and he did not have a problem attracting admirers. Yes, he had been married; his two young children were dropped off for one weekend a month. The marriage had only lasted a few years. He still enjoyed female company, just as he had when his wife was pregnant. He liked the attention he got, and he knew that the girls just loved his blue eyes. He lifted his right foot and, placing it on the rear of the car, adjusted the running shoes that he'd bought online for going over mountains. He swung the compact backpack easily around and it landed on his back. He clipped it across his chest.

He knew the route he was going to take; he'd done it before. He closed the boot of the car and looked at his watch, making note of the time. He reached into his pocket for his phone and took a picture of the mountain. He was smiling as he looked upwards, breathing deeply. Walking towards the road, he replaced the phone in the zip pocket of his running leggings. Today was going to be a good day. He looked over his right shoulder for an obvious break in the traffic. The stone wall that separated the road from the carpark was only three feet high, which was great - you could see them, and they could see you... Less than a hundred metres down the road was the metal tube gate. Beyond it, the road led up towards the hills. It did not take him long before he was over the gate and on his way up. He did not need a map; he knew the way well. The road went up towards the Bloody Bridge campsite. He was not even out of breath as he passed it and carried on. The road gradually turned to the right, but the track he wanted led off to the left. He had a good start. He ran on for a bit, then slowed and stopped, smiling. The weather had cleared, and the blue sky only had small patches of white clouds dotting it. He took out his phone and took two more pictures of the hills in front of him. He swiped the screen, then pressed the red button to record video footage. The timer at the side of the screen started counting. He lifted the phone up and began to slowly turn around.

"Another day in the beautiful Mournes." He carefully turned, panning the footage around to his right, "The sky is clear..." he was looking at the screen, at the footage he was getting. There was a large bird circling above the forest block over to his right. "Wow, look at that... looks like a buzzard!" He panned on until he was almost pointing back down the track. The rapid movement on the screen made him look over the top of the phone. "What the ...."

It looked like a large dog, not quite a husky but similar, and it was rushing towards him very, very quickly. He glanced around, searching for the owner; but he was alone, and it was coming straight towards him. He began to move backwards. What was it? His mind was confused; he loved dogs, he'd once had a dog, but he had never seen anything like this. It was closing in on him. He could now make out the face of the dog and it was angry. He quickly glanced behind himself looking for someone, ... anyone. There had to be an owner around here somewhere. Just as he looked back at it, it did something he had never seen any dog do - It started running on its hind legs and its front legs... were... not... legs .... "Oh my God, it has arms!" he heard himself say out loud. He tried to make sense of what was coming towards him; it had the upper torso of a human, the legs were moving so fast that he could not really make them out, but he could see the face .... that face, it was full of hatred. He had to run. He stepped quickly backward again. Fear was starting to take hold. He turned and ran for his life. He did not realize he'd dropped his phone, and then his foot slipped, and he crashed to the ground. He spun around, fighting with his backpack. He tossed it towards the creature. He did not see that the phone had bounced on the ground and come to rest against a stone, the camera pointing up the track towards him. He scrambled to his feet, and his body exploded with energy as he took off. Every fibre, every ounce of effort that he could produce, propelled him forward.

The creature cannoned into him, and he crashed to the ground. Pain exploded in his body. The creature rolled away and skidded, then righted itself. He rolled over onto his back, just as it leapt towards him. He could not hear his own wild screams of blind panic. He tried to kick it away with his feet but missed. Talons dug deep into his legs and, with one movement, the beast was above him. He tried to punch and push at the animal; his right forearm was grabbed with such force... he did not hear the bones break. He saw the creature snap its mouth, jerking its head to the left. The world went into slow motion as teeth sunk into his left forearm and the mouth closed around it. He looked into the bloodshot eyes - hate-filled, venomous eyes. The head shook, and his left hand flew off. It was tossed behind the beast and landed near the phone.

The phone had been splattered with blood, but it remained upright. It could not help him as the beast tore at him, it did nothing to calm the screaming, it did nothing to try and stop what it was recording. It just sat there, recording.

∞∞∞∞

Mike was looking over the printed pictures and text that Alan Dukesby had given him. He had printed out a set for each of them. They were in the portacabin with the TV. The chairs had been placed in a circle in the centre of the room. Mike glanced around at the group. He looked at Darren Forester, who was studying the documents in front of him. Then he studied each man in attendance: Alan Dukesby, Steve Minister, Chris Abbey and David Priest. He was gradually getting to know them better. It had taken some time, but he got the impression that these soldiers were slowly beginning to trust him. Everyone was engrossed in what they were looking at, Mike broke the silence.

"Okay, what I can see so far is that Mr Kris Martin isn't dead. There is some connection between him and the suspects from the bungalow, and the New Year's Day murders." They all raised their heads and looked at each other.

"Connection?" David Priest asked, Mike glanced at Darren.

"Well, he is certainly alive." Darren said.

"And," Steve pointed to the documents as he spoke, "has taken part in at least one murder that included rape and torture." There was a murmur among the group.

"Dermott said to start looking for a connection between this fella, Martin, and the girl." Alan said, and Darren looked over at Mike.

"Can you take that one on?" Mike nodded.

"There's something that I am not getting..." mused Chris.

"What?" Alan inquired, and Chris moved in his seat.

"When they came here, they kept referring to the deer farm as 'Dun' but said that all other wolfpacks around the world have 'Dens'..." he looked around and shrugged, "so, which is it? 'Dun' or 'Den'? I don't get the difference" It was Darren who answered,

"Well, 'Dun' is the Irish word for 'Fort', and the farm is built on the site of an old fort that dates back to the 1100's, so ..." he paused, and Alan joined in,

"So, the location is a 'Dun', ... didn't he say that they were the northern part of a larger 'Den' that covered all of Ireland?" They nodded in unison.

"Are we going to share this with M.I.T.?" Mike asked. Every head turned and looked at him; they all gave him the same look - it was the look given to someone who'd asked a stupid question; one they already knew the answer to. This lot did not share readily.

"There isn't anything here that would be admissible in a court of law," Darren replied, "but if you can confirm that link, then that would help them, yes ...." Everyone sat back in their chairs, and Chris Abbey asked the next question that everyone was thinking.

"So... Vampires, then?" the group looked at each other.

"Well," David started, "that would explain the video footage from the carpark at the Temple!" There was a nod from Steve.

"Hang on," Mike butted in, "are we actually discussing the possibly vampires are real?"

It was an exceedingly long afternoon for the group of professional men, at the end of which, Mike pondered what to share with his friend Sean. He could sure use his help, but... Sean was no longer in the police. The decision would weigh heavily on him for the rest of the day.

Chapter 18

Paul was just finishing off connecting the laptop to the TV in the living room of the farmhouse, and it had just gone 6pm. Dermott, Tony and Amanda had all taken their seats and were looking expectantly at the screen.

"What did Kyle say when you told him that we found out all the Nocs had moved where they were sleeping?" Paul asked. Dermott smirked.

"I sent him the message - he said to keep an eye on them, as normal, and let him know if there are any major changes," Dermott replied.

"So, this is what we got from 'them'?" Tony asked, pointing towards the screen. Paul pressed a button on the laptop and the screen came to life. Tony had called the police 'them' when, in the past, he would have said 'us'. Paul noticed he was finally making the distinction.

"Yes," answered Dermott.

"What are we looking at?" Amanda asked, as Paul landed on the sofa beside her.

"Two sets of footage, this ...." Dermott pointed towards the screen as he spoke, "is from the carpark at Mussenden .... when they took the last of the Latvians down." Everyone focused on the screen. The footage was taken through a light intensifier, which made it greyer than normal, but still clear. There was a small timer running in one corner of the screen. The carpark was about 100 metres away. Then the operator zoomed in on the image. From behind the stone wall, a tall woman suddenly appeared, running towards a car.

"Is that Gurin?" Tony asked.

"It is," answered Dermott. They watched as Yelina paused by the door of a parked car, fumbling for keys, then suddenly stopped and stared towards the far side of the screen.

"She has seen something!" Amanda stated. Suddenly Yelina's body spun. She had been struck by something with force. One hand went to her shoulder, as she slumped to the ground. From the far side of the screen, a tall woman with short, blonde hair walked forward, they could clearly see her face.

"Alison!" Tony recognised her straight away.

"You know her?" Amanda asked.

"Yeah, used to be a copper in Coleraine...left last month," Tony replied.

"Supressed weapon in her right hand." observed Dermott. They watched as Alison stopped by Yelina's feet. They were having a conversation which could not be heard.

"She is going to finish her off!" Amanda exclaimed.

"No, look, she is putting her weapon away," answered Paul. There was a reaction of shock from everyone in the room, as Alison pounced on Yelina. There was a struggle, but the wounded wolf on the ground was no match and could not keep her attacker away from her neck.

"SHE IS A FUCKING NOC!" Tony shouted. There were instant reactions from everyone in the room.

"Shit!" Paul said aloud. They watched as Alison continued to feed. Slowly the struggling arms underneath her weakened and then went limp, as the head at her neck rocked back and forth, feeding.

"You say you know her?" demanded Dermott. Tony glanced at him, then the screen,

"Yeah, but I had no idea about..." His right hand was pointing at the footage. The room went quiet again as Alison slowly stood up. She was covered in blood and took a step back, raising her head, a look of ecstasy on her face. They watched as she wiped her face with her left hand and looked down at the lifeless body on the ground. Alison suddenly turned and quickly walked over towards one of the parked cars, pulling her top off as she did so. She was wearing a plain tee-shirt underneath and used what she had just taken off to finish wiping the blood from her face. She stopped at the rear of the car.

"What is she going to do now?" Amanda asked. The others just looked at each other, then back at the screen; her question would be answered soon enough. The boot of the car was opened, and they watched as she leaned into it. They could not see what she was doing but after a moment, she straightened up and walked back towards where Yelina was lying.

"Right hand." stated Dermott, all eyes in the room focused on the long blade in her hand. Alison knelt over the body, with her back to the screen. She had turned Yelina over so the body was now face down; she was doing something, but they could not see what.

"What is...?" Amanda's question was obvious, and it was Dermott who answered.

"She is slashing her throat to cover what she has just done. ...She's done that before." Dermott looked over at Tony, "How long have you known her?" Tony continued to look at the screen as Alison slowly walked away, returning the knife to the boot of the car. Then she climbed into the driver's seat. She drove away, out of camera shot. The video feed ended. Paul walked over to the laptop and tapped a button, which froze the screen.

"Well," Paul understated, "that is a bit of a surprise." He turned to face the group. "So," Tony's eyes were darting around the room.

"So," continued Dermott, as he looked over at Tony, "tell me about the Noc that we didn't know about?" Tony glanced over,

"I ...." He started, "I didn't know ...."

"Well, let's start with what you do know." Dermott cut him off. Tony nodded.

"Right, sure." he moved from where he'd been sitting and started talking, as the others listened to what he had to say. Dermott was staring at him with a scowl on his face. "I know she joined the police back in 1989, when it was still the Royal Ulster Constabulary. She was first on scene when the IRA hit One Para at Mayo Bridge. That was a bloody one; we lost three guys."

"How long has she been at Coleraine station?" Dermott butted in.

"As long as I have. She has done her thirty years and just left when her time was up... left with a good pension." Tony pointed at the blank screen, "But I don't get it? When did she turn?" Confusion clouded his face as he sat back in the chair. Dermott looked at Paul, then back at Tony.

"So, none of the problems that they normally have?" Tony shook his head.

"No, nothing. She was in our section. She was really good with Kyle after he witnessed the wolf attacks in Coleraine with that journalist. She got him to really open up about what he had seen. It seemed she was the only one who could..." Tony let the sentence drift off as he realised what he had just said. Things were starting to make sense.

"And there hasn't been a Noc killing in the north the entire time she has been here?" Paul asked, Dermott shook his head. The group stopped talking. A heavy silence hung over the room, lasting for several seconds. "So, what does that mean?" Paul asked. Dermott looked up; there was growing anger in his face.

"It means she isn't a full Noc!" Dermott stated.

"Then what is she?" Amanda asked, "and how do we take her down?" Paul heard Dermott take a deep breath in before he spoke.

"She hasn't associated or had any contact with the Nocs already here ...." Dermott looked up and glanced at each one of them, "or we would know about that already." A chorus of heads nodded in agreement, "There hasn't been any Noc activity in the northwest at all," Dermott explained.

"So, if she isn't a full Noc, then what is she and what does that mean?" Amanda asked.

"It means she is extremely dangerous, could she know about us?" Paul asked. He looked at Tony, who returned the look, then glanced down.

"To be honest .... I have no idea."

"Do you know where she lives? Is there an 'other half'?" Dermott asked.

"All I know is that she lives just outside Bushmills, but I have never been there." Tony answered. Dermott looked up at Paul.

"Well, that shouldn't be too hard to find." Dermott stated, and Paul nodded.

"What else is on this?" Paul asked as he pointed towards the screen with the thumb of his right hand. The look on Dermott's face relaxed.

"It's the CCTV from the attack at the bungalow where that couple got torn up."

"The police think it is drug related." said Tony.

"Have they been told that it wasn't?" asked Paul, Dermott nodded,

"Yeah, when I met the army officer, I told him straight... gave him the envelope, as well." The screen began to move. It was CCTV footage but black and white, not quite the quality of that which they'd already watched. It was from outside, and there was no sound. They watched as the group approached the front of the house. Tony started naming each one as they came into the shot,

"That's that guy, Martin, the one they turned. That is Alison Wallace; that is Sabine ...."

"The one from the Salisbury coven?" Paul asked. Tony looked at him.

"Yeah."

"It seems she has *moved on* from there." Amanda was smiling as she spoke.

"I don't know who they are." Tony stated as he pointed towards two male figures who could just barely be made out on the screen. Dermott was staring at the image.

"Freeze that!" he said. Paul tapped a button; the image stopped. Dermott stepped towards the screen, studying the two men, and he pointed at each one in turn. "This one is a sapien; he's part of the security team. I think his name is Matt.

"And the other?" asked Paul, Dermott stared at the blurry image, then he spoke.

"Not 100% sure, but ...." he paused, "that could be 'The American.'"

"What is his name?" Tony asked, Dermott shrugged,

"'Don't know, but if it is him, then we have a fight on our hands."

"Why?" Paul asked.

"Not long ago he made a declaration he would 'free Europe from the grip of the Garou!'"

"Where did you hear that?" Paul asked.

Dermott took a deep breath, "It was at one of their larger covens somewhere near Little Rock in Arkansas. He was making a big speech just before they killed one of ours, publicly." No one had to ask for details; they could all picture what had happened.

"How come we don't have a name, then?" Tony asked, Dermott looked over at him.

"His security is very good. Over there, he is only referred to as 'him'; they never used a name... no idea why," he said.

"So, we have a major problem, then?" Paul asked, Dermott nodded.

"If he is here. Then yes, it was probably him who turned Martin."

"And broke the truce." Amanda spoke loud enough for them all to hear.

"And he broke the truce." Dermott confirmed. There was a pause in the group before Paul reached down to unfreeze the screen.

"We can watch the rest of this, then I will give Kyle a call." They watched as an extremely excited Kris Martin kicked at the front door. The four Nocs quickly rushed through; outside, the sapien, Matt, knelt by the front door. He slowly removed the small daysack that had been on his back, and opened it, but did not reveal the contents. He looked around. After a few moments, just visible through the partially open front door, they briefly saw Kris Martin with a woman whom he was dragging backwards. He had a firm arm around her throat; her hands were clawing at it - she was no doubt fighting for breath; blood was already coming from her nose and her screaming mouth. She was fighting for her life and losing. The excitement on his face was apparent. The doorway behind him gave way and she was dragged out of view.

Matt looked around, there was no sound. He slowly stood and closed the door, then returned to his watching post. He would stay there until morning. Dermott stopped the footage when there was a knock at the door. One of the farmhands appeared when it opened,

"Err, have you seen the news?"

Chapter 19

Mark was sitting at his desk, staring at the screen; he could not believe what he was looking at. The rear door of the office flew open and Cara-Marie burst in. She had a determined look on her face.

"'Morning." the door slammed behind her. He glanced over at her and paused the video footage he'd been watching.

"'Morning," he replied. She flung her coat over the back of her chair and the morning ritual of handbag being dropped, phone checked for messages, desktop switched on, and a general reorganisation of everything on her desk, commenced. The screen lit up and, as she was typing in her password, she raised her head and returned his stare.

"What?" she asked, "have I suddenly grown two heads or something?" He looked back at his screen.

"Did you hear about that fella who got ripped apart down in the Mournes yesterday?" he asked, eliciting a glare.

"Yes, it was all over the news; Keegan somebody, hillwalker," she replied, and looked back at her screen, then again at him. "The news just said murdered; it didn't say anything about being 'ripped apart'." Mark moved the mouse that was attached to the desktop computer and re-started the footage he'd been watching.

"This appeared online late last night. It's the mobile phone footage he was taking at the time of the attack." Cara-Marie's chair flew the short distance, crashing into his. She pushed herself forward as it began. Mark sat upright, joining her. The footage started by showing a view of the mountains. It panned to the right, not a single person in view.

"Another day in the beautiful Mournes," the male voice stated. The footage continued; there was open countryside with forestry blocks in the distance. It moved upwards to take in the sky, "The sky is clear… Wow, look at that! Must be a buzzard!" Cara-Marie was studying every frame as the camera zoomed in on one of the blocks of green trees. The footage started to shake as it zoomed in. There was something there, but it was unclear. The picture zoomed out and continued to pan around so that it was viewing back down the path. The image started to shake again and dropped so it was aimed at the ground. "What the ...." the voice trailed off. The image moved around and became blurred; it came up again from the ground, then began to move backwards, the screen jumping again and again. Whoever was holding the phone had looked behind himself. The only sound now was rushing wind, muffled footsteps, and panicked breathing.

"You should be interested in the next bit!" Mark exclaimed. She glanced over at him, then back at the screen…the footage was not great.

"Oh my God, it has arms!" The voice was now in a state of panic. He turned and started to run, showing a blurred image of the ground and the sky; then suddenly it was still. He had let go of the phone; it now lay on the ground, continuing to record. The figure of a tall, thin man trying to run and simultaneously shrug off a daysack from his back was silhouetted against the sky. Cara-Marie tilted her head slightly; he was running away! She narrowed her eyes to focus as a sudden movement came from the side of the screen and tackled the hillwalker, knocking him out of view.

Then came the heart-wrenching screams of the hysterical man, pleading; but there were other noises, too, and she could not place exactly what they were; growling, snapping, ripping… and the awful screams. She was listening to the last few moments of a man's life.

It lasted less than twenty seconds. The screaming stopped. The other noises continued, just off-screen. Cara-Marie continued to stare at the image, her eyes suddenly widened as the blurry shape of a fur-covered head rose and pointed its snout towards the sky. The long howl of victory was unmistakeable.

"It goes on for another ten minutes, but you don't see anything; just hear noises." Mark explained. She was in shock. Neither of them noticed that the editor had walked up behind them.

"What the hell are you watching, this time?" he demanded. Both spun around in surprise, it was Mark who answered,

"Footage from the murder in the Mournes yesterday. His mobile phone picked this up!" Cara-Marie stood up, excitedly pointing at the screen.

"This is first class; we have to run this story!" she exclaimed.

"What?" Kevin raised his voice, "since when have the Mourne mountains been in our catchment area?"

"But," she started, he quickly cut her off,

"But NOTHING! Local newspapers cover local stories!" He turned away from them and started to head back towards his office, "…and you need to remember that!" He walked on and turned back towards them when he was in his doorway, "Haven't you two got work to do? You know... WHAT YOU ARE PAID FOR!" The door to his office slammed shut. Cara-Marie stared after him; the two receptionists who had been watching the whole encounter suddenly became engrossed in whatever was in front of them. Cara-Marie slowly turned and sat back down in her chair.

"Nearly every newspaper in our 'wee country' will be running that story!" she said loudly.

"Yeah, they will...but not us."

"Who put that on the internet?" she asked, and he shrugged.

"I don't know, but the cops are trying to get it taken down."

"May I have a copy of that?" she asked. Mark smirked and held up a USB stick in his hand.

"Already done." He reached over and picked up several prints that were on his desk, "...and here are some stills for you." He was smiling as he passed them over to her. She looked into his eyes and mouthed a silent 'thank you'. Pushing the USB stick into her pocket, she lay the pictures face down on her desk. Mark closed the link and his screensaver came up. Cara-Marie glanced down at her handbag on the floor beside her. She looked at the envelope and, without thinking, reached down and opened it. As she was placing the contents face down on top of the pictures, Mark spoke,

"I forgot to ask; how did your meeting with 'The Earl' go, yesterday?" Mark was staring at his screen, his hand casually moving the mouse and the screensaver disappeared. He clicked on an icon and a different image filled the screen. She thought for a moment,

"Very well. It seems his family have been dealing with a werewolf problem for quite some time." Mark glanced over at her, "Really?" She met his look.

"I Yes, really!" A phone at the reception desk rang and was answered quickly. The small office radio was playing music that she neither recognised nor appreciated.

"So, did you, or did you not, get anything useful from his Earlship?" Mark asked.

"His 'Lordship' - Earls are addressed as 'his Lordship'," she corrected.

"Whatever," They both smiled. "but was it a waste of time?" She looked down at the small stack of papers that he'd given her. She had, of course, spent most of the night going over every detail, and had listened to the recording several times before she eventually fell into bed.

"No, no it wasn't." There was a pause. Mark turned towards her,

"So, ... care to share?" he asked. Her eyes darted around the office - no one was close. She looked at him.

"What would you do if I told you vampires are real?" There was a small smile on her face, and his mouth dropped.

"What?" She winked at him, then turned back to her own desktop.

"Yep... want to hear all?" She watched him put his fingers into his ears,

"Not listening ... la la la ... not real ... la la la, happy place, going to my happy place..." Then a notebook hit him in the side of his head.

∞∞∞∞

Dani was naked as she rearranged the four candles. She had cleared the dresser top in the hotel room earlier before she'd gone out. It had been easy to swipe the two small dishes from the bar area in the hotel. She positioned them beside each other with a candle at either end, and the other two candles behind them, between the dishes and the flat-screen TV. She opened the small plastic bottle and poured some of the clear liquid into one of the dishes, then replaced the top and returned the bottle to the side. She looked out the window of the hotel room; it was nearly lunchtime in Dublin. She heard movement and looked over her right shoulder at the bed.

He was bound. His hands were tight behind his back and his feet were tied back up towards his hands; he was arched to the point of pain. She had made sure that the thin rope was secured around his ankles to his wrists, so his arms were being pulled backwards. The rope then went up around his head. It dug into his face just under his nose, pulling his head rearward. He was completely helpless; he could not move any part of his body. She had cut up one of the small towels and used one of the strips to fill his mouth and another to keep it secure. No one outside the room could hear him, and he was now afraid. That contrasted with last night.

She had been shopping the day before. She made sure that the tight skirt she had purchased would show off the sexy lingerie she wore underneath, and the silk blouse left little to the imagination. Her hair and makeup had been good; everywhere she'd gone, she'd attracted attention. She would know which one she wanted when she met him. It had taken less than an hour before she was sharing a passionate kiss with him. He was slightly taller than she. She had spotted him taking off his wedding ring before he spoke to her, just the kind of deceit she enjoyed. They were back in the hotel room before 11pm. The sex had been fast and passionate. It was just after midnight when she had suggested he tie her up. He agreed, and he had certainly enjoyed himself. Then it had been her turn.

She stood by the bed and reached forward to stroke the side of his face with the tip of her forefinger. He tried to pull away from her touch, made a muffled sound and tried to struggle free, but to no avail. Her eyes moved over the marks she had left on him... over his back, his shoulders, down his arms. Yes, she had certainly enjoyed herself more than he had.

"Ssssh baby," she whispered, with a devilish smile, "I just need a couple more things from you." There was a muffled cry and strained movement from him. She patted him on the head and turned away. She leaned over her rucksack and rummaged around until she found the small black leather case. It was not large, only A5 size and only about half an inch thick with a zip around the edge. She walked back to the candles. He could hear the sound of the zip but all he could see was her naked back. He needed to get away from her... he needed to get away... but every movement brought searing pain.

When she turned around, she was holding a plastic syringe fitted with a needle. His whole body reacted, fighting against the ropes; but they held tight. He could feel the scream trying to force its way out, but the gag suffocated it. He was completely helpless.

"Oh, don't worry, my love," she leaned down so her face was only a few inches away from his, "this will not hurt a bit." But the smile on her face said something different. She pulled his arm so that he rocked onto his side. Climbing on top of the bed, she straddled him. Fear had taken him, and he struggled painfully. She giggled as she drew the needle down the side of his neck, knowing exactly where she needed to be. Then, with one quick movement, the needle pierced the skin. A muffled cry of anguish came from him as she slowly drew back on the syringe, watching it fill with his blood. She withdrew the needle and placed a fingertip over the puncture site. He was crying proper tears now. She smiled, tapping the plastic tube in her hand.

In one movement, she leapt off him and walked over to the candles and dishes. She pulled the needle from the end of the syringe, then slowly deposited an equal amount into each dish: the one with the clear liquid, then the other. She tossed the empty syringe to one side. Opening a small drawer in the dresser, she lifted out a box of matches and lit the dish containing the blood and the clear liquid. A blue flame gently rose from the dish. She stirred the other dish with the spent match. Stepping back, she sat down on the floor, crossing her legs in front of her.

His eyes widened as he watched her slowly start to rock back and forth. He did not recognise the language she was whispering, which frightened him even more. She had started to chant, the blue flame flickered, and the room filled with an unfamiliar smell. She lowered her head. Her hair fell over her face as she slowly raised her hands. The volume of her voice gradually rose. He thought he could make out some of the words, but most made no sense to him.

"Sleep, wolf, sleep." She continued to slowly rock back and forth, then raised her head, so she was looking at the ceiling. "Sleep, wolf, sleep," she repeated. She chanted in the strange language again, before repeating "Sleep, wolf, sleep." This time, she muttered something, slightly louder, and the rocking grew faster. Suddenly, she threw her arms straight up and let out a longer cry; no words, just the sound; and as suddenly she had begun, she stopped. She dropped her arms and lowered her head. She was whispering in that strange language before she stood up. She shook herself off and walked into the bathroom.

The blue flame was out. He could hear the sound of the shower. It would be several minutes before she walked out again and sat on the bed beside his head. She seemed pleased with herself, and again stroked the side of his face,

"Now darling, I haven't finished having fun with you!" The wicked smile and giggle were back. He screamed in terror, but again it was muffled by the gag. She had paid cash to have the room for another three days, but she would be leaving the following morning. What was left of him would be found then.

She had done what she needed to do, so she may as well have some fun in the meantime. She whispered softly to herself, *Really, what is life without a little fun?*

Chapter 20

Cara-Marie was sitting on her sofa with her laptop on her knees. The national evening news was over, the local news was about to start, and the killing in the Mournes had not even been mentioned. She had watched the footage that Mark had given her several times now and was convinced she had just watched a werewolf attack. The still prints were all over her coffee table and all the paperwork that the Englishman had given her was beside her on the sofa. She searched for more details, things she may have missed. The local news started. The reporter in the studio quickly went over the headlines, which included the killing in the Mournes. The condemnations poured in, along with demands for the case to be solved quickly. Cara-Marie watched as the politicians took turns voicing their outrage at the brutality of the attack on Craig Keegan.

"Did any of you pricks actually know him?" she said out loud. The reporter 'on the scene' was standing by some trees. Dusk was already surrounding her, and the light from the camera made her glow, Cara-Marie was only half-listening. They had not mentioned the video footage at all. The report switched to an interview with a uniformed police officer - she recognised the name of Chief Inspector Anderson. The interview had obviously been recorded earlier, as the day in the background was bright. It started off with him confirming the identity of the walker. The reporter was out of the camera shot.

"Our officers discovered an extremely distressing scene yesterday, and our investigation is at a very early stage," she sighed... how many times had she heard that catchphrase? It meant they currently had nothing to go on. "We would ask for anyone who was in the area yesterday morning to come forward and assist us with our investigation." She shook her head - they had nothing and were grasping at straws. She glanced back down at the screen of her laptop, but the next question made her eyes shoot up.

"What of the apparent phone footage of the attack that was uploaded to the internet?" The large foam-covered microphone was thrust back in front of the police officer's face, he smiled and chuckled at the question.

"Well, the investigation team is currently keeping all options open and pursuing several lines of inquiry at the present time. I would like to again ask if anyone was in the area between 8am and 2pm yesterday, can they please come forward and assist the police with their inquiries." He had said enough; they had nothing, she closed down her laptop and dropped it on the sofa beside her.

The reporter carried on, "Is this just the latest in a string of recent murders? Are these murders connected in any way?" Cara-Marie sat back with the empty mug; she had finished her drink without even realising it. She wondered how he would answer that one!

"No, I can confirm that the double murder in County Antrim and the New Year's Day murders are not connected in any way," he continued speaking, but he wasn't answering the question...what was she expecting? *'Actually ... werewolves and vampires are real and are currently running around Northern Ireland killing people and we have no idea what to do about it.'* She smiled at the thought, but no, that would never happen. Her phone buzzed with the arrival of a text message. She lifted it up and saw Kyle's name across the screen, then pressed the green button and read the short message.

'HI, STILL AWAY AT THE MOMENT BUT YES TO A COFFEE WHEN I GET BACK' Her eyebrows raised at his use of a smiley face. He had not answered her last question, but that would have to wait. She needed more; she wanted to find out more about the 'An Rua' wolves. In fact, the Englishman had mentioned that there are wolfpacks all around the world, and all she had to do was...prove it.

The phone rang. It was her mum. She pressed the button and put the phone to her ear with one hand and muted the TV with the other. Her mum was having some people 'round' the following night for dinner. The fact that she was determined to have her only remaining unmarried daughter join them could mean only one thing.

∞∞∞∞

Kyle was standing behind the sofa watching the news. He had been on the phone with Dermott, Paul and Tony throughout the day. They were going to send a team of four down to the Mournes to try to find out what had happened. They already had calls from the Southern den, *'it wasn't them and it wasn't one of us'* had gone back and forth a few times. Everyone had now seen the footage. There was a stray wolf on the loose and they needed to know more. But that had not stopped Tyler's punishing training. She'd wanted a walk-through demonstration in the gym as to how he had taken down the Mongol. She had given him a wooden training sword, and just stood at the side and watched. She said nothing as he slowly went through what had happened, she did not seem impressed. The afternoon had been about how to hold his short sword, how to defend and strike with two hands, then with one, as he had been 'doing it all wrong' and 'how the hell are you still alive?' was said more than once. He was reading over the message he had just sent to Cara-Marie, guessing what she wanted to chat about, but what could he tell her? Rhydian walked past him and plonked herself onto one of the comfy chairs, she began to watch the news,

"So, what's going on?" she asked, Kyle walked around the sofa and sat down,

"Just the reports about that fella getting killed down in the Mournes." Rhydian watched the screen until the interview with the very well-pressed police officer finished.

"Was it the Nocs again?" she asked. Kyle glanced over at her, then looked back at the news,

"No, not this one. It was a wolf."

"One of yours?" Kyle shook his head. "I thought you had taken care of all the Mongols?" Her question hit him like a brick. A stray Mongol was something that had not been considered yet. His phone was still in his hand, tapping out a message to the farm, he replied,

"That, little lady, is an excellent question!" She grinned at his response; his phone beeped to let him know that the message had gone. The news carried on to a different story, and he reached over to the controller to lower the volume slightly.

"Dinner will be ready in half an hour," the shout came from the kitchen. The two of them looked at each other.

"I guess that's our cue," Kyle stated. The grinning teenager jumped up and started to run towards the door.

"I'm in the shower first," she shouted. Kyle dropped the TV remote, jumped up and started to run after her,

"Not if I get there first, you aren't!" There was a crack of laughter as the two fought their way up the stairs, both pulling each other back to try and get past. It would be the teenager who got to lock the bathroom door first and would make him wait. Neither of them had spotted Tyler standing just inside the door of the kitchen. She had watched them being playful with each other as her face took on a severe look.

○○○○○○

"A Mongol?" Tony exclaimed.

"That is what he just messaged me: 'Could it be a Mongol that we missed?'" Paul asked, as Dermott walked in from the kitchen.

"What?" he said, walking towards the large chair. Paul was standing by the unlit fireplace and Tony was on the sofa.

"That is what Kyle just asked!" Paul replied, holding up the phone, as proof.

"No," Dermott stated as he sat down, "No way! They were *all* taken care of!"

"How sure are we about that?" Tony asked. Dermott's body reacted to the question.

"100%! We got the list of all their names from the two council members: the ones who first came here, and the ones who took part in the assault," Dermott's face contorted as he spoke, "and they got that from the pack in Latvia." Dermott looked towards Paul as he continued. "We got every single one of them!" Paul and Tony shared a glance; Dermott was being defensive.

"So," Tony started, "what are we going to do about a stray wolf running around the Mournes then?"

"Deploy a team," Dermott stated, "investigate as we would do for any dog attack." Paul nodded.

"I agree," Tony replied.

"Right then," Paul stood up as he spoke, "send a four-man team down and let's see what they find," Dermott nodded.

"Any idea who you will pick?" Tony asked. Dermott did not have to think about it... he already knew.

"Yeah, the twins, Emma and Gemma Silver and Will and Richard Gold."

"Silver and Gold," Tony whispered.

"The terrible twins!" Paul smiled as he spoke, "Well if there is anything to be found, they're the ones to find it."

"But what about the Nocs?" Dermott's stern expression was back, "We have found where they are sleeping. They have broken the truce and they are killing *on our lands,*" he glanced at Tony, then back at Paul, "We need to take them down!" Tony nodded in agreement. Paul thought for a moment and leaned back against the wall by the fireplace.

"And finding there is a loose Noc running around only adds to the problem!" said Tony.

"You mean the copper, Alison?" Paul asked.

79

"Yes, we have no idea who or how many she has killed," Tony said. As an ex-police officer, she is *'forensically aware'* and therefore will be able to remove or disturb practically all the evidence that could be gathered at any crime scene!" Tony had sat forward as he was speaking. Dermott followed suit,

"Tony is right." His voice was raised; he began using his hands to add emphasis to his statement. "We have her house, and we have where they are sleeping. We could take them all down at the same time!" Tony nodded in agreement. Paul was hesitant, as Dermott continued, "We have the people to assault her house and their lair tomorrow during the day...finish it all in one swoop!"

"We will have to run it past Kyle." Paul stated. Dermott seemed irritated.

"Tell him, yes," Dermott sat back as if to reinforce his point, "but we need to act NOW!" Tony nodded again and looked at Paul.

"We could set up both teams, do rehearsals once we know the layout of both locations, etc," Dermott sat forward again; he liked positive action. Tony carried on, "and once Kyle agrees, we can be in a position to do both at the same time."

"And end this crap they've started!" Dermott was making his intentions known. Paul thought for a moment, then stood up again.

"Okay, do it." There were physical reactions from both Dermott and Tony, as he continued, "Dermott, set the teams up. I want assault teams, cut-off groups and overwatch on both locations." Dermott was nodding; it is what he would have done. Paul turned towards Tony. "Do we have up-to-date plans of both houses?"

"The lair where they are sleeping? Yes. Alison's house? No, not yet, but I can get the communications team to sort that tonight." Paul nodded.

"Right, let's do it."

Chapter 21

He was standing with his back to the railings at the front of Belfast City Hall. Kyle looked around; the cold was starting to bite. He scanned the roadway in front of him. It was deserted. He looked up and down Royal Avenue. A few of the shops had lights on, but most were in darkness. The streetlights seemed darker than normal, but what was more unusual were the empty streets; nothing was moving. Apart from him, there was no one around. He dug his hands deeper into his pockets. He did not normally feel the cold as much as this, but it was getting to him. It had rained earlier, but he had been indoors, so that wasn't it. He shivered. His ears were tucked under the woollen beanie hat, but they were still cold. His jacket was zipped up to the top, but his body still felt the nip. He looked over to his left; there were no cars, no taxis or buses, nothing... just the darkness that seemed to be creeping over the buildings, trying to envelop even the lights.

The movement over to his right made his head shoot around. The man was walking towards him. Kyle stared at him. His woollen hat was pulled down and his face was lowered, as he was also trying to shelter from the cold. The thick jacket was buttoned all the way up; his trousers were of the older canvas type that hillwalkers would have worn twenty years ago. The man's pace slowed as he approached. He stopped about six feet away. Kyle looked at the familiar smiling face. It was a smile he was not expecting; certainly not around here, anyway. The words of recognition formed in his mouth, even before his mind processed who it was.

"Dad?" Kyle straightened and stood up. He moved towards the smiling man who now held out his right hand in greeting.

"Hello, Kyle. It's been a while." Kyle shook his father's hand; but he was still in shock.

"Yeah ... but Dad ... you're ...." Kyle didn't finish his sentence.

"Gone," his father finished the sentence for him, as he let go of his son's hand. "Yeah, that was unfortunate ... I wish I had known what was going to happen." There was a look of sadness on his face. He glanced down for a moment, but when he looked up there was a sparkle in his eyes, "I see you have grown up," and he smiled again, Kyle nodded,

"Yeah, yeah, a lot has happened since you... went ..." Kyle could not bring himself to say the actual word.

"That is why I'm here. I want to know what has been happening with you." his father said.

"Well," Kyle was a little taken aback, "where do you want me to start, Dad?" His father smiled reassuringly.

"From the day we left." Kyle looked up, recognising the question; the day *we* left. He was talking about Kyle's elder brother, who died the same day.

"Well ..." Kyle started, clearing his throat as he did so, "there were a few of us who went with Mum to the hospital." He paused as his mind fought for the memory, "I wasn't in the room, but I heard that Mum dropped dead on the spot when she saw what was left of you. I wasn't allowed in; they said I was too young." There was a sad look on his father's face as he listened.

"Yes, son, I know, she told me." Kyle's head shot up.

"Mum?" the shock was mixed with surprise.

"Yes, she told me that bit." Kyle's father took a step closer and placed his left hand on Kyle's shoulder, "There are things that you should not have had to deal with ... and that was one of them." Kyle lowered his head slightly, then looked up again. "But your mum is okay, continue." Kyle responded to the command without thinking.

"Yeah, well, I got sent off to Canada," he shrugged. "That was okay, I suppose." Both of them shared a small smile. His father listened as Kyle recounted parts of his life. "I was bored at school, so I joined the Air Force cadets, just for something to do; but when I was old enough, I knew I wanted to do something else; so, I joined the Legion."

"The Legion?" his father asked.

"Yeah, the French Foreign Legion - 2nd Foreign Parachute Regiment, or 2 ReP, as it is in French." A smile spread over his father's face. "I wanted to be with the best and I wanted a real challenge ... so off I went!" There was a short pause as they exchanged another smile. "French wasn't a problem, I mostly learned it in school. I really could not believe those other guys who turned up not being able to speak a word."

"How did they manage?" his father asked, Kyle smirked.

"As one of them told me once, 'you learn quick when you are being kicked in the head'," the two men shared a laugh.

"So, what did you do in the Legion?" his father asked.

"Well, first I became a sniper with 2 Rep," There was an understanding nod from his dad as Kyle continued, "and after four years I applied for Le Crap ... passed their selection without any real problems." Kyle did not mean to boast but he was obviously proud of what he had accomplished. His Dad looked somewhat perplexed.

"Le Crap? Doesn't sound so good."

"It translates as 'Deep Action and Reconnaissance Commandos', but they had a name change after a large exchange with the 82nd Airborne in America. Now it's called GCP or Commando Parachute Group, they are the Legion's Special Forces." The grin on his father's face widened.

"Special Forces ... I like it. We've shared similar roles, what did you do there?" he asked. Normally, Kyle would not be talking about his past like this, but there was something about telling his father that just seemed perfectly natural, so he carried on.

"Sniper again. Our biggest job during my time was in the Ivory Coast. President Chirac sent us in to evacuate over 5,000 French nationals because of the civil war. Then one night, they used two strike aircraft, SU-25's, to attack our location. They killed nine of us and wounded thirty-one, and one American. The following day, we took out their entire air force in one strike: both bombers, five helicopter gunships, all the airfield defence forces and anyone who got in our way," Kyle shrugged. "We didn't have a problem after that. There was some rioting, but we never got attacked again." Kyle was smiling, but then a memory crossed his mind as he remembered carrying a coffin onto the French Air Force C-160. His dad spotted it.

"One of them was a friend of yours?" he asked, Kyle nodded.

"So, what brought you back to Northern Ireland, then?" His father asked.

Kyle thought for a moment before answering,   "I did my time. I was offered an extension and promotion, but I decided to leave. I just felt like I had to come home."

"So, you did."

"So, I did," Kyle repeated. "I joined the police and was with the force until just before Christmas." Kyle's father was smiling again.

"You have done well, very well, I am proud of you."

"Dad, why didn't I know what the farm really was?" The smile dropped from his father's face. "Why didn't I know what I really am?" he asked.

"Kyle, my son," he took as small step closer, they looked into each other's eyes, "there is something else I have to tell you ...."

Suddenly his body jolted, he felt himself twist, then jump from the bed. The cold was gone, he was boiling; the sweat ran from him; the duvet had been thrown aside. He fought to control his breathing; he slowly stepped back and sat on the bed; the spare room gradually came back into focus. He placed both hands on the bed and looked down at the floor. He had never had a dream so vivid; he could remember every detail. He stared at the floor in front of his feet. He continued staring as his breathing slowly returned to normal, then he raised his head and looked at the clock on the side table. The alarm would be going off in less than two minutes; he turned his head. He punched the alarm button, rose and walked over to the window. Using his left hand, he pulled one of the curtains aside and looked out over the landscape of the island. He watched a flock of birds heading off in one direction and a single bird of prey circling nearby. Life was going on... but what had his father been about to say? It would bother him for the rest of the day. He had not noticed that a text message had arrived on his phone from Paul. The shower had been both soothing and rejuvenating and once he was dressed, he set about making sure his bedroom was neat and tidy. Some things from the Legion would be with him always, then he trotted down the stairs.

The living room was empty. He was about to head into the kitchen when he heard the noise. Two female voices echoed from the gym. There were angry shouts, both sounded at the same time and shouted one word. There was rapid movement and he could hear feet slapping the mats on the floor. He moved then and stopped just outside the partially open door. Stepping to one side, he was able to see them both. They were wearing gym wear and had their backs to the door. They had the same stance: left legs forward with their bodies side-on to the invisible target in front of them. Both sets of hands gripped the wooden training swords that pointed straight up towards the ceiling and, for a moment, both were still.

Suddenly, both right feet jumped forward, their bodies turned, and the blades swiped from the shoulders of their imaginary attackers and down through the bodies. The two warriors moved in unison as they danced like synchro dancers: both in perfect motion, speed and rhythm with each other. The blades swiped back, up, around, down with each turn. The dance continued for several more minutes. The single-word shout occurred twice more as they landed their weapons into their targets, the voices only adding to the force of the delivery. He watched.

Tyler moved with ease. She performed the exercise precisely, as did Rhydian. He would not expect a teenager with her body shape to be able to move as quickly or with the grace that she did, yet... here she was. She was still learning but was doing well. This was someone who could certainly look after herself. The story of what had happened on the Isle of Skye now made sense; he could see that she had been truthful. This woman would have been able to keep the Nocs contained in the room as Tyler freed herself.

Then they stopped. The two fighters turned to face each other and, maintaining eye contact, bowed slightly, then they relaxed, smiled and shared a short hug. He stepped back from view to allow them some family privacy.

"Yes, you can come in now," Tyler shouted from inside the room. Kyle, feeling somewhat sheepish, raised his hand and pushed the door open. They had separated and were sharing a private joke; both watched him enter.

"That was very impressive!" he said, as he took a few steps onto the mats. They looked at each other, smiles beamed, and they spoke in unison.

"What-ever!" Then they both burst out laughing. He just stood there, outside the conversation and outside of the joke. They composed themselves very quickly.

"Here, give me that." Tyler reached out for the training sword and Rhydian handed it over. "Now, go and finish off sorting out breakfast." Rhydian turned and smiled as she walked past Kyle. It was a huge smile... she was happy, she left the room, pulling the door shut. He watched her go, then turned back towards Tyler. She had turned away from him and was walking over to one of the large open black canvas bags. She dropped the wooden swords into it.

"I mean it, that was very impressive," he repeated. She looked back over her left shoulder in acknowledgement. She knelt down and zipped the bag up, then answered him,

"She has come a long way in a very short time." Tyler reached over for a dark-coloured sweat top, "but then, she's had to." As she stood up, she pulled it over her head and then pushed her arms into it. She turned towards him, adjusting it.

"What happened to her parents?" Kyle asked. Tyler glared at him before she answered.

"They are dead." She was walking past him as he spoke again.

"How?" She stopped right beside him and looked into his eyes.

"Nocs." She took one more step, this time he raised his voice,

"Right, let's get one thing straight here, I AM ALPHA, which means ...." Before he could finish his sentence, she had spun around. Her right hand gripped his throat as the palm of her left hand hit the centre of his chest. The force of the blow slammed his body into the wall and, for a moment, he was stunned. She had him up against the wall and it felt like, if she could, she would have pushed him through it.

"RIGHT, LET'S GET ONE THING STRAIGHT, YOU ARE *NOT* ALPHA HERE!" She pushed her face close to his; he could feel the force of her anger. He felt his wolf rise. His body tensed, ready for the fight. She let out a low growl from her clenched teeth and he felt his wolf back down. He could not win. Here, she was alpha. He felt his body relax and obey her. Her grip loosened, then she stood back and released him. He looked down towards the floor, then up at her. The anger had gone. She had established herself. He could see that, so far, everything he had heard about her was true. She took another step back.

"Sorry," he had said it quietly, she nodded.

"No problem." she said, placing her hands on her hips. She took another step backwards, opening the gap between them. "You run the fort. There, you are in charge. Here," she paused for a second, "here, it is me!" He nodded, her smile widened, "Cool... right then, how about you go and help Rhy in the kitchen and I will be in shortly." She turned and walked over to the far side of the room and moved one of the large plastic storage boxes. She knelt down in front of the long, dark-stained wooden box underneath, and looked back over her shoulder. "It is your breakfast as well you know, and this isn't a hotel!" The smile was still there but the sternness in her eyes let him know that it was not a request.

"Okay." His body moved without conscious thought and he walked out of the gym. As he was closing the door behind him, he heard the sound of metal being pulled against metal. He did not fully close the door. The sweat top flew off again and landed on the far side of the room and she took up the centre of the open gym. She was staring at the far wall. The sword was nearly hidden by her leg as she held it in her right hand. Her movements were slow, at first. She gracefully brought the straight ninjato sword up in front of her face and gripped it with both hands. He studied the craftmanship of the sword. It was not an ornament, it was not a decoration, but it was a thing of beauty. It had been crafted by an expert. Slowly, she started to dance around the room. There was a 'swish' as the sword parted the air. She turned, the blade moved faster, turning, gliding, parting. The speed of her movements increased. He was mesmerised. He had never seen such beauty, such deadly beauty. He watched. Each movement was a strike, each leg extension was a well-aimed and well-delivered kick. When she turned, extending her elbow, he could see the power that was being delivered. If it had been broken down, every movement was a precise strike, he knew he was watching a master.

Suddenly, the dance exploded. The sword launched in multiple directions - the speed was intense! He stood and watched as she dominated the entire room. She was engaging multiple targets; she was fighting for her life. Her grip was double-handed as the blade swiped around. Whoever her target was, they just lost their head! The sword suddenly spun as if on the face of a large clock as she kicked out to the side; her body ducked from an attack and her right foot came up like the strike of a scorpion; her fingertips briefly touched the ground as her body spun around, her foot clearing the area around her as her right hand extended. She caught the grip of the sword as if it had been suspended in mid-air. She forward-rolled as she jumped up, her limbs continued the frenzy of her defence against those around her. She dropped down onto her bum and, with speed and force, propelled herself backwards, landing upright on her feet. The sword parted the air and suddenly she stopped.

Her right eye stared down the blade and into his right eye. She did not blink, she just remained motionless. There wasn't a drop of sweat on her. In fact, she was hardly out of breath. She just stared at him.

"Breakfast is not going to get sorted with you standing there, you know."

Chapter 22

Mike Dear was sitting alone in the TV room of the hangar. It was busy outside; the military had been assigned an urgent task but, because he was not fully trained and hadn't obtained his full security clearance for this job, he was not allowed into the briefing. Whatever it was, everything else was shelved. Cars revved their engines and English voices barked; the hangar would be empty soon enough. The TV was off, he had the small coffee table covered in paperwork - most of it was what they had been given by Dermott. He could still not believe it all. He picked up one sheet of paper, rereading the information, he wondered if he should share any of this with Sean. The single door behind him opened and Darren Forester walked in, smiling.

"'Morning, dear!" Mike cringed - that joke ran its course when he was just a constable. He had hoped once he'd been promoted, he would never hear it again. It still irritated him.

"'Morning, Grey Fox," he said, and looked back at the information in his hands. Darren landed on one of the uncomfortable chairs opposite him.

"So, what have we here?" he asked, sitting forward, Darren seemed in a jovial mood.

"Dermott was right. There is a connection between Martin and the girl from the bungalow," Mike did not look up from the paper.

"Nice one! So," Darren started, "don't keep it a secret. What is it?" he asked. Darren's good mood was not infectious. He was sure happy about something. Mike was trying not to let it annoy him. He forced himself to relax. Reaching forward, he lifted one of the sheets of paper and handed it to Darren, who took it and sat back in the chair. Mike explained,

"They went to school together and over a four-year period she took out two different restraining orders on him." Darren looked up as Mike continued, "both of which, he broke; two arrests that resulted in one verbal and one written caution."

"Have you passed that on to M.I.T.?" Darren asked, looking down at the information.

"Yeah, they gave me a run-down of what happened in the bungalow." Darren looked up; Mike had paused. "Evidence points to a prolonged sexual assault with signs of torture."

"Shit ...."

"Yeah, that was for both of them, they said the husband's injuries point to the same, 'very violent male on male assault'; but there was one difference."

"What was that?" Darren asked.

"The girl only had one fatal wound to her neck, whereas he had several."

"So, it wasn't a drug hit then," stated Darren, Mike shifted in his chair.

"Well, if it was, he must have done something exceptionally bad. They said that the Drug Squad had a party to celebrate his demise." Darren looked up again. Mike glanced over at him and shrugged, "'Guess they are really pleased he isn't around anymore."

"So, are drugs still their main line of inquiry?" Darren asked.

"Publicly, yes. They don't want the nickname of 'vampire squad' following them."

"And what is that like?" Darren was smiling. Mike tried not to smile but he could not help it he had been a part of the 'werewolf squad' and had enjoyed being a part of something that everyone talked about.

"Yeah, not something I want to repeat," he reached forward and picked up some more of the paperwork in front of him. "But the big scandal they are trying to keep on top of is that one of the suspects from the CCTV is an ex-copper from Coleraine," Darren looked up.

"Who?" he demanded.

"Alison Wallace. She left the police in December, having completed her thirty years." Mike glanced over at Darren, who was staring past him.

"The tall, short-haired blonde one?" he asked. Mike nodded, and Darren continued. "Yeah, I knew her ex, they split a long time ago." Mike studied him; He was keeping something back. Mike could now spot it. It was part of his skill in reading an interviewee. The guilty always reacted, no matter how small, there was always a reaction. He learned how to recognise when someone was telling the truth or holding something back; and the Grey Fox was definitely holding something back. Darren dropped what he had been holding onto the table and sat forward again.

"Anyway," he started, "that's someone else's problem. I have good news for you ...

ooooooo

They had driven into the village of Bushmills; the traffic had been quite light. The road was open to the left with a small collection of houses just before the flat, concrete bridge that spanned the slow-moving river. Paul Hawkins, sitting in the passenger seat, looked down at his notepad and read the basic directions. There were four of them in the car; all of their equipment was in the boot. No one spoke except the driver who was keeping the communications room at the farm informed of their position. He pressed a small button on the dash.

"Papa, passing Green six." Before they'd set off, they had allocated each route a colour and each junction a number, according to the wall map back at the farm.

"Confirmed, Green six," the farm acknowledged. The two cars carried on. Paul looked around him at the white houses on either side, then ahead. There was only one car in front of them as they approached the small roundabout in the centre of the village.

"At the next junction, turn left," he motioned, the driver nodded. He knew the route; Paul was just confirming it. In the centre of the roundabout was a single stone plinth with a statue on top of it. The stone soldier was wearing an old-fashioned tin helmet and had a long bayonet fitted to the bolt-action rifle he was holding up towards the unseen enemy. Every town and village had a memorial to the First World War. Beneath the soldier were the names of everyone from the village who had not returned from the Great War of 1914 – 1918. Newer iron casts on the side held the names of those who had not come back from World War II. Paul had a childhood memory of his father buying him an ice cream in the corner shop, then the two of them walking over to the plinth. His dad had pointed out the name of a great uncle from his mum's side. He hadn't really understood the significance at the time. It had been a bright, sunny day and was still a happy childhood memory of him with his late dad. That contrasted to the grey overcast today; he hoped it would not rain again.

"Papa, now on yellow heading towards Yellow one," the driver spoke. Paul glanced at the side mirror; the other car was right behind them.

"Confirmed." The farm knew exactly where they were. The cars carried on past the small petrol garage and headed out into the countryside again. They were nearly at her house. The town had passed and there were low stone walls on either side of the road. Paul felt the car speed up slightly. They passed the farmhouse on the left where the walls were higher and hid it from the view of the road. As they carried on, the field on their left came into view.

"Next left." Paul commanded. The single-storey house was unobtrusive. Two round concrete pillars stood at the end of the single lane leading up to the house. The bungalow had an entrance door in the centre, with windows either side. The curtain was drawn back but there were still window blinds in place, blocking the view of anyone approaching

The. driver spoke again. "Oscar this is Papa, turning left on to target... now," he said, just as the car slowed and turned onto the lane.

"Papa, Oscar, roger, turning now," the car behind them was turning as well.

"I can see why a copper lived here," said one of the others from the back seat.

"Yeah," Paul confirmed, "perfect field of view, she could see anyone coming." They were all looking around. In front of the bungalow was an area that could easily hold at least three cars. The driver took a wide arc and turned the car, so it was pointing back down the lane, the other car pulled up beside it.

"If she is in, she will have seen us," a voice from the back seat remarked. Paul nodded.

"Let's go," both cars emptied. The doors were closed quietly. The drivers walked to the fronts of their cars and began scanning the area. The others gathered between the backs of the cars and the house. One of the boots was opened.

"Leave the long weapons," Paul directed. He pointed towards the busy main road, "too obvious from there, we will affect a rear entry. He pointed to the three from the other car, "Team two, to the left." He motioned towards the left of the house then looked at the two from his car. "We will go to the right -there should be a single door at the rear. We'll enter from there." His commands were acknowledged with a series of nods. As they started to walk slowly around the house, each one withdrew their own pistol; the long suppressors on each would ensure that any shots fired would not be heard back at the farmhouse at the junction. They met at the back door.

Paul scanned the surroundings; there were small wooded areas on either side of the open field. He looked at one of the men and nodded. It was answered with a nod and a weapon being returned to its holster. The man produced a black pouch from a pocket. Paul scanned around them again. He was standing on one side of the back door with the two from his car stacked up along the wall. Their weapons were drawn but, to the casual eye, out of sight. It was the same along the far side of the door. In seconds there was a loud click, and the door quietly opened. The three men from the far side quickly moved in. Paul was the fourth man through the door. The first two entered the doorway on the right, weapons drawn. The third stopped behind them. There was no sound as Paul stepped past him and knelt by the next door on the right. The next two did not have to be told what to do; the door opened and, without making a single sound, they entered the room. Paul looked up the hallway of the small house, watching for any movement at all. There was none. The room clearances were repeated until the house had been completely swept. No one was home. The six team members met back in the hallway; Paul unscrewed the suppressor from his pistol.

"No one here," said one of the others.

"Right lads. Quick sweep - look for anything Noc-related, and remember, don't leave any trace." There were shared smiles and knowing nods. Each one would be wearing thin latex gloves and the whole house would be searched before they left.

The fridge was empty and switched off, the TV had been unplugged, as had all the electrical appliances. No one had been home for a while. As they closed the back door, the small red light on the fire alarm that was on the kitchen ceiling started to flash. No one spotted it.

∞∞∞∞

Matt walked around the side of the small house again. The temperature had dropped, but it was February, after all. He was warm; the heavy boots they had issued him were perfect; the lined outdoor trousers not only kept the wind out, but they dried very quickly. With the fleece and the thick outdoor jacket, he could not feel the cold at all. His gloved hands swung the small hold-all onto his left shoulder. The double-barrelled shotgun inside was broken down - it would take him only seconds to assembly it. He had enjoyed the training; the thrill of driving fast, the anti-ambush drills, using a rifle, then a pistol, then finally a knife. They had done it again, and again, and again. His duty had been imprinted on him: Protection. He and the other sapiens were there to protect them. Them. He never used their name; it did not feel right. He was well paid and well looked after. It had taken a while for him to fully believe they existed but exist they did. The first time he had seen one of them feed, it made him sick and afraid. He had been 'marked'; the small, barely noticeable scar to the side of his left eye. He was marked; he would not be touched.

Matt could not actually remember how he had initially been introduced. He had not believed it, at first, but had been slowly convinced of their reality and their need for protection. He had played rugby when he was studying for his A levels; his size and speed made him perfect for the sport. He was a natural athlete, possessing speed and coordination that few could match. If he had gone on to university, sports would have been a natural path for him. But then he'd met them, and everything changed. Matt had stayed outside the bungalow that the American had taken them to. Kris had been so excited and could not wait to get inside. The man screamed for just over ten minutes, but the woman was screaming for over an hour. Matt's place was outside, so that is where he stayed. It was two hours before sunrise when Alison and Sabine took over his watch. The American was happy with the whole thing, and Kris had got his first kill.

When they had got back to this house, they all shared a meal to celebrate. That had surprised him about them. Yes, they needed blood and it had been explained to him that it was the vitamins C and D that they needed; but they still required normal food, as well. There was a lot of red meat in their diet. He had never met one of them who was a vegetarian or vegan; that thought always made him smile. He scanned every detail of the hedgerow at the far side of the grass field at the back of the house. Nothing moved. He paused. The soft wind blew gently along the back of the house. He walked on. All the doors were closed, every window shut. There would be no movement from inside the house for some time - sunset was over six hours away. He had never seen what sunlight does to them, but he had heard. They looked after him and the others, so they protected them.

He made his way around the front of the house. The view was lovely; this was a really nice part of the world, he mused. He was not expecting anyone anytime soon. Suddenly, his eyes darted over to his left. There had been a noise from the rear of the house. Matt walked stealthily around the side of the house, past the parked Land Rover and back towards the small back yard. He stopped at the corner of the house, and his grip on the straps of the hold-all tightened. Something had moved, but it was something small. His eyes searched every detail. His body tightened and tensed up, ready to react. The hold-all slipped from his shoulder - his left hand caught the straps. He was motionless. The only part of him that was moving was his eyes. Then he stepped to his left, so the house was directly behind him. He was considering opening the hold-all when the wall behind him was suddenly sprayed with warm fluid. Matt had not heard the suppressed stalking rifle fire from the far hedgerow; he had not seen the bullet tip pass through the air, nor had he felt it strike just below his right eye and smash its way out the back of his head. Matt, the bodyguard, the protector, was dead even before the bullet struck the side of the house and ricocheted off into the field, never to be found.

"Go, go, go," Dermott spat into the communicator. The shooter with the rifle stayed with his spotter as overwatch – the rest jumped up and ran en masse towards the house. All of them wore coveralls over their clothes; underneath, they wore vests that held the Kevlar plates snug against their bodies. They

87

all wore large woollen socks over their boots so they would leave no definable footprints. Their gloves were thin, allowing them to use their weapons without interference. Their heads were protected by Kevlar helmets, newly arrived from America -they had only just been fitted the night before. Their faces were covered with plain scarves and ski goggles for eye protection. Their black vests had pockets and pouches for all the tools they would need for the task. Everyone wore a belt with a suppressed pistol in it, but their primary weapons were the new G36 rifles. They'd constructed their own suppressors, which had been tested and retested.

The assault team was broken down into two sections of four - each one stacked up on either side of the back door. Dermott stopped by the front of the Land Rover. The dark eyes of the lead assaulter looked at him through her goggles. The one behind her placed his left hand on her shoulder to let her know they were all there and ready. Dermot nodded. She reached up with her left hand and opened the unlocked back door. She sprang forward, followed closely by the next three. The second team entered less than a second afterwards. One team would sweep the house and the other would go straight down the stairs into the basement, where they knew the Nocs were sleeping. Everything was done in silence. Dermott ran up to the back door, the house team was expertly clearing each room; they had gone over the layout of the house in the arena inside the main barn back at the farm. They had practiced the drill, several times, based on the floor plan the communications team had provided them with.

The assaulter at the top of the stairs held up his left hand in a fist. The three were at the door to the basement, ready to go. Dermott nodded - he wanted to see this. He made his way past the team member and moved stealthily down the few steps. The three at the closed door had removed their goggles and replaced them with the night vision goggles that were attached to their helmets. The lead assaulter looked towards Dermot as he went down onto one knee. Dermott was the cut off, no one would get out past him. She turned back to the task and the door quietly, but quickly, opened.

The three assaulters raised their weapons to their shoulders. As the first one in, she stood in the centre of the basement; one went to her right, the other, to her left. They moved precisely through the room, firing at the rows of sleeping bags. Dermott could hear the suppressed weapons spitting at the bodies, which convulsed and contorted as the bullets slammed into them.

The three assaulters moved with deadly efficiency and speed. The room was silent in less than ten seconds. Dermott could hear them coming back up the length of the basement. The occasional spit of a weapon let him know that none of the Nocs would survive. She approached the door as the main light of the basement went on. Dermott stood up. She lifted the night vision goggles and pulled the scarf away, revealing the face of a young woman, smiling excitedly. That smile he had known since she'd been a baby. He'd watched her grow up on the farm. She was not been much interested in working on the farm but, from a young age, it was obvious this 'tomboy' could look after herself. She had a strong, stalky build. Hers was not the 'hourglass' figure, nor had she wanted it; but he'd smiled when she had been marked on her first moon dance. The only ones smiling more were her parents; their little girl grown into a full Garou, There was no question what her ambition was: to work for Dermott on the assault teams.

"All done." Her voice echoed in his ear through the communicator as she stepped back to allow him to enter.

"All clear," the message was from the team upstairs.

"All clear, no movement outside," the overwatch confirmed. Dermott looked at her and smiled as he pulled his own scarf down. He reached up and pressed the communicator button.

"Okay everyone, all secure; commence site exploration." Three voices confirmed receipt of his message. The overwatch would continue to scan the outside to ensure no one would surprise those in the house; the team upstairs would remove any hard drives, laptops or anything that could give them information on what the Nocs were planning to do next.

"Well done, Ruth," Dermott placed his hand on her shoulder. The rifle hung across her as she removed her helmet. Her long hair tied in a bun at the back of her head came undone and dropped loosely down her back. The strip light in the centre of the basement lit up the room. One of the assaulters was at the far end of the room and the other was in the centre, weapons still at the ready. Any movement would get a swift response. "How many?" he asked, looking around at the twisted bodies that hung out of the bloodied sleeping bags on the floor.

"Twelve." Dermott looked at the young face of the first one that was nearly at his feet. He felt no remorse; he hated them; Ruth stepped forward to stand beside him.

"Is he here?" Dermott asked, looking over at Ruth, she shook her head.

"No... no sign of the American, Martin, or the two girls,"

"Good job, good job," Dermott shrugged. He could feel her smiling beside him.

"Thanks," there was pride in her voice. "I still find it funny that sapiens think this lot all sleep upside down!" There was a short laugh from all four of them.

"Hollywood has a lot to answer for," said one of the other team members.

"Yeah, it has," Dermott said. He looked at Ruth, "you know what to do?" she nodded. Each Noc would be photographed and a DNA swab done. All their possessions would be searched and anything useful would be taken; all mobile phones, cameras, anything that may contain information. Each one would be identified by name later. As they left, a fire would be set in the basement and upstairs. By the time the fire service got there, the house would have been in flames for over an hour and the An Rua would be long gone without any trace. They only thing they did not notice was the small fire alarm in the corner of the kitchen. The small red light had begun flashing when they had first entered.

Chapter 23

Kyle walked slowly into the kitchen, aware that his body would ache later. The training had been intense; he had to learn fast. She'd had him using the wooden training swords all day. The bruises were already visible on his upper arms - there would be more across his back. She had only hit him on the head once, but once was enough. He had learned to duck quicker. Tyler had gone upstairs; her mood having improved slightly as the end of the day approached. He looked out of the kitchen window at the darkening landscape as he filled the kettle.

"Whatcha doin'?" Rhydian's question nearly made him jump. She had bounded through the doorway, around the table, and looked into the empty pots on top of the stove.

"Making a brew...'fancy one?" Rhydian turned and plunked herself down on the chair that faced the open doorway.

"No, thanks... don't really drink the stuff." Kyle turned and placed the kettle on its stand, it would not take long to boil.

"So," he opened one of the cupboards and lifted down the first mug he saw. "What have you been doing all day?" he asked, dropping the teabag into the mug. Rhydian made herself comfortable and glanced over at him.

"What? Today? Mostly an assignment for my maths coursework." Kyle paused for a second, that was something he had not even thought about.

"You are not still at school, are you?" he asked, as he took the chair at the end of the table. The kettle started to bubble. She looked at him, smiled, then looked away.

"Me? What? Oh, no. I am seventeen you know!" she smiled as she spoke. He thought she was younger than that but did not say it. "Nope, I've been home-schooled since she took us in." Kyle thought for a moment but did ask about the other orphan - it was obviously still a painful subject. Rhydian continued, "I'm in my first year of A levels." Kyle thought about the education system he'd gone through before joining the Legion. In Canada, things were different. He tried to work out what she was talking about. "So," she tilted her head towards him, "are you looking forward to tonight?" Her question caught him off guard.

"Tonight?" he asked, she smiled and let out a short laugh.

"She didn't tell you? Okay, I won't spoil the surprise, then." She was now grinning, as the kettle clicked off. He stood to make the tea, then he looked over his shoulder at her. She was still smiling.

"It is not a secret, you know. You can tell me what she is planning!" She let out an adolescent giggle.

"Haha, no, nothing like that!" Rhydian turned and leaned over the table. "She doesn't do the whole romance thingy." Kyle poured the boiling liquid into the mug, then reached into one of the drawers for a teaspoon.

"So, what is happening, then?" he was watching the mug fill up. The teenager behind him giggled again.

"Well, tonight is the first night of this cycle of full moons, so she is going to take you through your first change." The words slammed into him. Of all the things he had expected her to say, it was not that! He was stunned. It took a couple of seconds for him to make the conscious decision to reach across for the bowl of sugar, then the milk. He was still stirring, as he sat down again. She was still smiling.

"Okay," he could not think of anything else to say. Rhydian sat back confidently in the chair.

"Well, from what I can see, you are alright at the training stuff." Kyle lifted the mug to his lips but could not taste it. His mind was in overdrive. Rhydian continued to speak, but he could no longer hear her. He stared down into the mug. She tapped his arm - the touch brought him back into the room. "Hey." He straightened up and placed the mug down on the table.

"Yeah, sorry," he heard himself say, his eyes darting around the room before returning to the happy face that stared at him through her large glasses.

"I said, don't worry, it will be fine .... just listen to Mum. She knows what she is doing." Kyle felt a part of him flare up. The alpha wolf in him raised its head - of course he would be fine; he could deal with any challenge. This was no problem; he would conquer this. He looked across at her, and the look in her eyes made him back down. It was a look of understanding; of knowing he did not have to prove anything. This was just another challenge for him to overcome. His wolf had answered a call once before, but now it would be allowed to come forward and take control. Part of him did not like that.

"So, the whole full moon thing?" he prompted. Rhydian laughed at his question. "It is a medical fact that the gravitation pull of the moon does have a physical effect on the chemical levels in the sapien brain." She was about to say something else, but she stopped herself. Kyle nodded once.

"Yeah, I know. There is a reason why they are called lunatics." She smiled at his statement. He lifted the mug again and an awkward silence filled the room. He fought for something to say. "What are we doing for dinner?" he asked. She looked at the ceiling, as if she could see through to the upstairs rooms.

"What is she doing now?" she asked. Kyle's eyes glanced at the open doorway towards the place he had last seen her.

"Taking a shower," he answered. Rhydian nodded.

"She will wait until after sunset... then, you two will head outside."

"Outside?"

"Yeah, well, she isn't going to let you change inside the house now, is she!" The defiant, confident teen was back. Kyle couldn't help smiling at her retort. What she had just said was obvious.

"Yeah," he paused and wondered for a second if he should ask his next question. *'Nothing to lose'*, he thought to himself. "So, what about boyfriends?" It was Rhydian's turn to be on the backfoot: she had not expected that question.

"What?" she asked, and Kyle repeated the question; Rhydian was flustered for a moment. "Err, me, no, no boyfriends, no time, anyhow!" Kyle smiled; the question had not referred to her.

"Okay, what about Tyler?" he relaxed. Her face tightened, and she became defensive.

"Mum, no," she turned back towards the table.

"Not ever?" he asked, as the uncomfortable teenager shifted in her chair.

"Well, not recently." Kyle did not say anything, he let her get relaxed again.

"Not recently?" they both smiled. Her trust in him was slowly building.

"Well, not that she would ever admit!" Kyle was intrigued.

"Do tell," Kyle had lowered his voice.

"Well, when we were on Skye, she would travel over to Inverness normally about three times a year, which, she would only say, was for farm business .... but it wasn't." there was a sly smile on her face.

"But it wasn't?" he asked quietly. Rhydian sat up in her chair again; there was a note of excitement in her voice now.

"Partly, yes, but she would also meet up with a guy she used to date. But that all went wrong."

"Wrong?" Kyle was using her own words to elicit more details.

"Badly wrong," Rhydian lowered her face to emphasize how badly the relationship had ended. "Yeah, a real mess."

"But she still goes back to him?" he poked gently.

"I think it was just a physical thing. She would always be depressed for days when she got back. I got the impression she just felt used." He nodded.

"So, does she still go there?" Her response was immediate,

"No, she stopped nearly a year ago. But you have someone; I know Amanda, remember?" They both smiled again.

"I was only asking. So never anyone when she was on Skye?" Rhydian let out a short laugh,

"There was this one night when the three of us went to a pub in Portree and this guy made a pass at her in the middle of the pub." Rhydian beamed at the memory, "big mistake on his part!"

"What happened?" Kyle was smiling as well.

"This one guy, a fat guy, kept shouting at her, about her bum ...you know." Kyle could guess what was said. He let her carry on. "We were at a table in the corner and Mum had walked up to the bar and this guy just barged into her," Rhydian giggled again. Her eyes were not focused on anything in the room, just on the memory she was recounting. "It was when he grabbed her ass, she reacted," there was another giggle.

"What did she do?" Kyle was smiling along with her. Rhydian looked over at him, straight into his eyes.

"Well, he lost consciousness and his mouth and nose suddenly started bleeding!" she laughed again, "As he flew across the room, one of his other fat friends took exception, but stopped when she had him by the throat up against the wall!" Kyle knew what that felt like. "After that, no one came near us." They were both laughing, as Tyler walked into the room,

"And what are you two laughing at? I could hear you from upstairs." Rhydian and Kyle looked at each other, then Rhydian answered.

"Just telling him about life on Skye." He glanced at Rhydian, then relaxed back in the chair,

"Yeah, island life sounds boring." He looked at Tyler, who had changed out of the gym wear she'd had on when they were training. She was now wearing an old, dark-coloured hooded top with matching bottoms. The bright colours of her trainers contrasted with her clothing He took note that Rhydian had not told her what they had really been talking about.

"Ready for ....?" he queried. She walked around the far side of the kitchen table and headed for the back door. She looked back over her shoulder with a stern look on her face.

"Well, don't just sit there looking gormless, come on!" The back door opened, and a cold blast forced its way in as Tyler disappeared out into the darkness. Rhydian looked at him and raised her eyebrows.

"That was your cue .... You are meant to follow her," she laughed as she spoke. He reacted quickly: the mug went down on the table and he stood up, pushing the chair backwards. He darted past Rhydian and out the door into the cold, not even shutting the door behind him. Tyler was striding straight up the middle of the grassland to the rear of the farmhouse. It did not take him long to catch up. She walked in silence as he fell into step with her. They walked in silence. He felt the cold of the night. Even though the moon was partially hidden behind a long cloud, the land was lit up. His eyes slowly adjusted to the greyness of the night, as more details came into focus. He could make out the far lights from the harbour on the island.

Suddenly, she stopped. He had taken another two paces before he stopped, as well. It was only now that he noticed she had been gently whispering the whole time. She was looking down at the ground.

"Take off your top." She commanded. He moved without thinking, as her eyes directed him to drop it on the ground. "Remove your footwear." Again, he did as he was told. He only felt the cold from the earth on his feet for a few seconds; then it did not matter anymore. He glanced up at the moon, which seemed to warm him as it was slowly revealed from behind the cloud. The whispering continued. The landscape sharpened in detail. The wind was soft and moved slowly bringing with it different smells. Some were familiar - the heather, the grassland, the smell of the sea that was not far away. Other smells were unusual. He did not notice that he couldn't smell her, or that she had taken a step back. "Remove your bottoms." He just barely made out the whisper. His body had followed the command before he even registered it. He was now completely naked, in a field, on an island, off the north coast of Northern Ireland in February. The frost was just starting to form but, for some reason, he could not feel it. He knew it was there, he was aware of it, but it did not feel cold. He looked around, feeling a strange connection. He turned towards the sound of the sea crashing onto the rocks. They were out of sight, but he could hear them, smell them. It was wonderful.

"This is ...." He could not form the words to describe what he could see, hear and feel. Then Tyler spoke.   "COME WOLF, COME."

His body exploded in pain. As he dropped to the ground, he couldn't even hear himself scream. His entire body contorted and convulsed. Pain burst through every part of him; he had never felt pain like it, all the pain he had ever felt had come back; come back all at once, in every part of his body. Everything burned. The cold of the ground offered no comfort, the woman who was staring at him offered no comfort. The pain racked through him. He tried to form words but couldn't. His hands fought for the source but found nothing. The lightening racked through every fibre, every organ, every piece of him. It burned; it burned, and made him scream, but nothing could make it go away. His body began to pulse; his eyes burned inside his head; his hands tried to claw at his face, but the very movement made his arms explode. It pulsed and pulsed and made him shake; he could not hear himself shriek as his body started to rock and shudder in tiny movements. He suddenly became aware of the whispering. His eyes were squeezed shut, trying to keep the pain out, but nothing worked. The pain continued to pulse from his head to his toes; pulse, pulse, pulse, every movement racked his body in pain, and it was a pain he could do nothing about.

Slowly, very slowly, it started to lessen, his body began to relax. Gradually, the pain grew less; he did not even know if the pain was still there...he was losing consciousness, and slowly he drifted off into the darkness.

Chapter 24

The trees had sheltered her from most of the rain earlier. The first full moon had been last night, but there had been no one up here. She looked up at the sky, she did not have to look at her watch to know it was only mid-morning. She went onto one knee and breathed in through her nose; she could smell the grass, the bark of the trees, the scent of field mice. It wasn't what she wanted. Then it hit her! A gust of wind whipped past the edge of the tree line and that scent filled her nostrils; they flared. She closed her eyes and touched the ground with outstretched fingers, her nose lowered towards it and she breathed in deep. That scent. She felt her pulse quicken; her body was reacting; the excitement in her physical body started to grow. Her eyes slowly opened, and she looked towards the pathway that was at the far side of the stone wall. Her body reacted and she took off like a sprinter. She ran. She ran as fast as her body would move. She ran towards the metal tubed gate that was in the corner of the ploughed field; she ran, her heart thumped with joy inside her chest, thumped with excitement at what was coming. She sprang over the gate with ease and landed in the track. She looked down to the left. She could see the farmhouse that had been converted into a café, with a camping area behind. It was empty now. The track carried on to the right. The scent was taking her that way. She went down on one knee again,

"Weniger al seine stunde!" she said aloud. Yes, it had been 'less than an hour' since they had passed - the scent was on the ground. A breeze blew against her face as she stood up. She slowly started to walk up the empty track towards another tubed metal gate, after which, it turned into a narrow path. She vaulted over with ease and looked around. There was an information board that was all in English; she could read it, of course, but she chose not to. Her eyes followed the path, with the stone wall on the left. It went all the way towards the summit of Binnian mountain. The mountain appeared empty, but she knew they were there.

She began to move at a walking pace, at first. She could feel her mouth start to salivate. Her pace quickened; her imagination flowed; her body tensed in anticipation. She loved this. Breaking into a jog, she covered the distance with ease, even as the path got steeper. She jumped from rock to rock over a small brook; her pace had quickened again, and the scent grew stronger. She was panting, not from the physical exertion, but from excitement. She made her way around an outcropping of rocks and spotted some rubbish that had been dropped: an uneaten crust of bread, an empty wrapper from a brand of instant snacks. She picked it up and sniffed at it. It was an older scent and it was not what she was following. She dropped it and took off again. The hill got steeper and she was now going along the side of the stone wall. Looking ahead, there was no one in sight, but there were signs on the ground: fresh footprints, a compressed area of grass where someone had sat down, recently disturbed rocks. She was catching up with them; the scent was growing stronger. She followed the wall as it climbed the side of the hill.

Up ahead she could see a wooden structure where a smaller stone wall met the larger wall at a right angle. She would stop there. Moments later, she was off again. It would normally have taken over an hour to reach the wooden steps that went over the wall, but she had done it in less than twenty minutes. She dropped her small rucksack and drank some of the water from the plastic bottle on the side. She unzipped her fleece top and walked around - the scent was gone. She brought her breathing back under control and closed her eyes. She went down on one knee and again reached out with her fingers. She closed her eyes and breathed through her nose. Her head spun around towards the direction of the laughter - it was from the far side of the wall. She slowly stood up and walked back towards her backpack. Staring down at it, she allowed the fleece to slide from her shoulders. She folded it and dropped it onto the top of her pack. She would need the large bottle of water to wash afterwards. She looked at the steps; she was breathing through her flared nostrils. The excitement grew... she loved this.

Cara-Marie sat on the sofa in her flat. The plate of half-eaten food was on the coffee table in front of her. The TV was on a news channel, but she was not really watching it; her mind was elsewhere. Meeting up with the English Earl had given her renewed vigour about what she was doing.. Her laptop was beside her. She had done an update on her blog; she was getting more followers, but most were fantasists from around the world desperate for the stories about werewolves to be true. She had asked the question, 'What if werewolves are real?' The responses made her smile: 'pour me a vodka and hope it's not the boyfriend!'; 'lock the cat flap and the windows'; 'call the journalist an idiot and move on!'. Some were more positive: Research more about the mythology surrounding it to try and prepare myself for protective purposes. She looked at her phone, picked it up and started scrolling through the names. She stopped at Kyle's.

She pressed the 'call' button and placed the phone to her ear. It was an automated voice that answered her. 'Sorry, the phone you are trying to reach may be switched off, please try again later or ...' she cut the call off before it finished. She looked at the screen. He was the new leader of the 'Northern den' and she knew it. She also knew he knew that she knew. She wished she had never sent that text when she challenged him about it; he had been very standoffish ever since. She dropped the phone on the sofa and turned up the volume on the TV. By the end of the programme she would have sent several texts and urgent calls to Mark and the editor. There was a lot to do.

ooooo

The evening news was on. The main stories were all about Afghanistan: a helicopter that had been flown by American Special Forces had crashed, and the Taliban were claiming they'd shot it down; the Americans were saying it had crashed and there were no survivors. 'It doesn't matter either way' he thought to himself… 'same result'. The next news story was about the ongoing fallout from the financial crash last year. There was still nothing about Northern Ireland. The news programme was coming to an end, when Darren Forrester walked in.

"Hi Mike." Mike Dear nodded in reply. The room in the portacabin was empty except for the few chairs that all faced the cheap TV. The walls were bare and there was a hum coming from the single strip light in the centre of the ceiling. "So, anything on the news yet?" Darren asked, as he approached Mike.

"Nothing on the main news." Mike spotted the thin hardback folder in Darren's left hand. "What have you there?" he asked. Darren looked over at him.

"Images from the scene," Darren stared at the TV screen as the main news finished and a weather forecast began.

"Is it bad?" Mike asked. Darren glanced at him, then offered him the folder,

"See for yourself." Darren tucked his hands into his pockets as Mike opened the folder. The first page had short, typed paragraphs, which he skipped over. "Just to warn you," Darren continued, "it's bad; worse than last year." Mike turned the plain sheet of paper that had 'POLICE EVIDENCE' in large letters stamped on it, as Darren continued, "…proper Jack the ripper stuff." The local news was starting. The camera zoomed in on the grim-faced presenter.

"We start this evening with the shocking murder of five hillwalkers in the Mourne mountains early this morning." Mike looked at the first picture, unrecognisable as a human body.

"Have the names been released yet?" he asked, as the presenter handed over to a reporter who was near the scene. There was a uniformed police officer standing in the middle of a pathway with stone walls running either side of it. The path was spanned by a single line of blue and white police tape. The reporter was wearing an outdoor jacket and, although it had not rained, the clouds in the background were ominously dark.

"Yes, thank you. The grisly discovery of five mutilated bodies was made just before lunchtime today." The reporter was looking directly into the camera, he was illuminated by a bright light.

"I don't think so," Darren replied. "They'll have to notify the families first." Mike nodded, then looked at the next picture. Darren heard his intake of breath.

"Shi ….it," Mike said, without thinking.

"*Have they been identified yet?*" asked the presenter in the studio. The screen was filled with the reporter, who was reading from a notebook in his left hand,

"*Yes, the names have just been released by the police in the last few minutes.*"

"Someone has been busy," Mike had not meant to voice his opinion out loud.

"*The first is fifty-one-year-old David Jackson, a Mathematics teacher,*" Mike looked at the picture in his hand. He closed his eyes momentarily and, for a moment, was back in the wooded area of Castleroe. The reporter carried on, "*Also among the deceased are forty-eight-year-old Amy Walken and her teenage son Michael. Amy was a nursing sister and her son was getting ready for his upcoming exams.*" Mike continued to flick through the pictures, each one as gruesome as the last.

"This isn't anything like what happened last year." he stated.

"The last two have been identified as forty-nine-year-old Fionnuala Cole, an I.T. consultant in Belfast and forty-one-year-old Lisa McCann, a charity worker."

"A maths teacher, a nurse, her son, an I.T. consultant and a charity worker… how did they all end up walking in the Mournes together?" Mike asked out loud as he continued to look through the pages in front of him. Darren nudged his side.

"Read the bio at the front." Mike glanced at him, then closed the folder and reopened it at the front page. "They are all from the same street in Lisburn and they all go to the same church …. common denominator." Mike studied the information in front of him.

"*So, who would want these people dead? It doesn't make sense!*" The reporter handed back to the studio as the first of a line of local politicians started condemning the murders.

94

"Well, Newry M.I.T. do not think it was a targeted attack," Darren commented, "just wrong place, wrong time."

"Any ideas who?" Mike asked. Darren looked at him and smiled,

"Now that... is the real question!" he surmised. As Mike started going through the pictures again, Darren said "Well, it certainly isn't your *friends* from last year - they are all dead."

"Where did it happen?" Mike asked quietly.

"Not far from the summit of Slieve Binnian," Darren answered as he pulled the buzzing mobile phone from his pocket, "Have you ever been there?" Mike shook his head. Darren put the phone to his ear and turned away slightly.   "Hello," Mike looked at the TV, recognising the face of the local politician on the screen. He despised him. *"...And I think it is about time the police get this figured out and bring all this killing to an end."* Mike thought for a moment; the person on the screen had not been this angry when the past killings had occurred.

"So, no name yet?" Darren said into the phone, "Yeah, sure, email me what you can, and I will see what I can do." Mike had heard that phrase many times in the past. He was glad he was not M.I.T anymore. The news was on a different story now. Darren replaced the phone in his pocket and turned back to Mike.

"Well?" Mike asked, Darren looked at the TV screen,

"Nope, no one local. Plus, there isn't anyone around who could do that." There was a pause and the only sound was from the TV. Mike handed the folder back to Darren.

"Any ideas?" Mike asked. Darren turned his head and smiled,

"Ideas? Yes, loads …. I think we need to speak to your 'Furry and Fang' club at that deer farm." Mike breathed in.

"Do you think they did it?" Mike asked.

"If they didn't, they may know who did." Darren slapped Mike on the shoulder and turned to walk out of the room, "Come on, we've got stuff to do before you head out." It would be some time before Mike realised the one question he had not asked, which would bother him for a long time: 'How did he get the pictures so fast?'

Chapter 25

Alison had been watching the news, as well. She was wearing a white hoodie and jeans; her shoes were on the floor; her feet tucked underneath her. She was comfortable. The door to the living room opened and Sabine walked in. Sabine was slim; her jeans could not have been any tighter and, as for the patterned top she was wearing, well, she had cut away the arms and taken a few inches off the bottom. Her flat stomach was visible. She had her hair tied up in a ponytail. She landed on the opposite end of the sofa from Alison.

"What's up?" she asked as she pointed to the TV.

"Just the news," Alison replied.

"Anything of interest?" she asked. Alison glanced over, then back at the TV.

"Oh, just the world is coming to an end because of the financial breakdown."

"Nothing much, then!" It was more of a statement than a question.

"Oh, the wolves have a problem." Alison commented.

"What?" Sabine asked.

"A wolf is running around the Mourne mountains, tearing hillwalkers apart!"

"Why are they doing that? Will that not bring more attention to them?" Sabine asked, as she made herself more comfortable. Alison shrugged,

"Yeah, I don't think it is one of their own this time." Sabine let out a short laugh.

"One of ours, then?" she asked.

"Not that I am aware of," Alison replied, "and that Englishman has been snooping around as well!" She kept looking at the TV as she spoke. Sabine tilted her head as she thought for a moment.

"Lord what's-his-name?" The look on Sabine's face made Alison smile.

"Earl Baskerville, from Devon," Alison corrected.

"So? What is that to us?" Sabine asked.

"Nothing," Alison sighed, "but his family has been fighting the wolves for a long time."

"Are you suggesting we should help?" The look on Sabine's face was one of annoyance. Alison looked over at her and relaxed. She tapped Sabine's leg as she answered.

"Oh, for heaven's sake, no!"

"What then?"

"Well, he has no love for them," Alison paused...

"The enemy of my enemy ...." Sabine said, out loud. Alison looked over again,

"...does not make him a friend." The two smiled at each other.

"Pity," Sabine sighed. "He was kinda cute." The news was coming to an end. "Anything worth watching on the TV tonight?" she asked, and Alison shook her head in a negative reply. Sabine was much younger than she but had a lot of sway with 'the American'. It wasn't anything sexual - he did not like girls; it was clear that, when he wanted a man, he wanted to take him; and he had certainly *taken* at the bungalow, much as Kris had with the girl. Alison despised those who *took* like that, but once they had overpowered them, she could not have stopped what happened next even if she had tried to. Matt, the sapien had gone up in her estimation. He had stayed outside the entire time, doing his job. When the two of them took over, he was offered what was left of the girl, but refused. She was already dead, and he did not do things like that.

"Pity," Alison quietly said, out loud.

"Pity about what?" Sabine asked. Alison glanced over and shifted in her seat.

"Pity about Matt - I kind of liked him."

"Kind of ... liked him?" There was a mischievous smile on her face. The two women shared a glance and a smile.

"No, not like that!" There was a short laugh from her. "Just liked him," she shrugged again. "Pity," Sabine straightened up.

"He did his job," she paused. A current affairs programme was starting, "as did the others, they were meant to be found." Sabine looked at the TV screen but met Alison's glance when she turned her head, "They had to die - it was what we needed to happen." Alison looked away as Sabine continued, "Besides, you didn't know them. Why should you worry?" Alison did not know what to say to that. The TV screen filled with the happy presenter who was excited about something. Alison wasn't listening to the TV anymore. "Plus," Sabine carried on, "if you had been at home, you would be dead now, as well." Alison was sullen at the thought. Yes, they had attacked her house. The alarm had sounded just as the wolves attacked. They had guessed that was what they would go for - the lair they knew about.

"Twelve is a lot to lose at one time," Alison stated, Sabine shrugged. "And why was there only one protection outside?" Alison folded her arms as she spoke. "Isn't there supposed to be at least four?" she was getting annoyed and Sabine knew it. Turning towards her, she placed a hand on Alison's shoulder.

"Ali .... they were bait; and the wolves took it .... Look what we learned about them." Alison unfolded her arms and glanced over before looking away with a nod. "We got excellent pictures of everyone who took part, their weapons and equipment .... and .... we were able to increase our file base information on exactly who does what at that farm of theirs .... all useful stuff." Alison's body relaxed.

"Well, he sure was pleased, wasn't he!"

"Yes. Between that, him getting a man and getting all of us over here without them knowing; it was some feat." Sabine smiled. The American was in a good mood at the moment.

"When is he going to Belfast?" Alison asked.

"Soon. There is a group coming up from Dublin that he wants to speak to, as well," They both shared a smile before Sabine jumped up, "Right, let's get some food in ya!" There was a playful tone in her voice, and Alison could not help but smile.

"Sure." As she stood, the smell wafted in from the kitchen. "Who is cooking?" she asked. Sabine looked back over her shoulder,

"He is," she walked on into the hallway, "and he is a great chef!"

ɔɔɔɔɔɔ

Kyle's eyes slowly opened. He was in his room at Tyler's house on Rathlin, under the duvet, and he was naked. He went to move, but pain shot through his body like electricity. He yelped. His movements were slow and deliberate. It took longer than usual to get up and get dressed. Every part of his body hurt; he was shuffling like a man four times his age. It seemed to take forever for him to get down the stairs. With each step, his range of movement increased, but it was still forced when he got to the door of the kitchen. Tyler was just coming in from outside, and Rhydian was sitting at the table with a mug in front of her. They were both laughing when he shuffled in.

"Welcome back to the land of the living, Sleepy Head." Tyler said, as her heel kicked the back door shut behind her, blocking the gust of cold night air. She let the outdoor jacket slip from her arms and dropped it onto the back of a chair by the table. Kyle muttered a response that neither of them could make out. He shuffled forward and pulled out the nearest chair. Tyler turned on the tap at the sink and began filling the kettle. Kyle slowly sat down.

"So," Rhydian began, as she sat back in her chair. "How'z you?" She had a huge smile on her face.

"I feel like I've been trampled by a herd of elephants!" was his honest response. Tyler looked over at him, sympathetically.

"You kinda have been." Tyler looked back at what she was doing. Kyle tried to make himself comfortable, but nothing seemed to work. Pain jolted through every part of him. There was a short giggle from Rhydian, and Kyle lifted his eyebrows at her.

"I had forgotten how funny this is," Rhydian exclaimed, laughing. Tyler clicked the kettle on and turned. She stepped forward and motioned with her left hand.

"Well, we'd better do something about it then." She was also smiling, as she walked past him towards the door. "Come on, then!" she exclaimed. Kyle was confused.

"What? Sorry?" He looked at Rhydian as Tyler left the room. Rhydian leaned forward.

"Mum wants you to follow her into the gym. She has some stretching exercises for you to do." Kyle felt his face contort at the very thought. "It will help – trust me," Rhydian continued.

"Come on, then," came the shout from the hallway. He carefully stood up, pushing the chair back with his legs.

"How long was I out for?" he asked, as he started to shuffle again.

"Just over a day," she was still smirking as she spoke. He could now see into her mug. "I thought you didn't like tea or coffee?" he pointed towards the mug with one finger on his right hand. She smiled again and held up the mug in a toast. "Hot chocolate!" She took another drink, as the repeated shout echoed again from the hallway. He let out a short laugh, turned and shuffled the short distance from the kitchen to the door of the gym. Tyler had taken off her outdoor boots and they were placed neatly by the doorway. She was wearing jeans and a small top, not her usual gym wear. He shuffled towards her.

"How come I feel like this?" he asked. Her eyebrows raised and she smiled.

"Because your body has just been through a physical change that has had a profound effect on every single piece of it." Kyle shuffled into the centre of the small gym. He stopped near her. He raised his

97

head and looked at her, then paused. He did not speak. Her explanation was not enough; he was as confused as he was tired. "Your body," Tyler carried on as she turned away from him, "has just run the equivalent of ten marathons, but in less than five minutes!" She turned her head and nodded for him to follow her. His movements were slow and deliberate; his body was stiff.

"So, what are we going to do, this time?" he asked. He was in no condition to fight. She had her hands on her hips and had been looking down as he spoke. His question raised her head only slightly, and she was looking at him through veiled lashes.

"We are going to do something about the stiffness." She relaxed her body and let her arms hang loosely by her sides; she closed her eyes and took a deep breath in. He opened his mouth to ask another question, but knew it was pointless. She wanted him to copy what she was doing. She closed her eyes, so he did as well.

"Take a deep breath in through your nose." He heard her take a long intake. As soon as he did the same, the smell hit him in the face so hard that he almost fell over.

"What the ..." his hands came up to his face as he bent over. It felt like there had just been an explosion inside his nose. He had not noticed the small scented candle that she had lit before he walked in. He fell onto his knees, his hands clasped around his nose. He looked up at her; she was smirking. "I don't see what's funny!" He was annoyed.

"Like I said, your first change has influenced every part of you .... your scent glands have woken up." He rubbed his face as if he was wiping away discharge from his nose. She got down on her knees in front of him. "Right, let's continue." For the next ten minutes she took him through various stretches and yoga positions that would have been difficult for him earlier. Tyler was very flexible; he wasn't. By the time they were finished, he was sweating again.

"I think I need another shower," he said, as he slowly stood back up again. She made no sound as she rose.

"Turn around and face the door." It was a command, not a request. He shrugged.

"Okay." He faced the door, his body tensed up; he was expecting an attack.

"Give me your hands," she said. He was reluctant to do so but he slowly moved his hands behind his back. He was not sure what it was she tied them with, but it was tight enough for him to know it would take him a while to get out of them. "Turn around and face me." Again, it was a command. He did so, she had taken a step back. She looked him up and down, with that stern look on her face. It was a look that he recognised now - there was about to be a fight. She met him eye to eye. "Attack me!" she said quietly. His arms tugged at the restraints. He looked from side to side, then at her, confusion showing on his face.

"With what?" he asked. She started to pace around him, speaking as she did so.

"Now that you are a wolf, your primary weapon is your mouth."

"Wha ...." She slapped his face. She never took her eyes off him as she circled around.

"You have shown that you can fight with your hands, ... but as a wolf, your primary weapon is your mouth." Suddenly, she jumped forward and slapped the side of his face again. She jumped back and continued circling her prey. He spun around as she came around to his right. He bared his teeth. "You have to learn to fight differently!" She jumped forward and slapped him again. He jumped forward, his arms fighting to be free. His mouth snapped into fresh air as she side-stepped and used her left leg to trip him. His forward momentum carried him on, and he crashed into the mat at the side of the gym. There was fury in his eyes as he fought to free his hands. He struggled on the ground and tried to lift himself. She slowly walked around and helped him to his feet. She pushed him gently into the centre of the room. He spun around and glared at her.

"If I wasn't ..." She held up her forefinger. It silenced him. She stared at him for a moment. "Turn around." She commanded. He did so. It only took her seconds to untie him. Once released, he stepped away and rubbed his wrists, then turned to face her. "Well, that is certainly something we are going to have to work on." There was a confident smile on her face as she walked past him and out of the gym. "You are going to need another shower," she shouted back from the hallway. "We will head over to the mainland tomorrow." Kyle stood there, staring at the empty space in the doorway, his anger now reduced to irritation. He continued to rub his wrists as he walked out of the door. He did not realise, at first, that he was not hobbling anymore. Rhydian came out of the kitchen, holding a phone up in her hand.

"It's for you...It's the farm."

∞∞∞∞

The car ride had been uncomfortable, to say the least. Dani had been blindfolded, then they'd put old foam headphones over her ears. They had been driving for about an hour and had stopped twice. Twice, the wolves had gotten out, then got back in again. She knew what they were doing - it was all to disorientate her, and it was working. She was not to know the exact location of the den of the alpha of all the Rua Garou in Ireland. This was only a *truce*. They were, technically, still at war with each other. Dani was pulled from the back seat of the car and the headphones, then the blindfold, were removed. The smell hit her first. They were either on or very near a farm that had cows. The car was now empty and the two wolves in front of her were not the same ones she had met in the town of Swords, near Dublin. She had waited exactly where she had been told to be. She looked around the large barn. For a farm, it was clean, but that smell turned her stomach. The two in front of her just glared at her. There was another behind her; none of them spoke.

A single door at the far end opened and a male figure walked in. He was an older man with shoulder-length hair. He had not shaved that day and was dressed for working outdoors. He did not seem to be in a good mood. One of the wolves standing in front of her turned his head to acknowledge him; he nodded back. He stopped near them and stared at her. He had authority over the others here. When he spoke, it was with a strong southern Irish accent. She couldn't quite place it, but she already knew that, even on such a small island, the accents differed markedly from place to place.

"When my alpha approaches, you will not make any moves towards him *at all*". Dani nodded as he continued, "If you do, you will die within seconds, *do you understand?*" he stressed his point. She nodded. "He will ask the questions and you will answer, *do you understand?*" Again, she nodded. The older man then spoke in what she knew to be the Irish language. She did not understand but knew the two in front of her did. They removed pistols that had been hidden under their clothes, cocked them and stood staring at her. They held their weapons in their right hands; their arms were relaxed in front of themselves. The wolf behind her moved to one side, giving them a clear line of fire. If she moved, the instruction had been clear. The older man turned and started to walk away.

"Wait, what is your name?" she called after him. He stopped,

"None of your fookin' business!" Then he walked away. She stood still as he reached the far doorway. It opened again, and several people walked in. She counted seven of them. The protection team formed a box with a principle bodyguard beside the tall well-built man with silver hair. The teams knew what they were doing; these were no amateurs. The woman beside him walked with authority. She was stylishly, but practically, dressed for the countryside. Dani could see by the way she walked that she was armed as well. The older one who had spoken to her stayed by the door. As they approached, Dani knelt down on one knee and lowered her head, so she looked at the dirt that was in front of her boot. She could feel the anger, emanating from everyone, towards her. The thought made her smile. She listened as they stopped in front of her.

"Rise," the silver-haired one spoke. She obeyed. She glanced up, but did not look them in the eyes, as that would be challenging. She made a point of not looking at head height.

"I am Dani, second princess of ...."

"I KNOW WHO YOU ARE!" he cut her off. Her eyes jumped from wolf to wolf. They had spread out so, if anything happened, they all had a clear shot at her. He lowered his voice when he spoke again. "It is why you are here that concerns me."

"You have nothing to concern yourselves with me," Dani had looked at his chest, not his face, then down again. Everyone stared at her. Her eyes moved over to the woman. Her dark auburn hair hung down over her shoulders. Dani could feel the hate emanating from her, but it was the alpha who spoke.

"So, explain yourself, what are you doing here?" he asked. Dani paused, she had rehearsed this, but she thought it over quickly again.

"I am no threat to you, your family or any of the southern den," she started. The woman grunted. She was not scared anyway, and obviously held Dani in the upmost contempt. Dani looked down again before she continued speaking.

"My issue is with your 'northern den'; they have done me great harm."

"By returning you to your own kind *after* you had run away?" It was the woman who spoke. Dani looked up at her, but only briefly. The woman continued, "And ran away from a solstice .... the very ceremony you were supposed to take part in!" This time Dani looked up in anger and looked into the woman's face.

"I was to be *given* to one of our hunters who had just collected a great trophy"!

"Your coven rules are the rules. You do not get to pick and choose which ones you follow" The alpha spoke; everyone remained motionless. Dani's face started to well up.

"I didn't want nearly 1,000 people watch me get raped over an alter!"

"There aren't 1,000 Nocs in the Salisbury coven - no coven is that large!" the woman interjected. The alpha looked at her, then back at Dani.

"She is right, there are only 200 Noctrailis in all of southern England!" Dani looked down again before she spoke,

"Yes, 200 Noctrailis with 800 sapien members." That got a reaction from the wolves - it was news to them.

"So, what is your problem with the north? Handing you back is exactly what would be expected of them. They did as they should have done."

"My mother is ...." Dani started.

"I know who your mother is," the alpha cut her off, "and, as Queen of the Black Witches, she set the rules .... and you broke them! If you were a 'prize', then that is up to her." Dani's eyes rose, but she did not look into his eyes. She was mad.

"But they have broken the truce; it was not us," she said. There was anger in her voice.

"Handing you back is not breaking the truce; it is honouring it," the alpha explained.

"They killed one of our teenagers," Dani said.

"When?" he asked abruptly.

"When we heard that the Mongols had arrived. We were just watching them." Dani looked up, "We did not intervene; it was your own pack business." The woman whispered to the alpha. Dani heard what she said but she could not understand spoken Irish; the alpha nodded.

"So," he replied. Dani looked up at him before she answered,

"And they murdered twelve of ours while they slept." There was a reaction from the wolves. They certainly did not know about that. Dani continued, "They took down one of our sapien protection outside first, ... *they* broke the truce ... not us!" The woman and the alpha looked at each other. The attitude of the wolves was changing, and Dani was trying not to smile.

"When did that happen?" the alpha asked.

"Yesterday."

"And what are you going to do about that?" he asked. Dani paused.

"Just hurt them," she glanced down, then up again, "just to even things, ...nothing more." Her voice was softer than before. One of the younger ones in front of her smiled; he was warming to her.

"And what then?" the alpha asked. She looked down again.

"Leave."

"Leave?" he repeated. She looked up.

"Yes, leave. All I want to do is even things with the north, then leave ... We have no interest here." The woman whispered again, and again he nodded. Dani was beginning to feel that the attitude of the whole group was changing; the danger to her was diminishing.

"Keep us informed of your movements, and what you are doing." He commanded.

Dani looked down and nodded. "These are your lands," she said submissively.

"Have you fed since you have been here?" the woman asked.

"Yes," Dani replied.

"Where and when?" the alpha demanded.

"On the ferry coming into Dublin and again in the hotel I phoned you from." The woman reacted, but the alpha didn't. She carried on. They would have known about the suspected murders so, by showing honesty about that, they may believe her about this: "I fed from their legs, not their necks; I caused injuries that will make your police believe it was just a killing." Dani kept looking down. The alpha did not speak for a few seconds. Dani could hear the sound of the wind around the barn and the sound of distant voices outside. Then he spoke.

"You will provide details of each before you leave."

"Of course," she nodded as she spoke.

"And you will inform us of all feeding while you are here," he commanded.

"Of course. These are your lands," she repeated. With that, he suddenly turned and started to walk away. The protection team quickly followed suit, leaving the original three staring at her. She watched as they headed back towards the door. The woman was talking to him She could not hear what she was saying, but she concentrated on his response.

"Not our problem," he said to the woman. Dani smiled; she had achieved what she needed to today. The blindfold would be replaced and the headphones as well before she was put back in the car. This time, she asked if they could not put on the local radio station, as the anchor was annoying, and she did not understand any of his stupid jokes.

Chapter 26

Kyle was in the passenger seat of Tyler's 4x4 as she drove off the ramp of the car ferry into Ballycastle. She had told him to pack a change of clothes, a bottle of water and a towel. She had been brief with her instructions about what was going to happen. They were heading over to the mainland, to a farm that was *friendly*; but she would not say any more than that. They would hunt as wolves and he had to follow her lead. Apart from that, nothing. He had many questions she'd left unanswered. She drove away from the ferry and slowed almost instantly with the traffic. She sat in silence and waited for a gap in the passing cars. The radio wasn't on, so there was no noise inside the car. He looked around outside. People walked back and forth, the line of cars seemed endless, and the silver BMW behind them was getting impatient. A dark-coloured hatchback stopped and allowed a gap to form. A quick flash of their lights signalled Tyler that they were letting her go ahead. She waved her thanks and moved forward. There was an angry blast of a horn from the car behind when they were not let out, as well.

"Someone isn't happy!" he remarked as he looked in the wing mirror. He glanced over at her expressionless face. She did not respond. She just slowly followed the road out of town. The traffic finally lessened as they neared the town limits. She sped up. Kyle reached forward and pressed a button on the music system and the CD that was in came on. It was a track by Queen. "Wow, I love Queen! This is ..." Tyler extended her left arm and turned the CD player off. Again, she remained expressionless. "Okay, so no music, then," he remarked. The darkness of the night covered everything; the lights of the town were long behind them, only their headlights broke the darkness. The land was grey. He picked out details from the fields to his left. Tyler just kept driving. He thought he had known all the roads around here, but he was unsure of the road they were currently on. Their speed slowed and she pulled into the entrance to a field on the right. The hedge had gone along the side of the road, blocking any passing motorist from seeing the field. It was only broken by the grey metal tubed gate that currently barred their way.

"We are here," she stated. She turned the lights of the 4x4 off, released her seatbelt and stared at him. There was a pause of a few seconds before he spoke.

"What? You have not said what we are doing next?" he asked. She glared at him as she answered,

"Well, let's start with you getting out and opening that damn gate." There was anger in her voice. He looked at the gate and cringed at himself for not realising that sooner.

"Yeah, sure," he released his seat belt, opened the door and jumped out. As he pulled the gate inwards his feet squelched in the soft ground; his training shoes were already dirty. Once the gate was fully open, she gunned the engine and the 4x4 jumped forward. Kyle closed the gate. There was no chain or lock to secure it. He looked at the rear lights of the vehicle as it headed off to the side of the field. "'Guess I am walking, then," he said out loud, and started off after it. She had parked beside the hedge at the far side of the field. The 4x4 was in darkness and Tyler was standing at the front with both of their daysacks on the bonnet. She was looking inside hers as he approached. He looked around; there was another field on the far side of this hedgerow and a small wood off to their left. To the right, the farmland stretched out into the darkness. The glow of Ballycastle could be seen nestled in the far hills; they had come farther than he had thought.

"Well," she stated. Kyle looked at her stern expression in the darkness. "Take your clothes off, then!" she looked back into her daysack, "you can leave them on top of here." As Kyle pulled off the sweat top he was wearing, he glanced at her.

"So, are you going to tell me what we are going to do next?" She stopped what she was doing and stared at him, as he finished his sentence, "...please?" She nodded.

"Once you have changed, we will have a run in this field, then we will go into the next one. You will pick up the scent, then you will follow my lead as we hunt the beast." She was concentrating on folding the clothes she was taking out of the daysack. They were being placed neatly on the warm bonnet, away from his daysack.

"Okay." He lifted his right leg and started to untie his footwear; it did not take him long until he was standing naked in a field outside Ballycastle. And it was winter. He felt the cold almost immediately. It looked like Tyler wasn't getting changed, as she had not taken anything off.

"Kneel," she commanded. He did. He was facing the 4x4 but was looking at the grass in front of him as she walked behind him. She had started whispering something that he could not hear and, as if by command, the cloud moved and the moon shone brightly. A strange warmth enveloped him. "Come wolf, come," she whispered. His body jolted! "Come, wolf come," she repeated, this time louder, so she was almost speaking it. The pain returned. Every part of his body exploded. He felt the coolness of the grass as he fell onto his side. The pain shot though his body like a constant flow of electricity. He opened his mouth and a sound came out, but it was not a scream, nor a shout; it was a cry of anguish. He wanted the pain to stop, but it wouldn't. Every part of his body jolted, contorted with small jumping movements, each one as painful as the last. But this time it was different; this time there was no comforting darkness to take the pain away. There was just the pain. His body seemed to burn - all of it, all at the same time. Every part of him felt wave after wave of pain pulse through him. His eyes started burning. He tried to raise his hands, but the movement made him cry out from the pain in his arms. His eyes burned hotter; he strained as he tried to keep them closed, but nothing could take the pain away.

As quickly as it had started, the pain slowed and lessened. He felt the welcome relief. He had no idea how long it had been; it had seemed like it had gone on for hours. His body ached as he opened his eyes. The field was still grey, as he looked around. He tried to move and get up, but he fell straight over. It was as if his body was no longer able to stand. He felt a weakness like he had never known. He fought for breath; he was exhausted; it took enormous effort just to get onto his hands and knees. His hands. He looked at his hands. The hair on the backs of his hands had grown. His nails were slightly longer. He looked at his forearms. The skin seemed 'different'; the hair was certainly thicker. He started to look at the rest of him when a breeze blew across him. Pain was electric behind his nose! His hands shot up as he nearly slapped himself in the face. But it wasn't his face. His face had changed - it had changed shape. The front of his face was protruding out. The wind blew again, and he looked over towards the distant lights. The wind carried smells; some he did not recognise; some he did. He could smell the earth, the recently cut grass.

He looked around as the confusion in his mind swirled. What was this? What had happened to him? He could not fully make sense of what he was seeing; smelling; the way his body felt. Still on all fours, he moved forward slightly. His head turned towards the front of the 4x4, to where she was kneeling. He raised himself up onto his knees and looked at her. She looked majestic. Her fur seemed trimmed to perfection; her body totally adapted to the form she was in. He was looking at a wolf, but he could still recognise her features. He reached out with his left hand towards her. She suddenly sprang away from him and burst into a run. He felt his body rise; he was unsteady - very unsteady, as he stood upright. She had stopped a short distance away and was looking back at him, wanting him to chase her. He stepped forward, then again. He was learning to walk again. He was trying to concentrate on the skill of walking; his body wanted to run. His mind fought with what his eyes could see, the noises of the small animals in the trees of the wood, and the smell coming from the ground. He could smell her. He stepped tentatively and slowly gained speed. She turned and was off again. She was on all fours now, moving with incredible speed until she reached the far hedgerow. He pushed his body to try and catch up. He was gaining speed, but she was too far ahead. He would not catch her. She was looking at him over her right shoulder. Even in the darkness he could see her hair hanging down over her shoulders. He had never seen anything so beautiful. She was kneeling, with the hedge to her left. As he approached, she pointed to the ground where she was with one finger from her right hand. He looked down and she was off again.

She took off down the hedgerow towards the far corner. He looked down towards what she had been pointing at - then it hit him. Her scent seemed to slap him in the face, and it led away into the greyness. He knelt down and breathed in. His nose filled with the scent. He could smell it again a few feet away. It was leading him down the side of the hedgerow. He took off after it. She was kneeling in the corner as he got to her. This time she did not move. His aching body came to a stop beside her. He looked at her. She looked at him. Was she smiling? He did not know, but he could feel it rising. The lust, the wanting; he wanted her, and he wanted her now. His body moved; instinct drove him as he tried to take her.

Her response was as fast as it was furious. She spun and propelled him backwards. Pain shot through his chest and right arm; he did not know what had connected, but something had. The ground was solid as he landed on it. He looked straight into angry eyes. Her teeth were on both sides of his neck. His right arm was being pushed with great force into his chest and one of her knees was painfully keeping his legs pinned to the ground. Her left eye stared at him; the message was clear. *'Don't try that again!'* She held him there for a few seconds, and the lust subsided. His body relaxed, as did hers. Very slowly, she released her grip and backed away from him. He rolled over onto his hands and knees again. She was also on all fours - ready to attack again. He felt his body react; his wolf laid down onto his side, an act of total submission. He would not try that again. Tyler stood up on her hind legs and motioned with her right hand for him to do the same. He tried to ask what was happening next, but he just choked and coughed. She let out a noise that was almost laughter, pointed to her own neck, then shook her head. They could not speak. He nodded in understanding. She turned and looked back towards the 4x4 and motioned with her head for him to follow. She was off again. He wanted to keep up, but his body was not moving as fast as she was. She was way ahead of him. He struggled but his arms and legs seemed to be in knots. He tripped himself up and landed on his face, then rolled over on the ground. It seemed running on all fours was not something he could do naturally. He pushed himself up and stood on his legs. He started walking at first, then slowly started jogging. He looked over at the 4x4. She was standing at the rear of it. He increased his pace. She was looking over the hedge into the other field. He slowed to a walk as he approached. He wasn't out of breath; in fact, he wasn't tired at all.

He looked around himself: at his arms, his legs and the way his feet and hands had changed. He looked up at her. She looked majestic standing there, but this time he felt admiration, not lustfulness. He walked up beside her and raised himself up to see into the empty field. She looked at him; then with two fingers of her right hand pointed at her own eyes, then into the field. He was being told to look over there. He did and saw nothing. He shook his head. Her face moved. Was she laughing at him? She moved behind him and went down on all fours and started off towards the corner of the field. He followed her. As he arrived at the corner, she was already climbing through a gap in the hedge. He followed her. On the other side, she was on one knee; he did the same. She looked at him and pointed to the ground in front of him. He looked at the ground, then at her...he did not understand. She went onto all fours again and got her nose right down at the grass; she was smelling the area. She raised herself up, then pointed at the ground again. He lowered his head and placed his nose close to the grass, taking several deep breaths. The smells made his head raise each time. He could smell the frosted earth; he could smell the grass; he could smell .... Wait, what was that?

He looked over at her and she nodded. He moved forward to where it was slightly stronger. The smell was there, but it wasn't anything he had smelled before. He moved his head to the left, then to the right; each time the smell lessened. He came back to where it was and moved forward again. He looked up; it was almost as if he could see where the smell was on the ground. He could not describe the smell, but it was something alive. It was totally different than the other smells on the ground. He started moving from one part of the grass to the other; it was leading him up the small rise of the field. Whatever it was, it was at the far side of the hill in the centre of the field. He looked back at her, and she motioned for him to carry on. He looked at the ground and smelled again; it was slightly stronger over there. He was now moving at a walking pace. The scent was laid out like a trail. He began to pick up speed. He stopped at the crest of the hill and dropped flat on the ground, Tyler did the same, beside him. The wind blew behind them, and he felt it sweep over him. He could smell the deer that was slowly walking from the right side of the open field. He was downwind, which meant the deer could not smell him. He looked at the beast as it moved. It was slow, but graceful. He was strong and alert. Tyler tapped his shoulder once. She motioned with her fingers that he was to watch.

She used her forefinger to draw on the ground what she wanted him to do. He would go to the right and chase the beast towards the far side of the field, but he was to 'observe'. He did not know how to take a deer down; she would show him how. He nodded in understanding. He watched as she moved back, out of sight from the beast. She was moving quickly and there was no sound. He blinked; she was a hunter.

He moved back so he was out of sight and started off in the direction she had wanted him to go. He was staying as low as he could, but he knew he was making noise. As he came into view, the beast was looking at him and it was angry. Kyle felt a surge of power as he stood up and ran towards him. The deer turned and started to run. It quickly got away from him, as it was much faster. It stopped a distance away and turned back to face the approaching danger. The stag lowered his antlers; he was going to fight. Kyle slowed as he approached, he did not know exactly what to do next. He extended his arms and growled at the face of his opponent. The stag let out a loud grunt and breathed heavily out of its nose. Kyle could see the breath in the cold night air. He looked into the eyes of the beast in front of him and started to walk towards him.

It happened so fast Kyle could hardly believe it. She had launched herself through the air. The deer had not seen her until she impacted with its throat; her hands pulled the antlers rearwards as her mouth dug deep. The force of her momentum sent the two of them skidding along the ground. The stag's legs kicked, and a sound came out of his mouth, but he was already dying. She threw her head backwards, ripping open the throat. Blood splashed over the ground. It pumped from the open wounds. The stag kicked and bucked, and Kyle watched as the movements slowed, then stopped. He was transfixed. Tyler looked at Kyle and beckoned him over. He walked walk forward. She knelt down and motioned with her hand for him to do the same. She started to trace lines down the side of his neck; Kyle realised he was being shown where the main arteries were. He nodded. She stood up and started to walk away. Kyle looked at the dead animal, then at her, *'surely they were not going to leave it here?'*

She started to run back over the centre of the hill. He followed her. By the time he reached the 4x4 she was kneeling by the front of it, washing herself with the bottled water she had brought. She looked at him and started making a circular motion with her right hand. He did not know what she meant; she did it again, he shook his head. She stood up and pushed his shoulder to turn him around. She prodded him to propel him forward, then walked to the rear of the 4x4. She pointed at the ground. He was to stay here. He nodded. She walked out of sight. He looked over the landscape. He could see such detail in the darkness. The wind blew across him from the woods and he closed his eyes as his nose filled with new smells. He breathed them in. He looked up at the full moon that seemed to be shining down on him. He felt a comfort and a warmth he had never known before. Yes, it was nearly the end of January and it was cold, but he could not feel it. When he opened his eyes, Tyler was dressed in her bottoms and a sleeveless training top and back in sapien form. She dropped his daysack at his feet and repeated the circular hand motion.

"Change," she commanded, he nodded as she walked away. He went down on one knee and thought for a moment. He stood back up away and walked back towards the front where she was washing the blood from her arms. He looked at her. When she looked up, he shrugged, no one had ever told him *how* to change! He did not know. She laughed and nodded again. "Kneel." He did. She walked up to him and started to stroke the top of his head; she was petting him. He could hear that she was whispering, but he could not understand the words. He suddenly felt very tired ... so sleepy, and his body started to relax. He laid down on one side, curled up and fell asleep. When he woke, he was mostly dressed and back in sapien form in the passenger seat of the 4x4. He looked at his bare feet – where were his trainers? Tyler was chatting on the phone; she was in a good mood. "That is great, thanks, no problem. See you then!" she ended the call. Kyle moved in the seat and looked at the clock on the dashboard. It was not late. He tried to stretch out, but he was confined by the space in the car. He looked over at her.

"Who was that?" he asked. She dropped the phone into her bag, then placed it on the back seat.

"The farmer. He will have the beast cleaned and he'll drop some of it over to the farmhouse for us. You like venison, yes?" He nodded. She started the vehicle and, as they moved off, looked over at him. "Seat belt."

"Well, that was an experience," he said, as he clicked the buckle into place. She glanced at him as they reached the gate at the edge of the field. He did not have to be told twice. Once they were back on the main road, she turned the opposite way from Ballycastle and headed out into the countryside. "We are not going back to Rathlin?" he asked. She smiled.

"We got the last ferry on the way over; next one isn't until tomorrow morning." He looked around, and she carried on, "We are booked into a small B&B near here for tonight."

"Okay," was all he could muster. He sat in silence as the dark countryside passed outside. He was not even noticing where they were anymore. He was calm. It was a calmness he had never known before. In no time they were pulling up outside a white farmhouse with a single light out front. There was a soft glow coming from the small window in the front door.

"Grab the bags, will you," she said, and jumped out once they had come to a complete stop.

"Where are my trainers?" he asked.

"On the back seat!" she did not look back as she walked towards the single door. He looked between the two front seats and spotted them. It only took seconds to put them on, but he never would find his socks!

As he opened the rear door of the 4x4, he could see Tyler was chatting with a woman who looked to be at least eighty years old. There were smiles and handshakes; he heard Tyler being addressed as 'Mrs Reynolds'. The front door closed, and she returned. "We are in two apartments over there!" Tyler pointed towards the white painted outbuildings that had obviously been converted into rooms. He nodded as she handed him a key. He handed her one of the daysacks. "I am in number three, you are in number four!" again he nodded as she walked away from him. He jogged for a few steps to catch up.

"Can we have a chat?" he asked. She looked at him as they approached her door.

"Sure," she smiled, "in the morning. You are knackered, so keep your questions for after you have slept, and we've had breakfast." She smiled a happy smile and her door opened. She quickly stepped through it and, just as it was about to close, held it open slightly. He was still standing there. He had a confused look on his face. She smiled back. "Sleep well."

"Sleep well," he nodded; and she shut the door. He felt exhausted, but his mind was racing. He had so many questions; questions that would now have to wait until morning.

Chapter 27

Spelga Dam – Mourne Mountains

She glanced at the watch on her wrist - it was nearly 9am. She was tying the lace of her walking boot resting on the rear bumper of the car. The boot was open, and her pre-packed daysack was inside, as was her sister's. Emma Silver stood up and looked over her left shoulder, she looked out over the open water of Spelga Dam. She turned to face it as a cold breeze blew in. She was warm; the wind did not bother her. She stepped forward to the edge of the small car park. A paved path led down to a small concreted viewing platform with a metal tubed safety rail on three sides. It was empty. Across the far side of the reservoir she could see the mountains they were going to cover today. The wind blew past her again. Her long blonde hair flowed down her back. She was tall - they both were. Her twin sister was identical, except for one obvious thing - their hair. Her sister had their father's jet-black mane, while she had her mother's golden blonde hair. She glanced to her right as Gemma walked up and stood beside her. The twins did not speak at first, just exchanged a glance. They were similarly dressed: walking boots, dark-coloured outdoor trousers and brightly-coloured Gore-Tex jackets – same brand; different colours. They were ready. They glanced back at the two parked cars; music blared from the boys' car.

"Bob Seger," Gemma said.

"What?" Emma asked. Gemma smiled at her sister,

"That Old Time Rock and Roll' by Bob Seger and the Silver Bullet Band. It's one of his favourites." They shared a smile. Emma looked back over the water, it was not common knowledge that her sister had started dating Will, one of the Gold twins.

Will and Richard Gold were, like them, twins. The resemblance was obvious, but their personalities were as different as chalk was to cheese. The girls were ready; the boys still fumbled around in the car. It would be several minutes before the four young hillwalkers set off from the otherwise empty car park down the road, away from the dam. The small, single-storey building on the opposite side of the road from the carpark housed public toilets, but they were locked; there was no displayed opening times. Both Emma and Gemma tied their hair up and pulled woollen hats over their heads. Gemma and Will walked in front - the body language between them was intimate. Emma smiled. She could tell that Richard wanted to be somewhere else; this whole task was 'such a waste of his time'. He was an academic. Emma was convinced he was slightly autistic, having difficulty relating to people. She walked beside Richard, along the side of the road. The low stone wall defining the edge of the road was a safety barrier between it and the drop, where the hill fell steeply down to where the narrow river flowed away from the dam. It had obviously been a lot higher at one time.

Will and Gemma could not take their eyes off each other. Emma was genuinely happy for her sister but couldn't help feeling slightly jealous. She was still single. Every time there some something on in the bar at the farm, it was almost a fight to keep some of the alphas away; but she was not interested in them.

"This is pointless!" Richard grumbled. "We've been here two days now, and nothing... absolutely nothing. I mean, what are we supposed to be doing?" he said sharply. She looked at him as a car drove past them towards the dam, then off into the rolling countryside heading north.

"Looking for a stray wolf that should not be here!" she walked on, "remember what Dermott said? You were there as well, after all." He looked down and shoved his hands into his pockets.

"Tasks like this are for lesser minds." His eyes shot up towards the blanket of grey clouds that covered the sky. He was not hiding his annoyance.

"What?" Anger was rising in Emma, Richard looked over at the mountain to their left.

"And over that is where we are going, is it?" Emma looked up at the mountain.

"Yes, first to Slievenamiskan, then on to Richard's mountain." She spoke loud enough for the other two to hear. They both glanced back, guessing what was coming next.

"Richard's mountain? I don't remember seeing a mountain called that on the map!" The two in front were smiling; Emma winked at her sister.

"It isn't. It's really called Cock Mountain but, hey ho, same difference!" There was a giggle from the two in front as they turned back and continued walking. Richard did not get sarcasm, but knew he was being mocked.

"Well, I will not react to your pathetic attempt at humour."

"'Surprised you understand it," Emma replied. Richard spun around and glared at her.

"Emma, I have an advanced degree from Oxford; I already understand everything that is worth understanding." He was being condescending, and she knew it.

"I have a degree, as well. You are not the only smart one around here, you know." She was starting to get angry. Richard looked down his nose at her, as he answered,

"Jordanstown is a trade school and the social sciences are nothing but a waste of time for lesser minds." Her punch into his side was not a playful one. He winced and almost lost his balance as she jumped forward and gripped his throat with her left hand. She extended her arm so her grip forced him upwards as he was almost on his toes. Will came between the two of them,

"Hey, hey .... everyone .... we are on the same side here!" Emma did not relax her grip. She glared at him as his eyes widened.

"You *EVER* call me a lesser mind again and I WILL nail your testicles to your forehead, you prick!" She stepped forward as she spoke, forcing him backward as his hands gripped her fingers trying to release her grip. Will tried to step between them, but Emma pulled Richard towards her, so his face was only inches away from her own. "Do .... you .... understand, ... Prick?" He nodded his head without making eye contact. She released her grip and stepped back. Will stepped in again, extending his arms to increase the distance between them.

"He didn't mean it like that," he started to explain, and looked at his brother. "Say sorry!" Richard looked around in anger and disgust. He liked to tell people that it was only the weak who said sorry. "Rich ...." Will continued, as he placed his left hand on his brother's shoulder, "there is no problem here. You are sorry. You didn't mean it like that. Remember what we talked about before?" His brother nodded. Emma was turning away as Richard spoke,

"Sorry." Will relaxed as Richard regained his composure. "I didn't mean to point out that you have a lesser mind." Emma spun where she stood just as Gemma's arms grabbed her and pulled her into a vice grip.

All four stopped suddenly and looked up towards the summit of the mountain, as the sound of a long howl echoed, Will stepped forward, staring up the slope.

"It must be at least two miles away," Gemma released her grip and both the girls relaxed.

"What is on the other side of Cock Mountain?" Gemma asked.

"Rocky Mountain," Emma spoke quietly. Will stepped forward and looked back at the three of them.

"Right! We have a job to do. This is the first trace we've had ... let's get on with it." Will started off down the road with the others just behind him. They were running as they reached the small metal gate in the break in the wall. Then, they were off the road and onto the dirt track that cut into the side of the hill. It only took seconds for them to reach the footbridge that crossed over the river. It was a metal construction but was designed for only one person to cross at a time. The rocks at the far side were open and bare, the side of the first mountain rose above them.

"Come on," said Will as he started up the hill. They were not quite running, but they scaled the side of Slievenamiskan in a quarter of the time it would normally take hillwalkers; but they were committed and now they were now in a hurry.

At the top, they all paused. Emma looked over to her left at the dam and the reservoir. She could make out the small car park and their two cars. A heavy blanket of clouds filled the sky, leaving only a few gaps. They continued on. Beyond, lay the rest of the Mourne mountains. It really was breath-taking. There had been frost on the ground, and it became slippery. Will stopped at the far side of the summit. The others soon caught up. It took a few seconds for them all to catch their breath. Gemma pointed to the smaller hill with exposed rock on its summit that was off to their right.

"It that Rocky mountain?" she asked

"No," Will answered, "that's Hen Mountain, Rocky is the other side of it." He pointed to the mountain in front of them.

"Is that Cock?" Emma asked, pointing at a further peak, its' summit hidden in the clouds.

"Can I video you saying that?" Will smirked. Emma could not help herself from smiling at the juvenile comment.

"Err, no." Three of them laughed, Richard extended his left hand and pointed.

"Look at that!" he said, walking ahead. Emma could not see what he was pointing at. He stopped and was looking down at something just out of sight. They all walked over to where the dead lamb lay.

Will went down on one knee beside what was left of the animal. It was lying on its right side. The rear leg was missing from the hip joint: it had been torn off with excessive force. The massive wound on the neck exposed everything from chin to chest. The damage was too extreme to be caused by any normal predator.... They had found the first evidence in their search. Will extended the palm of his right hand, so it was just over the carcass. "Still warm, less than an hour." He stood up as the two girls studied the lamb. Richard was looking at something else.

"Blood trail!" he stated, Will looked over.

"Where?" he asked. Richard walked around the lamb and stopped a few feet away. He looked down at the ground and pointed. The other three gathered around.

"There... tracks as well." He indicated the trail, easily visible through the frost. "Blood there and there! Single, non-human, but upright." The evidence would not last long. Will went down on his knee again and looked closer at the paw print in the frosty ground.

"Well, at least we know it is definitely a Garou."

"But what are they doing here?" Gemma asked, Will looked up at her.

"Let's go and find out, shall we!" He stood, smiling. His brother's face was grim. Emma nodded before she spoke,

"Let's get moving." She began pacing between each print. She moved from side to side, following the winding trail closely.

"From the size and depth of the prints, I would say that it's a 'she', and she was running!" The others followed. Emma looked up at the top of Cock Mountain - she could not see through the mist that still covered it. Their pace increased as they ascended the mountain in silence. Out of the mist appeared several slabs of rock, forming what looked like a natural bench. The four trackers stopped beside it. Visibility had reduced to less than thirty metres. Emma took off the hat she'd been wearing and tucked it into a pocket, not noticing her sister had already done the same. They were only slightly out of breath, but no one spoke. Emma searched across what she could see. The whole atmosphere had changed; something was wrong here. She glanced at her sister, who had a nervous look on her face. She felt it too.

Will slowly unclipped his daysack and placed it on the ground in front of him. The others quietly did the same. Gemma stood beside her sister, as they scanned their surroundings. When Richard stepped closer to Emma, she glanced at him. Whatever was there, he felt it as well. He kept looking over to the left. Will slowly paced around the rock slab, walked forward a short distance, and stopped. He stood and stared in front of him; then, without turning around, slowly stepped backwards. He turned. There was a concerned look on his face. He nodded down at the daysacks. Everyone knelt down and, opening their packs, withdrew their sheathed short swords. They followed Will's lead, as he slowly walked back around the rock slab. The two girls were just behind him on either side, with Richard following. There was only a short distance between them as the diamond formation moved forward, slowly and quietly. They passed an upright boulder, apparently guarding the entrance to a broad, bowl-shaped dip in the ground. At its deepest point, the bowl was only about two feet deep, but it was deep enough. The lamb was not the only thing that had been killed. Emma looked around as the small group made its way towards the centre of the bowl. She counted at least three adult sheep that had all been torn apart. Ahead of her, Will stopped and slowly unsheathed his sword. The sound of the blade leaving the sheath broke the stillness. One by one, the others did the same. There was a nervousness among them.

"Gemma," Will whispered, just barely audible.

"What?" she quietly answered. Emma was listening, her eyes searching in the mist for any detail, any movement. She sensed danger.

"Get in touch with the farm," he was being as quiet as possible. Gemma went down on one knee and, taking her sword in her left hand, fumbled in the pocket of her trousers for her phone. She tapped the buttons, then whispered,

"No signal." There was a pause before Will spoke again,

"Can you send them a message?" Emma could hear her sister rapidly tapping the buttons.

"Yes," came the quiet reply.

"Send them this, then." Gemma tapped, then paused, waiting for the message.

"We have a female rabid." There was a gasp from Gemma, Richard started to breath forcibly through his nose, and Emma could feel her heart thump inside her chest.

"The message is sent ... but I don't know when they will get it!" Emma could hear how scared her sister was, and she tightened her grip on the handle of her blade. Taking a deep breath in, she readied herself for the coming fight.

A light breeze passed over them. They all reacted to the smell. She was close; she was upwind, which meant she knew they were there, and she wanted them to know it. Emma felt fear grip her, eyes fighting against the mist as the breeze cleared it slightly.

"Did you say exactly where we are?" Will asked, his voice somewhat louder than before.

"N-n-no," she stuttered.

"Send it quick!" he commanded. Gemma fumbled with her phone as the others searched in different directions.

"I don't want to be here," Richard stated quietly. His voice had changed, this time it was not annoyance, but fear. They all knew what rabies could do to a single wolf... they'd never seen it, but it was their greatest fear.

The noise stopped them. All four turned towards it... a low growl. Emma took an unconscious step back, as Gemma and Richard turned and raised their swords defensively. Will stepped closer so he was on Emma's left side. He had a determined look on his face.

"Pairs... always stay in pairs," he stated.

"What?" asked a nervous Richard.

"Do NOT let yourselves get separated. If we stay together, we can survive; we will live." Will held his sword in both his hands, his determined look was turning to anger, as the dark shape appeared out of the mist.

She was on all fours and stopped a short distance away from them. She was well-built and the short fur around her face was splattered with blood. She lowered her head and each of them recognized the madness in her eyes. There would be no reasoning, no compassion; there was only rage in the bloodshot eyes. Slowly, saliva dripping from her mouth, a low growl emanated. She raised her head slightly and took a long breath in through her nose. She knew that smell; she knew what they were, and the rage in her eyes now mixed with excitement.

"WHO ARE YOU?" Will shouted, just as she suddenly leapt forward. He stepped to one side, and her mouth snapped at the space he had been standing in. Her body slammed into Emma, sending her flying backwards. She lost the grip on her sword and it skittered harmlessly away. She landed on the rock, and pain shot through her body. Rolling over, she lunged towards where her sword lay on the ground.

The rabid was jumping back and forth between them, snapping and grabbing at them. They fought frantically. Emma jumped up and ran forward, just as the rabid swung around with an open hand, claws outstretched, towards Richard's face. He ducked and brought his sword up. The blade and the claws clashed. The rabid jumped back, narrowly avoiding a full impact. Everything was moving so fast! The rabid launched another attack, this time aimed at Will. He rolled sideways and brought his sword up, just missing her face. The rabid was mid-air, as her right hand caught Gemma's arm. She landed and turned, flinging Gemma around like a rag doll. Gemma's body slammed into the vertical rock with such force that the scream she had been making stopped as suddenly as it had begun... Rage. Emma was filled with rage, as she launched at the rabid. She missed, the rabid spun and launched back. Emma was caught by her shoulder and thrown backward. She landed on her back, her body exploding in pain.

She righted herself just as Will spun around and deflected another swipe. In that second, Emma realised, just as Will did, that he had not been the target. Richard's sword found its mark and the fur parted... but he had made a catastrophic mistake! She let him get close. He had overextended his blade and, for less than half a second, had left himself vulnerable. Her mouth had found his throat even before his fingers let go of the blade. She drove at him with such force that his head bounced up into the air like a football. The rabid spun around at the far edge of the bowl and stopped. She now focused her attention on Will, Not taking her eyes off him, she slowly paced around the edge, circling. Emma jumped forward to his side.

"Come on then!" he was shouting, beckoning her with his sword. The rabid's eyes were full of hate. She snapped at them as she changed direction, never taking her eyes off them. Emma was about to shout something but, before she could form the words, the rabid launched the attack. Both of their blades missed, and the right hand of the rabid swatted her away as if she was a fly. Emma landed just outside the bowl. She had lost her sword. She fought the pain and righted herself. Suddenly, Will came into focus. The rabid was on top of him. Emma watched as the wild animal tore into him with more savagery than she'd ever imagined! His anger had turned to squeals of pain and anguish. She was transfixed. Emma had never seen anything like this before. The rabid was tearing at him with her mouth... her hands... ripping, tearing, shredding. His clothes were gone; his body was being ravaged in a way she had not thought possible. She froze. Will's body stopped moving. The rabid wasn't eating it; she was destroying it.

Suddenly, she looked up and met Emma's eyes. The fear took her, and she was running. She had never run that fast before, everything inside her screamed at her to get away, run, run, run, run. It was absolute, uncontrolled panic, and it had taken her. She cried, she sobbed, she screamed; her body fought, and the panic ran wild. She heard the double thud of the feet that were chasing her. She screamed. Thud, thud. They were closer. Thud, thud, closer still, thud, thud. She ran....Run, run, run; she had to get away. Her mind held only one thought. The fear had overtaken her; it drove her, pushed her on. Thud, thud. The footfall was gaining; she had to run, run, run, thud, thud! Panic made her scream. She had forgotten about her sword, about her daysack, thud, thud, closer... Then silence.

Emma Silver never even heard the rabid wolf jump through the air. It landed on her back, sending her face down into the cold ground. The panic would only last a few more seconds, the pain would last longer... but not much longer.

Chapter 28 –

Coleraine Town Centre

Cara-Marie was still annoyed. She was sitting on the bench with her back towards the entrance of the Church on Church street, absentmindedly watching the different people walking past. Her phone bleeped in her pocket; she would read that later. She slowly drank some more of her rapidly-cooling coffee. She barely noticed the old man hobbling his way towards the end of the bench.

"May I sit?" She glanced at him. His clothes were old, his shoes were scuffed but clean. His trousers had seen better days, as had the plain jumper he wore. The blazer looked like it had been part of a suit from years gone by, and he was balancing on a painted 'Blackthorn' walking stick. His face was old, as was his voice. She looked into his eyes and saw weariness; but there was still respect there. He did not need to ask her permission; he was just being polite. She nodded and looked away as a soft smile came across his face. She knew if she had said 'no', this old man would have shuffled on and found somewhere else to sit. He gave his thanks, but she did not hear the words. The old man placed the end of the walking stick between his feet and rested both his hands on it. She glanced over at him. He sat motionless, except for his eyes that looked at each person walking by. Cara-Marie noticed the walking stick when he raised it in recognition towards another pensioner, walking slowly in the opposite direction on the far side of the street.

"I like your walking stick." The words came out of her mouth before she even realised it. The old man turned his head and looked at her with a polite smile.

"It's not a walking stick; it's a Blackthorn," he corrected. He had lifted it up in his right hand to show her. She looked closer at it. The polished handle had a stained wooden pattern on it, but the stick itself was painted black.

"Oh, I'm sorry," she said, meekly. Part of her wanted to get up and walk away, but curiosity stopped her. "What is a Blackthorn?" she asked, "and where did you get it?" The old man smiled and looked around.

"We all got one when they disbanded the battery in 1945, at the end of the war," he replied. Cara-Marie was thinking this probably wasn't a conversation that she was going to get anything from, but something made her ask,

"Which unit did you serve in?" She edged slightly towards the old man. A warm smile spread across his lips. She glanced at her watch and made a note of the time. This guy had five minutes: if he rambled on more than that, she would be off.

"6 Light Anti-Aircraft battery, Royal Artillery. Most of us were from around Coleraine." She thought for a moment; that could be a story; maybe this would not be a total waste of time.

"There is a reserve Artillery unit still in Coleraine… is that the same?" she asked, thinking of the remembrance parade from the previous year. She smiled as she asked her question, and he let out a small laugh. Returning the smile, he replied,

"No, no they are field guns, we were Anti-Air." He paused thoughtfully, before continuing, "I got there the start of '42. We were in the desert, you know." She nodded, regretting her hesitancy to speak with him. He now had a captive audience. "We had the Bolfor 40 millimetre," he glanced over at her. "Do you know it?" She smiled and nodded. She had no idea what it was, but she knew that if she had said no, she would have got a full explanation of something she could not imagine. "Well, Operation Crusader was finished but the DAK certainly were not!" the old man explained. She thought for a second, then asked,

"Who are the DAK?" The old man smiled again.

"The Deutsch Africa Korps…. Rommel's boys." She smiled in understanding, she remembered something about them from history but could not recall any details. The storyteller continued. "We were heading for Tobruk to relieve the siege there; we had by-passed most of the panzers, but we took out a few of them." The old man sat back and, releasing his grip on the stick, started to use his hands to describe his memories. "We stopped near a wadi. It had been a real hot one, that day, when a pair of One-Ten's appeared… sent everyone scattering," his face changed. She looked at the concern on his face. In his mind, he was no longer on a street in Coleraine with overcast clouds, he was back in the vastness of the North African desert.

"What is a 'One-Ten'?" she asked. Her question brought him back to the present. He looked at her, then glanced around again before returning to his tale.

"Messerschmitt One-Ten. It was a really good ground attack plane … and when you are in a truck in the desert, you stick out like a bumblebee on a bulldog's arse!" The mental image made her laugh, but the concern was back on his face. She watched as his hands started to move, turn handles and operate something invisible. He was back at war.

"We saw them start diving towards us," he explained. "They could chew up entire convoys, the one-tens!" She listened to the old man recount firing his gun at the planes as they attacked from the air. "Some of the trucks were already on fire when they were coming back around again ..." he moved his hands to show what the plane was doing. "I could see his attack line ... I aimed ...then," he paused for dramatic effect, "we let him have it! Got him! He went down in flames, smoke trailing behind him." His gnarled hand dove towards the ground, then opened-up to show what happened. He was smiling at the victory, "The other one buggered off before we could get it, too!" Cara-Marie looked at her watch.

"Wow, that sounds really exciting," she said. The old man sat back to continue his story.

"It was, it was."

"Well, it has been really nice talking to you," she started.

"We sent a raid in that night..." The old man was staring straight ahead. Then the look on his face changed as she stood up to leave.

"Well, thank you again."

"Tear them apart, Foster could!" the comment stopped her. Her head spun around to stare at the old man, who was unaware of her reaction.

"Foster?" she exclaimed.

"Yeah ... the officer let him go in; sent three with him ... tear them apart, he could ... The Germans thought we were sending a hundred but, in fact, it was just him." Cara-Marie sat back down and looked at the old man, who was still deep in thought.

"What do you mean, 'tear them apart'?" she asked. The old man let out a single laugh.

"Tear them apart... never went with him but saw afterwards ... never actually believed it myself until I saw him." The old man stopped. His eyes widened. The street was busy with people walking by, but Cara-Marie could focus only on him, and he had stopped talking.

"Saw him do what?" she spoke quieter. Only the old man heard her question. He paused and stared into the distance.

"Do what he could do ... We weren't allowed to watch. He had to be naked for it, you know," he explained.

"Do what?" again she spoke quietly.

"Change." The single word made her heart race. She had to control the journalist in her.

"Change into what?" The old man's eyes narrowed.

"The creature." She took a deep breath in, and the old man continued, "He could tear them apart, really put the fear of God in everyone." He nodded at his own understanding, "Especially the Italians ... If he went near them afterwards .... they just ran ..." The old man turned to look at her. The look on his face changed to a wise smile, "...and that could only be a good thing."

"What type of creature did he become?" she asked. He looked over at her for a few seconds before asking his own question,

"You believe me?" She nodded. He fidgeted a bit and got comfortable again. "well, lass, you're the first. We don't even talk about it when we get together anymore."

"Where is Foster now? I would love to meet him; I could do a story on him." Cara-Marie could feel her body react with excitement at the very thought of meeting what was being described.

"Foster?" the old man exclaimed, "Oh, he went off to Italy before we all got sent to Normandy ... 'heard the Germans got him near Monte Cassino."

"He was taken prisoner?" He looked at her and shook his head.

"We heard the German paratroopers there had at least one, as well ... you know .... a creature .... like him. 'Heard they tied him to a post and burned him." She could see the anger and unresolved resentment in his face and hear the bitterness in his voice.

"Was he related to the Fosters who used to live in Coleraine?" she asked. The old man glanced at her again, "There aren't any Fosters from around here ... Kilrea direction... farmers, they were." Cara-Marie's heart nearly exploded and her whole body reacted as she knew a Foster who had family near Kilrea that had a farm. It was a deer farm.

∞∞∞∞

The editor was annoyed. She had spotted that as soon as she walked back into the office. Mark's desk was empty and, as she dropped her bag and coat over the back of her chair, she wondered where he was. The editor motioned her over. As she got to the open door of his office, he spoke,

111

"Just what the hell are you doing here?" He was not shouting but was close to it. Cara-Marie was confused,

"Err, I work here?" The phone on the desk started to ring and he reached for it.

"You are *supposed* to be at the police press conference in Belfast .... That Chief Inspector Anderson guy!" He picked up the phone and spoke. He looked up at her and waved her away with his hand. She walked back to her desk and turned on her computer. She had no idea what he was talking about; she did not know anything about that, or she would have been there. She started scrolling through her emails. Her eyes searched the title line of each one. She stopped at 'Police Press Conference tomorrow'. It was from Kevin and addressed to everyone. She looked along the side of the screen. The email had been opened by her login, but she did not remember reading it.

She quickly read over the contents, then looked at her watch. It would be starting in less than an hour. She would miss it. Kevin had put in his comments for her to attend. She closed it down and looked at her sent emails. She had replied last night. It must have been when she was going through all the crap emails from horror fans wanting details about what had been happening around Coleraine. She had just deleted them. Her blog was getting more attention. Most of it was junk, but it was keeping her busy. She quietly cursed herself for missing the press conference. She looked at her watch again. No, it was too late. She stormed out the rear door of the office with her handbag over one shoulder and her laptop bag over the other. She did not want to be around when Kevin was in a foul mood; and she knew from experience he would be miserable to her for the rest of the afternoon. She could get more done sitting in a coffee shop with her laptop.

Cara-Marie looked at her phone again, Kyle still had not replied. She walked through Coleraine and into the brown coffee shop at the bottom of Long Commons. There was no queue, so she got her vanilla latte quickly and headed upstairs. Once she'd made herself comfortable, she started going through other emails. The junk was just getting deleted. She looked at her phone again, still no reply. She'd been there twenty minutes already. She had hardly touched her coffee, but at least there were fewer emails now. She sighed and glanced at her phone again.

"Well, what do you have to say?" It was the young woman who was sitting at the table beside her. She had not noticed her nor the man in his twenties arrive and seat themselves. He had a small laptop open in front of him. The woman was angry. Her arms were folded. She was staring at him. He continued to stare at his laptop, then looked up.

"What?" he asked, with a blank expression on his face.

"Have you not been listening?" she replied. Cara-Marie was trying very hard not to listen either, but the volume of their conversation had just increased. She looked around the upstairs room. There was a woman in her late forties wearing a trouser suit and tapping away at a laptop; a man in the corner was reading a book; two teenagers to the right of the door were engrossed in their own world, unaware of their surroundings. Cara-Marie tried to concentrate on the email in front of her.

"What?" he repeated. The young woman got even angrier.

"Look, I have been telling you everything wrong with this relationship." She tutted, then looked away. He just looked tired. "I really wonder sometimes why I even bother with you!" she glared at him. He did not answer; just looked back down at his laptop. "Haven't you got anything to say?" she demanded. He slowly looked up.

"What do you want me to say?" he replied. Cara-Marie could see what was about to happen, even if he couldn't. She started a search on the internet for the press conference, then clicked on a link. The screen displayed a descending countdown. *'Press conference starting in 3:41 ...'* she watched as the seconds continued to count down.

"Look, I am breaking this up. I've had enough of your crap." The young woman was not getting the response she wanted. He was more interested in what he was doing on his laptop. There was a kick under the table that made him look up.

"What?" he asked.

"You are not listening to what I am saying!" she stated. He looked down again.

"I heard everything you said," he replied. She sat forward.

"You are ignoring me. I mean, what are you doing on that damn thing that is so important?" he looked up at her, his face still emotionless.

"Just updating my recently single profile on a dating website. Why?" Cara-Marie tried not to smile; she watched the screen as it passed 2 minutes. The woman stood up and stormed out in a rage. Her companion just watched her go, then returned to what he'd been doing. The whole conversation hadn't seemed to bother him in the least. Cara-Maire thought about making a comment but chose not to. She looked around the room; the older man returned to his book, the businesswoman went back to whatever she had been doing and the teenagers had left. Everything returned to normal.

The countdown continued. As it reached one minute, the young man closed his laptop, pushed his chair back and stood up. He walked slowly out, seemingly without a care in the world. He did not clear the mugs of coffee from the table. Cara-Marie reached into her bag and took out the small headphones. She plugged them into the laptop, found her note pad and opened it at a fresh page. She was not expecting anything but, just in case... The screen came to life. Seated at a cloth-covered table, nameplate in front, was Chief Inspector Anderson. His uniform was well-pressed, and he had a very solemn look on his face. An open folder containing documents lay in front of him. His elbows were on the edge of the table and his folded hands rested on the papers. He was introduced, and the audience was advised the Inspector would make a brief statement and then answer a limited number of questions.

"Good afternoon, everyone," he started, "I would like to thank you for attending this press conference." He went on to describe the murder of the single hillwalker, then the group that had been murdered on Slieve Binnian, he named each one in turn. "This is a very distressing time for the families, and all those involved in the case." Cara-Marie sighed; he was already deflecting future questions. "We are looking for a very violent offender, who should not be approached by the public," he continued. She did notice that he was calling them 'murders' and not killings, as he had done before. There was no new information. She started to relax about missing it; then the questions began.

"Are these linked to the 'New Year's Day' killings or the couple who were found murdered in the bungalow?" He shifted in his seat.

"No, there is no evidence to link them. They were murdered by an entirely different method, which points to a different offender." Cara-Marie smirked. He pointed to someone in front of him.

"Are these, in any way, connected to the werewolf attacks around Coleraine last year?" It was a female voice that Cara-Marie thought she recognised. Chief Anderson smiled at the question,

"Well, as we have previously stated, there was no 'werewolf' running around the north coast. Those crimes were part of a feud between very violent eastern European organised crime gangs. The evidence indicates that those responsible were found deceased at the Mussenden temple." He let out a short laugh. "There are no 'mythical creatures' running around, I assure you!" he laughed again. "Trust me, if we find the Loch Ness monster in the River Roe, we will let you know." He smiled again, deflecting the question. Cara-Marie had heard enough. She cut the feed and closed her laptop. What happened on New Year's Day and what happened in the Mournes mountains may not have been 'Nessie', but it certainly was not 'Organised Crime Gangs', either.

She looked at her phone again. The screen was still blank. The sooner she could get to Kyle Foster, the sooner she may get some answers.

∞∞∞∞

Dani was standing in the middle of the bridge, looking up the busy waterway. The volume of traffic behind her was constant. The phone in her pocket started to ring. The screen indicated a withheld number; that could only be one person. She smiled as she answered.

"Hello,"

"Hi." She recognised the American's voice;, she glanced around before she spoke again,

"It is done, the wolves are asleep." There was a positive reaction down the phone. "The spell worked; they will not intervene; well, not at first, anyway." She paused, as a large truck rumbled by behind her.

"Good, good, where are you now?" he asked. She glanced to her right and looked up the street that lead away from the bridge.

"Near O'Connell Street, in Dublin."

"Good. Come back north. The others are arriving soon."

"Okay," she replied.

"Get rid of your phone and anything that can be used to trace you." Before she could reply, he ended the call. He did not ask about what had happened at the den; he did not ask if she knew where it was or any details about how much danger she'd been in, with a den full of wolves.

She looked at the cheap phone. Then, with a flick of her hand, she watched it fly through the air, splash, and sink into the river.

113

Chapter 29

Kyle had watched from the window of his room as the farmer drove away down the narrow road. He had dropped off several cuts of fresh meat. Tyler had joked with him about needing a bigger freezer. The farmer said the payment had already gone through and he was pleased, she waved goodbye and returned to the kitchen.

Over breakfast, Kyle said he'd been told she had a horse when she was on the isle of Skye. He immediately regretted the statement. From the reactions of both Tyler and Rhydian, he realized their two horses had been killed along with the capybaras. The conversation upset them. They missed those horses, they had loved the freedom and companionship of riding over the countryside, at least the comment didn't make his nose bleed - he remembered Tony's tale about making jokes about her animals. He also remembered the conversation he first had with Tony about Tyler. It had all been true. She seemed to be very organised. Things were run so smoothly that Kyle wondered what she did for an occupation beforehand. He had come upstairs to use his phone. As it booted up, the phone pinged several times with the arrival of messages: there were a few from Amanda, two from Paul and one from Tony. He opened Tony's, smiling as he read the short message. 'HI MUCKER, HOPE YOU ARE HAVING FUN, REMEMBER PAIN IS ONLY WEAKNESS LEAVING THE BODY!' There was no mention of the farm, the police or, more importantly, Karen, so things must be on the up. Kyle sent a thank you.

The first message from Paul was mostly about farm business and the different orders they were following up on. He re-read it; farm business was something he was going to have to learn, and quickly. The second one said Paul would be coming to Rathlin that night for the barbeque. Kyle smiled, knowing it meant Amanda would be coming as well. He read on, 'THERE HAVE BEEN A FEW DEVELOPMENTS WE NEED TO CHAT ABOUT FACE TO FACE, NO WORRIES, WE HAVE SORTED THEM, JUST NEED TO LET YOU KNOW'. Kyle looked at the message; it must be about what had been on the news, but *We have sorted them* was plural; there must have been more than one. 'Okay,' he thought. He'd wait for that one to be explained to him. Before he started to read through Amanda's many messages, he spotted Cara-Marie's name, so he scrolled to that one and opened it. 'HI, WE DO NEED TO CHAT. THERE IS SO MUCH TO CATCH UP ON. CAN YOU TELL ME MORE ABOUT YOUR GRANDFATHER PLEASE?' Kyle's brow creased. His granddad? How could she possibly be interested in him? He had no idea what that was about.

He sat back on the edge of the bed and clicked on the first of Amanda's messages, already smiling, as it opened.

∞∞∞∞

Rhydian was in the front room with the TV on as Tyler walked past. She headed into the kitchen, towards the ringing mobile phone on the table. It was a withheld number.

"Hello," she answered.

"Hi Tyler, it's Paul here." She smiled in recognition, walking towards the back door and stepping out into the cold day.

"Hiya Paul, how are things there?"

"Yeah, busy, but mostly okay." 'Mostly okay'? She knew that wasn't good. Paul continued, "How is he doing?" She glanced back at the house. Kyle could not see or hear them.

"Better than expected, we hunted a deer for the first time, last night."

"Already?" he exclaimed.

"Yeah, he is doing better than most. Oh, what time are you guys arriving?" she asked, there was a pause before he answered,

"The ferry gets in just after teatime, so we will be with you shortly after that. But..." Paul paused. Tyler did not speak, allowing him to continue. Whatever was coming next was the real reason for the call. "I will need to have a chat with him first .... We have a serious problem!" She thought for a moment before asking the next question.

"Anything to do with what has been on the news recently?" Her eyes scanned the landscape of Rathlin Island, as the silence continued. That answered her question before Paul spoke again.

"Well, yeah ...." Paul had just been about to say something but stopped himself.

"Is it the Nocs?" she asked.

"As well, yes, but they are not the main concern at the moment .... Look, we can chat when I see you later." Tyler felt her wolf rise; there was danger here.

"Okay," she said sternly. "We'll chat later, then."

"Okay, until later," and Paul ended the call. He was concerned, and that was not like him. What could concern him more than the Noctrailis? What was really going on down in the mountains that she did not know about? She thought about it before turning and walking back inside the house. Kyle was in the kitchen, filling the kettle. He had a relaxed grin on his face.

"Cuppa?" he offered.

"No thanks," she walked past him and headed around the table. "I was thinking of having lunch at the hotel."

"When?" he asked. She looked back over her shoulder as she left the kitchen.

"Now! Get your coat." Kyle had the kettle in his right hand. He looked at it, then replaced it back on its stand. He could hear Tyler telling Rhydian about the new lunch arrangements, then heard the excited teenager bouncing up the stairs. He smiled and headed towards his hooded jacket hanging in the hallway, thankful they would be driving down. The rain was just about to start. He was looking forward to this. He had never been inside the small hotel overlooking the harbour; plus, eating out meant no dishes to wash up!

ထဝဃ

Rupert Baskerville had just returned to his hotel room. He had extended his stay for at least another week. Things back at his home were okay and the estate business was running smoothly, which was great; he could concentrate on what he was doing here. The police press conference had been a waste of time, but at least he knew where the police were coming from. He didn't ask any questions, so as not to draw any attention to himself. He used the remote to switch the news on as he walked towards the large window and looked out over panoramic Belfast. He knew the retired policeman would not, or could not, help him; but which one of them had been under surveillance in the coffee shop? He had not seen any others after that, which pointed towards the ex-detective being the one surveilled; but he would keep his eyes open.

The journalist may be of some use, but he would keep an eye on her articles and, more importantly, her blog. She had seen a Garou, that much was clear; and she liked what he'd given her. She was open to the idea of vampires, but not totally sold .... yet. The low, grey clouds threatened rain. He thought wistfully of home, some of the higher parts of the estate would be covered with snow by now. It was nearly the end of January and he was in Northern Ireland; it would not snow here until mid-February.

The evening news headlines started, but he wasn't listening. He reached into his pocket and retrieved his phone. He looked at the screen; he was waiting for a call. He tossed the phone on the bed, then looked out again over the skyline. Suddenly, he turned towards the TV screen.

"Following the deaths of several people in the Mourne Mountains, it has been reported that there have been sightings of a large animal on the loose. Our South Down reporter, Alice Newstead, has more."

Rupert turned and sat on the edge of the bed. The channel changed to an outdoors broadcast. The young, blonde woman wore a heavy outdoor jacket and looked wet. It had obviously been raining. Rupert did not recognise the background, but the sky was darkening. She wore an excited look on her face she was trying to restrain. The large microphone seemed out of place in her hand.

'Thank you, Donna," she started. Rupert glanced out the window at the clouds, then back at the TV. "The Mourne Mountains are immensely popular with hillwalkers and trekkers all year round ..." Rupert stared anxiously at the screen; she was time-filling; "and the nearby Tullymore Forest Park was the inspiration for C.S. Lewis's 'Narnia'...." She continued.

"Was it?" Rupert spoke; he hadn't known that. The reporter continued her broadcast,

"But, following the death of Craig Keenan, there have been several reports of a 'wild beast' in the mountains." Rupert was interested again. "There have been several sheep found ripped apart at various locations around the mountains; and the multiple deaths of a group of hillwalkers near Slieve Binnian is fueling local speculation that there is a 'beast' in the Mournes." The camera moved back slightly and, as she turned to her left, an older man came into view. Rupert guessed he was in his mid-sixties. "Here is local farmer, Donal McGuken." The farmer stepped forward and looked at the reporter as she asked her first question, "Mr McGuken, you say you have heard 'the beast'? The camera zoomed in and focused on his face. His name appeared at the bottom of the screen. His thick accent was that of a country man. Rupert could just barely understand him.

"Aye, heard da beest da furst time just after ta fella was torn up."

"Was that Mr Keenan?" the reporter asked, the differences in their accent very apparent. The farmer nodded.

"Aye, aye ... long howl it was ...."

"And where were you the first time you ..." the reporter was suddenly cut off; the camera spun round and pointed at the darkening hills. She let out a short scream at the sound of the long, low howl in the distance. Rupert straightened up. He knew that sound. It stopped, then came again.

"IT'S DA BEAST, IT'S DA BEAST!" shouted the farmer, who was now out of the shot. The camera was shaking, and very heavy breathing could be heard coming from the camera operator.

"OH MY GOD, WHAT WAS THAT?" screamed the reporter. The farmer appeared at the side of the screen, pointing into the darkness.

"It's da beast, It's da beast!" Repeated the farmer, the voice of the anchor back in the studio came on.

"Alice, what is happening there? Can you give us an update?" The camera panned over to the left and a very shaken reporter came into view. Rupert could see the fear on her face. She was not looking at the camera, but up towards where the sound had come from.

"Oh my God, oh my God ...." she repeated.

"Alice, what did you see? What was that?" the anchor asked. Alice' was visibly shaking.

"I .... I don't know,"

"It's da beast, I'm tell ya ... dats it!" The camera zoomed towards the reporter, who was reacting to what she was hearing from her earpiece. Rupert looked at her eyes, her face - he recognised the look of fear.

"I don't know what that was ...." A third howl echoed around them; the farmer started shouting again.

"Da beast, da beast, it's killed again!" The reporter stepped out of view of the camera.

"Screw this .... Get me outta here!" The feed from the outside broadcast stopped and the shocked face of the anchor filled the screen. She paused, looked down at the keyboard in front of her, then back up at the camera.

"Well, we seem to be having some technical difficulties with our outside broadcast at the moment. We shall return to that as soon as possible ...." The next news story started, but Rupert was not interested. He reached over for the remote and lowered the volume.

The reporter did not know what the sound was, but he did. The 'Beast of Mourne' was born. Yes, he knew what it was, but now he realized there was a very serious problem here in Northern Ireland; one that no one was prepared to deal with. He glanced down at the floor, then out the window again. Things were starting to make sense; the wolves here had kept to themselves; they were hiding and doing well; and now the vampires had arrived, which always meant trouble. He stood and walked over to the window again. He took a deep breath in and considered what to do next. His stomach rumbled. It was teatime and he hadn't eaten since breakfast. He would head into the city for dinner. His mobile phone started ringing so he picked it up from the bed and looked at the screen. It was a landline number from back home.

"Hello," he said quietly.

"Hey boss, long time no hear." He recognised the male voice at the other end.

"Marcus! Hey, how are you getting on?"

"Not bad since I left the squadron." There was idle chit chat as the two old friends reacquainted. Marcus had an accent, very few could place it exactly. It had been a long time since he had been 'home', but the accent was still there.

"So, Boss, tell me about this idea of yours ... and why do you need trackers in England?" Rupert sat back down on the bed.

"Well, I am offering you the job of Head Ranger in a new project on the estate. Are you interested?" There was a pause before Marcus answered,

"Interested, yeah, but what kind of project are you talking about? I need details." Rupert thought for a moment.

"Not the kind of thing I can discuss down an open call, so we'll need to speak in person," Rupert responded.

"Okay, can you give me anything?" Marcus asked, and Rupert thought about what he had told the journalist.

"Some, yes. I want to create a Fire Force of rangers for the estate."

"Like what we had back in Rhodesia with the RLI?" Rupert smiled. Marcus had only been a child when his family had left, but he had kept his accent. "Or is it more of a Selous Scouts thing?" Rupert nodded. Marcus's father had been with the Rhodesian Light Infantry before joining the famed Selous Scouts. After the war of independence and Rhodesia became Zimbabwe, his family had left for South Africa, never to return.

"More of an RLI thing, but you get the idea," Rupert answered. He could almost feel Marcus smiling down the phone.

"Okay, Boss …. but what are we hunting in England?" Marcus asked again. Rupert looked at the TV screen.

"Now, mate, that is for a face to face discussion."

"Okay, I can be at your hall tomorrow, if you like," Marcus suggested. Rupert looked out the window again.

"Sorry, big guy, but I am in Belfast at the moment."

"Belfast! What are you doing there?" Rupert stood up and walked back to the window.

"Oh, just tying up a loose end, I should be back there in a few days, may I call you then?" Rupert suggested.

"Ya, sure. You gat my number?"

"Yes, thanks, Marcus …. Oh, by the way," Rupert looked into the darkening night sky, ".… how much do you know about rabies?" They chatted for a few more minutes before Rupert hung up. Now would be real progress; Marcus, he could trust. His Fire Force would become a reality.

The news had moved on, but he wasn't listening anymore. The smile on his face was a satisfied one. His phone bleeped with the arrival of a message. He looked over to where he had dropped it on the bed. He reached over, picked up the phone and read Steve Minister's name on the screen. He pressed the green button and read the message; 'POLICE DEPLOYING TO MOURNE MOUNTAINS: FOUR HILLWALKERS FOUND TORN UP NEAR ROCKY MOUNTAIN. THOUGHT YOU WOULD LIKE TO KNOW.'

Earl Baskerville's plans for the evening had just changed.

Chapter 30

Kyle was standing by the rear door of the kitchen. The others from the farm were late. They had missed the ferry but were finally on their way. It would not be long now. He watched the sunset; the land was fading into darkness. Lunch had been excellent; both the girls were in a good mood. Rhydian, especially, was very chatty. Kyle noticed when they were around others, the farm, wolves or anything about that side of their past, was never discussed. He asked what she used to do as an occupation and was surprised by her reply.

"Environmental Scientist." That opened-up a whole new conversation, he knew she was educated but would never have guessed something like that. Her focus had been on environmental engineering. Kyle made a mental note to do an internet search on that. As they were leaving the restaurant, Rhydian hugged him, then went to the ladies' room, leaving him and Tyler by the front door. He did not know if she had kissed him or he had kissed her; but kiss they did. It had been a passionate kiss, before she pushed him away. There'd been a few moments of awkward silence before Rhydian returned. It was not mentioned on the way back to the farmhouse.

∞∞∞∞∞

He had watched the police press conference; he knew the name of Chief Anderson but was glad he did not know the man. As he watched, he missed being in the police, then thought about where he was now. If the two of them had not been loaned to Limavady District Command Unit, they would not have found the murder victims in the bus station. What would have happened from there? The journalist would not have been interested in them, the M.I.T. from Belfast would not have been interested either, especially after the Castleroe incident. He thought about his vision. Tyler was right; his eyes were getting better at low light, but was he a becoming a little bit colour blind? He was not sure. He pondered the kiss. Since getting back to the farmhouse, Tyler had busied herself with preparing the meal for those from the farm who were coming over. Paul and Dermott wanted a face to face chat; he had questions for them, as well. No, Tony wasn't coming. He would have liked to, but he needed to be with Karen. Kyle understood that. The lights of the Land Rover coming up the road cut through the darkness, they were here. He threw the last of his coffee over the ground then turned and went back inside, closing the door behind him. The smell from the kitchen made his mouth water. Delicious! As he entered the room, Rhydian was just walking out of the far door. Tyler was in front of several simmering pots on the stove. There were two venison roasts in the main oven. She was concentrating on cooking.

"They're here," he said, as he stopped by the table. Tyler glanced over at him and paused. Her eyes darted over to the far doorway.

"Well, don't just stand there .... go let them in! I am a bit busy." She looked back at the stovetop. He understood. He walked past her and out of the kitchen towards the front door. As he passed the open door of the living room, he glanced in; Rhydian was laying along the sofa, engrossed in her new phone.

"They are here!" he repeated, as he headed towards the front door. Opening it, he was briefly blinded by the headlights coming up the drive. He stepped outside just as the vehicle stopped. The rear passenger door burst open and a very excited Amanda jumped out. She rushed towards him; arms outstretched. He suddenly felt a wave of emotion envelope him as they met. They locked themselves in each other's arms and shared a passionate kiss. Kyle could not take his eyes off her; there was fire in her eyes and warmth in her embrace.

"I have missed you!" she stated, as they kissed again.

"I have missed you, too ...." Kyle went to say something else but was cut short.

"I really hate to break this up, but..." Paul emerged from the front passenger seat, and Dermott was walking around the front of the 4x4. Kyle released his embrace and took the extended hand that Paul offered.

"Good to see you," the smile was real. It was good to see him again.

"I hear you have been out hunting?" Paul asked, Kyle looked surprised at first and glanced over at Dermott as he approached.

"It wasn't Kyle who got the kill, but I will concede that he was there." Said the female voice from behind him. Everyone turned towards Tyler. Her arms were folded, but there was a welcoming smile on her face. Dermott and Paul stepped forward and greeted her warmly. Kyle could see the obvious respect they had for her. Rhydian appeared from behind Tyler, and that got a reaction from Amanda, who threw her arms up and squealed,

"Rhydian!" She was met with a beaming smile and a hug. They were close.

"Well, dinner was ready half an hour ago so, shall we?" Tyler stepped back and allowed everyone to enter. It did not take her long to have Paul setting the table and Dermott looking after the potatoes. Amanda and Rhydian were in the front room having a catch up.

"Where are we sleeping, since we are not getting the ferry until tomorrow morning?" Paul asked. Tyler looked over her shoulder before opening the oven door. The smell of the prepared venison filled Kyle's senses .... making his mouth water.

"There are two rooms booked for you at the hotel .... If you don't want that, you can have sleeping bags in the gym." The heavy pan was set on top of the stove... It smelled delicious. There was a burst of laughter from the front room.

"I wonder who they are gossiping about?" Dermott asked, without turning around, both Tyler and Paul looked at Kyle.

"Yeah, I wonder." stated Paul. Dinner took an hour and a half. They'd all eaten well, and conversation was jovial, especially between Amanda and Rhydian. Kyle guessed he was the only one in the room who did not know how they knew each other. He was pleased Amanda had made sure she was sitting beside him. He noticed Dermott and Paul did not seem relaxed. Something was troubling them, but he would have to wait to find out. The table had been cleared, the dishwasher loaded for the second time and glasses of wine had been poured. The first bottle had only given them one glass each, but Tyler had two more in the fridge. Kyle looked at his watch; the evening was getting on and, now that dinner was finished, he assumed Dermott and Paul would want to chat. Amanda and Rhydian returned to the front room as Tyler finished the clean-up. Paul had tried to help, but had put things in the wrong places, which got him a playful slap across the back of the head.

Dermott lifted his laptop out of the daysack. He was sitting at the end of the table with his back to the sink. The screen jumped to life.

"Right, so what's been going on since your last visit?" Kyle asked. The mood in the room became sombre as Paul walked over and closed the door. Paul walked past Tyler and sat facing Kyle on the opposite side of the table.

"Well, we've got some good, some bad and," Paul started.

"Some really bad," stated Dermott, who was now tapping at the keyboard in from of him. Kyle glanced over at Tyler. She closed the cupboard, then took a seat at the far end of the table. Whatever was going to be discussed, she wanted in on it. Dermott stopped typing and looked up.

"First thing: do you remember we told you about that English Earl who is over here trying to find out what he can about the Mongols?" Kyle thought for a moment.

"Can't say I do .... Remind me." He sat back in his chair, as Paul continued.

"His name is Rupert Baskerville ...."

"Him!" exclaimed Tyler, and Kyle looked towards her.

"You know him?" he asked. Tyler shrugged,

"I've never met him, but I've certainly heard all about his campaign." Paul fidgeted in his seat. Kyle was watching Dermott, expectantly.

"Yeah, he's a big landowner down in Southern England. He has a small group of Romano-wolves on the top of his estate. They've made trouble for over a century."

"Romano-wolves?" Kyle asked.

"Yeah," replied Dermott. "They aren't connected to any of the worldwide packs. They used to have a lot of land around Romania and Bulgaria but were mostly wiped out in the war with the Nocs." Dermott didn't look up from the screen in front of him.

"What war?" Kyle had asked the question even before he thought about it. The others stopped and stared at him. He looked at each one before speaking again, "Look, I don't know what you know ...." Paul and Dermott shared a glance that slightly annoyed Kyle. He sat upright. "Hey, I am here to learn, correct?"

"Yes, yes you are right," Paul said, as Kyle's eyes darted between the two men.

"There are packs all over the world?" Kyle asked. That got a reaction from Tyler.

"Of course, there are! How can you not know?" Kyle glared at her, she stopped what she was saying. These two were from his pack and he was alpha. She nodded once.

"No, I don't know .... but I want to learn," he sat back again. "So, this English Earl... what about him?" Paul continued,

"Well, he has gone public a few times in the past about the wolves on his land. Thankfully, no one believed him." There was a nod of agreement from Dermott.

"So, what is he to us?" Kyle asked.

"Nothing," Dermott shrugged. He looked up, "but he has been over here chatting to the retired cop that investigated the Mongols. He's been at the different sites taking photos, and chatting to the lass journalist from Coleraine, Cara-*what's her name.*" Kyle looked at Paul.

"So, what does he know about the farm?" he asked.

"Nothing we know of. The army major warned him off," Paul stated,

Kyle looked confused. "Why use them?" he asked, Paul shrugged.

"They know each other. He's ex-SAS, as well." Kyle nodded; Dermott cut in. "The SAS are British special forces ...."

"I know who the SAS are!" Kyle interjected, "continue." Dermott looked at the screen.

"We did the 'Close Target Recce' on where the Nocs were sleeping," he looked up. "All good, so we hit it." He was about to say something else before Tyler spoke up.

"How many did you get?" she asked, a smile on her face. Dermott smiled back at her.

"Twelve."

"Twelve?" Kyle asked, Tyler had that eager grin again, as Dermott continued,

"Yes, twelve in the basement, and one sapien protection outside." Dermott turned the laptop around and pressed a button, the screen came to life.

"What is this?" Kyle asked. The camera was perched inside a hedge, but the small bungalow could clearly be seen. The tall lone figure had walked around the side, then out of sight.

"Footage of the assault." Dermott stood and walked over beside Kyle, Tyler leaned forward, studying the screen.

"Only one protection?" she asked, and Dermott nodded. "That isn't like them; normally, there are at least four," she stated. Paul sat back; he had seen this before. The video continued as the lone figure reappeared beside the parked 4x4. "Something's not right," Tyler muttered.

"We had two cut-off groups, either side." Dermott narrated, Kyle watched as the screen zoomed inward and the face came into focus.

"What's in the bag?" Kyle asked, as the figure slipped the holdall from his shoulder. The camera slightly shuddered as the head of the figure exploded, Dermott's voice came over the footage as the assault team ran forward.

"There was a broken-down shotgun," Dermott said.

"Who is leading the assault?" Tyler asked. She moved closer to the screen, her eyes studying every detail.

"Ruth McDonal is the leading assaulter and the overwatch is 'Wee Jimmy'. Matthew Cairns is spotter." They watched as the rear door of the house opened and the assault teams entered.

"Well done, Ruth!" exclaimed Tyler. Kyle cast her a look.

"Have you made *her* nose bleed?" he asked, Tyler looked into his eyes.

"No... she didn't ask any stupid questions!" Both Dermott and Paul smirked.

"Who is Cairns?" she asked, looking at Paul. But it was Dermott who spoke,

"Jenny Cairns' boy .... He's only seventeen, but already a great shot." Dermott continued to look at the screen, as he finished off. "Not much of a farmer, but he will make a good stalker." He folded his arms.

"Wolf?" Tyler asked, looking up at Dermott.

"Yes. You should get him in about a year's time." Both nodded and returned to the screen. The camera zoomed out then panned from side to side. No movement was detected. Dermott reached forward and pressed the stop button. "There is not really anything more than that," he said.

"You said there were twelve of them?" Kyle asked. Dermott pushed the laptop around back to face where he had been sitting.

"Yes." Dermott sat back down at the table. Kyle looked over at Paul,

"I thought there were only ten in Ireland – five of those, here in the North." Paul nodded.

"Yes, that was right. We took DNA samples from all of them. We already knew about most of them, but there were a few that must be new arrivals.

"Was 'he' among them?" Tyler lowered her tone to ask the question.

Dermott looked at her. "No."

"Who is 'he'?" Kyle asked, as he eyes glanced around the room.

"The American." Paul responded.

"None of the main targets were there," Dermott stated. Kyle looked over at Tyler who was staring at the screen. She was angry.

"Something's not right there," she repeated.

"What?" Paul asked, she sat back in the chair.

"There should be two outside and two inside at all times. Having only one? That isn't right. Something is amiss. Who were your main targets?" she asked, as her eyebrows lowered, and her face tightened. There was obvious hatred for them. Dermott shifted, then answered,

"Four in total: The American, the two girls, Sabine and Alison, and that one they turned, Kris Martin."

"Martin?" Kyle asked.

"He was from the New Year's Day murders on the Strand in Portstewart," Kyle nodded. "Who are the others?" he asked. Dermott typed into the keyboard then turned it around just as more footage was starting. "What is this?" Kyle asked.

"CCTV from the bungalow they attacked." Both Kyle and Tyler leaned forward to study the footage, and Paul continued his narration.

"That, we believe, is Kris Martin ...there is the American. The two girls are ..."

"THAT'S ALISON WALLACE!" Kyle shouted as he pointed to the screen.

"Yes, we know," replied Paul.

"But she is a copper from Coleraine!" The footage continued.

"Aye, Tony told us," stated Dermott as he turned the laptop back around.

"She is helping them?" Kyle asked, Paul looked at Dermott.

"Show him." Dermott nodded.

"Show me what?" he asked, Tyler leaned forward and looked at what was on the screen.

"What is this?" she asked.

"Footage from the carpark at Mussenden Temple last year," Paul said.

"Where did you get it?" Kyle asked.

"From the military," stated Dermott. Both Kyle and Tyler watched as Alison attacked the helpless Yelina Gurin. Kyle was shocked; Tyler did not move.

"Hang on .... She is a Noc?" Kyle's shocked face looked at Paul, then Dermott. "I mean, I have known her for over two years .... This ...." he pointed towards the screen, "this cannot be!"

"We have studied her in detail," started Paul.

"And we hit her house .... She has not been home in some time," stated Dermott.

"But she can't be a Noc!" Kyle exclaimed in disbelief.

"We don't think she is. Not fully anyway," said Paul.

"But what about the daylight thing?" Kyle asked, "I mean, I have been in the same section as her for the last two years."

"Is she still in the police force?" Tyler asked. Kyle looked over at her, and Paul answered.

"No. She finished her thirty years in December, then .... whoosh, gone." Kyle started to shake his head.

"But what was she doing with the knife at the end?" Kyle asked.

"Covering the evidence," stated Tyler.

"I can't believe she is a Noc," stated Kyle, shaking his head.

"We don't actually know what she is, but," said Paul.

"She isn't Noctrailis," interrupted Tyler. All three heads turned towards her.

"Any idea what she is then? As we are a little 'in the dark'," replied Paul. Tyler paused for a moment, her eyes darting between each of them before she spoke.

"She could be a Valkyrie." Three mystified faces stared back at her.

"A what?" It was Paul who asked the question, but all three were thinking it.

"A Valkyrie," Tyler repeated. She sat there, looking back at the three of them.

"A 'hand maiden to the gods'?" asked Kyle. Tyler smiled and shook her head.

"Haha, no, nothing like that." There was another pause.

"Well, if you know something we don't, would you care to share it?" Dermott asked. Tyler looked down at the table, then raised her head. The smile was gone.

"The name comes from 'Old Norse' and it means 'chooser of the slain'." Paul and Dermott looked at each other, then back at her.

"So, what exactly is she?" Paul was concerned now, "I mean what are we dealing with? A Noc who can walk around in daylight?"

"No," Tyler shook her head.

"And how come I've never heard of them before?" Paul asked.

"Yeah, me neither," Dermott added.

"What .... exactly .... is .... she?" Paul repeated his question.

"Well, I have never come across one, but I heard about them when I was in Canada." Paul and Dermott looked at each other again as Tyler continued, "There is an old Norse poem that describes them as 'biting the neck, the breast, then hating you for eternity!' Unlike the Noctrailis they don't need to feed on blood to survive, but they are recorded in legend from across Scandinavia, Europe, even here in Ireland ...."

"That does not answer the question!" Paul stated. "What is she and what are we dealing with?" Tyler looked at him.

"I don't know much, but I heard they have sided with both Noctrailis and Wolf in the past."

"But this one is with the Nocs!" stated Dermott, as he pointed to the laptop.

"Yes, it seems so," Tyler replied, Kyle was still in shock.

"And having been a police officer for thirty years, she would know how to leave a crime scene with little or no evidence," Kyle added. Paul nodded.

"Any idea where she is now?" Tyler asked. "Because if you find her, you find the rest of them." Dermott agreed, as he turned the laptop back towards himself again.

"So, what happened at the bungalow? What happened there?" Kyle asked.

"We passed what we knew on to the police and the military," Paul answered.

"And got this in return," Dermott butted in.

"Yes," said Paul, "officially they say it was a drug gang 'feud', but we know it wasn't."

"Young Martin getting his first kill." A look of disdain was back on Tyler's face.

"Yes," stated Paul, watching as Dermott was doing something on the laptop. Kyle asked the next question.

"So, what about this 'Monster of Mourne' that's all over the news?" There was a physical reaction from both Paul and Dermott.

"That's the bad news." Paul stated.

"Is it a Mongol that was missed?" Kyle asked, and Dermott looked up.

"We didn't miss any of them!" Dermott was adamant.

"We sent a team of four down to see what they could find," Paul started, as Kyle leaned forward intently. Whatever was coming next was not good.

"And ....?" Kyle asked. Paul cringed.

"The only message we received said they think there is a female rabid down there."

"WHAT!" Tyler shouted, as she slammed her hands down on the table. "Who they hell did you send?" Paul looked away.

"We didn't know. We had no reason to even think ...." Kyle remembered what Tony had said about rabies... that it was the only thing that scared them.

"WHO THE HELL DID YOU SEND?" Tyler was shouting now. Paul and Dermott shared another look. It was Dermott who answered.

"The Silver and Gold twins." He had lowered his voice, but everyone heard what he'd said. Kyle did not recognise the names, but Tyler did. She jumped up, sending her chair crashing into the cupboard behind her.

"YOU SENT FOUR TEENAGERS AGAINST A RABID WOLF? ARE YOU INSANE?"

"Tyler, wait ...." Paul lifted his hands to try and calm her down. It didn't work. She slapped the table so hard the two in the front room would have heard.

"SO, WHAT DID THEY HAVE TO SAY WHEN THEY GOT BACK?" Dermott and Paul shared another look. Paul turned and looked at her.

"They were found last night near Rocky Mountain." Tyler started to pace around the space in the far side of the kitchen near the back door.

"AND YOU HAVE NO IDEA WHO THIS WOLF IS, I SUPPOSE ... GOD YOU LOT ARE STUPID!"

"Actually, we do," Dermott stated.

"Do .... what?" Kyle asked. "You know who it is? Is it one of our own?"

"No, not one of ours. We heard from the Chernsci just before we left the farm to come here," Paul stated, and Kyle looked at him.

"You heard from who?" he asked.

"The Chernsci." Paul repeated.

"Who the hell are they?" Kyle asked. Tyler was standing with her hands on her hips, glaring at the two at the far end of the table, she answered for them,

"They are the second largest den in Germany." Kyle was about to ask another question, but before he could, she picked up her chair, sat down and glared at Dermott and Paul. "So, who is it?" Paul took a breath in and nodded towards Dermott, who turned the laptop around again,

"Her name is 'Ute Fessler'. She comes from the town of Garbsen, which is just north of Hannover." He paused, as Tyler pointed to the screen. The image was frozen.

"What is this? Did you get it from them?" Paul shook his head,

"No, this is mobile phone footage taken by a hillwalker, who, we think, was her first kill here." Dermott pressed the button and the footage started.

"Who is he?" Kyle asked.

"His name was Craig Keenan. We got this from the cops." The room fell silent as the footage began.

"Another beautiful day in the Mournes," the voice said. The footage continued into the attack. Kyle felt himself flinch as the wolf pounced on the victim. Tyler did not move. When the video stopped, she asked for it to be repeated, which Dermott did. She leaned in closer, studying as much detail as she could. When it stopped again, Dermott turned the laptop around. He and Paul were silent. Tyler was furious.

"So," Kyle started, "I am asking, as I don't know," he looked over at Tyler. "How do we take down a rabid wolf?" Tyler looked at him, then back at the others.

"You send two teams of eight …. at least!" Paul nodded.

"We didn't know …." he started; Tyler exploded.

"YOU DIDN'T KNOW!" She slammed the table again, "YOU DIDN'T KNOW! AND SENT FOUR TEENAGERS WHO WERE OUT OF THEIR DEPTH TO THEIR DEATHS!" She stood up again, unable to contain her fury.

"Tyler," Kyle spoke softly. She glared at him, and he glared back, "TYLER!" he said sternly. Tyler paused, then sat back down. "Well, having never dealt with this before," Kyle looked slowly around at them as he spoke, "I don't think this is something I can do from here. So tomorrow," he looked at Paul, "I will go back to the farm with you," Paul nodded, "and we'll sort this situation out there, okay?" He looked at Dermott, who also nodded.

"I am going, as well!" Tyler almost spat out the words. There would be no argument. There was silence in the room for a few moments, then a knock at the door. All four heads turned towards it. The door slowly opened to reveal Amanda and Rhydian, who were smiling amiably.

"Is it okay for the kids to join the adults yet?" Amanda asked.

∞∞∞∞∞

Kyle looked at the small clock on the table by the bed. It was nearly 5am. He turned his head and gazed into the sleeping face of Amanda. They had not stayed up long. In fact, as soon as Paul and Dermott had left, she'd almost dragged him to the spare room. They didn't get a lot of sleep. He listened to her breathing now. It was soft and peaceful. He thought back to how passionate their lovemaking had been; they had missed each other. Tyler had said nothing about the kiss they had shared outside the hotel earlier. That had been unexpected. Rhydian had shouted 'have fun' as they had been going up the stairs. Amanda had squealed in delight at the news that he was heading back to the farm the following morning. She was happy. He wasn't. Hitting the sleeping vampires had been an overreaction; and sending only four teenagers to the mountains had been an underreaction. This rabid had to be stopped.

The late news stated the police had deployed armed search teams looking for a wild animal after the live news report broadcasted the howling. The internet exploded with different stories and theories. Farmers and hillwalkers suddenly came forward with various sightings, none of which fit the description of a rabid wolf. Tyler was furious with them; they lost four. It shouldn't have happened. There were two grieving families at the farm now, Kyle was looking back at the display on the clock.

"Hey there," Amanda whispered. He could not keep from smiling at her. Her hair was a mess and she looked tired, but there was a smile he could not help but respond to. He felt her hand move over his chest, as she moved on top of him. "Is the wolf awake?" she asked seductively. His hands moved up the sides of her body, then around her shoulders.

"I'm awake," he whispered. She groaned and he closed his eyes. Right now, he did not care if they woke the others in the house.

Chapter 31

Sean had not eaten much for breakfast. He hadn't felt like eating. He was sitting in his front room; the coffee was on the table and the news was on the TV. The clock beside him had just gone 9am and the headlines just finished. Four more hillwalkers had been murdered in the Mournes, and the broadcast that had picked up an animal howling, scaring the reporter half to death, was being replayed...again. It sent nearly all the local media into a frenzy.

Sean thought for a moment about M.I.T. dealing with this, missing them only slightly now. He had seen the news last night. Over dinner, his wife hardly spoke to him. The consultant job recommended to him for a security firm with contracts in the Balkans, had gone to 'someone else'. Well, that is what he had told his wife. He did not want the job, really; he was just looking for something to do. He hated this...sitting around the house all day, every day, not achieving anything. His wife had not long left. She said what she would be doing, but he hadn't heard; she would be out most of the day. He had seen the mobile phone footage of the animal attack. His mind went through all the 'scene of the crime' investigating that would be happening. That scene would have been similar to the one in Castleroe.

Time passed. The news ended and then there was a programme about buying old houses, doing makeovers, and then selling them. He never believed the amount they claimed to have spent; it probably was at least three times that, which would have resulted in a loss, not a profit. He reached forward and turned the TV off. He found he really didn't like daytime TV - all the adverts were the same; no, he did not want to adopt an animal on the far side of the world; no, he had not been in an accident at work; and yes, he was quite happy with the toothpaste he was using. He picked up the cold coffee and headed into the kitchen. The new coffee machine used pods; the coffee was a lot better than instant, but not as good as the percolator. Sean found himself looking out the window of the kitchen over the rear of the house; he had fond memories of when the kids were young, but both were married now and living their own lives; he seldom heard from them. He could hear the coffee machine working, then the sound of the doorbell abruptly echoed through the house. He almost jumped. He was not expecting anyone; who could it be? He looked through the security camera at the single figure standing there. He threw open the door and welcomed Mike Dear inside. His excitement was matched by Mike's; it was so good to see him!

"How are you doin'?" The two men shared a hug on the doorstep, then Sean backed inside and allowed Mike to walk past. Mike was smiling as he headed towards the kitchen and the inviting aroma of coffee.

"I see the missus is out," he said. Sean closed the front door and followed him into the immaculate kitchen.

"Yeah, how did you know that?" Sean asked. Mike stopped by the kitchen table and turned towards him.

"You know, detective thing..." he was smiling as he spoke, "your car isn't there, and your blinds are open meaning, someone is in." Sean felt that old familiar warmth inside him; it was good to see his friend again.

"Coffee?" he offered, pointing towards the machine.

"Well, I wasn't expecting a glass of water, in this house!" There was a short laugh, and the two men chatted briefly while Sean prepared the drinks; biscuits were offered but declined. Sean nodded towards the kitchen table and both men were soon comfortable.

"So how is life in Special Branch, these days?" Sean asked, watching Mike look out the window.

"Well, we are getting a name change; we are to be called 'Intelligence Branch' from now on, and M.I.T will be called 'Major Investigations Team'. I am off to some training centre in England for three months," Mike explained. Sean drank from his mug, letting Mike continue. He'd nearly missed the comment about the M.I.T. "Some place in southern England called 'the Fort' ...." Mike looked up, "But they won't tell me where it is." Sean smiled, but did not intervene. "It makes day to day stuff kinda difficult."

"How so?" Sean asked.

"Well, since I haven't completed the course, I am not cleared for some of the stuff that they do, especially the military. So, I am not included in the daily briefings...." Mike paused and looked away again; he was holding back. Sean reached out to his friend.

"I think the military stopped trusting us when the PSNI was formed." Mike smiled at the comment.

"They are certainly not like any military that I've ever worked around before."

"How so?" Sean asked, Mike sipped from his mug,

"They don't use rank .... all nicknames. It can be amusing," he was smiling as he spoke.

"Really?" Sean commented.

"Yeah, really," Mike replied. "It's all 'Dusty', 'Chalky', 'Smudge', 'Taff' and two of them are just 'Zero Three Seven' and Zero Six Nine'" Mike started to laugh.

"And why are they called that? Is it some sort of code?" Sean asked.

"No," Mike replied, "I asked them, and the answer is simple." He took another sip of coffee before attempting a Welsh accent, *"They're bot' Welsh, y' see!"* Mike placed the mug down. "Three Seven said they were both ex-Welsh Guardsmen and both were named Jones. Apparently, there are a lot of 'Guardsman Jones' so they are called by the last three digits of their army serial numbers."

"'Makes sense to someone, I suppose." Sean said. Mike looked uncomfortable; he wasn't as chatty as he normally was. Sean could see he was stressed about something but was not saying what. Sean changed the conversation.

"Did I tell you, that English Earl fella was asking questions again." he stated.

Mike looked up. "Really? That Baskerville fella?"

"The very one."

"What did he want?" Mike asked. The detective was back, Sean knew the tone of voice, the body language. This was a subject he was interested in.

"We met for coffee near City Hall," Sean started, deciding not to reveal that the surveillance had been compromised. "I think he just wanted more info .... I kept telling him I'm not with the police anymore." Sean watched him; Mike was definitely interested in this. "Have you had any more dealings with him?" Sean was turning the questions around; he wanted to discover what was bothering his friend. Mike answered nervously,

"Me? No, no, I heard that he knows some of the military." Sean knew Mike was holding something back. "They got together for a 'group hug' as they call it, but apart from that ...." Mike trailed off. Sean nodded. "Did I hear right that you have a job in the offing? Something in the Balkans?" he asked. Sean smiled. Mike had turned the conversation away from the one subject that he did not want to discuss.

"Yes, and no."

"Yes and no?" Mike repeated.

"Yes, I was offered a job by Calin United Royalties ... but they wanted me in the Balkans for nine months straight and .... I had to sort my own travel, hotels etc .... So, I said 'no'."

"Calin?" Mike asked. "The company that was set up by Dominic *what's his name* from the police depot?"

"The very one."

"And he only recruits those who were in the RUC..." Mike sat back in the chair.

"Yeah, he took the name of 'Royal Ulster Constabulary' and turned the letters around so ex-RUC would spot it." Sean explained.

"It's obviously working," Mike stated, Sean shook his head.

"What?" Mike asked.

"He emailed first, but when we spoke on the phone, all he wanted to know about was 'the werewolf squad' and how come the PSNI were now investigating mythical creatures." Mike spotted the way Sean's face fell, "It seems being the 'Inspector in Charge' of that mess is how my thirty years' service is going to be remembered." Mike nodded; he now knew the real reason Sean had said 'no' to the job offer. "So," Sean looked at Mike, "what's going on in the Mournes? Another four murdered last night?" Mike looked around.

"Newry M.I.T. are heading that one; nothing to do with us," Mike wasn't looking at him, Sean could always tell when he was lying.

"The news just said 'teenagers'; Any idea who they were?" Sean asked.

"Yeah, two sets of twins. They worked at that deer farm O'Brien used to own." Mike explained, Sean reacted,

"What?" He nearly dropped his mug onto the table. "That certainly wasn't on the news!"

"No, but they don't think it was linked." Silence fell between them. Mike lifted his mug and drank some more. He wasn't looking at Sean.

"Mike," Sean said sharply, Mike looked at him. "What actually happened up at Mussenden Temple?" Sean saw the reaction in Mike's body at the question, and continued, "they weren't eastern European organised crime gangs, were they?" Mike was tense.

"No, they weren't," Mike looked away, he was not going to expand any further.

"Let me guess ...." Sean started, "Forester has slapped you with a thirty year 'D-Notice.'" Mike looked up, sadly.

"One-hundred-year D-notice." He replied quietly.

"A hundred? Mike, what ...." Sean stopped. He did not ask the question he now knew his friend could not answer. Mike looked away, that was as far as he would go, Sean changed the conversation again,

"So, how is life with the missus these days?" Sean's question helped Mike relax; here was something he could talk about.

"The pendulum has certainly swung fully the other way." Mike almost smiled.

"How so?" Sean asked with a small grin.

"Now I am home for teatime nearly every day and if there is something going on at work that I can't see, I get a 'STAY AT HOME TODAY' message. So, I am around a lot more of the time at home," he smiled as he spoke.

"And she is hating it," Sean finished the sentence for him.

"Yeah, yeah she is." The two friends chatted for another hour; the subject of what Mike was now doing was not raised again. Sean enjoyed having his friend call 'round; but every time Mike asked how Sean was getting on, the reply was the same: *'fine'*. He wasn't, and Mike knew it. As his friend got up to leave, Sean realized it was almost 1pm. Time had passed quickly. He watched Mike drive away. Mike was heading to England the following day; Sean missed his friend already.

∞∞∞∞

Alison looked at her watch; it was nearly 8pm; it had been dark for over an hour. She folded her arms as she stood outside the double doors. She looked down the street. It was only wide enough for single traffic, as the old red brick buildings were so close together. She looked up Hill Street in Belfast. It was in the old Cathedral Quarter, and it seemed nearly every building here was being renovated. There were plans for new pubs, clubs and restaurants; apparently, this was to be the new night life destination in Belfast. That meant they could not stay much longer. The door opened, and Kris Martin walked out. He was in a good mood,

"So, where is he, then?" Alison looked him up and down. The tee shirt was too big for his thin frame, the denim jacket was far too small, his jeans had rips in them and there was dirt around his ankles. It looked like he had not washed in days. She looked away when he stopped beside her. The door behind him slammed shut.

"He is late," she said, leaning back against the wall. Three women came around the corner. There was an obvious age difference between them; they looked like a mum and daughter with one of mum's friends. They'd been out for a while - they were loud and obnoxious. The smell of cheap perfume did not hide the underlying smell of body odour. The mother was the loudest of the three; her bright top was loose; she would describe herself as 'cuddly'; others would say 'fat'. Her jewellery was cheap and there was lots of it; her hair had faded blonde streaks which were overdue for a 'touch-up'. It was not a good look. Cheap necklaces and gold wristbands jangled as she waved her arms, just passing Alison, who scrunched up her face and turned away from the armpit smell. The woman's friend was not much better. The slim, well-turned out daughter was certainly quieter and better dressed than her companions. She wore a short, black top and black jeans. She had straight black hair, and her face was dominated by black-rimmed glasses. Alison watched as they carried on down the street; The two older women were certainly having more fun than the daughter. Kris made a noise, and Alison glanced at him. His hands were in his pockets and he was staring after the younger girl.

"Hey!" she barked. Kris turned his head to look at her; his eyebrows were raised, and he had a lustful look on his face. He looked back down the street, as he spoke.

"Yeah .... now there is a twig I'd like to 'snap,'" he grunted, amused at his own comment. The back of Alison's right hand connected with the side of his head in a slap. It wasn't a playful slap - it was done with force. She re-folded her arms as he recoiled, rubbing the side of his head.

"Don't .... do that again," she stated, looking in the opposite direction.

"Hey, I was only ...." Her hand connected with his face this time, the force of which sent him reeling back into the doors. She did not look at him.

"Do your job!" Just then, a 4x4 with tinted windows came around the corner at the far end of the street. The three women were walking past it, and it slowly made its way towards them. "Here he is," she glared at him. There was a look of angry defiance as he rubbed his face. "Get back in there and let them know." The 4x4 carried on towards them, but he did not move. Alison stepped forward and lifted her hand as if to strike him again. "Now!" she commanded. He turned swiftly and went back inside. The silver 4x4 pulled up and stopped so the rear door was beside the entrance. She nodded at the driver, who nodded back. She would not open the door; it would be opened from the inside only when they were ready. She stepped to the side to give him room. The door opened, and the American got out. He was very smartly dressed – an expensive black suit, a black silk shirt and matching tie. She smiled as he straightened up.

126

"Alison! Hi," he greeted her. He stepped forward. There was a polite embrace, but only at arm's length. To anyone watching, they were two acquaintances saying hello. Alison stepped back, allowing him access to the doorway. Sabine shuffled out of the back seat while Alison opened the door for him. "Is everything ready?" he asked.

"Yes, they are waiting," she smiled.

"Have the ones from Dublin and England arrived?" he asked. She smiled back,

"Yes, as have those from France. They got here just before sunrise this morning."

"Excellent, excellent." He walked towards the doorway but stopped as he got there. He turned and pulled out a picture from his inside pocket. It was a photograph of a woman. Alison paused for a second. She had seen the face before but could not place her.

"Who is she?" Alison asked, looking at the small picture.

"Her name is Karen Fallon, and she is the wife of a Garou called 'Tony'." Alison took a breath in - of course she knew her, and what had happened to her. Alison's feeling of pity suddenly changed to concern, as she looked up at the American.

"Why are you showing me this?" she asked, apprehensively. "She has done nothing wrong," she stated. The American reached out and took the picture back.

"Only married the wrong kind .... but no, nothing is to happen to her .... She was part of a ruling; she is not to be touched during our mission. We need Salisbury to support us, not turn against us. See that she is protected, will you," he said, as Sabine closed the door of the 4x4 behind her. It moved off slowly. The two women looked at each other and smiled; this time the embrace was more friendly, the American walked inside.

"Hiya," Sabine said, and it was returned. She stepped forward into the building and Alison followed, closing, then locking, the doors behind her. They were in a small room, dimly lit by a candle on a side table. Walking through the foyer, the American reached into his pocket again and produced another picture.

"This one, on the other hand," he looked at both of them, "see that harm comes to this one personally, will you?" It wasn't a question - it was a command. Alison took the picture and looked at the pretty face on it. The picture had been taken from distance. She turned it over and read the details on the back. Sabine stepped closer and looked at the picture over Alison's shoulder; a small smile spread over her face.

"Amanda, mate of An Rua alpha," Sabine read aloud.

"That way?" The American asked, pointing towards the single door.

"That way," Alison confirmed. He nodded. After a short pause, he opened the door and entered. The light from inside filled the doorway and he stepped forward into the large room. Sabine followed and, upon entering, immediately moved to the left of the doorway. Alison followed her, closing the door behind her. The crowd-filled, rectangular room was illuminated by bright strip lighting down the centre of the ceiling. There were no windows, and only a single closed door at the far end of the room. The gathered crowd hushed to silence as the American stepped forward. Alison looked around the room. He held everyone's attention. This was a serious gathering.

"Everyone is here," announced Kris, who was on the right side of the room. The American was smiling as he turned and nodded towards him, then focused his attention on the patiently waiting crowd. He extended his hands.

"Gathered coven!" He intoned, loud enough for everyone to hear; he was no stranger to being in front of people. "Those who walk by night... this is an exciting time for all of us." There was anticipation in the faces of everyone watching him. He relaxed his arms and stepped forward.

"For many a year, in these lands, our kind have been hunted to near extinction." There was a rumble from the crowd. "Our enemies think we are weak; they think we have been defeated." Several heads nodded. "But the time is nearly upon us to drive the wolves from the green lands," The American was looking into the upturned faces. "They took one of our own last year," heads nodded again, "and they recently took twelve of our number as they slept!" The nods were accompanied by murmurs. "The time is nearly upon us to let these *wolves* know they no longer dominate this land." Cheers of agreement rang from the crowd. The American looked around the room,

"I have news for you: Dani, our princess, has ensured, ... at great danger to herself, I might add... that the southern wolves will not intervene here in the north!" There was a cheer from the group. Alison looked over at Sabine, who was smiling. Sabine looked at her and nodded. *'How the hell did you do that?'* Alison mouthed the words. Sabine just winked at her in reply. The American carried on,

"A difficult time is ahead of us." He began to slowly pace the floor in front of him, "I want you all gathered here tonight," he raised the volume of his voice, "to rally behind our Dani! She will lead you in the coming times ….” Alison glanced over at Sabine, who was beaming. She obviously knew what he was about to say.

“FRIENDS,” he was louder again, “THOSE WHO WALK BY NIGHT,” and he extended his arms, “WE ARE AT WAR!” A cheer rose up, “WAR WITH THE GAROU!” The cheer became even louder. Alison watched as excitement overtook the crowd. The American stepped back and lowered his arms.

He looked through the faces. “Maya, where are you?” he shouted. Alison watched as the crowd parted and a young woman appeared. She wore plain trainers, jeans, a nondescript shirt and an open jacket. Her light brown hair was shoulder-length and she wore small, plastic-rimmed glasses. She walked slowly towards the American. Her appearance was athletic, but unremarkable. That is, until she smiled. Alison saw her enlarged, extended canines…. she was excited! The American nodded in appreciation as Maya stopped in front of him.

“So, my warrior,” he shouted, stepping towards her. He raised his hands to her shoulders and turned her to face the others. His right hand remained on her right shoulder and he gently pulled her towards him. There was no objection from the smiling girl.

“Have you been preparing them for me?” She looked up at him, still smiling and snapped the fingers of her right hand. Suddenly, everyone, apart from Kris, moved and produced weapons. Most were M-16 type rifles, some were pump-action shotguns. Coats and jackets were opened to reveal pistols.

They were all heavily armed with illegal, military-grade weapons. Alison watched as they deftly manoeuvred their weapons. They obviously had trained with them, they displayed determination on their faces and in their demeanour.

“For the twelve!” came a shout from the crowd. The American lifted his right hand into a fist and punched the air.

“FOR THE TWELVE!” he shouted, and the room exploded into rapturous joy. Alison looked at Sabine, who smiled back.

Chapter 32

Cara-Marie turned the TV off; there was nothing on the news that she didn't already know. She looked around her flat; the laptop was on the coffee table in front of her, screen paused on the footage of the attack on the hillwalker. She had heard about the other four before she'd left the office, but Kevin had forbidden her doing anything about it. She sat back into the sofa and pulled the laptop onto her legs, clicking on the link that brought her blog up. She now had over ten thousand followers. Unfortunately, most of them had their own conspiracy theories about what was going on; some of the screen names she recognised as journalists from other papers - they never commented, just read her posts. She knew what they were doing: they were watching, looking for anything they could use. One post had made her giggle: 'they are not werewolves, or vampires but an alien reptilian species that is planning an invasion of our planet. They were after all of our water.' She told Mark about it and he suggested she write a screenplay... he'd watch that film! She added a new entry about the four hillwalkers. She'd heard they were from the deer farm, but that wasn't confirmed. Two families had received the worst news that day, so she did not recount the details they heard from one of the police.

The doorbell rang. She glanced at the small clock on the wall and set the laptop down, then made her way to the front door.

"What time do you call this?" she demanded when she opened the door.

"What?" Mark looked at her blankly. She stepped back to let him in.

"You were supposed to be here an hour ago!" Mark cast her a confused look as he walked quickly past and headed towards her bathroom.

"'Been busting for a pee since Castlerock." The door of the bathroom closed behind him. Cara-Marie closed the front door and walked into the kitchen to put the kettle on, not wanting to hear whatever he was doing in there. The kettle was starting to boil when he re-appeared. She already had two mugs with milk and coffee in them, just waiting for the addition of hot water, he patted her shoulder,

"Brilliant." He headed back into the living room, and dropped onto the sofa, right where she had been sitting. She didn't say anything while she poured the kettle and stirred the mugs. "What are you watching?" he asked, as she dropped the teaspoon into the sink.

"I *was* watching the news," she stated, then turned and walked back into the living room with a mug in each hand. She extended one towards him, which he accepted.

"Ta," he said. She walked around the coffee table and stopped beside him, expecting him to move. He looked up and she stared at him. She watched him clue in, then move along down the couch. He pointed towards the laptop screen. "Light viewing, I see." He lifted the mug to his lips and reacted, "Ach, no sugar!" He looked over at her expectantly. She looked back at him,

"You know where the sugar is, don't you?" Her face was blank. He looked around then placed the mug on the table before standing up. As he went into the kitchen, she lifted the laptop and shut it down. When he returned, she was drinking from her mug, the laptop was off, as was the TV.

"So," he started, and sat down.

"So," she repeated back to him.

"What has got you in such a foul mood, then?" He wasn't looking at her when he asked the question, but she was tense. "And don't say 'Nothing, I am fine!' because I know you are not." Her face changed from blank to annoyed.

"No, really I am, it's just ...." she stopped herself. Mark sat back and held the mug with both hands in front of his face.

"Just?" he inquired. Her eyes bounced around the room. Something was bothering her, he could guess but didn't, so he let her talk.

"Look, those last four hillwalkers who got torn up down in the Mournes yesterday, they were all from that deer farm ...." She turned towards him, "Why is no one talking about that? I mean, what were they doing down there?" Mark sipped from his coffee, listening as Cara-Marie exploded. "There is *something* going on at that farm. First those attacks last year *were* done by an animal .... No one believes it was 'eastern European gangs' .... I mean .... I saw one, for fuck's sake!"

Mark watched as she nearly dropped her own mug, her arms were flying in the air as she spoke. "Then, five get their throats ripped open on New Year's Day and one of them just 'disappears.' I mean, he gets up and just walks out of the mortuary ... And now we have more murders... and Kevin isn't doing a damn thing about this! I mean, this is one of the biggest stories and we hardly even mention *them*, at all!" Mark drank more of his coffee; he listened, knowing there was something else... this was just the surface. She carried on. "There is something not right about that deer farm .... The head guy just dies and everything gets left to Kyle .... Then I find out that his granddad was in the war and could turn into some sort of creature that could 'tear the Germans apart!' I mean, that, in itself, should be investigated." Mark continued to drink; he had not heard that name in a while... could that be what was bothering her?

"So why don't you just ask him?" he suggested. She spun where she was sitting, nearly shouting now.

"Don't you think I have tried that?" her arm flung to one side in frustration. "All I keep getting is 'I AM AWAY AT THE MOMENT', 'REALLY BUSY RIGHT NOW' 'MAYBE SOMETIME SOON'. I know that he hasn't been at the farm for quite a while now." Mark was convinced that he'd found what was really upsetting her.

"How do you know that?" he asked, she slumped back into the sofa in anger,

"'Because I went down there and asked. He is 'away', but they would not tell me where!" She folded her arms, frustration apparent in her face. Mark thought for a second.

"Cara," it was almost a whisper. She did not move.

"What?" she demanded.

"What's going on between you two?" he asked, and she tensed.

"Nothing! Absolutely nothing... anymore," she stopped herself as soon as she had said it. Mark had heard.

"Anymore?" he turned towards her, "Okay, Cara, what *was* going on between you two?" She sat back; she was annoyed with herself. She'd not wanted to say anything.

"No, nothing really." Mark was staring at her. She knew he would not let it go. "Okay, we just hooked up a couple of times... nothing serious."

"Nothing serious?" Mark repeated.

"Yeah, we would just message each other and ask to pop 'round." She could tell by the look on his face that he did not approve, but he would not say anything. She knew she had to give him something. "Look, he sometimes talks in his sleep. I got the name of the 'An Rua' from him. But the last time he was here, he just left without even saying goodbye." Mark drank more from the mug, then set it down and looked away.

"Okay," he said quietly.

"Hey!" she snapped, "you can't judge me; not after everything you've done!" she glared at him again.

"I wasn't," he started. "So, you've not heard from him at all?" he asked.

She relaxed slightly. "No." She was about to say something else, but Mark's phone started to ring. He placed the mug down, leaned back and fumbled about with the pocket in his jeans to get the phone out. He looked at the screen, then cut off the call. "'Not going to answer that?" she asked. He shook his head. Cara-Marie could guess who it was; there was only one person he did not want to hear from, these days. "When is the baby due?" she asked. It was his turn to be uncomfortable. He retrieved he mug from the table.

"Sometime in July." He closed his eyes before he drank again, then took a deep breath in and looked at her. "So, my friend," She looked at him; he had never called her that before, "what are we going to do about these creatures of yours, then? Did you get any more from 'his lordship'?" It was a total change in conversation; a welcome one, at that.

"Nothing I can use at the moment. It seems he has his own problems back in England.".

Mark nodded "So," he said.

"So," she repeated.

"So, what are we going to do about all this?"

Cara-Marie thought for a moment, "Well," she started, "that is what I brought you here tonight for; so we can discuss what we can do next!" Mark smiled and nodded.

"Okay, then, since the body count is certainly going up, what do we know for definite?" Cara-Marie smiled. She had her friend back.

ooooo

Kyle looked at his watch; it was nearly teatime. They had been driving for almost an hour. The extreme weather had slowed them down. The storm had caused problems all over Northern Ireland. Kyle heard on the news one person had been killed when a tree fell on him. The previous day was emotional when they returned to the farm. He had to meet two grieving families; the bodies would be returned to them within a few days. They'd identified what was left of their loved ones. There was no doubt now; they were dealing with a rabid wolf. There was a lot of pain and anger. Dermott was able to tell them that the police search over the mountains found nothing and was cancelled because of the weather. Paul and Dermott left Rathlin early. Tyler was going to follow tomorrow after she met with the clan chieftain. Paul talked through what was going to happen, but Kyle had not heard half of it. He was thinking of everything that had to be done around the farm.

Amanda was happy he came back with her. He did not realise it, but he had missed being on the farm. Tony was right; 'there will be a time when you need us, as we will need you'. He now felt 'the pull of the pack'. He had only seen Tony and Karen briefly; 'no, Tyler had not made his nose bleed' was his answer to Tony's first question. He wished he had been able to spend more time with Tony, but the families needed his time, and rightly so. The pack had lost four young members, four wolves, and the whole pack felt the loss. They'd received a video call from Germany later in the day and spoke with the clan chief and his number two. Heinz Staudegger and Franz Gartner had told them as much about Ute Fessler as they could. She'd been chased out of Germany and driven from the pack; they had not realised she was infected, or they would have dealt with her. The offer to send teams over to deal with her was politely turned down, but they would send recent images of her within the hour. She was here now, so it was their problem and they would deal with her. Paul mentioned before the call started that they may make an offer, but the South would not allow another pack on their lands.

Kyle looked around the darkening landscape; his mind had been wandering; the wind was still shaking the vehicle. He looked over at Paul in the driver's seat.

"Why are we not going to the Southern pack's dun? You said why before but I missed it"

Paul glanced at him. "After your first change, your hearing is supposed to get better not worse," he retorted. The rain pleated on the windscreen. Kyle thought for a moment.

"Remind me," Paul glanced over at him, "please." They both smiled, Kyle did not have to say please. Paul would have done what he was told anyway.

"So," Paul started, "we have to go to 'The Hill of Tara' so you can be initiated into the pack, as the alpha of the Northern Dun!" Kyle thought for a second before he asked the next question.

"And who was 'Tara' and what did she do that got a hill named after her?" Kyle heard Paul take a breath in, then laugh.

"Tara wasn't a person; it was a province." The car slowed as the wind picked up; Paul continued, "Ireland – both north and south, presently is comprised of four provinces: Munster, Leinster, Connacht and Ulster. But in ancient times, there were five, the fifth being 'Tara'. It is where the Great Kings of Ireland governed from. All great Irish leaders have gone there through time, as recently as Eamon De Valera, in the 1960's."

"Interesting," Kyle said, without thinking. Paul glanced at him; the rain was slowing, and Paul was able to speed up a bit. They sat in silence for a while, as Paul drove off the motorway and up to a roundabout. They were now heading into the countryside.

"Not long now," Paul stated. Kyle nodded. He looked around, trying to pick out landmarks. He was making a mental note of the road numbers so he could keep track of where he was going.

"So, what exactly is going to happen tonight?" he asked. Paul grinned, as the car slowed down and turned right onto a narrower road.

"A formal greeting to the pack, mostly ceremonial, but," Paul paused.

"But what?" Kyle asked.

"But you will still have to take the ancient route of the kings," Paul smiled as he spoke.

"The what?" Kyle asked. "I don't have to be 'naked with bells around my ankles' or anything like that?" Paul cast him a look of 'don't be stupid.' He shook his head before answering,

"No, nothing like that. You will have to place the bare sole of your right foot on the Stone of Destiny in front of Connor, then kneel in front of him and repeat the oath to the clan. It's as simple as that." Paul kept driving.

"And Connor is the Clan .... 'Chief'?" Kyle asked.

"Chieftain," Paul corrected, "and yes, he is." He did not expand any further, Kyle glanced at him, then continued to study the surrounding countryside.

"So, you have no idea what a Valkyrie is then?" Kyle asked, without looking over at him, Paul shrugged.

"I heard a rumour once about something like that. 'Never thought we would have to deal with one." Kyle nodded, and they drove on. Paul waited for a bit before he spoke again. "But our pressing problem is the rabid; if she infects others...." Paul's voice trailed off. This was the first time Kyle had ever heard him sound nervous. Tony had been right; it was the only thing that scared them.

"Well, Tyler is on the case now, and she has dealt with one before." Kyle reassured. He did not know if what he had just said was totally true, but he had guessed from her reaction when they were on Rathlin, that it was. They turned again and made their way up the hill to a T-junction, where Paul stopped. On the left was a brightly lit pub; in front of them was a row of parked cars, all of them reverse parked. Kyle spotted a few people around, most of whom were now taking an interest in them. In the darkness, he could make out the spire of a small church.

"We are here," Paul stated. He pulled in behind another car that was parked tight up against the hedgerow. He turned off the engine and looked at Kyle. "Everyone here knows who you are." Kyle nodded, releasing his seat belt, "also," Paul stated, "some of the older ones may not 'keep their tongue'. If any of them have a go at you, try not to react .... They are just pushing you to see if you'll fight back; they don't want a hothead running a dun." Kyle nodded in understanding and opened the car door. The cold night air rushed in. Kyle stood up and closed the car door behind him.

Out of the darkness, two figures were walking towards him. Kyle looked at them. He did not know how, but he could tell they were Garou. They slowed as they approached. Kyle guessed them to be in their early twenties. The girl had dark auburn hair and wore an outdoor jacket that was partially done up. She stopped about six feet away from him. The guy had dark hair and was wearing a similar jacket, but he had mud around his ankles. The girl was very much in charge, here. They were quite standoffish, as Kyle would describe later; not unfriendly, but there was a feeling of *distance* from them. Neither was presently smiling. Paul walked from behind the car, pulling on his Gore-Tex jacket, when he saw the two of them, a smile broke over his face,

"Saoirse!" he exclaimed.

"Uncle Paul!" she smiled broadly, as they shared an enthusiastic embrace. When they broke off, Paul shook hands with the young man.

"Jack, great to see you," Paul stated. The three obviously knew each other well, but Paul had not mentioned that he had family here. Paul would explain later that they were not blood family, but he had known them since birth. They had always called him 'uncle', Paul stepped back and extended a hand towards Kyle.

"Right, may I introduce you to Kyle Foster, Alpha of the Northern Dun." Paul was about to say something else, but Saoirse quickly extended her hand in greeting, Kyle shook it. She had a firm grip.

"Oh, I know who this is," she said, releasing her grip. "I have heard a lot about you!" she exclaimed. "I'm Seersha." She stepped back; Kyle let a small smile spread over his face, at the way she had pronounced her first name.

"Hello," he answered.

"This is Saoirse O'Connor and her younger brother, Jack," Paul continued with the formal introductions. Jack stepped forward and looked into his eyes. He had a strong southern accent.

"Mister Foster, welcome to The Hill of Tara. Father is looking forward to receiving you."

"And I am looking forward to being received by him," replied Kyle. Jack nodded once; he was being respectful. Then he turned and extended his hand towards a metal gate.

"Follow me, please," he said. Saoirse took a step back; she shared a look with Paul.

"So," she started, "How are things 'up north'?" She spoke directly to Paul. Kyle started to walk towards the gate, but Paul stopped him.

"Hang on," he said. Kyle half turned as Paul opened the rear passenger door of the car. He leaned inside and produced a dark-coloured waxed outdoor jacket. Throwing it towards Kyle, he said, "'Better put this on." They shared a smile, and Kyle pulled the jacket on. Paul continued to chat with Saoirse, "Things have certainly been busy since I last saw you." They both laughed, as Kyle adjusted the jacket.

"I heard you took the head off a Mongol?" Jack asked.

"Yes, I did," Kyle answered. Jack nodded, turned and walked towards the gate.

"I wish I could have seen that," he said, wistfully. Kyle looked at Paul, who nodded once. He was to follow him. Kyle walked after the young man, who had just opened the metal gate. Kyle looked around; he could not see the others but he knew they were here. There was a strange comfort to that; he knew he was on safe ground. Paul came through the gate after him and Jack started off across the grass ahead of them. Kyle looked to his left; in the darkness, he could see the silhouette of the small church. There was a bronze statue in front of it.

"Who is that?" he asked, pointing towards it.

"Saint Patrick!" Saoirse replied, as she came up on his right side.

"And why would there be a statue of Saint Patrick here?" he asked. The three of them were following Jack into the darkness. Kyle could make out the shapes of a group of people up ahead, all of whom were reacting to their approach.

"This is where Saint Patrick challenged the druids of the High King. They cast a fog over the land and Saint Patrick asked God to lift it. It is said the fog disappeared instantly. They then had a battle of miracles, and Saint Patrick won all of them. Afterwards, the High King had the druids executed and ordered the land to convert to Christianity." She did not look at him as she explained, "The rest is, as they say, history." When they neared the group, Jack stopped and spoke to them briefly, then he turned towards Kyle,

"You are to come with me." He was not loud; this was someone who was used to giving commands; he was a natural leader. Kyle glanced at Paul, who nodded once.

"After you," Kyle answered. Jack turned and headed off to the right, and Kyle followed. In the darkness, he could see a mound of earth that stood higher than himself; he could not see over it. Paul was just behind him, but Saoirse had stayed with the others. At the end of the mound, they walked around to what Kyle could now see was a second trench of earth which formed a passageway, leading up the rise of the hill. Jack stopped and looked at him.

"Will you remove your footwear? You have to do the Procession of Kings barefoot." Kyle nodded and leaned down to undo his boots. The three of them stood in silence as Kyle pulled off his socks and stuffed them inside the boots, which he then handed to Paul. Kyle turned and looked expectantly at Jack, who took a step back, turned and pointed up the passageway. "You are to make your way up the hill. From there you are to follow the path to your right, around the hill, then up to the stone," Jack explained. Kyle listened as he could see the figures in the darkness silently take their places, lining both sides of the path. Jack continued, "Once you are there, you will place your right foot onto the 'Stone of Destiny'. My father will then welcome you into the pack." Jack was watching him. "Is all that okay?" he asked. Kyle nodded. Jack smiled briefly and stepped back. He turned towards the passageway, shouting, "THEN, KYLE FOSTER, ALPHA OF THE NORTHERN DUN, I INVITE YOU TO TAKE YOUR PROCESSION OF KINGS." There was no cheer, no sound. Jack stepped back and extended his left hand toward the route. Kyle looked at Paul.

"I will see you up there," Paul stated, "I cannot go with you." Kyle nodded and stepped past Jack. As he did so, everyone who was standing on top of the earthwork suddenly switched on their torches. The beams of light lit up their legs making them resemble marble pillars in a giant hall.

Kyle looked ahead and slowly started to walk forward. He did not look at any of them as he made his way up the hill, but he could feel their eyes on him. He was not walking fast, but he got to the end quite quickly. The line of people stopped. He could see the way the path went around the hill. As he started, people began to appear along the top of the hill, as if guiding him, one at a time. Unlike the passageway, there was no light here. The grass was wet and soggy from the rain and his feet sank slightly into soft mud. He was aware of the cold ground, but it was not uncomfortable for him. He walked on. He looked up at the sky; the clouds were parting, and it was slowly clearing; there would be no more rain. He continued until he came to a lone figure blocking his path. He looked up at Jack. As he approached, Jack held up the palm of his right hand to stop him, then lowered his arm; Kyle could see that he was trying hard not to smile. Jack pointed towards the summit.

"Ascend from the earth and claim your place!" Kyle looked at him, then nodded.

"Thank you," he said quietly. Kyle looked up the side of the steep hill and started to make his way up. As he got close to the top, he saw that it was flat. There was an upright, standing stone off to one side. In the centre of the summit stood a semi-circle of nine people - men and women. No one was smiling. Kyle stopped at the edge of the small plain. Out of the darkness he could make out people coming up the far side and starting to line the circumference of the summit. He stepped forward as the circle closed behind him.

He looked at the nine people, easily making out the alpha in the centre. He did not look into his eyes. Silence descended; the only sound was that of the wind around them. He looked up as Alpha looked towards the standing stone with his eyes; Kyle was being told what to do. He walked over and stood in front of the stone. Kyle remembered what Jack had said, and lifted his right foot, placing it on the stone. When he did so, there was a single cheer from the crowd around the side; but nothing from the nine.

"Foster!" the Alpha spoke. Kyle lowered his leg and turned towards them. The Alpha stepped forward and moved his right hand in a wave. "Come forward." Kyle walked towards him and stopped several feet away. The nine closed around him, forming a circle. None of them spoke. Kyle looked down at the earth, then knelt in front of the alpha.

"I am Kyle Johannes Foster and I am my father's son. I am of the Northern Dun of the An Rua of the Garou and I make this sacred oath that I will serve the pack unto death to defend these lands; I will follow our laws and commands, as you have directed me so." Kyle felt a wave of emotion sweep through him as he repeated the words of the oath he'd memorised. He stared at the feet of the one standing directly in front of him. He felt a hand placed on top of his head. Soon, the hands of the rest of the nine rested on his shoulders; only Connor's hand was on his head,

"I am Connor, Alpha of the An Rua." Kyle felt himself welling up inside; he had not expected this to be so emotional. Connor raised his voice for all to hear, "LET THOSE GATHERED HERE ACKNOWLEDGE THIS ONE." There was warmth coming from all the hands that were placed on him. "HE WILL DEFEND THESE LANDS. HE WAS TAKEN FROM US WHEN BUT A CHILD, BUT HE HAS RETURNED! HE STEPPED FORWARD

AND TOOK THE HEAD OF ONE WHO WISHED US DESTROYED!" There was a roar of approval from the crowd. The hands on him lifted, and they all stepped back; all, except Connor, whose hand remained on Kyle's head. Kyle continued to look at the boots in front of him. Then the last hand was lifted, and Connor stepped back. "ONCE AGAIN, A FOSTER RULES IN THE NORTH!" Kyle was now fighting back the tears. "Foster," Kyle looked up as his name was quietly spoken. He looked into the clear blue eyes that looked back at him. Connor shouted once more, "RISE!" Then he looked up, "AN RUA .... RECOGNISE A WARRIOR OF YOUR OWN!" Kyle stood, and as he did so, he realised that, apart from the nine, everyone standing around the edge had all changed into their wolves. The roar rose again sounding like a single howl, all in unison.

They looked magnificent! As he looked around, heads lowered; some of the nine were smiling, but Connor was not. Kyle went to speak, but Connor's right hand came up suddenly to stop him. Kyle remained silent at the command. Connor stepped forward and placed his right hand on Kyle's shoulder, speaking directly to him. "I recognise you as alpha of the Northern Dun, may you defend the North for many years." Kyle looked into Connor's eyes. Connor stepped forward and embraced him. There were barks from the wolves and clapping from the nine. Connor stepped back and turned towards those closest to him. "Let me introduce you to the elders of the clan ...." Each one stepped forward and shook his hand in turn. "This is Jason .... Sam .... my wife, Orla, ... Ronan.

The wolves behind them all retreated down the hill. Paul walked forward, carrying his boots. Connor turned and acknowledged him. Paul was smiling.

"Well done, Kyle," he said. Kyle smiled and they hugged. Paul dropped the boots on the ground and Kyle reached inside for the socks.

"So, Paul," Connor started, "tell me why you and your new alpha took down twelve sleeping Nocs, thus breaking the truce, without my permission?" Both Paul and Kyle looked up. Connor was not smiling; neither were any of the others.

Chapter 33

Dermott held the handpiece of the old phone to his ear. He looked up as the farmhouse door opened. Ruth walked in and closed the door. She smiled and stopped in the middle of the living room. Dermott acknowledged her, then returned to the call. She stood there for a moment and enjoyed the warmth; it very quickly penetrated her rubber wellington boots and her wet trousers. She opened the zip of the waxed jacket to let the warmth in. It had been cold out in the storm. They'd had quite a job getting as many of the livestock as possible under cover of the barns before the main part of the storm hit. There might still be a few out on the loose, but they had accounted for most of them. A full head count would be underway.

"Right, got that," Dermott started to write something on the small notepad that was beside the phone. Ruth watched as his body tightened. Whatever he was being told, it was not good news. "Right .... okay ...." Dermott had turned his back towards her, his tone was one of anger. The text message that he sent her calling her here seemed urgent. "Okay .... we will deal with this, ... don't worry, we will sort this tonight." Dermott turned back towards her, and nodded, "Okay .... Slan," after saying goodbye in Irish he replaced the handpiece and stepped towards Ruth. "Right, just heard that the Nocs are on the move down in Belfast!" She straightened up; there was a serious look on her face.

"Okay," she said quietly. Dermott dug into the pocket of his trousers and retrieved his mobile phone. He looked at the screen, then up at her.

"Right, still nothing from Paul, so we will sort this ourselves," he stated.

"What is up?" she asked, Dermott returned the phone to his pocket.

"Five of them, including that fella, Martin, are openly moving around Belfast. Matthew thinks they are on the way to feed." Ruth nodded, as he repeated what he had just been told. What I want you to do is head down there with a team. See what they are doing. If you suspect anything, then take them down!" he paused and looked her straight in the eyes, "Do you understand what I want?" he asked.

"Yes," she replied.

"Take one team down and sort this." Dermott walked past her and headed towards the entrance, chatting as he did so, "plus that English fella, Lord basket-case."

"Baskerville," she corrected. Dermott looked at her and smiled.

"Baskerville," he repeated, "he was spotted nearby taking photographs, so keep an eye out for him, as well."

"What do you want me to do about him?" she asked, Dermott stopped by the door.

"Nothing, unless he gets in the way."

"And if he 'gets in the way'?" she asked, smiling conspiratorially. Dermott smiled back.

"Make sure the body isn't found." He almost laughed as he had said it, "I will get someone to keep an eye on him from now on."

"Any news from Paul?" she asked, as Dermott opened the door. The cold wind from outside blew in around the room; the storm was not over yet. He looked back at her.

"No. Get this done as soon as you can." Dermott was giving her a command. "Have you got Matthew's number?" She nodded, Dermott turned and walked outside, leaving the door open for her to follow. There were two vans parked facing down the entrance lane with several people standing around them. Dermott headed towards the communications building. She watched him stride away, then turned and walked towards the waiting farmhands. They gathered around her and she spoke.

"Right; blue team...stand down, red team...mount up. There are five Nocs we need to deal with in Belfast." A ripple of excitement went through the group. Several turned and walked away as they were not needed, but those who were required stepped closer to find out more information. Ruth continued with her briefing.

"What are we dealing with?" one asked.

"Five, including the one they turned... Martin. He was one of the targets we missed when we hit their lair, so we want to take him down for sure!" she looked around as she spoke. "Just remember, we don't engage them in view of the public - short weapons with suppressors, and blades." She was answered by nodding heads.

"Who is watching them at the moment?" another asked, and Ruth looked at him.

"Matthew and one other," she answered.

"Where are they?" someone else asked.

"Near the Kings Hall, at present," she looked around again. "We move in ten minutes .... Everyone know what to do?" She held her hands out, palms up, looking for any other questions. There were none. "Right, get to it." With that, the group exploded with activity. Ten minutes later, and after she had changed out of her wet clothing, both vans were heading down the lane towards Belfast. The communications building would be in constant contact with them.

It was nearly midnight before Dermott received a short data message from Ruth over the secure communications system. 'TWO TAKEN DOWN IN CAR PARK AT MUSGRAVE PARK HOSPITAL. OTHERS RAN AWAY. MAIN TARGET NOT SEEN.'

ထထထ

Sean ended the call. It had rung until the automated voice told him the phone was switched off. That was unlike Mike, but he had said when he was at the Fort for his training course, he would not have his phone on him. Sean put the phone down on the table. He turned towards the door of the living room as the sound of his wife thumping up the stairs seemed to echo throughout the house. She'd made her views very clear. He should do it. He, on the other hand, wasn't convinced. He did not like talking to the press, no matter what newspaper they represented. But this time they had been persistent. He repeated several times he was no longer serving and could not comment on the present investigation. It would have been easier if he had spoken with them first. Unfortunately, his wife answered the first two calls.

The TV was off. He scanned the room; everything was tidy and clean and in its place. He could hear his wife moving around upstairs. Yes, he had received their email with the offer in it; yes, it was more than enough; but a big part of him still did not want to go through with it. He really wanted to speak with Mike. He needed to talk to his friend. His wife was delighted. In fact, he heard her on the phone with one of her friends; she was 'over the moon' with the offer. An hour's work and getting nearly three months wages for it...of course he should do it! He did not share that view. He knew which hotel he had to be at; 'yes, 10am was fine'; it would take no longer than an hour; there would be still pictures taken, but no video footage. 'Yes, he was happy to answer their questions', but he had repeated he would not answer any questions that may compromise any current investigation the police service was conducting.

He tried the number again. He lifted the phone to his ear and listened to the ringing sound. He counted the rings, each one bringing him closer to the automated voice again. As soon as it started, he cancelled the call; he did not want to leave a message. Sean slowly stood, then walked into the kitchen. He looked out the rear window. No, he didn't want coffee. He took out his phone and started to scroll through the pictures. The faces on the screen made him smile. Most of his recent pictures were taken at his leaving function, where the M.I.T. team had all turned up. He scrolled on. He stopped at the picture of Mike and him, with their wives. Four smiling faces looked up at him. He scrolled on. His thumb stopped at a picture of Mike and Simon; both were smiling, both had mugs in their hands. The picture was taken in his old office, and he was seated behind his desk. He could not remember what they were chatting about, but it made him smile at first. Then he was filled with sadness. He studied the smiling face of Simon. The image of what had been done to him flashed in his mind. The contrast was stark. From smiling, happy face to tormented terror.

Sean remembered how much Margaret cried at the funeral; they were closer than Simon ever let on. They had been together longer than he let on, as well. She hadn't believed the story about criminal gangs, either. Someone told him she left the job, but he could not remember who. His wife shouted something from upstairs, but he didn't hear what she'd said. He walked to the bottom of the stairs. He stopped. He looked at the phone again, then shut it down. He left it on the small table near the front door and turned off the downstairs lights. Then he slowly ascended the stairs. No, he was not looking forward to tomorrow; yes, he wished he could talk to Mike. He did not know what was going to happen next. Sean Parrish felt cold. It was nothing to do with the weather outside; he felt cold in his soul. A lifetime of direction, a lifetime of service, a life that meant something. Now he was an 'ex'; a 'had been' investigator with the police. 'Was'; 'had been'; He could feel the very words dragging him down. He got to the top of the stairs and looked at the open door of the bathroom. The decision to brush his teeth took effort. No, he was certainly not looking forward to tomorrow.

ထထထ

Cara-Marie looked at her watch; it was almost 1am. The laptop was shutting down, and there was nothing of interest coming from any of the news outlets about the shooting in Belfast earlier. 'TWO UNKNOWN SHOT DEAD IN A CAR PARK AT MUSGRAVE PARK HOSPITAL' had been the first message she'd received. The second one sparked her interest. One of the first people on scene, a journalist she knew, stated one of the dead had really strange teeth - the canines were a lot longer than usual.

It was also rumoured that Kris Martin, the one who had returned from the dead, was now on a killing spree and had been seen there, as well. She looked at the photo again. No, she could not use it, but

.... and it was a very big 'but'...she may be able to sometime later, possibly on her blog. The picture was of an open mouth; the journalist's hand was holding the jaw, indicating the abnormal canine teeth. But these two had been shot dead. Both shot through the heart, and at close range. Whoever did it, they knew what they were doing. The police had announced that one of the dead was from France, the other, from England. So far, there was no record of them even entering the country, which raised the questions: How did they know each other? What were they doing in Belfast? Why were they killed?

The rumours had already started saying it was between drug gangs, which she did not believe. She knew not to even raise the issue with Kevin, the editor. She already knew the answer: 'Not a Coleraine story!' Cara-Marie was looking at the pictures already online. She spotted the English Earl in the gathered crowd. He had a habit of that. She had spotted him only the day before at the scene where the four teenagers had died in the Mournes. What did he know that he was not saying? He had been very forthcoming to her with a lot of information - none of which she felt she could use. The stuff about the vampires could be interesting, but it was not where she wanted to focus.

She knew the werewolves were real. He knew they were real. He had told her about the 'clan' that his family had been fighting for a century and a half. She knew that he totally believed what he was saying. Yes, she had believed him, but it was no help to her. The question was *how* could she prove to an unbelieving world they were real? She felt a tiredness creeping over her. With slow, deliberate movements, she moved around her flat, switching everything off. The last thing was the lights. Soon, she would be pulling the duvet around her.

She picked the phone up and looked at the screen. Her mum stopped trying to introduce her to people. 'Isn't she the one who believes in werewolves?' was said to her mum too often now. She read the last text. She scrolled the messages she had sent before. He still had not responded. She would try again in the morning. She needed to speak to Kyle as soon as she could. Her eyes closed and sleep slowly drifted over her. In what seemed like just a moment, her alarm was sounding, and it was time to wake up. Today was going to be a long day.

Chapter 34

Sebastian MacAulay had been walking in the Mourne Mountains for years. At least once a month he was up there; it was his escape from working in the office all week in Belfast. He camped out in the hills; he had been over every hill and mountain several times and loved the feeling of freedom it gave him. He would bring friends sometimes, for short treks, but only certain people for longer ones. He was not fast... in fact, he looked deceptively unfit...but he had endurance.

He always had all the latest walking gear. The waterproofs, handheld GPS markers, the latest phone. The front of his hair was curly, but he kept the rest short. He could no longer hide the fact it wasn't dark anymore. In fact, he had gone from being known just as 'Seb' to 'Silver Fox' around the office. He liked the staff talking about him. His busy social life was always a source of good gossip. 'Who was he with, this month?' The tubby blonde only lasted two months, the leggy redhead from last Christmas lasted even less. One of his female friends warned him to stay away from 'that stuck-up bitch', but he met her anyway. Their first date in Belfast went so well, in fact, that she had booked them into a hotel for the night. She didn't notice him place his phone on the nightstand beside the lamp, so he could record them. He liked doing that. The guys in the office enjoyed keeping up with his sexual exploits, and he liked being known for picking up women. His collection of 'date videos' continued to grow.

He watched his friend climb over the small gate. He and Nath Campbell had been friends for years. Nath looked a lot younger than Seb. He'd gone the other way and married the girl he had been with since they were teenagers. Twenty years later, they were still together. Seb knew Nath's wife could not stand her husband going for a night out with him. The very thought made Seb smile.

Nath Campbell was also an experienced walker. He knew the mountains well and he enjoyed walking with Seb; the routes he chose were always challenging. He liked that. Seb had stopped a few feet down the pathway. His hands were on his hips, the straps of the daysack on his back clung to his shoulders. The earlier rain had stopped. His face was damp with both rain and sweat. Seb smiled as Nath struggled with a strap on his daysack that had caught on the gate.

"Having problems there?" Nath looked up at the smiling face that was making fun of him. He righted himself and, with one hand, released the offending strap.

"No, not at all. Are you feeling the pressure of walking with a younger man?" Nath retorted, as he repositioned the daysack on his back. Nath's hair was jet black; he had a classic facial structure and a personality that easily attracted women, but even when Seb kept encouraging him to 'go for it', Nath never strayed from his marriage. That fact always earned him a ribbing from Seb in the workplace.

"With, you? The virgin incarnate himself? I don't think so!" Nath laughed as Seb turned and began to lead the way up the narrow path. It was only wide enough for one person, hugging the side of the small hill. Off to the right was the open vista of County Down. On a clear day you could almost make out the cranes in Belfast docks. But that was for a clear day and this certainly wasn't one of those days.

"Did you see that news report about the 'monster'?" Nath asked the daysack in front of him. Seb looked back over his left shoulder.

"Really?"

"Yes, really." Nath said. Seb walked on.

"I'm surprised you are taken in by that crap. I have been walking in these hills for over twenty years .... There is no 'Mourne monster'.... Trust me." Seb turned away and carried on.

"But what about all the murders?" Nath asked.

"Yeah, *someone* is killing people .... but it certainly isn't some sort of Bigfoot creature." Seb carried on walking around the side of the hill. He looked up at the low clouds, "Let's move," he started, "we should get to the carpark before the rain starts again." Nath looked up at the cloud base. Seb had a knack for being able to tell which clouds were full of rain. At some point in his past, someone had taught him well.

They carried on and the pathway opened-up so they could walk side by side. On their left was the hill they had just walked around; on the right was a small dam. On the far side of the dam was a forestry block. The main road was further on past the trees. It led up the rise of the small mountain to the Ott carpark, where they had left their cars that morning. They started early and were over Slieve Loughshannon, then over the summits of Meelbeg and Meelmore. When it rained, the fog and the rain closed in, but when it was clear, the views were amazing! Nath took several pictures he would upload to his social media later. He looked down at the small stream on his right. The track followed the side of the reservoir and met at the edge of the forestry block.

"What is that?" Nath asked.

"Fofany Dam," Seb knew exactly where they were, and he slowed down.

"Did you get that stuff sorted for the presentation on Tuesday?" Nath asked. He looked at Seb, who was staring at the water. Nath poked his arm. "Seb!" Seb looked at him, then turned his head back to where he'd been looking at the far side of the dam.

"What? Err, yeah, yeah, all sorted." Nath looked over the water. He could not see what Seb was looking at.

"What is it?" he asked. Seb had slowed down.

"There is someone swimming in that!" he stated. Nath's eyes searched the surface of the water.

"Really? It must be freezing in there!" Seb slowed almost to a stop. He lifted his right hand and pointed to the far side of the reservoir.

"See that gap in the trees, about halfway?" Seb directed.

"Yes," Nath's eyes followed the directions.

"Look in front of that. See the fallen tree along the shore?"

"Yes,"

"Blonde hair, just to the left of the tree." Nath's eyes picked out the blonde bump, just as it surfaced.

"There's a woman in there?" Nath asked.

"Yeah." They had come to a stop as the blonde head reached the water's edge.

"I wonder who ...." Nath started, but Seb cut him off,

"Fucking hell!" he exclaimed, as the naked woman stood up and, with her back to them, slowly walked up to the fallen tree and the towel that was laying over it. The whiteness of her body stood out against the green background. She had a gorgeous figure they could easily make out, even from this distance. As she wrapped the towel around her, she walked into the wooded area. Seb took off at speed along the path. Nath had to jog for a few paces to catch up.

"Where are you going?" Nath asked, Seb glanced at him with a smile on his face.

"Just going to drop in and say 'hello.'"

"Hello?" Nath questioned. They were now covering distance easily, the path was wide enough for a tractor, and Seb wanted to get to the trees as fast as he could.

"Well, as experienced hillwalkers, we should just make sure she is okay and not suffering from hypothermia, for example." He explained with a grin, Nath looked at him.

"Really?" he stated, and Seb grinned again.

"She might be stuck .... or lost ...."

"And you are the 'knight in shining Gore-Tex, here to help her out." Nath shook his head; Seb was at it again. They arrived at the end of the path and the edge of the treeline. They could easily make out the domed tent in the middle of the trees. The front flap was open. "For the record," Nath stated, and Seb looked at him as he spoke, "this is a bad idea."

"What? Being concerned subjects? And just making sure a fellow hillwalker is alright?" his sly grin said something else. Seb started towards the tent. As they got closer, there was movement inside. Nath looked around. He spotted the circle of stones, where there had been a small campfire. The area around the tent was tidy; there was no rubbish. Seb spoke as they approached. "Hello, anyone home?" A fallen tree partially blocked their path. Again, there was movement from inside the tent. A pleasant, smiling face appeared. She had blue eyes and her wet hair was hanging around her face.

"Gut after-noon," she had an accent and a smile that lit up her face.

"Good afternoon," Seb started. The woman stepped out of the tent. She wore a thin, white tee-shirt that clung to her damp body and, as she stood up, Nath's eyes were drawn to the small blue shorts, which displayed her long, slim legs. This girl liked to work out. She was not a bodybuilder, but her shape was almost perfect. He had to concentrate to look only at her face. Seb was off. He stepped over the fallen tree and held out his hand. "Hi, I'm Seb." They shook hands. The girl seemed pleased to see him, nearly as much as he was to see her. Nath knew what was coming next. He'd seen it enough when they were on a night out.

"Hallo, I am Ute!" she replied, Seb did not let go of her hand.

"Is that a German accent I hear?" she blushed and giggled at the same time. Nath cringed. She released her hand, and Seb relaxed his posture.

"Ja, Ich bin," Ute paused, looking up, as if searching for something; "sorry, yes, I am German" she smiled a broad smile. Nath could not see Seb's face, but he could guess; he watched his friend's head move he looked her up and down, not hiding his ogling.

"Excellent," Seb exclaimed. Nath noticed that he had not been introduced.

"Ja," she replied, she looked at Nath, "and who are you?" Nath blushed.

"Hi, I am Nath," he smiled, and she tilted her head.

"Nate?" she repeated.

"It is short for 'Nathan,'" he explained. Ute stepped past Seb and held out her hand in greeting. Nath took it. She had a firm grip.

"It is nice to meet you." English was obviously not her first language. Nath had smiled as they shook hands; again, he had to concentrate to look only at her face. Her feet were bare; walking in the forest did not seem to bother her. She stepped back; Seb had not moved. His hands were on his hips again.

"So," Seb started, "What brings you to our 'wee' country?" he asked. Ute paused; Nath could see that she was translating what Seb had just said in her head.

"Urlaub," she replied. She lifted her right hand to her mouth and smiled, "Sorry... holiday," she explained.

"Really?" said Seb, "Just you, or have you a pack of friends nearby, or something?" Seb was smiling as he spoke. Nath thought he detected a slight change in her facial expression. She smiled again.

"Nein, just me. What brings you both here?" she asked. Seb was now totally entranced.

"Well," he started, "we were walking the far side of the dam and we spotted you swimming," Seb slightly turned to Nath for confirmation. Nath nodded, knowing he would be dismissed soon enough. Seb carried on, "and we just wanted to make sure you were okay." Seb looked her up and down again. She did not seem to mind. In fact, Nath thought she was enjoying the attention.

"Ja, I am gute," she extended her left hand towards the tent. "In fact, I was about to have something to eat. You are welcome to join me," she offered. Seb's faced beamed and Nath cringed again.

"I would love to!" he exclaimed. Nath leaned forward on the fallen tree that separated them. Ute looked towards him and Seb turned his head. Seb looked at him and moved his eyes upwards towards the carpark; Seb was telling him to 'get lost'. Nath grinned. He had seen this so many times before... Time for him to go.

"Well, I have to get going," he said. Ute looked hurt, but Seb was grinning. Nath straightened up. "So, I will leave you two to it." Seb winked at him.

"Okay," she said. Then she turned and bent down, pushing her head into the tent. Her bum was sticking up in the air, right in front of Seb, whose eyes nearly popped out of his head. The perfectly formed rear end had been squeezed tightly into the tiny, blue shorts. Nath turned and started to walk away, as he reached the edge of the trees he looked back. Seb had dropped his daysack and followed the girl into the tent. He said something incoherent, and the girl was laughing. Nath smiled and turned away. He followed the small track up the side of the treeline to a wooden stile that connected the stone wall. The gate was slimy from the earlier rain. Nath took his time climbing over it. Once he was on the road, he started up the hill towards the carpark. The grade was not steep, but it did take effort. Ott carpark was up ahead on the right. He made his way towards it. The clouds had become darker; it was going to rain again, and it looked like it was going to be a heavy one.

Nath took off his day sack as he approached and dug his car keys out of his pocket with his right hand. He pressed the button and the car bleeped, unlocking it. He opened the boot and dropped the daysack in it. He picked up his trainers, not wanting to drive in his walking boots. Their cars were the only two in the carpark. The storm and the 'monster' stories had kept a lot of the regular hillwalkers out of the mountains recently. Nath sat on the back of his car as he changed out of his dirt-covered boots and into the comfortable trainers. He looked at his watch - it was nearly 2pm. They had covered the distance quicker than he'd thought they would. He looked up at the sky again and made a decision. He would leave Seb to it and make his own way home. He took out his phone and looked at the screen. No signal. He pushed the phone back into his pocket and closed the boot of the car. He would tell him personally.

The walk back down the hill took much less time than the journey up had. He was over the stile and in the woods in no time. He could not see Seb or the German girl outside the tent but, as he got close, he heard them inside the tent. Nath shook his head. He could hear the rhythmic slapping of body flesh. Their sex was fast and loud. Both Seb and the German were certainly vocal, Nath looked around; it was a good job there was no one else nearby.

The girl started shouting something in German. She was having a great time. Seb was loudly grunting in time with the slap of flesh on flesh. Nath turned and started to walk away. As he got to the stile, he could hear his friend shouting about a god that he knew he did not believe in. Nath climbed over the stile and walked back up to his car. When he got there, he remembered that he had not finished his lunch. Nath Campbell took the steel flask out of his daysack and poured some of the warm hot chocolate into the mug. He sipped the drink and looked out over the surrounding hills. He sat on the back of his car, enjoying the quiet serenity. There was another shout from down the hill; Seb was having a great time. Nath shook his head and emptied the last few drops of hot chocolate onto the ground. He dropped the flask into the boot of the car, closed it and walked towards the driver's door. He was about to open the door when something made him look up. He straightened and tried to focus on the rapid movement on the track they had walked earlier. There was a naked guy running, and he was running fast. Nath smiled, realising it was Seb. He was running along the track, away from the carpark. Nath took a step forward. There was something after him. Nath had to squint his eyes at the blurry, fast-moving shape. Was that a dog? Nath heard the scream of terror as the animal caught up to his friend. He began to run.

Nath Campbell and Sebastian MacAulay would never walk the mountains of Mourne again. It would be nearly four hours before another group of walkers on their way to the dam would discover the remains.

The 'Monster of Mourne' had struck again.

Chapter 35

The car turned into the lane that led to the farm. Kyle smiled; he was happy to be back. He'd hardly noticed the second car behind them with the four protection team members in it. They had remained with the cars when they were parked at Tara and had missed the ceremony at the top of the hill.

Paul used the communications system to let the farm know they were close and that they had now arrived. Kyle looked at his watch; it was just gone 6pm. As they reached the top of the lane, Kyle spotted Tony's car, and smiled. Paul just said something, but Kyle didn't hear; his mind was elsewhere. Paul turned the car around, and reverse parked it as the second car reached the top of the lane. The two farmhands who'd been on the far side of the hedge stood and waved at the second car; their greetings were returned. Kyle studied them as he climbed out of the car. Both wore green rubber boots, jeans that had mud around the ankles and old camouflage jackets. The first one swung the bolt-action rifle onto his shoulder; the other carried his weapon in his hands. Kyle smiled and nodded towards them, he was greeted with smiles and a single wave. The door of the farmhouse opened, and a serious-looking Dermott filled the doorway, he wanted to talk. As Kyle closed the car door, he looked up at the windows of the farmhouse; his bedroom light was on; his was the upstairs spare room. The living room and kitchen windows were lit up as well; there was a lot of activity in the house. Paul lifted his hand in a wave, which Dermott returned.

"He is the first person we need to chat with," Paul stated, and Kyle agreed.

"Let's get something to eat first," Kyle suggested. Paul looked over the car at him.

"Yeah, that's a good idea." Kyle walked across the yard towards the farmhouse. Dermott smiled as he approached, then stepped to one side.

"'Evening," Kyle held out his hand as he spoke, and Dermott shook his hand.

"Aye, how did it go?" Dermott asked. Kyle released the handshake and headed towards the open door.

"Not bad," Kyle went inside, and Dermott watched Paul approach. He paused in front of Dermott.

"The ceremony went well; it's what happened after that could be a problem," stated Paul. Dermott looked at him, "Why? What happened?" Paul shrugged.

"Connor tore into him about the Noc teenager that the Mongols took down near Castlerock; then slapped him for the house assault and taking down twelve of them." Dermott reacted angrily,

"What the hell was wrong with that?" Paul looked ahead into the farmhouse. Kyle and Amanda were locked in a passionate embrace; he would give them a few more minutes.

"They are furious that it was not sanctioned by them; we 'broke the truce'; we failed to see all the Nocs arrive..." Paul's voice trailed off.

"WHAT?" Dermott raised his voice, "They broke the truce, not us. We had a chance to take them down, so we did!" Dermott was about to say something else, but Paul raised his hand.

"The south are furious; I think they've been in touch with Salisbury." Paul lowered his arm, and looked at Dermott, "They are not going to help us if this kicks off; we are to get permission from now on for any direct action we are going to take against them." Dermott looked away in anger. "Plus, they are very concerned about this German; they have a containment plan; but she is ours to take down, before she infects anyone." Dermott looked up and nodded; Paul spotted it. "What?" he asked. Dermott twisted his face,

"We took down two Nocs in Belfast, last night."

"WHAT?" Paul stepped forward, "please tell me you are kidding me!" Dermott shook his head; Paul closed his eyes and slightly raised his head before he looked at Dermott again. "What the hell were you thinking?" Dermott was defiant,

"We had a team watching them. That fella, Martin, and four others went out on a hunt. I sent Ruth with a team down to stop them." Dermott looked away.

"And?" Paul stared at Dermott.

"And we got two, but he got away." Paul continued to stare at Dermott, who said, "Look, two less Nocs can only be a good thing, I think."

"I don't care what you think!" Paul cut him off; he was angry now. "We have been made to look like idiots; that was the first time Kyle was meeting them." Dermott shrugged; he could not see the problem. "Connor made it clear that if Kyle cannot control things up here, then he will take direct control of us!" Dermott straightened up, Paul carried on, "and you know as well as I do, that means he will replace all of us. We will not be able to do *anything* without his direct say so." Dermott gritted his teeth. Paul looked in through the open doorway. "Right then," he said, and walked inside. Dermott paused for a moment, then followed him. Amanda was happy; very happy, in fact. The smell from the kitchen attracted Paul's attention straight away. "Wow, what have you got on?" he asked her once they had separated. Amanda smiled at him.

"Me? Nothing!" she replied.

"Nothing?" stated Paul. Amanda looked at Kyle, then back at him.

"It is Tony's doing; he is *chef-ing* this evening; nothing to do with me, at all." She was holding Kyle's left hand, beaming. Kyle turned and pointed at the large, new TV that was on a new wooden corner stand. The wood was unstained and had two drawers; the new digital box was connected and sat underneath it. The TV took up the entire corner. It was more than twice the size of the old one.

"And what is that?" he asked.

"A treat from me; a new plasma TV." She was almost jumping with excitement.

"It was installed yesterday," Dermott explained. Kyle turned and smiled at him.

"And what was wrong with the old one?" Paul asked, as he took off his outdoor jacket.

"You mean what was right with it?" Amanda exclaimed, "you need to join this century, and this is the most up-to-date TV there is!" She smiled as she spoke, and Paul and Dermott shared a glance, Paul turned and hung his jacket on one of the pegs behind the door.

"Anyway," he was grinning as he spoke, "shall we see what's for dinner?" Paul looked at Dermott, who nodded, then followed him through to the kitchen. Amanda threw her arms around Kyle's shoulders again.

"So, you are now a full-fledged member of the 'An Rua'." She smiled as she snuggled into him. Kyle pulled her close, and the kitchen door opened again.

"Oi!" Kyle looked up; Tony was happy to see him. "If you can't control it, then get a room!" Kyle laughed and Amanda stepped away from him. He turned and shook Tony's hand; they were happy to see each other.

"I have a room... upstairs," Kyle stated, Tony looked at Amanda.

"I wasn't talking to you!" He got a playful punch from her on his arm.

"It's good to see you," Kyle said, and Tony agreed. He stepped back and motioned towards the chairs,

"Shall we have a catch up? It has been a while," Tony mused.

"It has," Kyle agreed, sitting down in the large chair that Carl used to sit in. "So, tell me about Karen. How is she getting on?".

"Yeah, she is good." Suddenly there was a crashing noise from the kitchen; all three looked at each other. Amanda stood up and started towards the door.

"I'd better find out what those two are up to."

"Check on the beef in the oven!" Tony shouted, as the kitchen door closed.

"So, you were saying about Karen?" Kyle said.

"Yeah she is good. Her mum has, thankfully, backed off. She was getting to be quite overbearing."

"Understandable," stated Kyle, Tony nodded.

"Yeah, it's a slow mend... but we're getting there." Tony looked down; this was still sore for him. "So, tell me about Tara. How did that go?" he asked. Kyle relaxed back into the chair and started to describe what had happened the night before. Tony nodded as he listened. "You know, I have never actually been there, myself." Tony said.

"Really?" That surprised Kyle, "You should go sometime."

"Where did they have you staying?"

"In a local pub that was a B&B as well." Kyle answered. "Had the first 'telling off' last night; then got another one with a slap in the face at lunchtime today."

"What was the problem?" Tony asked. Kyle shifted in the chair. He repeated what Connor had said, then added,

"They were furious that we took down the twelve Nocs; they didn't see them turning one first as breaking the truce."

"...Even though it was." Tony stated, Kyle nodded.

"Yeah, they were furious that we did not spot a load of Nocs arriving. He stressed it is a 'northern problem' and, if I cannot deal with it, he will take direct control of the north." Tony looked at Kyle; the smile was gone. He knew the implications of the threat.

"Connor would not have a problem doing that," Tony stated. "After all, he has done it before!" Kyle looked up.

"Has he? You mean here?" Kyle asked, Tony shook his head.

"No, down south. Apart from the main den, there is only one smaller one; there used to be two. He shut one of them down and basically disbanded it."

"What happened?" Kyle asked, Tony sat forward.

"I'm not 100% sure, but elements of the pack went wild and had to be brought back under control," Tony explained.

"That makes sense. Well, the new ruling is that we cannot make any more moves against the Nocs without first informing Connor." Tony glanced up.

"Did you hear about the two Nocs we took down last night?" Tony sat back.

"What?" Kyle's head shot up.

"Dermott sent a team down to Belfast. There were five of them, including that fella, Martin."

"The one they turned?" Kyle asked.

"Yeah, him; same one from the bungalow." Tony continued, "Wee Ruth led the team. They intercepted them; took down two, three got away, including Martin."

"Did we ID them at all?" Kyle asked, and Tony nodded once.

"Yeah, we got DNA samples from the two dead ones."

"Do we know them?" Kyle asked. Tony looked over at him; he was learning fast.

"No, , but one was from England, and the other from France." Kyle thought for a moment.

"Is that normal for Nocs to band together like that?" Kyle asked.

"Nope. Something is up." Kyle nodded at Tony's reply. There was a murmur of voices from the kitchen. Amanda's voice could be heard giving instructions, and Dermott and Paul complaining about whatever they had just done. The two of them smiled. "So, how was everything with Tyler? I heard you had your first change."

"Yeah, that was an experience," Kyle said, thoughtfully.

"So, did she make your nose bleed?" Tony joked, Kyle smiled,

"Nope...though it was close a couple of times," they shared a knowing laugh.

"Either you are getting better at tact, or she is getting soft." Tony retorted.

"Of all the words I would use to describe her, 'soft' isn't one of them!"

"Did you take down the deer, or did she?" Tony asked.

"She did," Memories of that night flooded back; he let out a short chuckle.

"What?" Tony asked with a smile. Kyle paused for a few seconds, then answered,

"Well, afterwards she was telling me to change back, but I didn't know how to." Kyle chuckled again, "I mean, no one has ever taught me anything like that before; how do you change from a wolf back to a human?"

"I never actually thought of that," said Tony.

"Speaking of which, where is she?" Tony looked at the living room doors then back at him.

"I haven't seen her yet, but she is around." Tony smiled, then sat forward again. "Kyle," Tony had lowered his voice.

"What?" Kyle asked. Tony looked up at him.

"Have you seen the footage of Alison Wallace?" The happiness was gone from his face. Kyle nodded; Tony looked directly at him. "How did we miss her? How did we not see she is a Noc?"

"Tyler doesn't think she is one."

"Yeah, I heard... What the hell is a Valkyrie?" There was a look of genuine confusion on his face. Kyle shrugged,

"I have no idea; you will have to ask her!" They both smiled nervously. Suddenly, the front door of the farmhouse burst open, and Tyler bounded in. She was angry,

"You're back, great." The door slammed shut. The kitchen went quiet. She strode to the middle of the room and pointed at the TV. "Turn the news on; there's been another one!" she said, hurriedly. The kitchen door opened, and Dermott and Paul appeared.

"Problem?" Paul asked. Tyler was in no mood for pleasantries.

"If you call that rabid wolf killing two sapiens and leaving what is left for all the world to see, then yes, there is a *fucking* problem!"

Paul walked forward, followed by Dermott and Amanda. Kyle shifted uncomfortably in his chair as Tony stood up, walked over to the plasma TV and tried to turn it on. After a few seconds Amanda stepped forward and took the remote control. It did not take long for the large screen to display a 24-hour news channel. Paul and Dermott sat and Tyler moved near the fireplace. Amanda stood at Kyle's chair, as the headlines started. Two more for the 'Monster of Mourne'. The reporter stated police were on the scene but names had not yet been released.

"Do we know where that is?" Kyle asked. All heads turned towards him.

"Yes," said Dermott. The news report continued. There was an interview with a uniformed police inspector near the car park. The rain had soaked her earlier; her face was still wet. She looked very concerned. The investigation was still 'at an early stage', she kept repeating. Then she asked for anyone who had been near the area to come forward.

"They won't find her." Paul stated. "But we need to check everyone she's attacked, just to make sure she has not infected anyone."

Everyone looked at each other, then at Kyle, who spoke. "Right," he started, "How do we take down a rabid wolf?" Tyler stepped forward and looked at everyone. She placed her hands on her hips.

"I know how .... but I will need at least two of your teams," she stated,

Kyle looked at her. "You got it."

"...following my lead!" she continued.

"Agreed."

"Good," she relaxed, "then I want to see them in the main barn in an hour."

Kyle stood up. "Dermott!" he said loudly, and Dermott stood. "See to it!" He nodded once and walked over to the front door, reaching for his jacket. Kyle looked at Tyler. "But first," he said. Tyler looked at him quizzically, and he smiled.

"But first what?" she asked, he sniffed the air...

"I want to have dinner; I'm starving!"

Chapter 36

Rhydian and Tyler hugged each other and said their goodbyes. Kyle was watching from the doorway of the farmhouse. Just before Rhydian climbed into the car, she had looked over the roof and smiled at him. She'd waved excitedly. One of the wives from the farm was going with her back to Rathlin Island, and Tyler would head back there once the rabid had been dealt with. Kyle had been surprised by how many people here at the farm knew Rhydian, but he did notice none of the teenage males would try anything with her. She had not expanded on 'they know better', but he assumed she'd made herself perfectly clear. The car drove off down the lane.

Tyler was dressed like any other hillwalker. She had instructed several of the farmhands who turned up that morning wearing camouflage or military style clothing that, if they met the police search teams, or anyone else for that matter, they were just groups of hillwalkers who were sticking together for safety. Kyle liked that approach. Tyler had done some slow time walk-throughs with both teams last night. Each team was composed of ten people. They would all carry suppressed pistols and at least two in each group would have shortened shotguns, which were to be kept in their daysacks and out of sight until they were needed. They would not be taking any long-barrelled weapons along, as it would attract too much attention. The vans and two 4x4s were all packed and ready to depart. They would be camping out, taking turns guarding while they slept. Kyle watched as Paul walked around the side of the main barn, carrying a large whiteboard with a map and a photograph on it. He spoke to Tyler as he walked past. Kyle did not hear what was said, but Tyler agreed.

"Right, everyone into the barn for a final briefing!" she shouted. Kyle glanced over his shoulder into the empty living room. Amanda had gone back upstairs after breakfast. Tyler had stayed in another spare room; 'she must have heard us', Kyle thought. He looked over the group of people entering the barn. He followed them in and closed the doors behind him. Paul had set the map up on a stand just inside the arena. Tyler was studying it and chatting quietly with Paul, as the teams gathered around them. Kyle looked over the arena. Even though it was only a few months since he had beaten the Mongol in here, it seemed like a lifetime ago. The funeral service for Carl had taken place here, as well; nearly 500 people had turned up. They'd understood that most of the southern den would stay away. They'd held their own service for him down south, and several of the families from the north attended. Tyler called for everyone's attention. She looked at Kyle and smiled, then the serious look returned to her face. Paul was studying the large photo of a woman with blonde hair in the corner of the board. Then he turned and looked at Tyler.

"All set?" he asked, she nodded, and Paul stepped back. The group had formed a semi-circle around her; the murmur of conversation stopped. "Right, then," she started, looking around at those gathered in front of her. "We have a serious situation that must be dealt with immediately." There was no sound from the group. Kyle tried not to smile. "We know that the rabid is called 'Ute Fessler', and she is from the Chernsli pack in the northern plains of Germany," she indicated the face staring at them from the whiteboard. Kyle glanced at Paul as he made his way around the outside of the semi-circle towards him as Tyler carried on. "The Germans have told us they did not know she was infected ...." Several people looked at each other; Kyle felt the atmosphere change. Tony was right again, there was only one thing that frightened them, and they were now being confronted with it. As Tyler spoke, Kyle noticed she did not say the word *rabies*. "This is what she looks like. She has already taken down four of our own and it is up to us to take her down." Some of the pack members shuffled uneasily and glanced at each other, but still no one spoke. "We have gone through *how* we take her down," and several heads nodded; "what we have to do now, is decide *where* it will be done." Tyler stepped back and stood at the side of the map. With her right hand, she pointed out each location, describing what had happened, "The first attack was here, near Bloody Bridge. The next ..." Tyler pointed to the map, indicating the small markers that Paul had put there beforehand, "was here .... near the summit of Binnian ...." Tyler looked around the group again. "From there, she struck near Spelga dam, then recently beside Fofany dam ...." She looked at the map again, "here." She looked up at them, "and although there have been repeated sightings, none of them have been confirmed." She brought her hands to her hips, "Looking at her hunting pattern and the locations of her kills, it looks like she has found a den to hunt from." She pointed towards the map again, "I would say the central area is probably somewhere around here ...." Her finger stopped on the map, "Around Ben Crom Reservoir." She lowered her arm and looked at all of them. "So that is where we will start our search." She paused. Kyle could see she was studying those in front of her. "Most of her prey has been male, so we will use males as bait. As we went through last night... no one does anything alone! It will require all of us to take her down." Some of the heads nodded again, Tyler looked over at Kyle and Paul, "We have been told the southern den has containment teams their side of the border to stop her heading south," Paul nodded. "BUT," she raised her voice, "this is still up to us!" she extended her hands, "Any questions?" Some shook their heads. "Remember, there will be hourly communications between us and the team here at the farm." Again, she glanced at Paul, who nodded in agreement. "Right!" she exclaimed. "Let's get to it!" The crowd moved and started to make their way towards the exit, talking quietly amongst themselves. Kyle briefly lost sight of Tyler and looked over at Paul.

"By the way," Kyle asked, Paul turned his head,

"Yes?"

"The German pack ...."

"The Chernsli," Paul stated.

"Yes...are they the only pack in Germany?" Kyle asked, Paul looked at him, mystified.

"No," he was walking towards Tyler, who was dismantling the whiteboard and stand. Kyle walked with him. Paul continued, "Magna Germania' are the largest pack, but they are mostly in the south." Kyle began to ask a question, but Paul guessed what it was. "There are over twenty main packs worldwide .... The Mongols and the Siberians cover most of Russia .... The Diamondbacks are in Australia .... The Arverni are in France ...."

"You forgot the 'Saka'!" stated Tyler, with a grin. Paul scrunched his face.

"They are extinct," he replied. Tyler folded the stand and handed it towards Paul.

"You mean wiped out!" They both smiled, Kyle was the odd one out in this conversation.

"Wiped out?" he asked. Tyler and Paul looked at him, as Tyler turned away, Paul answered,

"The 'Saka' were an ancient pack from over modern-day Iran and Israel. The wolf part of that race was wiped out by the Roman Empire over 2,000 years ago."

"Enjoy your history lesson!" shouted Tyler, walking away from them. Kyle watched her go, he looked at Paul.

"Do we have a map of where everyone is?" he asked.

"No," stated Paul as he picked up the white board and stand, "we don't need one. I'll talk you through it later if you really want." Paul started to walk away from him again.

"No thanks. I am supposed to be heading to Belfast with Amanda this afternoon; she has more shopping to do." Kyle said, as he caught up with Paul. The sound of engines starting up filled the air. As they got to the large door, the first of the vans took off down the lane. It was not long before the convoy was on the main road, heading away from the farm. Paul looked at him.

"Belfast?" he asked.

"Yeah, in fact," Kyle looked at his watch, "she wanted to take off shortly." Kyle looked up. Paul was staring at him. "What?" he asked.

"Did you forget about the military coming here this morning .... to see you?" Kyle thought for a moment.

"When did that happen?"

"I told you last night; you were obviously distracted." Paul looked at his watch, "They will be here in half an hour."

"Do we know what they want?" Kyle asked. Paul looked at him and shrugged.

"Your guess is as good as mine. All I know is there are two of them coming, the officer and one other."

Amanda would be going shopping in Belfast by herself.

∞∞∞∞

Alan Dukesby was in the passenger seat as Steve Minister drove up the lane. The other car, driven by David Priest, had already gone past. He would not be far away. They were not expecting trouble, but the van with the support team would be parked at the roadside, just over a mile away.

"'Looks nice, doesn't it," Steve stated, Alan looked at him.

"Yeah, you would never guess what actually lives here." Steve pressed a small button on the dashboard.

"ZERO, THIS IS THREE THREE NOW ARRIVED AT LOCATION ONE," he released the button, he was answered straight away.

"ZERO, CONFIRMED," the control room had received the message; everyone else would have heard, as well. As they reached the top of the lane, a single figure stepped out of the hedgerow on the right side. The young man was wearing a camouflage jacket and had a bolt-action stalking rifle over his shoulder. Steve slowed the car down and lowered the driver's window. The young face leaned towards him.

147

"What-a-bout-ye?" it was a country accent, Steve nodded in reply. The farmhand pointed to the space in front of the barn, "Youse can park da kar der." Steve nodded again, and the car slowly moved forward. The farmhand retreated into the undergrowth.

"Do you get the impression they don't like visitors?" Steve asked, as he turned the car around to reverse park.

"You can ask Rupert about that one," Alan said. Steve looked over at his boss, and chuckled. As they climbed out of the car, the front door of the farmhouse opened, and Paul Hawkins emerged, raising his hand in greeting. Alan waved back. The car alarm beeped twice, as they two soldiers walked away from it towards the farmhouse. From the hedgerow, the farmhand pointed an instrument that looked like a hairdryer at the car and pressed a button. There was a reaction back at the control room; they were using countermeasures again. There would be no live feed from the stationary car. At the farmhouse, Paul greeted both men with handshakes.

"Hi... welcome." He stepped back, allowing them to walk through the open door. Alan spoke to him as he walked past,

"I was chatting with my father the last time I was home, and he said to say 'hello' to your father and hopes he is well." At that, Paul stopped, and looked down, Alan knew straight away it was not good news.

"Thank you," Paul paused, Steve looked at them, then walked through the doorway. "My father passed away in 2001," He looked up solemnly at the Major. Alan was saddened by the news.

"I am sorry to hear that," he said, "he spoke highly your father; he was well-respected."

"'As was your father. I only ever heard Dad talk about the Radfan in detail once." The two men held a gaze for a few seconds.

"Then you know it was true!" Alan commented.

"Yes, I realised that at the time." Alan relaxed and walked through the door, as Paul continued, "I heard your father led an SAS squadron up a cliff face and took the Adoo totally by surprise." Alan smiled. Paul spoke again, "...and he got a DSO for it."

"Yes, he did," Alan reached out and placed his hand on Paul's left shoulder. "I also heard what your father did ... he should have got a VC for that!" the two men nodded, as Kyle's voice came from inside,

"By all means leave the door open; it's not like it's cold outside."

Alan and Paul shared a smile. "It seems your boss is keen to get started." Alan stated as he entered.

"You have no idea," whispered Paul, and he walked in after the Englishman, shutting the door behind him. Kyle was standing in the middle of the room and Steve was off to one side. Alan and Kyle shook hands.

"Please, have a seat. Can we get you anything? Coffee? Tea?" Kyle offered as he sat down. Steve sat on the sofa. Alan paused for a second, then took the other chair.

"No, thank you," Alan answered. Paul walked over and stood by the fireplace so he could watch the soldier's reaction to the conversation. Kyle sat forward.

"So," Kyle started, "what can we do for you?" Paul watched as the two visitors glanced at each other. It was the officer who spoke.

"Oh, not much really, we just stopped by to let you know we are leaving."

"Leaving?" asked Kyle, Alan nodded.

"Yes, our tour is up, and ...." the Major paused. Paul watched as Kyle let him continue, "we are not being replaced."

"We are needed elsewhere in the world," added Steve.

"Afghanistan?" asked Kyle. There was a physical reaction in them both. "I do watch the news, after all!" Kyle added.

"We are not at liberty to say," Alan continued, "but this is the last time you will see us. We thought we could have a final pooling of information before we go."

∞∞∞

Kris Martin was excited. He shut the door to the room full of sleeping bags; several of them were snoring. He pulled the drape over the doorway, just to make sure no light got in. The second doorway was only a few feet away; they were never to be opened at the same time during the day. Daylight still was not a problem for him. He was told that it was only a matter of time, so he would enjoy walking during the day while he still could. He made his way through the second door and into the large room where the American spoke to them all only two nights ago. It was empty now. The American, Sabine and Alison were somewhere else; it annoyed him that he was not told where, and now Maya kept barking orders at him. He almost ran across to the far door, then outside. The two sapien protection team members were outside the outer door to prevent anyone getting in; the other two were on the roof. They were doing their jobs.

Out in the street, he looked at his phone again. The messages were from Sabine, saying she had a job for him, and he would *enjoy* it. That could mean only one thing. He had seen the picture last night, of the young dark-haired Garou female that the American wanted taken down. Sabine said it may take time for them to isolate her; it must have happened sooner than she'd expected. His phone bleeped again. He opened the message. 'SHE LEFT THE FARM AN HOUR AGO AND SHE IS ON HER OWN.' Kris could not believe how easy it would be! The phone beeped again. 'TAKE HER ALIVE. LET THE COVEN FEED ON HER AND RECORD IT WITH HER OWN PHONE. WE NEED TO SEND A MESSAGE TO THE WOLVES.'

Kris Martin was almost jumping with excitement. He was to take her alive, but there were no instructions as to how it should be done. He looked up and down the street, then went back inside. He would take some of the sapiens with him. They would drive the car so he could keep her hidden and bring her back here. Kris could feel himself salivating. His heart was thumping so hard it felt like it was going to burst out of his chest. He had never had a wolf before! The phone bleeped again. 'SHE HAS PARKED IN CASTLE COURT. WE THINK SHE IS UNARMED.'

Chapter 37

Sean walked back into the living room; it was already dark outside. He picked up the remote for the TV and switched it on. The evening news would be on in a few minutes. He placed his coffee on a small coaster on the table and sat down in his chair. The magazine interview lasted over an hour; they had done a bank transfer that afternoon, so at least his wife was happy. He, however, was not. 'No, I cannot comment on current police investigations'; 'they will be looking at collecting science-based evidence that can be presented in a courtroom'. He lost count of the number of times he said that.

He'd gone to the hotel as they directed, and was met at the entrance, then taken upstairs to the room they'd set up. The whole conversation was recorded, and they had taken several pictures. The guy doing the interview seemed hurt Sean had never heard of him; he repeated the title of a show he hosted, as well as other news outlets he did work for. Sean had no idea who he was. 'He sure thought he was important', was how he would describe him afterwards to his wife. She was more interested in what she would do with the fee the would be forthcoming. The TV was on but he was not paying attention. He stared at the mug of hot liquid. He was numb. He'd been numb since receiving the phone call just after he'd returned home. He hadn't seen it coming; neither the call itself, nor the content. Chief Inspector Anderson was furious: The interview was not authorised, and Sean had spoken to the press about an ongoing police investigation without the knowledge of the police. Sean knew what he was really saying - he had not gone through him, nor advised him beforehand.

When Sean pointed out he was no longer in the police it just made matters worse. The shouting continued for several minutes. The Chief said at the end of the call that he told the new inspector at Belfast M.I.T. to have nothing to do with Sean. His last words before he hung us were 'Police officers who talk to the press without authorisation will not be tolerated'! Right now, Sean was glad he was out of the service. Even though he still had the phone numbers of some of the detectives who still worked there, he knew the drill. They would be told to cut all contact with him so as not to feed the press any details about their current investigations, especially now he was doing it for money. He looked around the room; everything was still. He pressed the button and the screen went blank. He looked towards the door. There was a rhythmic thump of footsteps as his wife trotted up the carpet-covered stairs; he'd not even noticed she had been downstairs. He looked at the coffee again. The only thing moving in the room was his own chest. He breathed quietly accentuating the silence.

He regretted the interview now. He had not given them anything; it seemed he'd just kept repeating himself throughout the hour-long interview. Sean took out his phone and started to scroll down the names; no, he did not want to speak to him; no, not him either; no... his thumb continued to scroll. He stopped at Mike's name and smiled. He pressed the green button, then held the phone to his ear as the ringing started. He relaxed in his chair, listening. The smile slowly fell from his face with each ring; it should have been answered by now. The automated voice started, and Sean ended the call. He did not want to leave a message. He set the phone down on the table and sat back.

He sat there. The silence of the room was deafening. He could feel the walls, just slightly squeezing the room, compressing the air, pushing down on him... squeezing, drowning, suffocating. His eyes moved; they were the only part of him that could. The only sound was his own forced breathing. It took conscious thought to move; everything felt heavy; everything weighed him down. It felt like there was a big black dog, sitting on his chest, staring at him. He reached for the remote again, and the screen flickered to life. The news came back on. He turned the volume down, but it still seemed like it was screaming at him. The main news was about the continuing effect of the worldwide financial crash that happened last year, then the war in Afghanistan. The US military claimed to have killed 15 Taliban in Laghman when they were targeting a Taliban leader, and the new president was trying to close the US military prison in Cuba. None of it affected him. Finally, the local news began. He turned the volume up slightly. The main news was that the local assembly approved planning permission for the National Trust in Northern Ireland to build a new Visitors' Centre at the Giant's Causeway. Sean watched the report as a woman with shoulder-length blonde hair was being interviewed. Plans of the new building were shown. Whoever she was, she was very excited about the whole project. He had been to the Causeway, but it was years ago. He reached for the remote as the final story appeared. He stopped. For a moment, it felt like he had been hit in the face with a wooden bat. He could only stare at the screen.

"And in other news, Sean Parrish, the former police inspector who was in charge of the investigation into a series of very brutal murders across the country last year, has given an interview in which he reveals that the PSNI were, in fact, looking for werewolves around the north coast." Sean was astonished, "It is claimed in the interview that will be published tomorrow, that the DNA evidence they'd gathered was being used to hunt for these mythical creatures," the anchor continued. Sean shook his head... that wasn't what he'd said, the screen changed to Chief Anderson, looking stern as always.

"The Police Service of Northern Ireland is committed to investigating all murders and pursuing evidence-based inquiries that can result in guilty verdicts in a court of law. The PSNI, does NOT pursue mythical creatures!" Sean looked up at the angry man who filled the screen. The phone call made sense now. A voice beside the camera said,

"In the interview, Inspector Parrish claims that last year his team was given the nickname of the 'Werewolf Squad', and that some of the murders they were investigating were perpetrated by something that wasn't human!" The Chief's face contorted. The interviewer asked Sean if they had been given that nickname; all he'd said was 'yes' - nothing else.

"Well, first of all," Sean closed his eyes briefly; his name would be dragged through the mud. "That former inspector was medically discharged from the police service with severe stress, and it was later proved that the very brutal murders you are referring to were, in fact, part of a feud between violent eastern European organised gangs!" Sean looked up in disbelief. He was not 'medically discharged' from the police; he had taken early retirement. In fact, he asked for it! He noticed the Chief had not even used his name; he was now 'that former inspector'. Chief Anderson continued, "He'd had to deal with the death of one of his team members, and we believe he took it personally, that it was a part of his stress reaction." Sean looked away again as the report went back to the studio. At least he had not said 'breakdown'; that would have been even worse.

"And finally, let's have a look at the weather. So, has the storm passed us by, yet?" Sean's thumb moved and the screen went blank. He sat there and did not move. No one in the police department would take a call from him now. He was totally alone. Nothing he could say would change that.

Sean's eyes moved around the room. Thirty years in the police force - he had survived terrorist attacks, buried friends, and seen violent criminals sent to prison for their crimes. But he now knew this 'werewolf story' is what he would always be remembered for. He felt himself well up. The TV remote dropped to the floor. His eyes looked at the space on the carpet between his feet and the legs of the coffee table. He stared. The sound of his phone ringing brought him back to where he was. He looked at the screen; it was a withheld number. Apprehensively, he pressed the green button.

"Hello," his voice was quiet; reserved. He didn't know who it could possibly be.

"Sean?" Mike exclaimed. Sean sat up,

"Mike!" a smile broke across his face. He was pleased to hear from his friend, "How are you?" he asked, "and how are things over there?"

"Sean, what the hell is going on?" Mike was almost shouting down the phone, ignoring Sean's greeting. For a moment Sean was confused.

"Mike, what? Wait ...." He stuttered.

"I have just had Anderson on the phone, and he is furious with you!" Sean felt himself shrink; he now knew what this was about.

"Mike ...." Sean felt himself welling up again,

"YOU DID AN INTERVIEW WITH A JOURNALIST? WHAT THE HELL WERE YOU THINKING?" Mike was angry, Sean felt his soul sink even further.

"I didn't say any of that ...." Sean started, "They are taking it out of context."

"Of course, they are!" Mike shouted. "That's what journalists do!"

"But Mike, ... I didn't ...." Sean could feel the tears building up. The one person he could turn to was turning on him; the one person he could say anything to was shouting at him; the one person ....

"Sean, you of all people should have known better, you, of all people!" Sean felt himself starting to nod at what Mike was saying.

"I know that now," Sean looked at the blank TV screen. "I don't actually know which part they have focused on; we were chatting for over an hour," Sean tried to explain. "They did not give me a copy of what they were going to print."

"I have seen it!" Mike exclaimed.

"What?" Sean straightened up.

"I have a copy, Anderson just sent it to me, everyone is being told to cut ties with you." Sean felt his eyes would burst anytime.

"I ...." he stuttered.

"Sean," Mike was quieter now. Sean didn't respond. "Sean," he repeated louder this time.

"Y-yeah," replied Sean. There was silence for a few seconds.

"Sean," Mike repeated, and Sean tried to compose himself.

"Yes," he was firmer now.

"Don't worry about this," Mike stated. "Give it time and it will all sort itself out." Sean was not convinced.

"Yes, yes of course it will," Sean looked down as he answered hesitantly. In his mind, his friend was standing in front of him and, for the first time ever, he was embarrassed. "At least the missus is pleased by the fee I got." Sean was grasping at straws.

"Yeah, I bet she is. She'll have spent it all, already!" Mike exclaimed, his forced attempt at humour falling flat.

"Yes, probably," replied Sean quietly.

"Look, I've got to go," Mike stated.

"Okay," Sean answered, looking up at the ceiling. His eyes were now red and brimming with tears.

"I will be back next weekend, we can meet up then," Mike suggested, Sean felt the first tear roll down his cheek.

"Yes, I'll look forward to it," Sean was forcing himself to sound confident.

"Okay, I have to go," said Mike.

"Sure, chat to you then," replied Sean.

"Yes, we'll talk soon," and Mike ended the call. Sean sat back into the chair. He dropped the phone on the floor, then sat forward, covering his face with his hands. He started to sob. The tears quickly soaked the inside of his hands, and his nose began to run. His whole body shook with each sob, as the pain flowed out of him.

The sound of his wife walking across the floor of their bedroom made him look up. He sat back and reached into his pocket for a tissue. He wiped his eyes and face. He looked around the room, then at the phone on the floor. The thud, thud, thud of her footsteps echoed across the ceiling once more. Sean stood up. He stood there for a few seconds, then went down on one knee and picked up the phone. He looked at the screen and slowly placed it in his pocket. He looked around the room again, then moved without thinking. He walked into the hallway and stopped by the coats that hung beside the front door. It was dark and cold outside but he decided against grabbing a jacket; he probably would not need it anyway. Sean looked up the stairs. He could hear running water; she was running a bath.

"I am just heading out for a while," he heard himself say flatly. Then he reached out with his left hand and opened the front door.

"Where are you going?" came her voice from upstairs.

"I'm just going outside," he whispered. "I may be some time." He stepped forward and quietly pulled the door closed.

Chapter 38

Cara-Marie was sitting in her car. She was the only one in the carpark on the hill overlooking Portstewart. The car pointed towards where the sun had set behind the Inishowen peninsula. The convent that dominated the landscape, stood out against the sky, was in darkness. She could still see the shoreline of Portstewart Strand.

She had not been there since the New Year's Day murders, but many folks had been, the 'wolf tourism' had continued. The local tourist board was loving it; every hotel and bed & breakfast was having a bumper season, and every single day, tourists would come into the office looking for her. Thankfully, Kevin had finally reacted and done something about it. She had pointed out that, with the constant interruptions, her normal work was suffering. Her coverage of the local stories was taking far too long, as she was continually fending off these people. The wind had picked up again, and the car gently shook. She could still smell the fish and chips she'd eaten in the car while she waited. All he'd said was "as soon as I can get there".

She opened the door and the cold rushed in. She swung her legs out and stood up. She was wearing a thick top under her outdoor jacket, but the wind still cut through her jeans. As she closed the car door behind her, she took the knitted woollen hat from her pocket and pulled it over her head. She slowly wandered over to the small, red building that once was a lookout post. She pushed her hands deep into her pockets, and stepped closer to the wall, searching for cover from the wind.

She looked up at the sky. Most of the clouds had cleared; it would be a cold night and not long before the snow came. She hugged herself to keep out the cold. She searched the landscape; the lights of the promenade only went so far; she could hear the sea but could see very little of it. She loved living here; in fact, she could not imagine living anywhere else. She could not live like Fiona - in Belfast, surrounded by concrete and brick. Fiona had a small flat but didn't know anyone around her. It seemed a lonely existence. Cara-Marie thought for a moment, then took out her phone and tapped a short message. 'WE STILL NEED TO HAVE A WINE CATCH UP SOMETIME SOON'. Anyone reading that would just think it was about two friends from university, but Fiona would know the real reason: Cara-Marie wanted to talk about the murders. She put the phone away in her pocket and looked over the landscape again. Even though it was cold, she felt the warmth of familiarity. Kevin was still not listening to her. Yes, he was right about what was happening around the Mournes not being a local story, so she had been posting the details on her blog. It had grown. She was now getting messages from USA, Canada, across Europe and beyond; but none of them were what she was looking for. True, she had numerous bits of information, but not enough to piece together the whole story. She wanted to link them so she could finally prove what she knew, what she had seen; but she knew no matter what she believed, it wouldn't be enough; she would need absolute proof.

Her phone bleeped, indicating a message. She fought with her pocket for it. It was either Fiona replying, or .... she looked at her Mum's name on the screen and sighed. Reluctantly, she pressed the button: TOMORROW EVENING HILARY IS COMING OVER FOR DINNER, SHE WANTS TO CHAT WITH YOU, BE HERE FOR SIX WILL YOU? She closed her eyes, then reread the message. Her mum's friend would not be alone; her son was Cara-Marie's age and had recently moved back home. He was now a doctor in a local surgery, and her mum had once again taken it upon herself to find Cara-Marie a husband. She would go, and she'd make sure the conversation got around to 'werewolves' as quickly as possible. That normally had the desired effect. Her mum was furious the last time she had done it. If Hilary's son was cute, that could be a different matter but, from what she remembered of him growing up, he was not the one she wanted to spend her life with.

"Cara," the voice made her spin around, so she was facing the opposite direction. Kyle was standing about six feet away. He was wearing baggy jeans and a thick outdoor jacket that was zipped up at the front and a woollen beanie hat pulled down over his head. His hands were in the pockets of the jeans, which made the jacket look bigger than it was. He was smiling. Not an excited smile, but a polite one. Behind him, four figures were disappearing into the darkness. She had not heard any of them approach.

"Oh, h-hello," she stuttered, he looked past her at the landscape.

"Beautiful, isn't it?" he stated, she looked back out into the semi-darkness.

"Yes," she almost whispered, "I love where I live." A small smile broke over her face as she said the words, then she looked over at him. "It's been a while," she said. No hug, not even a handshake had been offered, he glanced at her and smiled as well.

"Yes, it has," he replied and looked away again. The wind swirled around them, Cara-Marie fixed her eyes on a point in the darkness and asked her first question.

"So, how is life as the Alpha of a pack of werewolves?" She turned her head towards him, "An Rua isn't it?" Kyle looked at her seriously.

"Careful," he whispered.

"Or what?" she raised her voice. "You are not going to 'just pop round' for the night anymore, then?" she folded her arms. "It has been a while since you did that!"

"Well," he started, "I wasn't exactly made to feel welcome the last time that happened." He looked away, "I was asleep, then you came poking me in the shoulder and telling me that I was not staying and to get out," she looked over at him.

"Yeah, I went into the kitchen to make some tea, then all I hear is the front door closing …. Just the 'wham bam'; not even a 'thank you ma'am'!" Kyle looked over at her, then away.

"So, where did you hear the name 'An Rua'?" he asked.

"From you," there was a pause before he spoke again,

"No, you didn't."

"Yes, I did!" she replied.

"When?" he asked, she looked away and smiled.

"Sometimes, after sex, you talk in your sleep." She unfolded her arms and pushed her hands into the pockets at the front of the jacket.

"But that name means nothing to you," he had lowered his voice, she noticed the change in conversation, but this topic was the reason she was here.

"The An Rua, …. ancient defenders of the 'High Kings of Tara'," she said, and watched as his body reacted. She carried on, "once a part of the 'Red Branch warriors'; there are Irish legends of their feats and daring in battle," she paused. He was looking out to sea. She changed tack, "and I know that Carl O'Brien wasn't killed by a deer." Kyle's head spun around. It was the confirmation she needed. Kyle didn't answer but his body had certainly reacted; he was no poker player. "So how many werewolves do you have under your command?"

"What?" Kyle stared at her in disbelief.

"There are over seventy people registered as 'working' at the farm, are they all werewolves?" she was staring at him now. He briefly looked at her, then away.

"Why would you want to know that? Are you looking for more stuff for your blog?" She looked back out to sea.

"I just want to know the truth."

"The truth about what?"

"About what I saw when you and I found that woman by the riverbank!" Cara-Marie slowly reached out with her left arm and touched his right arm. He looked at her. They stood there for a few seconds, staring at each other, not speaking. Cara-Maire moved first and lowered her arm. "I don't believe for a second that what I saw was part of an eastern European crime gang," Kyle looked away.

"He wasn't." Cara-Marie felt her eyes dilate and her own heart beat faster. 'He' was confirmation. She had a list of questions, a list of 'what about this?', 'what about that?' The journalist in her was about to take over, but it had been hard enough getting him here and she did not want to scare him away, so she would listen. She stepped closer to him, hoping for more revelations. She waited. The wind continued to sweep past them; she was not expecting what came next.

"His name was Davidov Sprogis, and he was from a wolf pack in Northern Latvia," Cara-Marie was ticking the information off in her head.

"He was found with the others at Mussenden Temple last year; his head off," she said. Kyle glanced at her, then looked away again. She "I did a report on that story!"

"Not quite," Kyle was looking out to sea again. "He killed his alpha at Mountsandel …." Kyle paused again. He was considering how much to tell her.

"Chernov?" her question was louder, "I thought that was a suicide?" Kyle shook his head,

"Sprogis is the one you saw at the riverbank," Cara-Marie thought for a moment.

"But why kill Chernov? That doesn't make sense!" she looked back at him; a reassuring smile spread over his face.

"You are missing the first, and most important, question." Kyle looked into her eyes.

"What would he gain by doing that?" she asked, and Kyle shook his head again.

"No, the first question for you to ask is 'what were they doing here in the first place?' and 'why did they have to leave Latvia?'" Cara-Marie's mind was in overdrive. Of course! That was an excellent place to start!

"So, the Castleroe murders?"

"Sprogis and the girl, Nikitin,"

"But why? They were only kids?" It was a genuine question from her.

"Sprogis and Nikitin were having an affair; she was with Chernov at the time. They met up there and the kids spotted them having sex. They made sure there were no witnesses."

"But they were seen!" she stated, Kyle nodded.

"Yes, the lass who works in the coffee shop... I forget her name," Kyle said.

"Boyd," offered Cara-Marie, "Rachel Boyd."

"The very one."

"So, the footage on her phone was real?" she asked, Kyle almost laughed.

"You also have the footage from the Mournes," she nodded, "Well, have a look and compare the two." ...Why hadn't she thought of that? It was a brilliant idea!

"So, the 'monster of Mourne' is one of your werewolves, then?" This was exciting; this she could use.

"A wolf, yes."

"So, you have lost control of one of your own?" Kyle's head snapped over; she had just crossed a line... she got a reaction.

"NO," it was nearly a shout. He looked away and let his anger subside. She looked at him, studying him. She prodded once more for more details; it was worth a try.

"So, who is it then?" There was a long pause.

"We don't know her name," Cara-Maire listened; 'her' it was a girl. "But she arrived a few weeks ago. We don't know where she is from." Kyle's tone of voice had changed.

"How?" she asked, Kyle glanced over at her.

"How what?" he replied.

"How did she arrive? Boat, car, plane?" It was a gentle prod.

"She landed at the city airport we think only a few days before the first killing." Cara-Marie widened her eyes again; that gave her enough to go on. She was happy. Silence fell over them both again. The sky had darkened.

"Isn't there a full moon soon?" The question made him look over at her.

"No," he smiled, "there isn't one until February 10th."

"Then you all 'turn furry' and 'bark' at the moon?" She smiled as she asked the question, Kyle looked at her and scrunched up his face; then he let out a short laugh.

"Hollywood has got it all wrong," he looked away. "It is nothing like that."

"What is it like, then?" she stepped closer, hoping for an invite that did not come. Out of the darkness behind them, a figure stepped forward, they both turned.

"I have to go," he stated.

"Are you not concerned I might have recorded this whole conversation?" It stopped him. He turned back and looked at her, smiling a genuine smile.

"Look at your phone," he said. She fumbled in her pocket and looked at the blank screen. She looked up at him with a mystified look on her face, he was still smiling. "It is called 'countermeasures'; nothing electronic will have worked the entire time we've been chatting," she stared after him as he walked away.

"Call 'round some night," she shouted after him. He stopped and looked at her, she was smiling, "It would be good to have a proper catch up again," They both smiled. Kyle nodded, turned, and walked into the darkness, joining the figure. Cara-Marie watched him go. She looked at her phone again. Yes, she had tried to record it, but now saw she had got nothing. He told her enough though and also told her where to look. She was happy with that. She would get home before she realised she forgot to ask him about his grandfather and World War 2.

∞∞∞∞

Kyle walked with his companion across the small carpark to the steps that led down the far side of the hill towards the promenade where their vehicles were parked. The protection detail closed in on him. He was handed his phone.

"It's Paul." Kyle nodded and took the phone as they started down the steps.

"Hi," he said.

"Hiya," Paul replied, "how did that go?" Kyle glanced over his shoulder.

"Well, I gave her a couple of tidbits..."

"Like?" Paul asked,

155

"Like the approximate date the German arrived, if she can get access to the CCTV from the airport, that will be at least three days of footage for her to go through; and a few bits about the Latvians - that should keep her busy for a while." There was a short laugh down the phone.

"Right, are you coming back here, now?" Paul inquired.

"Yes," Kyle thought for a second, 'was there something in the tone of his voice?' He was not sure, so he asked. "Why? Is something up?" There was a brief pause before Paul spoke again.

"Well, yeah ...." Kyle and the protection team walked around to where the two cars were parked, and the teams split up. The principal bodyguard walked with Kyle. She was very unassuming, but she knew her job well. The driver, who'd been standing by the car, climbed in as they approached. He had once stood and held the door for him, but Kyle put a stop to that - if they were under surveillance, that action could give him away.

"Yeah, what?" Kyle asked, as he opened the rear door of the car.

"Amanda's gone missing in Belfast...it looks like there was a struggle."

Chapter 39

"Where exactly are they?" Tyler asked.

"Just south of Hare's Gap, they say it is a strong scent." Tyler watched as the young man continued to relay from the radio he held to his ear. He was in touch with the other search team. The young man looked up, "they say, less than an hour ago." There was a buzz of excitement in the group, they would all pass as hillwalkers; their weapons were hidden, but could be brought to bear quickly, when needed. The search was going well. Tyler walked towards one of the girls who was holding a map. Tyler placed the map on the ground and bent down,

"Right, everyone close in!" The group gathered around her, Tyler turned the map around, so it was orientated to the area. She took the rectangle compass and pointed to the map with the corner of it. "We are here .... at Buzzards' Roost." She moved the compass across the map to where it said, 'Hare's Gap'. "They are here," she moved it again, "and if the scent trail is correct, the rabid is moving this way, towards the Ben Crom Reservoir." She looked up at the young guy with the radio, "tell them to move quickly down past shelter stone and get to Ben Crom Dam as fast as they can, we will meet them there." he nodded and began passing on the instructions.

"They are on the way now and are moving at speed!" he confirmed.

"Will she not pick them up?" a voice asked. Tyler stood up, as did the girl with the map,

"Yes, of course she will. She'll have picked up our scents as soon as we arrived." She looked around the collection of faces, then pointed to the map again. "She will also know why we are here. She will not directly try and tackle a pack, so we need to move from here." She stepped back and pointed down the side of the hill, "We will extend in a line down this side of the hill, we should get to the dam before she does. Then, with the others coming up behind, she will have nowhere to go." Tyler adjusted the straps of the daysack on her shoulders.

"Then we take her down!" came one of the voices and a chorus of agreement.

"Remember what we practiced." Tyler looked at each face in the group of people around her. "No one gets inventive," she paused, "we *cannot* let her infect anyone or there will be a national crisis on our hands, and the sapiens will descend on us in a way we have not seen for centuries," she paused again, "and I don't know about you, but I have no intention of spending the rest of my days in a cage, undergoing experiments," she looked out on the solemn faces again, "right, let's go." Tyler stepped around the group and headed away from the large rocks shaping that part of the slope of Slieve Binnian. The others fanned out and soon formed a line, then headed over the crest of the hill. Tyler looked up towards Hare's Gap. A strong scent meant she was close, the scent around Binnian was almost gone. They were moving at speed now, not quite running, but certainly moving quickly. Everyone here had known the twins, and they all wanted their own justice for what happened to them.

As they moved around the side of the hill, Ben Crom reservoir came into view. This was part of Silent Valley with the Silent Valley dam just a few miles further down to their left. Tyler had paused here earlier. It was beautiful. The grade soon became much steeper, and they slowed right down, they were now carefully picking their way down the precipitous slope.

"Tent!" one of them said, and everyone stopped. Tyler looked over to her right, towards where he was pointing.

"Where?" one of the others asked.

"'Far side of the dam," Tyler's eyes followed the indications that were shared with the group. "Far end of the dam, left end of dam, flat area ...." She found it easily; the directions continued. "Right side of area, with branches over it, there is a single domed tent." She could see it now, the tent was there, and someone had placed some branches and moved a fallen tree in front of it, so it was not clearly visible. It wasn't fully camouflaged but hidden well enough.

"THAT'S IT!" Tyler shouted. She made her way around a large rock. She looked down at the pathway she was following. The smell of the brambles and the heather filled her nose; it was beautiful, and, for a moment, she forgot why she was there. She felt a strong connection with the land. Each step was deliberate, as they carefully made their way down the steep side of the hill. A wooden stile connected the wire fencing but there were obvious signs of damage. There was a small open area beside it. The group was descending towards it.

"THERE SHE IS!" shouted one of the team from over to her right. Tyler's head shot up; everyone had stopped. There, around the side of the hill and along the path, was a blonde-haired woman, running. Her hair was flowing free and she had a light blue top on and light-coloured trousers with a small daysack on her back. She suddenly stopped. She froze where she was. She made a noise and lowered herself, as if to attack. She knew instantly who they were.

"NO ONE MOVE!" Tyler shouted. Everyone stopped and stared at the rabid. She stared back, looking at each one of the team in turn. She recognised what they were and why they were here. Her face twisted in hatred. She raised herself up, aggressively. She would not go quietly. She looked straight into Tyler's eyes. Tyler met her glare. Tyler slowly dropped her daysack. "Remember what I said," she wasn't shouting but everyone heard her. She jumped and sprinted the last twenty metres down to the gate. The rabid had started walking slowly towards her, never taking her eyes off her. Tyler was in charge, so she would be the one to take down first. Tyler slowed, and then stopped. There was some space, but not much. The hill fell away to her left down to the water's edge and the team forming an extended line was up to her right.

The rabid suddenly turned and looked behind her. As the first of the other team came into view, she realized there was nowhere for her to go. She turned and jogged a little towards Tyler, as more of the other team came into view. Tyler held her hand up and they stopped. She extended both of her arms horizontally as an instruction for them to form an extended line. They did. The rabid stopped about thirty metres away.

Tyler stared at her. The rabid started tearing at her clothes; she was changing, and this had just become a challenge. Tyler looked up at one of the team and nodded. They nodded back, and quiet instructions were passed. Tyler slowly started to remove her own clothes in order to change herself. Her clothes would be folded neatly; the rabid's clothing was tossed to one side. Tyler knelt on one knee and embraced her wolf. This was daylight and was, therefore, breaking so many rules; but the rabid had to be dealt with.

The others watched as the rabid stood up, extended her arms and made a bark-like noise at them. It was defiance. She began to walk towards where Tyler had changed and was now slowly standing. Tyler flexed her arms, then her legs and took a step forward. She looked at the creature coming towards her: the way she walked, the way she snapped her mouth and licked her lips, the grotesque gestures she made with her hands... Tyler could see the madness in her eyes. She took a step forward, then stopped. The rabid came to the end of the path where the wire fence started; she was now ten metres away. Her attention was totally focused on Tyler. She relished the coming fight and snarled again. Tyler saw the rabid's muscles tense - she was about to launch herself forward in an attack.

Suddenly, Tyler dropped to the ground. She lay on her stomach with her hands under her shoulders, ready to jump up if she needed to. The rabid straightened up. There was a confused look on her face for just a second; then she turned and looked up the hill. Tyler watched as time seemed to slow down.

A look of shock appeared on the rabid's face as the first bullet struck. Her body rocked, then spun as bullet after bullet found their mark. Tyler glanced up. The extended line had moved closer, everyone had their pistols drawn, suppressors on. Every single team member was firing. No one... nothing... could survive the barrage of firepower coming from the group on the hill.

As quickly as it started, it ended. Tyler lay where she was until she heard a voice shout,

"Clear!" She lifted herself onto one knee. She looked at the body that lay at the end of the path. It was riddled with gunshot wounds. The body twitched, then relaxed as the last breath was exhaled. Tyler needed to change back, and quickly before they were seen.

Tyler looked at the team on the hill, they all were reloading. Two of them moved closer, weapons extended. One stopped, aiming directly at the wolf on the ground. The second moved off to the right, maintaining the field of fire but closing in on the wolf at the same time. He stopped, only a few feet away. The one closest to the wolf took careful aim and fired twice. Tyler watched the head of the rabid explode as the bullets tore through it. The rabid was dead. She needed to change back, and quickly before she was seen.

The team on the hill slowly descended as the second team ran towards the kill. Tyler turned and started to change back to her sapien form, it was not long before she had dressed and was tying up the laces on her boots. The group was elated; they were proud of their accomplishment. Tyler was smiling.

"Did you see the look on her face?"

"She wasn't expecting that!" the comments were flying; the excitement was obvious.

"Has anyone bothered to inform the farm yet?" Tyler asked. Several heads turned towards her, there was a collective 'no'. "Right!" she exclaimed, "I want her bagged up as fast as possible. Remember to wear gloves; we don't want any contamination." They looked at each other as she continued, "I want that tent of hers collapsed and everything gone through, then taken back to the farm. We clear the area! Make sure we collect all the empty bullet casings and leave no trace that we were here, and Michael..." A dark-haired male stepped out from the rear of the group.

"Yes?" he asked, as Tyler stood up.

"I want you and three others to go and get the 4x4 and bring it in as close possible, and then I want the decoy in place. …. We have to give the police their 'monster'." Tyler stood up and stepped towards the happy group as one of them handed her the daysack that she had dropped up the hill. "Does everyone know what needs to happen?" There were murmurs of agreement. "Okay, let's do it, then." There was a flurry of activity, while they discussed the reception awaiting them back at the farm.

Tyler watched as one of the girls knelt near the rabid's head and took out a small hunting knife. She took a firm grip of some of the unspoilt fur with her gloved hand and scalped a fistful.

"Nice one," a voice said, and the girl was patted on the shoulder.

"Make sure that is bagged and cleaned before you mount it!" Tyler instructed. The girl looked at her and nodded. "It is still diseased." Tyler turned away; she didn't see the single tear roll down the girl's face.

"For Emma and Gemma," the girl whispered.

"For Richard and for Will," her companion added. They shared a look and then a rueful smile as the girl stood up. The Silver and Gold twins would be mourned for some time. Tyler opened the top compartment of her daysack. The screen on her phone indicated a message had arrived. She pressed the green button and read the single line.

'URGENT: PHONE THE FARM AT ONCE'

ooooo

Cara-Marie read over the email again: 'WEREWOLF SQUAD INSPECTOR DIES IN SINGLE VEHICLE TRAFFIC COLLISION'. She read the details and could picture the scene that was being described. 'Mr Sean Parrish, former detective inspector was pronounced dead at the scene of a single vehicle incident near Ballymena.' She read the rest of the article, not recognising any names except that of Chief Inspector Anderson. Cara-Marie remembered them both from the press conference. Sean had been the quieter one; the Chief Inspector had been the one who shouted her down and told her to stick to school fetes and flower shows. They were calling it a traffic collision, as it was no longer correct to call them traffic accidents: 'an accident implies there is no one to blame', someone had told her. The report did not mention the one word that should have been in there: 'SUICIDE'. There were no other cars involved; it was a straight road; it had been dry, no ice, yet he managed to leave the road and hit a very prominent signpost.

She took out her phone and looked around the office before placing the call. Beside her, Mark was engrossed in something; she listened to the phone ringing. Her eyes were reading the words on her computer screen, but the information was not registering. The phone continued to ring, her desktop pinged with the arrival of another email. The ringing stopped, and the automated voice clicked in. Cara-Maire ended the call.

"Who were you ringing?" Mark asked, she looked at him.

"Umm?" there was a confused look on her face, almost as if she did not understand what he just said, Mark stopped what he was doing and looked at her.

"You were just trying to call someone …. You had it on speakerphone," she looked at the phone, then back at him. She had not realised she'd done that.

"Oh," there was another pause.

"Well, you certainly have something on your mind," he said, as he looked down at his work again. Cara-Maire looked at the phone, tapped the screen, then placed the phone on her desk. Her fingers were poised over the keyboard, but they did not touch the keys. She stared at the screen; the desktop pinged again. She looked over at Mark. He had just said something that she had not heard.

"Pardon?" she asked, Mark was staring at her again.

"I said, what has got you so engrossed?" The camera in his hand bleeped. He looked at it, touched a button then looked back at her, she looked at the screen again.

"Sean Parrish committed suicide last night near Ballymena," she could see Mark thinking about what she had just said.

"Parrish …. The inspector in charge of the 'werewolf squad'?" he asked.

"Yes, the article is on your feed," she answered. Mark set the camera down and moved his mouse.

"Is it? Okay." For a moment he became engrossed in what he was reading, nodding once. "It doesn't say suicide," he remarked. "What makes you think that?"

"Well," she started, "first he did that article a few days ago in which they claimed he said the police had been looking for werewolves last year."

"And the police denied every word," Mark added.

"They did, and then they launched an attack on him for doing the interview."

"So? That doesn't mean he killed himself!"

"By itself no, but ...." She saw Mark look back at his screen, then glance at the camera he had been working on. He was losing interest. "...look at the article, it says there was no other car involved; it was estimated he was going nearly twice the speed limit and,"

"And?" Mark asked.

"And .... he had disabled the airbags.... and he was not wearing his seat belt!"

"Okay, suspicious? Yes, but doesn't prove he did it himself, even if he did ...."

"Why would someone want him out of the way?" she asked, "or why would he feel there was no other way out?" She was staring at him as she asked the questions.

"Because he'd been institutionalised!" Neither of them had spotted Kevin walk up behind their desks.

"He was what?" Mark asked.

"Institutionalised!" repeated Cara-Marie, "someone who's lived in an institution or environment for a prolonged period and is governed by a rigid set of rules. They gradually become less able to think and act outside of it," she explained.

"What?" Mark looked confused, glancing between the two of them.

"Like spending thirty years in the police force, being retired, then suddenly having nothing to do with yourself all day," Kevin added, he looked over at Cara-Marie.

"And then giving an interview that is taken completely out of context and all your former workmates suddenly cut ties with you," she finished the sentence.

"I think you have something there .... I like it. Keep looking, let me know if the police are treating it as a suicide." Kevin walked away, leaving Cara-Marie smiling, Mark looked at her.

"By the way, you did not answer my question."

"What question?"

"Who were you phoning?" Cara-Marie looked over as Kevin suddenly turned and walk back towards them.

"Just remembered why I came over here in the first place." They turned to look at him as he continued, "That fella, Martin, who survived the New Year's Day murders, has struck again." There was an instant reaction from both of them.

"As in ...Kris Martin?" Cara-Marie asked.

"The very one. 'Seems he killed a woman in Belfast last night, then chopped her hands off as some sort of trophy. The police just released some CCTV footage ...." He turned and headed back towards his office again, "Find out what you can, will you?" Mark and Cara-Marie would be busy for the rest of the day.

Chapter 40

Alison looked at the large TV screen. Her arms were folded, and she had an intense, angry look on her face. Sabine walked up and stood beside her. Despite the huge sectional couch and numerous chairs scattered about the TV room at the lair, they remained standing. The only lighting, aside from that of the TV, was a single strip light.

"What's this?" Sabine asked, Alison glanced at her, then turned back to the news report.

"Lunchtime news," she stated angrily.

"As bad as we'd thought?" Sabine enquired Alison took a deep breath.

"Worse, he was caught on CCTV and they've released it!" The news anchor finished one story, then a still picture of Kris Martin appeared at the side of the screen.

"And police are urgently wishing to speak to Mr Kris Martin, following yet another incident last night in Belfast…"

"Oh, for fuck's sake …." Sabine started. The news presenter handed over to a young male reporter with wet hair, who was standing in the rain. He was obviously cold. Alison glanced over at the annoyed look on Sabine's face, then back at the screen.

"The young female, who is yet to be officially identified, was found late last night. Initial reports indicate she had been dead for several hours and had taken a severe beating. Sources reveal the victim's hands were cut off, prompting suspicion of a 'trophy killing'." The reporter continued, interviewing a middle-aged woman, who stated she found the body while out walking her dog.

"And it was the girl, Amanda?" Sabine asked.

"Yeah," replied Alison.

"That is certainly going to get a reaction!" Sabine retorted.

"It will bring fury from Kyle; the kind of attention we don't need right now. He was never one to back down," Alison stated.

"We need to control Kris. He is psychotic! He was intending to bring her here!" Sabine exclaimed, as she looked back at the TV screen. The reporter was interviewing a local politician.

"So, what are we going to do about him?" Alison asked.

"He needs to be dealt with," Sabine stated and turned back to the screen. The reporter continued,

"Police have released two images taken by CCTV in the hopes of tracking down Mr …." The reporter paused as he read from a notebook. The two images filled the screen. The backgrounds were dark, but you could clearly make out Kris's smiling face. He continued "…Kris Martin, whom the police are describing as 'extremely dangerous'. They are warning the public not to approach. If anyone sees him, they should call the police immediately." Sabine sighed out loud as the report went back to the studio. The anchor continued, "At a police press conference, the family of Mr Martin made an appeal directly to him." The screen changed. There was a covered table with police recruitment screens in the background. Sitting at the table were an older couple and a young woman, with the Chief Inspector sitting officiously at the end. The older couple filled the screen; they were in tears; their names scrolled across the bottom of the screen.

"Who are they?" Sabine asked.

"His parents," Alison answered.

"Kris, please come home," his father pleaded, while the mother looked down, quietly subdued, Sabine's phone bleeped with a text message. She read it, then looked at Alison.

"We may have a solution to our problem," she said, showing the message to Allison.

"What time does she get here?" Alison asked, as Sabine looked at her watch.

"They should be here now," she stated, Alison unfolded her arms and stood.

"Shall we get everyone up?" she asked, Sabine shook her head,

"No, let them sleep. She isn't happy about our little problem."

"I bet she isn't!" Alison replied. "Let's hope she's come up with a plan to deal with him."

"We will find out what it is, soon enough," Sabine stated, then turned and walked away. Alison picked up the TV remote and pressed the red button. Sabine knew more than she was letting on and Alison was not happy about that. She dropped the remote onto the sofa and followed Sabine quietly through the lair towards the front door. Two protection team members were standing outside the front door, one of them had his eye pressed up against the spy hole in the middle of the door.

"That's them, now," he stated, and stepped back. The other one opened the door and daylight flooded in, slicing through the darkness. Sabine jumped out of the way, just in time.

"DON'T DO THAT AGAIN!" she shouted. "You announce before you open a door in daylight!" The two protection team members looked at each other blankly, then stepped inside, as the dark-coloured car stopped. The rear door opened, and Dani stepped out. As she stood up, she turned and reached back inside for a large rucksack. She pulled it over one shoulder and walked into the house. The car door was shut by another member of the protection team, then it slowly drove away. The front door of the lair was closed behind them, Dani dropped the rucksack onto the floor.

"Where did you get that?" Sabine asked with a smile, as she stepped forward. Dani looked at her, then Alison, ignoring the two behind them.

"From a hillwalker in Wicklow," she shrugged. "He didn't need it anymore." There was a shared smile; they all knew what that meant. Then the smile fell from Dani's face. "Right, where is that fucking idiot?" she spat, angrily.

∞∞∞∞

Dermott opened the front door of the farmhouse to admit Tony. The room was a warm respite from the cold outside. Dermott closed the door behind him.

"What the hell happened?" Tony asked, Dermott walked past him and stopped near the coffee table.

"The good news is Tyler got the rabid."

"Not surprising...I heard they were going to leave a decoy." Tony added, and Dermott nodded.

"Yeah, the vet had a Husky dog with some sort of bone condition and was going to put him down. It will be positioned so it looks like it fell from a height." Tony looked at Dermott, who continued, "A couple of dead sheep torn apart by two of the hunting team, etc.; everything the police will need to shut the 'monster' stories down." Dermott lifted up a large envelope from the table. It contained several 8 x 10 photographs.

"Yeah, the police will be all over that; sounds good," replied Tony. Dermott slid the pictures out of the envelope, and Tony stepped forward. "So, what else is happening? Is it true about Amanda?" Dermott handed him the pictures.

"The first two are the stills released by the police. The rest ...." Tony shuffled through them and stopped. The photograph had been taken in an alleyway. Amanda's face was covered in blood; the wounds to her neck left no doubt what had killed her. Her clothing was torn; she was partially naked with trauma wounds on her shoulders and the exposed side of her chest. The next picture was a closer shot of the neck wound; Tony studied the bite marks.

"Not a normal Noc," he said.

"Or else, one who didn't know what he was doing!" Dermott was looking at him, expectantly. Tony understood.

"Was it definitely Martin?" Dermott nodded, then motioned towards the pictures.

"Keep looking." Tony flipped to the next picture, there were more than one set of footprints around the edge. The next picture was a head shot of Kris Martin; he was rapturous. His mouth was covered in blood, and he was holding up two severed hands, as the trophies they were.

"He cut her hands off?" Tony gasped, Dermott looked down at the floor,

"Look at the last photograph." Tony flipped again. His eyes moved over the image. His wolf came forward; he could feel the anger in him rise. There was no doubt who had done it. Amanda's body was on its side and Kris was kneeling beside it, with her hands held up in a mock surrender. Around him stood a group of male and female Noctrailis. Most were smiling... it was as if they had been on a safari and this was their prize. Tony looked at the faces, then at their weapons. There was a mix of military rifles and shotguns.

"Oh shit," he whispered.

"Oh shit, indeed," Dermott replied, and Tony added,

"I don't recognise any of them." Dermott walked towards the kitchen door,

"Neither do I." He stopped and turned back towards Tony, voicing what they were both thinking. "We have no idea who this lot are!" Tony looked down at the picture again,

"Are they not sleeping in the usual place?"

"Nope," replied Dermott, "and we can't hit that, anyway, without permission from the south!" Tony looked at him, "it seems they were not happy about last time." Tony could see the anger in him. Dermott hated them and did not hide his opinion that every single one of them should be hunted down and destroyed.

"So, where are they sleeping?" Tony asked.

"'No idea," Dermott shrugged. Tony looked towards the door.

"Where is Kyle?" Tony asked.

"After battering one of the manikins in the training room for half an hour, he is now down at the range... target practice." Tony looked back at the pictures.

"Where did you get these?" he asked.

"From her phone," Dermott replied.

"Whose phone?" Tony looked up as he asked the question.

"Amanda's."

"Really? Where the hell did you get it?" Tony was shocked.

"It was in a jiffy bag that was dropped at the bottom of the lane, first thing this morning!" Tony could feel his anger rise again.

"They wanted us to know about this!" Tony spat.

"Paul and I had to wrestle Kyle to the ground when he tried to attack one of the manikins." Dermott said, "I actually thought he was about to change, right there!" Tony looked back at the photos; he could just imagine that reaction.

"So, what are we going to do about this?" Tony asked, slowly gaining control of his anger. Dermott turned towards him and answered,

"We have already sent a four-man team to Belfast to see if we can find the new lair." Dermott pointed with his finger towards the pictures as he spoke.

"But?" Tony inquired.

"But the south has said that it is just an isolated Noc attack, so no council members needed, and we are to tell them first about anything we do ...."

"The restraints are on, any direct action will take time to get approval," Tony concluded.

"Then the little feckers will be long gone," Dermot said, his hands on his hips.

"There is a lot more to this than what we thought there was." Tony stated, and Dermott nodded in agreement.

"Yes... and look at the weaponry they have! This isn't just an attack; it's an incursion!"

"When is Tyler back?" Tony asked.

"This afternoon, things there, at least, went well. The south is pleased that we were able to deal with the rabid," Dermott was still angry.

"Are they going to help?" Tony asked.

"Who?"

"The south... Are they going to help?" Tony expanded his question.

Dermott shook his head. "Nope, we are on our own. It's like they are totally ignoring what is going on up here!" Tony thought for a second; he did not want Dermott flying into a rage.

"Then it is up to us," he stated.

"Then it is up to us," Dermott repeated. "Paul was talking about sending down two teams; one led by me, the other by you. Are you okay with that?" Dermott asked, and Tony nodded.

"No problem, where is Paul?" he asked. Dermott half turned away and waved towards the front door.

"He is with Kyle." Tony felt his anger begin to subside. He looked over the photos once more, then walked over to the table and picked up the envelope. He put them back inside and dropped it onto the table, then he turned and walked outside.

The cold air hit him as soon as he opened the door. He zipped up his jacket, and stopped, as the sound of rapid gunfire echoed through the yard. Even though the range was at the far end of the complex, the sound bounced among the large buildings. The speed and rate of fire reflected Kyle's anger, he had a right to be angry. Though he had never said it, Tony knew that Kyle had felt more for Amanda than he'd let on.

Two farmhands walked past, greeting him; he responded in kind. One of them had two of the farm's Irish wolfhounds on leads; they were heading towards the main open area. Tony was thinking about what he had just heard. His phone bleeped with a message. He fumbled in his pocket; it was a brief message. He scrolled through the contacts and stopped at Karen's name. He held the phone to his ear, as it started to ring.

"Hello," just the sound of her voice brought a warm feeling inside him.

"Hiya," he said, as he looked around; there was no one nearby.

"Is it as bad as we'd thought?" she asked, Tony answered,

"Yes. They killed Amanda last night," Karen gave a brief cry down the phone.

"What is going on? How is he taking it?" Tony straightened up.

"I am just going to go and see him now; it was a group we didn't know about."

"How could that happen?" she asked.

"Not sure... but we'll find them," he paused; this wasn't the reason he had called.

"Will you be home tonight?" she asked quietly. Tony felt his insides tighten at the question; there was nowhere he'd rather be than by her side.

"I'm not sure, but I'll let you know," he closed his eyes.

"It's okay, darling, let me know, either way," she spoke softly. She was so supportive, even after what she had been through. She was the woman he loved, and he felt the feelings well up inside.

"I love you, sweetheart," he whispered.

"You better do, or this marriage is in serious trouble!" she said playfully, attempting to lighten the mood. He knew she wanted him home, needed him around; but she knew he had to deal with this. He gave a short laugh before saying goodbye in Irish. He pushed the phone back into the pocket of his jeans, then walked over to his car. He would drive down to the range to see his friend.

Chapter 41

Kris slammed against the wall. He hit with such force that he bounced off and landed on the floor, rolling over once. He shook his head in disbelief. It took a couple of seconds to get his bearings. He fought for breath and tried to suppress the pain, he looked around the room for support; there was none.

Alison and Sabine stood just inside the door, watching him, scornfully. Dani's blow struck him in the centre of his chest; he had never felt anything like that!

"YOU LITTLE PRICK!" Dani shouted, "GET UP WHEN I AM TALKING TO YOU!" Kris moved slowly, righting himself. She jumped forward and sent him backwards into the wall again. Grabbing him by the throat, Dani lifted him, so he was on his tiptoes. She pushed her face close up against his and shouted again, "YOU WERE TOLD TO GRAB THE MATE OF THEIR PACK ALPHA AND BRING HER BACK HERE .... DID YOU DO THAT?"

"N-no," he whispered, fighting for breath as he struggled against her.

"YOU WERE SUPPOSED TO DO IT QUIETLY .... SO, NO ONE WOULD KNOW IT WAS US! DID YOU DO THAT? NO!" He tried to shake his head. "NO. INSTEAD YOU TAKE A TEAM, START A FIGHT, THEN ...." Dani looked over at the other two, "ACCORDING TO THE REST OF THE TEAM, YOU TRIED TO RAPE THE WOLF!" Dani pressed her face even closer to his, as she shouted, "AND IT ALL GETS CAUGHT ON CCTV .... AND WHAT THE FUCK IS THE WHOLE 'CUTTING HER HANDS OFF'? HUH?" Kris's hands came up and tried to loosen the powerful grip; he was struggling to breathe.

Dani let go and stepped back. Kris collapsed into a heap on the floor. He fell forward onto his knees and his left hand, as his right hand clawed at his throat. He gasped for breath. Dani was not done with him. "You fucking idiot! Why would you give them her phone? Do you realise what you have done?" Kris was slowly regaining his breath. He looked up. She paced away from him, then turned around. "They had no idea what we were doing; no idea that we had gathered strength." Kris managed to pull himself to his feet. Then he took a step forward, as she continued. "They had no idea we have armed ourselves; they thought there were only a few of us. Now, thanks to you, they have photographs of our entire Forward Combat Team!" Kris rubbed his throat and started to speak,

"I-I-I only wanted to show them..." Dani moved so fast that even Alison and Sabine were surprised, she leapt towards him. The palm of her right hand connected with the side of his face. The force was so great that he struck the wall again, and landed, motionless, on the floor. He lay face down. A small pool of blood began to form beneath his head. Dani stared at him. Alison paused, then unfolded her arms and walked towards him. She knelt beside his head and placed her hand on the centre of his back.

"Is he dead?" Sabine asked. Alison glanced over at her, then looked at the very angry Dani.

"No, just unconscious." Alison stood up, and Kris groaned.

"Pity," Dani spat.

"The wolf girl fought him off for nearly half an hour," Sabine stated, "'turns out, she wasn't a full Garou!" she explained.

"But she was Foster's girlfriend," Dani said. Sabine nodded,

"Yes, she was."

"It would have been better if he had done what he was told," Dani was still angry.

"...And we also found out that Reynolds is now living over here. She was recorded leading one of the teams in the mountains." Sabine continued to explain, "I have not seen the footage myself, but I hear it is very good." Dani stared at Sabine.

"Who is Reynolds?" Alison asked, "I haven't heard that name before." Dani stepped towards where Kris was lying on the floor,

"Tyler Reynolds is one of their top assassins. She took down over twenty of ours in Canada a few years ago, and several in the USA; then she came to England." Dani continued, "After a couple of years ...."

"And two whole covens destroyed!" interjected Sabine.

"...and two covens destroyed, then she disappeared. We found her last year hiding out on the Isle of Skye. So, we sent a team to take her down." Dani looked straight at Alison, "None survived." Alison nodded.

Kris twitched, then shook his head. Alison stepped away as he slowly stood up; there was blood coming from his nose. He turned and faced the others; still looking shocked. The flow of blood was constant; he held his nose with his left hand, and looked around, searching. Alison stepped forward and offered him a tissue. He nodded without speaking and held it against his nose.

"Go and clean yourself up. Then get back here as soon as you can," Dani commanded. Kris glanced at the other two then made his way out of the room. As soon as the door shut, the atmosphere in the room changed. Dani relaxed, as did the others. They gathered near Alison.

"So," Sabine started with a smile, "what else is new?" Dani grinned.

"Things are moving; slowly coming together."

"Slowly?" Sabine asked. Dani explained,

"Yeah, Salisbury found out 'he' was over from the US, so now he has moved. They weren't too happy that they hadn't known." Sabine laughed, and Alison glanced at them. They were talking about the American.

"I have never been," Alison stated. Dani looked at her.

"Where? Salisbury?"

"Yeah... 'never been," Alison answered.

"You aren't missing much." Sabine joked, sharing a knowing look with Dani.

"Are they going to get involved?" Alison asked.

"They have no idea what we are doing!" Dani snorted.

"It's better that way," Sabine said, secretively.

"Yeah, that's why he had to move on; we don't want them interfering." Alison was now concerned about the coven in Salisbury.

"And now that the wolves have caught that stray wolf running around the mountains, things should quieten down." Alison stated.

"Yeah, pity about Ute, but that was always going to be the end result." Sabine replied. Dani nodded and Alison looked over towards Sabine.

"You knew the wolf?" Alison was confused; Sabine had not said anything before.

"Ute Fessler, from the Chernsli pack in Germany," Dani stated. Sabine looked up and nodded once.

"Wait, you knew about this?" Alison asked Sabine, Sabine looked over at her, but it was Dani who answered,

"Of course, we are the ones who brought her here," Alison looked at Dani as she continued to explain. "Once her own pack found out she was infected, they gave her twelve hours to leave. When we found out there was a rabid wolf up for sale, we jumped at the chance!" Alison was now in shock. "And Sabine, here, helped with getting her here; first, across the channel into England, and then she sorted a car for her when she got here," Dani disclosed casually.

"You said she was 'infected,' What was she infected with?" Alison asked. Dani looked up and a small smile spread across her face.

"Rabies! It scares the shit out of them," she let out a short laugh, and Sabine joined in. Alison thought for a second, and lowered her voice,

"You knowingly brought *rabies* to Ireland?" Dani started to walk away,

"If it kills wolves .... then I don't care."

"And look what we managed to get," Sabine started; Alison raised her eyebrows as she continued, "up-to-date pictures and video footage of their assault teams; names, faces, weapons, tactics .... We got quite a scoop!"

"So, the German fulfilled her purpose - she drew them out, we found Reynolds, we now know our enemy." Dani smiled as she spoke.

"An enemy that is now awake!" answered Alison. She turned and watched as Dani headed towards the door. Sabine raised her eyebrows, then followed, stopping by the door as Kris came back in. He had washed his face but still looked sheepish. Kris walked past Dani and Sabine, then stopped.

"In fact, ..." Dani started, "there may be a way he can redeem himself." She pointed at Kris's back. He turned and looked at Dani. Sabine was staring at her, communicating silently. She nodded. Dani turned towards him and let the door shut. She reached into her pocket and produced a single picture. "Right, I have a job for you ...."

She handed the picture to him. Kris looked at it, then looked up at Dani, uncomprehendingly. "Simple job... so even you should be able to handle this." Kris did not move or react; he just listened. Dani pointed towards the picture. "This," she explained, "is one of their assault team leaders; and we've found out where she'll be this afternoon."

Dani looked at Sabine, who nodded once, Dani continued. "You are to go there and take her down as quickly as possible." Alison watched as his face reacted, but he did not speak. Dani was almost shouting now, "I just want her dead! No 'cutting off hands'; no raping; just DEAD ... YOU GOT THAT?" Dani walked up and held her face only a few inches from his. "So, let me be clear. I want her dead .... quickly ... and out of the sight of any sapiens …. You got that?" Kris nodded; Dani glanced at Sabine then stared back at him. "Fuck this one up and I will make sure the police here find what is left of your body!" She stepped back, then walked towards the door again, stopping by Sabine, "He is to go alone, no weapons." She glanced back at him as she opened the door, "I mean it, fuck this one up and I WILL feed you to the wolves!" Kris nodded. Dani turned and walked out the door, allowing it to slam behind her. Sabine smirked, then looked over at him.

"She is going to be in Dromore this afternoon and will be alone. She led the team that took down the twelve. Like Dani said, get it done, then get back here. Okay?" Kris nodded once. "Right," she handed him a slip of paper, "the location is written on that, be on your way." Sabine clicked her fingers and Kris walked out the door. "Oh and leave your phone. We don't want it tracked to the location, either," she shouted after him. Kris looked back and nodded. The door closed and Sabine smirked, Alison spotted it, Sabine walked over towards her.

"Who is he going after?" Alison asked.

"Exactly who she said - the one who led the assault on the lair," Sabine smiled. Now Alison knew for sure she was not being told everything.

∞∞∞∞

An hour later, Kris was driving down the A1 dual carriageway, approaching the turnoff for Dromore. At the junction, on the left, he spotted an old grey-painted tractor. His grandfather had owned one like it when he was a child. He remembered old pictures of his father sitting on it. This one was in the middle of arranged flower beds with a welcome sign. He turned the small car and started up the hill towards Dromore. He had searched the internet to find the 'Dromore Motte and Bailey'. He learned about such fortifications at school and had had taken field trips to several dotted around Northern Ireland; but it never really interested him, and he retained no information. Following the GPS, he drove through the town, taking the left turn when he was directed to do so. On the far side, he travelled up a tree-lined road. Above the trees on the right, he could just barely see the large mound of earth. It was the famous site where the old Fort had stood. He turned into the unobtrusive lane that served as the entrance. He looked around, there were no other cars here; this could be a wild goose chase.

He opened the car door and stepped out into the cold. The rain had stopped, so frost would be settling in soon. He reached back into the car and lifted the small daysack from the passenger seat. He swung it over his left shoulder and slammed the car door. If anyone was here, they now knew they were not alone. Kris walked over to the gap in the hedgerow where the entrance was. There were two green metal gates that, if opened, would barely let a single car through; but they were chained shut. To the right of this was a single passage swinging gate, which allowed access, but prevented livestock from getting out. He walked through the gate, taking the daysack from his shoulder and, gripping the strap in his left hand, opened the zip across the top. He found the large hunting knife easily, he changed his mind and left the knife inside - if he needed it, he could reach it quick enough.

He had been told 'no weapons', but he could argue that it meant 'no guns'; besides, a knife could not be traced. He looked around; the ground was covered with grass. The large earthen mound loomed in front of him; the steep mass was obviously man-made. He thought to himself that it must have taken months, if not years, to build it up, using only rudimentary tools. Kris followed the ramp across the defensive moat. The path led around and, gradually up, the massive mound. It had been well-fortified. Anyone approaching would be identified and dealt with long before they reached the top. As he followed the curve the plateau eventually opened up before him. This was the top of the Motte. It was obscured from the road but gave a commanding view of the countryside.

There, sitting cross-legged in the middle, eyes closed… was Ruth McDonal. He smiled. He recognised her from the photograph; this was who he'd been looking for. Slowly, she opened her eyes and stared at him. He looked at the unsheathed straight sword that was lying on the ground beside her. Grinning, he took the daysack from his shoulder and brought out the hunting knife.

"So, you are the wolf that took down twelve of ours while they were defenceless, then!" Ruth reached out with her right hand and slowly gripped the hilt of the ninjato sword. With slow, deliberate movements, she stood up. Her eyes never left him, Kris dropped the daysack and began to circle the young woman. "Do you know what I am going to do with you?" He laughed ghoulishly as he spoke, all the while moving around the circumference of the summit, to her left.

Suddenly, from the far side of the hill, three other women appeared. Kris knew instantly that they were wolves; all were young females with swords drawn. They stared at him. "Well, well, what have we here?" he joked, "Looks like I am going to get *four times the fun* I was expecting today!"

Ruth turned and slowly brought her sword up. The three who had just joined them did not move. They stood there silently, swords by their sides. This was Ruth's fight. Kris moved the knife in a slashing motion in front of him; he stopped moving to the side and took a step forward. He held the knife up and motioned with his left hand, "Don't worry, little pup .... you will be smiling by the time I have finished with you," he chuckled as he spoke. Ruth stared at him.

"Amanda was my friend." She spoke softly, but he heard. He stopped; then smiled again.

"Well, I certainly enjoyed the last half an hour of her life. You should have heard the way she screamed!" He was baiting her. She did not move; he stepped closer. "Come on, then!" His body tensed up, then he jumped forward, thrusting the knife towards the centre of her body. The knife found nothing but air; she had jumped back, bringing her sword up in a double-handed grasp in front of her. He thrust again and the blades clashed; the two combatants circled each other. Arms moved, flexed and reacted; metal clashed on metal. One would jump forward in attack; the other would defend. The circling, attacking and defending continued.

Watching from afar, it would seem like two people dancing. Ruth's face remained focused, concentrating on her task; Kris's face twisted ghoulishly, taunting. His blade moved, twisted and sliced; Ruth's head jerked backwards, the blade just missing her face. Her sword came up, hilt first; Kris side-stepped, as the blade sliced into the gap where he had been. They twisted and turned and faced each other again, both weapons held up, defensively.

Then they stopped. Both suddenly were still... only the wind blew past them. Quiet descended over them all. A car horn sounded in the distance; birdsong came from nearby trees; life carried on. The two stared at each other. Then Ruth slowly raised her blade. Kris stepped to one side, and his right foot stepped backwards. He kept the large knife in his right hand and brought it close beside his hip; he extended his left arm, defensively. His eyes moved over the young wolf in front of him. She took a small step forward. The wind blew around them. His scent filled her nostrils; it was a stench; she hated him. She hated him for what he had done, for what he was, for what he wanted to do. He would not stop on his own - that much was clear, she must stop him.

His body tensed, then pounced. She moved to one side; his attack missed; then her blade found nothing but air, he was as fast as she had been warned. They circled each other; first he attacked, then she did. Her feet shuffled forward, and her blade came straight down; but was stopped. The clash of metal on metal echoed. The others did not move. Again, he struck; again, he missed. She launched strike after strike; each one fended off by his blade. They moved in circles. He stopped. She kept her defence up, the blade still firmly in both her hands.

"First blood to me," he boasted. She glanced at the slice in her right sleeve. He had cut the fabric, but not the flesh. She kept her composure, eyes staring back at the face of her enemy. She spotted his body tensing up again - he was getting ready to strike. Ruth jumped forward; her blade moved with speed. Kris leapt to one side; blade clashed with blade again. Kris spun around, raising his knife up, searching to find flesh; it found the space where her shoulder had been. She spun as well, turning inside his defensive stance and brought her blade around like a scythe.

Using all the force she could muster, she extended the half circle in front of her, and swung fully around, separating the head neatly from the shoulders. Kris's body paused then fell onto its knees, dropping the knife. then it collapsed to the dirt. The bloody head landed with a thud, bounced once, and rolled to a stop, eyes staring, unseeing, at the sky.

Ruth stood, still gripping the hilt of the sword in both hands. She felt tears welling up inside her and her throat became tight. The three others slowly walked over to her. They formed a small semi-circle around the lifeless body of Kris Martin. Ruth turned her sword around, so the tip touched the ground in front of her. Keeping both hands on the hilt, she went down onto one knee; the others followed her lead. She closed her eyes and bowed her head, as tears carved tracks down her cheeks.

"Sleep well, my friend, he can hurt you no longer."

Chapter 42

Cara-Marie was driving past the entrance to the site in Dromore. She looked over to the right; two uniformed police officers were standing guard. She glanced at the clock on her dashboard, it was ten minutes to six. She recognised the line of transit vans from M.I.T. Several people were walking back and forth. She was looking for a place to park. The line of vans nearly blocked the opposite side of the road and a small crowd gathered on the left at the entrance to a small housing estate. She drove on. She pulled in at an approach to a small field; the impatient silver Land Rover behind her wanted to get past. The engine roared as it accelerated away.

Cara-Marie looked out over the field; there were no livestock, so she took a gamble at leaving her car there. It did not take long for her to be walking at speed back up the hill. The small crowd was assembled at the far side of the road. She stepped around the first of the line of transit vans; someone in a white disposable forensic suit was walking towards her along the outside of the line of vehicles. Cara-Marie had to step around him as she passed. He did not speak. His face was covered with a mask, so only the eyes could be seen. She walked on.

When she got to the end of the line of vans, she was met by two police officers. She was about to start her introduction, hoping to gain access to the site, but one of them spoke first,

"Hello, Cara, what brings you down to these parts?" Cara-Marie paused for a second as she studied the face of the first police officer; the other said nothing. It took a second before she recognised him,

"Billy Banford! As I live and breathe!" Billy smiled and stepped forward, holding out his hand as he did so. It was warmly taken.

"Hiya Cara, it's good to see you," he replied as they released each other's grip. Billy turned slightly and introduced the other officer. "Cara, this is Alan Fair," she shook his hand.

"Hi," Alan said quietly.

"Alan, Cara is a journalist with the Coleraine Herald," Alan smiled politely. Cara-Marie looked at Billy.

"No need to say it like that, some of us are human, after all." They were both smiling as she spoke. "So, what are you doing down here?" she asked, "I haven't seen you since the Mountsandal murder." Billy straightened himself as she spoke.

"The suicide of that eastern European fella," Billy corrected, then looked at Alan. "Well, I moved from Coleraine station just after that," he looked back at her, "I've been in Lisburn since."

"And not looked back," Alan stated.

"Really? Wow! Any reason why?" she asked. She would use this polite conversation to get through some barriers. Then she would see if she could get past the line of blue and white police tape and onto the site.

"I am now in my last five years," Billy started, "so it's time to sort the rest of my life out," he was smiling as he spoke, "how are things back up the road?" He was asking about Coleraine, quickly changing the subject.

"Well," she shrugged, "things got a wee bit busier after what happened at Portstewart Strand at the New Year, so ...." she paused, "Coleraine is full of every conspiracy theorist and horror fan looking for things that are not there," they both laughed.

"I bet the local council are loving that!" Billy replied.

"Every hotel and bed & breakfast is almost always full; there are so many people coming to the town now..." Cara-Marie glanced to the side as another person in a white suit walked past, heading out towards the vans. Then she continued, "but, there are constant complaints from places like the golf clubs and caravan parks about all this lot walking around .... Oh, there is even a 'Werewolf Tour' you can take!" She smiled. Billy smiled back, but Alan's face did not move.

"I thought you believed in werewolves," Billy stated, she was about to answer but Alan cut her off.

"That's where I know you from; you are the journo that keeps doing the werewolf stories!" Alan suddenly became excited, Cara-Marie looked away, then back at him.

"Just trying to report the truth .... Speaking of which," she motioned with her right hand towards the large earth structure behind them, "what is happening here?" She wanted to steer the topic of conversation away from herself.

Both coppers turned to look behind them. There was a dark blue transit van that had been reversed in; the front of it was pointing back out of the closed gates. There was movement behind it, but she could not see much. From where she was, she could make out the white forensic tent erected on top of the hill. There were several figures moving about; everyone onsite was dressed in the same white disposable suits. They turned back towards her, glancing at each other before Billy spoke.

"We are just site security for the investigation team; you'll have to speak to one of them." It was a standard answer and she knew it. Billy would not say anything to her in front of the other police officer.

"Yes, no problem. Is there anyone available for comment?" she asked. Billy looked over at Alan, who nodded.

"Sure, I'll grab someone for you," Alan turned and walked through the swing gate and headed off towards the back of the van. Cara-Marie stared at Billy as he glanced around. No one could hear him now; he lowered his voice and stepped closer to her.

"It *is* that fella, Martin, the one they've been looking for!" he was almost whispering, her eyes widened.

"Wow!" she said out loud, "So, what happened to him?" she asked. Billy looked to either side, then continued in a quiet voice.

"You have not heard this from me..." She loved those words; she may not be able to quote the source, but it usually put her on the right track, and gave her direction regarding which questions to ask. "There was some sort of fight - he had his head chopped off!" Her mouth opened in disbelief.

"Really?" she exclaimed.

"Yeah, whoever did it put his head on a pole about three feet off the ground. The body was laid out in front of it like they had done some sort of ceremony." Cara-Marie was nearly drooling, as her mind pictured what he was describing. "Yeah, he ...." Billy was suddenly cut short, as Alan returned with someone in a white suit and face mask. As Alan started to introduce them, the woman pulled back the hood and deftly removed the face mask. She shook her head, revealing a long dark ponytail. The detective was not smiling, as Alan spoke,

"This is Detective Sergeant Wells, with the investigation team, and this is ...." Alan turned towards Cara-Marie who stepped forward and held out her hand. It wasn't taken by the stern-faced woman looking back at her.

"Hi, I am Cara-Marie McKenna, Coleraine Herald," Cara-Marie introduced herself but, judging from the austere glare, she knew she would get nothing from her. In less than five minutes, she was walking back to her car, having received nothing from the young detective, apart from 'A full statement will be released in due course'. She was not allowed onto the site... but she had got something from Billy.

A head on a pole... now, that was familiar! The images were racing through her mind so much she didn't realise rain had begun to fall. The car beeped and she opened the driver's door. She tossed her large handbag onto the passenger seat, along with the heavy outdoor jacket she'd been wearing. She jumped in and slammed the door. Several heads from the small crowd looked over at her; she had not meant to do that. She pulled out her phone and scrolled through the numbers. When it started ringing, she held it to her ear.

"What?" was how Kevin, the editor, answered.

"That is no way to answer the phone," she stated, and he sighed.

"Cara, what do you want, this time?" he sounded tired.

"I am just down in Dromore and got confirmation that the body is Kris Martin." She paused; there was silence down the phone. She waited for a few seconds more before continuing, "Okay, well this should interest you – I learned he was beheaded, then the head was placed on a pole, and his body was arranged in front of it!" She tried to hide her excitement and waited again. Kevin gave another sigh.

"Okay," he started, "write it up, quote your sources and put it in the dropbox," She rolled her eyes; that is exactly what she'd planned on doing. "Did you get any imagery?" he asked, his voice picking up slightly. She was disconcerted.

"No, I didn't. I could not get on site. I got a few from the cordon, on my phone," There was another pause before he spoke again.

"No problem, see you tomorrow." He ended the call and the phone went dead. She was annoyed. She was not sure why, but his reaction pissed her off. She would be giving him the best story he'd seen in a while. She looked over at the dwindling crowd starting to disperse; the rain probably had something to do with that. She secured the seatbelt, then started the engine.

It was not long before she was well on her way back to Coleraine. The rain was now only a light shower. She was going over what Billy told her. She thought about phoning Mark, but then dismissed it. No point in phoning Kyle or Tony - they were not police anymore, so she would get nothing from them. Then she had an idea. Her phone connected to the car's audio, and the ringing sound came through the speakers. It stopped with a single word.

"Hello," the accent was English.

"Lord Baskerville? This is Cara-Marie. We met in Coleraine a short time ago," she re-introduced herself, even though she was quite sure that he would remember her.

"Cara, yes, good evening. I hope things are well with you?" The sharpness of his accent was in distinct contrast to what she heard every day. "And please, call me Rupert."

"Okay, Rupert."

"There is a reason you are calling?" he got to it before she did.

"Yes," her eyes glanced up at the dark sky; the rain was slackening off. "I was wondering if you are free to have a meet and a chat." She was hopeful, "you will have heard what has happened today. I am just getting onto the M1; I should be passing Belfast in about twenty minutes." If anyone could make sense of what was going on, he could.

"Oh dear," he started, "I am afraid I am no longer in Belfast. I came home yesterday." She was disappointed, then annoyed, "I have not seen the news today as I am back on the estate, catching up with what has been happening here in my absence." She quickly went through what had occurred in Dromore. "Well, that all makes sense!" he stated, when she finished, she was confused again.

"Really? How?" she asked, slowing down for a lorry in front of her.

"Yes, this recently-turned Noc... what's his name?"

"Kris Martin," she replied.

"Yes, yes of course. Martin turns; it is not unheard of for the recently-turned to become psychotic. He killed the mate of the alpha and then, to prevent an all-out war, they serve him up to the wolves so they can exact their revenge .... Simple politics, my dear." Cara-Marie pulled her car into the outside lane and accelerated past the lorry.

"Yeah, that kind of makes sense," she said out loud, repeating what he had said. "But how do I prove it?" she asked. Rupert laughed before answering,

"You don't." Cara-Marie was confused again, "do you have any connection with the farm?" Rupert asked.

"I saw Foster the other night, but did not really get much from him," she stated.

"...and you won't, so don't try," Rupert advised, "a former police officer, and now pack alpha, will not give anything to a journalist about his pack being involved in murder. Do you know of anyone else?" he asked. She thought for a second.

"Well, sort of," she had not meant to say it out loud.

"Then, go to them, see if you can get any information from a different source. You won't get anything from Foster that he does not want you to know. It's a control thing - quite common with alphas, especially pack alphas," Rupert explained.

"Yes, that makes sense. I will try someone else. Thank you." She only had one other person she could try.

"Well, do not forget the invite over here still stands," Rupert sounded pleased with himself.

"Thank you, I will remember that" she smiled as she spoke, even though she had no intention of ever taking him up on the offer.

"Brilliant.... Well, happy hunting!"

"Oh, did you hear the police found the dog that was killing walkers in the Mourne mountains?" she asked.

"That was no dog," he stated.

"No, I didn't believe that either," she replied.

"What was reported on the news?" he asked. She paused, then spoke.

"They said it had been a large husky dog with some sort of bone disease that drove it insane. But it had been found dead, so everything is back to normal." she paused then spoke again, "but that howling was no normal dog!"

"Well, huskies do howl as a main form of communication, but I agree with you: the footage from the news report was no husky."

"So, what was it, then?" her voice lowered as she asked the question.

"It would only be a guess, but I would say that it was a stray from somewhere else. If it had been one of the An Rua, then they would have dealt with it sooner and a lot quieter. It would not have been allowed to do what it did."

"A stray?" she asked, as a sports car tore past her in the outside lane of the motorway.

"From another pack, yes," she felt her body react to what he was saying; she had not thought of that.

"There is more than one pack in Ireland?"

"Good lord, no, the An Rua would not allow that at all. It would have come from another pack, but it would be up to the An Rua to deal with it. They would've had to take it down, especially after losing four of their own to it. It's a matter of pack pride."

"How many packs are there?" she asked, without thinking. She looked into the darkness; the rain had almost stopped.

"The An Rua cover Ireland and parts of Scotland; the Iceni, most of Southern England, with the exception of the ones I have a problem with here. But I know they have nothing to do with main Garou culture. As for the rest around the world .... I am not sure."

"Around the world?" her question was almost a whisper, but he heard it.

"Yes, there are at least twenty packs, and they are just the ones I know of." Her mind raced again; this was far bigger than she had ever imagined.

"Thank you," again, it was only a whisper, and again, he heard it.

"No problem. Remember, you are always welcome to visit over here."

"Thank you, I may do that one day." She could almost hear him smiling down the phone, then the line went dead.

She drove on through the darkness and on up the M2 towards home. She was not sure how to make the approach to the farm, but she knew she would have to. "Over twenty!" she heard herself say out loud.

Chapter 43

The TV room of the lair was packed; they were furious! Alison looked around from where she was standing by the door; everyone was there. In the centre of the room, Maya was shouting, venting her fury at Kris's death. The news was received with anger and resentment. Sabine was the one who told them once they'd received confirmation.

"Why was he sent down there by himself?" Maya demanded; her hands were on her hips. Sabine turned to walk away; all eyes followed her.

"Because we had to."

"HAD TO? .... HAD TO??? .... WE DON'T 'HAVE TO' DO ANYTHING!" Maya screamed. Sabine stopped and looked back at her.

"He killed, then mutilated, the mate of their alpha. He did it publicly; he was caught on CCTV and the sapien police were looking for him. If they had found him, they would have found all of us .... plus," she paused, and turned to face the gathered crowd, "if we hadn't, that would have given them reason enough to fully mobilise...here in the north, and down south as well!" All was quiet, Sabine's gaze moved around the room. Every face she looked at, looked away. "And we are not yet strong enough to take them head on .... not quite." Sabine waited for a few seconds, then turned and walked towards the open door, where Alison was standing. Very few noticed Dani's arrival at the far side of the open door.

"He was *told* to go for the girl." Maya did not shout this time, but her voice was loud enough for everyone to hear; she was furious. Alison unfolded her arms and walked the few paces towards her.

"Yes, he was, but he was *told* to bring her here. Not kill her, not cut her hands off, or..." Alison looked around as she spoke. Several faces looked down, "or try and rape her. If he had done what he was told to do, we would have a top prize, and ...." she stopped and folded her arms again, "he would still be alive. But Sabine is right, ..." Maya turned away in disgust, as Alison continued speaking. "With the police looking for him, it would only be a matter of time before he was spotted by someone and the sapien police would have descended on us." Maya turned and burst out angrily,

"AND WHAT WOULD YOU KNOW? YOU DIDN'T KNOW HIM! YOUR NOT EVEN ONE OF US!" Maya was in a rage.

"I spent thirty years in the police; I have a fair idea of how they will react," Alison stared at her. Maya spun on her heels and turned away again. She muttered something that Alison did not hear, but all the faces around Maya suddenly started smiling. "Sorry, I didn't hear that," Alison raised her voice. Maya suddenly turned, screaming, as she lunged at Alison. Sabine turned as Alison's right foot stepped back; her body was now at an angle as Maya flew towards her. Alison's right hand was closed in a fist close to her chest, but her left was extended, with the palm held up in a 'stop' signal. Maya stopped a few feet in front of her and stared.

Sabine only saw the knife when it stopped. It hung motionless in the air, just a foot away from Alison's hand. There had been a gasp from the crowd, as no one had seen Maya throw it. Everyone stopped and stared.

Alison relaxed, reached forward, and took the knife like it had been sitting on a flat surface. Maya's eyes widened in shock. Alison dropped the knife on the floor, as if it had suddenly remembered what gravity was. Shock rippled through the room. Maya quickly went from shock back to anger. Her face contorted with rage, and her body tensed for the attack.

"I've had enough of your shit!" Maya jumped forward and let loose a flurry of kicks. Alison stepped back and used her arms in successive blocking motions from side to side, as Maya tried first two kicks with her right leg, then one with left. Then she spun on her left heel and swung her right leg around, aiming for Alison's head and upper torso. It missed. Alison ducked and, with lightning speed, rammed the palm of her right hand into the centre of Maya's chest, sending her flying backwards. Maya skidded along the floor and crashed into the base of the sofa along the far wall. She screamed - first in pain, then fury. She spun around and jumped onto her hands and feet. Her fingertips touched the ground, her left knee was outside her arm and her right one inside; she was readying for attack. She let out another scream and threw herself forward. This time, Alison stood her ground and let Maya get close. Maya threw a flurry of punches and attacks with her firsts and elbows; Alison defended with such speed; Sabine could barely make out her movements. A palm push sent Maya backwards. Alison crouched in a fighting stance.

Maya shook herself, reformed her fists and opened her mouth - her incisors were extending. "You're gonna die, bitch!" she shouted, lunging forward again. Yelps and cheers emitted from the crowd. Maya was the favourite. Another flurry of high kicks and punches were all deflected by Alison. Maya was full of rage; Alison's look was intense. Maya was repelled again and again. Sabine breathed in as Dani stepped forward. She was standing beside her, silently... but there was a small smile on her face. Maya spun and her legs were taken from under her; she hit the floor with a resounding 'thud'. The cheering was louder now. Alison stepped back as Maya jumped up again, this time with the knife in her right hand. Again, she threw it at Alison and again it stopped in mid- air, at Alison's command. Maya stared in disbelief as Alison raised her left hand and turned the knife around, pointing towards Maya. It was just there...suspended in space. The room fell silent.

"Never trust your life to a weapon," Alison stated. With that, the knife flew towards Maya, who twisted her body sharply, so the knife flew past her and bounced off the far wall. Maya screamed and threw her right fist towards Alison's face.

Everything suddenly slowed down for Sabine. She watched as Alison moved to one side, her right-hand catching Maya's extended wrist. She stepped back, pulling Maya's body forward. Maya slammed into Alison as if she'd hit a rock. She yelped. Alison turned abruptly, so Maya completely lost balance. Alison kept the turn going and, as Maya started to fall, Alison's left hand grabbed the back of her hair and pulled Maya's head backwards. They both landed on the floor, on their knees. Alison had complete control and Maya could do nothing except scream as Alison bit into her neck. It was over with one bite. Alison shoved Maya's struggling body forward as the blood spewed from her neck, Maya writhed on the floor while audible gasps filled the room. The cheering had stopped.

Alison stood up and stepped back. She slowly took out a tissue and started to wipe the blood from her face. She wore a determined look. Two of the group knelt at either side of the struggling Maya. It was a fatal wound; they all knew it. Maya's hands fought with the pulsating blood, as the jerking movements of her body began to slow. Words of comfort from the two on either side of her body did not concern Alison. She put the tissue away in her pocket and watched as Maya's body twitched. She made several gasps, fighting for breath; they slowed, then stopped. She was dead.

Alison looked around. No one met her eyes. The two who had been beside Maya stood up. There was silence in the room. Alison looked over at the shocked Sabine and smiling Dani. She looked at each face in the crowd. No one spoke. She turned and walked towards the doorway. Sabine moved out of her way; Alison flashed her a smile as she walked past. Dani just nodded at her and stepped forward.

"Right," she started, pointing at Maya's lifeless body. "I want that disposed of in the usual way, I want this place cleaned and gutted. We still have work to do tonight." She looked around, nodded, then walked back towards Sabine, who stopped her.

"What the hell just happened?" Sabine asked, as the rest of the room slowly filled with murmured conversation. Dani looked at her and shrugged.

"Alison just defended herself. Maya *was* going to kill her." Sabine reached out her hand and touched Dani's arm.

"No, I mean, *what just happened* with the knife? .... I've never seen anything like that before!" Sabine looked baffled. Dani smiled, raising her voice so everyone heard.

"She is a Valkyrie!"

"So?" Sabine was confused.

"Most Valkyries are telekinetic," Dani was smiling in her own superiority.

"What?" someone asked, she turned towards him,

"Telekinetic; it means they can move things with their minds." Dani looked back at Sabine, "I wonder what else she can do?"

"I have never seen that before," Sabine was in shock.

"Well, I have only heard, to be honest. She is the first real Valkyrie I've ever met," Dani grinned in excitement.

"But she still needs to feed, so she is one of us," Sabine stated. Dani looked over at her as Maya's body was lifted up.

"No, she doesn't." Sabine looked confused, so Dani continued. "That is just one way they kill. That is why she does not have a problem with ultraviolet light." Sabine thought for a moment, she lowered her voice and moved out of the way as the group shuffled past, carrying Maya.

"So, what else can she do?" Sabine repeated Dani's earlier statement. Dani looked around, then back at Sabine.

"I have no idea .... But I want to find out!" Sabine watched as Dani smiled and walked out the door. There was something else going on and she did not like it. It had been the American who'd introduced Alison to them all and brought her into the coven. So far, everything had gone through her; she knew about all the different plans and ideas but finding out that Alison was not all she seemed unnerved her. Sabine felt the phone in her pocket buzz with a text message.

ooooo

Mike was sitting in the hire car. The darkness of the night had closed in around him. He was in the small car park beside the pebble beach on the south coast of England, where he walked earlier. He found the small memorial with a Canadian Flag on it. It had been dedicated by a Canadian prime minister with a French name he had never heard of.

According to the inscription, these were the beaches that the Canadian Divisions had launched from, for the D-Day invasion in June 1944. He walked along the beach for over an hour before returning to his car. He had gone the required distance away from where he was studying before he could switch his phone on. Technical security was something they took very seriously. He was waiting for the call from Darren, but it was late. Mike decided he would wait until after he spoke with Darren before calling his wife. Darren had seemed keen to speak with him, so he assumed the call would take a while. He looked at the screen of his phone, then dropped it on the seat beside him. He looked around. He had done anti-surveillance before, but what they had been doing here was on a whole new level; the people teaching him were experts.

He looked around the carpark again; it was still empty. The lights of the Isle of Wight could be seen across the water. He hadn't been there yet but would certainly visit before he finished this course. His mind was wandering. The ringing phone brought him back to the present. He looked at the screen; it was a withheld number.

"Hello," his voice was almost a whisper.

"Hiya mucker, what about yea?" Darren's familiar accent made him smile.

"Hiya, yeah, I am good... you?" he asked, peering out into the darkness. He could see the boat lights out on the water, but his mind was not registering it; he was concentrating on what Darren was saying.

"Aye, have you seen the news over there?" Darren asked, Mike shifted his position.

"No, there is no TV here at all .... Why? What has happened?"

"Well," Darren started, "first of all, Sean's funeral is happening in two days' time. Can you get back for that?" Mike nodded, then answered.

"Yes, I have already checked with them, it's no problem."

"Good. I've emailed you the details."

"Great, what else is going on?"

"Well, remember Kris Martin?" Mike thought for a second.

"Got killed on New Year's Day walked out of the mortuary and went on a killing spree?"

"The very one!"

"What has he done now?" Mike asked.

"Killed the wrong girl, and got his head chopped off for his troubles."

"What?" That made Mike sit up.

"Remember Foster, from the deer farm?" Again, Mike paused; this was an open phone and he knew Darren would not say anything private over it.

"The ex-Foreign Legion guy, who was a copper in Coleraine?" Mike did not mention what they had found out about the farm.

"That's the one. Well, Martin attacked his girlfriend."

"Shit!"

"Yeah, cut her hands off, ...proper nasty stuff."

"What he did at that bungalow was also pretty gruesome," Mike stated.

"Yeah, it was, but this time, he really overstepped the mark. Do you know the Motte and Bailey site in Dromore?" Mike thought for a second then answered.

"Yeah, I do. We went there on a school trip, learning about Norman castles when I was about fourteen years old."

"Well, that is where he ended up," Darren explained.

"Was it..." Mike paused, thinking how he could phrase his next question without compromising what they knew, "the farm? Or someone else?"

"M.I.T. is looking at feuding drug gangs. They went after him for taking down one of their suppliers at the bungalow."

"Was it?"

"Apart from slicing his head off, there was not a mark on his body, whoever did it, knew what they were doing."

"Where did it happen?"

"On top of the Motte. His head was on a pole and body laid out like a crucifix."

"Is that where it happened, or was it transported there?" the detective in Mike was back.

"It happened there but it certainly wasn't a drug gang!" Mike smiled at Darren's answer.

"Yeah, they would have been in a street with pump-action shotguns, blowing holes in everything!" They both chuckled, imagining the scene.

"So, what else have your military friends found out?" Mike asked. Darren would not give anything away down an open phone. He chose the words of his question carefully.

"They are off ...." Darren stated.

"What?" asked Mike.

"They are off. They are going 'elsewhere in the world'." Darren did not have to say any more; Mike could guess they were off to Afghanistan; there would be no more input from them.

"Okay, so anything else with the Martin fella?" Mike asked.

"Yeah, he had help .... A lot of help," Darren stated.

"What do you mean?" Mike asked.

"The CCTV footage we got showed nearly twenty others with him. The young lass put up a hell of a fight, though."

"Any idea who they are? Have we identified them yet?" Mike asked.

"Nope. All totally new faces, nothing came up with the facial recognition software."

"Nothing?" Mike was surprised at that.

"Nope, not a thing! Whoever they are, they are not from around here!"

That got Mike thinking, "Are they from down south?" Mike was asking if these people were from the Irish Republic.

"Nope, nothing from them, either" Darren continued, "but I can tell you more when I see you," There was more to this than Darren could say. Mike understood.

"Sure, I will message you the flight details when I have them."

"Brilliant," Darren answered. "See you then!" With that, the line went dead. Mike relaxed and looked around again. His was still the only car in the carpark, the lights on the water still blinked and the lights of East Cowes glowed in the distance. The fact that there was one less serial killer was a good thing, but the way it had happened was not. It would have been better if the police had gotten to him first; there were so many unanswered questions about New Year's Day, and then the events at the bungalow. Mike stared into the darkness. He sighed and looked at the screen of his phone again. Scrolling through the numbers he stopped at his wife's name. He pressed the green button and held the phone to his ear, as it started ringing.

"Hi, Darling," he said, when the call was answered. "Could you do me a favour and book me a flight home for tomorrow? I have the details of Sean's funeral."

Chapter 44

Dermott was standing outside the farmhouse when the first of the cars pulled up. He glanced at his watch - it had just gone 4pm. Kyle opened the rear door and climbed out. He was wearing a black suit, white silk shirt and a black tie. Tony got out of the front passenger door and Tyler, the far side. Other cars moved past and parked. The minibuses were not far behind.

Everyone was dressed in black. He nodded at Kyle, who responded with a single nod, then walked straight past him without speaking. He extended his hand which Tony shook firmly.

"How did it go?" Dermott asked. Tony had stopped beside him, Tyler nodded and followed Kyle into the farmhouse.

"As funerals go," Tony replied, "badly." Dermott glanced around as everyone emerged from the cars, all dressed in black. There was a sombre mood over the farm, he looked back at Tony.

"How so?" he asked. Tony looked around, then at Dermott.

"Well, we got to Castlederg without a hitch, but that is where the problems started," Tony paused. "She did not have a lot of family left. In fact, there were only five of them." Dermott nodded, and Tony carried on, "We got stopped outside the church by a cousin. Her grandmother knew who we were, and they would not allow us inside for the service."

"What?" exclaimed Dermott, "Did Kyle not demand ...." He stopped himself, and Tony looked at him.

"He respected the families wishes. The grandmother hissed at us as she was going inside. The cousin had told the family we were a 'cult' and had brainwashed Amanda and taken her away from them. .... Everyone heard him."

"'Bet that got a reaction," Dermott stated.

"It did. Several of the younger ones were about to go for him; Kyle just held up his hand and stopped them."

"What did he say?" Dermott asked.

"Nothing, he did not say a thing. We all stood there. Then, when she was carried out of the church, we followed around to the side where the graveyard was."

"Was it a family plot?"

"Yes." Tony nodded, "She had ancestors there going back several generations."

"And her family? Do they know about us?" Dermott asked.

"Some do, yes." His phone in his pocket buzzed, "The grandmother, definitely; the cousin, I would say, probably; as for the others, I am not sure." Dermott nodded.

"Okay. How is he?" Dermott asked.

"Seemed okay, hardly spoke on the way there and didn't say a word on the way back."

"Did we pay for the entire thing?" Dermott asked. Tony nodded. "'Any press there?" Dermott continued; Tony shook his head. A horn sounded as the first of the minibuses entered the yard from the lane. "Right," stated Dermott, "I have work to do." The two shook hands again.

Dermott walked over to where the vans were parking and Tony walked into the farmhouse. The front room was warm. There had been a fire in the fireplace, but it was out now. The room was tidy and quiet. Sounds of movement came from the kitchen and Tony walked towards it. Tyler was busying herself with the kettle, and there was a large metal teapot on the stove. The smell of toasting bread filled his nostrils. She looked over at him.

"'Fancy a cuppa?" she asked, Tony smiled and nodded. She turned towards the tap on the sink, as he took off his jacket and hung it over the back of a chair beside the kitchen table.

"I take it he's upstairs?" he asked, as he sat down, she looked at him again.

"Yeah, he'll probably be there for a while."

"It figures, I suppose." Tony made himself comfortable as she readied two mugs and a small plate of biscuits. He took out his phone and read the message. He stared at the screen, thought for a second, then typed in a reply. As he pressed 'send', Tyler placed the plate of biscuits and a mug in front of him. "Thanks," he said. She sat down opposite him.

"So," she said. Tony looked up.

"So, what?" he asked.

"So, what is next?" she asked. Tony peered into the hot liquid, then up at her.

"I think we have dealt with quite enough, so far. Don't you?"

"Yes, but there is something else going on." The harsh look was back on her face. Tony rested the mug on the table.

"What do you think is going on?"

"Well, the rabid was not here by accident."

"No, no she wasn't."

"Did Paul show you what was on that phone?" she asked. Tony shook his head. "The pictures on her phone showed a whole load of Nocs we didn't know about, and ...." Tony sat back in the chair as she continued, "they are very well-armed."

"What did you see?" he asked. Her eyebrows shot up.

"What did I see?" she reacted. "Well for starters, the group that were standing around all looked like they knew what they were doing with their weapons; they've been trained." Tyler was starting to get annoyed; Tony did not speak. "Plus, look at the weapons! Remington eight-seventy pump-action shotguns, the rifles looked like Colt M-16s; they all had Sig Sauer pistols," Tyler stared at him, intently. "Tony, that is military firepower ... You cannot get any of that in a shagging shop. Someone got all that for them, and they got it for a reason." Tony sat forward.

"Yeah, I agree, plus, we don't know anyone in those pictures; they have all come from somewhere else."

"And Martin's phone was in his car. From that, we found out they were the ones who brought the rabid over here. The text messages indicated it was 'Sabine' who organised it." The anger was back on her face.

"So, what should we do?" Tony asked.

She had spotted his reaction at the mention of the name, Sabine. "We need to take her down. She is obviously organising and leading them. I hear you know her from before," she lowered her voice when she asked the question. He looked up at her.

"Yeah, a long time ago." Tyler nodded. The question made him uncomfortable, and he changed the topic. "But what should we do?" Tony repeated his question.

"Gather a full assault team. We need to take them down before they hit us."

"Not a chance in hell!" the voice came from the far side of the door to the living room. It opened and Paul walked in. They both turned to face him. Paul Hawkins had not been at the funeral. He was wearing green rubber boots covered in mud, dirty jeans, and a dark-coloured outdoor jacket with a woollen jumper underneath. He had been outside most of the day. Tony pushed his chair back, smiled and held out his hand. Paul stepped forward and took the firm handshake with both hands. He smiled back. "Hey Tony," as they released the grip, Tyler smiled and nodded towards him. "Hiya Tyler, where is he now?"

"Upstairs. He'll probably be there for a while." Paul stopped by the table; Tony remained standing beside him. Paul nodded and looked towards the two mugs on the table.

"Is there a pot of tea on?" he asked, with a smile on his face. Tyler returned the smile,

"The kettle has not long boiled. If you'd like one, you can help yourself." Tony let out a short chuckle at her retort. Paul looked at Tony.

"Guess I will, then." He headed over towards the kettle, Tony retook his seat.

"So, 'not a chance in hell', then?" Tony repeated.

"Connor would never allow it," Paul replied, without turning around. He reached up and lifted a large mug from the cupboard and began to prepare his tea.

""They didn't just kill Amanda; they mutilated her," Tyler pointed out, turning in her chair.

"And they gave us the Noc who did it, so we could deal with him," Paul still did not turn around, "and we did."

"We've discovered a group of them that we did not know anything about," stated Tony.

"A fact which Dermott is furious about," Paul poured the tea into the mug.

"And they are very well armed, obviously planning to use those weapons shortly!" Tyler was staring at Paul as he turned around. He held the mug in one hand and stirred with the other. He did not look phased at all. He tossed the teaspoon in the empty sink. It landed with a clatter. Paul took a taste before he took the chair at the end of the table. "We should push for a ruling!" she stated.

"The south sees this just as a Noc skirmish, nothing more. Therefore, council members are not needed at this time."

"So, we do nothing?" She was getting angry again. Paul smiled.

"On the contrary. We put all our resources into finding out exactly what this lot are up to. We put names to every single face; we gather an inventory of all their weapons... Once we know all that ..." Paul drank from the mug.

"What?" Tony asked as he sat forward, placing his arms on the table. "What do we do once we know all that?" Paul relaxed, smiled and put his mug on the table.

"We stop them! We 'defend these lands, not govern them'. Never forget that." Tony and Tyler looked at each other, then at Paul. "We don't yet know where their lair is; nor its layout;" They were watching him, "we don't fully know their strength; or even why they are here... It would be wise to find that all out first." Tony nodded in agreement. They were all silently contemplative.

Tyler agreed but was of the opinion they should act fast to bring down the Nocs as they are discovered; before they can become stronger. Tony agreed with Paul's more deliberate approach of analysing all the information, before forming and carrying out the plan. After several minutes of internal reflection, Paul looked towards Tyler, "Oh, have you seen what he's done with the third bedroom upstairs?"

"The wee one that was the storeroom?" Tony asked.

"Go have a look." Paul grinned.

"Okay," Tyler said as she stood up, pushing back her chair. She left the mug on the table and walked around behind Paul, heading towards the stairs. Tony stood up,

"I'll have a look, as well," and he trotted up the stairs after Tyler. They walked past the spare room where she was staying. She opened the door to the smallest of the three bedrooms and walked in, Tony following close behind. They stopped just inside the room. It contained a single bed pushed up against the wall on the left side. There was a set of drawers opposite, made of dark stained wood. On top of it were two featureless manikin heads - one wearing a white peaked hat, and the other, a green beret. The cap badge was over the right eye and it was pulled down over the left side of the head. Where the white hat was in pristine condition, the beret was old and worn, having been well-used. Directly above the busts was a large wooden plaque with a background of green felt and a metal emblem in the centre. The rest of the walls were covered with smaller plaques and framed pictures, but the large plaque was obviously in a place of honour. Most of the pictures were of groups of soldiers, some in parade dress, others, in camouflage with various weapons. It was all very impressive.

"What is that?" Tyler asked pointing to the large plaque.

"It is two ReP's cap-badge."

"What?"

"Second Foreign Parachute Regiment of the French Foreign Legion," Tony explained, Tyler stepped forward and studied the pictures closer.

"Wow!" she said. Tony moved to the opposite wall. He was looking at a photograph of three soldiers, all wearing parachutes and reserves, one of whom was Kyle.

"They were about to do a jump with the Americans," he said, pointing towards the photo.

"How can you tell?" she asked.

"They have American parachutes on... plus, the background looks like Fort Bragg," he answered. Tyler moved closer to a photo of a sunset. It had been taken on a mountainside; there were trees to one side and the rugged ground fell away down to a clear blue body of water.

"I wonder where this is?" she asked.

"They are Cedar trees," Kyle said from the doorway, "in Lebanon." They turned towards him. He was still wearing the black trousers and white shirt, but he had taken off his tie and jacket. He smiled. Tony looked back at the other picture.

"Is this Bragg?" he asked. Kyle walked forward until he was standing between them.

"We did an exchange with the Eighty-Second Airborne. That's where I got my US wings."

"And Lebanon?" Tyler asked.

"I did two UN tours there," she nodded and looked over the other photographs.

"Impressive," Tony said.

"What is happening here?" Tyler asked, as she stopped at another photo. Kyle walked over and looked where she was pointing. The picture was of a group of heavily camouflaged soldiers; Kyle was at one side. Most of them held the French-made Famas rifle, but he was holding a longer weapon with a scope attached. Their faces were all covered in different shades of green. At the far side of the group was a large soldier carrying a different machine gun, one that she did not recognise. The faces were a mix of races: white, black, Hispanic, Asian... Kyle pointed them all out.

"This was an operation in Central Africa. We were the assault team."

"What happened?" she asked. Kyle spoke while staring straight at the picture.

"Well, they grabbed four French UN workers - two husband and wife teams - and demanded a ransom." Kyle looked over at Tyler, and continued, "They emailed family members video footage of them being tortured." He looked back at the picture, then shrugged, "We went in, took down all the bad guys and got three of the hostages out." Tony walked up behind them.

"What happened to the fourth?" Tony asked, and Kyle glanced over at him.

"The wife of one of them was ...." he looked back at the picture, "already dead." Kyle tapped a face on the picture. "That is Ian Kojima," he looked back at Tony again, "He's the Japanese guy who taught us sword fighting," he smiled and moved along the photographs.

"Ian? That isn't a very Japanese name," Tyler said.

"It was his nom de guerre. Everyone who joins the Legion gets one."

"What was yours?" she asked. Kyle looked at her and smiled.

"Kevin Fitzgerald." He looked away again, "The recruiter thought it sounded more Irish than Foster." Kyle smiled at the memory.

"So, how come this guy got Ian?" Tony asked.

"Because they could not pronounce his real first name," Kyle almost laughed. He looked around the room, then at them. "Anyway, I am hungry... anyone fancy something to eat?" It was a question meant to end the current conversation. He walked past them and headed out of the room. They heard his footsteps on the stairs. Tony looked at Tyler,

"That's the first time I've seen him smile in days."

"Yeah, he's not had much to smile about, lately."

"No, he hasn't," Tony said softly, Tyler turned and slapped his shoulder.

"Right! Well, let's do what the man says. I am getting hungry, as well." She smiled and headed to the door. Tony listened to her going downstairs. He looked around the room. His eyes picked out faces, people, soldiers. He did not know them, but he recognised them. How many similar pictures was he in, doing exactly the same as they were? The weapons, the uniforms, the backgrounds were different, but the proud smiles were the same. For a moment Tony smiled, then whispered the only word that was appropriate.

"Airborne."

Chapter 45

Mike was walking along the gravel pathway that led down the far side of the graveyard. He looked back at the plot still surrounded by people. Sean's wife was calmer now. She was almost hysterical last night, and Chief Anderson hadn't helped. Mike was furious at what he had come out with in front of her. The police piper walked past and nodded. Mike did not know him personally but his version of 'Flowers of the Forest' seemed to hit the right mark. Mike slowed to a stop where the path turned sharply to the left. Sean did not have much family. Mike had not seen his children in quite a while; he was amazed at how much they'd changed. 'Road Traffic Collision' was the term everyone used. No one would say *suicide*, even though that was plainly what it was.

Mike was angry at himself for not picking up on what Sean had been saying. He was angry because he knew he could have done more for his friend. If he'd died on duty, there would have been a long line of senior police officers and politicians making sure they were seen on TV but, because Sean was an ex-officer and had taken his own life, none of them wanted anything to do with it. Mike was furious.

Mike's wife, Joanne, had been at the service in the church, but they had decided it was best if she did not go to the graveside. There were a few members of the press outside. All the team was there. Mike managed to dodge most of their questions about what he was now doing. Darren Forrester was there as well; he would jump in when the questions got too precise. Mike looked at the scene surrounding him. The path led down to the single road that opened to the carpark. Several people in dark suits milled about in twos and threes. The single road split the two sides of the Lisburn cemetery. They were in the 'new side'. The original graveyard was on the far side of the main road. It was full.

Sean had purchased a new plot for his family. Mike had no idea when he did that - it was not the type of thing you discussed. His wife managed to locate all his paperwork for the arrangements. His wish was that no one be in uniform, except him. In the house, Sean laid in the open coffin, wearing his dress uniform with his medals. Sean had looked at peace. Mike tried but could not stop the tears when he first saw his friend. He stood now, at the graveside, staring but not seeing anything. The wind blew past; he did not notice the chill. The trees were bare and swayed from side to side, but he did not see. There was morning birdsong, but he could not hear.

"Mike!" the voice catapulted him back into the present. He blinked as if he was waking up and looked towards the voice to see a man walking towards him. Mike smiled at the familiar face.

"Eddie," he said, shaking Eddie Cargill's hand.

"Sorry I did not get a chance to chat with you, earlier," Eddie explained.

"No problems," Mike replied.

"Sad time," Eddie looked down at the ground.

"Yes, it is." There was a moment of silence between them.

"I would never have imagined ...." Eddie stopped himself from saying the word. Mike looked at his friend, his own eyes welling up. Redirecting the conversation, he asked,

"How are things with you and the team?" He looked away.

"Mostly," Eddie started, "since the end of January, nearly all the team have been moved; I mean, we have been scattered," he looked at Mike and added "I'm starting to think it is deliberate."

"It probably is," Mike stated, "who is in charge now?"

"The newly promoted Inspector Pelan."

"Pelan? 'Used to be in Armagh?" Mike asked, as Eddie looked over at him.

"The very one, she certainly made her presence felt from the very beginning."

"How?" Mike asked.

"Well, Chief Anderson walked in with her in tow and demanded everyone stop what they were doing and gather together for a briefing."

"Nothing unusual about that," Mike pointed out.

"No, but when they walked into the boss's office, she dropped her coat onto the desk then stood there and started laying down the law!"

"Again, there's nothing unusual about that. It is common for a new boss, especially a recently promoted one, to want to make their mark." Eddie tilted his head slightly,

"Aye, I suppose."

"What did she say?" Mike was curious now, and Eddie responded,

"I'm surprised you don't already know." There was a small smile on his face.

"And why would I already know?"

"I thought the 'all-knowing, all-seeing' Special Branch knew everything!" The two of them shared a laugh.

"Yeah, I wish...but I am not Branch, yet" he stated.

"So, what are you doing?" Eddie lowered his voice. Mike looked at him, then glanced around. "Training,"

"What for?" Mike smiled at Eddie's fast response; he was a detective, after all.

"Training with MI5 and MI6; but it is just that... training." Eddie nodded; he would not ask for any details, Mike returned to the previous conversation,

"So, tell me about your new Inspector's first day."

"She started off by tearing into us: sloppy; poor crime scene technique," Eddie paused and looked him in the eye, "You can guess the rest." Mike could. "Then she went off about the nickname: 'You will NEVER refer to yourselves as the 'werewolf squad', ever again! That stops NOW!'" he mimicked.

"Was that it?" Mike asked.

"No," Eddie replied, "she went on for nearly twenty minutes with the Chief standing behind her nodding all the way through it." Mike could picture the scene. "She does all the briefings and all the public addresses; any contact outside of the team goes through her." Eddie and Mike shared a knowing look. "She made all that very clear. The following day, the first of the moves came."

"Who are the sergeants?" Mike asked.

"Only got one, so far. Sergeant Michelle Keyes," Eddie said resentfully, Mike thought for a second before he could put a face to the name.

"Only ever met her on a training weekend up at Magilligan a few years ago, she seemed okay. What are they like?" he asked.

"It has become very apparent that if you are male and a detective, you will not be getting promoted. Our new Inspector made it clear she is going to redress the lack of senior female detectives. The four she has brought in are all women."

"'Nothing wrong with that," Mike stated.

"No, there isn't, but when you are told that, there is no point in even putting in for promotion if you are male," Eddie looked around himself before he continued, "there is something wrong with that!"

"Have you completed your sergeants' course, yet?" Mike asked. Eddie looked at him, then shook his head. "Well then," Mike looked away as he continued, "she cannot stop you doing the course and, if another vacancy comes up in another team, she cannot stop you applying for the post. In fact, she has to support you - blocking promotion on account of your gender is illegal." Eddie looked at him.

"I miss working for you." The two men shared a look and smiled. "What did you think of the Chief's little speech this morning about how to behave in front of the press?" Eddie asked.

"I didn't hear it," Mike spoke quietly.

"Really, I thought ...." Eddie did not finish what he was saying, Mike looked him in the eye, then looked back up the path they had come down. Mike was telling him to look back up that way. Eddie turned and saw Chief Anderson walking towards them. With him, was a woman in a pressed black suit. They stopped when they reached the two men. Chief Anderson spoke first,

"Detective Sergeant Dear, this is Detective Inspector Pelan." No hands were offered in greeting. Mike nodded but did not speak.

"Sergeant Dear," the Inspector addressed him, keeping her hands behind her back, "let me start by saying congratulations on the Henderson case last year. I followed that closely."

"Really?" Mike's eyebrows raised. "Why? Did you know him?" he asked, Eddie shuffled where he was, obviously uncomfortable.

"Yes," she started, "I was in uniform in that part of Belfast. I got to know him and his cohorts quite well, but we were unable to get anything on them."

"Thank you, but it was not just me; it was a team effort," Mike replied. There was a pause. The atmosphere had become tense since they arrived. Mike watched as the two of them shared a glance. The Chief had his little prodigy, and he was going to mould this one into what he wanted. "I wasn't aware you knew Sean." Mike stated, expectantly. He was really asking 'why are you here?' and everyone knew it.

"You had met him before, hadn't you?" the Chief interjected, she nodded once.

"Yes, we met at the training college when we hosted the Israelis a few years ago," she paused, then looked at Mike directly. "My condolences... I understand the two of you were close." Mike could feel anger rising inside him, and he looked around before he spoke again. More of the team members were slowly making their way down the path towards them.

"Thank you. Yes, we were a good team." Mike was about to say something else, but the Chief cut him off,

"Yes, well, it is unfortunate things ended the way they did."

"WHAT?" Mike had raised his voice. "What is that supposed to mean?" His volume and his anger were both rising.

"Detective, do I need to remind you that you are speaking to a Chief Inspector?" the Chief pointed at him with one finger of his right hand.

"I want to know what you mean by 'the way it ended'," Mike demanded. The Chief frowned in annoyance.

"Do *NOT* take that tone with me, Detective."

"I want to know what you meant by what you just said!" Mike was furious now. Eddie had taken a step back. Inspector Pelan raised her hands, trying to come between them.

"Gentlemen, please," she lowered her voice. It did not do any good.

"What I meant was that Mr Parrish was ill, but that is no excuse for breaking the rules on talking to the press."

"WHAT?" Mike's shout was heard across the graveyard. "He wasn't *ill*; nor, by the way, was he medically retired." Mike's right hand pointed towards the Chief, "He completed thirty years of exemplary service. Plus, he was no longer in the service, so there were 'no rules to break', and if you had read the transcript of that interview, you would know he did not say anything at all to reflect poorly on you or the department!"

"DETECTIVE!" the Chief straightened up, "I will not tell you again. DO NOT take that tone with me!" Eddie moved and turned so his back was to the Chief and the Inspector,

"Mike, this isn't solving anything." He had lowered his voice, but the Chief continued,

"He obviously was medically unfit ...."

"HOW CAN YOU SAY THAT?" Mike shouted at him.

"WE DON'T INVESTIGATE MYTHICAL CREATURES!" the Chief shouted back. Eddie placed his left hand on the centre of Mike's chest; he wasn't exactly pushing him away, but he did use pressure.

"We were not investigating mythical creatures," Mike lowered his volume, but not his tone.

"Gentlemen, please," the Inspector said, as the first of the team came alongside of them.

"It is no surprise, then, that he took the cheap way out when he realized he ...." The Chief had just finished the word as Mike's fist landed square in his face. No one saw him move; no one could have stopped him. The passing team broke up the scuffle, quietly and efficiently, but they had attracted the attention of everyone in the graveyard.

Standing beside one of the cars, Cara Marie was holding her new phone up and looking at the screen. She was dressed for the funeral and had kept the phone in her pocket through the service and the committal. She had not expected this! The red dot at the bottom of the screen indicated she was still recording. She had heard the start of the argument and had recorded most of it. She was far enough away for them not to notice her, but the zoom feature of her new phone was better than she'd expected it to be. She stared at the screen as the two groups of people separated the shouting men. She had a smug smile on her face.

"Excuse me," the voice came from the older man walking towards her. He was dressed in a black suit with matching plain black tie. His sliver hair was neatly brushed back. Cara Marie knew by his demeanour that he was with the police. She looked at him. He recognised her as a journalist.

"Yes?" she replied. He was reaching out with his right hand, eyeing the phone. She backed up as he closed the distance between them.

"This is a funeral. Can you please show some dignity to the grieving relatives?" He continued towards her, and she tapped the red dot, then pushed the phone into the pocket of her coat.

"Yes, of course," she said, apologetically. He lowered his arm and stopped only a few feet away. The commotion grabbed his attention. "I am terribly sorry," she said, before turning and walking around the parked cars towards her own. She would look at the footage in detail later. She climbed into her car, then slowly navigated her way around the other cars and the groups of black-garbed mourners. The car made its way up the incline and through the ornate metal gates attached to red brick pillars on either side of the entrance. She pressed a button on the audio in the dashboard and waited for the traffic to clear and her phone to link up. The car moved forward, turning left. She accelerated and caught up to the van ahead of her, glancing over at the entrance to the main graveyard as she passed. The sound of ringing blared through the audio. A male voice answered,

"Coleraine Herald."

"Mark!" She slowed at the traffic lights at the bottom of the road.

"Oh, hiya Cara," he replied. "I see the assassins have failed again!"

"Yeah, you really should try harder." She smiled; he seemed in a good mood.

"So, how did it go?"

"As funerals go, okay, but the fight at the end was pretty good." There was a laugh down the phone. Her car moved off and she turned right just past the bridge.

"When my uncle was buried, there was almost a mass brawl outside the church hall," Mark was saying. She could picture the scene. He carried on, "So, did you get anything at all?" he asked.

"Yeah, I confirmed that Parrish was not medically retired and was not ill, as Chief Anderson had said. Plus," she paused, moving over into the next lane. She looked up at the road sign that directed her back towards the motorway.

"Plus, what?" Mark asked.

"Plus, the fight was between none other than Mike Dear and the aforementioned Chief Inspector!" She smiled, triumphantly.

"Did you see it?"

"I not only saw it, I recorded it on my phone!" There was a moment of silence.

"Cara,"

"Yes,"

"I don't care what everyone else says about you .... I like you." She laughed.

"Well, I don't like you!" and he laughed with her.

"Yeah, you do - everyone likes me!" That made her eyebrows raise.

"Really? Well, I can think of at least one person ...." The phone went silent. Cara-Marie was turning onto the on ramp of the motorway. She had not asked him about his pregnant ex-girlfriend in a while, and it was a subject he had not raised. She instantly regretted her retort.

"If you mean Kevin, he doesn't like you either." It was a good well-deflected response.

"Kevin does like me," she insisted.

"What? The way you two argue?" Mark stated, "I don't think so."

"We don't argue!" she responded.

"Err, yeah you do."

"No, we don't; it isn't arguing."

"What is it, then?"

"I am just explaining why I am right." She heard another short chuckle from him, then she accelerated into the faster lane.

"Where are you now?" Mark asked.

"Just got onto the M1 at Lisburn. I'm heading back there now," she explained.

"Okay, see you soon." Mark hung up before she could say anymore. Yes, the ex-girlfriend comment had stung him, but he was excited to see the footage she had of the fight. It would make more of a story than the funeral. She would write it up, Mark would select some stills from it, then she would submit it into the dropbox. That should keep the editor busy and off her back for a while. She had another contact to pursue.

Chapter 46

Tony started the car; he had not felt this good in ages. Pulling away from the front of his house, he could not help but look in the rear-view mirror. Eyes front, he pulled out onto the Ballymacrea road. There was no other traffic. The road dipped and rose with the contours of the hills; he loved living here. There wasn't a cloud in the sky. It was going to get colder tonight, but he didn't mind; at least the storm had passed.

Beyond the main junction, the traffic was heavier. He watched the cars and vans drive past. His mind wandered. For the first time in months, he was happy; glad he was out of the police force. Things seemed to be going well at the farm; he was glad his family was less stressed about what happened last year. He remembered their astonishment when he told them they were all targeted by the 'eastern European gang' because he had become a thorn in their side. That was all he'd disclosed. They could never have accepted the truth: that a pack of Garou had arrived from Latvia and targeted him as part of a larger plan to take over the north. None of Karen's family knew what he really was. He liked that, and he intended it to continue.

A car shot past at speed, much faster than the speed limit... but he wasn't in the police force anymore. A small smile spread across his face as he watched the car disappear over the hill. A white van drove by, heading down the hill. There was a small hatchback driving the other way. He only caught a side view of her face; it was just a glance as the hatchback sped by. Recognition jolted him. He looked both ways, then threw the car into first gear. The hatchback was already out of sight. His car shot forward, turning in the same direction. Using the controls on his steering wheel, he scrolled through the numbers and made a call. He fought to get past the infuriating driver in front of him. A gap in the traffic coming in the opposite direction opened up and he gunned the car; power surged from the engine and he manoeuvred around and into the open road. The car filled with the sound of a ringing tone. The road curved to the left as the ringing stopped and a male voice spoke,

"Hello."

"KYLE!" he shouted, feeling his heart rate quicken.

"Tony, I..."

"Shut up and listen! I'VE FOUND HER!" Tony shouted at the car audio.

"What? Found who?" Kyle's voice replied.

"Alison. Alison Wallace. I've found her!" On either side, the road was bordered by boundary hedges, with occasional breaks. His car slowed behind another car. More traffic was coming in the opposite direction. The road curved slowly to the right; the break in the hedge on his left revealed a view of the countryside. This time, he had no interest in it. He only had one focus, and this slow driver in front was not helping.

"What? Where?"

"Driving away from Portrush along the Ballybogy Road."

"Where is she going?"

"I have no idea, but I intend to find out."

"Tony!" Kyle's tone had changed.

"Yes?" he asked.

"Follow her, but do not try and tackle her alone, I will get Dermott to mobilise a team."

"No time!" Tony responded. Another gap in the traffic appeared and he took it. The engine roared as he accelerated past. She was out of sight. He dropped the car down a gear; power surged through the engine as it accelerated up the road. Cars passed in a flash going the other way. He controlled the car around corners, going as fast as safely possible. Power was nothing without control. There was a large road sign on his left. The road carried on towards Ballymoney. There was a left turn coming up that went back to Coleraine; the right turn went to Bushmills. "Of course!" he exclaimed. He now knew where she was going. "Kyle!" he shouted.

"What?" Kyle's voice boomed from the audio.

"She's going back to her house!" Tony slowed the car down and took the right angle turn onto the quiet road heading towards Bushmills.

"What makes you think ...." Kyle stopped himself. There was noise in the background; Kyle was outside. "Okay, we will meet you there," and he ended the call. Tony turned onto the Priestland road and opened-up the car engine again, surging forward. The country road was empty, and he was soon slowing down to enter the small town. There was traffic about, but not much. It still annoyed him, though, as it was slowing him down.

It would be several minutes before he was turning into the lane that led up to the small house where she used to live. He slowed the car down, his eyes searching for her. Her car was parked to the left of the house. As he approached it, he slowed down to a crawl, reaching the top of the lane. His right hand was on the steering wheel as his left hand released the seat belt. He took in every detail of the house. It looked like nobody was home. He turned and stopped the car alongside the hedgerow. Slowly, he opened the door. His movements were quiet and deliberate. He got out.

Closing the door softly, he reached under his shirt with his right hand and felt the comforting grip of the pistol. He moved swiftly but stealthily; the way he'd been taught as an Airborne soldier. He moved past the windows looking in for any movement; there was none. the drapes covered the inside of the windows so he could not see anything beyond. His foot placement was deliberate; his fingertips traced a line along the wall of the house as he made his way around the right-hand side. He quickly scanned along the hedgerow that separated the grounds of the house from the fields. She was not there. He came to the corner at the rear of the house and stopped. He pressed his back against the wall and peered around the corner. The rear of the house was clear. He looked over the surrounding area and could see nothing. He moved along the back of the house, lowering himself under the windows so he would not be observed from inside. Silently, he approached the back door. He withdrew his pistol, raised his left hand and tried the door handle. It moved; there was a click. He opened it an inch. He moved his hand away from the handle and brought the pistol up, so it was central to his body. Lowering himself on to one knee, he gently pushed the door. It moved slowly, swinging inward. His right elbow was bent, and he gripped the pistol firmly, pointing it down the empty hallway. His eyes took in every detail; there was no movement from inside the house. Noiselessly, he raised himself and entered. Then he stopped. He slowed his breathing as the rest of his senses concentrated on every minute detail. There was danger here. He started to move again but stopped abruptly. He turned his head slowly to his right... and saw her.

She was at the far corner of the room. He looked directly into her right eye and saw the concentration there. She had him in perfect sight with the pistol she was aiming at him. The blade foresight was in the middle of the notched rear sight; she stood sideways to him, so her silhouette was reduced. She had a perfect aim and was less than ten feet away. She could not miss; she had him.

"Slowly, ... with your left hand, lay it on the ground," she said quietly. He nodded once. The only part of him that moved was his left hand...slowly, deliberately. Once his pistol was on the floor, he straightened up. "Both hands, palms up on top of your head." Again, it was just a whisper. He did as she instructed. "Stand up and take two steps backwards." He looked straight ahead, down the hallway. He silently cursed himself. How could he have missed her?

"Alison," he said her name out loud, but kept looking forward. Then he looked over at her. "Alison," he repeated, but quieter this time. Her aim was still true.

"What?" There was annoyance in her voice, he was looking at her.

"I don't get it," he stated.

"Get what?" she asked, "Why I'm pointing a gun at an armed intruder? Sounds like the 'right to self-defence' to me."

"Well, that could be argued in court," he paused, "but no," he looked back into the house again. "I don't get how you can move around in daylight," she relaxed her stance.

"What do you mean by that?" she asked, he was looking straight at her.

"I saw the footage from the car park at Mussenden Temple." She lowered her weapon, he lowered his arms and turned to face her.

"What footage?" She looked at him sternly.

"The SAS had subterranean surveillance on the carpark. You obviously know they took down the last of the Latvians at the temple that night. We all saw what you did to the girl, Yelina." Alison did not move; she just stared at him. "How long have you been a Noc?" he asked. A smile spread across her face.

"I'm not," she replied.

"I saw what you did; only the Noctrailis feed like that!" she watched his body tense up.

"I wasn't feeding; I don't need to," she took a single step towards him. He did the same, closing the distance between them to a few feet. "Tony, I have no quarrel with you, personally."

"I don't get it?" he asked.

"What is there to get?"

"Don't play me for dumb!" Tony was getting angry, she smirked.

"Would you rather I throw a stick for you and shout FETCH?" She was letting him know that she knew what he was. Tony jumped towards her. She stepped back and brought the pistol up again. The palm of his right hand slapped the inside of her wrist, while his left hand slapped the back of her hand, sending the pistol flying off to his right. It clattered on the floor. He went to grab her wrist, but she was already ducking and turning away from his grasp. She pushed the palm of her right hand into the centre of his chest, sending him flying backwards. He landed hard on his back. Pain shot through his body. He instinctively rolled over to his right, just as her foot slammed down right where he had been. Tony sprung up and leapt towards her with a flurry of kicks and punches, the speed of which would normally defeat anyone. But Alison was not just anyone. She stepped back, blocking each kick and punch in turn, and responded with high kicks of her own. They danced backwards and forwards: punches blocked, kicks ducked; bodies attacked and defended. They moved out the door and around the rear of the house. Her fist struck the left side of his face, but he ducked out of the way of the second blow. The speed with which they fought was intense. Tony threw himself at her, but she ducked and defended against each attack. High kicks, low kicks, palm strikes; they went for each other with incredible speed that no normal human could have fended off for long... but they both kept going. She attacked, he defended, he replied, she blocked, they danced back and forth. Another of her blows connected. It focused him. They jumped back from each other, fighting for breath, both with their fists up in defence, staring at each other.

"If...you...are...not...a...Noc, then...what...are...you?" Tony fought for the words between each breath. She stared at him as her breathing began to slow down. Her body relaxed and she straightened up.

"That...isn't...your...concern," she replied, Tony stepped out of his fighting stance. He was still breathing heavily but was recovering much faster now.

"If you are not one of them, then why are you helping them?"

"Who said I was helping anyone?" she was not answering his questions.

"How long have you known?"

"About you? The first day I met you in the station," she smiled as she spoke. "However, I did not spot Kyle at all."

"No, me neither," Tony replied.

"Where is she?"

"Where is who?" Tony responded.

"Reynolds,"

"Tyler? What do you want with Tyler?" Tony asked, his voice raised.

"Not your concern."

"Actually," Tony said, stepping towards her, "it is."

"Not for much longer," Alison answered, just as she attacked again. Tony fended off the first of the blows and the kicks. He attacked again, extending a kick aimed at her head. She ducked and pushed on the ground with her right hand. Her right foot was firmly planted as her left foot thrust into his side. The force of the kick sent him backwards, then the body blow made him collapse and roll on the ground. Pain wracked his body as he came to a halt near the perimeter hedge. He'd rolled over, trying to fend off the blur of arms and legs that assaulted him. Another blow landed on the side of his head; he was starting to tire and slow down. The ferocity of the attack continued but, with his back to the hedge, he had nowhere to go. He aimed his right fist at her head and threw all the speed and power he had left towards it. He missed and, in doing so, committed the ultimate sin in hand-to-hand combat - he had overextended himself. Pain bolted from his wrist as both her hands gripped it, pulling him off his feet. The sky and the ground blurred as one for a moment. His body crashed into the ground. His right hand was forced up his back, and his face slammed into the gravel, as she landed on top of him. He could do nothing. The world came back into focus and the pain of the assault shot through his brain.

Her left hand gripped the hair on the back of his head and yanked it backwards. His neck was completely exposed, and he knew there was nothing he could do. His feet fought in the open space near the hedge; his left arm was pinned underneath his body; his right arm could go no further up his back; his head was forced backwards towards his spine. The right side of his neck was exposed, ready for the final blow. She stopped.

Tony's mouth was wide open as he fought for each breath. His body tensed up, but her grip did not weaken. Tony tried to look at her; her grip was lessening. Her head came into focus. She was staring over towards the woods - her attention, riveted. Then he heard it for the first time. The noise. She loosened her grip, seemingly transfixed on the woods.

"Oh shit!" she exclaimed. She released him and jumped up. Tony rolled over and got onto all fours, expecting another attack. But she was running over to where her pistol was lying on the ground. She grabbed it and turned back towards him. She wasn't looking at him; she was looking at the forest, and she was afraid.

She was backing away, cradling her weapon in her hands, "Oh shit," she repeated, before she turned and ran around the side of the house. Tony righted himself and stood up. His body was in pain, but he could still fight. What had just happened? Her car started and reversed at speed. He walked over towards his own pistol. There was the sound of spinning tyres and spitting gravel, as her car took off down the lane.

Tony bent forward and picked up his pistol. He turned towards the forest and stared. The noise came again. He did not know what it was, but it had scared Alison. Tony limped to his car, feeling pain throughout his body. There was electric pain every time he breathed in. Her kicks must have broken some ribs. He would inspect the cuts and grazes later. The pain in his side was not going to go away anytime soon.

He opened his car door and grabbed the phone that was on the passenger seat. There were two missed calls - both were withheld numbers. He scrolled through his contact list and selected a name. As he held the phone to his ear, it started ringing.

"WHERE THE HELL ARE YOU?" screamed Dermott.

"At her house. She's gone." Tony held the phone away as he was blasted with aggressive swearing. It would be another half an hour before Dermott and the team arrived. When they searched the woods, there was nothing there.

∞∞∞∞

It had been two hours since he first called Kyle from his car. He reverse parked it beside the barn. Kyle was standing in the doorway of the farmhouse with his arms folded. He watched his friend slowly climb out of the passenger side and hobble his way towards him. He was in pain, there was no doubt of that. As he got closer, Kyle could make out the light bruising that was starting to form around his left eye socket. Tony looked down as he approached. He only looked up just as he arrived beside him.

"Hey," Kyle said.

"Hey," Tony replied. Kyle moved to one side and Tony shuffled past, heading inside. Kyle looked around the farm. People moved about. One of the farmhands had two Irish wolfhounds trotting beside him as he walked around the corner of the barn. Another lifted his hand in a wave, which Kyle returned. He turned and walked back inside, shutting the door behind him. Tony lay gingerly on the sofa. This was not an act. He was in pain. He had taken a beating.

"So," Kyle started, as he walked over and took his chair.

"So," Tony repeated. Kyle looked at him.

"I got the feedback from Dermott; there was nothing at the house, or in the woods." Tony winced again.

"There WAS something there," Tony said, "and whatever it was scared the hell out of her!"

"Well, she certainly isn't scared of you!" Kyle was smiling as he spoke. Tony let out a short laugh, which made him wince again.

"No, she certainly isn't."

"Any idea what she was doing at the house?" Kyle asked, Tony shook his head. "You should have waited for Dermott." Kyle had folded his arms again, Tony looked over at him.

"If I had, she would have killed several of them before she was put down," Tony looked away. "She would not have been taken alive, that much I am sure of." Kyle nodded in agreement. "But they are certainly up to something."

"Yes, they are," Kyle confirmed.

"Has Dermott found anything more out yet?" Tony asked, and Kyle shook his head. Tony was adamant, "Something is coming, and it is something big." He looked around the room, "and that is not the only thing that is happening," he stated.

"What?" Kyle frowned.

"Yes, what?" Tyler walked in from the kitchen. Tony smiled and tried to stand up as she walked over to him. Pain jolted his body back into the sofa. "What the hell happened to you?" she asked as she sat down on one of the armchairs.

"I ...." Tony started.

"Tony took on our friend, Alison," Kyle explained. Tyler let out a short laugh.

"You will not do that again in a hurry, will you?" Tyler looked at Kyle who wore a wry smile. "So, what happened, then? Tell me everything." Tyler demanded. Tony went over what had happened while Kyle sat and listened; he had heard this already down the phone from both Tony and Dermott, but it was good to hear it again. He could concentrate on the details more.

"Why did she let you live?" Tyler had a concerned look on her face.

"She said she 'had no quarrel with me'," Tony explained.

"And what was in the woods?" She sat forward, placing her elbows on her knees and bringing her hands together. She rested her chin on them, listening to every word Tony was saying.

"I can only describe it as a noise. I don't know what made it; I really don't."

"Did we search the woods?" she asked, looking at Kyle.

188

"Yes. The team was unable to find any tracks. As far as they could tell, nothing had been there," Kyle replied.

"There *was* something there." Tony insisted.

"I believe you," Tyler said quietly. She was looking down at the floor.

"What are you thinking?" Kyle asked. Her eyes shot up.

"I'm not sure. I want to look around there myself."

"Are you asking or telling?" Kyle asked, Tyler paused before replying,

"Asking."

"You're not going by yourself after what Alison said about you!" Tony said Kyle nodded,

"Yes, he is right, there will be a team going with you," he confirmed she nodded and looked down again. There was a short silence in the room before she spoke again.

"I am really surprised she let you live; that is not like her kind, at all." Tony shifted uncomfortably.

"She said she had no quarrel with me," he repeated.

"Not like a Valkyrie, at all," she whispered.

"What actually is a Valkyrie?" Tony asked. He glanced at Kyle, then looked back at Tyler, she sat back in the armchair.

"I have never actually met one, so I am not totally sure."

"Well, I want to find out." Kyle unfolded his arms as he spoke. It was more of a command than a statement. Both Tyler and Tony looked at him.

"It is a great name, though ...." Tony started, "you get a picture of a beauty, not wearing much, with long flowing hair, riding a flying horse with a huge sword in one hand..." Tony was smiling as he spoke.

"I think you should keep your fantasies to yourself, Mr Fallon," Tyler was smiling, there was a short, communal laugh among them.

"There is a lot in a name," joked Kyle.

"You mean, like Cerberus?" Tyler asked.

"Who?" asked Tony.

"Cerberus, the hellhound," Kyle answered. "According to Greek legend, Hades, Lord of the underworld, had a hellhound called Cerberus guarding the gates." Tyler looked at him and smiled.

"Yeah, and Cerberus is a Greek name from the Latin, Kerberos which means 'spotted',"

"Spotted?" asked Tony.

"Yes," she replied.

"So, Hades, Lord of the underworld, is guarding the gates of the underworld with a dog named SPOT?" Tony was laughing, the mood in the room lifted.

"Yeah, pretty much," Tyler laughed.

"That kinda changes the mental picture you get of the hellhound now, doesn't it!" Kyle chuckled.

"So," Tyler said as she sat forward again, and looked at Tony.

"So," Tony replied.

"So, what is the other thing you were about to say when I walked in and disturbed you?" Tyler looked straight at him with raised eyebrows. Kyle looked at Tony. She was right, he had forgotten completely and, judging by Tony's bright red face, so had he.

"Well, yeah, there is something else," Tony looked around the room. Whatever it was, it certainly made him uncomfortable.

"Okay, don't keep us in suspense," Kyle said, sitting forward. The smile beamed from Tony's face,

"Karen is pregnant!"

Chapter 47

"Hey, it's lunchtime, let's eat!" Mark was certainly happy about something. Cara-Marie glanced at the clock on the wall, then back at him.

"You know, I wasn't hungry until you said that!"

"Well," he started, "good thing I did, then," the smile lit up his face. He had been in a good mood all morning, and it was getting annoying.

"So, where do you suggest we go?" she asked, then looked past Mark. Kevin had just walked out of his office and was heading their way. She caught Mark's eye and glanced at the approaching editor. Mark picked up on the warning. She could not tell exactly what the folded sheets of paper were in his left hand, but he caught her eye as he approached.

"Cara," he stopped at Mark's desk. Mark turned in his chair and looked up at his boss.

"Yes," she replied, her fingers poised over her keyboard. She had finished the article but did not want to send it to him yet.

"Right. I like the story about the fight at the funeral, but we aren't going to use it." She just stared at him. He was not allowing anything even remotely connected to last year's events past him. Her blog, on the other hand, was getting more hits than ever. "Can you follow up on that golfer from Portrush and the other one from Bangor who are playing in Dubai next week?" She was already bored. He carried on, but she was not listening, "Mark, can you locate recent pictures of the two of them? Cara, I want three hundred words. Thanks." He turned and walked back towards his office. Mark grinned at her.

"That should keep you busy for a wee while."

"That will take twenty minutes." She picked up her coat, "You were saying about lunch?"

"Yeah, and I think it is great that you're paying this time!" He, too, stood up and pulled his jacket from the back of his chair.

"Who said anything about me paying?"

"Yeah, thanks for that. Let's go!" Mark headed for the back door, looking back over his shoulder with a smile. She grinned, then pulled on her coat and scooped up her handbag, feeding her arm through the strap. The door of the office closed behind her and she jogged a few paces to catch up to him.

"So," he started, "are you going to tell me what the 'wolf investigator' is up to now?" He zipped up his jacket and pushed his hands into his trouser pockets. She looked around; there was no one nearby to hear them.

"So, after the fight in the cemetery, I spoke with the English Earl on the phone."

"What is his lordship up to now?" She looked at him. He was looking at the ground, a short distance in front of his feet.

"He is back in England; he has a pack of werewolves on his estate he needs to deal with." He glanced at her.

"Is that all?"

"Nope. He invited me over to spend a weekend on his estate." Mark looked directly at her; his eyebrows raised.

"Are you going?" She ducked around a lamppost,

"Of course not."

"Why not? He obviously likes you. You could be the next 'Lady Baskerville'," Mark giggled, as he walked on. She glared at him and he carried on with his ribbing, "Surely your mum would love that one .... OOWW!" The punch landed hard on his left arm. He looked hurt, "What?"

"Less of that from you. I get enough from her."

"So, no real progress then," he carried on.

"Not really. Well, nothing I can use." She let out a sigh.

"Sorry to hear that. I take it you are going to carry on, then?" She tightened her left hand on the strap of her handbag and pushed her right hand into the pocket of her coat.

"Of course! I know what I saw, I just want to ...." she stopped speaking as her fingers touched an object in her pocket. She stopped and reacted, "What the ..." Mark had taken another step, then turned towards her.

"What?" he asked. Cara-Marie looked puzzled as she pulled the small object out of her pocket. She held up the computer pen drive. She looked at it, then at him.

"Did you put that there?" she demanded. He moved closer to inspect it.

"No," he reached out and took it. He studied it closely. There was a small, round, yellow smiley face on it. "I don't recognise the type. I'm not sure if they are even for sale around here." Cara-Marie grabbed it back and studied it.

"Well, it certainly isn't mine." She paused, looked around, then back at Mark.

"Who has been close to you today?" he asked.

"No one."

"And it's definitely not one of your own?"

"Absolutely not."

"When was the last time you wore the coat?"

"Yesterday, at the funeral."

"Could someone have slipped it into your pocket then?"

"Don't be absurd!" she replied.

"Well," he turned and started to walk away, then looked back over his left shoulder. "I guess you won't know until you look at it," he turned, "after lunch!" She looked at the pen stick, then at the back of the photographer walking away. No, it would not have been him, but he was pinching at her curiosity. No, it was not one of her own, and no, no one had been that close to her. How did it get there? Now she was curious.

What she most wanted to do was turn and head back into the office. It could be nothing after all, just be a blank stick with nothing on it that she had forgotten about. She would look after lunch. In the meantime, she had to catch Mark up as she was certainly not paying for lunch this time.

∞∞∞∞

Kyle was driving the Land Rover along the edge of a field. Tyler was beside him. He stopped at the top of the hill, then got out and walked around to the front of the vehicle. He climbed onto it, turned and positioned himself so he was sitting comfortably. Tyler joined him; neither spoke. Kyle surveyed the landscape. There was a small forest at the bottom of the hill on the right; the field stretched out in front of them. Several deer moved slowly around the bottom of the field. There was a single farmhand on a quad bike, nearby. Kyle looked beyond at the rest of the landscape; the hills rolled on to the horizon. Each field seemed to be a slightly different shade of green than the others. The few clouds were gathered in a small clump. There was a chill in the air - the frost was coming. He looked at the position of the sun. It had already started to set behind the distant hills. A contented smile spread across his face.

"Now what kind of thought can cause a smile like that?" she asked. He looked over at her, then back at the sunset. He could feel the warmth on his face.

"I was just remembering," he spoke quietly.

"Remembering what?" she asked, he looked at her again. Her dark auburn hair was tied back in a short ponytail. The dark blue padded jacket was zipped all the way up and she had a thin scarf tied around her neck, patterned in blue, yellow and white. Her jeans were clean and showed off her shapely legs. She was wearing a pair of well-worn brown walking boots. Tony had joked, just as he was leaving, that it gave her a rather rugged look. The jovial banter flowed between them; she pointed out that fashion was not his thing... *"I mean, look at you!"*

It was great to see Tony happy. The news that Karen was pregnant again was brilliant, especially after what had happened last year. Kyle smiled again.

"I was here when I was a child," he used his hands to help with his descriptions. "I remember the ground being covered in deep snow." She looked at him, noting his eyes were almost glazing over. He was not sitting on the front of a 4 x 4, anymore. He was a child again. "I had a thin, black bin liner and I was using it as a sled to go down this hill." The smile was back on his face. "Dad was pushing us as we both slid down. Then we ran back up the side and did it all again." It was a happy memory for him.

"When was that?" she asked quietly, looking at him.

"I was only little. The wall ...." He pointed towards the small stone wall at the edge of the field, "I was not even half the size of that, so I must have been really young." There was an excited look on his face. "I could get up to quite a speed going down this."

"How did you stop?" she asked. The question raised his eyebrows.

"Badly, normally, but it was always a race to get back up, so I could be the first going back down the hill again." There was warmth in his smile, as he stared down the hill. She was looking at him when the smile started to fade. There was a sadness in his eyes now, and he frowned. "Dad laughed and laughed at the state of us."

"I have never heard you talk about your dad before." She looked away. Her comment brought him back to the present. He looked at her, then back at the hill.

191

"No, it's not something I normally want to chat about." He jumped off the front of the Land Rover and stood up straight. He watched the sun slowly disappear behind the distant hills.

"Great news about Tony and Karen!" she said, as she jumped off the front of the vehicle herself, changing the subject.

"Yes, I..." Kyle was cut off by the handheld radio that was clipped to his belt. It was set on the main farm channel.

"ALL STATIONS, ALL STATIONS, ALL NON-ESSENTAL STAFF ARE TO REPORT TO THE MAIN BARN AT ONCE!" It was Dermott's voice and there was an urgency to it. Kyle reached around and pulled the small black radio from his belt and held it up.

"Base, this is Alpha. What is happening? Over," Kyle looked at Tyler. There had to be something very wrong for Dermott to be calling everyone together without speaking to him first. The very tone of Dermott's voice said that.

"ALPHA, ROGER, THERE IS AN URGENT PROBLEM THAT WE NEED TO DEAL WITH," Dermott paused, but spoke again just before Kyle pressed the talk button. "PLEASE RETURN TO THE FARMHOUSE AND I WILL BRIEF YOU."

"Roger... on the way now. Can you give me an idea what the problem is? Over." Tyler stepped closer and looked at the small device in Kyle's hand. There was a pause before Dermott answered.

"ROGER," Dermott paused, "KNOCK, KNOCK." Kyle's eyes widened; Dermott had just told the entire farm what the problem was.

"The Noctrailis!" Tyler said, running to the passenger door. Kyle had turned and was running, as well.

"En route!" he replied, into the small radio. As he landed in the driver's seat, the passenger door slammed shut. Tyler was still faster than he was. The engine coughed to life as Kyle looked over his left shoulder out the rear window. He reversed a short distance, turning the steering wheel as he did so. The Land Rover stopped, then he threw it forward, turning back up the way they had come. The radio was full of different voices.

"ROGER, KILO TEAM ON THE WAY."

"LIMA TEAM, NOW MOBILE!" The whole farm was responding. It did not take Kyle long before he was at the gate that led back into the main farmyard. Two of the hands were nearby and opened it for them. There was a flurry of activity. Kyle drove forward, acknowledging them as he went past. The gate was closed behind them. Kyle brought the Land Rover to a stop by the farmhouse and they both jumped out. Dermott was standing near the back door of the farmhouse. Paul Hawkins was beside him, and they were surrounded by a small crowd. Dermott was barking orders at them. Kyle and Tyler ran towards them. Dermott looked serious. Paul looked angry.

"What is going on?" Kyle demanded. The crowd went quiet. Dermott looked at him. They all looked towards their alpha.

"The Noctrailis have mobilised. They have all left their lair in a convoy of vehicles and are heading north out of Belfast!" Dermott was loud enough for everyone to hear, "Our overwatch team is following them."

"All of them? Where are they going?" Tyler demanded.

"Yes, all of them. We have to assume they are coming here," Paul answered.

"DERMOTT," Kyle raised his voice so everyone could hear; a command was coming. Dermott straightened up. "IS THE DEFENCE PLAN READY?" Kyle was staring at him, intently.

"IT IS," Dermott shouted his reply.

"THEN SEE TO IT!"

Chapter 48

"That should give them something to think about!" Dani smiled. Sabine zipped up her jacket - the cold was starting to bite. She looked around the carpark and watched as the minibuses that had dropped them off began to drive away. Only a single car was left. There were just over twenty of them. The car park was lined with trees on one side and a raised bank on the other. Just over the rise was a single building that was being used as a youth hostel.

Sabine glanced up at the darkening cloudless sky. That would benefit the wolves, not them, she thought to herself. She looked at the others. If anyone walked past, they were just a group of young people, all dressed for hiking. Some carried small rucksacks, and a few carried large ones, which contained the weapons they were planning to use later.

"Yes, heading towards the farm, then splitting into three groups was a good idea," Sabine replied. "It will have split their surveillance on us." The others started to gather around. Dani turned towards them.

"Right, then," she started, "we are to head down to the beach and wait until we're called." Several of the group nodded, and Dani carried on, "Tonight, we are going to get our first strike at the wolves. Security is important, which is why we did not do a central briefing."

"What is going on?" one voice asked. Dani looked at the group and smiled.

"It's simple," she glanced around, "we allowed them to see us all leaving and heading in one direction. They will assume that we are going straight to the farm for an all-out assault." Sabine pushed her hands into the pockets of her jacket, the frost nipping at her exposed flesh - it would be cold tonight. Dani continued, "We split into three separate groups to confuse them. They will deploy a team thus weakening their overall den."

"How?" another voice asked.

"Each team they deploy, we will track, lure into a killing ground and take down. Every time they deploy, we kill them - one group at a time, gradually weakening the pack." Dani was pleased with herself.

"What are the others doing?" another asked.

"We are Assault Team One. Team Two is being dropped off at the far side of the Giants causeway. We'll have a decoy in place near the ruins at Dunseverick Castle, which will draw them in," she explained. "The vans are going to be driving around to keep the wolves guessing, and only coming to pick us up when we are summoned."

"Why there?" the same voice asked.

"Simple, the natural bowl there makes it perfect for an ambush. Once we lure the wolves into it, we can dominate the high ground and make sure none of them leave there alive!" A small cheer rose from the crowd.

"Right, let's head to the beach and get a couple of fires going. Dave, you get the tent set up so we can all get comfortable until they call." There was a sea of smiles - everyone was happy...except Sabine. The group moved towards the entrance gate at the far corner of the carpark. Beside it was the signpost with an information board. Sabine could just make out the name, 'White Park Bay'. A small pathway led down the side of the hill on their left; to the right were thick bramble bushes. The path was laid out in a Z shape, enabling hikers to traverse the side of the steep slope. It zigzagged down the hill, then rose gently before dropping sharply away down to the beach.

Sabine was looking over the ground. Dani came up beside her. "What?" she asked. Sabine looked at her as they followed the pathway.

"Why down on the beach? Would it not have been better to wait in the carpark?"

"The beach is obscured from view so we can remain out of sight until it is time to go. If any sapiens walk past, we are just a group of friends out camping." Dani explained. "If we had stayed at the carpark, we would have been visible from the main road. Being out of sight ...." she paused, "is what we want." Sabine stopped suddenly and peered into the darkness.

"Wait!" she said loudly. Everyone stopped, searching the darkness. Sabine was tense. She lowered slightly and raised her arms in a fighting stance. The rest did the same. She stared at the white building to their right. "There is something moving over there," she whispered. For a few seconds the only sound was the crashing waves, and the wind. Dani straightened up.

"Rabbits!" she declared. Everyone relaxed. Dani walked around Sabine's left side and pointed towards the white building. "That is a half-demolished Victorian schoolhouse. There are several rabbit warrens around it." She walked on, "They will also help distract the wolves if they do come here." She stopped and looked back at Sabine. "...which they won't. We have the upper hand."

"Is there a bounty on wolf pelts?" a voice asked, bringing a ripple of laughter.

"If there is, we are about to make a load of money!" someone replied. Dani raised her eyebrows and tilted her head. Sabine smiled, then looked down. When she looked up, Dani was still smiling at her. Sabine nodded and walked towards the rise and a small wooden bench.

"Right, then," Dani raised her voice again, "let's go down to the beach and get comfy." There was another ripple of excitement. The group quietly made is way down to the beach, where they lit campfires and huddled around them. Sabine had gone for a walk along the beach. There was a natural bay with high cliffs at one end and protruding rocks on the other. A small river cut the beach in two, as it met the Atlantic Ocean. Sabine's hands were shoved deep into the pockets of the jacket. She pulled out her phone and looked at it, the screen lighting up her face. There was no signal. Pushing the phone back into the pocket she looked back at the group. Everyone was cheerfully confident; they were finally getting direct action against the Garou.

Sabine spotted Dani moving around the different groups. Everyone welcomed her; she was the focus of attention. Sabine took out her phone again and scrolled through the numbers. She stopped at Alison's name and pressed the green button. Hopefully, she held the phone to her ear; but there was no connection. Sabine did not know what Alison was doing, or exactly where she was, which infuriated her. Dani didn't hide her hatred for the wolves, nor her intention to wipe them out. However, she had not been forthcoming with details of *how* they were going to do it. All the American said was 'follow her lead'. Sabine folded her arms.

Suddenly, there was a buzz of excitement, as a group of four crested the hill with two struggling sapiens who'd been camping nearby. They would feed on the teenagers before any fun and games with the Garou.

∞∞∞∞

Alison hated that Dani had not told her everything. Of course, she understood operational security, but she felt she should have an idea of the part they would be playing in the bigger picture. Brooding, she stared out the window of the minibus. She barely knew the guy driving; she did not know his skills nor how he would respond to any threats. Yes, she knew where she was; she had policed this area for years.

She took out her phone and looked at the blank screen. She had no idea what Sabine was doing. All they were told was to drop her team off at White Park Bay carpark. They had 'something else to do' before picking them up. She surveyed the empty minibus and looked down at the canvas bags laying on the floor. If they were stopped by the police, it would be tough to explain the M-16 assault rifles and pump-action shotguns; they were all illegal. She turned back towards the front. The driver was silent, as he followed another minibus. They were heading back into Coleraine again; Alison had no idea how Kyle or Tony would react. Dani had certainly been angry when she was not able to answer her questions about them. Yes, she had known them both for two years, but had never socialised with them off duty. How could she not have seen what Kyle was? She had spotted Tony easily enough, but not Kyle. That had been a surprise. But how would they react to what was happening? She had no idea... which made Dani furious. The minibus slowed, as did the red taillights ahead. The area to their right was brightly lit, dominated by a large supermarket.

"What are we doing?" she asked. The driver stared straight ahead; he had barely acknowledged her since they'd started the journey.

"Petrol," was the single reply. Since killing Maya, Alison had found herself ignored by most of the coven and stared at by the rest. She could live with that. But she worried about them turning on her. "It's all about how you handle Plan B," Sabine had said to her; she'd just smiled and nodded. Alison needed to come up with a Plan B now.

∞∞∞∞

Tyler listened to the communicator in her ear. Ruth's voice instructed them all to turn right, then left into the carpark. She felt the small daysack on the floor between her feet. She looked around the back of the van; this part of the assault team was sitting in silence. Two of them wore plated body armour under their outdoor jackets; they held the bolt-action rifles between their legs, pointing towards the roof. 'Accuracy International AX338 Lupua Magnums with 10 x 42 scopes... perfect for stalking,' was the answer she'd received when she'd asked about the rifles. She certainly got the impression they knew what they were doing. The rest of the team carried pistols. Everyone was silent; The only sound was the engine of the vehicle.

They had carried out the defence plan for nearly three hours before it was agreed the Nocs were not going to the farm. In fact, they had split up, which did not make sense. You should never split your forces! Kyle had remained at the farm to keep it secure and Dermott was in the communications building, controlling all movement. The communications team had kept the Nocs under surveillance and discovered that one group of minibuses had stopped at the carpark, before moving on. The subsequent weight on the axles indicated that a considerable load had been dropped there.

When Kyle had asked what was at White Park Bay, the answer had been 'nothing that interests us.' Tyler knew there had to be a reason they were here, which was why she'd insisted on coming with this assault team. Ruth would be in charge. She, herself, was just an added bonus. Tyler tightened her right hand on the strap of the daysack - the only thing inside was her short, straight sword. She knew she would need it before the night was out. The van stopped and everyone looked expectantly at each other. Ruth's voice came over the communicator again.

"TEAM TWO, TEAM TWO, TWO ALPHA, PULLING INTO THE CARPARK, SLOWLY" The back of the van had not been warm, but when the side door opened, the chill from outside swept in. All the lights were out in the back of both vans and they were in complete darkness. Their movements were slow and quiet.

Tyler moved forward and stepped out of the van. The others were standing around and there was a low murmur of conversation. The van had reverse parked beside the other van on the far side. Ruth was talking to two team members from her van and she was pointing in the direction of the sea. They both nodded and headed off quickly. Tyler looked around; she had never been here before. Swinging the daysack onto her left shoulder, she pulled a pair of black cotton gloves out of her jacket pocket. She looked around the empty carpark. Their two vans were the only ones there. Ruth had tasked three pairs to various points around the carpark. One pair opposite the entrance, another to the far side and one on top of the rise behind the vans. The pair by the entrance would remain there, but the other two would patrol the surrounding area, ensuring nothing got close to the vehicles or surprised them from behind.

The drivers remained in their seats. Tyler watched as Ruth motioned for everyone to come closer. When they were all huddled around her, she began her briefing in a hushed tone.

"Right, everyone, listen up," the gathered crowd listened in silence. "Michael and Davey have gone ahead. I want to know exactly what is here, so we can find out why the Nocs were so interested in it."

"Where are we?" asked one voice.

"White Park Bay - Right: the lay of the land…" stated Ruth as she turned and stepped forward into the darkness. She was facing the sound of the waves crashing on the shore. "To our left is the cliff and just over there," she pointed to the left corner of the carpark, "is a youth hostel, currently un-occupied." She lowered her left hand and raised her right towards a small gate. "Over to our right is the entrance to the pathway, leading down to the beach. It is tarmac with stone steps to the bottom of the hill, then sand dunes …" Ruth turned back towards them, "If it all goes wrong, this is the rally point," she pointed to the front of the vans. "Is everyone okay, so far?" There were nods. Tyler was impressed by the little wolf. "Right, once the other two get back, we will make a start." Everyone relaxed and stood in groups in front of the vans. Each conversation was just above a whisper.

They did not have long to wait. Out of the darkness ran a single figure. He was out of breath. They all closed in around him, and Ruth stepped forward, placing a hand on his shoulder. He stopped beside her and bent over, fighting for breath as he told them what he had seen.

"NOCS! … AT LEAST … TWENTY OF THEM … DOWN ON THE BEACH!"

"Michael, what are they doing?" Ruth asked. He looked up at her as his breathing started to slow down.

"They have a tent set up …. and a few small campfires …. but they are just sitting around

"Any security?" Ruth asked, he shook his head.

"Not that we could see; they seem to be waiting for something." Ruth straightened up at the information.

"Thanks Mike, that is first class, where on the beach, are they?" she asked. Michael was regaining his composure; he straightened up and turned towards the gate.

"Down the path, then over the dunes… There is a large crest, so they are out of view …" Michael used his hands to help with his description. "They're on the far side of the crest, so they will not see us coming!" There was a murmured reaction from the team.

"Any visible weapons?" Ruth asked, he shook his head,

"Not that we could see."

"They will be in the tent," Tyler spoke out loud. She was looking at Ruth as she said it, Ruth nodded once.

"Yes," Ruth paused, then, with a stern look on her face, issued her plan. "Right, they are obviously here for a reason, so let's not wait around to find out what it is. Our direct action will be broken down into phases." Tyler, again, was trying not to smile. Although young, this wolf was well-trained. Ruth turned and looked at the four with the stalking rifles, "Overwatch, I want you along the cliff edge, so you have a good view over the target area. Engage any target that presents a threat." The four of them nodded, then smiled at each other - they would get a kill tonight. Ruth turned back to the rest of the team, "I want Charlie team on my left, so you go down the path first; I will be in the middle, with Delta team on my right." Ruth looked around at each one of them, "I want two team members with pistols in sapien form at each end as cut off. The rest of you ...." a smile broke over her face, "you will be in our true form." There was an immediate reaction to her statement; excitement filled the air. "We will form up at the bottom of the hill, where I will wait for confirmation from overwatch," she pointed towards them as she spoke. Tapping her right ear, she said, "When I hear from you, we all go over the rise at the same time." The ripple of excitement grew. "I will stay as I am and will have my pistol with me, so watch for my signal." She scanned the jubilant faces in front of her, "Once it is all done, I want every one of them searched and everything we find brought back to the vans, so we can take it back to the farm. Let's learn as much as we can about what they are up to!" she stated. There was a chorus of agreement.

"What will we do with them afterwards?" a voice asked. Ruth smirked,

"Strip them and lay them out on the sand. Leave them for daylight - there will be nothing for the sapiens to find. But everything else comes back here... no traces ...does everyone understand?" Ruth looked at Tyler, who was listening with a grin on her face. "Can you stay with me, just in case there is something we cannot deal with, or if there is a serious problem?" Ruth was asking publicly; she was showing Tyler respect.

"No problem. This all sounds perfect to me." Tyler slightly raised her voice to confirm everything Ruth had said.

"Right, does everyone know what they are doing?" Ruth looked around. There was a series of nods. "Right, then, let's go!"

∞∞∞∞

Sabine was sitting on the sand looking into one of the campfires. The large sand dune was behind her and the cold wind blew in gently from the sea. Most of them had fed off the two sapiens earlier. When they had finished, Dani had taken one other with her to dump the bodies. But that had been some time ago, when they had walked off along the beach with the bodies slung over their shoulders. They had not yet returned.

There had been a party atmosphere on the beach; everyone was in a great mood. The real reason they brought a tent had become obvious. Various pairs went inside, the first couple had emerged to applause and jeering. They were followed by others, taking their own turns, but the current ones were making so much noise, it was concerning Sabine.

"'Any chance they can they keep it down; we are NOT to attract attention!" she implored the small group that was sitting around this particular fire.

"Why? 'Getting jealous that no one has taken you in there yet?" said the young, excited face on the far side of the fire. There was a collective chuckle at his comment -none of them would dare propose that to her. She stared at his young face. His dark hair flopped over his forehead; he was lying on his left side facing the fire, a small brown bottle of cheap beer in his hand. The fire seemed to light up his smile.

"I would eat you alive," she replied, as she looked over the tops of her knees.

"Well, here's hoping!" he laughed. Sabine chuckled at his audacity.

"Be careful!" she warned, raising her eyebrows and pulling her legs in closer.

"Why?" he asked, looking around for support, "do you bite?" The small group shared a laugh, Sabine could not help but smile - she did like him.

Suddenly, her eyes darted to the left; her head slowly turned as she looked up at the cliffs in the distance, then at the sand bank behind her.

"Has anyone seen Dani come back yet?" she asked.

Chapter 49

Tyler was lying prone facing the top of the crest. She looked behind her. Ruth had tasked two guards to remain a short distance back, near the half-demolished white building that was once a schoolhouse. They were the rear protection for the assault. The cut-off pairs had fanned out and the two groups of wolves moved across the ground in stealthy silence. Ruth was on one knee. It was getting dark, but they could see where everyone was. Ruth held the Sig pistol in both hands as she looked to her left and to her right. She silently directed the wolves into place with her left hand, re-establishing her firm grip on the pistol after each movement.

Tyler had left her daysack with the neatly laid out piles of clothes. Her sword was in her right hand, unsheathed. She smiled as the two groups of wolves silently moved off. The hunt was on! Ruth looked at her and raised her fingers to her ear. She looked over to her left towards the cliff edge. The overwatch was in place. Ruth nodded, then looked from side to side. With the pistol in her right hand, she extended her left arm out from her side and, keeping the palm of her hand uppermost, slowly raised it. All the wolves moved as one. Slowly, they raised themselves onto all fours, then waited for Ruth's lead. Tyler rose as Ruth stood and quietly moved to the top of the crest. They looked down at the scene on the beach.

Off to the left was a single domed tent. There were at least two in there and, by the level of noise, the sex was fast and aggressive. There were five small campfires, each surrounded by a group of Noctrailis. Tyler knew what they were; she could instantly tell the difference between a Noc and a sapien. Her grip on her sword tightened and they all came to the top of the crest in unison. Tyler looked into the face of a male Noc who was standing at the farthest fire. The look of shocked surprise was wiped out the instant his head exploded - the first bullet found its mark. The overwatch had their first kill. Tyler was bounding down the side of the hill; everywhere around her there were frenzied movements. Ruth had stopped at the top of the hill with her pistol extended; she was maintaining overall control of the situation.

The wolves cannoned into the Nocs. Tyler chose the nearest campfire, which had six Noctrailis around it - a mix of males and females. They all jumped up, screaming. The battle had commenced. Tyler approached the nearest Noc, who was on his feet, the knife gripped tightly in his right hand. There was hatred in his eyes. She brought her sword up, gripping it with both hands. He lunged at her, totally overextending himself. It was too easy. The sword slammed into his chest and thrust out his back, as his body thudded into her. She pushed him away with her left hand and withdrew her sword.

All around her the wolves tore into them. There was a mass of fury as teeth and claws ripped and shredded. Some of the Nocs tried to fight back; everywhere, there was the flash of metal. The tall woman in front of her screamed, then lunged towards her. Tyler spotted her elongated incisors - she was going for her neck. Tyler planted her left foot and thrust forward her right foot in a frontal kick that hit the centre of the woman's torso. Her momentum switched from charging forward to being thrown back like a rag doll, straight into the path of a wolf, who pounced on her just as she landed on her back, skidding in the sand. The wolf's attack was so ferocious her face and neck were mutilated within seconds. Another wolf pounced on another Noc; Tyler's sword sliced through the air and a head came neatly away from the body it had been attached to. The head landed on the sand with a thud. The headless body stumbled forward and collapsed onto the campfire, arms and legs twitching, sparks flying.

Tyler looked to her right, to see a wolf fly backwards. Another yelped loudly. She turned towards the ongoing fight at the far campfire. A female Noc came at her; Tyler's left hand shot out and grabbed the struggling woman by the throat. The strength of her grip put an immediate end to the attack. Her fingers dug into the neck - the scream had gone from anger to gasping, and the Noc's hands fought to release the grip. Tyler was lifting her up, so she was on her tiptoes. Her sword passed easily through her abdomen. In seconds, the struggling stopped. Tyler pulled the blade away from the corpse and released her grip to allow the lifeless body to drop to the ground. The sound of a shotgun blast made her head spin to the left. A single Noc was staggering rearwards, the pump-action shotgun in his hands. There was fear in his eyes. The wolf that had, only a moment ago, been standing in front of him rolled forward onto the ground. He pushed the front grip of the weapon upwards and the spent shell flew out the side. The Noc pushed the slide forward again; the teeth of another wolf sunk into his upper right arm; another attacked his upper left leg; and a third jumped towards him. He would not get to fire the weapon again.

Tyler was not listening to his screams, nor those of the other victims struggling around the campsite. She spotted a group of wolves encircling a tall, blonde woman who sent a series of furry bodies flying backwards, yelping in pain. Others still surrounded her - some on all fours, others standing; all snarling, growling, snapping and barking at the single Noc who refused to give up. Wounded wolves lay on the ground in the wake of the slowly moving circle. Tyler fixed her gaze on the tall blonde who gripped a long knife and stood expectantly. Every wolf that attacked was cut, sliced and thrown off.

Tyler knew instantly this one had fought wolves before. She was taking small steps gradually moving the circle of wolves away from the campsite. Tyler glanced back at the rest of the scene. The dome tent had been shredded; various wolves leaned over their prey. Most of the Nocs were already dead, and those still struggling would not live for long. Ruth stood up and pressed her finger to her ear, listening to the overwatch. Tyler looked back at the circle. This Noc was different.

"STOP!" Tyler shouted. All the wolves went silent. Some glanced over towards Tyler, others stared at the lone woman in front of them, still baring their teeth. "STEP BACK!" Tyler commanded. They obeyed.

Sabine turned and looked at Tyler, remaining in her stance, knife at the ready. Her face emitted venomous hatred. If she could kill them all, she would. Sabine looked at each wolf in turn, and then watched as Tyler walked towards them. The circle of fur parted as Tyler approached. She stared at the vampire in front of her. "No one kills her but me." It was a quiet statement, Sabine's eye's widened in recognition, then a sneer spread over her face.

"Reynolds!" she hissed. Tyler was standing, facing her, the sword in her right hand hung loosely by her side. The hatred went both ways.

"You must be Sabine," Tyler did not take her eyes from her. Sabine's eyes widened in excitement, her mouth slightly open, her incisors elongated.

"We have been looking for you for a long time!" Sabine was panting as she spoke, almost in ecstasy.

"Well, the last time you found me, it did not go well for your little team." There was a ripple of amusement from the growing circle of wolves. More were joining to see what was happening. Ruth appeared beside Tyler. She aimed her pistol at Sabine.

"Lower your weapon." Ruth demanded.

"Or what?" Sabine replied sarcastically.

"Leave it," Tyler said. Ruth looked up at her. Tyler was watching the vampire in the centre of the circle. "She is mine... and mine, alone."

"Do you want to know how he died?" Sabine almost spat the words. Tyler's face tensed at the question.

"What? Do I want to know how *who* died?" she asked. Sabine was staring into Tyler's eyes and Tyler returned the stare.

"Your husband!" Tyler reacted as if she'd been punched. Her eyebrows lowered. There were various reactions from the circle. Some snapped their mouths; others growled. Sabine looked around with a nefarious smile of her face, before settling on Tyler. She was pleased with the reaction. "Way mishta taci gutchi lana,"

"What?" Ruth said loudly, not understanding what Sabine had just said. Tyler's head moved slightly.

"She is speaking the ancient language of the Noctrailis," Tyler explained.

"Do you understand it?" Ruth asked.

"Da," Tyler replied, "it is a form of ancient Russian, I believe." Sabine smirked again.

"Socki tuaam, huu tuaam sta wamama Koch!" Sabine stated.

"Agreed!" Tyler replied. Ruth looked over at her.

"What did she say?" Ruth asked. Tyler's eyes fixed on Sabine.

"She wants a one-on-one challenge, and I agreed." Ruth looked back at Sabine. She was looking at the circle of wolves, with total defiance on her face, as if she knew she could beat them all. Some of the wolves reacted - snapping or snarling, but all obeyed the command to stay back.

"Cue eta weetana, bouko ryevera roussline cassanti!" Sabine spat on the ground after she had spoken. Tyler did not react.

"You are not leaving here alive!" Tyler stated.

"What did she say?" Ruth asked, Sabine smirked again.

"Where?" Tyler was speaking directly to Sabine; she did not answer Ruth's question. Sabine motioned d towards the sea. "What else?" Tyler asked. Sabine seemed to relax.

"Mootai," Sabine paused, "kasta cunti wanna wak!" Tyler did not move, nor respond. She just stared at Sabine.

"Why should I?" Tyler finally asked, Sabine shrugged.

"What have you got to lose?" Sabine reverted to English; Tyler let out a short laugh.

"Okay," Sabine smiled and turned to walk away. She stopped in front of two wolves who were standing upright, barring her exit. She stared at them.

"MOVE!" she demanded. One of them looked towards Tyler.

"She isn't going far. Let her pass," she commanded. The wolves moved aside, and Sabine walked past them, heading towards the shore.

"What is happening?" Ruth demanded, "I am actually in charge here!" She was annoyed. Tyler stepped forward, then looked back over her shoulder at her.

"You are to do everything you said you would when we were up at the carpark, but in this ...." Tyler pointed towards the back of the tall blonde who was walking away from them, "you are not to intervene."

"She isn't leaving here alive!" Ruth stated to the back of Tyler's head.

"She will if she beats me." There was a shocked reaction from everyone. Ruth stepped forward and touched her left arm.

"Beats you? Are you serious? You're ...." Tyler glanced at her, this time with a serious look on her face.

"No matter how good you are, there will always be someone better." Ruth looked confused. "If ...." Tyler said, "this does not go as planned, no matter what happens, you are not to intervene ...." Tyler looked around at the growing number of wolves, "Is that clear!"

"I am in charge here!" Ruth was adamant, Tyler turned took her hand.

"You will do as I say. If she beats me, it will take most of those here to take her down," Tyler looked around her as she continued speaking. "Do not intervene .... Is that clear?" Tyler let go of Ruth's hand and turned away. One of the wolves placed a hand on Tyler's right shoulder, amid barks and motions of support. Tyler smiled and winked at the wolf, then looked back at Ruth. "Besides, haven't you got enough to do here?" Ruth smiled, but it was not a happy smile,

"Yes."

"Well then, the sooner you get started, the sooner you will be finished." Tyler turned and walked after Sabine. Ruth watched her go. Sabine was only thirty metres away; they could all see her. Ruth stared at Tyler's back.

"Right everyone, you all know what to do, so get on with it." There was a flurry of activity as they set about clearing up and searching each of the bodies. One wolf stopped beside Ruth and looked at her; a second one came up and stopped as well. Ruth looked into their faces. The first wolf turned towards Tyler and let out a soft growl before looking back at her. Ruth nodded. "Good idea. The two of you wait here - if Tyler wants help, then you two, respond!" They nodded. Ruth holstered her weapon, then set about organising the clean-up.

◌◌◌◌◌◌

Sabine stood facing her as she approached. The knife was in her right hand. Tyler stopped about ten metres away. Sabine looked at her sword, then at her own knife. She smiled and, with one motion, threw the knife away towards the water's edge. Tyler nodded and turned, throwing the blade back behind her. She made a mental note of where it landed, knowing she would want it back...but this was hand to hand combat.

"Ott-valee suka!" Sabine spat; Tyler looked at her.

"No, fuck you .... Bitch!" Sabine hissed, then slowly walked towards her, peeling off her jacket as she did so. Tyler hesitated, then did the same. She tossed the jacket behind her, then focused on the fury in the eyes of the vampire in front of her.

Tyler brought her hands up in a defensive pose and Sabine did the same. Her mouth opened, displaying the sharp incisors. The look of near ecstasy was back in her eyes; Sabine was loving this. The distance between them closed. Sabine extended her left hand, so the palm was flat towards the ground. Tyler understood what she was doing. She reached out and their fingertips touched; the two fighters acknowledged each other. There was electricity between them. Suddenly, the fight was on.

Both launched simultaneously with punches and kicks, blocking with incredible speed. They closed in on each other and dug their feet into the sand, as they both threw a flurry of punches. The blocking stopped - the punches were hitting their marks, landing in each other's face, head, chest, shoulders.... Punch, punch, punch, punch - it was turning into a slugfest. The power of each landed punch soon drew blood, which flowed from their noses and mouths. The speed suddenly picked up – they moved closer still...slam, slam, slam, slam, as the punches landed. Sheer force of will drove them at each other. Sabine was leaning forward to add weight to the power of her blows, when suddenly Tyler side-stepped. Sabine's forward momentum was increased by Tyler's punch slamming into her side, then pushing her body. Sabine lost her balance.

Tyler planted her left foot, so her left leg was at an angle to trip her. Sabine reacted by throwing herself into a forward roll. Tyler spun around and launched at Sabine, as she rose up. Tyler extended her right leg in a front kick; Sabine knocked the lower limb to one side as she moved out of the way, and the

199

force of the kick expired into the air. Sabine twisted her body, and her right elbow connected with Tyler's right shoulder. Tyler spun in the opposite direction. There was a yelp of pain, as Sabine continued to spin, then stopped, so she was facing her opponent. Tyler had done the same. There was a pause as they faced each other. Both pairs of eyes stared at each other, both fighting for breath. Their fists were up in front of themselves, defending, but also ready to strike. Tyler moved forward a single step, and Sabine launched at her with a front kick. Tyler jumped to the side so the kick missed, sending Sabine's boot through the space where Tyler's body had been. Tyler turned and threw her arms around the leg, picking her up. Sabine swung her left fist, striking Tyler on the side of her head, but it was not enough to stop her from raising Sabine up and slamming her down hard onto the sand.

Tyler grappled with the struggling Sabine, who thrust her right knee into Tyler's torso, buckling her body, so Tyler was thrown off her. Both scrambled, then jumped up at the same time. Tyler landed a roundhouse kick with her right leg to the side of Sabine's face. Sabine cried out as she fell to the ground. As quickly as she had fallen, she rolled and jumped up again. Tyler was launching another kick, and this time, Sabine blocked it. Tyler kicked with her left leg, and Sabine ducked. Then Tyler jumped up as Sabine hit her with a leg sweep. Tyler landed on the ground and Sabine attacked with a series of kicks and punches. Tyler blocked each one. Ruth watched from where she was standing, her pistol in her hand. Everything she wanted to do was forbidden. Tyler had been clear, and Ruth would stick to her promise. There was movement all around her. Some of the pack had changed back into sapien form; others were still wolves. Although everyone was busy, they were also watching what was happening at the water's edge.

"Holy Cow!" Ruth glanced at Michael, who'd stopped beside her. He was just zipping up his jacket. "Look at them go!" he exclaimed. Ruth felt her hand tighten on her weapon.

"Yeah," she said, watching the fight. Tyler flew backwards and landed on the sand; Sabine jumped forward, but her knee only hit the empty space where Tyler had just been. A side kick from Tyler sent Sabine rolling off in the opposite direction.

"I think we should..." Michael stepped forward.

"NO!" Ruth cut him off. We have our instructions." She turned to complete the tidy up of the beach. She tapped her ear. "Overwatch .... close down and return to the rally point," she said, holstering her weapon. Michael turned to watch the two women in the darkness battle on.

The speed and ferocity had not diminished; blow after blow landed in Tyler's side; she spun, and her right elbow crashed into Sabine's head, throwing her back. Tyler pressed on. She threw punches, which Sabine either ducked or blocked. Tyler had started a side kick when Sabine's face suddenly jerked forward; her forehead connected with the middle of Tyler's face. Her hands came up. Sabine's right boot landed in the middle of her chest, sending her flying backwards. Tyler's back skidded on the sand. She instinctively rolled over and up onto her hands; her feet dug into the sand. She was ready to defend whatever assault Sabine was about to launch.

Tyler was dazed - she blinked and looked at Sabine. The attack did not come. Sabine was looking past her, her mouth open. This time, her eyes were wide with fear. Tyler did not turn around. Sabine staggered back; her whole demeanour changed. The defiance was gone. She stepped away.

"Oh, shit," Sabine whispered. Sabine looked at Tyler, then back up towards the cliffs. Then she turned and took off as fast as she could run along the water's edge, away from her opponent. Sabine was sprinting now, desperate to get away.

Tyler shook her head, which slowly cleared, and the dizziness passed. Tyler stood up and watched Sabine disappear into the darkness. She was still out of breath when Ruth and the others arrived. They erupted with congratulations, which Tyler quickly supressed.

"What the hell just happened?" Ruth asked. Tyler glanced up towards the cliffs, then looked at Ruth.

"I have no idea." One of the others handed her a small piece of cloth. "Thank you," she said, and started to wipe the blood from her face.

"We could go after her," someone suggested.

"No," Tyler looked in the direction Sabine had run, "let her go."

"That was brilliant! You scared her off!" another exclaimed, the group was still joyous about their triumph on the beach.

"No, no, I didn't," Tyler handed the cloth back to him, "right, let's get this beach sorted and get out of here!" The group turned and headed away, excitedly replaying the events of the night. Ruth stayed with Tyler.

"What happened?" Ruth asked quietly. Tyler looked at her,

"I don't know."

"Why did she run off like that?"

"She was scared of something."

"What?" Ruth asked. "Was it you?"

"No," Tyler shook her head, "definitely not. It was something else." She looked back at the cliffs. "Have you still got your overwatch up there?"

"No, they are back at the vans." Ruth looked confused. "Why?"

Tyler turned and started to walk away from her. "I need to talk to them."

"They would not have seen your fight." Ruth stated.

"Whatever was up on the cliffs with them is what interests me."

Chapter 50

Cara-Marie was getting comfortable on her sofa. Her mother had just left, after giving her a lecture about 'modern girls' and the need to 'settle down'. The real reason for her visit had been revealed just before she got up to leave. Different people in town were commenting on her blog about werewolves and vampires, and her mother was not happy. 'How do you think this makes me look?' she had said, more than once. Her mother was not interested in investigative journalism, nor ground-breaking research that could change the way we, as a species, view the world we live in. Her mother was concerned with the way the family was viewed around the town.

Cara-Marie had not noticed that her brother hadn't called her for some time. According to her mother, it was because he was asked questions at his work about his fantasist sister and her horror stories. Her mum was fed up and she felt she had a right to say something. Cara-Marie disagreed with everything her mother said. She hadn't meant to raise her voice, but she did, and so did her mother in response; so, she shouted louder. Her mum slammed the door when she left.

Turning on the television, Cara-Marie recalled being told about the change to the crime watch programme tonight, and that Chief Anderson was going to be on. Kevin hadn't known exactly what the content would be. The programme was starting. She reached forward and picked up the glass of wine. Her notebook and pen were beside her, as usual, but she was not expecting anything of importance. The first story was about a jewellery robbery where they'd used a digger. She was not interested. The next story was even less captivating. She got up and refilled her wine glass in the kitchen. The phone in her pocket buzzed just as she was about to sit down. It was a message from Mark, the photographer. She landed back on the sofa, took a sip of wine, and opened the message. 'ARE YOU WATCHING THE CRIMEWATCH PROGRAMME?' Her face contorted. She took another sip, then tapped out her reply,

'OF COURSE, I AM WATCHING'. Cara-Marie had just about enough grief tonight; she did not need any from him. The camera panned around, and the presenter introduced Chief Anderson. He was wearing a pressed white police shirt and seemed quite pleased with himself.

"So," the presenter started, "to give us an update of several current investigations, I am pleased to welcome Chief Inspector Anderson of the Police Service of Northern Ireland. Chief Inspector...welcome." Cara-Marie noted that other police officers who'd been involved with previous stories all had used their own first names, but not him. This was very formal.

"Thank you," Chief Anderson started. Cara-Marie's eyes narrowed as the camera focused in on the career police officer. "Yes, we have several serious crimes we are investigating at the present time. We would like the outlying communities to come forward and help the police identify and stop these very dangerous people before they act again." She glanced at the notebook, then back at the screen. There was nothing new here. She picked up her phone and scrolled to the last message Mark had sent her. A map appeared on the TV screen, then zoomed in on Portstewart. They reviewed what was now referred to as 'The New Year's Day Murders'. The young faces of those who'd died appeared on the screen. She looked at them and paused; she glanced back at the phone, then set it down again.

"And there was a survivor who has also come to an unfortunate end, I believe?" the presenter asked, playing his role to perfection.

"Yes," the Chief Inspector answered, "we have always believed that Mr Kris Martin was not acting alone. We wanted to speak to him about other incidents, as well, before he was murdered not long ago, and we believe he was murdered by the very people he was associating with." Cara-Marie was cringing. Her phone bleeped with a message. It was from Mark.

'THIS IS ALMOST PAINFUL' The message made her smile; he was feeling the same. They showed still pictures from the bungalow and from the carpark in Belfast: there was nothing here she did not know already. They showed grainy photos of people they would like to speak to. This was the same Chief Inspector that had told her to 'stick to fetes and school sports days', and now here he was, asking the media for help. Her resentment of him continued to grow.

"So, there has been a recent incident, I believe, on a beach?" the presenter asked the scripted question.

"Yes, only yesterday, in fact," the Chief Inspector started. "A young couple out camping were discovered at White Park Bay, which is along the north coast," he explained. "Both were brutally murdered, but we currently do not think this incident is related." Cara-Marie raised her eyebrows.

"You mean you don't know the connection, even though they are all linked!" Cara-Marie retorted towards the screen. She had seen a photograph of one of them. The bite wounds were the same as the New Year's Day murders.

"I heard there were guns recovered. Could there be any terrorist links there?" the presenter asked. The face of Chief Anderson filled the screen again.

"No, we have already confirmed that the weapons were not linked to any local group, but we are looking towards organised crime." The presenter seemed appeased. Chief Anderson was thanked, then the camera moved as the presenter filled the screen again.

"So, if you have seen or know the current whereabouts of any of these people, please get in touch. Let's help put an end to these barbaric murders." He was reading from an autocue. She picked up her phone again and started to tap in a message. The presenter handed over to the female correspondent, who was with a different police force. Cara-Marie had lost interest.

'WELL THAT WAS A WASTE OF TIME!' She hit 'send' and dropped the phone on the arm of the sofa beside the unused notebook and pen. She was just reaching for her drink when the phone bleeped.

Mark had replied, 'THEY DON'T HAVE ANYTHING.' She nodded, then replied,

'I THINK WE HAVE MORE THAN THEM ☺ ', adding the smiley face at the end, mostly as a joke. The phone bleeped again.

'WHAT WEAPONS WERE FOUND?' he asked.

'THREE PUMP-ACTION SHOTGUNS, ONE OF WHICH HAD BEEN FIRED AND AN ARMALITE RIFLE, ALL WITH THEIR SERIAL NUMBERS FILED OFF, BLAMING ORG CRIME GANGS AGAIN! WHICH IS TOTAL CRAP.' The phone was quiet for a few moments, then Mark replied. He did not acknowledge her comments about the guns... how could he have missed that from earlier in the office? A couple murdered at White Park Bay had kept them busy most of the day, but how could he have missed the police finding the guns?

'IS HE LETTING YOU DO A STORY ON THE FIGHT AT THE FUNERAL?' She knew he was referencing the editor. Her thumbs tapped the screen, and she sent her reply,

'NO, NOT REALLY A COLERAINE STORY .... APPARENTLY.' She placed the phone down, then picked up her drink. Before she could take a sip, he replied. She lifted the phone and read his response.

'PITY, THERE WAS A TIME WHEN TWO COPPERS FIGHTING AT A FUNERAL WOULD HAVE BEEN A STORY. SO, THERE IS NOTHING HAPPENING THERE THEN?' She sighed and replied,

'THE SERGEANT, MIKE DEAR, WAS ARRESTED THIS MORNING AFTER THE CHIEF INSPECTOR MADE AN OFFICAL COMPLAINT OF ASSAULT.' Cara-Marie drank with one hand and held her phone with the other. This time, there was a pause before Mark answered,

'REALLY? WOW, WHAT HAPPENS NEXT?' Cara-Marie raised her eyebrows. Had he not been at the newspaper long enough to know that already?

'P.S.D. WILL INVESTIGATE THEN REPORT TO THE P.P.S. IF THAT HAPPENS, HE WILL BE SUSPENDED FROM DUTY PENDING A COURT CASE.' Cara-Marie placed the phone down and looked at the TV screen; she had not been following what else was happening. The phone bleeped again.

'OK, WHAT IS P.S.D. AND P.P.S.? JUST TO BE CLEAR.' Cara-Marie could not believe what she just read.

'WHAT? YOU ARE KIDDING ME? WHAT HAVE YOU BEEN DOING SINCE WORKING WITH US? HOW CAN YOU NOT KNOW THAT?' His message had annoyed her. She read it again, then answered his question,

'P.S.D. – PROFESSIONAL STANDARDS DEPARTMENT OF THE POLICE ... WHAT THE AMERICANS CALL 'INTERNAL AFFAIRS' THEN THERE IS THE P.P.S. – PUBLIC PROSCUTING SERVICE .... HOW CAN YOU NOT KNOW THAT?' She placed the glass down and waited; the phone bleeped.

'I DID, JUST CHECKING IF YOU DID ☺ .' She did not believe him, and did not hide her anger in her reply,

'JUST WAIT UNTIL I SEE YOU TOMORROW!' She scrolled through to Tony's name. She stared at it, then tapped out a short message,

'HIYA, ARE YOU AROUND FOR A COFFEE AND A CATCH UP? IT SEEMS AGES!' To sit and gossip was not on her agenda; she had not got much from Kyle. Rupert was right: he had become very defensive since becoming alpha. His visits to her flat had stopped. She watched as the word 'sending' scrolled across the screen. She placed the phone down and drank some more, her mind racing with questions to ask him. The phone bleeped. Excitedly, she picked it up, but felt let down when she read Mark's name.

'YEAH WE PROBABLY DO ☺ ' She didn't realise at first Mark was answering her earlier comment about them knowing more than the police. She did not respond. She guessed that Tony would not reply to her this evening. The phone landed on the coffee table and she changed the TV channel; she wanted some escapism for a while.

Suddenly, she remembered about the pen drive. Cara-Marie set her drink down and fished in the pocket of her jacket for the pen drive. It did not take long before her desktop computer was fired up; she pushed the drive into the USB port. A small hourglass symbol appeared as the computer linked up. Cara-

Marie got comfortable and, using the mouse, clicked on the link to the pen drive. After a few seconds, the document opened. The page was filled with numbers, symbols and letters; whatever it was, it was corrupted. She sighed, then closed down the desktop. There was nothing on the pen drive, so she took it out of the USB port. She went back to the sofa and, lifting her drink, got comfortable. She scrolled through the available films and smiled when she read the description of one of them.

"Six men, a full moon and no chance! Why not?" she said out loud. 'A bitch of a werewolf movie!' she read from the review. Cara-Marie sat back and let the film start. She would update her 'werewolf blog' later.

∞∞∞∞

Tony walked over to the landline phone in the living room of the farmhouse. He looked at the message on his own phone, then slowly punched in the number. There was movement upstairs, but the room was empty. As the ringing tone started, the front door opened, and Paul Hawkins walked in. He nodded towards Tony as he closed the door. Tony nodded, and then became engrossed in the call he was making. Tyler appeared at the entrance to the kitchen. She patted Tony on the shoulder as she walked past.

"Hey," she said, stopping beside Paul.

"Hiya," Paul looked her up and down, "are you not getting dressed up for tonight?" he asked. She scrunched up her face.

"I will once they are off." Paul nodded once. He looked at Tony, who looked like he was getting angry. Tyler turned towards Tony but spoke to Paul. "I thought Kyle had already talked to Connor down south?" she asked.

"He did."

"And what was the response?" Tyler looked at Paul, who shrugged his shoulders.

"Connor was not happy, but Kyle told him we were responding to what is happening." Paul glanced at Tyler, "Although Connor wasn't happy, he let it go."

"He let it go?" Tyler's tone rose. "What is that supposed to mean?" she demanded.

"Well, as you know, he told us if we stepped out of line, he would shut us down and run things directly from down south." Paul's face revealed what he was thinking. Tyler did not interrupt him so he continued, "We can 'respond' to any Noc incursion, but any backlash is on our own heads." The two looked into each other's eyes, "and Connor made it very clear he would not intervene."

"Even though we have identified a large group of them, on his lands... he is not going to 'intervene'!" Tyler placed her hands on her hips and shook her head.

"So, what was on the cliffs that scared the Noc away? The overwatch said there was nothing there when they were in place." Paul said. Tyler looked at him, then glanced at Tony.

"I don't know," her answer was almost a whisper.

"You don't know?" Paul had raised his voice, and Tyler shook her head.

Tony's voice rose in the background, "Look, I'm just letting you know where she is!"

"So, who is he talking to?" Tyler asked.

"The coven in Salisbury," Tony quietly indicated. Tyler's whole body reacted as she shot a look at Paul. Paul returned the look and raised his eyebrows. "We still have a pact in place, and we are letting them know where their precious princess is." He explained. Tyler was angry - her feelings were clear on the matter. As Tony replaced the handset, Kyle appeared in the doorway of the kitchen. He was wearing a baggy tracksuit and was smiling excitedly. They turned towards him.

"So, are you ready?" Paul asked, crossing the room, holding out his hand. Kyle stepped past Tony and took the handshake.

"As ready as I'll ever be!" Kyle was smiling as he spoke. Tyler stepped forward,

"Remember, a deer in a straight line is faster than you; it will be able to outrun you and the team. You need to get it into the woods and force it to stop and turn." Tyler passed on her knowledge. Kyle nodded and Tyler continued, "Have you done a walk-through with the rest of the hunting party?" she asked.

"Yes, we finished that an hour ago," he acknowledged. Everyone was smiling, except Tony. Kyle turned towards him. "So, what did they say about their precious princess?" Kyle asked. Tony paused before answering,

"They claim they know nothing about her being here. They say she is in France, then on her way to Italy."

"You put them right, then!" Tyler was annoyed again. Tony looked over at her.

"Yes, they repeated if it *is* her, she is not sanctioned by them," Tony explained.

"So, if we take her down, they cannot react!" Paul exclaimed; Tyler smiled.

"At last!" she said.

"So, the truce will still be in place?" Kyle asked, and Paul nodded.

"Yes," Paul looked towards Tony. "Were you able to record the conversation?" Tony smiled and lifted his left hand to show the small Dictaphone that he was holding.

"Hell, yes," he smiled as he spoke. That lifted the mood of the room. Kyle nodded and smiled in return.

"Has there been anything on the blog of that journalist in Coleraine?" Kyle inquired. Tony noticed that he did not use Cara-Maire's name, just her job title.

"Nothing that concerns us," Tony stated. "She just messaged me asking to meet for coffee sometime." Tyler looked over at him.

"She only wants to find out what she can from you," she stated.

"Of course, but I can also turn it around and feed her info of no use to her!"

"Isn't she an old school pal of yours?" Paul asked.

"Yes," Tony nodded.

"No problem with that," Kyle said, "go for it and see what else you can find out for us," he instructed. There was movement outside. Paul looked towards the front door,

"Well, we have a hunt and a moon dance to attend. There is lots to celebrate." He looked back at Kyle, "Okay, boss, it's time to lead your first hunt!" Paul stepped back and motioned with his left hand towards the door. Kyle walked over to the door. He opened it and walked outside. They all followed him out.

The front yard was full of people; most where dressed for a black-tie event, but there were some still dressed for farm work. Kyle was greeted with handshakes and pats on the shoulder. Paul stepped forward and shouted, and the group went quiet. Kyle was standing at Paul's side; Paul knew what he was doing.

"HUNTING PARTY, COME FORTH!" Paul shouted. Smiling faces parted and four excited teenagers stepped forward. One at a time, they filed past Kyle, nodding once as they did so, then formed a line on Kyle's right side. All were dressed in similar baggy track suits. Paul raised his voice again, "BRING FORTH, THE BEAST!"

The crowd turned as one, towards the opening barn door. Then they moved back to form a path, as one of the farmhands led the stag forward, stopping a few feet in front of Paul and Kyle. Kyle walked around the deer, breathing deeply as he did so; the rest of the hunting party followed him. Kyle held out his hand and gently caressed the animal's hide with his fingertips. The deer did not move. Each breath filled Kyle's nostrils with the deer's scent. He'd never felt anything like it; Tyler had been right. His heart rate quickened, and the excitement of the coming hunt grew inside him. His wolf wanted out. Kyle stopped at the front of the deer and looked into its eyes. The large, brown eyes stared back. Paul spoke quieter this time to the farmhand who held the rope. "Lead him to the field." The farmhand nodded, and the crowd parted. The five members of the hunting party walked slowly after the animal, led by Kyle. The gate to the field was already open. The crowd stopped and gathered by the fence. Paul nodded at Kyle; he had told him what to do earlier. Kyle followed the stag into the field, and the gate was closed behind them. "RELEASE THE BEAST!" shouted Paul, and a cheer rose from crowd. The farmhand removed the harness and the deer bolted forward towards the centre of the darkening field. Paul turned towards the crowd, "Let us retire to the bar!" Kyle looked back; his eyes found Tyler and Tony, who were both smiling.

Tyler leaned towards Tony, and said, "I am going to go and get ready." It was loud enough for Kyle to hear. Tony smiled, then said something in reply. Both turned and walked away. The farmhand walked past them, then turned around, walking backwards for a few steps before they reached the gate.

"Fiach maith, An Rua!" they all shouted. Kyle looked back at them and nodded. They had shouted 'good hunting' in Irish. The four teenagers were all motionless, they were looking towards him, waiting for his lead. Kyle looked intensely at each one, in turn.

"Remember what we discussed earlier," he stated, and started to undress. The others followed suit. Once he was fully naked, Kyle knelt on one knee. He placed his fists on the ground and looked at a patch of grass in front of him. "Come wolf, come," he whispered... and his body exploded in pain.

Chapter 51

Kyle opened his eyes. The evening had gone grey and he no longer felt the cold. The field was now in sharp contrast; he could make out details farther away than before. Then the smells hit him. He breathed in through his nose; he could smell the grass, the earth. He looked to one side, then the other; he knew each wolf by the scent. The wind blew gently into his face and he lowered his head. The deer had left footprints, each heavy with scent. They led away like steppingstones over a pond. He could see them in a different colour leading over the rise towards where the deer was grazing.

Kyle stood up; the pairs of wolves on either side of him did the same. He focused on his prey. His eyes narrowed; his body tensed. He glanced to his left, and motioned with his head; the two replied, then turned and headed off at speed. They would be bringing up the left side, preventing the deer from heading to the lower fields. He looked at the two on his right and did the same; they replied, then ran in the direction they had rehearsed earlier. Kyle straightened up and looked over his shoulder at the few who stayed by the wall. The group was made up of several people dressed for a formal dinner and the more casual hands who would work on the farm that night. Smiles, claps and cheers wished them on their way. Kyle nodded, then turned and slowly started to walk away from them. His ears twitched; he realised he could hear the footfalls of the running wolves. He looked down at his hands, the way they had changed; the hair on the backs of his hands, on his fingers, the way the nails had grown slightly but, he remembered from before, the nails on his toes had not. He lifted his left hand and touched the side of his face. He could feel where the contours had changed, from sapien to Garou. His fingers continued through the short fur around his neck. He closed his eyes and breathed. His mind processed everything his senses were telling him. He could see, hear and smell the other four wolves and, most importantly, he could see, hear and smell exactly where the prey was.

That's what it was now. It was no longer a deer; it was a beast, it was prey. His hands were by his sides, and his walk increased to a trot. As he went over the rise, the beast turned and looked at him. It showed anger in its eyes, then its head lowered to attack. The beast was not afraid.

Suddenly, it looked to its left, then to its right; it had spotted the other wolves. The beast turned and ran. Kyle broke into a run. He was sprinting as fast as he could towards the deer. Tyler had been right; the deer was easily outrunning them in a straight line. He was upright and running as fast as he could, but the distance between them was increasing. The beast crashed into the forest, bounding from side to side, just as the others entered behind it. The trees would slow it down; and the wolves would move faster. Kyle jumped through the gap in the trees, where the beast had gone. His vision seemed to be in shades of grey, but everything was in fine detail. The scent led him through the forest; it was a strong scent, fresh; it led like a path through the trees. On either side of him, he could hear the others crashing through the trees at speed. They were driving the beast. Kyle stopped. He bent down on one knee and placed his fists on the ground. He lowered his snout. He easily found the scent and looked up in the direction it was leading. The beast had slowed down. Instead of running, Kyle was now stalking. He raised himself up and looked around. He could not see the others, but he knew exactly where they were, doing precisely what they had planned.

He moved off at a trot. There was a loud crashing noise to his left. The beast had turned and had tried to head into the centre of the woods but the two wolves on its left had cut it off. The beast was coming back towards him. He slowed. His keen eyes picked out the sudden movement about seventy metres ahead. The stag was moving at speed, crossing in front of him. It was about to encounter the other two wolves and would be forced back to the centre of the wood block. Kyle slowed now to a deliberate, slow, stealthy walk. The beast was turning back towards him. He stopped as the beast skidded to a halt in front of him. The other wolves appeared through the trees; they split, forming a perimeter around the animal - it had only one way out. It had to get past Kyle.

Kyle stepped forward, slightly lowering his head as he did so, looking the beast in the eyes. He recognized defiance there; this animal was not afraid of him, it would fight. The deer lowered its head, never releasing his glare from Kyle. He scratched at the ground with his right front hoof. Kyle nodded; he was being beckoned forward. Kyle did not have to look around, the other four would prevent the beast from running away, but this deer had no intention of doing that.

Suddenly, it jumped forward, thrusting its antlers to push Kyle back. The deer opened its mouth and a low-pitched noise came out - Kyle had a fight on his hands. He looked at the antlers; they were sharp enough to do him damage, if not kill him. He would have to move fast. Kyle spread his arms and opened his fingers. He growled, then barked at the deer. He was not afraid either. Kyle stepped towards it, just as the deer attacked with a leap. Kyle sidestepped the attack into empty space. Kyle swiped with his right hand, aiming for the beast's neck, but missed.

The deer moved slowly in a circle; Kyle kept the antlers in front of him. The deer beckoned with its hoof again to entice him closer. They were surrounded by a chorus of barks and growls from the other four, with the occasional snap of teeth. The deer fixed its gaze on its attacker; the jostling continued. One of the others suddenly barked a warning. Kyle quickly realised what the beast was doing; he had been turning them so that it was on higher ground than Kyle. It jumped forward again. Kyle jumped back, then responded with an attack of his own. The antlers missed the side of his face by only millimetres. Kyle's teeth snapped open space as the deer tried to push him further down the gradual slope. The thrust of the antlers forced him to roll to his right. One of the other wolves jumped forward and the deer snapped its antlers towards it, and, for a brief moment, the left side of the deer's neck was exposed.

It was all Kyle needed. His hind legs propelled him forward with such speed that his first bite only tore open the beast's skin but, as the deer hit the earth, Kyle found his target. The deer bucked and fought with its head and forelegs, but Kyle's teeth were embedded in its throat. Kyle's left arm was wrapped around the deer's neck, as he tucked his legs in to deflect the flailing legs. The hooves were sharper than they looked.

Blood splashed over Kyle's face; it was warm and tasted metallic. Kyle held on, his grip tightening while, with each pump of blood, the deer's strength waned. The others pounced; the beast was overpowered. Its movements slowed, then stopped. The blood stopped pumping; the body went limp; it was dead. A hand patted Kyle on the shoulder; he could relax. He rolled away from the dead animal and stood up, his body surging with excitement; he felt jubilant. He'd never felt anything like this before. The others were standing now; the excitement flowed through them like electricity. They were waiting for his lead. One stepped forward and motioned towards the sky. Kyle understood. A feeling of pure euphoria flowed through him as he pointed his snout skyward and put his whole body into the long howl that came out of him. The others joined in with a joyful chorus. Kyle gulped, took a deep breath, then howled again. When he stepped back, the wolves crowded around him in exaltation; they were victorious! Vehicle headlights cut through the trees. The Land Rover stopped at the edge of the wood. Kyle could hear slamming doors and watched as torchlights cut through the trees. One of the wolves turned and barked twice. The torchlights veered towards them. Four of the farmhands approached; there was a joyous welcome!

"Well, that was quick!" one of them commented, as the hunters were applauded. The torchlights illuminated the beast on the ground. Kyle's shoulders were patted again.

"Well done boss, that was a good one! Leave the rest to us; all of you need to head back so you can get cleaned up and dressed for the dance." Kyle nodded appreciatively at the smiling face.

The joyous hunting party walked to the edge of the wood. When one of them broke into a run, they all responded. Kyle felt himself take off at speed. The younger wolves were faster than he was, but he relished the sense of freedom, the sense of belonging. He was a pack member, and this felt like one of the most natural things he'd ever experienced. His lungs fought to suck air in as he ran with all his strength. He could feel the ground move under his feet, and he increased his speed; he was loving this.

The gate at the far side of the field appeared all too quickly. The wolves slowed and came to halt. Kyle looked around as the elated team congratulated each other. They shared the moment; they had worked as one; achieved what they set out to do. They'd felled their target; the hunt was successful. They each found their own clothes; it was time to change back. Kyle walked over to his pile. He knelt down and closed his eyes. He felt himself strain; his wolf wanted to stay. He strained again, and felt the change begin. He closed his eyes, and pain shot through his body. Suddenly, he could feel the cold again. It was not until he stood up that it became obvious to him how much blood there'd been. It was not just over his face and neck, but the entire front of his body, across his arms and splashed onto his legs. Kyle looked at his human form, how different from his wolf. His body was twitching from the change; it was still painful for him but, with each change, it became less so.

"At least one of us needs a shower!" one of the hunting party said as he pulled on his shirt. Kyle looked up at the smiling faces; he smiled and nodded.

"We all do," shouted another, and laughter rippled through them. The Land Rover behind them gunned its engine; it was on the move.

"We'd better hurry up, then!" Kyle exclaimed. He had completed his first hunt and it had been a success. He leaned down and pulled on his briefs, then picked up the rest of his clothes. "See you lot at the barn, then." The gate opened. The others had dressed quickly, but Kyle did not. He kept his clothes bundled under his left arm and as soon as he'd walked through the gate, he broke into a run. He was not quite sprinting, but it was fast enough. He headed towards the front door of the farmhouse. The rest of the hunting party broke off in different directions and headed off to get changed. The front door was unlocked, and Kyle closed it behind himself. The farmhouse was empty, and it was warm. He padded his way up the stairs and went straight into the bathroom. He dropped his clothes on the floor and closed the door behind him. He was now sticky from the drying blood. He reached forward and switched the shower on. The water flowed over him, into a red pool at his feet. He watched the water slowly change from dark to light red, then clear.

In the last twelve months, everything he thought he knew had been challenged. He had done things he'd never thought he could. His mind flashed over what he'd seen. The bus station in Limavady, the Castleroe killings, what stood at the top of the hill, finding Karen on the floor of the kitchen, watching a change for the very first time in the arena, then the Mongols. In a moment, he had gone from being an item of curiosity to becoming the one in charge. In the months after Carl's death, he had to start from scratch. The one voice that objected was gone; Kyle guessed he would meet Sean Lefebvre again.

In the days following Carl's funeral, Kyle had been unsure what kind of reception he would get; but it was nearly all positive. Carl was alpha for so long; it would take time for them to grieve properly. Kyle made it clear when he was around the farm, anyone who had a problem could talk to him. Paul said afterwards it was a very good way to get to know the individual members of the pack. Kyle had stood up to the Mongols and beat them in such a way no one could doubt his formidable prowess. It was Carl's decision to open up to the British military; and, letting them take down what was left of the Mongols at Mussenden Temple had proven to be a good idea. Kyle remembered the exchange when he met Connor and the rest of the clan leadership. They had reacted with anger at the recent actions taken. They would not be coming north to help. Kyle reached for the shower gel. It was time to get on with tonight's celebration.

∞∞∞∞

He closed the door of the farmhouse. He looked over at the entrance to the barn, where the rest of the hunting party waited for him. Kyle had pressed the dinner jacket, shirt and trousers himself. The heels of his shoes clicked on the stones as he approached. He was trying to suppress how good he was feeling, but the electricity from the others was infectious. He was met by handshakes and embraces from the guys and a peck on the cheek from each of the two girls. Kyle complimented them all on how good they were looking; none of them could contain their excitement. They had just completed their first hunt! The barn door was pulled back and a well-dressed farmhand poked his head out.

"Everyone here?" he asked, the hunting party looked towards their alpha.

"Yes, we are," the farmhand beamed and pushed the heavy door open,

"Everyone is seated in the hall and is waiting to receive you." Kyle stepped forward and placed his hand on the farmhand's shoulder as he walked past him.

"Thank you." The others followed. Kyle went through the door that led towards the bar area. The bar was empty except for three people working behind the bar. It was cluttered with empty glasses. While they were hunting, the rest of the pack was partying. The curtains that hid the double doors leading into the hall parted, and Dermott emerged. Kyle and the others walked over to him. Dermott held out his hand, which Kyle took in a firm handshake.

"Well done; very well done, indeed!" Dermott walked down the line greeting and congratulating each one in turn. Kyle stood by the curtains. There was a buzz of conversation coming from inside the hall, through the open doors. Kyle tried to mask his apprehension with a confident demeanour, but inside he was nervous. This was a huge step forward for him as leader of the pack. He did not fear a challenge but for him to be fully accepted this would be an important step. Dermott came back towards him and asked,

"Are you ready?" Kyle nodded, "right," Dermott explained, "I will go in first and announce you. As you walk in, head along the right side of the room, and stop when you see the chalk mark on the floor." Dermott looked down the line, "Each of you line up beside Kyle, in order." He looked back at Kyle, "Stay there. Paul will do the marking ceremony then you can take your seats." Kyle nodded again. Dermott looked at each one of them. "'Everyone got that?" he asked. Nodding smiles answered him. "Right, then," Dermott reached out with his left hand and stepped towards the curtain. He looked back over his shoulder, "Good luck, everyone."

"Luck is not a factor!" answered one of the groups, and Kyle smiled at the response. Dermott smiled again, gave Kyle a nod, and stepped through the curtain, allowing it to close behind him. The hall went quiet as Dermott started.

"GAROU OF THE NORTHERN DUN OF THE AN RUA, PLEASE BE UPSTANDING TO WELCOME YOUR HUNTING PARTY!" The room exploded in rapturous appreciation as Dermott pulled the curtain back. Kyle stepped forward through the doorway and into the hall. The tables were formed in the usual 'M' shape; everyone was standing and turned towards them. There was clapping and cheering. Kyle tried to contain his pride and excitement as he walked forward. He glanced around, not making eye contact with anyone; he walked on. His eyes searched for the mark on the floor. As he neared the top of this leg of tables, he spotted

208

the single white line on the floor. Kyle stopped beside it and turned to face where the top table was. The others formed the line to his left. The standing ovation continued until Paul shouted to quiet them.

"AN RUA … … PLEASE TAKE YOUR SEATS." Kyle stood with his hands behind him, and the others followed his lead. After a few seconds of shuffling, everyone except Paul sat down. Kyle eyed the line of faces along the top table. There were two gaps on either side; he knew the one in the centre was for him. Paul was standing to the right of his seat and Tyler was sitting on the left. Her hair was down, and she looked happy. Paul turned to the seated crowd. Kyle spotted him looking over at the curtains again, waiting for an agreed signal. He shouted again. "AN RUA … … WELCOME THE BEAST!" Everyone remained seated, but the applause and cheering started again. Kyle looked over to his left, as did the rest of the hunting party, and the curtains were pulled back. The lights in the bar had been switched off.

They heard the piper before they saw him. He was dressed exactly the same as he had been at Kyle's very first dance. The piper marched in and the applause turned to clapping in rhythm with the tune. The piper turned to his left, marched a few steps, then stopped. He turned towards the rest and continued to play as two others carried in the massive silver platter holding the stag's head on their shoulders, their hands firmly gripping the edges. They briefly paused and tilted the platter, so it looked like the deer was lowering its head; then they straightened up and walked on towards Kyle. The head was dressed, and it looked good. It passed in front of Kyle and over towards where Paul was standing. They stopped and the platter was tilted again. Paul raised a small sherry glass in salute. The pair then turned so they were facing everyone seated. The piper went silent. Paul reached down to the table and picked up a knife that was about four inches long. He held it by his side as he walked towards the head. He stopped when he got there and turned towards everyone, then raised the knife. A cheer echoed around the room. As Paul turned towards the stag's head, he looked at Kyle and smiled. Paul nodded once; Kyle responded the same. Paul gripped a piece of the skin on the neck and started a sawing motion until a piece of flesh came away in his hand; he placed the knife on the platter. Paul looked at Kyle, then walked over to him. Paul was beaming.

Kyle would never be able to describe how he was feeling in the moment. He closed his eyes, and slightly lowered his head. He felt Paul wipe the flesh down one side of his face, then the other. Kyle opened his eyes, and Paul stepped back, almost in tears. Kyle nodded towards him. Paul then stepped down the line and repeated the ritual. Paul walked back past them again and replaced the meat on the platter. He turned to the room again. "AN RUA, PLEASE BE UPSTANDING AND WELCOME THOSE WHO HAVE COMPLETED THEIR FIRST HUNT!"

The room once again exploded in joy. Paul looked at Kyle and extended his right hand towards his seat as everyone stood up again. Kyle made his way toward the centre of the top table. Walking behind them, he was greeted with smiles, pats on the shoulder and congratulations. When he got to his seat, he saw Tyler look back over her left shoulder. She was applauding, and she had a look of joy on her face. Her hair hung over her shoulders. The dark blue satin dress showed off her figure. It was sleeveless, with an open back. His chair had been moved to one side. Kyle manoeuvred his way, so he was standing in front of his place setting. He looked over his shoulder as the others from the hunting party made their way past. Kyle stood there and looked around the room. Tyler leaned in and spoke into his ear.

"We are all waiting for you to sit down." Kyle looked into her eyes, and she winked. He was still learning. He smiled, then reached behind him. As he pulled the chair up and took his place, the applause quietened down. Everyone took their seats. Paul walked up and stood in front of him. The murmur of conversation gradually slowed. Kyle looked over to his left as the head of the stag was carried out. The piper remained standing, obviously waiting for his next cue. Paul lifted the small sherry glass one more time.

"AN RUA … TONIGHT, WE FEAST!" This time, Kyle joined in with the applause, as he used the napkin that had been neatly folded beside his wine glass to wipe the blood from his face.

∞∞∞∞∞

`The last of the final course had been cleared away. Everyone had eaten very well. Paul knocked hard on the table and the room went quiet. Kyle watched as Paul stood up. All eyes in the room turned towards him. Kyle reached into his pocket for the small cards with some basic handwritten notes on them and placed them on the table in front of him. Paul looked over the room; this time, he spoke quieter than he had before.

"An Rua," he paused, smiling around the room, "first, I would like to thank everyone who helped set up and organise this evening." There was a murmur of conversation. Kyle's eyes darted over to his left as, from the corner of the room, a chef dressed in white appeared. Paul carried on, "I would like to take this opportunity to thank our catering team for, once again, providing such magnificent food for us." Paul raised his glass towards the smiling man in the corner, who nodded as the applause started. Kyle looked back at Paul as the room went quiet again. Paul once again looked over the room. "An Rua," he started, then looked over at Kyle, "our alpha!" The applause started again; Kyle pushed his chair back and stood up beside Paul. The two exchanged a firm handshake and spoke quietly to each other. Paul let go of the embrace, then took his own seat. Kyle looked over the room; everyone was looking at him.

"Firstly, may I add my own thanks to the catering team – they were outstanding!" there was a small ripple of applause. Kyle glanced down at his notes. He looked up before he spoke again. "I would like to say a few words before the entertainment starts," he glanced down and then scanned the room. "Where is Ruth McDonal?" he asked, there was excited movement to one side as his attention was drawn to her smiling face. She raised her right hand to let everyone know where she was. "Ruth," Kyle continued, "please stand." The embarrassed woman slowly pushed her chair back and stood up, looking around. There was a cheer as she did so; Ruth was popular.

"Ruth," Kyle spoke directly to her. She turned and looked towards the top table. "Over the last few weeks, you have twice led operations against those who mean us harm," Kyle did not have to say the word 'Noctrailis', but everyone knew who he was talking about. "First twelve, then over twenty just a couple of nights ago." The room again burst into applause; a few took to their feet, clapping and cheering for Ruth, who smiled and glanced around. She was not used to being the focus of attention. The room quietened down and, apart from Kyle, everyone retook their seats. "Ruth," Kyle said to her, "For your outstanding leadership, please accept this small token from me." The curtains opened and one of the bar staff walked in with a large bouquet of flowers. Ruth's hands came up to her face and she blushed as the flowers were handed over. The applause started again, and Ruth, holding the flowers, whispered her thanks, and sat down again. As the room quietened down, Kyle said to her, "Ruth, there is also a bottle of champagne waiting for you behind the bar." Kyle smiled as said the words. Ruth was still being congratulated.

"Nice touch... I like that," whispered Tyler from beside him. He glanced over at her then rearranged the cards in his hands and looked back over the room,

"So, before we enjoy the entertainment, one thing I would like us all to acknowledge," the room went quiet, "is that, although we have scored successes, there has been a cost to our pack." The mood in the room became sombre. Kyle looked at the sea of faces in front of him. "Carl was taken from us, as was Amanda. You all know Amanda and I were close," Kyle felt himself start to well up. He had planned to say this, but his body was reacting with the memories of her. "I would like us all to stand and raise our glasses." There was a flurry of movement as everyone in the room stood. Kyle waited for the noise to stop before he raised his glass. "An Rua ... ... to our absent friends." Kyle toasted, then drank a sip. They all did the same and a ripple of applause went around the room. Everyone sat back down. Kyle remained standing. Once the room was quiet again, he looked towards Paul. "I believe there is entertainment planned?" Paul nodded.

"Yes, there certainly is!" Paul responded loudly. Kyle turned back to the room; he had read the last line of his notes. Paul had told him what to finish off with:

"THEN, LET THE ENTERTAINMENT, BEGIN!" Kyle replaced his glass and re-took his seat. The curtains to the bar opened and the casually dress piper walked in with a set of Irish pipes under one arm and a small stool under the other. He was followed by two others, one with a bodhran drum and the third with a penny whistle. They positioned themselves against the far wall and soon started up a tune. Kyle found his right foot tapping away as the pace of the tune increased. He looked down at Tyler's right hand, reached over and squeezed it.

"Well done," she whispered.

"By the way," Kyle leaned over towards her.

"What?" she asked. Kyle looked at her.

"You will have to tell me in detail about your fight on the beach!" Tyler looked at him, then turned her head towards the musicians.

"Later," she replied. Kyle looked over the room, as well. There was a pause before the musicians started a different tune, equally toe-tapping. The curtains flew back, and three female dancers leapt forward. Their outfits were of thick black felt with elegant Celtic patterns on them. Their arms hung stiffly by their sides, as their black-stockinged legs began to tell a tale in perfect unison. Kyle knew there were another three dancers waiting for their turn. The dance would be in two parts and would be rewarded with ecstatic applause at the end of each tale.

Afterwards, everyone would be in the bar and the disco music would play into the night. For now, Kyle forgot about all the problems facing the pack. For one evening, he did not concern himself with what Connor and the southern pack may do in response to what they had done. He cared even less what the vampires would do. They had been dealt a blow that would take them some time to recover from. For this one evening, they were all on safe ground, and they could relax.

Chapter 52

Cara-Marie zipped her coat up a little bit more as she walked away from her car. It had gotten colder; it would not be long before the snow would fall. She studied the flow of traffic while she stopped at the crossing. The lights stopped the cars, vans and lorries, then the beeping sound let the pedestrians know it was safe to cross. She walked forward, avoiding the bald-headed man coming towards her. He looked angry and he did not notice her at all. She walked around the corner and headed to the back door of the office. Mark was standing outside with one of the receptionists. Something was wrong.

"What are you two doing out here?" she asked, checking the watch on her wrist. She was not late. They both turned towards her. The receptionist smiled in greeting, but Mark looked bored.

"We can't go in yet." Mark stated, as she stopped beside him. The door was partially open, and she was able to see inside. Rubbish, paper and other items were scattered over the floor. Kevin was standing in the middle of the office with his back towards them.

"What the hell?" she asked out loud.

"We've been broken into!" the receptionist exclaimed. Cara-Marie looked at Mark, who shrugged.

"Really?" Cara-Marie asked.

"Really, really," Mark replied. Cara-Marie stepped towards the door and pushed it open with her left hand.

"What has been stolen?" she asked, looking at the mess on her desk. Kevin turned at the movement of the door. The anger on his face subsided slightly.

"Cara!" he exclaimed.

"Kevin, what ..." she started, stepping over the threshold and into the room. It had been completely trashed!

"Don't touch anything," he snapped, as he put his hands on his hips and turned towards the main office. "Have a quick look around your desk and let me know if anything is missing." Cara-Marie walked towards her desk. The drawers were open, the contents scattered over the floor and the desk. She prided herself on always keeping her desk neat and tidy. It was a disaster! She reached out towards one of the drawers, and Kevin snapped at her. "I said don't touch anything! The cops are on their way!" She withdrew her hand.

Her office chair was on its side and had been pushed underneath the desk. She took a mental inventory of everything in sight. She wanted to immediately sort through it all, put it back where it belonged. It was an effort not to. She unzipped her coat, looking around the floor and back over the desk. She exchanged baleful looks with Kevin. "Well?" he asked. Cara-Marie looked at him and for a moment, was silent. Kevin raised his eyebrows. "Well," he repeated, "is anything missing?" She surveyed the mess, then looked back at him.

"Not that I can see, no," she replied, Kevin was scanning the destruction.

"What were they after?" he asked of no one in particular.

"Is anything gone?" she queried, Kevin looked over his left shoulder at her, then shook his head. He looked away again.

"You'd better wait outside," he suggested. Cara-Marie nodded and walked outside again. She closed the door and looked up at two more staff members who'd just arrived. They all seemed to be in a state of shock.

"Anything missing?" Mark asked, Cara-Marie shook her head.

"Isn't it awful?" someone said.

"Yes, it is," Mark responded. The rest of the staff started an intense discussion about what might have happened.

"I mean... there is no money there, so it could not have been that!" exclaimed one. Mark looked at Cara-Marie.

"Well?"

"Well what?" she answered.

"What do you think?" he asked. She looked at him quizzically.

"Who could have done it?" another member of staff asked the group.

Cara-Marie looked at Mark. "I have no idea," she replied, her mind was racing, but she was not coming up with any answers.

"Did you look at that pen stick you found?" he asked, she looked at him blankly.

"What?" The pen stick was the last thing on her mind right now.

"The pen stick you found in your pocket; did you get a chance to open it?"

"Yes, last night…and no, it was blank, there was nothing on it." Cara-Marie looked to her left as two uniformed police officers approached. She studied them; the one on the left was older. She recognised the face but could not remember his name. The other officer was much younger. Her uniform was perfectly pressed, and her boots shone. Cara-Marie was guessing she had not been out of the police college very long. The older one was introducing them all to the younger officer.

"This …" he held out his left hand towards the gathered crowd, "is Mark Scott, the Herald's resident photographer," Mark did not look impressed but gave a brief nod. "And this is Cara-Marie McKenna, reporter. Watch what you say in front of her, as it may end up in print," he chuckled. The younger police officer's face reddened slightly. The older officer was smiling; Mark was not.

"If you are looking for Kevin, he's inside," said Mark, pointing towards the back door with his right hand.

"Aye, no problems," the officer said, his partner remained silent. The staff moved out of the way as the two officers walked past them and headed into the office.

"Right, then," Mark started, "since we are not going to get into the office anytime soon, we all might as well go for breakfast."

"I've had breakfast," Cara-Marie answered, and Mark turned towards the town.

"Well," he adjusted his coat collar, "we may as well head to the wee café just down the street. This is obviously going to take a good part of day." He turned to the others, "'Anyone else fancy a cup of tea?" Mark looked around, "At least it'll get us out of the cold." There was a chorus of agreement. Mark smiled, Cara -Marie smiled back,

"Why not."

∞∞∞∞

The darkness was closing in fast. Tony slowed the car down; he was looking for a right turn that he knew was along here somewhere. He had never been to Dunseverick Harbour before, but he remembered driving past the entrance. The moon dance last night had been a good one. Kyle had done very well - first with the hunt, and then with his address to the whole pack. They all had accepted him as alpha. It may be a while before they trusted him fully, but he'd proven himself a true leader. Connor, and the main pack down south… well, that was another matter altogether. Tony noticed Tyler had let Kyle know she was interested, but Kyle had walked away. Tony knew that, after falling for Kelly, and the way she had treated him, he had not let Amanda get too close to him. But it was unusual for an alpha to be single.

Single. It made him smile, and he thought of Karen. He felt like he was absolutely glowing on the inside and hoped it didn't show too much. Several people passed on comments and congratulations on Karen's pregnancy, especially after what happened last year. He wanted this meeting to be over soon, so he could head home to be with his wife. The road rose-up, then dropped away, following the contours of the land. Even in the darkness, he could make out the sea in front of him. He slowed the car and took the next turn. The road narrowed to one lane now. To his left were the crashing waves; the grass verge rose on both sides of the road. On top of these, the landowner had put up thick, round wooden posts every ten metres. In his headlights, Tony could make out the barbed wire strung between them. The road twisted and turned.

Suddenly, over the rise in front of him appeared a single light. There was a passing point on his side of the road, so he pulled in. The motorcyclist roared past at high speed. Tony tried to catch a glimpse of the rider or the bike, but they were too fast. He had to think. He knew who he was meeting but was unsure if anyone else would be there. This could be just a ploy to get him on his own. He turned off the engine and the main headlights of his car. The night around him was dark. After a moment, he quietly opened the driver's door.

The cold of the night blew in. Tony stepped out of the car and slowly pushed the door shut with a click. He reached around his waist and found the familiar grip of his pistol. If anything was going to happen, he could at least defend himself. He looked back along the coast - he could just make out the looming cliffs; the glow of Portrush was beyond them. The sound of the motorcycle was fast disappearing into the distance. He looked ahead at the road. It rose slightly, then dropped down the far side of the rise to the right. The harbour itself was just out of sight. Far out to sea, he could make out the lights from Rathlin island. He left his jacket unzipped and, placing his right hand on his pistol, walked along the right side of the road. He slowed, then stopped as the harbour came into view. It was a small harbour with a natural rocky breakwater, and a slipway to accommodate small boats. The road ended at the open area just before the slipway. On the left side was a single-story building that had once been an outhouse. On the opposite side was a larger white-painted building that looked like it had once been the farmhouse. There were two lights that lit up the front yard, but the house itself was in darkness. To the right of that, was a carpark with a metal frame over the entrance which prevented vehicles over a certain height from entering.

Tony looked around; there was no movement. His eyes slowly took in every detail. He knew she was there, but he could not see her yet. Tony stood in the darkness; his body shielded from view. Then he noticed the single car at the far end of the carpark. There were no lights or any movement around it. He scanned the surrounding area to make sure there was no one else around. He sensed they were alone. The phone in his pocket bleeped, making him jump. He turned and walked quickly back to the car. He knew better than to take it out and have his face lit up by the screen. He would be visible to anyone watching the harbour.

He slowly closed the door of the car and pulled out the phone, keeping it well below the level of the windows. It was a text message...just one line.

'YES, I AM ALONE, HURRY UP, I AM FREEZING.'

He deleted the message without answering it and smiled. He switched on the car engine but did not turn on the lights. He slowly drove the short distance to the end of the road, then turned right into the carpark. The small hatchback was reverse parked up by the long single-story building. As Tony passed through the metal gate posts, he noticed the two overturned wooden dinghies laying on the grass to the left of the carpark. The familiar shapes of lobster traps indicated whoever lived in the farmhouse was a lobster fisherman. He turned the car around and reverse parked next to the hatchback. He switched off the engine and climbed out of the car, quietly closing the door behind him. He adjusted his jacket as the driver's door of the hatchback opened. He watched as she stood up, shut the door, and rested her arms on the roof of the car.

"Hello Sabine, it's been a while," Tony said with a smile. Sabine smiled, then walked around the front of the car. Tony walked to the front to meet her. He noticed the walking boots she wore. His eyes moved up; she had on leather trousers with no pockets and an outdoor jacket. She wore thin gloves on her hands. Tony looked at her face. She was pleased to see him.

"Hi, well, we couldn't really talk the last time, could we?" She smiled cheekily and stopped in front of him, she placed her left hand on his right clavicle and, stepping closer, pecked his right cheek with a kiss. She looked into his eyes, then went to kiss him on the lips. Tony stepped back and brought his hands up to keep the distance between them.

"Don't," he whispered.

"What?" she asked, looking hurt.

"I didn't come here for that." Tony turned away from her stare, when he looked back, she was annoyed.

"Don't you remember what we had?" She pushed her hands into the pockets on her jacket.

"That was before I got married."

"Yeah, I heard .... a sapien?"

"Yes."

"And how is that working out for you?" she asked, Tony paused. The only sound that broke the silence was that of the waves crashing against the rocks. He looked at her,

"Great! We're starting a family." Tony could not help but feel pleased.

"Congratulations," she replied, tersely. Tony knew she didn't mean it.

"Thank you," he responded. Sabine sat down on the bonnet of the hatchback.

"I heard what the Mongols did to her last year," Sabine looked away as she spoke. Tony suddenly felt anger rising in him.

"What?" He tensed at the memory; Sabine turned her head towards him.

"I heard what they did... I am sorry." Tony took a single step towards her as she looked down at her feet. He stared at her, she looked back at him. "It is a pity you and I never had a child," she said quietly and looked away again, she wore a tight smile.

"I didn't think your kind could have children. Something about your body losing too much blood at childbirth?" He felt his hands tighten into fists, then relax again. "Has there ever been a successful Noc birth?" Tony asked.

Sabine glanced over at him, and said, regretfully,

"No, not that I am aware of." She looked away again. The two didn't speak for a few seconds. Then she looked at him and motioned for him to sit beside her. Tony thought for a moment, then did so.

"Well, it is nice to see you again," Tony said, as he placed both his hands between his legs to keep warm. He wasn't wearing any gloves. Sabine shifted closer. They briefly looked into each other's eyes, then away. Tony noticed her shiver slightly.

"I heard your friend, Foster, took down a Mongol alpha in front of your whole den," she stated, Tony considered what to tell her before he answered.

"He did."

"That fight must have been a good one to watch."

"Well, Carl had been killed first, so it was a bit of a mix."

"He beat an alpha when he himself wasn't fully a wolf yet?" Sabine rubbed her left shoulder into him, "still some feat." Tony did not respond to the physical contact.

"It was."

"We'll have to keep an eye on him," Sabine stated.

"Why is Dani here?" Tony raised his voice with the question. Sabine looked at him; the serious look was back. "I spoke with Salisbury last night and they were under the impression that she was in France or Italy. They are not happy that she is over here causing trouble." Sabine shrugged. Tony stared at her, "What .... Is .... She .... Doing .... Here?" Tony's question could not have been more direct. Sabine looked around; she could not look at him, as she answered,

"She wants to get her own back on you and Foster for handing her back in the carpark." Tony remembered the exchange following the fight outside the harbour bar in Portrush. Sabine carried on, "I loved the ruling you worked in for your family, that was really good." Tony looked away.

"All we did was follow the rules," Tony took a deep breath. "If we hadn't, it would have triggered another conflict. Besides, what is she doing here in the first place? They told us she ran away." Sabine looked down, then around the harbour.

"She did."

"What was she running from? Isn't she the second daughter of the Queen, down there? And it was the night before a solstice," Tony wasn't looking at her as he asked the question. Sabine took her time before she answered,

"Yes, that's right."

"So," Tony turned towards her, "what was she running from?" Sabine was hesitant. She nodded once.

"Okay, we are not supposed to discuss this, but..."

"We need to know," Tony interrupted, Sabine looked at him.

"You don't 'need' to know, but..."

"But you are going to tell me anyhow." Sabine stood up and walked a few paces away from him. Tony rose and walked towards her, she glanced back over her shoulder.

"One of our hunters had scored a great feat...." She turned away, "and was asked what he wanted as a prize," Tony's eyes never left her.

"And what was the feat?" he asked. Sabine stopped and her head spun around.

"Coven business...which means, it is none of yours!" Sabine started to slowly walk away from him, Tony caught her up.

"So, what was the prize?"

"He wanted her."

"So, why run?" Tony asked, Sabine stopped and glared at him.

"What? Are you kidding me? Finding out that you are going to be tied over a stone altar as a prize and raped in front of two hundred .... Yeah, I can see why she ran!" Sabine snapped. Tony stopped. She turned and started to walk away again.

"Why her?" Tony followed her. Sabine stopped, just as she reached the metal frame at the entrance to the carpark.

"As a princess, for him to be able to even suggest anything like that means he has rank, plus," they both stopped and looked at each other, Tony finished the sentence, "Plus, she can move around in daylight, which means she isn't fully Noctrailis!"

"No, she isn't." She went to turn away again, but Tony's hand shot out and grabbed her arm. Sabine looked at it, then at him. Tony held her gaze and his grip.

"Tell me," Tony spoke quietly, she nodded, and he released his grip.

"She wasn't turned...she was born."

"But your kind cannot have their own children," Tony interrupted.

"Not within our own, no," Sabine turned away.

"So, how does that work?" Tony asked. Sabine turned back toward him.

"Her mother wasn't; her father was."

"Wait," Tony was surprised, "the 'Queen of the Black Witches' isn't a Noc?"

"No, she isn't. She's the first one in quite a while, all three of her children were conceived during rituals," Tony thought about what she had just said.

"You said it happened to her?" Sabine walked towards the harbour, and Tony followed.

"When she was taken back there, she was punished. The Queen was furious with her for running away." Sabine explained.

"How was she punished?" Tony asked, Sabine gave him a meaningful look.

"She was tied to the alter and all ten from the hunting party were given her. 'From ten minutes after sunset to ten minutes before sunrise'."

"What?" Tony asked.

"That was the declaration from the Queen to the whole coven; they could do whatever they liked during that time," Sabine stopped and stared out to sea. Tony could tell she was describing what she had witnessed. "Her wrists were bound with leather straps and no one was to intervene .... And no one did; they were brutal with her." Tony stood beside her and looked into the greyness of the night. Sabine had stopped talking. There was an agonized look on her face. Sabine had not agreed with the ruling.

"So, why is she here? When I spoke with Salisbury, they thought she was off to France," he asked quietly. Sabine smirked at his question.

"She blames you and Foster for handing her back." Sabine turned and leaned in towards him, "She wants you dead, my dear wolf...you and your friend. She will not stop until she gets what she wants!" Sabine leaned forward and kissed him on his cheek. "You need to be careful; forgiveness is not in her nature," Tony looked at her.

"I will." Tony paused before he spoke again, "I've seen the footage from the bungalow; I didn't know about Alison."

"But she knew about you. You are not great at hiding your wolf, by the way,"

"Why is he here?" Tony asked.

"Why is who here?" she replied.

"The American." Sabine's body reacted, she stepped away from Tony.

"I could ask the same about Reynolds."

"What about Tyler?" Tony asked, as Sabine walked towards the parked cars.

"We want her," she said, Tony caught up with her again. The wind whipped past him as he looked around the harbour again.

"I hear she kicked your ass recently. White Park Bay, wasn't it?" Tony was smiling; it was a dig at her. She looked at him, her eyebrows furrowed in anger.

"Actually, I was winning, until we got interrupted."

"Yeah, I heard, by what, exactly?" Tony asked. Sabine's pace had slowed, she looked down, then over at him.

"'Nothing that concerns your lot!" He had touched a nerve, and he knew it.

"Okay, so tell me about the American, then." Sabine let out a short laugh.

"Gladly," Sabine took his left hand in her own, "but that will cost you."

"Cost me?" Tony was surprised, then he saw the lascivious look in her eyes.

"Yeah, but I'm sure you'll have just as much fun as I will." There was a wicked look on her face. She pushed up against him and went to kiss him. He grabbed her arms and stopped her.

"No," he said, pushing her away. She stared into his eyes.

"I will tell you everything you want to know, but I get what I want, first!" There was passion and fury in her voice. Tony felt his own body react, he looked at her intently.

"If I even think you are going to bite me, you will not leave here alive." Her eyes widened with excitement. "Understand?" Tony was threatening her, but she seemed to enjoy it. He watched, as her incisors grew. She was passionate, in full lust. His right hand grabbed her throat and squeezed. Her own hands came up to loosen his grip. "I mean it!" His grip relaxed. Her eyes were full of excitement. She was panting as her fingers moved from his hand to the side of his face. Her fingertips drew lines down either side of his neck. Her voice changed to almost a hiss; he had heard it before. Her lips quivered as she spoke,

"You are the only wolf, you are..." Tony grabbed her hand and marched her over towards the parked cars.

Behind the wooden dinghies was a short stone wall. It divided the carpark from the first of the fields that ran along the coast. Just where the wall met the side of the farmhouse was the green-painted wooden gate. On the far side of the gate was the small plastic box. Two of the stones from the wall had been placed on top of it, with another in front, so it was almost obscured. The lens of a remote camera protruded. The small microphone on the side of it had picked up most of the conversation, apart from when they had walked down to the harbour. The lens whirred slightly, and focused. Less than half a mile away, Mark was laying in his car, with both seats folded back. To passers-by, the car would appear empty. The screen was sitting on the other seat, a small red dot in the corner. It was recording everything. His phone vibrated slightly, he lifted it to his ear.

"Hey Cara, you were right, your friend was meeting someone...and you are not going to believe who!" he paused. As the voice at the other end spoke, he nodded. "Yeah, I have a remote camera out. No, I hacked the voicemail on his phone. There was only one message. It was a woman's voice, saying to meet at Dunseverick Harbour." He listened to her next question. "No, I didn't, but I guessed something was definitely going to happen, as different cars and bikers kept driving down here, then leaving." He watched the screen, and a small smile spread over his face, "Well, he met up with a tall blonde who, I think, is the same tall blonde from the bungalow .... Yeah, yeah, I got most of the conversation, but not all of it..." Cara-Marie was getting excited down the phone,

"What are they doing now?

"Are you sure you want to know?" He focused the camera again, "well, currently the blonde is leaned over the bonnet of his car and he is going hell for leather behind her .... Yeah, and judging by the amount of noise she is making, she is having more fun than your friend Tony is .... yeah, got the whole thing on tape ...." He smiled and refocused the camera. He watched as the rigorous sex continued. "Yeah, I can... yeah, sure, see you tomorrow." Mark ended the call and pushed the phone back into his pocket. He went back to his voyeurism. He watched for a few moments more, then reached for his phone again. He tapped in a message and scrolled through his list of contacts. He stopped at one name, and pressed 'send'.

He would not have long to wait for the two he'd been watching to go their separate ways. Then he would head off towards Coleraine. He read his message again with a smile. 'HEY BABE, OK IF I CALL ROUND?'

∞∞∞∞

Cara-Marie pushed the front door with her left hand. She was sure she had found the lair in Belfast. She moved slowly, going through the second door. She felt along the wall for the light switch. The single strip light lit up the room. She looked around. There were no windows, the walls were painted a dark colour. The old furniture that was pushed up against the right side of the room had been well used, she walked towards the centre of the room. There was nothing... no rubbish, no evidence of people currently in residence. But she knew that someone had been there. Mark had used facial recognition software and had found local CCTV footage that had Kris Martin, the tall blonde and Alison Wallace all nearby.

Could this actually be the lair of the vampires? She stopped in the middle of the room and looked at the floor. There was something about the floor that was unusual. For an unused building, the floor was exceptionally clean. She turned and walked back to the light switch. She switched it off, and dug around in the pocket of her jacket, producing a small torch. She adjusted the settings, then switched it on. The ultra-violet light lit the room with an eerie glow. Cara-Marie walked back towards the centre of the room. The UV light showed where the pool of blood had been; someone had died there. The floor was covered in different footprints. There had been several people walking around, through the blood, covering the floor with footprints from various types of footwear. They led off towards the far door, and she followed them. Cara-Marie walked through the door and moved cautiously around the rest of the lair. It was empty. Everything was tidy; everything was clean. It was as if someone had removed all evidence that anyone had ever been there. They had been incredibly careful not to leave any trace, almost as if someone with forensic knowledge had instructed them. Someone like an ex-police officer.

As she was leaving, she looked above the main entrance door. There was a smoke detector with a small red light flashing on it. Someone, somewhere, knew she was there. Cara-Marie guessed the vampires would not be returning to their lair in Belfast.

Chapter 53

"I know why they are here!" Tony was excited, as he burst into the living room of the farmhouse. Kyle, Tyler and Dermott were all seated comfortably in the room. It was Paul who had let him in. Tony stopped in front of them. Everyone looked at him expectantly, and Kyle motioned with his hand for him to sit down.

"Okay, so what is happening?" Dermott asked, Tony excitedly took a seat.

"Well, I met up with Sabine and she spilled quite a bit."

"Did she?" Tyler remarked.

"Yeah," Tony said, Paul walked past him and took a seat.

"Well, go on then," Kyle encouraged. Tony sat forward and began to fill them in on the conversation, it did not take long.

"So," Dermott responded, "this princess is here for revenge and she has brought a load of Nocs from all over Europe; we still don't know the real name of this American guy; all we do know is that he wants to wipe us all out and make Ireland a Noc sanctuary; Alison is not fully with them; and we have no idea what scared them away from the house at Bushmills or the beach." Dermott looked around, "Is that basically it?"

"They also know that Tyler is here," Tony glanced over at the stern-faced woman who had not said anything. "They still are very keen on getting their hands on her."

"Would they try a direct assault on the farm?" Kyle asked, without looking at Tyler, Tony shook his head.

"No," he sat back in his chair, "they know what happened to the Mongols."

"So, what exactly is their plan?" Dermott asked, Tony looked over at him.

"To draw us out in groups and take us down bit by bit," Tony was not as excited as he first was, the group was thoughtful.

"Do we trust this source?" Paul asked, "I mean, who exactly is this coming from and why would she help us? She is a Noc, is she not?" Paul was serious. Dermott nodded in agreement. Tony took a deep breath before answering,

"Her name is Sabine, and we know she comes from the main coven in Salisbury. When the American came over last year, and they were searching for Dani, she was part of his personal security detail, which means she has rank."

"But why would she help us? That is the bit that is missing!" Tyler asked.

"This could be a complete lie or a bluff to divert us away from what they are actually doing," Dermott added. Kyle looked at Tony.

"Well," he questioned, "is it a lie or a bluff?"

"I don't think so," Tony looked around, the others seemed unconvinced.

"Do they know I have a place on Rathlin Island?" Tyler asked as she leaned forward.

"I don't think so, but they know you are here at the moment."

"Do they know about Rhydian?" Kyle asked. Tyler's eyes shot over to him, then immediately back at Tony.

"She wasn't mentioned."

"So, why did this 'Sabine' want to meet you?" Dermott asked. "What she has told you, we had already guessed. There is nothing concrete we can use." Paul looked towards Kyle as Dermott continued, "but we have confirmed that Tyler is here, and we will react to anything they do .... Not exactly breaking their codes now, is it." Tony looked dejected.

"No, not really."

"Do we know where they are sleeping, presently? Do we know their intentions? Did we find out what they are going to do in the next forty-eight hours ...." Paul let the question hang, Tony did not need to answer, they all knew it was no.

"I think I am missing something," Dermott stated.

"What?" Kyle asked, Dermott looked at Tony.

"How did she know to get in touch with you? And how did she know you would expose yourself like that? It could have been a trap!"

"Yeah, it could have been, but it wasn't."

"How, exactly, did you know that?" Tyler spoke quietly, she stared at Tony; he was evading the questions. Tony looked at her, then at Kyle. Kyle nodded once.

"Okay," Tony started, "Sabine and I once had a relationship." Tyler's eyes widened, Dermott sat upright, but Paul and Kyle did not move.

"You WHAT?" Dermott shouted.

"It was long before I was married," Tony said, defensively.

"And why did we not know this already? Carl would have had your head if he'd known!" Dermott was not hiding his anger, Tyler stared in disbelief,

"You had sex with a Noc?" It was more of a statement than a question.

"Yes, I did. We were together for just over a year, and ...." Tony turned towards Dermott, "Carl *did* know, he also knew it was over before I got married."

"No way!" Dermott raised his voice again, "Carl would not have allowed that to happen!" Dermott turned towards Paul who had not moved. "I mean, Paul, surely not!" Dermott was looking for support. All eyes turned towards Paul, who was looking at Tony.

"Yes, I remember that. Carl did know, but he also knew it was in the past and .... Carl allowed them to communicate as a back-door channel between the coven and us." Kyle tried hard not to smile. Tyler glared; she was less than happy with that.

"Well, what's in the past is in the past; it's the present I am concerned with now," Kyle declared, "were you able to attach the tracker to her car?" Tony smiled at Kyle's question.

"Yes."

"Did she see you do it?" Tyler asked.

"No.

"So, we know where she is now?" Dermott asked. Tony started to speak but there was a sudden banging on the door.

"COME IN," shouted Kyle. The door burst open as one of the farmhands rushed in. She had been running.

"We just heard from the communications room that there are three groups of Nocs now circling the complex!"

The room exploded in activity. The farmhand was bombarded with demands for information but there was no more coming. They all went outside. Suddenly, it had become a hive of activity. Dermott stepped forward as he placed the communicator into his ear. Kyle was standing by the door with Tyler on one side. Tony had walked to the wall beside the farmhouse and was staring down the lane towards the entrance. Paul appeared behind them and handed each of them a communicator. Dermott was already issuing instructions. Kyle fitted the device into his right ear. He recognised some of the voices.

'ROGER, ONE X-RAY HEADING WEST ALONG THE PERIMETER, JUST SOUTH OF FARM FOUR.'

'ROGER, THREE X-RAY HEADING AWAY FROM THE PERIMETER NORTH OF FARM SIX.'

'TWO X-RAY TAKING PICS OF FARM TWO, NOW HEADING AWAY AT SPEED, I THINK THEY SPOTTED US. ADVISE ACTION. OVER.' Kyle turned towards Dermott, who spouted orders.

"All stations, all stations, this is Delta Mike, action Defensive Plan Bravo. I repeat, action Defensive Plan Bravo." As Dermott spoke, two farmhands ran around the side of the barn; both were carrying bolt-action stalking rifles and had small backpacks slung over their shoulders. They sprinted for the metal ladder at the side of the barn that would take them to the roof. From there, they could observe an arc to the front of the farm. In minutes, the entire perimeter would be under surveillance.

Dermott nodded towards Kyle as one of the 4x4s raced up to the farmhouse. The driver was already wearing body armour and the three in the back climbed out. All wore all-weather boots, outdoor trousers, camouflage jackets with the same body armour, and carried G36 rifles. All three wore rolled up face masks. "Right," Dermott started, "you are Reaction Team One." They all nodded. Dermott looked towards Paul as a second 4x4 came up behind them. "Paul, can you take Team One?" Paul shook his head.

"No...Tony can." Dermott glanced at an expectant Tony, who nodded. "I will stay here," Paul motioned towards Kyle. He would stay by his alpha's side. As he spoke, Paul took out his Sig pistol and cocked it then returned it to the concealed holster.

"Right," Dermott put his right hand to his ear before speaking to Tony, "there is a vest and a rifle in the back of the wagon." Tony took off towards the rear of the vehicle to get ready, and Dermott continued to instruct the rest of the team. "Team One, you will cover the northern half of the farm, understand?" He was met with a series of nods. The farmhands from the second 4x4 arrived, all dressed the same. Dermott turned his head,

"Tyler, could you go with Team Two and cover the southern half?"

"Hell, yeah!" she exclaimed. Team One was climbing back into their 4x4 as Tony walked around to the passenger side. He nodded at Kyle as he climbed in. One of Team Two smiled at Tyler and patted her on the shoulder, before turning to lead her to their Land Rover. It would not be long before they were on their way, as well. Paul walked over by the wall and looked towards the entrance; Kyle walked up beside him. Dermott was still busy with all the chatter over the communicator. Kyle pulled it out from his ear.

"What do you think they are doing?" he asked, Paul shrugged,

"I have no idea," Dermott was concentrating on what he was hearing, and more instructions followed, Paul glanced at Kyle.

"Have you any thoughts?" Kyle pushed his hands into his pockets and looked up at the clear night sky.

"Well, they know not to try and hit us here," he glanced at Paul. "They would lose too many," Paul nodded, "and they have lost enough recently," Kyle continued. He looked towards the top of the lane and noted every detail on their way to the entrance. He spotted the still forms of the Frontal Protection Team, and his eyes moved on. "I think ... they are just probing us and will be watching our response." He looked up at the hill across the road from the entrance. "Dermott?" Dermott turned and walked over to where the two of them were standing.

"Yes," Kyle lifted his hand and pointed to the hill.

"Do we have anyone on top of that hill?" he asked. Dermott let a small grin spread over his face.

"Remote cameras." Kyle watched him, as he explained. "We have several out; all monitored by communications. They all have motion detectors, so we know if anyone goes near them. It was one of the cameras that picked this lot up!" Dermott looked satisfied. Kyle was about to ask another question, but both Dermott and Paul became engrossed in what they were hearing. As Kyle was replacing the device in his ear, Paul explained.

"We've found a track in the northern half; Team One is on their way." Kyle tapped the device into place and voices filled his ear.

'ROGER TEAM TWO, I HAVE EYES ON YOU. KEEP GOING TO THE NEXT GATE ALONG THE WALL TO YOUR RIGHT AND STOP THERE, TRACKS ARE AROUND THERE.'

"That is wee Ruth; she has the assault team deployed at the armoury," Dermott explained. Kyle nodded, as he heard Tony's voice.

'ROGER, YES, YES. WE CAN SEE THAT. STOPPING NOW. TEAM TWO NOW FOXTROT AT GATE FOUR.' Kyle looked at the field in front of him. The frost was already starting to form; it was going to be a cold night.

∞∞∞∞

Tony crouched beside the wall. The butt of the rifle was in his right shoulder; he pulled the thin face mask over his head. The engine of the 4x4 went quiet. The driver would stay there while the four of them moved quietly along the wall.

Matthew Cairns was in front of him; he was a far better tracker that Tony. He had stopped, as did Tony and those behind him. Tony searched to the front and to the left of Matthew, who was staring at the ground. The two behind him had their own arcs covered. Everyone knew what to do; they were well trained and practiced this regularly. Matthew turned his head. He kept his rifle in his right hand and used his left hand to pass the message. He held up two fingers in a V shape: there were two tracks. He made a karate chop motion towards the far side of the wall: they had come from that direction. Matthew pointed to the ground and, with one finger, drew a circle motion: they had stopped here. Matthew held one finger up, then, using the hand chop signal, pointed off to their left towards the middle of the field: one of them had headed off in that direction, the other had doubled back the way they had come.

Tony nodded. He looked back at the driver, who had seen it, as well. Tony listened as the driver spoke into the communicator; the rest of the farm had gone silent. They were watching, but they would only speak if something was happening. This allowed the radio to remain clear if they needed the assault team in a hurry. There had been an incursion onto the farm. Matthew turned and very quietly stood up. He held his rifle in both hands. The four moved off silently, following the single track. Tony had patrolled like this many times when he was in the army; he remembered why he had loved it. He moved quietly, sweeping arcs with his weapon. He covered Matthew, who slowly made his way along the single track of footprints, careful not to disturb them. They made no sound. Matthew stopped and went down on one knee; the others did the same. The radio in his ear was quiet. Matthew turned towards Tony; the tracks had changed direction, moving to the edge of the field. Tony nodded. Matthew stood again and moved off along the set of footprints.

As they approached the wall at the edge of the field, Tony turned to the two behind him and, with his left hand, motioned for them to spread out. If there was anything ahead, they could bring more firepower towards it. Matthew stopped. Tony stopped. Matthew was looking from left to right. He kept looking up, then over to his right and then to his left. This continued until Matthew looked back and motioned for Tony to come towards him. Tony quietly moved alongside him. Matthew leaned over and whispered,

"This does not make sense."

"What?" Tony asked.

219

"These tracks are a young male, moving at speed; they came down the centre of the field, then turned right to here," Matt pointed to the ground as he spoke. Tony looked at him and shrugged. Matthew continued, "Then from here, it looks like he ran about ten metres up the field, turned and came back down to about ten metres heading down the field and back again." Tony could see Matthew was confused. "It does not make sense, at all."

"Where does the track lead from here?" Tony whispered, as quietly as he could. Matthew leaned towards him and whispered again,

"I don't know .... they just seem to .... stop." Tony's head suddenly came up; he looked beyond the wall.

"Baseline, baseline," he spoke out loud; the stealth of their actions was gone. The two from behind ran up so they were all level. Tony stepped to one side of Matthew, so all four were in a line with gaps between them. Their weapons pointed in the same direction; all of them were on one knee.

In his ear, Tony heard the driver telling everyone what they were doing. "Advance!" Tony commanded, and the four rose simultaneously and moved forward. Tony's eyes spotted the single movement to his extreme left just as the force hit him in the chest. It felt like he had been kicked by the hind legs of a horse. His body flew backwards, and his hands released the rifle; his arms folded over his chest to contain the pain, as he flew through the air. His body slammed into the earth and all his breath left him. His body screamed in pain as he fought for breath, aware of the cold, hard ground beneath him.

Tony could not hear the other three engaging the movement that had been off to his left; he did not know the reaction back at the farmhouse or at the armoury. Nor could he hear the driver's voice in the communicator that had fallen out of his ear.

"CONTACT – SHOOTING – MAN DOWN MAN DOWN"

∞∞∞∞∞

"It is called Behind Armour Blunt Trauma and it is a classic resulting injury such as this." Tony could hear the voice, recognise it, but could not remember the name. He heard the voices first... then the pain hit. There was extreme pain all over his chest, and suddenly the world came back into focus. He was lying on the sofa in the living room of the farmhouse and every breath intensified the pain across his chest.

"So, he is going to be fine, then?" Kyle asked. Tony opened his eyes and looked around the room. Paul was standing by the front door, which was slightly ajar; he was interested in whatever was going on outside. Tony coughed and the pain hit him again. He let out a grunt and his face contorted with the pain. Kyle was standing nearby with his arms folded. Tony's hand shot up to his nose and his fingers found what had made him cough. He pulled the rubber tube out. The voice he'd woken up to was coming from the figure kneeling in front of him. Smiling at Tony, he held out a piece of white gauze. Tony took it to wipe at his nose. It took him several more seconds to put a name to the face.

"John, isn't it?" he croaked.

"Hi Tony."

"John is our resident paramedic," explained Kyle. Tony nodded; he knew that.

"What the hell is this?" Tony asked, holding up the rubber tube, which John took.

"This," he explained, "is a Naso-Airway. It has been keeping your airways clear." John turned and started to pack away some of the medical paraphernalia that had been on top of the open trauma pack on the floor. "Yeah, his chest sounds clear. The armour took most of the impact, but at least two of the ribs are broken; the trachea is central, there is no evidence of a tension pneumothorax and there is no surgical emphysema; no penetrations to the chest but, from what I can tell without a chest x-ray," John looked up at Kyle, then at Tony, "he should be okay. But you're going to hurt like hell for a few weeks." John efficiently repacked the trauma kit and zipped it closed. "I've given him some intravenous paracetamol that will take the edge off the pain," John looked reassuringly at Tony, "You should sleep well tonight, at least."

"Thanks, John," Kyle said, relieved. John stood up to his full height, over six feet; his large frame revealing his immense physical strength. Effortlessly, he hefted the trauma pack onto his shoulder.

"The bruising should fade in a week or so, but if you are having any breathing problems, get yourself to the causeway hospital for a chest x-ray, okay?" John nodded towards Tony, who smiled painfully. Paul thanked him again at the front door, and he left. Tony struggled to sit up. He leaned forward and placed his elbows onto his knees; it made breathing slightly easier.

"What the hell happened?" Tony asked, looking down at the two massive bruises on the left side of his chest.

"You got shot," replied Kyle as he sat down.

220

"Okay," Tony was talking between painful breaths, "any chance for more detail than that?" Paul started speaking to someone outside, and Tony looked at Kyle.

"Short version: you walked into a trap and got shot; the plates in the armour took the brunt of the force, the others took down the two Nocs who shot you."

"They are okay?" Tony asked, "the rest of the team?"

"Yeah, they are fine, and it seems you will be, too, in a few weeks." Paul looked at Kyle and nodded. Kyle stood up and, as he walked away, he looked back at Tony. "You can crash here for the rest of the night if you want to; then tomorrow, go home and stay there. You're no use to me in this state." Tony tried to stand, but the pain forced him back.

"Home... but ...." He started.

"No buts! Three members of the protection team will go with you, plus," Kyle paused, "you have a pregnant wife to look after!" Tony looked into Kyle's eyes and smiled. He pulled the throw blanket over himself as Kyle and Paul walked outside. Tony closed his eyes; the medication was starting to take effect.

∞∞∞∞∞

Paul and Kyle walked around to the back of the Land Rover, where several of the farmhands were milling about, still wearing body armour and carrying their weapons. The rear of the Land Rover was open, and two bodies lay there with their feet sticking out. Beside the rear door, Ruth McDonal was standing, with her weapon hanging by her side and her helmet in the other hand.

"So," Kyle asked, looking at the two bodies, "What have we got?"

"Both are full Noctrailis." Ruth pointed to the one on the left, "He was carrying French ID, probably fake, and this one," she pointed to the second body, "was likely English."

"Names?" Kyle asked.

"Not confirmed yet, like I said the IDs look fake, but we are checking."

"What about the others?"

"We did a full perimeter check, all other Noctrailis have escaped. They had cars waiting for them at various points." Kyle looked at the two dead faces. Both had elongated incisors. Ruth continued, "These two were not properly trained."

"What makes you think that?" Paul asked, as Ruth studied the bodies.

"First, the location of their firing point. It was not where someone trained would have chosen, extremely poor arcs, no cover from the side. Plus, why engage a superior force with no possible beneficial outcome? Their rifles weren't even prepped." Kyle looked at Paul, then towards Ruth as one of the other members of the assault team handed her an M-16 rifle. Ruth placed her helmet inside the vehicle, then took the rifle. There was no magazine fitted, so she cocked the weapon once. She held it in one hand with the barrel pointing up to the sky. "This rifle has the serial number removed and has not been cleaned in months. It had not been properly prepared for firing. It just seems completely unprofessional to me."

"So, what is the plan with these two?" Kyle asked, motioning towards the bodies.

"We can dispose of them here, no problem," answered Paul. "Remember, what happens to a sapien body in 12 weeks occurs in 12 hours with this lot!" There was a murmur from the gathered wolves.

"You know," Kyle said, turning to the assault team, "I have never actually seen what sunlight does to them!" There was quiet laughter from all of them.

"No problem," Paul said, smiling. "That can easily be arranged."

"Speaking of burning things, where is Tyler and the rest?" Kyle asked.

"They are at the armoury, cleaning and returning their weapons," Paul replied. "We can have our little bonfire in the morning!"

"Just as well," stated Ruth. Kyle and Paul watched as she looked up at the sky. "It is going to snow tonight."

Chapter 54

Cara-Marie was sitting in the coffee shop at the bottom of Long Commons in Coleraine. It was two days since the break-in at the office, and the police had not come up with anything. Nothing was taken; it had just been trashed. But it gave her a chance to spend time on her favourite subject. She was convinced they found the vampires' lair, but it was now deserted. She guessed they would not be returning. Something happened down at White Park Bay and it had nothing to do with organised crime and drug dealers, this time. She watched Mark's footage from Dunseverick Harbour. It was not great - a lot of the conversation was inaudible. But Tony had met up with the tall blonde, who'd been at the bungalow where two people were raped, tortured and murdered. The camera caught Tony and the tall blonde having sex over the bonnet of one of the cars; then they stood and spoke again. At least she now had a name... Sabine.

Cara-Marie also discovered Tony and Sabine had once been in a relationship. She had so much to ask him. Cara-Marie looked at her watch; he was late. She was seated facing the entrance to the upstairs room. Her mind wandered. Not long ago she was in this same room with Kyle, when a girl had thrown a glass at the wall, her brother had been murdered at Castleroe only days before. Her eyes caught a movement outside the coffee shop. She looked below at the opposite side of the street. A pair of teenagers were both wearing hooded tops with wolves on them; they each had the same black peaked cap with an emblem from one of several new 'wolf tours' that had sprung up recently. They were unsteady in the snow but seemed excited about something. She was sick of these kinds of tourists. They wanted the gore, the horror. A lot of her recent evenings were spent deleting emails with requests for information from just such people.

Her eyes shot over to the top of the single staircase, as Tony arrived. She stood, smiling. Tony smiled back and pulled off his gloves and hat. Cara-Marie stepped to the side of the table and chairs, as he approached.

"Dia Duit, Cara," he greeted her in Irish.

"Dia Murie Duit, Tony," she replied, and they shared a brief embrace. She reverted to English as he was taking off his jacket. "So, would you like a coffee?" Tony dropped the jacket over the back of one of the chairs. He motioned towards the stairs.

"Got one coming up," he looked at her partially consumed drink, "would you like a refill?" he asked, pointing at her mug.

"Yeah, a refill would be nice, thanks." She noted he seemed happy to see her, but she felt a tenseness when they had hugged, almost as if it had been painful. He took a seat directly opposite her and, just as they got comfortable, one of the staff appeared with a large mug on a tray. The coffee had a flower drawn in the foam; 'latte art' was starting to take off.

"Thank you," Tony said, as the mug and a small plate with a tray bake on it were placed in front of him. He looked over at her. "What would you like?"

"Vanilla latte, please," Cara-Marie said to the server, whom she did not recognise, the young girl nodded and left.

"So," she smiled, Tony lifted the hot drink to his lips.

"So," he replied, and placed the mug back on the table.

"So, how is life in the 'expectant dad' world?" Cara-Marie was smiling as she asked her question, it had the desired effect. Tony beamed, as he exclaimed,

"It is amazing! We are so excited!"

"How is Karen getting on? Especially after ...." She stopped herself from saying the words; it stopped Tony in his tracks. The smile disappeared, and he glanced down briefly before continuing,

"She is grand...doing really well. The doctors say everything is exactly as it should be." His eyes welled up.

"That is brilliant news! I am over the moon for you both," Cara-Marie smiled, then realised what she had just said. Tony let out a short laugh, reaching for his coffee again. Cara-Marie looked over to the doorway, watching as the server reappeared with a single mug on a small tray. "Thank you," Cara-Marie said as the mug was placed in front of her. When the girl left, Cara-Marie lifted her coffee, and Tony raised his.

"Cheers!" they touched their mugs lightly together. Again, he flinched; something was wrong. "So, what has been happening in the exciting world of local journalism?" he asked.

"Well, the break-in caused quite a few problems, but all we keep getting from the cops is 'we are investigating ...'" She looked over the rim at him, "I don't suppose you have heard anything from your former colleagues, have you?" Tony looked confused,

"What break-in?"

"The break-in at the Herald's offices a couple of days ago."

"Really?"

"Yes, really," she let out a short laugh; he really didn't know.

"What was stolen?"

"Nothing."

"Nothing at all?"

"No. Whoever it was got in through a window and wrecked the place."

"And nothing was taken?"

"No."

"Was anything damaged?"

"Apart from the window frame, no... nothing," She looked at his face; the police officer in him was concentrating.

"Who is investigating it?" She had to think for a second to remember the names.

"Mike Hutchinson and Laura Patterson." Tony scowled, lifting his coffee again.

"He is an idiot! Don't expect much from him," he advised. Tony obviously had no respect for him whatsoever, he looked at her, "What was the other name?"

"Laura Patterson," she repeated.

"Nope, 'don't know her."

"I got the impression she is new."

"Well, she isn't going to learn much from him!"

"You really don't like the guy, do you?" she was smiling as she asked the question. Tony did not look up as he replied,

"You don't like him either."

"What makes you say that?"

"When I called him an idiot, you didn't disagree," he looked at her and smiled. She grinned; she could not argue with that.

"Okay," she said. It was time to change the direction of the conversation. "What happened down at White Park Bay last week?" She eyed him over the rim of her mug, "and don't give me that crap about 'organised crime' or 'drug dealers'." Tony paused, looking around uncomfortably.

"I have not been to White Park Bay in years," he shrugged. She looked at him pointedly. There was a moment of silence between them, then he said, "Why don't you tell me what you think happened?" She smiled and sat forward. Even though they were alone, upstairs in the coffee shop, she still lowered her voice,

"Okay, I think there was a battle."

"A battle?" Tony quizzed, "between whom?" The smile had gone from her face and she looked at him intensely,

"Between the Noctrailis and the An Rua." Tony stopped abruptly. She carried on, "which, from what I can gather, the wolves won very convincingly."

"The who?" he asked.

"Don't insult me!" she fired back at him. He wasn't looking into her eyes anymore, so she continued. "There is a group of vampires called 'the Noctrailis' and there is a group of werewolves called 'An Rua', who have been very successful at keeping themselves out of sight for centuries." Tony still wasn't looking at her. "And your friend, Kyle, became alpha a few months ago!" She stopped. That made him look up.

"Why do you think that?" he asked.

"He sometimes talked in his sleep," she smirked.

"When?" Tony demanded. It was her turn to feel uncomfortable.

"Before Christmas."

"Crap! I didn't think he was seeing anyone then," Tony retorted.

"No, we were not 'seeing' each other, as such. He called 'round to mine a couple of times and I went around to his; nothing more than that." Tony went to say something but stopped himself, so she carried on, "It was never going to go anywhere; he was infatuated with that physiotherapist, at the time." Cara-Marie knew she had his attention. "There was one time, when he'd been fast asleep, I woke him and went to make a coffee. I was expecting a chat, but he left. The only thing he'd muttered was 'An Rua ... An Rua.'"

"He wouldn't," Tony was being defensive. "He..."

"He what?" she interrupted. "Oh, for fuck's sake Tony! We were both adults; it was nothing more than that!" Tony looked annoyed. "He isn't the only one who's done that, you know."

"What do you mean?" he asked. Cara-Marie decided to go for what she wanted.

"You!"

"What about me?"

"You and a tall blonde who is wanted in connection with two murders!" Tony's mouth opened. "Don't try to deny anything!" she almost shouted, "I know you met that lass, Sabine, two nights ago at Dunseverick Harbour." Tony was in a state of shock, "Mark, our photographer, had a camera covering it and got video footage of the two of you having sex over the front of her car. I hear she's an ex of yours, tell me, can a Garou and a Noctrailis actually have a child?" Tony went from shock to rage in an instant. His hands slammed down on the table, his body lurched forward, his face contorted with anger. Cara-Marie jumped back into her seat.

"DON'T, ..." His mouth was open, but words did not come out. He gritted his teeth and gripped the edge of the wooden table. Then he looked towards the floor.

"Who is she? And what are they ...."

"I SAID DON'T!" Tony released his grip on the table, sat back and stared deep into her eyes. "Cara .... please, don't."

"You having an affair is not exactly front-page news," Tony looked away, "but an ex-police officer meeting up with someone wanted for murder is something I may have to look at more closely." Tony glared at her again.

"I am NOT having an affair; it was just a one-off," he explained, "I needed to find out what they were doing, and that was the price."

"They?" she repeated, "you mean these Noctrailis?"

"You don't know who or what you are dealing with." Tony was being serious. She wasn't afraid, but she knew he meant what he was saying. "Cara, do not pursue this. You don't know them."

"Acquaint me with them," she sat forward, looking into his eyes as she spoke.

"No," he whispered.

"Tony," she had lowered her voice and her tone, and he looked up. "I know that werewolves are real; I have seen them. I am convinced vampires are real, as well .... And those murdered on New Year's Day were not killed by wolves or organised crime gangs."

"Stick to writing your blog," he retorted.

"Tony, help me, please."

"To do what?" he demanded, she took a few moments before she answered.

"All I want to do, is prove that both really exist; that's all!"

"No,"

"I will not identify you by name, you and Karen will be okay."

"No."

"Tony, please..."

"You do not know what you are asking."

"I do."

"No, you don't," Tony lurched forward, "Let this go, you need to walk away right now."

"Why?"

"You don't want to look into the darkness."

"You only fear the darkness because of ignorance," she smiled at her own reply.

"Who's that? Shakespeare?"

"No," she replied, "Plato .... I think."

"It doesn't change anything," Tony said.

"Why will you not let me help you?" she asked.

"Because we don't need any help."

"We?" she quoted. "So, you are finally admitting what you are," she was forcing herself not to grin. Tony just stared at her; he had not meant to say that.

"I do not want to end up in a cage, or being used as a weapon," Tony sat back in his seat, and he relaxed.

"What? Who said anything about ...?"

"EVERYTIME..." Tony cut her off, "every time we have revealed ourselves throughout history, that is precisely what has happened!" Cara-Marie looked confused. Tony carried on, "Every time we open ourselves up to the sapiens, we are put in cages, or hunted and killed, just for being what we are. Sapienkind can never accept us. To them, we are monsters that have to be killed...destroyed."

"If you did go public, people will respond. People are smart."

"What? Listen to yourself," he snapped. "People are panicky, paranoid and believe everything they see on TV! How many films have you ever seen where a wolf is portrayed as the good guy? We are ALWAYS the horrible beasts that must be killed! People believe that crap!"

"You could change that."

"No. People fear what is different; they fear what they don't understand. The Nazis convinced a whole country that one race of people was totally to blame for all their troubles. Millions died in a conflict caused by division, fear and suspicion."

"Eighty million," she whispered.

"What?"

"Over eighty million people died during the Second World War," she said quietly. Tony sat back and stared at her. There was a noise behind him, as two teenagers carrying mugs appeared at the top of the stairs. They still had their outdoor coats on, and they were shaking off the snow, chatting between themselves. They hardly noticed Cara-Marie or Tony, as they got comfortable around a table at the far end of the room.

Neither Tony nor Cara-Marie spoke. The teenagers were engrossed in their own world and paid no attention to them. "All I am asking is for you to help me, help you," Cara-Marie spoke quietly. Tony's eyes slowly moved from the floor up to meet her gaze.

"I cannot, and will not, help you," he paused. "You need to drop this and walk away. This is so much bigger than you could ever imagine," She shifted in her seat.

"Well, I can always head over to England. There is an English lord who has a pack of werewolves on his land. He wants help getting rid of them, so," she said clearly, "if you will not help me, he certainly will!"

"Who is that?" Tony inquired.

"What? You don't already know about Rupert Baskerville and the wolves that have been on his family's land for over a hundred and fifty years?"

"I can't say that I do."

"Come on. You need to learn to lie better than that!" she dropped the smile. He reached for the mug in front of him. The two teenagers behind him burst into laughter. Tony glanced over his shoulder, then replaced the mug on the table.

"Well, it's time I was off. I've got things to do."

"Like hunt a pack of vampires?"

"Like look after the mother of my child." Tony stood up and reached for his coat. Cara-Marie stood up, as well. As Tony was pulling his coat on, she reached out her hand.

"It's been nice. We'll have to do this again sometime." She raised her voice loud enough for the teenagers to hear, but they ignored her. Tony took her hand,

"Yes, we will. It has been nice to see you." Tony released his grip, then turned and headed towards the exit. Cara-Marie sat back down and watched him go. After he disappeared down the stairs, she reached for her large handbag and switched off the Dictaphone. She did not get exactly what she wanted, but an admission that the Garou were real was at least a start. The downside was that Tony would never meet her for coffee again. She had lost a good source of information. Tony zipped up the coat before he stepped outside. The cold hit his face, as the door to the coffee shop closed behind him. He turned left and started walking up Long Commons. He reached into his pocket for the ringing phone; he already knew who it was.

"Did you get all that?" he asked.

"Yeah," Kyle's voice was at the other end. Tony could hear voices in the background. "No problems, you head home, and we'll sort it from here." Tony walked on.

"I didn't know about the photographer, or that they had footage." A car beside him blasted its horn; the traffic was backed up all the way from the petrol station and the driver was impatient. It made Tony look around and increase his pace.

"Don't worry. Like I said, we can deal with it," he could make out Tyler's voice in the background, but not what she was saying.

"Okay," Tony could not think of anything else to say.

"Give my love to Karen." Kyle's comment turned his insides. He had been unfaithful to his wife; the one who loved him more than anything...and it was on video.

"Yeah, I will do," Tony felt bile rise in his throat. He briefly closed his eyes to stop the tears from welling up. Kyle ended the call, and Tony pushed the phone back into his pocket. He stopped and looked at the traffic. It was now stationary. He walked between cars to the other side of the road.

Tony did not know how he could regain the trust of Kyle, the pack, or, especially, Karen. It would only be a matter of time before she found out what he had done. His insides turned again as regret engulfed him.

∞∞∞∞

Kyle turned and looked at Paul. Tyler was pacing back and forth in the farmhouse living room. The door opened and Dermott walked in, nodded at Kyle, then closed the door behind him.

"So, the journalist is still grasping at straws?" Kyle asked the collective group.

"Good news! Apart from putting up stories on her blog that she cannot prove, she hasn't got anything," Dermott stated with a smile.

"The video footage could hurt Tony." Kyle stated.

"Then he *shouldn't* shag vampires!" Tyler spat. Kyle and Paul shared a glance.

"Yeah, that could be a problem, but only a minor one," Paul reassured.

"Not for his wife, it isn't!" Tyler was not happy with what Tony had done. The loud knock at the door made them all turn their heads.

"Come in," Kyle shouted. The door opened. A young face appeared. It was one of the communications team. He stood in the doorway and passed on what he had to say.

"The Nocs have been sited and they are on the move, we know exactly where they are!" There was a reaction in the room. All eyes turned towards Kyle.

"Their strength is what we think it is?" he asked, the young face nodded.

"Let me finish this," Tyler stepped towards him as she spoke. Kyle looked at Paul, then Dermott; both nodded. He looked at Tyler,

"Take what you need." Tyler turned and rushed for the door, almost pushing the young man out of the way as she did so. "TYLER!" Kyle shouted. She stopped in the doorway and looked back at him, excitedly. "Keep me informed and *do not* make an offensive move without letting me know beforehand." Tyler smiled and was about to say something, but Kyle stopped her. "Understand?" Tyler nodded, and the door slammed behind her. Kyle looked at Dermott.

"Do you think she will stick to that?" Dermott asked. Kyle smirked.

"Probably not. Can you send someone with her to make sure we know what she's up to?" Kyle asked Paul. "We need to keep the south informed of our actions, even if we are on our own."

"Yeah, good idea," Paul said.

"I can send Matthew Cairns," Dermott suggested.

"Do we know where they are heading?" Kyle asked the young man.

"Presently, yes," he replied.

"Right, let's have a look, then," Kyle stated, as he turned towards the front door to look at Paul, "Paul, can you phone the south and let them know what we are doing?"

"And what exactly is that?" Paul asked.

"Defending these lands!" Kyle replied. Dermott smiled; he knew what that meant.

Chapter 55

Sabine looked up at the sky through the trees; it was going to snow again. She shivered. She could not zip up the jacket any further. That was mostly okay, but the cold bit at her face and she regretted wearing jeans – they weren't much protection from the wind. She looked at the snow-covered ground; her boots were stylish, but not practical for being in a forest. She leaned back against the tree and folded her arms. In the past, the cold had not bothered her, but this year it was different; she was really feeling it.

"Your boyfriend is dead!" Sabine exclaimed as Dani approached. She had a blatant scowl on her face.

"I thought you would be pleased," Sabine said. Dani stopped beside her and looked around. Everyone was huddled in small groups around various fires throughout the forest. Some were making hot drinks; others just huddled together. Canvas bags containing weapons lay beside each group.

"I wanted to do it myself!" Dani had not hidden her desire for revenge.

"Are you sure? Then what was the point of going to the farm?" Sabine was still unsure about their recent action. Dani glared at her.

"I don't have to explain myself to you!" Dani was openly hostile.

"I'm not asking you to explain yourself. I just want to know what we achieved, apart from losing two of our own in an act of aggression where the wolves only lost one?" The two stared at each other. The group closest to them stopped talking - their heads all turned towards the conversation. Dani spotted it, and spoke loudly,

"We achieved a great deal! We probed their defences in three places and watched their response. We know where their reaction force will gather, we know where all their overwatch positions are now, and we know how they check their perimeter. Best of all, we took down one of their top-tier dogs." The group of faces all grinned. "And all of that is stuff we can use against them." Dani was being defiant; Sabine was not convinced.

"We don't know if he was killed or not," she stated.

"We saw Davie shoot him. He was hit, he went down, and they carried a lifeless body away. What more do you want?"

"Was he not wearing body armour? He could have survived."

"Aww, missing your boyfriend, are you?" Dani was being condescending.

Sabine knew it. "He wasn't my boyfriend. I used him for information, that's all." Sabine shivered again and looked away.

"What? Finding out Alison is not with them at the farm is hardly ground-breaking, is it?"

"We still need to find her." said Sabine. Dani half turned away from her.

"Why? She was nothing but trouble; we had no further use for her."

"But" Sabine started,

"But what?" Dani demanded.

"But we still need to find her!" Sabine repeated.

"Why?" Dani shrugged. "She isn't one of us and, for all we know, she was working with the wolves the entire time." Some members of the small group nodded. "And don't forget about what she did to Maya!" Dani was now speaking directly to the small audience, and there were murmurs of agreement. She turned back to Sabine, with a venomous smile on her face. Sabine could not disagree with what Dani just said.

"But she isn't with them. She's just disappeared," Sabine spoke loud enough for all to hear. Dani had started to walk away from her, but now looked back over her shoulder.

"Good riddance to her! We are better off without her." Sabine wanted to say something else but chose not to. She was concerned for her friend. She changed the subject,

"What about 'him'?" There was a reaction from the small group. Dani spun around and shot a glance at them before speaking directly to Sabine.

"'*He*' doesn't exist!"

"He does. He was on the cliffs and saw what the wolves did."

"Did you actually see this fictious character?"

"No," Sabine conceded.

"So," Dani glared at her again, "how do you know he exists, then?"

"I..." Sabine hesitated. She had heard the stories. He was the only thing they were afraid of. None who had met him had ever survived. Many thought it was just that - a myth, a legend, that he was not real... just a bogeyman. Dani did not believe it and would never be convinced.

"You what?" Dani stepped towards her, verbally pushing her, daring her. Sabine had felt that he was there. She had felt his anger, his hatred... but Dani had not. Sabine backed down. She looked at the snow on the ground, then back up at Dani, who smirked. She'd won, and she knew it.

"What about the wolves?" Sabine asked. Dani stopped and turned around, extending her arms, as if in a welcoming embrace.

"We have the minibuses leading them on a wild goose chase tonight. They will not get a lot of sleep following empty vans!" She said, smiling. Then she turned away and walked off through the forest towards another group, huddled around their fire.

"She is right," said one of the those who had been listening. "We found the trackers they'd attached to the minibuses and we've had a team following them since they left the farm. We have the upper hand," he explained. "We will be picked up in a few hours, after we've ditched their surveillance." He looked around, then back at Dani. "Everything is coming together just as it should. It won't be long now." The faces around the small fire were illuminated by the light from the flames.

"They'd better hurry! I'm freezing!" stated one of them. Sabine agreed; they were all cold.

"And I am starving," stated another. There was sudden movement from the edge of the forest. All attention turned towards the noise.

"Someone is coming," came the whisper from a different group to her right. Sabine dropped to one knee and took cover behind the tree. Her right hand moved under the jacket to the small of her back. Her fingers found her leather belt and followed it until they located the pistol.

She peered towards the sound of snapping branches and careless movement. Whoever it was, it wasn't one of them. Sabine slowly brought the pistol around and had it firmly gripped in her right hand. Her left hand was against the tree, using it as both support and cover. The fires had been quickly extinguished. Everyone now lay on their stomachs, looking towards whoever was crashing about in the forest. Sabine controlled her breathing and focused her senses. She strained to hear what was coming. The noise continued; It was coming towards them. Sabine narrowed her eyes - there were two of them. She could now make out their shapes. The one on the left was male, taller than the girl. Both were wearing padded jackets, gloves and woollen hats, carrying rucksacks. They were campers, but they'd picked the wrong forest to camp in.

Sabine heard the growing excitement in the group nearest her. This was a young couple; she could now hear their voices. They were excited about something. They shared a laugh, seemingly quite happy to be together. The ground near her started to move; slowly, quietly, stealthily. The pair were heading directly towards their deaths and had no idea what was about to happen to them. Sabine didn't move as the forest around her suddenly burst to life. The predators jumped to their feet and rushed towards them. There was no one else for miles. Sabine stood up and replaced the pistol back under her clothing; she would not be needing it now. There were squeals of excitement mixed with screams of terror. She stood, watching as Dani ran back towards her. They shared a glance; Sabine's face was emotionless. Dani was thrilled with excitement, and she rushed to join the frenzy. Sabine watched as the rest of them arrived amid the chaos. A single boot was tossed away to one side. The terror-filled screams were mixed with the sounds of tearing and shredding of clothing...and flesh.

Sabine readjusted her jacket; she was still cold. She looked up as the snow was starting to fall. The guy would be screaming for less than ten minutes, the girl would be screaming through the gag made from her own clothes for some time to come. Sabine's eyes focused in on a single snowflake that was gently falling past a branch above her. Her eyes followed it, watching as it fluttered slowly towards the ground. Yelps and squeals of excitement filled the forest as the snowflake made its way down. She watched it land and disappear on the forest floor. She looked upwards and focused on another snowflake. It seemed so peaceful... the slow movements of the falling snow...

∞∞∞∞∞

Kyle's eyes opened and he looked around the bedroom of the farmhouse. There was light behind the curtains covering the windows, but the alarm had not gone off yet. His left hand worked its way out from underneath the warmth of the duvet and found the small clock. He lifted it and turned it so he could focus on the time. It was later than he'd thought; the alarm had not been set. It was time to get up.

The shower felt good. As he was returning to the main bedroom, he looked towards the door of Tyler's bedroom. It was closed. It only took a couple of minutes for him to get dressed; then make his way down to the kitchen. He made his breakfast in silence. The toaster popped and the single slice bounced up. He slathered salted butter on it and sat at the table. He had finished it without even thinking about it. His elbows rested on the table; he had a mug of tea between his hands. He looked around the quiet kitchen and suddenly realised what was missing. He set the mug on the table, then pulled his phone out. Amanda had bought it for him for Christmas, then had to show him how to use it. He was not used to the new smart phones, but he was getting there. He tapped the side and started to scroll through the pictures he had saved. He looked at Amanda's face and smiled at the memory. For a second, he could see her in her dressing gown, hair a mess, smiling, and handing him a mug of tea. The fire in her eyes; the warmth of her smile...

He felt the intense emotional loss hit him like a tidal wave, like a dam bursting. He choked, then started to sob. His body shook. As quickly as it had started, it stopped. He fought to control himself. The house was empty. No one saw his moment of weakness. As alpha, if he showed weakness, he could be challenged. In that moment it had hit him how much he missed her. Kyle started to compose himself. He wiped his eyes and turned to reach for a paper tissue. He wiped away the tears, discarding the tissue in the small bin near the sink. He scrolled through more pictures and stopped at the one of her in the dress at his very first dance, when he had met her. He smiled at the memory; she'd led him away from the bar so he could watch the dun running as a pack for the very first time. The first time they kissed... the fight in the bar... They were happy memories. He flicked out of the photos and pushed the phone back into his pocket. The farmhouse was quiet without her. The stillness was broken by a knock at the front door. Paul opened it and walked into the living room.

"In here!" Kyle shouted from the kitchen table. Paul appeared in the doorway.

"Mornin'," he greeted. Kyle nodded towards him, and Paul stepped forward to take the seat opposite him. Kyle looked a mess. "Did you not sleep well?" Paul asked.

"What? Why?" Kyle looked up quizzically.

"You look like shit," Paul smiled as he spoke. Kyle lifted the mug of tea,

"I'm grand," Paul did not believe him. He looked like he had hardly slept; his eyes were red with lack of sleep. "So, what did Tyler get up to last night, then?" It was a quick change of conversation.

"Did you make a pot of tea, or just in the mug?" Paul asked, pointing towards the drink in front of Kyle.

"Kettle's not long off the boil. Help yourself." Paul walked over to the kettle flicked it on and started to prepare his own mug
of tea, chatting as he did so.

"Well, it did not go as well as she had wanted it to."

"Why?" Kyle asked.

"They followed the tracker signals until nearly four this morning. It looked like they were driving around, stopping at different carparks." The kettle started to boil, so Paul poured the steaming water into the mug and stirred the teabag with a teaspoon. The used tea bag landed in the sink with a smack. "Then suddenly they all stopped."

"For how long?" Kyle asked.

"Well," Paul turned around and seated himself opposite Kyle. "They had not moved for some time and the assault team had stayed well back. Dermott wanted to find out how many they were dealing with, so he got a car to drive by where they all were." Paul drank from the mug and looked up at Kyle. "There was a plastic bag pinned to a tree with all the trackers names in it and a handwritten 'Merry Christmas!' note inside the bag." Kyle smirked; Paul drank some more.

"So, no sign of them, then?" Kyle asked.

"None," Paul replied, "and they completely dumped all of our surveillance. Dermott is absolutely furious!"

"I bet he is. What about the tracker Tony placed on the blonde's car?" Kyle asked. Paul shook his head,

"After leaving the meeting with Tony, it was driven to a pub near the Giant's Causeway, left in the carpark there, and has not moved since."

"Almost as if she knew," Kyle paused. "Which pub?"

"As you go past the entrance to the Causeway, you keep going until you reach the next junction. It is just across the road from there."

"Yeah, I know it," Kyle nodded. "So, everyone got back here with no problems, then?" he asked, Paul nodded once.

"Yes, just after six."

"I won't wake her for a while then," Kyle straightened up in his seat. "So, we have no idea where they are or what they're going to do next?" Paul shook his head, Kyle took a deep breath, and looked directly at Paul. "'Any ideas what we should do?" Paul paused, thinking.

"Well, there are a couple of things," he started.

"What would Carl do?" Kyle asked, that got Paul's attention, Kyle had never asked that question before.

"He would listen to all available courses of action, then make a decision."

"Well, give me all available courses of action, then."

"We will need Dermott as well, for that," Paul smiled as he replied.

"No problem, we can get together later on then, after they have all had a sleep." Kyle sat forward again, "What about Rhydian on Rathlin? Is there any chance they know about them?" The smile dropped from Paul's face. Of course! He had forgotten about the orphan and the other two female security there.

"I don't know, it's a possibility."

"Right," Kyle started, "they are really exposed, have them brought back here. They are just too tempting a target for them."

"I agree," answered Paul. "I will get that sorted today," he glanced at his watch, "which reminds me, we have an order from Scotland to sort out this morning, as well." Kyle looked confused.

"Scotland?"

"Yes, Scotland," Paul tried not to grin, "in case you've forgotten, we are a business, and we have clients in Scotland whom we supply."

"Of course," realisation dawned on Kyle's face, this was a deer farm, after all.

Chapter 56 –

Lisburn Courthouse.

Mike looked at his watch as he walked outside. The cold hit him; he was only wearing a suit. It was nearly midday, and he was angry. He took out his phone and stepped to one side. The sound of a train could be heard from the far side of the white-painted wall. Lisburn train station was on the other side of the fence that ran from the wall, along the side of the building, then across the front, effectively restricting access to the courthouse. Mike pressed the button on the side of the phone; the screen lit up. He paced a short distance from his car he'd parked in the small carpark beside the courthouse. He heard voices as the courthouse doors behind him opened and Chief Anderson walked out.

The Chief glared at him, then turned and headed towards the car park exit. The new Inspector of Belfast M.I.T. followed her boss towards the turnstile. Mike glanced around at the fence. It had been put there long ago to stop a rocket attack but, as far as he knew, Lisburn Courthouse had never been attacked. It was not the same for the Law Courts in Belfast. In the early 1990's, it was under constant attack. Mike looked at the back of Chief Anderson with contempt. He'd had his day in court and, although the legal proceedings were over, Mike knew Chief Anderson wasn't finished with him yet.

"That wasn't too bad now, was it?" Mike looked up at the familiar face of Darren Forrester. Darren was not dressed for a court appearance: woollen hat, outdoor jacket, gloves and walking boots. He looked more like he was heading to the Mourne mountains than a courtroom.

"I didn't know you were here!" Mike exclaimed; Darren shrugged.

"Here to give you a lift, plus, I didn't want to advertise that we are here," he replied. Mike was not sure, but did he just wink at him? "So, a two hundred pound fine - that is okay," Darren stepped past him and nodded towards the parked cars. It was only when Mike spotted the movement inside that he realised the car was still occupied.

"Well, I still have the P.S.D. investigation to go yet. The Chief will not let it go that easily!" Mike said. They turned and watched as the Chief Inspector and Inspector Pelan were let out the pedestrian entrance.

"We will just have to keep him out of our business then, won't we?" Darren looked back at him; eyebrows raised.

"Are you saying Special Branch can make P.S.D. 'go away'?" Mike asked. Darren let out a short laugh,

"Hell no! There have been plenty of times when I wish we could." Mike saw that Darren was now looking past him, back at the front of the courthouse. "And here comes one person that does want to speak to you!" Mike turned and looked over his left shoulder at the approaching journalist. He recognised her face but had forgotten her first name. She had jet black hair and was smartly dressed in a thick outdoor jacket. A brown leather handbag swung from her right shoulder. She had a notepad and a small electronic device, probably a Dictaphone, in her left hand. She smiled a sweet smile and stopped a few feet away from him. "Detective Sergeant Dear," she held out her hand, which he took. She had a firm handshake. "So nice to see you again." Mike smiled as he released her grip, he paused,

"I'm sorry, I know we've met, but I can't remember your name."

"Oh, that's okay, I would not remember me either!" She was trying to put him at ease, make him relax, hoping he would be more agreeable to answering her questions, and he knew it. "Cara-Marie McKenna, Coleraine Herald," she smiled, and gave a small nod of her head. He suddenly remembered. She was the 'wolf girl'; the journalist from last year who had published the werewolf stories, for which she had been publicly ridiculed. What he could not tell her was how close she'd been to the truth. Simon had interviewed her about sightings around Coleraine, which had given them accurate CCTV footage of the Latvian called Anna, and Anders Dusmanov. His body was one of those found at Mussenden Temple after the shootout with the SAS. Part of him wished he could sit down with this woman and have a 'tell all' chat. But that, he knew, could never happen. The disclosure notice prevented that.

"Ah yes, I remember you now. Sorry, I meet a lot of people."

"I am sure you do."

"What brings you here?" he asked. Get her on the backfoot - that would give him more time to answer her questions when they came. "I didn't think any Coleraine media would be interested in this."

"Well, just following up," she lifted the notebook and glanced at it. "'Any thoughts on today's proceedings?" Mike took a deep breath. He had been briefed by Media Branch what he could say and, more importantly, what he could not.

"Yes, well I have publicly given the Chief Inspector a full apology for the minor incident that occurred, we both consider the matter resolved."

"I was at Inspector Parrish's funeral. I saw what happened," she interrupted his prepared statement. Mike stopped, and she carried on, "I know the two of you were friends. I am sorry for your loss." Mike looked into her eyes.

"Thank you," he said quietly. Then he looked at the small group of barristers carrying briefcases and folders. It was both the defence and prosecution teams. They all seemed happy. Well, they had reason to be... two hours in court would be a good pay-out for them. "Sean was ...." Mike stopped. For once in his life, he did not know what to say next. Cara-Marie nodded, smiled politely and picked up the conversation.

"It was said in court that the Professional Standards Department of the police are still investigating the assault. Is that even possible ... to prosecute for the same offence twice?" Mike straightened up.

"The court appearance today was to answer an assault charge, for which I was found guilty and fined two hundred pounds... which, I may add, I am happy to pay." Cara-Marie stood motionless, listening. This was a prepared answer, and she knew it. Mike continued, "The P.S.D. is carrying on with normal police procedure in a situation like this. No, they are not investigating an assault, but an offence while in public office and the behaviour of a police officer in a public place." Cara-Marie thought for a moment before asking her next question.

"How do you feel about that?" She studied Mike. He wasn't giving anything away.

"Well, I will fully co-operate with any inquires the P.S.D. wish to make." Mike shifted his stance, and continued on, "Like I said, it was a minor offence and the P.S.D. have to wait for all legal avenues to be resolved before they can close the case. It is normal procedure." He had not answered her question.

"What did he say that provoked that reaction from you?" Her question stopped him. His eyebrows shot up, he glanced away; the question made him uncomfortable.

"It was an emotional event. It was a minor offence and I regret my part in it," he still was not answering her question. She was about to say something else but was interrupted by the sound of a car horn from one of the parked cars. Mike turned and waved at the two people who were looking at them through the fence. "Sorry, but I have to go," he said, as he started to turn away. She held out her hand, which he took.

"Thank you for chatting with me," she said, he released her grip and started to turn away,

"No problem," and he left. Cara-Marie found herself standing alone, outside the courthouse. She watched Mike climb into the back seat of the parked car. It moved off and drove slowly past her, the balding man in the front seat of the car looked at her, then looked away. The car slowly made its way towards the front barrier. She watched it stop to give the security guard time to open the heavy gate. The car moved forward. The guard gave a single wave, then slowly pushed the gate closed. The car moved into the one-way circuit of traffic.

Cara-Marie recognised the face of the police officer in the front seat. She started to walk slowly towards her car, which she had covertly parked by the train station. The guard smiled politely as he opened the gate and wished her a pleasant afternoon. She nodded and smiled in reply. She walked gingerly on the compact snow covering the pavement. She unlocked her car and threw her handbag and jacket onto the passenger seat, then took out her phone and climbed in. She started the car and, shivering slightly, turned on the heater. As the car moved off, her phone connected to the audio system. She waited for a space in the traffic, then drove up Railway Street and stopped at the traffic lights at the top. When the lights changed, she followed the road to the left, as it dropped down past Lisburn College. Suddenly, she was able to put a name to the face!

At the next set of traffic lights, she had time to make a call. The sound of ringing filled the car, then stopped, and she moved off again.

"What?" the answer from Mark was abrupt.

"That is no way to answer a phone. I could have been anyone!"

"Your name comes up on the screen when you call. It's a modern thing called technology; you should check it out sometime."

"Piss off!"

"Okay I will, but you'll only call back if I hang up now."

"Good to see you know who is in charge here!" Cara-Marie said out loud.

"Anyway, what do you want?" He was distracted by something. Cara-Marie slammed her brakes on as a cyclist cut in front of her. Her right hand hit the horn. "Wow, someone's tired!" Mark had obviously heard the horn.

"I'm fine."

"That'll be a first." Cara-Marie's car moved off. The cyclist gave her a dirty look as she overtook him. Her left hand gave him a single finger reply.

"Anyway," she said.

"Anyway," Mark repeated.

"Can you do something for me?" Cara-Marie was forced to slow down again in the traffic. This would be better once she got onto the motorway.

"Well, you never phone just for a chat now, do you?" Cara-Marie did not say the first thought that was in her head.

"Does the name Darren Forester mean anything to you?" The phone was quiet for a few seconds.

"No, should it?"

"Superintendent police Special Branch, used to have the nickname 'Grey Fox'."

"And how, precisely, would I know him?" Mark asked, "when were you talking to him?"

"I wasn't, he drove past me at the courthouse, just as I was leaving."

"How did that go? Anything interesting?"

"No, not really. Can you do a check on him for me?"

"What's the magic word?" Mark stated. She accelerated and just got through the traffic lights as they changed to red, stopping the car behind her.

"What?" she asked.

"What's the magic word?" he repeated.

"Now!" she said, grinning. She was just getting onto the M1 motorway.

"That's not very nice." Cara-Marie looked to her left and stared at the driver passing her very slowly. He was positioned so she could not pull out to overtake the traffic in front of her. The driver just smirked at her; he knew what he was doing. "But hey," Mark continued, "you do know I am the photographer and you are supposed to be the investigative journalist?"

"Yeah," this driver was starting to really annoy her, "can you do it, or not?"

"I'll see what I can do. Where are you now?" Mark asked. She glanced around.

"Just got onto the M1 at Lisburn."

"So, you are about two hours away, then?"

"An hour and a half... not everyone drives as slowly as you do!" she retorted. There was a short laugh down the phone.

"Well, if you make it alive, I should have something by the time you get here. 'Any reference what this is about?" Cara-Marie thought for a second then answered him.

"Nothing I want to say down a phone, but we can chat when I get there." Mark could now guess the subject. There was only one thing that she would not discuss over a phone call, but Mark had no idea how a superintendent in police Special Branch could be connected with werewolves.

∞∞∞∞

The landline phone in the living room of the farmhouse was ringing. Tyler had not been awake long and was walking down the stairs when the ringing started. The living room was empty, as was the kitchen. It was already dark outside. She picked up the handset.

"Hello," she spoke quietly.

"Hi," said was an excited male voice, "is that Tyler?"

"Tony?" she recognised his voice once he had said her name.

"Yes, is Kyle there? I need to speak to him. It's urgent!" Tony sounded stressed.

"He isn't here. I can only guess he is out on the farm. Why? What's up?" she asked. There was a pause. Tony's heavy breathing indicated he was stressed about something.

"Right, I can't say too much, but"

"But what? Are things okay there?" she asked. Tony coughed.

"Well, no, something might be up." Tyler relaxed; for an instant, she'd thought he had told his pregnant wife about his infidelity and was now paying the price. She was quickly losing interest.

"When I see Kyle, I will ask him to give you ring, would that do?" She was about to put the phone down.

"No, look, they are here! They are driving past outside," his voice picked up an octave as well as volume.

"Who are?" Tyler was still unconcerned. He had been unfaithful to his wife, so whatever was happening, he probably deserved it. She was not expecting what he said next.

"They ...them ...the Nocs! They are driving past really slow." Tony was obviously concerned, and Tyler's attention had picked up,

"How do you know? Are you sure?"

"I know one when I see one. They must be close - it started just after sunset." There was real concern in his voice. Tyler's mood changed. No matter what he had done, he was still one of them. He was still a wolf.

"Right, what is the security team doing?"

"What?" he asked, his voice strained.

"The security team, I thought there was a team of two with you and your wife at all times." Tyler turned and looked at the door, willing it to open. It did not.

"What? Oh, right. No, they are not here at the moment," Tony answered. Tyler heard a woman's voice in the background. She had met Karen, but she did not know her well. Tony's reply had her confused.

"What? Where are they?" she demanded, Tony was hesitant,

"They are in Coleraine, doing shopping." Tyler's eyes closed and her grip tightened on the handset. She knew Karen was being very careful after what happened to her last year, and Tony was told to stay indoors in case the Nocs thought he was out of the picture. But they still needed to eat.

"Okay," she opened her eyes. Her hatred for the Nocs, took over. "Are you armed?"

"Of course! I have my pistol and a double-barrelled shotgun here, as well."

"Are they just looking, or do you think they are hostile?"

"I WOULDN'T BE ON THE FUCKING PHONE IF I THOUGHT THEY WERE JUST LOOKING!" Tony screamed down the phone, Tyler nodded once.

"Right... stay there! We are on the way." Tyler slammed the phone down and ran towards the door. She flung it open and she ran outside; there was no one there. A sense of urgency gripped her. She ran towards the corner of the barn... no one. A farmhand, carrying a sack of grain over his shoulder, casually walked around the far corner. "Where is Kyle?" she demanded. The farmhand stopped and stared at her.

"I, err," he stammered.

"Where is he?" Tyler shouted this time.

"I-I don't know..."

"What about Paul or Dermott, then?" Tyler stepped towards him

"They're down at the 400-metre range." There was a look of surprise on his face.

"Right," Tyler pointed at him, "get a hold of all of them and tell them Tony is in trouble! The Nocs are at his house!" She turned and ran back to the farmhouse, not waiting for a response. She flew through the living room, through the kitchen, then up the stairs to her room. She ripped at one of the bags and grabbed her sword. She was back outside in seconds and jumped into one of the Land Rovers. Her sword landed on the passenger seat as the engine roared to life. It lunged forward and took off down the lane.

Tyler knew what happened to families when the Nocs showed up. She forced the image of her husband outside her burning house in Canada from her mind. No one was going to cut the heart of Karen Fallon out, not while she could do something about it... and she was going to do something about it!

∞∞∞∞∞

Cara-Marie looked around the newspaper office. She was the only one left. It was dark outside, but nice and warm in here. She looked her desktop screen; the story was done. She filed the short article about what had happened in Lisburn Courthouse into the drop box of the newspaper group. Kevin had not been interested in the story, but perhaps someone else in the group would be.

She sat back in her chair with satisfaction and looked at the clock on the wall. It was time to go home. She closed down the computer, pushed her chair back and stood up. She packed her personal items into her handbag and switched off the main lights. She stopped at the back door and looked around the dark room. Nothing had been taken during the break-in and, apart from minor damage, they'd just made a mess. It did not make sense. She tapped in the code for the new alarm system Kevin had installed. She zipped up her coat, pulled open the rear door and stepped outside. The door slammed shut and she listened for the three beeps. Then the office went quiet: the alarm was set. Cara-Marie headed quickly towards her car. The female voice behind her made her jump, she turned around.

"Excuse me. Cara, isn't it?" Cara-Marie looked at the young woman who was walking tentatively towards her. She did not recognise the face. She was young, with short, bobbed hair and a smile that hid what she was thinking. There was a moment of recognition, but Cara-Marie could not quite place her. The woman did not offer her hand, as she stopped in front of her, "I'm glad I caught you."

"Hi," Cara-Marie stopped, the girl looked around her before she spoke.

234

"Hi. I'm not really supposed to be talking to the press but, hey ho, here I am." The woman wore thick mittens on her hands and shiny black boots on her feet.

"Hi. I'm sorry but, do I know you?" Cara-Marie asked. The woman paused, then looked around again.

"Well, we only met briefly once, I am Laura Patterson, I was one of the police officers who responded to the break-in here at the offices."

"Oh yes!" Cara-Marie exclaimed. Now she extended her hand and they briefly shook. Laura stepped past her, obviously wanting to walk and talk. "You have not been at Coleraine for long, have you?" she asked. Laura glanced at her,

"No, this is my first station out of the training centre," she was walking slowly; she was here for a reason. "I have two years' probation to complete, then I can apply anywhere I'd like." Cara-Marie knew this already - it was normal for new police officers.

"Are you enjoying it, so far?" Cara-Marie made small talk, hoping to gain her confidence. This could be her new source inside the police station.

"Yes, I love it," Laura said excitedly. Then she looked directly at Cara-Marie, "Let me start by saying that I have been following your stories and your blog for some time," Cara-Marie let her continue, "I did a presentation during training about the Castleroe murders. It went over very well." Cara-Marie raised her eyebrows; she did not know that.

"Really? Well, I suppose it was easier to find when I changed the name on it."

"Yes, really, well, all except the werewolf bit," she said, smiling.

"Yeah, most people have a problem with that part," Cara-Marie chuckled.

"I believe you," Cara-Marie stopped suddenly and looked at her; she guessed she was telling her the truth.

"Thank you." Laura had stopped as well. They looked at each other, "is there any particular reason why?"

"Clear, concise reporting... and I agree with your blog...what happened at New Year's wasn't at all what they passed it off as."

"Thank you," Cara-Marie repeated, unsure where this conversation was going.

"Anyway, I was on the early shift today and I just heard about the body they found near Mussenden Temple."

"What body?" This was news to Cara-Marie, and she stepped closer. Laura leaned towards her slightly, lowering her voice. Her right hand went into her pocket and pulled out a smart phone which was similar to her own.

"Well, I just received the message half an hour ago: somebody walking their dog found a male who had been stripped naked and had his heart cut out." Cara-Marie's mind was racing ... this was certainly news to her.

"What? Where exactly?"

"Do you know the forestry block, just across from the entrance?"

"Yes."

"Officers arrived there after a 999 call. The throat had been ripped out, as well. First reports..." Laura held up her phone, indicating this was how she knew; coppers were messaging each other. "...say he was staked out on the ground and there is blood all over the place. M.I.T. has already been advised and are on their way." Laura spoke confidently, "It sounds a lot like what happened at Portstewart Strand on New Year's Day." The journalist in Cara-Marie was exploding; she wanted to get there as fast as she could.

"Thank you, thank you!" she stepped past the girl and walked quickly towards her car. Her hand was already in her pocket, fishing for her phone to call Mark.

"By the way," Laura said. Cara-Marie turned back towards her. Laura was smiling, and Cara-Marie noticed the small piece of folded paper she was offering to her. "This is me. Message me when you get a chance. We should meet for a coffee sometime." Cara-Marie had her source! She took the note, then raced towards her car. Mark was not answering his phone.

Chapter 57

Tony had the phone to his ear as he walked back into the darkened living room. He stopped just short of the main window. He could make out the headlights of a car cutting through the night. He had forgotten about the pain in his chest, for the moment.

"There is a car approaching my house; if that is you, flash your lights twice," he instructed. His eyes focused on the single car. It did not slow down, but the main beam flashed twice.

"Can you see me?" Tyler asked. He was guiding her; she hadn't been to his house before.

"Yes, take the next entrance on your left; that is me."

"Okay, yes, I see it." The car slowed down and turned into the driveway. She turned off the headlights. Gripping his pistol, Tony opened the door slightly and scanned the darkness. There was no movement there. Tyler came bounding up the steps, holding the sheath of her sword in her left hand. Tony stepped back and she flew past him. The door slammed shut and he immediately locked it. The house was in darkness.

"Right," she started, "what is happening?" Tony walked past her and headed into the living room; she followed.

"It started just after sunset," he looked over his shoulder at her, "which means, wherever they are sleeping now, it is nearby." With obvious concern, he walked over to the edge of the large window. Tyler agreed… they had to be close. He motioned with his left hand as he spoke. "I spotted the first car driving by, slowly, three up. They had a really good look at the house, then sped up." Tyler listened; the grip of her left hand tightened around her weapon. "Then, a couple of minutes later, a different car; again, three up, came past heading the other way. This time, I spotted someone with either a phone or a camera taking pictures as they slowed down. The one in the driver's seat was grinning like a Cheshire cat and held up a pistol when he saw Karen at the window!" There was anger in his voice.

"Have they seen you?"

"I don't think so." Tyler turned her head towards the door of the living room as Karen walked in. They smiled uneasily at each other; then they embraced.

"Hey you,"

"Hey you," Karen repeated. She had her hair tied back in a ponytail and the side-by-side shotgun strap hung over her right shoulder.

"I hear congratulations are in order," Tyler said, smiling. Karen beamed.

"Thank you," Karen looked at Tony, "it is the most amazing thing." She stepped closer to him and reached out her left hand. Tony took it; he was welling up. Tyler could see their connection; Karen obviously did not know what he had done recently. Tyler pointed at the shotgun.

"Do you know how to use that?" she asked, and Karen smirked.

"Yes, she does," Tony answered. "In fact, she is better at clay shooting than I am!" he declared, obviously proud of his wife.

"Well, that probably isn't a hard thing to do," Tyler looked at Karen and winked; she grinned back.

"You two are not supposed to gang up on me," Tony protested.

"You'd better get used to it," Karen said, giving him a playful punch on the arm.

"Right, then," Tyler stated, "to the matter at hand."

"Yes," Tony let go of his wife's hand.

"What security do you have?" she asked, Tony's face became serious.

"This way," Tony turned and walked out of the living room and headed towards the kitchen; the women followed. Tyler placed her hand on Karen's shoulder.

"Are you okay?" Her concern was real.

"Yeah, I'm good," said Karen, poking Tony in the back, "I have my wolf to protect me!" She was smiling. Tony opened one of the cupboard doors to reveal six small monitors. They showed different angles around the exterior of the house.

"Black and white?" Tyler asked.

"Passive infrared," Tony replied. On top of the monitors sat four small black boxes, about three inches long and half an inch high. Along the front of each was a line of lights that went from red to green.

"What are they?" Tyler asked, pointing to them.

"Motion sensors." Tyler grinned at him.

"When is everyone else coming?" Karen asked, expectantly, Tyler stepped back.

"I'm not sure," she replied.

"What did Kyle say when you told him?" Tony asked, Tyler glanced at him.

"I didn't see him," she looked back at the screens, "after we spoke on the phone, I told a farmhand to find him and tell him. Then I came straight here."

"Did they see you arrive?" Karen asked.

"If they're watching the house they would have," Tyler stared at the screens.

"Then they would be nuts to try something, with you here." Karen's mood lightened. "Anyone want a coffee, then?" she stepped back and smiled

"Yeah, great, what have you got?" asked Tyler. Karen smiled and switched the kitchen light on. It would not be long before the smell of freshly brewed Kenyan coffee would fill the kitchen. The vibe was improving.

ooooo

"Right, okay, no problems," Kyle said into the handset of the landline. He looked around the living room. Paul and Dermott were seated, and Ruth was standing behind one of the chairs. "Keep me posted. If you need anything, call, okay?" Kyle replaced the handset, then walked over to his chair. Dermott spoke first.

"Okay, so what is happening?" he asked. Kyle got comfortable before he answered,

"The Nocs started slowly driving by his house just after sunset, taking photos and, in one case, brandishing a firearm." Kyle looked around, "It seems they have not tried to hide what they're doing.

"Intimidation." Ruth stated. Kyle glanced at her and nodded.

"But to what end? They would not try an assault now." Dermott wondered aloud.

"They are not going to assault the house," Kyle replied, "I think they were not sure if Tony was there, and just wanted to scare his widow."

"Who would probably be defenceless," Paul added, and they agreed.

"Just like a Noc!" Dermott spat.

"Tony thinks they must be close, as he first spotted them just after sunset." Kyle looked at Ruth, and asked, "Who is with him as security?" he asked.

"Becky and Fiona."

"Are they back at the house now?" Paul asked, Ruth shook her head.

"No, they were out doing the shopping when this started. I have spoken with them. They returned and, after chatting on the phone with Tony, took off to follow the next car that went past with the Nocs."

"Where did they go?" Kyle asked. Ruth shifted uneasily.

"They are still behind them, updating me with data messages every few minutes."

"Good," said Kyle as he sat back in the chair. "Are they armed?" he asked.

"Both with pistols, and one G36 in the car." Ruth looked straight at Kyle, "They know the rules about using them in public...only as a last resort," she confirmed.

"Great. Keep me posted on that," Kyle nodded as he spoke, then looked at Paul. "What do you think they're up to?" Paul took a deep breath before he spoke.

"Well, they got quite a slap in the face, losing so many down at White Park Bay." Dermott let out a small laugh; Paul carried on. "So, whatever their overall plan was, It's had to change. But this," Paul pointed towards the landline phone, "I think, is just intimidation against one of our families. I cannot see what they hope to gain." He looked at Dermott, "If they thought Tony was dead, they'd have to know that taking down his wife would only bring a reaction from us!" Dermott blinked, then nodded once in agreement. What Paul was saying made sense.

"Have we told everyone who lives off-site about this?" Kyle asked.

"Yes. There've been no other sightings." Dermott answered.

"And Rathlin?"

"Rhydian and the two security there are packing up and will be on the ferry, tomorrow," Ruth stated. "They should be here around lunchtime."

"And the Nocs have definitely left Belfast?" Kyle asked.

"Definitely," Paul replied. He motioned towards Ruth. "We sent a team down to go through the lair and there was absolutely nothing!"

"Yes," Ruth confirmed, "the place was spotless. No trace they'd been there, at all."

"And we don't know where they are sleeping at the moment, then?" Kyle's question had Paul and Dermott glance at each other.

"Not at the moment, no. But now we know it is close to Tony's, so we can concentrate our search around there," Paul answered. "Is Tyler going to stay with Tony and Karen tonight?"

"As far as I know, yes," Kyle answered. "Has there been anything from any of the other off-site families?" Kyle asked.

"Not so far," Dermott answered, "but I'll phone around and tell them to be on their guard."

"Ruth," Kyle sat forward. She stepped around the chair and looked at her alpha,

"Yes?"

"I want an assault team ready to move at a moment's notice, just in case they try anything," he instructed.

"Already done. We have assault team one in the barn. They've already completed comm checks and are doing rehearsals." Ruth did not take her eyes off Kyle as she reported the actions. "All the wagons are fuelled up, and we are going to go over route checks to all the off-site locations. If anything happens, we are ready." She tried not to smile, "all we need is the word to go!" Kyle looked at her and smiled.

"Good," he said. He slapped his hands on the arms of the chair and stood up. Dermott and Paul stood, too. "I have not had dinner yet. Is anyone else hungry?"

oooooo

"CAR!" Tyler shouted from the front living room. Karen grabbed the shotgun from the kitchen table and followed Tony, turning the light out as she went. Tyler was standing with her back to the wall by the main window, staring at the car that had turned into the short driveway. The headlights were turned off and it rolled to a stop beside Tony's car. It reversed, then manoeuvred into a reverse park.

"It's Becky and Fiona." Tony relaxed and replaced his weapon in the holster. Karen sighed, turned and walked out of the room. Tony coughed and winced at the same time; he was still in pain. Tyler looked at him.

"You okay?" Tony looked at her and coughed again.

"No, I've been shot twice in the chest, and it is killing me!" In the darkness of the room she could see him smile, but she knew he was still in pain. The front door opened, and she heard Karen admit the new arrivals. They stopped in the hallway, exchanging greetings. Karen switched the hallway light on, and Tyler moved towards the entrance; she still had her sheathed sword in her left hand. She recognized the two women from the last moon dance, but they'd never been properly introduced. Both of them were young, still in their twenties; Fiona had long, dark brown hair and Becky had long, mousey blonde hair that hung down over her shoulders. She seemed to be the older of the two. Both wore outdoor jackets, jeans and walking boots. Fiona was carrying what looked like a thick briefcase with a long metal handle.

"Where is the shopping?" Karen asked.

"It's still in the boot of the car. Do you want it in now?"

"It can wait," Karen reassured them with a smile. They looked at Tyler, and Karen introduced them. "Tyler, this is Becky and Fiona. They have been keeping me company for a few days now," Becky extended her hand.

"Hi, I'm Becky,"

"Fiona," Tyler shook hands with each of them, they knew who she was.

"Right, let's get a coffee on!" Karen said, as she turned and headed back towards the kitchen. She seemed more relaxed.

"Tea please," Fiona said, as they started taking off their jackets. Tyler did not realize that she was staring.

"You have not been for training with me, have you?" she asked, Becky hung her jacket up and smiled a response.

"No, I was with you in the Mournes when we took down the rabid." Tyler's eyes glanced down at the belt on her jeans; or, more importantly, at the SIG 226 pistol on one side, and the pouch containing two magazines on the other side.

"Yes, I remember." Tyler was about to say something, but Tony interrupted from behind.

"Where did you follow the Nocs to?" he asked, Fiona had placed the briefcase between her feet and was still wrestling with her jacket. The two of them wore matching fleeces, and Fiona wore her pistol and magazines in the same place as Becky.

"We lost them the far side of Ballybogy," she replied.

"So, they are close, then?" he asked. Becky headed off towards the kitchen as Fiona hung her jacket up.

"Yeah, we're pretty sure they spotted us, so we had to cut the surveillance." Tyler looked at Tony; the concerned look was back. Fiona picked up the briefcase and walked towards the kitchen. Tony started to walk forward but Tyler did not move; he bumped into her. She was looking over her right shoulder at him, and he stepped back. Then she turned around to look directly at him,

"They know we are all here now, they will not try anything," Tony did not respond, so she continued, "Your family is safe; nothing will happen to them." Tyler turned and walked away, "I will not let anything happen!" Tony stood in the silence of his own living room. It was lit only by the light from the hallway, and it was so quiet. The kitchen light was on and the four women were chatting. He heard the sound of mugs on the table and the kettle being switched on. The mood in the house was lifting. His right hand came up and touched the top of the pistol at his side. He took a deep breath, then walked through the doorway to the kitchen.

Karen was by the side counter making tea and coffee, and Becky was at one of the cupboards, filling a plate with biscuits. It was not long before they were all enjoying the hot drinks and chatting. Tony was beside Tyler. He could see her eyeing the briefcase Fiona had been carrying. He knew what it was but guessed she did not. The shotgun was on the floor along the rear wall beside the back door, right behind Karen. Tyler's sword was up against her chair. The mood was convivial.

"So," Tyler asked, "what do you two do at the farm, then?"

"We are part of Dermott's security team," Becky answered, then took another drink from her mug. Fiona nodded in agreement.

"Okay, but what are your normal jobs? If you were not here, what would you be doing at the farm?" Tyler spotted Tony and Karen glance at each other. They shared a smile; they obviously knew something she didn't.

"Well," Becky placed the mug on the table. "I am a schoolteacher."

"And I am a criminal psychologist," stated Fiona with a wide grin.

"Oh," the answers had caught Tyler off guard; she had not expected that.

"Many on the farm do lead normal lives." Tony advised. There was a collective giggle.

"So, how come you are both here, on the same security detail?" Tyler lifted her mug and watched as the two of them again looked at each other, then back at her.

"We are sisters." they answered in unison. Tyler's face reddened. She looked at them. Only now as they sat beside each other, could Tyler see the family resemblance.

"Nice one."

"You know Keith, the guy in charge of logistics at the farm?" Tony asked,

Tyler glanced at him, "Yes?"

"His two girls," Tony extended his right hand towards the girls smiling back at her, Tyler motioned towards Becky.

"Oh God, I remember when you were born!" There was another collective laugh, then, "Thanks for making me feel old!" Suddenly, the smiles on the girls faces dropped as they looked past Tyler and Tony towards the security cupboard.

"MOVEMENT!" All heads turned and looked at the red flashing lights on one of the displays. Tony jumped up and went to the door of the kitchen that led to the front of the house; Karen flicked the light out, grabbed the shot gun and knelt beside him, facing the door to the living room. Tyler was down on one knee with the sheath of the sword in her left hand and her right gripping the handle of the blade. She was staring at the back door, waiting for any sign they were there. Becky came down beside her, her pistol was firmly gripped in her right hand, and she was staring at the monitors. Fiona had her back to her sister and had quickly opened the briefcase. She gripped the long rifle butt and attached it expertly to the G36 rifle.

Tyler looked around. They had obviously practiced this; the security team knew what they were doing. Both entrances to the house were covered. The kitchen was the secure room and it was in darkness. Becky slowly stood and pressed a button on the control panel. Suddenly, the outside of the house lit up with bright security lights. Becky knelt back down and pressed her back against her sister. Tyler glanced at the rifle. Fiona had the butt securely against her shoulder; she had a good grip on the weapon and was looking over the top of the sights. There was something attached to the front grip, which Tyler did not recognise. It had a small torch and another lens protruding from it. She would ask later what it was; but not now.

The room went quiet. After a few moments, Becky's left hand started to move. She told everyone in a whisper what she was seeing. Becky held up two fingers in a victory sign, then clenched her fist and pointed to the ground with her thumb. She tucked her thumb into her hand then, keeping her fingers together, formed a cup shape and motioned to her right. "*Two .... enemy .... moving to the right,*" her eyes studied the screen. She held up one finger, then again pointed to the floor with her thumb. "*One .... enemy .... moving to the left,*" Tyler saw her glance at Tony. He nodded in understanding. Becky looked at her, and she nodded once, as well. Tyler spotted the small movement of Becky's left elbow as she prodded Fiona. Fiona kept staring over her weapon, searching for a target. She gently leaned back to indicate that she understood. Tyler looked out over the back garden. Something was not right. To carry out an assault with only three fighters against a prepared superior force did not make any sense at all. Becky moved again. Tyler looked at her.

"Two .... enemy ...." Her hand performed a karate chop motion towards the screen, *"moving away .... returning to vehicle...."* Tyler did not take her eyes off her, as she continued. *"One ... enemy .... moving .... to rear of house...."* Becky turned around, looked over her sister's shoulder and raised her voice, "We should be able to see her now!" All heads turned and looked out of the windows into the back garden, and watched Sabine slowly walk into the light. She stopped. She gripped an unsheathed sword in her right hand and wore a vengeful look on her face.

"Report all targets." Tyler stated.

"Only one observed, rear of Red Papa One." Tyler guessed that 'red papa one' was how Tony's house was marked on the main map back at the farm.

"Right, maintain secure room here and get in touch with the farm." Becky reached into her pocket and brought out her smart phone. She held it in her left hand, away from her face; it was on speaker. She turned around so she was facing Tyler, with her left side pressed into Fiona's back. She looked up at the monitors.

"REYNOLDS!" screamed Sabine. Tyler stood up to see her, clutching the sword with her left hand. Tyler looked at Becky as the sound of the ringing tone echoed around the room.

"Stay here and protect the family!" Tyler commanded. Becky nodded once. Tyler looked out the back window. "No one kills her, but me!" Tyler paused, and looked directly into her Becky's eyes, "If she gets the better of me, do not leave the house! Understand?"

"Roger," Becky responded.

"Communications," the male voice answered the call. Tyler walked around the table and opened the back door.

"Tyler, wait," Tony went towards her. Tyler's right hand shot out and held up her palm.

"Stay here, defend your wife and child, this could be a ruse to lure us all into a killing area."

"But"

"No buts!" Tyler looked at Karen, whose eyes were filling with tears, "stop him from doing anything stupid, will you?" Karen nodded twice.

"Control, this is Papa One Zero, CONTACT," Becky was talking to the farm. Karen nodded. Tyler stepped out into the cold night and closed the kitchen door behind her. The room filled with Becky's voice, "One hostile towards the rear of location, armed with a sword; we are in the secure area."

Sabine stared at her without moving. Tyler slowly walked forward, gripping the handle of her sword. There was metal scraping as the blade was withdrawn. Tyler dropped the sheath onto the light crust of snow that covered the ground. Sabine had a look of absolute venom in her eyes.

"Ott-valee .... Suk-a!" she spat.

"No," Tyler replied, as she let a smile spread over her face, "fuck you .... Bitch!"

Chapter 58

Cara-Marie looked at the watch on her wrist; it was just after 11pm, and she was freezing. The snow had begun to fall before she arrived and it was still coming down, two hours later. She stomped back towards her car. It was parked along the side of the road behind a row of police vehicles. She'd already been told to move once by M.I.T. when they'd arrived. The C.S.I. were different from M.I.T; they, at least, were happy to chat. They did not give much away, but she did get some bits she could use.

The C.S.I. were nothing like the TV show. But then, that was America, and this was Northern Ireland. She slipped and nearly fell; she was wearing the wrong footwear for this kind of terrain. Regaining some of her composure, she righted herself, then looked around; no one had seen her. The uniformed police officers at the cordon were cold, as well. They had been professionally polite, but they all knew who she was. There had only been one comment about there not being any 'mythical creatures' involved in this, from one of the M.I.T. members. But the uniforms could be chatty when on their own. She followed the path that had been trodden into the snow. Cars slowed down as they went past on the main road. One of the C.S.I., dressed in a disposable paper one-piece suit with her face covered, was walking down the side of the row of transit vans. She stopped where the path met the road to allow Cara-Marie to pass.

"Thank you," Cara-Marie said, but she was not acknowledged. Here was another person who wished she were somewhere else. She stopped on the road and looked back down the path. Her eyes followed the white suit as it trudged back into the forest block. The path went on for another twenty metres before the first cordon. Cara-Marie looked around; the forest seemed to be dark and consuming, as if it was trying to hide what had happened there. She was tired and cold. She looked up; the night sky was a sea of white flakes gently falling towards the earth. Cara-Marie turned and made her was along the snow-covered grass verge where the vans were parked one behind the other. Her small car was at the end.

She slipped again, as she was coming around the back of her car to get to the driver's door. The car was facing away from the vans and down the hill towards the steep slope of the Downhill. She opened the door and shook the snow off her coat, then threw it on the passenger seat. Next, she pulled her gloves off and tossed them onto her coat. She stomped her feet to shake off as much of the snow as she could, then landed on the seat and slammed the door shut. The inside of the car was as cold as the outside. The cold nipped at the exposed skin on her hands. She fumbled with the ignition keys before the engine roared. The heater blew cold air, but it would only take a few minutes to warm up. She shivered. She had to stretch herself so she could reach her phone in the right-hand pocket of her jeans. The light from the screen lit up her face as she looked up and searched for the light in the roof of the car. She flicked it on. She pushed the button on the car's audio system and waited for the icon on the edge of the screen to indicate her phone had connected. She scrolled to a name on the screen and a few seconds later, the sound of a phone ringing filled her ears. She dropped the phone beside some CD's and turned the light off. Clicking the seatbelt into place, she looked around, then slowly moved off into the falling snow on the road.

The car made its way down the steep slope, then levelled out. As she drove past a collection of buildings huddled together at the bottom of hill, she remembered the old hotel there, that was now closed down. It had been in the middle of nowhere; no wonder they couldn't make a go of it. Her speculation was interrupted when the ringing stopped and the male voice answered,

"What?"

"What do you mean, 'what'? I have told you before - that is no way to answer a phone!" she protested, "Is that how you answer it to everyone?"

"No, just you," Mark replied, she was about to ask how he knew it was her, but she remembered what he said last time.

"Anyway, since I finally got you," she started.

"You do know I was actually asleep..."

"No, you weren't!"

"Actually, I was."

"At this time? It's not that late."

"Cara, it has gone 11 and, yes," Cara-Marie's eyes glanced at the clock on the dashboard of the car; the green digital display showed 11:17. Mark carried on, "I was asleep," she heard him take a deep breath, "I may have not been for long, but I was asleep."

"Okay, well you are not now," she said.

"Just so you know, ... I am about to hang up!"

"Mark, no! I was just going to tell you about the murder near Mussenden Temple." The road was dark; there were no streetlights. She passed the occasional house on the left side of the road; there was a hedgerow and trees blocking the view of the fields on the right. Beyond that, was the wild and windy Atlantic Ocean.

"What? You are kidding me! Cara, that can wait until the morning," he said, irritated. Cara-Marie slowed the car down as she approached the small bend in the road, then clattered over the railway tracks.

"Mark, wait, I ...."

"NO, YOU WAIT! That happened months ago. The police said it was 'organised crime gangs. No one is going to believe your wolf stories!" Mark was getting irate.

"I'm not talking about that; I am talking about the body that was found earlier today!" she snapped back. The road straightened; the snow was falling faster, and visibility was deteriorating.

"What body?" He was quieter now.

"I sent you a text earlier; there was a body found by a couple out walking their dog in the forestry block, across from Mussenden Temple." There was a pause.

"No, you didn't."

"Yes, ... I did."

"I didn't read it, I was in the bath, so I've not seen my phone," Mark was still not interested.

"Well, this is something that we will be covering, so you need to know!"

"Alright," he sighed, "Who, what and where?" Cara-Marie was concentrating on driving in the snow. She continued,

"Right, the body of a male named Colin Daly was found there; he was naked, and they had cut his heart out!"

"Really? Shit, that's not good."

"He also, apparently, has massive injuries around his neck."

"His neck?"

"Yeah, I got it from one of the coppers; it was very similar to what happened on New Year's Day." Her eyes were searching for details of the road and the hedgerow in the falling snow, but her mind was picturing the body. "They said that he had been laid out spread-eagled among four trees, and it was a real mess!"

"I bet it was, do they have any idea who is responsible?" he asked.

"Not yet, but there was more than one; in fact, they are looking for a large group, and M.I.T. are looking at a possible link to Portstewart Strand."

"How do they know his name?" Mark asked, Cara-Marie responded quickly,

"They found an English driver's licence nearby and he matched the picture. According to C.S.I., the family in Bournemouth has been notified already."

"That was quick!"

"For them, yes," she agreed.

"So, he is not local; that will add to the media interest," Mark stated. She agreed.

"But the mystery is... what happened to the girlfriend?" Cara-Marie slowed down as the road rose and fell with the contours of the land. It bent around to the left, then past the turnoff that went down towards Magilligan Prison and the ferry across to the Republic. Everything was covered in a blanket of white.

"Okay, do tell," Mark encouraged. She had finally tweaked his interest.

"Right, the police were called by a couple walking their dog. It seems the body was there for at least a day, stripped naked, heart cut out and neck mutilated." Mark listened silently. He knew this would hit the national news, so they would be bombarded by English press again, first thing in the morning. "They have found shredded clothing belonging to him and the girlfriend," Cara-Marie paused, slowing down to go around a sharp corner.

"Do you know her name?" Mark asked.

"Yes, Amy something."

"Amy something?" Mark let out a short laugh, "That is not like you!"

"I do know what it is." He had riled her a little, but she carried on, "It's in my notebook, but I am driving at the moment!"

"And she was not there?" Mark asked.

"Nope, they found a load of her stuff shredded, as well, but no body, yet."

"What were they doing? Do you have any ideas?"

"Yes, they were on holiday, he was a landscape photographer and they were staying in a bed and breakfast, not far away."

"Did you speak to the B&B?" Mark asked.

"Of course, I did! I've been doing this a while now, you know!" she paused. He did not react this time, so she carried on, "the owner said she had not seen them since breakfast yesterday. I got the impression she was not overly impressed with them."

"Why is that?"

"Unmarried couple, sleeping in the same room." She smiled as she spoke, remembering the old woman's reaction. The road straightened and she could go a bit faster.

"Really?"

"Yes, really!" she replied.

"I didn't think anyone still thought that way," Mark stated, then continued, "but the police are looking for a gang or something?"

"Yeah, for some reason, there were a lot of people around. I could see the mass of footprints and tracks in the snow."

"I take it you have not spoken with Kevin?" she looked at the clock again.

"No, we can chat in the morning, when I have more done."

"But it was okay to phone me, was it?" Mark was not going to let this go.

"I know how much you like to know what is going on!"

"Oh, for ...." He stopped himself from finishing the sentence.

"Right, text me what you've got, and I will get on it," he acknowledged.

"Sure, no problems!"

"Where are you now?" he asked. She looked out, studying her surroundings.

"Passing Bellarena,"

"Bellarena? Where are you going?" his voice raised an octave with the question.

"Home," she replied, without thinking.

"Home?" he asked.

"Yes, why?" There were a few moments of silence before he spoke again.

"So, you were at the Downhill and you are going home to Portstewart, and you are passing Bellarena?" She thought for a few seconds before she answered.

"Err, yes."

"Cara,"

"What?"

"You're going the wrong way; that heads into Limavady!" she heard him laugh as he spoke.

Cara-Marie looked around; he was right...she was going the wrong way. She had got into the car and headed out, but she was concentrating on phoning him and not paying attention to the moment she was in. He was never going to let her forget this mistake! She knew he'd be ribbing her tomorrow morning, from the moment they both got into the offices of the Coleraine Herald.

Chapter 59

Tyler was standing a short distance in front of Sabine. She gripped the handle of her sword in her right hand; the tip of the blade pointed towards the ground by her side, showing Sabine the edge of the blade. Her left hand hung by her side; Sabine stood the same way. Silently, they both fought to control their breathing, after the fury of their initial assaults on each other. The sweat had already cooled and evaporated into the cold night air. It was still snowing.

Their struggle had cleared a space in the snow in the backyard of the house; they certainly had not finished. Sabine glared at her with sheer hatred. Tyler broke the silence.

"Sorry for spoiling your attempt to finish Tony off, you must be disappointed to find us here." There was contempt in her voice, Sabine's facial expression changed,

"He's still alive?" for a moment, she seemed relieved.

"He's alive," Tyler did not take her eyes off her opponent, "but that is not for lack of trying, on your part."

"I didn't want him killed," Sabine protested, "it was just unfortunate he was there; but you," Sabine snarled, "I've been wanting you dead for over twenty years."

"That's a long time," Tyler spoke quietly.

"To wait for revenge, yes but, looking at you now, worth it." The savagery was back; she emanated hostility. Tyler's breathing was returning to normal.

"And what do you want revenge for?" Tyler asked.

"You assassinated an elder in Canada; he was like a father to me."

"I didn't 'assassinate' anyone!" Tyler's voice rose.

"You went after him and four others, murdered them in their sleep!" Sabine spat.

"First of all, it wasn't 'murder', you lot have the monopoly on that!" Tyler was getting angry. Sabine had touched a nerve. Tyler stepped forward, pointing at her with the forefinger of her left hand. "Secondly, if they had not 'murdered' my husband, then I would not have needed to react, at all!" Sabine stared at her.

"A sapien?" Sabine screwed up her face as she asked the question, "they are our food. How can that be 'murder'? Plus, you could have got another one!"

"I was happy with the one I had," Tyler lowered her voice again.

"They are all the same," Sabine retorted.

"You are not supposed to try them all," Tyler sneered at her, Sabine narrowed her eyes. Behind Tyler, there was movement inside the kitchen. She could make out the shape of one of the security team standing and heading out of the kitchen. The one with the rifle was aiming it at her. Sabine looked at Tyler and a small grin appeared.

"Okay," she whispered, as she slowly raised her sword. She grasped it in both hands and held it out in front of her. The tip of the blade pointing directly at her enemy. Tyler did the same... challenge accepted. Sabine took a small step to her left, and Tyler followed suit. The pair circled each other, Sabine focused on her target, readjusting her fingers into a tighter grip. There would be no let up this time. Nothing would come between her and this wolf.

∞∞∞∞

Kyle was sitting in the rear of the 4x4, his sword was in the small daysack that was on his lap. He removed the communicator from his ear. The constant updates from the two small convoys and the communications building back at the farm, was getting annoying. He couldn't think. Dermott stayed at the farm to control the defence, should they attack there. Paul was driving as quickly as he could. Ruth was in the front passenger seat, her rifle pointing into the footwell. A full daysack, heavier than it looked, rested on the floor between her feet. She had her phone to her right ear and was speaking to Becky at Tony's house. Kyle was annoyed he let Tony go home. He should have made them stay at the farm. The Nocs were obviously closing in to finish him off. He could not let that happen. The vans behind him had briefly stopped to drop off the two teams that would provide overwatch on the east side of the house. The other convoy was circling around, so it was closing in from the other side. Kyle wanted to get to the house as quickly as possible.

"Yes... Roger, we are on the approach road and will be onsite in less than one minute," Paul spoke into the communicator.

"Right, we are on the Ballymacrea road now... single vehicle," Ruth confirmed into the phone. She glanced at Paul, "yes, we will flash main beams on approach." Paul gave a confirming nod. Kyle could feel the pistol digging into his side, under his jacket. He looked around outside the Land Rover. The snow had continued, which made finding the Nocs easier, but it also made them easier to track. Kyle looked at the clock display on the dashboard... 11:29. His left hand tightened on the strap of the daysack. If anything happened, he would use his pistol first. He peered out the windshield. The headlights only illuminated the continuous starburst of falling snow. Paul flashed the lights once,

"Turning left...now!"

"Yeah, okay...cheers." Ruth took the phone away from her ear and dropped it into her pocket. She held the pistol grip of the rifle, searching all around outside the vehicle.

"Becky is at the front door; the rest are in the kitchen. Tyler is in the back garden, with the Noc, Sabine," she stated, and Paul nodded.

"What?" Kyle reacted, Paul had turned off the headlights and was easing the vehicle into the driveway. Ruth did not look back; she kept her attention focused on the surroundings. All the security lights were on; the house was completely lit up.

"That is all she said," Ruth explained, as Paul stopped beside the other 4x4 that Tyler had driven. Kyle's door was already open; he was out and running. Ruth and Paul slammed their doors behind them, but Kyle was charging up the stairs towards the opening front door. They would be inside in seconds. Kyle headed straight for the darkened kitchen.

∞∞∞∞

The tip of the blade passed in slow motion, only inches away from Tyler's face. She had moved out of the way, just in time. She brought her own blade, edge upwards, vertically until it connected with Sabine's blade, knocking it out of the way. Tyler took a short step forward with her left foot, then her right, balancing her body as she struck vertically with her blade. Metal clashed on metal. The blade lifted a short distance and struck again, and again. Each blow was blocked by Sabine. They attacked and counterattacked. Sabine had speed - that much was noticeably clear. She had also been well taught how to use a straight sword. Metal clashed with metal again, and again, and again. Tyler did not even notice the gently falling snow, as her blade sliced through it. She stepped back and gripped her blade in both hands, left foot forward... she was perfectly balanced. She held the blade vertical, perfectly centred; her eyes focused on her panting opponent. Sabine was a mirror image of her - the stance, the blade, everything. It was only when they paused that Tyler realised that she, too, was panting. She fought to control her breath and felt her eyes tighten, her body tense. She was preparing to strike. Tyler launched forward with a series of frontal, left and right strikes, all blocked by Sabine. Then Sabine launched an assault of her own. The two danced in the snow. Tyler saw Sabine had overextended herself and brought her blade up, just missing Sabine's forearm; Sabine countered with a swipe of her own. The material in Tyler's left shoulder parted and a small red line appeared. She righted herself, then stood, defences back in place; Sabine did the same.

Tyler registered the pain, but she had to concentrate on the vampire who moved to one side in front of her. They maintained the circle, attacking each other again and again.

∞∞∞∞

They all saw the wound, everyone in the kitchen reacted.

Kyle's voice got everyone's attention, "BE STILL!" They were transfixed by the battle going on outside.

"We can..." Becky started to speak, as she stood up behind her sister, Fiona was still on one knee with the rifle in constant aim out the rear door of the kitchen. Tony and Karen were at the sink, watching out of the rear window.

"We can do nothing!" Kyle cut her off, then said to Becky, "You .... monitor the perimeter and ensure this is not a distraction for an assault." He checked the CCTV screens, then instructed Tony to watch the front door. Tony looked at him, nodded once, and walked through the doorway of the kitchen.

Kyle stood just inside the doorway. From there, he could cover the front, and keep an eye on everyone in the kitchen. Karen was up against the side of the unit, her right hand gripping the edge. She held the shotgun in her left hand and was intent on what was happening outside. He was about to command her, but stopped himself; she was not trained, and was not obligated to react. Kyle looked at Fiona, who still aimed the rifle. "Have you got her?" Kyle had lowered his voice. Fiona moved her head but did not look at him.

"Yes," she whispered. Kyle looked back outside at the flurry of blades.

"If Tyler goes down... you drop her," Kyle was watching the fight. Fiona maintained her crosshairs on the enemy.

245

"No problem," she whispered her reply. Silence returned to the kitchen.

∞∞∞∞

Paul could see Tyler and Sabine at the rear of the house. Becky was relaying instructions from Kyle. Paul was by the long hedgerow that separated the fields; the rest of the pack where kneeling out of sight, either side of him. The other team were at the far side of the house. They had been instructed to secure the area and ensure there were no other Noctrailis about to attempt an assault. If there were, it was down to Paul to deal with them. The overwatch was in place; they would advise him of any movement.

"Why are we stopping here?" Ruth asked, Paul looked at her.

"You heard the instruction as well as I did."

"But what if...?" Ruth stopped herself; her anxiety was mixed with rising anger. She shifted uncomfortably. Paul looked back towards the sound of clashing blades. Everyone along the hedgerow wanted to join in but were practicing restraint.

"But nothing, you have your instructions," Paul muttered. Ruth was jumpy, itching to get going. "Ruth," Paul said suddenly, "Take two others and make your way along the road to the other team." Ruth rose quickly. There was an angry look on her face.

"You, and you, come with me," Ruth pointed to the two who were beside her. They both nodded and jumped up.

"Ruth," she looked back at Paul.

"Yes?" she asked. Paul looked concerned.

"Remember to keep your long weapons out of sight. We don't want anyone phoning the police, reporting people running around the countryside carrying guns!" Ruth nodded. She folded the butt of the weapon and tucked it into her right armpit, the glove of her right hand gripping the front of the rifle. In daylight, it would be easy to spot; at night and in falling snow, less so. The other two did the same. They were heading off when Paul stopped them. "If you come across *any* Nocs .... deal with them!" Ruth's eyes widened and she smiled, as did anyone within earshot. There was a communal reaction from the rest of the pack, Paul's attention returned back to the fight, Ruth stepped up to the hedgerow to see what was happening.

"Tyler knocked the sword out of her hand!" whispered one of the wolves, excitedly, everybody was grinning.

"It's now a slugfest!" said another, "look at them go!" Paul glanced at Ruth.

"Get going," he said, Ruth nodded, and they sprinted off into the falling snow.

∞∞∞∞

Tyler glanced over to where the swords had landed. She ducked as Sabine's right foot passed through the space where her head had just been. She had overextended herself again. Tyler moved her weight onto her left foot and, as Sabine's body steadied itself, she launched a front kick that landed in Sabine's right side. The force threw Sabine rearwards with a squeal of pain. She crashed to the ground.

"Finish her!" Tony had nearly shouted, Kyle looked at him, then back outside. Tyler was running over to where the swords had landed, and Sabine scrambled to get up. Everyone had heard the pained scream from Sabine. Tyler grabbed her sword and threw Sabine's over the hedge into the field behind her.

Tyler stopped, holding her sword in both hands with the blade uppermost. Sabine was full of rage; her face was bruised from Tyler's blows. She screamed loudly as she threw herself at Tyler, mouth open, incisors elongated. Her fingers extended as she ran straight towards Tyler, grabbing at her. For Tyler, everything moved in slow motion: Sabine's footfalls crunching in the snow, her arms reaching towards the neck of her prey, eyes full of fury. Tyler dropped to one knee, pointing the tip of the blade at the vampire who was propelling forward. With one movement, Tyler rose slightly and side-stepped. Then she launched herself towards her attacker.

Sabine's right hand missed. Tyler gripped the blade with her right hand and, with all her might, slammed it into, and through, Sabine's body. The tip of the blade burst out of Sabine's back. Tyler stopped and stood upright. The fatal blow had frozen Sabine's momentum. Her scream ceased; her attack ceased. Sabine's right arm, strength lost, bounced off Tyler's body. Her expression went from rage to shock. The two stood together. Tyler stared at the face that was now only inches away. From a distance, it would almost have looked like they were hugging. Sabine, wide-eyed, looked down at the handle of the sword protruding from her chest. Tyler saw the look of fear and disbelief on her face. Sabine's eyes welled up and her lips quivered. Neither of them could hear the cheering coming from the field.

246

"I-I..." Sabine stuttered, Tyler kept her grip, Sabine looked into her eyes. Grey eyes looked back at her. Both faces were bloody and bruised.

"You will die soon," Tyler stated quietly. Sabine started to gasp and fight for breath. She looked away; her body was starting to shake.

"I am sorry for the loss of your sapien," Sabine whispered, and her eyes darted around as if searching for a rescue that was not coming.

Tyler did not answer. She watched as all colour drained from Sabine's face. Then she released her grip on her sword, and Sabine dropped lifelessly to the ground. Tyler knelt and fought for breath. The rear door of the house burst open. Tyler looked at the snow in front of her and tried to compose herself. She was close to collapse.

Chapter 60

Mike Dear switched on the hallway light and closed the bedroom door behind him. His phone was still in his left hand and he raised it to his ear again, readjusting his dressing gown.

"You do know that it's gone midnight?"

"I'm fully aware of that," Darren Forester's voice was at the other end.

"My missus is really pissed off at you, right now," Mike said.

"Well, it's not the first time for that and probably not the last. Anyway, now I have you...we need you to come in." Mike stopped and stared at a framed print that was on the wall at the top of the stairs. He could not believe what he'd just heard.

"What?"

"We need you to come in. How soon can you get here?" Mike was dumbstruck.

"I ...."

"I wouldn't be calling if it was not urgent!" Darren explained. Mike felt his spirit sink. He could not say no.

"I am supposed to be flying back to England tomorrow, I need to finish the course at the Fort," Mike explained.

"Yes, that is still happening, we just need you here for a wee bit, that's all." Mike couldn't hide his disappointment.

"Can whatever it is not wait until morning?" said Mike, looking around.

"A body has been found near the Mussenden Temple.,"

"Err, so? I am not M.I.T. anymore!"

"Neither are we. The throat has been ripped out, it is very similar to the New Year's Day murders," Darren paused, "you need to come in, Mike."

"Okay, I will head there as soon as I can." Mike knew he would not be getting any sleep that night, but his most pressing task was to try not to awaken 'Grumpy'.

∞∞∞∞

The kitchen of Tony's house was abuzz. Tyler was sitting on one of the chairs, holding an ice pack wrapped in a cloth to the left side of her face. She was hoping to reduce the swelling. John, the paramedic, was kneeling in front of her with his trauma bag open on the floor. Tony and Karen were with Becky and Fiona in the hallway. Paul, Kyle and several others were gathered around Tyler. Her sword had been cleaned and was back in its sheath on the table. The back door was open, a large group had gathered; everyone was excited. Sabine's body had been wrapped in a plain bed sheet that Karen had produced. Kyle had forbidden them from taking photographs, and Karen had forbidden them from bringing the body inside her house.

"She was a foe, an enemy, but still should be respected in death!" Kyle had told the pack when they all assembled at the house. The farm had been told; they, also, were celebrating the victory. It had been such a long time since a prominent Noctrailis had been taken down, and they all knew the significance. John stood up and looked at Kyle and Paul. Then he looked at Tyler, then back at Kyle again and spoke,

"Right, she has minor head injuries, soft tissue trauma to her shoulders, arms and face." Kyle nodded once, and John continued, "She has at least three broken ribs on her left side and bruising on the lower legs ...." John smiled, "in short, nothing that a couple of days' rest will not sort out."

"What about the slash on her shoulder?" Paul pointed to her injury.

"It's a clean laceration. I've cleaned it and closed it with steri-strips, so, daily dressings and ..." John looked at Tyler,

"And?" she asked.

"And you will have a nice scar you can lie about for the next few years, at least!" There was a ripple of laughter.

"Thanks John," Kyle patted him on the shoulder as Tyler closed her eyes, wearily. John zipped up the trauma bag and effortlessly swung it onto his back. He turned and headed towards the open door, grabbing his jacket from the back of one of the chairs. Outside, the snow had stopped for the moment. Tyler looked up at Kyle.

"Any chance of a bit of peace and quiet?" she asked, Kyle nodded and turned to the crowd.

"Right, everyone who does not need to be in here, make your way outside!" There was a chorus of nods. The back door closed on the muffled chatter, as the last one left.

"So, what are we going to do with the body in my back yard?" Tony asked. All eyes turned towards Kyle.

"Leave her for sunrise." He looked at Tyler who gave a wry smile, then he looked back at Tony, "I mean, legally she does not exist, right?"

"Right," confirmed Paul.

"After daybreak there will be nothing left, but dust," Kyle explained. "Have you ever seen what direct sunlight does to them?"

"Yes, I have!" Tony replied, the mood in the kitchen was still triumphant.

"Right," Paul said, "what shall we do with this one?" He was looking at a very tired Tyler.

"A shower, then bed is on my agenda," she replied.

"You can do that here," offered Karen, as she walked into the kitchen. She was as excited as everyone else. Tony filled the doorway, with his hands touching the top of the frame. He was smiling, as well. Tyler looked up, as Karen stopped by the table.

"Thanks, but I want to head back to the farm, if you don't mind." Karen nodded.

"Of course." Tyler stood up with an effort, but batted Paul's offer of assistance away.

"I'm exhausted, not crippled!" she exclaimed. Tyler reached over and picked up her sword with her left hand, she looked at Kyle, "If you have no objections..." Kyle beamed; he did not.

"No problem," he looked at Paul, "can you run her back to the farm?" Paul nodded, "Take one more of the security team with you, just in case you run into any problems on the way."

"But what of *them*?" Tyler asked, looking at everyone. Tony relaxed his arms and stepped into the room as Tyler continued, "They were up to something." She pointed towards Tony, "they did not know he was still alive, and they certainly did not know I was going to be here. They are still up to something!" Kyle straightened up at her comment.

"I agree," he looked around, then back at her, "but for tonight," he pointed at Tyler, "you have done enough, and I am grateful." He looked over at Paul, "Now, take her back to the farm." Then he looked back at the dishevelled Tyler, and smirked, "plus, I'm not sure what else you could actually do!" She stepped forward and raised her arm to give him a playful punch. This time she winced, and her hand went to the broken ribs at the side of her chest.

"Well, that is something we both have in common now!" Tony laughed. Tyler looked at him, and grinned. Karen stepped in closer and looked into Tony's face; her adoration shone for everyone to see. Tyler looked away.

"Oh, I forgot to say... Rhydian will be at the farm tomorrow," Kyle said. Tyler looked excitedly at him, and he carried on, "I felt they were too exposed and, if anything happened there ...." He paused.

"We could not get there fast enough," Tyler looked away as she finished his statement.

"Unless we had a helicopter!" Tony said, excitedly. Everyone looked at him.

"Do we have a helicopter stashed away that I don't know about yet?" Kyle asked, chuckling.

"Nope." Paul joined in; Kyle looked towards Paul.

"Have we anyone who can fly a helicopter?"

"Nope."

"Have we got anywhere we could keep and maintain a helicopter?"

"Nope," they were all laughing now.

"Well," said Kyle, folding his arms, "that is something we can look into some other time."

"It was just a thought," Tony said, dejectedly.

"Okay, let's get out of here," Tyler said, as she turned and reached for her jacket on the back of a chair.

"I'm driving," stated Paul.

"You're driving," confirmed Tyler, shuffling past him. Kyle stepped back to let her pass. He gave a nod to Paul as he followed her to the front door. Fiona stood at the doorway, holding the rifle across her body. She wore a confident smile on her face. Kyle nodded for her to come closer. She walked into the room and stopped.

"Fi, you and Becky will stay here, one awake at all times; two hours on, two hours off, until sunrise," he commanded. She nodded once, then turned to tell her sister.

"I can help with that," Tony offered, but Kyle looked at him as the front door of the house opened. Becky was saying her goodbyes to Tyler.

"You are going to bed." Kyle smiled at Karen, "Make sure he does will you."

"I've never been *told* to take my husband to bed before!" she laughed as she spoke. Tony did not know where to look; his wife took his hand, "you look exhausted," there was real concern on her face. The front door shut as Karen stepped towards the door that led to the rest of the house. Tony and Kyle shared a smile and he followed his wife. Kyle walked out after them and headed back into the living room. It was still in darkness. Becky and Fiona were standing by the edge of the large window. Kyle walked over and joined them. He looked out at what they were watching.

Tyler was walking around to the rear door of one of the Land Rovers. Several members of the security team had gathered around and were applauding and congratulating her. Kyle watched as she shook hands and acknowledged the accolades. Paul walked through them to the driver's door. The lights outside the house lit up the area.

"She's amazing," whispered Fiona.

"Yeah, she totally kicked that Noc's ass!" Becky replied. The two sisters shared a look as if Kyle was not even there. The vehicle roared to life and drove off down the short driveway and into the night. The security team members retreated into the darkness.

"Do you two know what I need you to do?" Kyle spoke quietly, the two girls turned and looked at him.

"Yes, it will be done," Becky stated.

"Are you staying here?" Fiona asked. Kyle had not thought of that, he looked around. There were three bedrooms in the house, and all would be occupied. He could command one of them to give up theirs, but he decided against it.

"Yeah, I will crash on the sofa."

"I'll grab you a duvet," said Fiona. Becky lifted her hand to the communicator in her right ear. She paused for a few moments, then looked at him.

"Ruth is at the back door; she wants to talk to you."

"Tell her I'll be right there." Kyle turned and headed back towards the kitchen. Behind him, Becky relayed the message,

"Roger, zero alpha en route." Kyle went into the kitchen; Ruth was opening the back door as he arrived. She had snow on the shoulders and hood of the jacket. There was snow and mud on her boots, and she carried her rifle in her right hand. She stopped just inside the doorway. Kyle stood near her; the crowd was still gathered outside. They were all looking towards Ruth, who had her left hand to the communicator in her left ear. She listened with a concerned look on her face. Her eyes shot up to meet Kyle's,

"Overwatch says there are four Nocs moving towards us across the fields to the rear."

"Where?" Kyle's tone changed. Ruth turned and pointed out the rear door.

"Five hundred metres that way, moving very slowly."

"Do they know we are still here?" Kyle asked. She looked back at him.

"Probably," she answered.

"Don't guess. Confirm." Kyle walked past her and outside. The crowd stepped back. He looked back at her, she followed him outside. "Where is the overwatch?" he asked, Ruth lifted her left arm, and pointed,

"Hillside over there." Then, she looked the other way and pointed to the right, "second overwatch on the rise, that way," she touched the device again. Kyle felt the cold of the night. Everyone else was dressed for the outdoors; he wasn't. He glanced down at the sword that was still in his left hand. "They are in a diamond formation, no visible weapons seen by either." Ruth looked back at him, "They've stopped at the corner of a field four hundred and fifty metres away... yes, it seems they know we are still here."

"They are looking for her," stated one of the security team, pointing towards the wrapped body of Sabine.

"What do you want us to do?" Ruth stood beside her alpha and waited for instructions. Kyle looked back at her.

"Defend these lands from those who mean us harm!" he stated. A small cheer went up from the group. Kyle looked around at his wolves; they were excited. "Right then," he started, "we will split in two. Ruth, you take team two, and I will lead team one." The excitement was growing.

"What about the long weapons? Paul said earlier to keep them out of sight in case someone spots us and phones the police!" Ruth said.

"And he was right; stay as you are with that," Kyle pointed at the rifle she was holding. Then he turned to the rest of them, "All of you .... will hunt in our true form!" Excitement rippled through the group. They were happy with the decision. Kyle looked back at the open doorway where Becky was standing.

"Becky, we will leave the weapons here. You keep an eye on them, will you?" he asked, but it was a command.

"No problem."

"Right," Kyle started, "leave all your weapons in the kitchen, and change as quickly as you can." The crowd moved into action, Kyle and Ruth walked past where Sabine and Tyler had been fighting, and on to the end of Tony's rear garden. They were still lit up by the security lights. Ruth stopped beside him, and they both knelt down. "Okay, where are they?" he spoke, quieter than before.

Ruth was listening to her earpiece, then looked up and used her left hand in a karate chop motion, "They are that way," Kyle looked into the greyness of the night. Everything he could see was covered in a blanket of snow. Finding them would not be a problem. Ruth continued. "They have stopped; one of them is looking in this direction."

"Where have they come from?" Kyle whispered. He did not have to look at the young woman who was briefing him, using her left hand to help with the descriptions.

"Axis, from here," Kyle eyes followed a straight line going away from where they were, "right of axis, hill."

"Seen," he confirmed.

"Left of hill, forestry block."

"Seen,"

"Behind the hill is a road; overwatch reports a single car parked there." Kyle thought for a moment, then made his decision.

"Right, I will take team one from here," Kyle used his right hand in the same karate chop motion. Ruth listened to his instructions. "We will go right of axis and sweep up the hill; as we are doing that, you take team two straight down the axis and head for the far side of the forestry block," She nodded her head, but did not speak. Kyle continued, "Once there, we will sweep through the trees." Kyle glanced at her, "Any Nocs that make a run for it... are yours." Kyle looked at his watch. It was just after 1am. "Start line is this fence. Be ready to move in five minutes." Ruth looked at her own watch, then at Kyle,

"No problem!"

"Exactly how many have we here?" Kyle asked.

"Just under forty."

"Great," Kyle stood up, and Ruth joined him, "Let's get this done!" Kyle turned to walk back towards the house with Ruth. Standing upright at the back of the house was a group of wolves... moving, swaying. They parted to let the two of them through and, as they approached, more wolves came out from the house. There was a chorus of growls and grunts of excitement.

"Right then, gather 'round!" Ruth shouted. The pack of wolves encircled her, eager to hear the plan for the coming fight.

Chapter 61

Kyle landed on the far side of the fence just as the lights around the house went out. The jacket he'd borrowed from Tony was zipped up, but he kept the hood down. He started off at a brisk walk, soon increasing his speed to a slow jog. Behind him, a group of wolves jumped the fence and moved as a pack. Gripping the sheath of his sword, he glanced over at Ruth and her group as they made their way across the far side of the field. She was leading the pack at a brisk pace, the rifle slung over her back.

Kyle looked over his shoulder. The pack of wolves behind him was a breath-taking sight. He slowed down to a walk as they reached the far corner of the field. Then he stopped and went down on one knee, to study the footprints in the snow. They were wearing boots and there had been a lot of activity in this corner. The wolves around him stopped and waited for direction from their alpha. Several of them lowered their heads and started sniffing. A larger wolf was on all fours, his nose was right up against the snow, head moving from side to side, taking each step carefully. He walked up to the gap in the hedge, looked through, then back at Kyle. He understood; they went that way. Kyle stood up and looked around the gap. The large wolf nudged him, he looked down at the wolf,

"We need to make sure there are no booby traps. The Nocs can be devious!" His comment was met with a chorus of approval, and the larger wolf lowered his head and took a single step back. Kyle moved closer to the gap - it was a perfect place. He inspected the edges, then looked back at the group of bright eyes, glowing in the night. "On my sniper course in the Legion, this is exactly the type of gap you would avoid when stalking." Kyle smiled as he looked back at the gap, "but we are not stalking, we are hunting!"

The gap was clear. Kyle launched himself through, and into the next field. He ran for about twenty metres before he stopped and again, went down on one knee. His eyes scanned everything twenty metres around him, then ten metres, then five. The track of footprints led off around the hill to his right. His wolves jumped either through the gap, or over the hedge, and gathered around him. He looked up at the summit of the hill, where a fence cornered. His eyes moved along the ridgeline until it met the edge of the forestry block. The tracks led towards the trees. Kyle looked to his left and saw Ruth and her group circling the far side of the large field. They would be in position shortly. Kyle rose and started along the trail of footprints, breaking into a jog. His wolves were on either side of him. Kyle motioned and they formed an extended line. They followed the tracks around the side of the hill. Kyle did not notice the chill in the night air. He was excited for the hunt; he felt so alive. He glanced to either side; the wolves were spread out horizontally with short gaps between them. Some ran upright; some ran on all fours. He looked ahead as they came around the side of the hill. The slope stretched down to the edge of the forest. There was nearly a hundred metres of open field.

They all saw the Nocs at the same time. Four Nocs were in front of the wood block. They were young males, wearing boots and outdoor jackets. One had a small daysack on his back. Three of them were kneeling around the fourth, who was lying on the ground. They looked up at the row of dogs now charging towards them.

"OH SHIT!" one of them screamed. The three who had been kneeling sprinted towards the trees. The one lying down scrambled to get up. Kyle was now sprinting as fast as he could. The pack broke into a full charge, barks and yelps echoing as they closed in on their prey. The fourth Noc made it to his feet just as the others got to the tree line. He slipped and fell. His feet tried to grip in the snow, but they gave way; his hands grasped at the ground in an attempt to propel himself forward. All the wolves focused in on him, he would not survive. Kyle was still sprinting, but the rest of the pack had overtaken him, closing in on their kill. There was now nearly ten metres between him and the last wolf. The Noc managed to get to his feet and began to run, just as the first wolf cannoned into him. Kyle sprinted towards them. The first wolf was joined by a second, then more.

Suddenly, Kyle's eyes caught the movement all along the tree line. A row of figures all appeared at the edge of the trees, both males and females. Kyle knew instantly they were Noctrailis. They all carried rifles, and stepped forward as one, weapons aimed. Kyle heard the sound of gunfire mixed with the yelps and screams of his wolves. There were eight, possibly ten, Nocs scything through his pack. It had been a trap! Kyle went from excitement to rage as he jumped over the first of the bodies on the ground. They were peppered with bloody circles.

The charge, though dwindling, continued. A few of them had gotten close enough to attack the vampires. The wolves were shredding the Nocs they could reach, blocking the view of the other vampires. The battle closed in. Kyle jumped through the first of the trees, gripping the handle of his sword, blade forward. One of his wolves was writhing on the forest floor. The Noc standing above him screamed with satisfaction, firing continuously. Too late, he saw the figure holding the sword close in. He tried to bring the

M-16 up, but it was too late. Kyle swiped the blade across the torso, then forced the sword, with all his strength, through the body. Kyle brought his right foot up and pushed the dying vampire off his blade.

All around him were clashes. Pushing the Noc to one side, Kyle crashed on along the edge of the treeline to the next vampire, who was too engrossed in the wolves in front of him to spot Kyle's approach. His head came neatly away from his shoulders. The body dropped to its knees before falling over. On the ground, a bloodied, dying wolf looked up at him, arms cradling the wounds on his body. Through the chaos of the fight, Kyle could hear the dying whimpers and cries of his wolves, but he had to carry on. Kyle went after the next vampire. Off to his right, the field was covered with dead and dying bodies. Behind the next vampire, an upright wolf was savaging one of his enemies. The Noc was desperately struggling with the cocking handle of his M-16. His eyes locked on Kyle, then widened with fear, as he threw the useless weapon at him. Kyle batted it to one side. The Noc threw himself at him in a futile attempt to disarm him. Slash, slash, slash... Kyle's blade swished through the air, and the body in front of him sliced open, bounced off a tree, and landed on the ground. The contents of the abdomen flowed dark red onto the snow-covered ground.

Kyle carried on. The last of the vampires was fumbling with the shells of the pump-action shotgun as fast as she could. Three wolves got to her at the same time. Kyle looked around, he was no longer interested in her screaming, the ripping of flesh, the snapping of bone. His sword was still up in front of him, held firmly in both hands. He saw the wolf kneeling against a tree nearby down on one knee, yelping in pain. He'd been shot and was using the tree for support. Kyle stepped forward and placed a hand on his shoulder. He recognised the dying wolf as one of the farmhands.

The volley of gunfire from the far side of the forestry block made him look up, searching through the trees and the darkness. There was screaming and yelping. Ruth's group had just been hit, as well.

"Bastards!" Kyle spat, as he tried to make out what was happening. The gunfire ended as quickly as it started. He turned and knelt beside the wounded wolf, trying in vain to stop the bleeding. The remaining wolves were still tearing away at the bodies of their enemies, angry and enraged. Kyle looked at the field beside the trees; some wolves lay still, others moved and moaned. "Right," he said, standing tall, "Everyone, listen up!" A wolf nearby stopped and looked at him. There was blood all over her mouth and down the fur of her neck. Kyle needed to regain control. Those who were left needed to help the rest of the pack.

Suddenly, it felt like he'd just been kicked by a horse. He was thrown off a tree and landed on the cold ground. The searing pain in his left shoulder made him scream. He slapped his right hand over the flowing wound. Another wolf screamed, thrown rearwards. Kyle rolled on the ground. His eyes caught sight of his sword laying near his head. His right hand shot out and grabbed it. He forced himself up onto one knee. His eyes searched for the source of the shot. As he raised himself up, he could see the shapes coming through the forest. There were three pairs, all carrying long weapons and they were coming towards them. Kyle dropped down; the larger wolf came up beside him. There was rage in his eyes and blood over his face. Kyle raised his head once more, looked around, then dropped down beside the wolf. "Right, they are coming to finish us off."

The wolf growled, and Kyle looked into his eyes, thinking for a few seconds, "this is not a fight we can win." The wolf bared his teeth, viciously. Kyle winced in pain. "Listen to me," he demanded. The wolf looked at him, Kyle glanced back at the hill behind them. "Do you see that summit, there?" Kyle nodded with his head. The wolf looked over to the right, then back at Kyle. "This is what I want you to do," directed Kyle, as he closed his eyes and strained against the pain. He opened his eyes. "Take those who can move and head to the rear of that hill." The wolf's expression changed. 'No...', he shook his head. Kyle still clutched the sword, but he was able to punch the wolf in the shoulder, "Yes! Take everyone you can. I will stay here." The wolf looked into Kyle's eyes; he was alpha, he must be obeyed. The wolf nodded once. "Any Nocs who get past me, take down as they come over the rise. Look after whatever wounded you can," Kyle looked up again in the direction of the approaching pairs, then back at the wolf. "Do you understand?" he demanded. The wolf nodded. "Right, get on with it then!"

The wolf turned, remaining on all fours. Kyle laid on his stomach. He could not feel the cold from the ground, as he crawled over to a tree. He raised himself up, using the tree as support. The Nocs had stopped. He could hear voices in the darkness that seemed to echo in the woods. Kyle looked back and saw the wolves making their way toward the hill. The larger wolf looked back at him, they met eye to eye. The wolf nodded. The group of wolves limped and shuffled their way as fast as they could towards the hill. Kyle tried to raise himself up again. The voices in the darkness continued; a female voice kept shouting at them. Kyle managed to get up onto one knee again, leaning against the tree. He could still make out the three pairs. He could tell by the way they moved they were Nocs, and he felt cold hatred for them.

They made their way towards him, pointing the weapons. Kyle could tell they were not soldiers. The pain pulsed through his shoulder. He wished he could turn it off. When he looked up again, the pairs had spread out, but the distance between them was not far. It looked like the pair on the left were heading straight towards him. Kyle did not move. The gloved fingers of his right hand tightened on the handle of the sword. He brought it slowly across his body. The six Nocs approaching were not quiet, obviously assuming no one survived the attack. Kyle sat quietly against the tree, fighting to control his breathing, so it would not be seen in the cold night air.

They were getting closer. His eyes picked out details now. The two heading towards him were walking, one behind the other. The girl had short, brown hair; her jacket was open, and she had a light-coloured top on underneath. She held the shotgun in both hands and seemed nervous. The guy in front of her was much older. He looked to be in his fifties. His dark hair was thickly threaded with silver. He wore dark-rimmed glasses and was chewing on something. Kyle's eyes could now make out the shape of the older model M-16. Kyle felt his body tense up, getting ready for the strike, as the pair approached. They were inspecting the carnage around them.

"Look what they did to Terry!" she said, a look of shock on her face.

"Look what Terry did to them!" the guy replied. Branches and twigs snapped under their feet as they walked on.

"How did we not kill them all?" she asked.

"Because he took too long to spring the trap," said a voice further down. "He let them get too close." Kyle looked over to the next pair. Again, one was leading and the other was a few feet behind; both had old M-16's. The lead Noc, who had answered the girl's question, was young - he looked to be in his early twenties and had a French accent. The Noc behind him was much older and heavier. The far two were a male and a female.

"There they are!" shouted one of them. He had obviously spotted the wolves heading up to the summit of the hill. The far pair opened fire, and all six started to run towards them. The pair closest to Kyle became excited and changed their direction, running off to his right. Kyle launched himself at the older man. The sudden movement startled him. Kyle's blade sliced through the air just has Tyler taught him, cleanly opening the neck. The Noc dropped his rifle and both hands shot up to try and staunch the massive flow of blood. He hadn't been able to alert the others; their attention was elsewhere; but the girl saw him. She screamed, and tried to run, but Kyle's blade thrust through her chest. She stopped and looked down at it. She fell to her knees, then felt a foot in her back, pushing her down the blade and onto the ground. It would take her a very long minute to die.

Kyle charged on. He glanced to his right; most of the wolves were near the top of the hill. He watched as one of them turned and charged the attackers. For a moment, the wolf was running upright, then several bullets hit him. The body jolted with each strike and was propelled rearwards. He fell on his back, arms outstretched. Kyle let his rage out on the two Noctrailis who were now only a few feet away. The head of the younger one came off neatly and bounced on the ground. The larger one tried to bring his weapon up, but Kyle attacked with savagery. The Noc waved his arms in a futile attempt to fight him off. Kyle landed slice after slice; the Noc would not survive.

Kyle turned his attention to the final two, who had just spotted him. They weren't far away; the male was struggling with the magazine on his weapon. He had fired all his bullets and was now desperately trying to reload. The girl would be the main threat; she was already firing, as she spun around. Kyle jumped forward, slashing as he went. She missed with her rifle. Kyle did not miss with his sword. Her body landed beside a wolf, still-bleeding out, lying near the base of a tree.

The last Noc took a step back, just as the magazine snapped into place. Kyle tried to close the space between them as fast as he could. The Noc had the butt of the weapon tucked between his hip and his elbow, and swung it in an arc, firing in automatic, screaming. Three of the rounds slammed into Kyle, sending him rearwards. His body bounced off a tree and he landed face down on the ground. Kyle brought up his knees into a foetal position, his arms cradling the burning pain. A boot tucked under his body and rolled him over. Standing over him, was the hate-filled face of the Noc. The rifle was pointed at Kyle's head. Recognition dawned over the Noc as he realised who was lying on the ground in front of him.

"Well, look who I have here!" Kyle watched him; he could do nothing. His mind was full of pain from the gunshot wounds; he was fighting for breath. "Pity I haven't the time, I would want to kill you slowly!" Kyle looked into his eyes. The Noc brought the weapon up. Kyle looked past the fore sight, and through the aperture of the rear sight at the evil smile. Kyle stared back with all the defiance he could muster.

With a sudden flash of fur, the Noc disappeared. Kyle was looking up through the trees into the clear night sky. His body tightened; his mind was racked with pain. A few feet away, the Noc was on his back, arms and legs useless against the massive werewolf on top of him, savaging him. Kyle could hear the screams and pleas for mercy. The large wolf let his full fury out on the enemy that was now splattered over the cold ground. The night grew quiet. Kyle was in the most pain he had ever felt in his life. He closed his eyes, and again curled up his body.

"Where is Kyle? Kyle?" His eyes flew open and he watched Ruth come crashing through the trees. Her jacket was half open, her face was splattered with blood, her hands and arms were red. She held the rifle firmly in her right hand. She was panic-stricken, "Kyle, oh my God!" She landed by his side and turned him over onto his back. She examined his body, then looked into his face. "Are you okay?" Even though his brain was racked with pain, he managed a laugh.

"I'm pretty far from okay," he coughed jolting his body. Ruth looked over at a larger wolf.

"You, come here and help me with him." She was composing herself. The wolf appeared at Kyle's side, the face and hands covered in blood. "Right, lift him up. We've got to get him out of here!" Her left hand went under his right shoulder, but it was the strength of the wolf that lifted him up with one movement. Kyle yelped.

"What of the others? What of your wolves?" Kyle managed to get out between breaths. Ruth was standing beside him. She looked around, then back at him.

"We heard them open up on you, which gave us the time to realise it was a trap. They were not fully ready for us, so we got the better of them," her eyes welled up as she looked into his eyes. "We have lost some, others wounded."

"Where are they?" Ruth surveyed the scene again.

"They carried the wounded and the others and headed back to the house; I came to find you." Ruth was nearly in tears. She had not used the word 'dead', but Kyle understood. The wolf carrying Kyle growled and nodded towards the hill. Ruth looked up, "Are they up there?" she asked. The wolf growled and nodded once. Kyle looked to hilltop, where a single wolf was silhouetted, cradling his wounded body.

A female voice began to shout furiously from deep inside the forest; the Nocs had not finished yet. All three heads turned towards the sound of a group making their way through the trees. The enraged voice was screaming at them to get moving. Kyle could see shapes in the distance, slowly making their way forward; most carrying long weapons.

"We have to get going." Ruth said, as she turned and raised her rifle, the butt in her right shoulder. She looked over the top of the weapon, as she had been trained. "You, move!" she ordered the wolf, as she faced the approaching Noctrailis. The wolf turned and took a step towards the edge of the trees.

"Stop!" Kyle commanded. The wolf stopped and looked at him. Ruth was stepping backwards, her weapon pointing back into the woods. "Where is my sword?" he asked. Ruth and the wolf both looked around.

"There!" Ruth rushed over to where Kyle had dropped the sword when he had been shot. She knelt and picked it up. As she handed it to him, he looked into her eyes. Behind them, the female voice screamed again.

"COME ON, WHAT ARE YOU PLAYING AT!" There was anger and venom in the voice, Ruth's face looked back into the woods towards where the voice came from. The sound of the Nocs crashing through the trees echoed around them.

"Leave me here," Kyle said, just above a whisper. Ruth stepped away.

"What? Don't be stupid." She turned and started towards the summit of the hill.

"Do as I say!" Kyle spat. The wolf carrying him stopped.

Ruth turned back at the two of them, "But ...."

"No buts!" Kyle looked at the wolf, then at her, "If we all try as we are, they will catch us in the open." He looked at them, intently, "You are to gather those who are left at the far side of the hill. If they get past me, when they go over the rise, you will be waiting for them." Ruth looked down, then back at him again.

"When they get close ...." he said to the two of them, "then, tear them a new one!" Ruth stepped nearer to him.

"I, ..." She started. Kyle stared at her.

"Do as you are told .... NOW!" It was a command from her alpha; she had to obey. The wolf moved towards the nearest tree and lowered him to the ground. He winced in pain again. They helped him to a standing position, his back was up against the tree. His sword was in his right hand. Ruth stared at his face; he was in agony. She was going to say something, but the sound of the approaching voices stopped her. They were getting closer. "I need to be standing up. We need them to think I am not injured; it will slow them down. They'll think it's a trap," Kyle stated, looking down. Ruth glanced behind her. What he said made sense. The wolf made a noise and nudged his nose against Kyle's face; it was a sign of obedient affection.

"He's right," Ruth said, "you can't stand up with your wounds." Kyle's head came up. He smiled at the werewolf on one side, then he looked at Ruth on the other.

"Then tie me to the tree. They need to be able to see me, to give you time." The wolf looked at Ruth. Before she could ask the obvious question, Kyle used his left hand to lift his jacket. "Use my belt and tie me to the tree." Ruth nodded. She rested the barrel of the rifle over her right boot, keeping it away from the snow on the ground. The wolf lifted Kyle's body and she pulled the long canvas belt through the double ring buckle then through the loops of his jeans, the belt came free. The wolf held him up as Ruth wrapped the belt around the tree and her alpha. Kyle's body swayed, then he righted himself. He looked up; he could now make out the shapes that were in pairs in an extended line. They were slowly coming through the forest, weapons raised. They were being cautious. "They can't see us yet," Kyle whispered. The wolf looked at them, then grunted; Ruth let out a short laugh.

"They can't see as well as us in the dark!" she said. Kyle took a deep breath, then righted himself against the tree. He brought the Katana sword up and looked into the forest.

"You two, get going!" Ruth looked at him. She wanted to say something but could not; then she did as she was told, the wolf followed her. Once they had cleared the trees, they broke into a run towards the hill, past the bodies of wolves lying in the snow.

"There they are!" shouted a Noc voice. They started to run, still not seeing him.

"IS MIS AN RUA!" Kyle shouted as loud as he could. He held the sword up with his right hand, above his head. All the Noctrailis stopped. Several of them went down onto one knee, raising their weapons as they did so.

"WHAT ARE YOU DOING?" screamed the female voice again, "THEY ARE RUNNING!" Kyle kept the sword pointing towards the sky. He could hear voices but could not make out what they were saying; the female voice was furious. Kyle lowered the sword; he took a guess at who the voice belonged to.

"DANI!" he shouted as loud as he could, "SABINE IS DEAD!" He had guessed the voice right. There was a scream of fury, and the single figure charged towards him through the trees. Kyle watched as she jumped through the gaps between the trees. He remembered her from the carpark. They had never really found out who the Bulgarians were and why they had tried to take her, but that did not matter anymore. She was dressed in a long black coat, open at the front. It flowed out behind her, like wings.

Kyle lifted the sword again, just to ensure she had seen him. She changed direction and was now running directly towards him. His eyes caught the glint of the blade in her right hand. It was a large knife with a slight curve on it. Her long, black hair flowed behind her; her face was full of venom and hatred as she was coming straight at him. He lowered the sword. She was screaming as she approached. The others behind her had stopped, unsure of what to do.

Dani crashed through the woods; eyes fixed on him. She wanted to tear him apart, and she wanted everyone to see. He was just standing there, the sword by his side. As she came towards him, he was looking down. He had given up; he looked as if he was asleep. She raised the blade up above her shoulder, the tip pointing towards him, preparing to ram it into him repeatedly. She was now only a few feet away, her first strike imminent.

She spotted the belt that was holding him up; he was sacrificing himself to her! Suddenly, he looked up and his upper body straightened. His sword sprang forward in a sudden, swift movement that surprised her. Her body slammed to a stop. Confusion spun in her mind; she could not work out what had just happened. She stood, her body twitching, her strength draining, her limbs limp. She looked at the pale face in front of her. He glared back at her. The fingers of her right hand opened, and the blade landed with a thud on the snow. She tried to speak; her lips moved, her mind formed the words, but nothing came out of her mouth. She looked down at the back of his right hand. He still had a firm grip on the handle of the sword that had pierced her. She looked along the blade, watching the blood flow off the bright metal onto the ground. She looked again at the solemn face that was looking at her.

"Just so you know," Kyle Foster was saying. She stared ahead, suddenly feeling lightheaded, he continued, "this is how Sabine died." She coughed, then felt her eyes close, and her strength gave way. Ruth turned and looked back down the hill. She had heard him shout that he was An Rua. She saw the group of wounded wolves that had gathered on the far side of the hill. The larger wolf who was silhouetted against the skyline, lowered himself onto all fours. Ruth knelt down beside him. They watched as the Noctrailis charged Kyle. He let her get close before he struck, and what a strike it was! Ruth felt herself welling up as the princess flopped over onto the ground, the sword protruding out of her back. She coughed, landing on the snow in a rapidly expanding pool of blood.

"IS MIS AN RUA, IS MIS AN RUA!" Kyle shouted as loud as he could again. Ruth could hear the vampires shouting and running, but she could only see a few of them. She felt her body tighten. The hair along the back of the neck of the wolf lying beside her rose; he bared his teeth, ready to launch himself. Kyle's body rocked with the bullets slamming into him.

The gunfire echoed, then stopped as quickly as it had started. Ruth wanted to cry out in anguish at what she had just witnessed. She closed her eyes, trying to force the scene below from her mind. Watery eyes opened as the first of the pairs of Nocs came into view. They were forming a semi-circle around him. She lifted the weapon to her shoulder and looked through the scope. Her finger moved to the trigger, as her first target filled the scope. The Noc was male, quite young, with dark hair. He had a pump-action shotgun in his hands. It was raised and pointing at the lifeless body hanging forward, tied to the tree in front of him. She took a breath in; he would be the next to die.

Suddenly, the Noc's body jolted and spun in an unnatural way. She looked up; the wolf beside her was reacting as well. There was chaos below, as panic gripped the Nocs. Some fell over, some screamed; bodies jolted, then fell. It started from the right side of the group. Her eyes shot over to the movement in the forest. They were in a line, moving quickly through the trees. She could make out the first one, followed by others. The figure wore a helmet, and she recognised the lens of the night vison goggles attached to it. Their faces were covered by mesh. They were sapiens; she could tell by the way they moved. The camouflage clothing was not normal military; neither were the rifles. From a distance it looked like compressed M-16's with modern suppressors. The body armour and equipment were used by very specialized troops. They were dropping the Nocs with deadly precision.

The soldiers moved forward with speed, aggression and surprise; they had done this before. The wolf beside her jumped up and turned to his right. She looked around him at Paul Hawkins and two soldiers, who were running up the side of the fence towards them.

"Stop, stop, it's me!" Paul shouted as he waved both his hands. The wolf looked at the first soldier, showing his teeth and growling. The soldier pointed his rifle towards the sky and, with his left hand, lifted the night vision glasses.

"British army!" he announced.

"Relax, they are with us," Paul stated, as he arrived, breathlessly, at the summit. He looked at the gathered wolves. "Oh God, no!" his face contorted as he knelt beside a wolf lying in the snow.

"Chris, see if you can help any of them!" the first soldier pointed to the group. The second soldier pulled at the strap underneath his chin and lifted off the helmet. Chris Abbey looked at Ruth,

"Hi, I'm Chris. I am a medic - how can I help?" Ruth looked at the two soldiers. She remembered when the military had come to the farm. Ruth nodded as he pulled his left arm through the strap of the medical bag on his back. He got to work, quickly moving among the wounded, triaging the injuries.

"Where is Kyle?" Paul asked. Ruth stood up and pointed to the treeline.

"Down there." Paul jumped up and ran past her.

"You look after them!" he pointed at the group of wolves she was with. The other soldier stepped forward. The larger wolf stood up and looked at him as he took his helmet off. He recognised him but could not remember his name. The soldier pressed a button on his weapon, looking down the hill at the activity in the forest. A flare from the far side of the trees shot up into the sky.

"Roger, this is three three, secure the site, commence S-S-E." Ruth studied his face. He was older than the other one, and his accent was vaguely Scottish.

"Who are you?" she asked. He let the rifle hang by his side and took off his right glove. He extended his hand, which Ruth took. The soldier introduced himself,

"Steve...Steve Minister." Ruth shook his hand. She now knew who they were. "Sorry we were not here sooner. We only just found out what they were up to."

"So, you guys are the SAS, then." Behind him, a sapien was coming up the hill. He had the same helmet and body armour, but different overalls and a pistol in a holster on his right hip. Darren Forester would introduce himself when he got to the top of the hill.

Chapter 62

Tyler was walking towards the front door of the barn, away from the farmhouse. There was a group of farmhands standing beside the Land Rover Paul had parked when they'd returned in the early hours. The mood around the farm was solemn. The main door of the barn opened, and a stern-faced Dermott walked out. He was issuing jobs to the farmhands. She glanced at her watch; it was nearly midday. The farmhands all moved off and Dermott turned towards her.

"They are all inside," he nodded back towards the open door. Tyler came to a stop beside him. For some reason, she could not look him directly in the face. She knew who he was talking about. She did not want to go and look at the bodies, but something compelled her. Movement behind her made her turn around. Rhydian had run from the farmhouse to catch up with her. Tyler smiled a sad smile, which was returned by Rhydian. Tyler's face still stung from the bruising.

"Oh, one question," Dermott asked.

"What?"

"When the army stopped you, why did just Paul go with them?" Tyler looked at him, he had a quizzical look on his face.

"I was exhausted, and we had no idea what was about to happen, Paul directed us to carry on back here, while he went in their van!" Tyler smiled, but she felt regret. If she had gone back, would Kyle still be alive? She did not know. "Are the army lot still here?" she asked quietly.

"No," Dermott replied, "they left just over half an hour ago." Tyler glanced at him, Dermott carried on, "It's probably for the best they don't meet Connor and the lot from the south. When are they due to get here?" he asked. Tyler looked at her watch again.

"In about half an hour... Where is Paul?" Dermott nodded again with his head, towards the open door of the barn. Tyler nodded once, then headed towards the opening; Rhydian followed close behind her. "Dermott, best call the pack together for the arrival!" Tyler said, looking back over her shoulder at him. He nodded and fumbled in his pocket for the handheld radio.

Tyler walked through the doorway of the barn. Paul was standing in the arena and was looking at something she couldn't see. They walked forward into the open area. Paul lifted his head and acknowledged them. Tyler looked slowly to the left. She came to a stop beside Paul. She was trying not to stare, but it was all she could do.

"Oh, my ...." Rhydian exclaimed, as she raised a hand to her mouth. Each of the bodies had been wrapped in a white sheet and lay beside each other.

"What is the final ...." Tyler stopped herself. What should she say? Final count? Final score? How do you quantify the dead?

"Eleven." Tyler looked up at him. "Well, twelve, if you include ...." Paul raised his right hand and pointed to the one figure that was a few feet apart from the others. Tyler felt her insides turn with painful emotion. She knew it was Kyle.

"How many hurt?" Tyler looked with concern at Rhydian as she asked the question.

"Twenty-eight," he replied. Rhydian's hands were shaking, and she was welling up. "John certainly had his work cut out for him. Thankfully, the army brought medics with them. Chris, the main guy, did say they had never had to wait for a casualty to change back to human before." Tyler looked at him. Twelve dead and twenty-eight injured; she felt herself welling up again.

"Is Tony here?" she asked quietly.

"No, he left just after the army," Paul answered. "The two girls have gone back with him." Tyler looked away. "He said he'd heard from some of his friends in the police that there were reports of distant gunfire." Tyler's eyes looked over the line of bodies. They were all wrapped the same, but she could tell each was different. "Tony received phone calls asking what he knew about it."

"What did he say?" Rhydian asked. Tyler and Paul looked at her. Rhydian looked back at them; her question made sense. Paul paused before he replied,

"Not much. They wouldn't have believed him if he had said there'd been a battle between 'werewolves and vampires' out back!" Rhydian shrugged and looked away. Dermott appeared in the doorway, and all three of them looked towards him.

"They are here!" He did not shout, but his voice echoed in the barn.

"Who?" asked Paul, Dermott looked behind him.

"The South." Dermott turned and walked back outside. The three of them walked back to the entrance, stopping just inside. Outside, the sky had cleared; the bright sunlight reflected off the white snow-covered hills. The four Land Rovers were in a line, driving up the lane. The first and last ones were older versions, used for working on the farm; but the two in the middle were newer and designed for road driving. They were more modern and a lot more comfortable. Connor had arrived.

"Dermott," Paul spoke loud enough. Dermott was standing by the barn. He turned his head and looked directly at Paul.

"Yes?" he asked.

"Call the pack together!" Paul directed. Dermott nodded, then turned away. Paul looked at Tyler. "Whatever he is going to say... everyone should hear it." Paul explained.

"'Already doing that," Dermott shouted back. The small convoy came to the top of the lane, Tyler looked over to the corner of the barn, where the pack was emerging. They were sullen; the loss of so many would take time to recover from. The convoy turned and the lead vehicle stopped in front of the farmhouse; the others pulled in behind it.

"I wonder what he's going to do about all this." Paul mused. The doors of the lead and rear Land Rovers opened; the security team all stepped out. The pack came closer.

"Well, he has not exactly been helpful so far, now, has he?" Dermott stated, as the rear door of his Land Rover was opened, and Connor stepped out. He had a serious look on his face. Other doors opened and senior pack members emerged. They walked over beside Connor, who was pulling on an outdoor jacket.

Tyler, Paul and Dermott walked forward, stopping a few feet in front of him. The pack came closer but was stopped by one of the security detail who'd raised his hand. The farm was silent, apart from the blowing wind.

Orla stood beside Connor and looked at Tyler, Sam O'Neil nodded towards Paul. Connor broke the silence.

"Where are they?" he asked, solemnly.

"In the barn," Paul replied. He stepped back and turned. Dermott and Tyler stepped to the side. Orla lowered her eyes as Connor walked after Paul. The security team formed a circle around them; Jack and Saoirse, Connor's children, followed. Jack reached out and placed his hand on Tyler's shoulder. She looked at them both. They had concerned looks on their faces. Tyler acknowledged them with a nod as the pack closed in, following the group into the barn.

The large metal door creaked as it was pushed open, and the crowd solemnly entered. Connor stopped in front of the dead; he looked sad. Orla was to his left, and Paul had stopped to his right. Tyler and Dermott made their way past the security team that had formed a semi-circle around their alpha. They looked at the gathered pack that shuffled in around them. The barn door closed noisily. All eyes looked at the young woman who bolted the door shut. She stared back at them. She had dark hair and was dressed for working on the farm. She walked a few paces, glaring at Connor. Connor looked at her, she stopped at the edge of the pack.

"Lower your gaze!" demanded Sam; the woman looked at him.

"Make me," she whispered. He moved towards her.

"STOP!" Connor shouted. Everyone stood still. Connor looked at the woman. "What is your name?" he asked quietly. Her glare was defiant. She breathed in deeply, before replying,

"Lynne M'Kane." Connor thought for a second and recognised the name.

"Paddy M'Kane's ....?"

"Sister," she did not move; she did not flinch. Everyone knew what her brother had done; but that was him, not her. Connor glanced at Paul, then looked back at the bodies.

"So," he started, "what exactly happened?" Paul took a single step towards him. He looked down at the wrapped-up bodies, then began to speak,

"Well, after White Park Bay, which you already know about, they probed our perimeter. They thought they had taken Tony Fallon down." Connor looked up, then away again, as Paul continued, "They were doing drive-bys past his house. They didn't know he was alive."

"How do you know that?" Sam asked.

"The Noc called Sabine told us," Paul replied.

"Just before Tyler took her down!" came a shout. A ripple of excited approval spread through the pack. Connor and Sam exchanged a glance. Connor looked at Tyler. She glared back at him with obvious hostility. He nodded once, to acknowledge her achievement, then turned to Paul,

"And what was someone so prominent doing here in the first place?"

"We are not sure," Paul replied.

"But she was involved in whatever they were doing," Tyler interjected. Connor turned away again and stepped towards Sam, who then stepped forward, as did Orla. The three looked at each other. Tyler glanced at Paul; something was going on.

"How many Nocs do you think were involved?" Connor spoke quietly.

"We took down over eighty!" Dermott raised his voice, so all could hear him.

"Impossible!" Sam spat. "There has not been a coven like that here in over a century! We would have known …"

"That is the number we have taken down, and it includes a Noc princess!" Dermott was not hiding his anger.

"No way!" Sam glared back at Dermott.

"He is telling you the facts," Paul concurred, Connor turned.

"How?" he asked.

"How what?" asked Dermott, belligerently.

"How did you take down a princess?" It was Connor's turn to look annoyed.

"Answer the question!" demanded Sam. Dermott looked at Paul and Tyler. Tyler turned so she was facing the three of them.

"After I took Sabine down,"

"Yes, Paul sent us the footage," Sam interrupted. Tyler paused and composed herself.

"After I took down Sabine," she repeated, "four Nocs were seen. Kyle deployed the pack in two teams, with overwatch." The front of the pack parted, and Ruth stepped forward,

"Yes, I was leading one and Kyle led the other." Everyone turned to look at her. She described the events, "He was following the tracks of the four, and we headed off to the right to cut off any who were in the woods." She paused, glanced at Tyler, then back at Connor. "We heard the first burst of gunfire, the Nocs in the trees in front of us were not expecting us from that direction. By the time I got to Kyle, he had already been hit a few times." There was movement from the pack behind her. Some shuffled, others nodded. Connor looked at her, then at Sam.

"We have been asleep," he stated, and looked back at Ruth, "Continue."

"There were Garou and Nocs all around. Kyle had taken down nearly all of them by himself. We realised that the ones remaining were about to charge, so even though he had been shot several times. he remained behind on his own." She looked around at the others, welling up with the memory. "He held them back. It gave us time to get over the hill." She turned towards Tyler. Ruth was almost in tears now, and Tyler looked at her with compassion. She was welling up, as well. "That was his plan - for us to be out of sight behind the hill. When they came up, we would be ready for them. He gave us a chance!" Connor stepped forward.

"What of the Noc Princess? How did she die?" Connor asked, raising himself up to his full height. Ruth looked up, then lowered her eyes and continued,

"Kyle raised his sword and shouted, 'IS MIS AN RUA! IS MIS AN RUA!' The Noc ran at him with a large, curved knife. When she got close, he got her right through the heart with his katana! We could see the blood flowing out of her as she hit the ground." There was a wave of emotion from the pack, Sam looked furious, Connor looked concerned and Orla looked worried. Tyler stepped forward and placed her arms around Ruth's shoulders, pulling her into an embrace. Ruth clutched Tyler and broke down in tears. She sobbed briefly, then let go. Ruth wiped her eyes and composed herself. Tyler and Ruth smiled at each other. A tall farmhand stepped forward; his eyes were red - he was fighting back tears.

"Kyle stood as they surrounded him like a firing squad riddling him at point blank range!"

"What the hell did he think he was doing?" demanded Sam, he tensed up, tightening his fingers into fists. Tyler's mood changed instantly.

"HE WAS DEFENDING THESE LANDS, JUST AS HE WAS SUPPOSED TO DO!" she shouted in reply. Sam was about to say something when Connor raised his right hand and stopped him. Sam restrained himself. He looked at Connor, then glared at Tyler. He didn't like being spoken to that way. Connor moved ahead and stood over Kyle's body,

"*And a warrior will rise from the green land, and the blood of his enemies will flow from his sword!*"

"*And from him all Garou will find new strength!*" Paul finished the quote. Connor looked at Paul and slowly nodded.

"This is bollocks!" Sam spat. "When the Noc came to the farm, all she said was they were taking down Kyle. The rest was all his fault, a complete overreaction on his part. This is all his fault!"

"Wait... WHAT?" Tyler shouted. She looked in disbelief at Sam, then turned towards Connor. He turned to face her. The atmosphere in the barn had changed. "She was at the farm?" Connor opened his mouth to speak, and Tyler stepped menacingly towards him. Paul and the pack all looked at Connor. Tyler shouted at him, "YOU LET A NOC LOOSE ON OUR LANDS?"

"Lower your voice!" Sam demanded, "remember who you are talking to!" Tyler briefly glanced at Sam,

"Shut your face, or I'll shut it for you!" Sam jumped towards her. He would not be spoken to like that. Tyler side-stepped using her left hand to block his fist as her right first connected under his chin. He was sent backwards, landing on the ground with a thud. The pack closed in; the security team drew their pistols.

"STOP!" commanded Connor. His voice echoed around the arena. Everyone stood still. Sam struggled upright and went for Tyler. Connor held out the palm of his right hand in a 'stop' motion. Sam stopped, obeying the command. "Lower your weapons." The security team slowly replaced their pistols. This had almost become a standoff between them and the pack in front of them. "We are all An Rua, and there will be no conflict between us." Connor spoke loud enough for everyone to hear. He looked around at the angry eyes that glared back at him.

"She cannot speak to you like that!" Sam was angry, Connor took a step forward and looked directly at him.

"You," Sam straightened up obediently, "...are not to say another word!" Connor's command restrained him. Sam stared at the ground in front of Connor, who stepped forward and looked at Tyler, Paul and Dermott. "Yes, I allowed a Noctrailis princess onto the farm, and yes, we agreed to terms." Tyler was dumbstruck.

"Do you realise what you have done?" Connor looked over at Orla.

"She said she was only after Kyle," he justified, Sam was close to bursting with anger.

"She was a Noc... Nocs tell lies!" Tyler responded.

Connor lowered his face but looked up at Tyler. "I made a decision."

"YOU BROKE THE LAW!" Tyler raised her voice. Connor glared at her; he was not used to be being spoken to like this.

"I did what was best for ...."

"It was against the law! To enter into terms with the Noctrailis against a Garou ...IT IS AGAINST OUR LAWS! .... To allow a Noctrailis onto our ground .... IS AGAINST OUR LAWS!" Connor straightened himself up again.

"She is right!" It was Orla who spoke. Connor spun around and stared at her. "It is against our laws," Orla confirmed. Connor looked back at Tyler.

"Remember your place, or I'll ...."

"Or you'll what?" Tyler lifted her arms, then flopped them down, as she stepped away, "You'll leave us to our enemies? Well, guess what? YOU ALREADY DID!" Connor stepped towards her. There was anger on his face, and his eyes narrowed, as Tyler continued, "You let a dozen of us die!"

"Are you challenging me?" he said, threateningly. His wolf wanted to come forth. Tyler turned and placed her hands on her hips,

"Don't be so stupid!" The pack reacted with astonishment; no one had ever spoken to a pack alpha like that before.

"So, what are you saying?" Connor demanded. Tyler glanced around; the pack was with her. Paul nodded once; whatever she was about to do, he was behind her.

"I demand ...." she paused, then made a decision, "I demand a RULING!" Connor stared at her. Tyler took a single step closer to him. "I demand a ruling from the Council, and, until such time, the North with be separate from the South."

"I won't let you split this pack!" Connor tightened his fists to reinforce his point.

"The North will always remain An Rua. We will recognise you as alpha, and we will follow our laws until the ruling." Connor stared at the wolf in front of him. She was binding his hands. Orla walked forward and stood beside Connor,

"The Southern pack acknowledges this ruling request. We will ensure that at least two council members will be present, but this will take place on the farm, in the south." Orla was looking at Tyler, but she saw Connor staring at her. He looked back at Tyler, who nodded to acknowledge what she had said, then at Paul.

Without speaking, he turned and stormed away from them. The security detail ran after him, as did Sam. The mood in the barn lifted. Orla looked back over her shoulder and watched the main door open to allow them outside. Some of the pack followed them, others closed in near Tyler. Orla stepped closer to Tyler. She held out her hand, and Tyler took it in her own. Orla lowered her voice. "We are sorry for everything. He is furious that he did not see this coming. Believe me, he is angrier at himself than he is with you!" she explained with a forced smile. Tyler returned the smile and released her hand. Orla turned and the pack members behind her parted to allow her to walk towards the open door. Paul put his hand on Tyler's shoulder,

"Well done, you!" Tyler smiled, then looked over at Kyle's shroud. She looked back at Paul and placed her hand on her abdomen.

"It is what he would have done." The pack gathered around and shook her hand or patted her on the shoulder. They were excited again.

"Right, we still have work to do," Dermott shouted. They followed him towards the door, leaving Paul and Rhydian standing on either side of Tyler. Rhydian looked at her.

"You didn't tell him, did you?" she asked. Tyler smiled at her, then pulled her into a comforting hug.

"No, no I didn't."

"Tell who? What?" Paul asked. The two women looked at him. Rhydian smiled, and Tyler blushed,

"Mum is going to have a baby!" Rhydian exclaimed. Paul was shocked.

"Really?" It caught him off guard. He had not been expecting this. "Who is the father?" he asked. Rhydian and Tyler shared a look of sadness, then Tyler looked over to where Kyle was lying, wrapped in a single white sheet.

Chapter 63

'How would we, as a modern society, react if it were proven that a human body could change or shift in shape? Throughout history, in all cultures around the world, there are legends and myths about people having the ability to partially or completely change their shapes'

. Cara-Marie studied the screen of her laptop, then clicked on the 'post' icon and added it to her blog. She looked around the office. Everything had returned to relative normalcy. She looked up at the clock on the wall. It was nearly 11am. Her eyes darted over to where Mark Scott was sitting, staring at her.

"What?" she asked. Mark shook his head and looked at the screen of his desktop computer.

"I didn't think you heard me," he muttered. She looked around again, Kevin was in his office, and the reception staff were busy, everyone seemed to have stuff to do.

"What?" she asked again, Mark looked up.

"Did you hear what I just said?"

"No," she shook her head, "Sorry," Mark started to tap at the keyboard, trying to refocus. She waited for a few seconds before she spoke again, "well, what was it?" Mark glanced up, then looked back at the screen.

"It doesn't matter," he muttered again.

"Fine," she whispered as she closed her laptop. She moved the mouse to her desktop, and the screen came into life. She started reading over the article she was about to place in the group mailbox. Mark sat back in his chair,

"So, on a different topic... what did Kevin say about your story on the gunfire reports from the far side of Portrush the other night?" Cara-Marie did not look up.

"We're not going to run it."

"Why?"

"Why?" she repeated, this time she did look over at him.

"Yeah, why?" Mark repeated, she looked away.

"It was just a couple of reports from some residents saying they heard what sounded like gunfire, but the police said all they found were a couple of old, damaged M-16 rifles. They thought it was probably some people out test-firing them...found out they were crap and discarded them."

"Case closed?"

"Case closed," she repeated. "The weapons had no serial numbers, no fingerprints, so nothing to investigate."

"But you think it was something else?" Mark was staring at her. Cara-Marie stopped what she was doing and looked over at him.

"Look," she started, "when I got out there the following morning, I saw that there had been a lot of activity on the ground. It was more than just a 'couple of people', and there was definitely blood on some of the trees."

"But you could not get close enough to confirm that, could you?" he asked. Cara-Marie was getting annoyed.

"No, but something was going on, that guy, Forester, was there."

"The Special Branch guy you saw at the courthouse in Lisburn?"

"Yeah, and he only shows up when there is something going on," she said.

"What do you think it was?" She stopped what she was doing and eyed him thoughtfully,

"I think there was some sort of gunfight."

"Between .... whom?" He had a quizzical look on his face. Her eyes darted around the room again, no one was close, so she lowered her voice,

"Between a group of vampires and the wolves they are trying to wipe out!" she paused. His face did not move; his look did not change. His eyes moved first, looking down, then at the screen, before going back to her.

"And you can prove that... how?" She felt her heart sink, she couldn't, and he knew it. She shrugged. "So, you are suggesting that there is some sort of war going on here between werewolves and vampires and the government knows all about it and is covering it up? .... No one will believe anything like that without concrete evidence!" Mark paused, "I mean, look at the Bigfoot stories. There are so many eyewitness accounts but, until one is caught and studied, the general public will still refuse to believe it!"

"Like the panda," Cara-Marie was staring into space as she spoke.

"Panda?" he asked, they had discussed this before.

"Yes, pandas. In the 18th century, explorers and scientists brought back stories of black and white bears, and horses that had stripes. We now know them as pandas and zebras, but at the time, it was considered so outlandish that the European scientific community laughed at them, until ..."

"Until they brought them back, yeah, I remember." She had made her point. Cara-Marie relaxed; she knew he was right, but how could she prove it? Mark carried on,

"So, until someone actually produces one of these ...." Mark waved his hands to emphasise his point, "*werewolves*... no one is ever going to believe you," she nodded, "so, what is your next plan?" he asked.

"I don't know," it was almost a whisper. Mark looked at her, he remained quiet and considered what he would say next.

"That fella, Foster... his funeral is this afternoon, isn't it?" Mark became engrossed in what was in front of him. He changed the topic of conversation deliberately.

"Yes, at 1pm."

"You going?"

"Yes," she looked at the clock again, "but I'll have to go home and change first."

"Wasn't it a car crash, or something, that killed him?" Mark did not look up as he asked the question.

"The Land Rover he was driving overturned at the deer farm and caught fire,"

"Mmmm... That doesn't sound like the kind of thing M-16-wielding vampires would get up to." Cara-Marie glared at him, she thought for a second before answering,

"Well, he doesn't seem like the kind of person to lose control of a Land Rover."

"You mean, like Lawrence of Arabia?"

"What?"

"You know, T.E. Lawrence. He got the Arabs to rise up during the First World War to fight for the British against the Turks."

"I know who Lawrence of Arabia was!" she retorted.

"He led an amazing life, only to die in a motorcycle crash when he got back to England!"

"So?" she asked.

"So, he could not have been at your shoot-out, then."

"He could have been, the crash happened the following day. The police said no one could get near it initially as there had been a stalking rifle and bullets in the vehicle at the time, and they were exploding. So, it was not safe to approach, and they had to wait for the fire to burn out. After that, there was not much left. They ID'd him officially from dental records."

"The post-mortem was quick, then," Mark stated. She shrugged and opened her laptop again. "There couldn't have been much of one." Mark looked over at her. She looked up, shrugged and started to type into her laptop. Then Cara-Marie stopped typing and looked over at him.

"Mark?"

"Yes?"

"When is it you are going to become a dad, again?" Mark's head shot up. She carried on with her change of conversation, "And how is your ex, these days? I have not heard you mention her in a while."

∞∞∞∞

The view from the graveyard was spectacular. It was on a slope that fell down to Portrush, then to the sea. The Ballywillan road went past the entrance and down the far side of the stone wall, in a straight line towards the town. The sea stretched to the horizon. There was a blanket of snow over the fields and the tops of the houses, but the roads were clear. It was cold, but the wind had died down. Cara-Marie was dressed head to foot in black. Black leather knee-high boots, black trousers, a black woollen jumper and a thick black coat. The only splash of colour was the red scarf that was tucked down into the jacket. There had not been a church service, but there had been a service at the farm. The details of that had not been made known.

The coffin was met at the gates by a line of old soldiers, most in their sixties. Their green berets perched proudly on their heads, the cap badge of the second Foreign Parachute Regiment of the French Foreign Legion was over their right eyes, which shone with pride. Each one wore a dark blazer, white shirt and a dark green tie. She did not recognise any of the medals they wore. One of them gave a command in French and they all saluted as Kyle was carried past. His grandmother from Kilrea was there. Cara-Marie noticed she did not speak to anyone from the farm. Tony acknowledged her, but they had not engaged in conversation. He and Karen left as soon as the service was over.

Cara-Marie was not introduced to the two young women with Karen. There were not many people in attendance, less than twenty, which was far less than she'd expected. There was only one police officer from Coleraine there, and he did not want to chat with her. As the coffin was being lowered, the former Legionnaires started to sing a melancholy song. It was French, and in a deep, sombre tone. At the end, one of them spoke for all to hear. She had to ask someone for a translation.

"Long live the Legion. The Legion lives, so the Legionnaire lives!" She asked if they knew Kyle personally: one did, most had met him at a reunion in London the previous year. "But we are all Legionnaires, so we are all family," he said. None of them had any comment for a journalist.

Cara-Marie was standing a short distance away from the open grave and watched the last of the mourners leave. Her eyes looked over the empty graveyard. She was trying hard not to cry in public, but she was welling up and it was becoming more difficult to fight back the tears. She looked out over the view in front of her. The movement of the last two former Legionnaires walking out the gate made her look over to her right. That was when she first saw her. She looked at the lone woman standing by the gate. She had not been at the funeral; Cara-Marie could not remember if she'd ever seen her before. She was wearing leather boots similar to the ones she, herself, had on; black trousers and a dark purple jacket that looked like it was made of felt. Her dark auburn hair hung down either side of her face. But it wasn't until she lifted the phone to her ear that Cara-Marie noticed the silk gloves she wore. She ended the call and replaced it back in the pocket of her trousers. Solemnly, she looked at Cara-Marie, who looked away. She turned her head back to the grave. The woman walked along the path and came to a stop beside her. Cara-Marie looked into her face. She was older and a little taller than her. Her eyes were red, as well.

"Hi." It was little more than a whisper. The woman looked at her, with a half-smile.

"Hello," Cara-Marie said, the woman reached out her hand in a formal greeting, "Tyler."

"Cara-Marie," Cara-Marie said, shaking the firm grip of the woman. She released her hand, then looked away.

"How did you know ...." Tyler paused before she said Kyle's name. Cara-Marie looked at her and felt herself welling up again.

"I first met him through a mutual friend," Cara-Marie answered.

"Who was that?... If you don't mind me asking," Cara-Marie looked at her. Something made her feel safe with this woman called Tyler.

"An old school friend of mine, named Tony. How did you know him?"

"Ah, yes, I know Tony Fallon well. I ...." Tyler paused, something stirred Cara-Marie's interest in her. "...knew Kyle's father quite well," Tyler looked at Cara-Marie, then looked away. "I've been associated with the family business for a number of years," Tyler explained. "Would you be the journalist from the Herald, by any chance?"

Cara-Marie looked inquisitively at her. "Yes... yes, I am," Tyler nodded. "I'm sorry, I don't know anything about you," Cara-Marie prodded, Tyler looked at the open grave.

"I moved back here only recently, I lived away for quite a while." Tyler was staring at the grave. Cara-Marie felt herself well up again. Her body shook; this time she could not contain it.

"I loved him," Cara-Marie said. Then the emotion burst from her, her hands came up to her face and the cry came from her mouth; tears rolled down her cheeks, as she sobbed. The woman she had never met before placed a hand onto her right shoulder and stepped closer to her. As quickly as it started, Cara-Marie brought it under control. She composed herself. Tyler spoke,

"I loved him too," the women exchanged a glance. Tyler smiled, "but I never told him." There was a gentle laugh from Tyler and a smile from Cara-Marie. They both looked back at the grave. "Anyway," Tyler lifted her hand and stepped away, "It's time I was somewhere else." Cara-Marie looked back at her again, eyes red from the tears.

"It was nice to meet you," she said, Tyler looked at her and smiled a polite smile.

"Yes, and you." Cara-Marie watched as Tyler turned and walked away, back up the path heading towards the entrance to the graveyard. Cara-Marie looked back in front of her. She moved, stepping forward and walking the short distance to the edge of the grave. She looked down at the top of the coffin. Several flowers lay over it where others had dropped them. Her eyes welled up again. She looked over at the headstone beside it. He was beside his mother and father, with his elder brother on the far side of his parents. "Look after him," she whispered towards them.

She stood there in silence for a short while, then slowly turned and started to walk up the path. She walked along the graves, then turned left at the top the path. She headed towards the metal gate that spanned the gap in the old stone wall that surrounded the graveyard. She slowly walked on, pushing her hands into her pockets. She could not feel the cold anymore. She looked at the trodden snow in front of her, putting one foot in front of the other.

"Excuse me, Cara-Marie, isn't it?" The voice made her look up. The accent was English. Standing just inside the gates, were a man and a woman. They looked like they were in their late twenties. Both were smartly dressed, but not for a funeral. She did not know either of them. For a moment, confusion ruled her mind.

"Yes?" The man had short curly hair. When she looked at him, he stared straight back, and held out his right hand, which she took.

"Hi, I am Sam." He released the grip and turned towards the tall woman whose long, blonde hair flowed over her shoulders and down her back. She extended her hand as she was introduced, "and this is Lucy."

"Hello." She was also English.

"Hi," Cara-Marie shook her hand. They were friendly, but she knew they were here for a reason. Sam turned back towards her.

"Let me introduce ourselves. We are from the SIS, and we would like to chat to you about your research," he said.

"SAS?" Cara-Marie asked, Sam and Lucy exchanged a glance, and a grin.

"No, not SAS, S-I-S," Sam spelled it out, "We are Secret Intelligence Service." Cara-Marie's eyes widened, and Sam carried on, "You probably know us better by our World War Two title," Sam paused, as if for effect, "MI-6."

"And what, may I ask, does MI-6 want with me?" Cara-Marie asked. Sam stepped forward and extended his hand towards the pathway. Cara-Marie stepped to the side, as he started to walk forward.

"We are very interested in your research, especially to do with ..." Sam stepped past her and looked over with an invitation to join him for a stroll, "things that most people do not believe exist." Cara-Marie turned and started to walk beside him; Lucy walked behind them.

"If you want a printout of my blog ...." Cara-Marie started.

"We already have that" Lucy said, and Cara-Marie glanced over her shoulder at her. Lucy finished with, "In fact, we already have everything from your computer!" Cara-Marie looked at Sam.

"And how, may I ask, did you get that?"

"Simple," Sam smiled. We put a pen stick with a back door on it, in your pocket." Sam looked at her, then looked away as he continued to explain, "so when you plugged it into your desktop, we got open access to your entire hard-drive." Cara-Marie was shocked.

"We had to be sure, so we had a look at the desktop in your office, as well," Lucy stated. Cara-Marie stopped walking and glared at Sam.

"It was you who trashed the office?" Sam smiled.

"Oh no, that wasn't us .... Forced entry and destruction of property is illegal." Cara-Marie did not believe him.

"So, if you have everything .... what do you want from me?" Anger was rising in her. Sam stopped and turned towards her.

"Your skills," he said with a polite smile.

"What?"

"We don't want anything from you," Lucy explained, Cara-Marie looked at her.

"Then why are we chatting now?"

"We are here to help." Sam said, and Cara-Marie looked at him.

"Help? With what? How?" Sam and Lucy exchanged a glance, and Sam spoke,

"Help with what you are doing .... sort of ... steer you in the right direction." Cara-Marie still did not believe him.

"And how do you intend to do that?" she asked.

Chapter 64

The Old Hotel, Ryazan, Russia.

Grishin held the phone to his ear as he walked out the front door of the hotel. The cold wind hit him, but he hardly noticed it. He walked forward under the entrance portico. The road to the front of the hotel was always busy. There was a row of parked cars along the side of the road, all facing the front of the hotel. To his left was the hotel restaurant, where they had eaten last night, after checking in. The walls were painted white, with wooden struts decorating the sides and the roof.

The uniform he wore was an older-issue dress uniform, no longer in use. The only ones who wore it were veterans. Rows of medals clinked together, as his boots crunched the snow on the steps at the front of the hotel. The sun broke from behind a cloud and reflected off the gold adornments on his shoulders. He held the sky-blue beret in his left hand, as he replaced the phone in his pocket. To his left, in front of the framed windows of the restaurant, were several small tables with chairs around them. Tatamovich sat at one of them. He was wearing the same uniform, the almost empty bottle of vodka in front of him. Grishin smiled and walked over to him.

"What took you so long to use the washroom?" Tatamovich demanded. Grishin looked at the faded beret beside the vodka bottle. The two of them had sat there most of the morning. He was looking forward to the Veterans' Parade at the Academy, later that afternoon, but Tatamovich was not. The Higher Airborne Military Academy was the home of his country's airborne forces and the special purpose troops, the Spetsnaz. All Russian special purpose troops started their careers here.

"I had to take a call," Grishin said, casually.

"Yeah, from that girl at reception, no doubt?" Tatamovich stated.

"No," he breathed heavily, "we may have a problem to deal with," Grishin explained, sitting down. Tatamovich looked over at the parked red double-decker bus that the hotel owner had bought in London. It was certainly one way to ensure everyone would follow directions to the hotel... 'find the red London bus - it's right beside that.'

"I have had enough of that idiot and that pipeline! Who put him in charge, anyway!" Tatamovich was angry, "It is moving from one problem to another. All things he should be able to deal with, without constantly whining to us!" Tatamovich was annoyed, "He needs to go!"

"No, it's not the pipeline," Grishin stated.

"Oh?" Tatamovich asked. Grishin looked over to his left, past the parked bus, at the four young men running across the road. They had long, dark coats on and were wearing the Ushanka hats issued to the Russian army. Grishin recognised the emblem on the front. They were officer cadets from the Academy. They were all laughing at something one of them had just said. Tatamovich looked at them, then at Grishin. The tall cadet at the front suddenly stopped and gaped in surprise. The other three behind him stopped, as well. There was an exclamation of surprise from the one at the back. The lead cadet looked at the two men sitting at the table. They both wore the rank of full Colonel.

The two veteran officers looked at them. The cadet turned and snapped an order. They quickly formed a line and started to march as if on a parade ground. They extended each foot and slammed it hard on the ground; arms swinging in wide arcs at their sides. As they approached the veterans, the tall cadet spotted the emblem on their arms; they were from the 14th Spetsnaz – GRU Brigade, some of the country's most elite soldiers.

The four marched as one along the pavement. As they came alongside the front of the hotel, the tall cadet shouted an order and all four heads snapped over, and four right hands saluted sharply.

Grishin stood up and, placing the sky-blue beret on his head, returned the salute. The four cadets then marched on. A couple coming out of the hotel stopped and waited for them to pass. Grishin lowered his hand and sat back down again as the young men marched around the corner, he dropped the beret back on the table.

"It takes a hard head to wear the blue beret," he smiled.

"That it does," Tatamovich agreed. Both men chuckled. Cadets were taught from the start of their Airborne training, that the venerable sky-blue beret was tough to earn. "So, what is the problem?" he asked. Grishin reached forward and lifted the bottle of vodka. He refilled the two small glasses on the table.

"We may have to go back to Ireland," he stated.

"Ireland?" Tatamovich straightened up in his chair, "I thought the An Rua had dealt with the Mongols?" Grishin smiled at his friend.

"They did, but now it appears they have a problem with the Noctrailis," he stated, looking around the front of the hotel. They were the only ones sitting outside. It was warmer inside, but here they could talk freely. "Are you ready to serve?" Grishin was smiling. He already knew the answer. Tatamovich did not have a choice; they would be going back to Ireland. He reached forward and raised the glass of vodka with his right hand, in a toast.

"I SERVE THE SOVIET UNION!" Tatamovich said, looking at Grishin. Surprise appeared over Grishin's face. Then he relaxed and smiled,

"I have not heard that in a very long time," Tatamovich leaned over and nudged Grishin with his right shoulder. He nodded with his head towards Grishin's glass, Grishin let out a short laugh, then raised his glass.

"Nostrovia!"

"Nostrovia!" Tatamovich replied. Both emptied the contents of his glass in one mouthful.

"We had better make our way to the Academy," stated Grishin, as he stood up.

Tatamovich grunted and reached for his beret. "If we must..."

ထ၀၀ထ

Alison Wallace was sitting in a dip on the slope of the sand dune that gave her some cover from the wind. She looked out to sea from Portstewart Strand. She hunched forward; her chin was nearly on her knees. She looked at her trainers. Most of the snow was gone from the beach, but the harsh wind blew in from the sea. She looked up and out to sea and let her mind wander...

The spot where they had found the group on New Year's Day was only a short distance along the edge of the dunes from where she was now. She looked over to her left, eyes following the coast to where the headland jutted out. She recognized the silhouette of the Mussenden Temple against the setting sun. Her eyes moved further along the horizon. The beach was empty, and the sea was rough. Alison remained deep in her thoughts. Suddenly, she sensed movement over to her right. Someone was walking over the dunes. She listened, closing her eyes to concentrate on the sound. There was just one person. She thought there might be a dog, but no, the walker was alone. She lost interest and looked out to sea again. Shifting her position, she felt the pistol at her waist dig into her. She moved again and settled comfortably. She looked at the small daysack beside her. The movement of someone coming down the slope to her right made her glance over with casual interest.

Suddenly, fear gripped her. Her whole body reacted. She turned to stare at him. Frozen, she couldn't even scream; she just stared in horror. It could be too late already. Her right hand grabbed at the pistol through her Gore-Tex pocket, ready to defend herself. He came to a stop, glanced at her, then turned to face the sea. He put his hands in his pockets and stared. He was standing less than ten feet away. How had she not realised it was him approaching? When he had been in the woods close to her house, she had known he was there. How had he gotten so close this time? Alison fought to control her breathing, trying to calm herself down. He just stood there. She stared at him.

Her mind tried to describe him, as if describing a suspect to a fellow police officer over a radio. Her eyes went over each detail. Age: late twenties; Build - slim; Complexion - fair, neatly- trimmed beard; Hair - dark ginger, tied back in a knot; Height - just under six feet; Dressed - dark green hooded outdoor jacket, large grey scarf around his neck, blue jeans, old trainers, small daysack over both shoulders. She looked closer for details, and spotted cigarette stains on the first two fingers of his left hand. He once had his ears pierced but wore no jewellery now.

He looked over at her...his face was emotionless. He slowly turned his head and looked back out to sea. Her heart thumped in her chest. She fought the fear, wanting to get up and run, but unable to move. He looked back at her again, then back out to sea. Was he playing with her? She felt her body move, and slowly stand up. She could feel her hands shake, but it was not from the cold. Her feet moved, unbidden. She walked a few short steps and stopped near him.

"Dani is dead, so is Sabine," she said softly. He continued to look forward. She went on, "The wolves took down nearly all of them," she fought to control the fear, clenching her hands. Her eyes looked down, then she turned to look out to sea, "From what I know, they took down several wolves, including their alpha, Foster." She tried to slow down her breathing; she could hear the fear in her own voice, "but the wolves overpowered them. If any got away, they would not get far." She watched him take a deep breath and studied the side of his face. It was impassive. There was nothing in his eyes, he just stared. "The bullets I got for them were substandard." His head moved slightly to look at her, then back at the sea. "They didn't know they contained only half the amount of powder, so they'd have been less effective." She stopped talking. She stood there, feeling her body shake. He blinked and looked down, then back at her. Then he

268

turned and just walked away. She stared at the back of his head as he walked back the way he had come, each footstep sinking slightly into the soft sand of the dune. Then he was gone... over the rise, and out of sight.

Alison collapsed onto her knees, gasping for air. Her fingers dug into the sand. After a few minutes, her hyperventilation slowed, and she straightened herself up. She was nearly in tears when the phone in her pocket started to ring. She forced a deep breath, then pulled the phone out of her pocket and looked at the screen. It was a withheld number. She pressed the green button and held the phone to her ear. She did not speak.

"Where the hell are you?" It was the American, Alison nearly broke down.

"HE WAS JUST HERE! IT WAS HIM... FOR REAL!" she screamed dramatically down the phone line.

"What? who? What are you going on about? Just what the hell is happening?"

"HIM! HE IS REAL... JASON IS REAL!... HE WAS JUST HERE!"

"What? No, he ...."

"HE IS REAL AND HE WAS JUST FUCKING HERE!" Alison screamed into the phone. "Jason Apollyon is real! He was just here, and he knows you are here, right now, in Ireland!" Alison straightened and lowered her voice, as she carried on, "He knows you are here, and he is coming for you!" Alison paused. There was nothing but silence from the phone, then the line went dead.

It took Alison Wallace a few moments to recover before she was able to stand. As she did so, she looked at the blank screen and pushed the phone back into her pocket. Her hand was still shaking. She looked over at the daysack that was lying on the sand. Then she took off, grabbing the daysack, and running as fast as she could to where she had parked the car. She had to get away... her life depended on it.

11 DIE IN FIRE AT YOUTH HOSTEL

by Cara-Marie McKenna

Eleven people have died in a fire at the youth hostel at White Park Bay. Fire and Rescue Service were called out just before midnight last night to reports of smoke and flames coming from inside the building. "The fire was well-developed by the time they arrived at the scene," stated Senior Fire Officer Crawford. "The roof of the single-story building had already collapsed, but the Service quickly got the fire under control. Unfortunately, eleven bodies were recovered from inside the building." Senior Officer Crawford stated that the fire had started in the kitchen and all the victims would have been overcome by smoke inhalation very quickly.

All those who died worked on a deer farm near Kilrea. A spokesman for the farm said they were saddened beyond belief at the loss of so many.

The names have not yet been released by the police, but the next of kin have been informed. A spokesperson for the police stated their investigation is at an early stage and is ongoing.

The End

Watch for
Moon Dancing Volume 3
coming soon.